more . . .

CAROL HIGGINS CLARK, a writer and actress, is the daughter of author Mary Higgins Clark. She has starred in television, film, and theater productions, and for many years worked as editorial assistant and researcher on her mother's best-selling suspense novels. Her first novel, *Decked*, began the highly acclaimed Regan Reilly mystery series. It was a *New York Times* bestseller and was nominated for an Agatha Award for Best First Novel. Carol Higgins Clark, a graduate of Mount Holyoke College, now divides her time between New York and Los Angeles.

Also by Carol Higgins Clark

DECKED

PUBLISHED BY
WARNER BOOKS

CAROL HIGGINS CLARK

SNAGGED

A DOVE BOOK

WARNER BOOKS

A Time Warner Company

Enjoy lively discussions online with CompuServe. To become a member of CompuServe call 1-800-848-8199 and ask for the Time Warner Trade Publishing forum. (Current members GO:TWEP.)

Publisher's Note: This is a work of fiction. Names, characters, places, and incidents either are the product of the author's imagination or are used fictitiously, and any resemblance to actual persons, living or dead, events, or locales is entirely coincidental.

If you purchase this book without a cover you should be aware that this book may have been stolen property and reported as "unsold and destroyed" to the publisher. In such case neither the author nor the publisher has received any payment for this "stripped book."

WARNER BOOKS EDITION

Cover design by Jackie Merri Meyer
Cover illustration and lettering by Bill Sloan/Three

Warner Books, Inc.
1271 Avenue of the Americas
New York, NY 10020

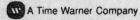 A Time Warner Company

Printed in the United States of America

Originally published in hardcover by Warner Books.

First Printed in Paperback: August, 1994

10 9 8 7 6 5 4 3 2 1

For my siblings and siblings-in-law,
Marilyn, Warren and Sharon, David, Patty and Jerry
With love.

Regan Reilly would like to thank the following people for assisting in her birth: Michael Viner, Nanscy Neiman, Larry Kirshbaum, Maureen Mahon Egen, Eugene Winick and Lisl Cade. She is also grateful to the author's mother, Mary Higgins Clark, for introducing her daughter to a life of crime!

SNAG—any obstacle or impediment

Ride on! Rough-shod if need be, smooth-shod if that
will do, but ride on! Ride on over all obstacles,
and win the race!

Charles Dickens

RICHIE BLOSSOM TUMBLED from the side of his bed as he bent over in an awkward attempt to pull on his brand-new pair of panty hose. "Birdie," he exclaimed, smacking a kiss in the direction of the enlarged Kodak of his late wife, snapped at their last picnic in the backyard, "I wish you were the one wiggling into these." His writhing contortions matted down the flecked, gold-and-sea-green shag rug that had been bought in celebration of their forty-fifth wedding anniversary.

"Yahoo," he yelled to his reflection in the mirror on the closet door as he kicked his heels in the air, "even the nails of the Wicked Witch couldn't put a run in these babies." Like a June Taylor dancer, he splayed his legs, then brought them together, practicing the scissor motion that had become so popular in aerobics classes, as he admired his satiny gams. "Not a run, not even a snag," he muttered enthusiastically. He grabbed the material around his right foot and pulled hard, knowing that the callus on his heel would normally be rough enough to split wood. He let go of the luxurious fabric bunched in his hand, started to sit up, and then, for good measure, gave it one more yank before bending his leg and pulling it close for further examination. "There isn't a mark," he whispered.

He looked around anxiously, as though someone could hear him. The run-proof, snag-proof, callus-proof panty hose was his invention. The realization of the dream he had had when Birdie, short for Bird Legs, had never been able to find hose that didn't blow in the wind around her matchstick ankles. She had tugged and yanked at them so much that no pair ever lasted more than one round of miniature golf.

"Birdie, Birdie, Birdie," he sighed happily, gazing at the picture that unfortunately had been clicked just as Birdie was about to yell at him to hurry up. It was the last picture on the roll, so no retake had been possible. Birdie's unexpected demise in her sleep that night meant that Kodak was out a sale and her panty-hose troubles were laid to rest. "But I've created this masterpiece in your memory, my little buttercup. Women will be able to buy it in any color, and each pair will last for years. Who in the world could have any objection to that?''

Maybe it was the way the sun slanted through the thick Miami air and reflected off Birdie's scrunched-up nose in the picture frame, but one thing was for sure. Birdie looked worried.

THE ROAR AND vibrations of the 747's engines underneath Regan Reilly's feet were no match for the snap, crackle and popping of her neighbor's gum. For hours she had tried to ignore it as they crossed the country, but the wad of Bazooka in her seatmate's mouth was continually being replaced with the next stick in an economy pack. The only respite was during the doll-sized "meal," which Regan picked at before abandoning the miniature fork, deciding that the dollop on her tray, grandly termed lasagna al forno, bore an uncomfortable resemblance to mystery meals she had endured in college.

Regan pushed the button to ease her seat back, hearing the annoyed sigh of the person sitting behind her, and closed her eyes. She bolted upright seconds later when the first bubble from a fresh piece of gum was enthusiastically decimated by her seatmate, who was now buried in a tabloid whose headline warned of UFOs bearing pregnant skeletons landing at Euro Disney. Where's Miss Manners when you need her? Regan thought. Probably riding in first class.

Feeling her body twitch as another bubble lost its fight for survival, Regan leaned forward and pulled her copy of *USA Today* out of the seat pocket in front of her. For some reason she always loved to read this newspaper on airplanes, checking out the weather map for the conditions of the cities all over the country, and especially the ones they were passing thirty thousand feet below. Not exactly like traveling in a wagon train, with the wind blowing off your bonnet, but with a little imagination one could conjure up a nasty day in Butte, Montana, or dismal skies, not too promising, in Chicago. But one thing Regan could never understand was why the captain would get hold of the microphone and interrupt the in-flight movie to announce that the speck below was the Grand Canyon. Oh, great. Let's all raise our window shades and make the actors on the screen a bunch of shadows and the people who paid their four bucks for the headsets a bunch of squinters yelling, "Pull down the shades!"

Once again Regan read the prediction for her destination—Miami, Florida. Muggy and hot. No surprise there. Regan, who had inherited the pale skin, blue eyes and dark hair of her Irish forebears, was not a sun worshiper, but she loved a swim in the ocean.

A thirty-year-old private investigator from Los

Angeles, Regan Reilly was coming to Miami to be a bridesmaid for the ninth time. This occasion was the nuptials of her childhood friend Maura Durkin. Maura's father, Ed, had worked for Regan's father, Luke, in his first funeral home in Summit, New Jersey, then decided to open his own place in Miami, where business was always good. The families had remained close and Regan's parents and Maura's parents always saw each other at the annual funeral convention, which, not so coincidentally, was being held in Miami this weekend.

"You know old Ed," Maura had told Regan. "He wants all his friends from the biz at the wedding, and what better time to schedule it than when they're all going to be down here anyway. Besides," she added, "I think he's getting a break on the flowers from a floral exhibitor at the convention."

"I imagine there are a few sample guest books floating around you could grab too," Regan replied, "not to mention limousines, cosmetologists who can do your makeup, hair . . ."

"Oh, I already asked the woman who does the hair for my father's clients if she'd be interested, but she says she has no experience doing the backs of people's heads."

"OH, GOD!" Regan had always laughed with her oldest friend at some of the absurdities of growing up with a mortician father, a bond they would share until death did them part. When they were little and discovered "The Munsters" television show, where Herman, the father, worked at a funeral parlor, Regan and Maura had gone through a stage where they called their fathers

Hermie. But their parents drew the line when the girls wanted to make telephone booths out of upright coffins.

"Ladies and gentlemen, please bring your seat backs to their upright and locked positions, stow away your tray tables, and make sure your seat belts are securely fastened. We'll be landing at Miami International Airport in a few minutes."

There is a God, Regan thought as she obediently complied, making sure that her carry-on bag, which weighed at least a ton, was completely tucked under the seat in front of her. If that thing went flying, Regan thought, someone would end up with whiplash. But if it could just be used to dislodge gum . . .

The plane swayed from side to side and finally landed with a thump, streamlining down the runway. Scattered applause and a wolf call from a college kid who'd enjoyed a few beers along the way resounded in the aircraft. With her long red fingernails, the bone-thin woman next to Regan, who Regan figured was probably in her early thirties, daintily plucked the pale-pink gob from her mouth, wrapped it in a tissue and proceeded to re-ruby her lips, powder her nose, and smilingly spritz herself with Jardin de Roses perfume that two seconds later assaulted the olfactory glands of everyone in a three-row radius.

"My boyfriend is picking me up," she said with a smile to Regan. "He hates it when I chew gum."

"Oh, really." Regan made an attempt at a laugh that to her ears came out sounding incredibly fake.

"Yeah, but I get so nervous on planes, it makes me feel better. It also helps your ears pop, you know." She fluffed her light-brown hair as she once again glanced at her pretty but tough face in the mirror of her compact. "My boyfriend has a really good job in real estate down here. So I'm gonna lay on the beach while he works. I can't wait."

"Sounds great."

"Ladies and gentlemen, welcome to Miami International Airport. Please remain seated until the aircraft has come to a complete halt and the captain has turned off the seat-belt sign . . ."

Before the announcement was finished, the clicks of unfastening seat belts echoed up and down the aisles of the 747 as impatient passengers shifted in their seats and began to gather their belongings.

"Sir, please remain seated until the aircraft has come to a complete halt," the flight attendant chirped in a cheerful but firm tone to a traveler already fumbling for his carry-on bag from the overhead compartment. "Federal regulations require that you remain seated—"

"All right, all right," the stout middle-aged man grunted as he snapped the compartment shut, his bowling bag now secure under his arm. As he reclaimed his seat, Regan gazed out the window at the hot tarmac, which from a distance looked as if it were hosting a jellyfish hootenanny. Squiggles moving up and down and bouncing back and forth similar to the kind you see right before you faint, Regan thought. It must be hot out there. A late-day swim and a jog on the beach sound pretty good to me. After sitting for over five hours, she was anxious to move and stretch.

Regan had a reservation at a hotel on Ocean Drive in the South Beach area of Miami, a section that had been renovated in the past five years and transformed into a pastel Art Deco wonderland, complete with trendy restaurants, hotels and sidewalk cafés right across from the beach, and great for people-watching. Modeling agencies had recently sprung up, as fashion photographers started to take advantage of the beautiful setting and weather.

Luke and Nora were staying a few miles away at the Watergreen, which would be filled with morticians who would be ready to boogie on Sunday afternoon in the Grand Ballroom.

"All the rooms at the Watergreen have been booked for over a year," Maura had said.

"Are there that many morticians descending on Miami this weekend?" Regan had asked incredulously.

"No, but get this. There's also a panty-hose convention coming to town."

"It sounds like a weekend to load up on free samples."

"Control top, thank you. Anyway, I made you a reservation at a hotel in South Beach. It's funky and more fun anyway. It's a few doors down from where my Uncle Richie lives—"

"How is he?" Regan interrupted. "Has he invented anything new lately? Those chunky earrings he sent me that held a 'big surprise' sure did. They started tinkling 'You Light Up My Life' when I was out on a date. Needless to say, I never heard from the guy again."

"He gave me the same pair. Luckily I was already

engaged. Anyway, now Uncle Richie says he's really outdone himself, inventing a run-proof, snag-proof panty hose.''

"If he did, it would be the Eighth Wonder of the World.''

"No kidding. Right now he's in the process of letting all the big hosiery companies know about it. I think he wants to start a bidding war.''

"Well, if they really are unsnaggable, I'm sure the big panty-hose companies will be after them in one way or another. The last thing they want on the market is panty hose that will last more than thirty seconds.''

"You're right, Regan. And right now he's also trying to save the Fourth Quarter, that's the old folks' place where he lives, from being bought out. He moved there after Aunt Birdie died. They all have their own apartments, but there's a community room where they socialize. Richie needs a lot of money by Monday, when their option on the place expires. That real estate on Ocean Drive has gotten really valuable. Naturally there's a lot of people who want to get in on it, but that means squeezing out the older people who've been there forever but can't keep up with the higher taxes. So with his new invention and the panty-hose people being around this weekend, God knows what he'll be up to.''

Regan waited until the plane emptied before getting up, preferring the seated position to the hunched-over variety that people were forced into while waiting for the people jamming the aisles to start filing out.

Everyone in a rush to go stand around the baggage-claim area. Regan's seatmate had said a hurried "Have a nice time,'' as she charged up the aisle on what Regan assumed were the wings of love. I guess if you have a hot date meeting you, Regan thought, there is more of an incentive to cut people off on your way out. But when the next person you'll end up conversing with is most likely a taxi driver in a bad mood, what's the hurry?

Down at the baggage carousel Regan stood for a good eight minutes before a buzzer went off and a red light started flashing, an oddly celebratory way to announce the slow arrival of everyone's goodies. The conveyor started to move and Regan watched as one suitcase after another was spit out of the chute, slid down the ramp before crashing into the wall, and silently rode on as each piece waited to be claimed, sometimes being chased by an owner not fast enough to grab it before it disappeared around the bend.

Regan shifted impatiently as baby seats, cardboard boxes, and suitcases tied together with twine, masking tape, and what Regan assumed was a prayer, all made an entrance. After what seemed like an eternity, her big blue-gray suitcase finally showed up. Regan broke into a big smile and realized that she must have looked as if she were greeting a lover as she lunged forward, throwing her arms around it, pulling it close to get it off the conveyor belt and over the hump. That accomplished, she swiftly retrieved her garment bag with one arm and wheeled her suitcase toward the exit with the other. Wheels on the bottom of suitcases were a great invention, Regan thought, except when they behave like the wheels on your average shopping cart, stopping dead or locking themselves in a position where the only thing they will do is make a never-ending right turn. Regan sometimes wondered if she'd ever get a decent shopping cart on the first yank from the bunch corralled together in the entrance to her local supermarket.

Outside the terminal the Miami air was hot and sticky. Regan felt her energy drain and longed to be in her hotel room already, relaxing with a cool drink. As her suitcase squeaked, she made her way over to the taxi stand and was surprised to find her seatmate at the head of the long line. Where's lover boy? Regan thought.

Their eyes met. Her fellow passenger shouted, "I'm going to the South Beach area. Where are you headed?"

"South Beach," Regan yelled back as the people in front of her glared.

"Wanna ride together?"

Regan debated fiercely. Did she want to share a cab? They hadn't even talked much on the plane. But the line was long.

"My boyfriend's paying."

That does it, Regan thought, and stumbling over the litter of suitcases on the sidewalk, hurried to the waiting cab.

As the driver piled the luggage in the trunk, Regan listened in awe to the instructions he was receiving.

"Put the blue one on the bottom. Don't crush the green one, it's got all my toiletries. Lay the garment bag on top. Don't get it too near that greasy tire. You know, if you're gonna be picking people up at the airport, you really should clean out your trunk."

The scrawny leather-skinned driver reminded Regan

of Popeye. Regan thought she saw him push the garment bag toward the offensive tire the instant before he slammed the trunk shut.

The luggage director, her voice sounding satisfied, said, "Okey-doke. Let's get on our way." She turned to Regan and extended her hand. "Hi. I'm Nadine Berry."

"Regan Reilly. This is really nice of you. That line doesn't look like it's moving too fast."

"That's because we're holding it up," the cabbie snarled. "Get in."

The interior of the cab offered an unlovely combination of dried perspiration and smoke, which was made worse by the Christmas-tree-shaped air freshener dangling from the mirror.

"Turn on the air conditioner," Nadine ordered.

"It's broken," the driver said as the car lurched forward and a lit cigarette magically appeared between his lips.

"Put that out," Nadine commanded, "or we'll have to take a different cab."

"I should be so lucky," the Popeye look-alike muttered as he squashed the butt in the ashtray.

Nadine turned to Regan. "If there's anything I can't stand, it's cigarette smoke. A terrible habit." She opened her bag and pulled out her gum. "Want some?"

"No, thanks. I thought your boyfriend was picking you up."

"He couldn't. You know how I told you he works in a real estate office. There's a meeting of the big shots at five-thirty and they made him stay to answer the phones. Where are you staying anyhow?"

"The Ocean View on Ocean Drive."

"Oh, that's right near the old folks' home!" Nadine exclaimed and then lowered her voice. "Everyone at Joey's office is sitting on pins and needles. An option expires on that home Monday, and there's a lot of money at stake."

Oh, brother, Regan thought. That's got to be Richie's place. The poor guy.

It took forty minutes to get to the Ocean View. By the time they arrived, Regan had heard Nadine's autobiography. Nadine was twenty-seven, sold stereos in a discount store outside of Los Angeles, and had met Joey at a Club Med vacation in Hawaii. She had been jetting back and forth to visit him for nearly six months. "He pays for every other trip," she confided. "It's easier for me to come here because he's been working so much on weekends."

As the cab neared the Ocean View, Nadine said, "What about you?"

Regan had to make it quick. "I live in Los Angeles. I'm here to be in a friend's wedding this weekend."

"Oh, I've been a bridesmaid so many times. All those dresses you never wear again, but every time they promise you'll get a lot of use out of them. I say yeah, sure, on Halloween. By the way, what do you do?"

"I'm a private investigator."

Nadine's eyes and mouth became perfect circles. "That sounds really interesting. Do you pack a gun?"

"I'm licensed to carry one but I never bring it on a trip like this."

"Do you ever get in real danger?"

"Sometimes," Regan laughed.

"Listen, Joey's apartment is only a few blocks from here. I'll be on the beach when he's at work. Maybe we can get together if you have any free time."

"Great," Regan said with a heartiness she hoped didn't sound forced. "Can't I help you pay for this?"

Nadine waved her hand. "Not at all. Joey's the greatest. Once I set foot in Miami, he tells me to put away my wallet."

The cab stopped in front of a pale-purple hotel with an outdoor café. In a few minutes I'll be in air-conditioning and drinking something cold, Regan thought.

BARNEY FREIZE WAITED nervously in the plush reception room of the Calla-Lily Hosiery Company. Across the wall a poster-sized edition of the ad that had appeared in all the fashion magazines showed a pair of exquisite legs clad in shimmering black panty hose. The copy began: "The Calla-Lily legs are in bloom again."

Freize knew that Calla-Lily hosiery enjoyed the position of being the number-one choice of well-shod women in America and abroad. Those women didn't mind paying through the nose to have their legs look good.

Barney studied the ad. "The Birdie stockings look better than them," he muttered. He pulled up his own socks and brushed the lint off his Hush Puppies. "Yup, if I were a dame, I'd be happy to get my hands on a pair of the Birdie specials.'' He looked up quickly. I've got to stop talking to myself out loud, he thought. They'll have me committed just like they did Cousin Vince. Now there was one crazy cat.

The Muzak piped in from a seemingly invisible speaker started to play "Luck, Be a Lady Tonight." Barney found himelf humming. Talk about luck, he thought. Whatever possessed him to take a walk past the old panty-hose factory that night he didn't know. He'd worked there in the maintenance department for years, until nine months ago, when they finally had to shut the place down. Business wasn't good enough. The owners never realized that specializing in panty hose for clerics just might be a slightly outdated idea. And now the place was going to be demolished.

But in the meantime his fellow maintenance worker Richie Blossom had been hanging around the place, setting up a little research lab, tinkering with the machines, up to his usual business of trying to invent something useless. But when Barney peered in the window that night and watched Richie fiddling with scraps of fabric, he just got a feeling that this time it might be different.

Barney's curiosity was piqued. He knew that if he knocked on the door, Richie wouldn't tell him what he was doing. So he went home and searched through all his maintenance uniforms, which he sentimentally kept heaped in the corner of his closet, and found what he hoped might be there. A key to the side door of the panty-hose factory.

The next night he waited outside until Richie had

left, gave him fifteen minutes in case he had forgotten something, then let himself in. Armed with his flashlight, he started looking around.

The old picnic table where they had gulped their coffee during their strictly observed five-minute breaks hadn't been moved; Richie was obviously using it as the command station for his project. Barney couldn't count the number of times he'd ended up with a burned tongue as he rushed to swallow the black brew that was passed off as coffee.

The gray time clock attached to the wall was still there, clicking away. Barney went over and gave it a punch, remembering all the misery it had brought him. "There," he smirked. "I didn't forget to punch in."

Stacks of cheap paper with a printed message, the kind that people force on you when you're running down the block late for an appointment, were lined up on the table. Barney picked one up, and with the glow of his flashlight began to read Richie's literature on his new invention. "One size fits all! Superior-quality hosiery that will not run or snag. You can't afford to pass up this offer!!" Give me a break, Barney thought. I wonder if he sat around all day suffering from writer's block as he tried to think that stuff up, or if those catchy phrases came to him naturally.

If you're going to try and sell something as unbelievable as run-proof panty hose, Barney mused, you better get someone like me, a born salesman, someone who could sell ice to the Eskimos, to do it for you. I'll write your ad, I'll even act it. Barney always thought he would have been a great salesman, but his mother said that one

Willy Loman in the family was more than enough and urged him to get into the maintenance workers' union when he had the chance. May she rest in peace, the poor soul.

Barney leaned over and shuffled through the papers. Photocopies of handwritten letters to various hosiery companies asking them for a few minutes of their time were scattered on the table. It doesn't look like he's had to start a file for responses, Barney thought. It'd probably be easier to get an audience with the Pope.

As he straightened up, he scanned the room with his flashlight, and started to walk toward the machines. Before Barney knew what was happening, he tripped over a cardboard box and fell to the floor, his flashlight cracking in the process, tiny pieces of its glass arranging themselves on the floor of the factory. Sharp pain stung his knee and shin. "Damn it! Damn it! Damn! Damn! Damn!" he repeated faster and faster into the sudden darkness as he rolled on his back, cradling his knee to his chest while he rubbed his shin. With his flailing arm he accidentally brushed the side of the cardboard box and grabbed it to steady himself. And then he felt it. And forgot his pain. A jumble of the smoothest, silkiest material skimming his fingertips.

Barney grunted as he lifted his back off the floor and arranged himself Indian-style, with his feet tucked underneath him, then greedily dipped his hands into the mound of luxurious fabric that turned out to be a couple of dozen pairs of panty hose. This must be the stuff, Barney thought. Richie's latest. Knowing that Richie had never been too organized, he helped himself to a few pairs, hoping that they wouldn't be missed. I'll get these home and test these out myself, see if they're what Richie claims they are.

He did.

As far as he could tell, they were.

Run-proof.

Snag-proof.

Which had led him to the Calla-Lily Hosiery Company, whose owner had hired Barney's nephew to do yard work. The only other hosiery company besides the defunct "Hose for the Religious" headquartered in the Miami area. That had been a month ago, and now Barney was waiting to meet with Ruth Craddock for the results of their lab tests.

"Mr. Freize, Ms. Craddock is going to be a little while longer," the receptionist reported to Barney, stirring him out of his thoughts. "Can I get you a cup of coffee?" The request did not sound as if it were coming from an eager-to-please waitress.

How about a life-insurance policy in case I die in this room? Barney thought, but what came out of his mouth was "Light and sweet."

DOWN THE HALL Ruth Craddock sat at the head of the gleaming conference table, panting in exasperation. An ashtray overflowing with cigarette butts smeared with orange lipstick was positioned to her right. She constantly flicked her ever-present cigarette in its general direction, only occasionally hitting the mark. Crushed cans of Coke littered the table. Her ranting speech was interrupted only for deep drags, tornadolike inhales that puckered her weathered cheeks and looked as though they had the force to leave major tar and nicotine deposits in her little toes. Exhales were followed by a swig of soda.

"We are going to get screwed!" she opined in her raspy voice. "We have got to buy the formula for that panty hose or else we'll be out of business! If someone else gets it first, then we may as well put out a sign that says GONE FISHING!''

The eight members of the board seated on either side blanched and shook their heads. They were all older men who had been with Calla-Lily since the early days and were called together now for the first emergency meeting since jeans started to replace skirts in the sixties as the fashion of choice, sending business into a tailspin. Women wanted to be liberated, and one thing they definitely wanted to be liberated from was garters. Garters that dug into the flesh on the backs of their thighs when they were seated, causing pain and leaving indentations. But garters held up stockings, Calla-Lily's bread and butter. That's when the idea of panty hose caught on, thank God, and kept women from adopting jeans or the dreaded pantsuit as permanent replacements for skirts and dresses.

Bra manufacturers had also gone through a worrisome period when their pretty laced cups were being used to fuel bonfires. Fortunately for them, most women realized you can't fight nature and the laws of gravity, and the bra business has held up since then, so to speak.

"I'm telling you," Ruth continued after another drag and swig, "we have got to buy out that Blossom guy before somebody else does. His Birdie Panty Hose is not to be believed. It's comfortable, sexy, can be made in all different colors and, worst of all . . .''

The board members braced themselves.

"IT DOESN'T RUN OR SNAG!''

"But madam," Leonard White, a distinguished octogenarian, began. "Five million dollars is an awful lot of money, and we don't want it to compete with our other lines."

Ruth slammed her fist on the table, causing the ashes to fly around like the fake snow in a watery Christmas-scene paperweight. "What, are you crazy? Who's competing? These panty hose will never see the light of day. Remember our motto: 'Repeat Business.' We buy the formula, own the patent, and then put it away for safe-keeping. Over my dead body will a panty hose be marketed that doesn't run. As for the five million dollars, we figured he could get a lot more than that if it goes to auction. We want to offer him a figure he'll take right away. It'll cost us a lot more than that if someone else gets their hands on it."

White, the only brave one in the group, cleared his throat. "But can we be sure it's so durable? You've only had them for a month."

Ruth narrowed her beady eyes and tossed back her shoulder-length brown hair. "I wore them for a week straight, and went down to wash them in the Laundromat's battered machines every night. Beach towels get chewed up in those things. The next morning when I put them on it was like they were fresh out of the wrapper. Then I gave them to the lab to test. Every test so far has come out positive. Irving is supposed to give us an update at this meeting. WHERE IS HE?"

The door at the back of the room opened and Irving Franklin, a thin, bespectacled man in his early fifties, wearing a white lab coat with a pair of black panty hose draped over his arm, stepped inside. Irving had been with Calla-Lily since the start of his career as an engineer and had seen them through the transition from stockings to panty hose and all the other crises in between, including the year of the fishnets. "Hello, Ruth. I'm here now." There was no trace of nervousness in his manner. He was the one employee Ruth couldn't bully, and she knew it.

"Talk to us, please," Ruth urged. "I've been trying to tell them . . ."

Irving walked to the opposite end of the conference table and reverentially laid the panty hose in front of him. He took off his glasses, pulled a tissue out of his pocket and began to clean them, holding each glass inside his mouth and giving it a good "hahhhhhh," before returning them to the bridge of his nose. The board members fidgeted in their seats and Ruth finally exploded.

"Irving, would you please hurry up!"

Irving stared at her.

Ruth slunk back in her seat.

"I have completed most of the tests," Irving began. "It seems to me we have a breakthrough. I liken this to the discovery of nylon, which of course revolutionized the stocking, for the most part replacing the use of delicate silk. I can't swear, but they seem to be perfect. I even gave them my own personal test."

"What was that?" an up-till-now silent board member croaked in a barely audible voice.

"I lent them to my mother-in-law. She hasn't been to the chiropodist in years."

Murmurs rippled through the boardroom, many of

whose members knew firsthand the importance of
monthly visits to the foot clinic.

"My mother-in-law wore these for three days, which
is an endurance test equivalent to any of us competing
in a triathlon," Irving pontificated as he walked around
the room, "and not even breaking a sweat."

More murmurs.

"These panty hose survived so well that my thirteen-
year-old daughter, who weighs about one hundred
pounds less than her grandmother, was able to borrow
them for a teen dance and not worry about bagginess.
These things snap right back into shape. Yes, I must
say that these are the first 'one size fits all' that don't
look cheap."

"I told you!" Ruth yelled. "We've got to buy them
before they do to us what nylon did to the silkworm—
put it out of a job—"

"However," Irving interrupted, "people's bodies react differently. There's one more endurance test we are
now conducting on the pink pair, and our results will
not be in until Saturday."

"Saturday!" Ruth screamed. "The panty-hose convention is this weekend. We've got to make a move
before Blossom presents them to our competitors. Or,
worse yet, peddles them to someone who isn't even in
the business, who will put up the money to manufacture
them and make a big killing all at once."

"We can't do that until we have the approval of the
other board members," Leonard White offered, "and
some of them are on vacation. Others are flying in late
Friday night."

Ruth crushed another soda can in her hands. "Then we'll have our meeting at the crack of dawn on Saturday . . ."

Several members of the board thought longingly of their golf clubs, which would now go untouched this Saturday morning.

"If we have to, we'll sit here and wait for Irving's results, and then we'll vote. Remember, everyone, we are lucky to be the only company that has the inside scoop on these panty hose. No one else bothered to check them out, probably thought it was some crackpot writing a dopey letter to them." Ruth took a final puff on the little beige stub that was threatening to burn her fingers. "Blossom is planning his fashion show at the convention Saturday afternoon. We've got to get to him before then." She got up and stalked out of the room as the board members gathered around the panty hose in awe.

"I'd a been a lot happier if we had stuck to garters," one was heard to mumble.

WILL EVERYONE PLEASE sit down and be quiet?" Richie Blossom urged his fellow tenants of the Fourth Quarter old folks' home. "We have a lot to discuss and not much time left."

"I've been thinking that for the past twenty years," Sam Joggins called out. And then, as everyone expected, went on, "They call this place the Fourth Quarter. I feel like I'm living in Overtime." He slapped his thigh and looked around to see who would laugh this time.

Flo Tides, the social director of the Fourth Quarter, handed Sam a glass of Gatorade in a plastic cup. "Eb would roll in his grave halfway to China if he heard you. That was his joke." Flo continued around the room, handing out the liquid refreshment. Her late husband, Eb, had always been an organizer, and he used to say that the best way to make sure people get to a meeting is to lure them with food and drink. She had met him at a church social fifty years ago, and when they were introduced they both knew they had found the right match. Eb and Flo. And that's what they did together for forty-eight years thereafter.

The twenty-seven people who lived at the Fourth Quarter didn't need to be lured to this meeting by the promise of Gatorade and sprinkled cookies, however, as there was serious business to be discussed. They were in danger of losing their home, the place they had retired to, the place where many of them had found companionship after the death of a spouse. Last year they had purchased an option on the property and that option was about to expire. They had to come up with the money to exercise their option and buy the property outright, but it had to be done by Monday. There was another buyer interested, who already had an offer on the table. And if they gave up their option before the weekend, everyone at the Fourth Quarter would get a bonus check of $10,000.

"Who took the last chocolate cookie?" Elmer Pickett whined as he wandered in and perused the confectionary offerings on the plastic tray. "That always happens to me."

"Well, that's what you get for being late," Flo admonished. "Just take one of the orange ones and sit down. We've got to get started."

"I don't like that kind. The dye runs all over my

tongue," Elmer muttered as he took a seat and crossed his legs.

Richie stood at the front of the room, by the bulletin board that held announcements of upcoming folk dances, poetry readings, and a sign-up sheet for the next outing to Sizzler. He smiled nervously. "Things are tough," he began, "but we've all been through bad times before. We have to stick together. We don't want to lose the Fourth Quarter."

"I say we should take the offer they've made to buy us out," Elmer yelled out. "That way we won't end up with nothing."

"Where we'll end up is living in some dump on the wrong side of the railroad tracks," Richie said vehemently. "I went to check out the place where they want to move us. It's broken down and it stinks."

"Well, at least we'll all go there with a check in our pocket," Elmer cried, still grouchy from not getting a chocolate cookie. "If we don't take their deal right now, then we'll all be tossed out of here with no place to go and no money to get there."

The group started shaking their heads and muttering as Richie called for them to calm down.

"My run-proof panty hose really works. I've got a patent on it. I'm showing it off this weekend at the convention. All the big companies will be there."

"But Richie, your last big invention bombed," Millie Owens choked.

"Do you call the Clapper a bomb? The guy who invented that beat me to the marketplace. My device worked practically the same way."

"Richie, it's easier to clap hands to shut off the television than it is to sneeze it off." Millie snorted.

"Not for people with arthritis," Richie protested.

Flo placed the tray of Gatorade on a side table. "Let's get to the point."

Richie agreed. "Now we all put money into the option. Of course none of us want to lose it. That's why we just have to sit tight until this weekend, when I show the panty hose at the convention."

"But you told us that the panty hose was wonderful and that all the companies would be lining up to buy it," Elmer accused. "What happened to that?"

"I sent them letters, but it's not until they see it that they'll know. That's why we're doing the fashion show. They'll all want it, I'll sell it, and we'll get to stay here. By the end of this weekend I'll be a millionaire and I'll buy this place for all of us. It's our only hope."

Flo interrupted. "Let's get a report from our treasurer."

Nonna Begster stood up with her clipboard in hand and walked to the front of the room. She had an angelic-looking face and graced the group with a beatific smile. Her white cardigan sweater was thrown around her shoulders and buttoned at the neck, leaving its arms dangling at her sides. She cleared her throat and began speaking in a voice that was clear as a bell. "As of three P.M. this afternoon, Eastern Daylight Time, our account at Ocean Savings contained eight hundred twenty-two dollars and seventy-seven cents. This is a result of our bake sale, door-to-door pot-holder drive, and paper-recycling effort. Given that we need one point one million dollars to purchase said property, that leaves us in need of one million, ninety-nine thousand, one hundred seventy-seven dollars and twenty-three cents. Thank you.''

"Give me a break,'' Elmer yelled. "We've got to win the lottery to raise that much money. Like I said before, we should just take what they're offering and not risk losing everything.''

"I can't stand the idea of leaving this place,'' Millie Owens moaned sadly. "My son and daughter-in-law would take me in, but they live in Montana and it gets so friggin' cold there.''

"Oh, I know what you mean,'' Wilhelmina Jackson said enthusiastically. "My daughter-in-law is a pain in my butt.''

Richie interrupted. "If we could all just agree to wait till the end of the weekend and my fashion show, which a few of you ladies have agreed to model in, then I promise you we won't have to leave . . .''

REGAN CHECKED IN at the front desk of the Ocean View Hotel. Walking in the door she felt as if she were stepping into another era. Overhead fans cooled Art Deco furniture. Black-and-white tile covered the floors. Old black-and-white pictures of bathing beauties from the twenties frolicking on the beach across the street hung behind the desk. She handed over her credit card as the dark-skinned girl smiled and looked up Regan's name on the computer. What would we do without computers? Regan thought. Wait on long lines while clerks shuffled through index cards, that's what.

Her room on the second floor was described as having an ocean view—that is if you got out of bed and walked over to the small window in the corner of the room and peered out through the venetian blinds. They should have handed over a periscope with the room key, Regan thought as the bellman placed her luggage on the steel foldout contraption with two army-green threaded belts that somehow held it all together. It screamed for a rest, looking as if it had been salvaged from a Girl Scout camp.

"Thank you," Regan said as she pressed a tip into the bellman's hand.

"You're welcome, miss. Thank you. Enjoy your stay." He shut the door behind him.

Regan looked around the room. It was soothing. A white cotton bedspread, blond pine furniture, an overhead fan above the bed, more pictures of Miami in the old days decorating the walls, all contributed to its charm. A small refrigerator with an ice bucket on top stood in the corner. Regan sat down on the bed and kicked off her shoes. "Thank God," she muttered as she lay back on the bed and stared up at the fan. She closed her eyes for a moment and listened to the faint whir of the blades as they continued on their ever-revolving course. Voices from passersby on the sidewalk one floor down registered in Regan's brain.

Suddenly the phone rang, an urgent double ring, quickly followed by another, as if to admonish the callee to hurry up and answer. Regan sat up.

"Hello."

"Regan, you're there!" It was Maura.

"I just got in a few minutes ago. How are you doing?"

"Well, I'm fine. We're just getting all the last-minute things together. I just talked to your parents over at the

Watergreen. My mother decided to have an impromptu supper here tonight for a few people who are already in town. Luke and Nora said they'd come over, so why don't you come too?''

"Well, sure, I was just going to give them a call to see about dinner.''

"Great. Was your trip all right?''

"Oh, it was fine.''

"How does the bridesmaid dress fit?''

"Like a glove.''

"Oh, that's good, because you know I really tried to pick a dress that you could wear again.''

There was a momentary pause. Regan laughed and so did Maura. "You don't have to worry about that, Maura. I'm thrilled to be in your wedding, you know that.''

"But really,'' Maura began, "if you just cut it down, you could wear it to a cocktail party . . .''

Given by who, Regan thought, the Salvation Army? "Maura!'' she said. "Stop worrying. It's your day.''

"All right, all right. By the way, do you think you could stop and see if my Uncle Richie is over at the Fourth Quarter? It's just a couple doors down from you. I called his apartment there and got his machine. Sometimes they just sit outside or gather in the community room. We'd love to have him come by tonight. He's been so preoccupied with this panty hose of his that we've hardly seen him, and he probably hasn't been eating right . . .''

"Oh, sure. Then we'll take a cab over to your parents' house.''

"Thanks, Morticia."

"No problem, Wednesday." Regan smiled, remembering their other favorite show, "The Addams Family."

"See you anytime after seven."

"Great." Regan hung up the phone and jumped up. Her jog would have to wait. Time for a quick shower and to pick out the least-wrinkled clothes from her bags. I'm also going to open up one of the bottles of water sitting on the dresser and check if there's any ice in the fridge, she thought. But not before I give Luke and Nora a call.

LUKE AND NORA sat in deck chairs on the balcony of their hotel room, which overlooked the turquoise-blue Atlantic Ocean. They had arrived a few hours before and, following their usual routine, unpacked immediately. Because they did so much traveling, they liked to feel settled in as quickly as possible. Somehow it made hotel rooms feel more homey when you had your own things around.

Nora Regan Reilly, a popular suspense writer, had just completed a book that she claimed had been the most torturous one yet for her to write. Her husband, Luke, and only child, Regan, had reminded her that this was what she said every time she was in the middle of writing a book, and her response was always the same. "It was never this bad." In any case she had happily

turned it over to her editor and was very glad to get on
the plane with Luke and head to Miami for the funeral
convention and Maura's wedding. While Luke attended
seminars dealing with the latest embalming techniques,
Nora planned to laze by the pool and even squeeze in a
massage or two at the hotel health spa. She felt like a
hunchback from sitting at her computer for endless
hours for the last three months as she revised and re-
wrote her latest yarn.

Nora looked over at her husband, who was reading
over his notes for the welcome speech he would give
tomorrow to his colleagues. Nora smiled as she watched
him move his lips, raise his eyebrows, and gesture with
his right hand, all without making a sound. "You'd
have made a good mime, darling."

"Huh?" Luke looked up from his notes.

"I said, you'd have made a good mime." Nora
chuckled and took a sip of her mai-tai.

"Sometimes I feel like a mime. Like when I try to
talk our daughter out of taking a dangerous case." Luke
shrugged his shoulders, half smiled, and shuffled
through his notes. They were both relieved that Regan
had just finished a case where she'd been tailing a rapist.
The family of one of his victims had been appalled when
he was released from prison early on good behavior.
They were terrified he would seek revenge on their
daughter for testifying in court, so they hired Regan to
keep a watch on him. He was moving back to their area.
Regan had set herself up as a potential victim in an
empty parking lot and nabbed the guy when he tried to

force her into her car. He was now back behind bars and wouldn't see the light of day for a long time.

Luke and Nora were proud of her, but still wished she had taken that LSAT course she had signed up for in college and gone on to law school. But one look at the workbook and a few practice tests made Regan realize that she didn't think like a lawyer. She had started training as an investigator when she graduated from college, which over the years had meant a lot of sleepless nights for her parents. They were both looking forward to seeing her and were happy for the chance to have a mini-vacation in Miami this weekend.

The phone rang in their room and Nora put down her drink. "This might be Herself." Nora stepped inside their luxurious hotel room and sat down on the pink pastel couch as she reached for the phone.

Luke cocked his head as he heard his wife of thirty-five years greet their daughter. He turned and saw Nora running her fingers through her short blond hair as she laughed into the phone. Regan, with her dark hair, took after her father, although Luke's had turned to a dignified silver. At six feet six, Luke towered over the five-foot-four Nora. Their offspring combined both sets of genes in the height department, coming in at five feet seven.

Luke stared out in the distance at a ship on the horizon, and then down at the shoreline at a young couple walking the beach with their three small children. He and Nora would have liked to have had a big family but it had never happened for them. That's why it's so nice,

Luke thought, to be down here to celebrate Maura's wedding with the Durkins, people who felt like extended family. Maura and Regan had always been close, and now Maura was marrying a nice guy. Now if only Regan could find someone like that . . . Luke shrugged himself out of his reverie. My God, he thought, I'm starting to think like my beloved wife! Give her a break. If I ever get my hands on that guy who didn't tell her he was engaged, only to let her find out about it by reading it in the Sunday *Times*, I'll kill him. And to think I bought him dinner the week before. He was even marrying someone else named Regan. I guess it makes it easier if you talk in your sleep. But Luke was glad it wasn't his Regan because the guy was such a loser. Regan, of course, had laughed it off, saying she'd been some detective, but in his day . . .

"Hey, Marcel Marceau," Nora said for the second time.

Luke looked up at her. "Very funny."

Nora took his hand and pulled him out of his chair. "We've got to get ready. We're meeting Regan at the Durkins's in less than an hour."

REGAN SHOWERED QUICKLY and immediately felt much better. A cool-water rinse at the end was refreshing and served to give her a second wind. Stepping out of the old-fashioned tub, she wrapped herself in a towel and attempted to wipe the steam off the mirror, only to watch it immediately reappear. I guess I'll get dressed first instead of fighting this losing battle, she thought.

Her garment bag was hanging in the closet, where there was also a safe and, surprisingly enough, a variety of hangers, the kind you'd find in an old closet at home. At least they don't lock them onto the rack the way they do in some hotels, as if anyone paying a couple hundred bucks a night for a room isn't entitled to make off with a few wooden hangers, she thought.

She pulled out a pair of white jeans, a striped blouse and her red leather flats, then looked at the alarm clock on the nightstand, which read six-thirty. Regan went over and picked it up. Boy, this really is a relaxed hotel, she thought. In most places this thing would be nailed down with industrial-strength screws. They must have good insurance.

Ten minutes later, Regan was ready to go. She'd done a quick makeup job and fluffed her hair with a pick. She transferred her wallet, keys and a cosmetics bag to an oversized purse and then decided to take advantage of the room safe. She placed her extra cash and jewelry on the shelf, slammed it shut and pulled out the key. There, she thought, the crown jewels are protected from any sticky fingers lurking in the vicinity.

She shut the room door and hurried down the one flight to the main floor. Outside, people were lingering over drinks at the tables on the sidewalk. One couple was going through models' composites that were stacked up before them. Like me going through mug shots, Regan thought, or police sketches. Only the people I deal with don't have one-word names like Autumn or Sapphire. South Beach had become the latest hot spot for fashion shoots. Several young girls with their portfolios in hand passed her walking down the Strip.

Maura had told her that this place jumps at all hours. She was right. Now, at six forty-five, it was way too early for most South Beach diners to have dinner, but the cafés along Ocean Drive were crowded with people enjoying a cocktail and checking out the scene. Some looked very European with their designer shades, and their cigarettes held at that just-so angle between their fingers.

As Regan strolled along the narrow sidewalk, a dark-haired guy on Rollerblades, wearing a Day-Glo orange outfit, zoomed by her and jumped over one of the small café tables. That lunatic must be getting ready for the Olympics, she thought. He certainly makes walking around here hazardous.

The Fourth Quarter was just two more doors down. There was no missing it. Whereas the other buildings had been transformed into trendy Art Deco pastel treasures, Richie's building looked like a large sea shack. But there was something inviting about it. It looked weather-worn and comfortable. Somehow Regan knew that the people she'd meet inside would not be anything like most of the people she had encountered thus far.

Beach chairs were lined up in a row by the screen door. Regan walked in and was immediately greeted by a diminutive old lady with curly gray hair who was sitting at the front desk with her knitting needles in hand.

"Hello, dear. Can I help you?"

"Yes. I'm looking for Richie Blossom."

"He's at a meeting right now." Knit one, purl two.

"Do you know when he'll be back?" Regan queried.

"He's here, dear." The needles clicked in her skillful hands.

"I'm sorry, I thought you meant he was out."

"Oh, no." The old lady shook her head as if in sympathy.

By the time I figure out Richie's location she'll have

finished an afghan, Regan thought. "Well, then, where
is the meeting?"

"Down the hall."

"Do you think I could stick my head in and ask him
something?"

"If I sat here all day, I couldn't think of a reason
why not." The woman held up the brown square in her
hands for inspection.

"Thank you. You say it's right down the hall?"

"Oh, yes. In the room we recently dedicated to Dolly
Twiggs, the former owner of the Fourth Quarter, who
passed away just a year ago. Keep her in your prayers."

"Of course." Regan smiled and walked toward the
back of the building and made a right turn in the paneled
hallway, immediately coming upon the Dolly Twiggs
Memorial Room. She heard Richie shushing people and
begging for order. Regan slipped in the back and took
a seat on a folding chair in the corner.

Millie Owens stood up and yelled, "Will everybody
please shut up?"

All heads flipped in her direction. "I say let's give
Richie a chance. I wouldn't mind a check for ten thousand dollars, but what I want most is to stay here. I've
lived here for years and have enjoyed every minute.
Like everybody else, I was afraid of getting old, but
moving here and being around friends all the time and
having socials, I tell you I felt like I was sixteen again.
I'd be heartbroken if we had to split up, with some of
us ending up in the dump across town and the others
being farmed out to relatives. If we take their offer on

the option right now, we might get a few dollars, but in the long run we'll have lost something worth a lot more . . .''

The room had grown surprisingly still. You could have heard a pin drop as some of Millie's companions stared at her while others looked down into their laps.

Millie's hands tightened on the chair in front of her. Her face broke into a wry smile. "Besides, people told me I could have been a model years ago, and now I've got my chance in that fashion show parading around in Richie's panty hose."

Everyone laughed and the tension in the air seemed to diminish.

Millie continued, "All of us gals have to get out there on that runway and kick up our heels. The men have to come and support us. And if they end up running us out of here, at least we'll have gone down fighting." She sat back down with a defiant look on her face.

Quietly Richie said, "Thank you, Millie. Now let's take a vote."

Everyone voted on index cards and they were quickly counted. Twenty-four were in favor of giving Richie a chance to sell the panty hose. Three wanted to surrender the option now. A cheer went up in the room when Richie announced the results.

"Tomorrow afternoon, let's have a rehearsal for the fashion show in here at four P.M. Thanks, everyone." Richie hurried to the back of the room and gave Regan a big hug. "You're here for all the excitement. How are you?"

"I'm fine, Richie. Maura called and they're having dinner at the house, but she couldn't reach you. Can you come with me now?"

"You bet, honey, you bet."

Regan and Richie walked arm in arm back up the paneled hallway. "Regan, do you mind coming up to my apartment for a minute? I want to grab a light jacket."

"Sure."

They walked up the curving staircase to Richie's second-floor apartment.

"Regan, I tell you, this is going to be some weekend for excitement," Richie said as he put the key in the door.

"Maura told me about your panty hose," Regan said as she followed him inside.

"I tell you, honey, they're unbelievable. Wait here a second," he said and disappeared into the bedroom.

Regan heard him rummaging around and sat down on the overstuffed couch, next to a black-and-white wedding picture of Birdie and Richie.

A minute later Richie was back, handing Regan several pairs of the magic panty hose. "Here, try them. This is one invention of mine that really works."

Regan held the luxuriant fabric in her fingers. "They're beautiful, Richie."

"They're not just beautiful. They last and last. There's a panty-hose convention over at the Watergreen Hotel this weekend, and I'm arranging a fashion show so the big shots can get an idea of what I'm offering here. All I need is the chance to show it off and I'll get the money to save this place. They'll all be fighting to buy the patent I have on them.''

''They're so delicate,'' Regan murmured as she admired both the ivory and pale-pink colors.

''They come in all different colors. Do you think your mother would like a pair?''

''Sure. She's always complaining that she can't find a pair of panty hose that fit decently and won't run.''

''Let me grab a few more.''

Regan pulled on the fabric and was amazed that something that looked so fragile seemed so resilient.

Richie reappeared with his hands full. ''I'll just carry these.''

''Here,'' Regan said. ''Put them in my bag. It's oversized anyway.''

''Oh, one more thing,'' Richie said. He looked over at the corner table and saw that the light on the answering machine was blinking. ''I'd better check my messages.'' He hurried over and pushed the playback button.

There were two messages from Maura, one hang-up, and one from the Models Models Modeling Agency. A gruff woman's voice barked, ''Richie, this is Elaine. If you weren't so adorable, I'd think I was crazy. I've got some of the models coming by your place tomorrow for you to see about the fashion show. I told them they won't get paid unless you sell the panty hose, but they're willing to take the chance. They're young, they like you, and what the hell, the show's on a Saturday anyway.

It's six o'clock and I'm going home. Give me a call tomorrow.''

Richie rewound the tape and chuckled. ''Regan, I bet you didn't know I'm about to become a star. A photographer needed some extras for a shoot they were doing on the beach and they wanted some of us old guys for authenticity and I got picked.'' He laughed as he gathered up his jacket. ''He said I was a natural, so I went down to this modeling agency to see if they'd be interested in representing me—and they were. Said they needed a few different types besides the gorgeous young girls. Elaine sent me out on a commercial audition for a local restaurant and I got the job! Now they're willing to help me out with my fashion show.''

''I'd better get your autograph now!'' Regan laughed.

Richie shut the door and they started walking downstairs. ''The commercial is supposed to start airing any day now. It's so much fun. I've become friendly with the people at the agency and it gives me something else to do, besides my inventions. Since Birdie died, I just like to keep busy . . .''

''I know,'' Regan said softly as they reached the sidewalk and felt the salty breeze blow up from the ocean. They walked quietly for a moment, then stepped off the curb to cross the street. Richie turned to her as they continued walking. From behind him Regan could see a dark car speeding up the side street. ''RICHIE, WATCH OUT!'' she screamed as she pulled him back to the sidewalk and they both tumbled to the ground. The car's front wheel screeched against the curb as it hurtled past them and disappeared around the corner and down Ocean Drive. For a moment they both lay dazed on the sidewalk. That guy deliberately tried to hit us, Regan thought, as she pulled herself to a sitting position. People were rushing over to assist them to their feet.

"Richie, are you all right?" Regan asked.

"Yeah, sure, thanks to you, Regan," he said fervently.

A pretty young girl who looked like a model was picking something up in the street. "Is this your bag?" she asked.

"What's left of it," Regan said as she studied the squashed white tote with the tire mark down the center. She bent down and gathered up the panty hose that had fallen out and had been run over.

"You two sure were lucky," a middle-aged man in the crowd called out.

"Did anybody get a good look at the car or the driver?" Regan asked.

People in the crowd shook their heads. "It all happened so fast," a waiter from the café nearby said. "It's too bad there wasn't more traffic. He'd have been slowed up, but he got away before anyone realized what happened."

"It was a he?" Regan asked quickly.

"Yes, a dark-haired guy in a blue sedan."

The crowd started to break up as the shock of what almost happened began to wear off.

"If anyone remembers anything about the car or the driver that might be helpful, please let me know," Regan called out. "My name is Regan Reilly and I'm staying at the Ocean View. That did not seem like an accident."

She turned to Richie and held out the stained ivory panty hose. "I'm so sorry."

"No problem, Regan," Richie replied and started to brush off the fabric. Amazingly the dirt disappeared. "See!" he said. "It's like the commercial with the gorilla who jumps all over the suitcase. You can't hurt it!"

"Too bad you can't say the same for us," Regan said as she rubbed her knee. The encounter with the sidewalk had torn her white jeans, leaving them slightly bloodied. "Let's get out of here. They're going to be wondering what happened to us."

"We can tell them we were testing my panty hose," Richie said brightly.

"That sounds like a good explanation for my parents," Regan said as she steered him across the street to the taxi stand, checking both directions before they moved an inch.

THE CAR THAT had almost hit Richie and Regan made a quick right turn off Ocean Drive. The driver raced the two blocks to Washington Avenue as he pounded his fist against the steering wheel. Heading north, a few blocks later he spotted a parking space and quickly pulled over. Within seconds Judd Green had peeled off his windbreaker, stuffing it into a gym bag on the floor of the stolen car.

He looked around quickly, made certain he was not being observed, then leaned down and yanked off the dark wig that was covering his blond hair, placing it in the bag with the windbreaker. Sliding over to the passenger side, he got out, picked up his bag, pulled off his gloves, and joined the thin stream of pedestrians, just another lean, tanned, good-looking male in his early thirties. A closer examination would have revealed the cold emptiness of his brown eyes, the raw strength of his shoulder and arm muscles.

He walked as quickly as he dared without attracting notice for a mile, until he reached the Watergreen Hotel. Sidling in the front door, Green took the stairs to his tenth-floor room, where he hid the gym bag in the closet, ran his head under the faucet and quickly changed into khakis and a sport shirt. He combed back his wet hair, sprayed on cologne, gathered up his wallet, and headed out to the elevator bank.

Two middle-aged couples were greeting each other, saying how quickly the year had gone since the last convention. They all wore badges indicating they were in town for the gathering of morticians. He smiled at them and pretended to be absorbed in his own thoughts as he listened to them yak about their plans for the weekend. I wish I could have served you up some business, fellas, he thought grimly, but I blew it. For now.

Downstairs in the lobby he ordered a beer at the bar and made it a point to flirt with the tawny blonde a few stools away who had placed her towel near his on the beach that morning. He chatted with the bartender, who told him he'd been at the Watergreen for thirty years and proceeded to ramble on about how many hurricanes he had sat out in this very lobby.

"In my time here," the short dark-haired man with a slight Spanish accent said cheerfully as he wiped off the bar, "I have seen some unbelievable things go on. My wife says I should write a book, but I don't want to lose my job."

"I bet," he said.

"Yeah, like this weekend, we've got two conventions. Funeral people and panty-hose people. Now if they're going to have a few fitting sessions with the girls in their panty hose, I say great. Which room? Can I deliver the drinks? But I can do without seeing people check out how good coffins fit. I guess we all have to go sometime . . ."

"Right, buddy." He laid his money on the bar and got up to leave. I've been here long enough to establish my presence, he thought. He headed around the corner, into the area where the pay phones were lined up. Sliding into a booth, he shut the door and braced himself for the call he had to make.

The phone rang three times before it was picked up.

"It didn't work," Green said flatly. "He was walking with some girl. She pushed him out of the way." He gripped the receiver and listened.

"No, I don't know who she was. But don't worry. It's not going to happen again. Next time I'll get both of them."

THE TAXI PULLED up in front of the Durkin home. A beautiful stucco ranch house, it reminded Regan of the kind of homes you find in southern California.

Richie insisted on paying for the cab, saying never in his life would he let a lady pay his way.

"Forget your inventions; you should start a charm school for men," Regan said as she got out of the car. "And I'll give you a few names for your mailing list."

They rang the bell and stood waiting as they heard voices on the inside. Mr. Durkin, an auburn-haired man of medium height with the map of Ireland on his face, answered the door and extended his arms. "Regan, Richie, come in. We've been waiting for you," he boomed in a voice never used at the Durkin Funeral Home.

He hugged both of them. They were barely in the door when Richie began telling him about their adventure. "You'll never believe what happened. We were almost killed. If it weren't for Regan's quick thinking . . ."

Nora and Luke, followed by members of the Durkin clan, hurried from the living room into the foyer when they heard the commotion.

"Hey, everybody," Regan said brightly and went over to kiss her parents.

"Regan, what happened to your pants?" Nora asked.

Regan looked down at her knee, which was bloodier-looking than before.

"She almost got killed trying to save my life," Richie said with enthusiasm. "You should be so proud of her."

"Oh, God, Luke, I thought this was going to be a vacation," Nora moaned. "Regan, are you okay?"

"Oh, Mom, it was no big deal. We were waiting to cross the street and a car came by going a little fast, that's all. I pulled Richie out of the way and we both fell down."

"What's going on?" Maura called out as she entered the room from the kitchen. "Oh, good, Regan and Richie are finally here."

"Regan just saved me from being killed," Richie insisted on repeating, much to Regan's chagrin.

"What?" Maura exclaimed.

"We were outside and a car came speeding by and Regan pushed me out of the way." Richie sounded as though he was just getting warmed up.

Ed Durkin suddenly urged everyone to move into the

living room. "Have a drink, for God's sake, tonight is a celebration."

As everyone wandered back into the large living room, Regan and Maura hugged.

"Let me get you a drink," Maura urged. "Still drinking white wine?"

"Of course," Regan replied and sat down on the couch next to her parents.

"You know, dear, you could stay in our room tonight. Maybe that would be a good idea," Nora suggested.

"Mom, chances are I'm not going to get killed escorting Richie back."

Richie plopped down in the chair across from them as Maura returned with Regan's drink. He began his fourth recitation of the near tragedy.

"My God, Richie, isn't it just about a year ago that Dolly Twiggs was murdered?" Maura asked.

"Murdered?" Regan echoed.

"We don't think she was murdered," Richie said, "but yes, it was just about a year ago she died. We're having a memorial service in the Dolly Twiggs Memorial Room on Monday."

"The cops think she was murdered," Maura reminded him.

"What happened to her?" Regan asked quickly.

"She liked to take early-morning walks on the beach. A group of sunrise swimmers found her face-down in shallow water. There was a bump on her head and some blood, but it could have been from hitting a rock when she went down. Dolly actually died of drowning, so she had to have been breathing when she hit the sand,'' Richie reported. ''She had a heart attack. Her jewelry was missing.''

''That's too bad,'' Regan murmured, as all her instincts warned her that it sounded like more than a mugging.

''We were just lucky,'' Richie continued, ''that she had signed the deal giving us the year-long option the day before she died. She wasn't supposed to sign it until the next day, but the nice young man from the real estate office brought it over for her on his way home from work. It gave us a year to raise the money to buy the place. Otherwise we probably would have had to get out right away. So now, if my panty hose takes off on Saturday—''

''Who was the guy from the real estate office?'' Regan asked.

''I was sitting at the front desk that day when he came by. We all take turns. I think he said his name was Joey.''

Regan immediately thought of her gum-chomping seatmate, Nadine, whose boyfriend Joey worked in a real estate office. She made a mental note to check it out first thing in the morning.

''Richie,'' Regan said. ''Get out your panty hose.'' She turned to her mother. ''Mom, what do you think of hosting a cocktail party on Saturday afternoon, before a panty-hose fashion show?''

NICK FARGUS SAT at his desk in the manager's office of the Watergreen Hotel. He liked to think of himself as the captain of a ship. The one-thousand-room hotel with its many conference rooms, ballrooms, restaurants and arcade of shops all hummed around him. It was always busy but especially in the winter months, when they were booked solid with conventions. One after another. Wanting to escape the dismal cold and slushy streets up yonder, conventioneers came down to Miami anxious to soak up the sun and play a few rounds of golf or tennis, often abandoning the idea of attending unnecessary seminars or meetings.

And it wasn't only the weather. Miami had become a real international hot spot, a center for culture. In the past few years it had experienced dynamic growth, and the future looked even better. Designers, musicians, dancers, photographers and models were all setting up shop down here. Celebrities were jetting in for the weekends. Even Madonna had bought an estate. Things were happening. There was a beat that was getting louder, and people from all over the world were hearing it.

So why did Nick feel so out of it?

Because of South Beach, or SoBe, as it was also known these days.

Just a few miles down the road, it felt like a different world from the Watergreen. It was where all the hip and beautiful people stayed, where they strolled, where they partied. Hell, the Watergreen made the best piña colada in Florida, but it wasn't as much of a draw anymore. Everyone was drinking all that goddamn mineral water. The Watergreen had a great piano bar but the models weren't interested in sitting around and listening to show tunes. They just wanted to go to those clubs where they pack you in and blare the music.

At forty-two, with sandy hair, mild gray eyes and a slight build, nothing about Nick attracted immediate attention. He made a good living and had socked away some money but he never felt content. Sure, on some days he felt like Donald Trump as he blustered around the hotel solving problems, his phone ringing endlessly. But on nights like last night, when he had gone down to South Beach for a drink and the models he met wouldn't give him more than three seconds of their time, he felt angry. If I were a club owner, they wouldn't treat me that way, he thought. He was feeling so bad he went into one of the shops and bought a hot new skin cream that cost a fortune.

Nick straightened the papers on his desk and took a final sip from his coffee. It was nearly eight o'clock. What should he do tonight?

Never having married, Nick was always looking for a woman who could advance his social position. Along the way there'd been a few nice girls he had dated, but they all wanted to settle down and have children, and that didn't cut the mustard with him. "I'm not ready," he told those types. One had recently replied, "You're going to have to chase your kids around the house with a walker."

Nick got up from his desk and turned out the lights of his office. One of the perks of his job was to have his own large apartment on the top floor of the hotel. Very impressive. If I could only get one of those models to see it, he thought, then they'd look at me with different eyes. So far, no such luck.

I'm not that hungry, he thought. And I don't feel like watching television. Maybe I'll put on that new flowery shirt I bought for $175 at one of those fancy boutiques and give South Beach another try tonight. Who knows? Maybe I'll finally get lucky.

R EGAN SAT IN the lobby of the Ocean View enjoying her morning coffee and a bowl of fruit.
Breakfast was an informal buffet where you helped
yourself to coffee and juice and chose from a variety of
cereals, bread and fruit. Bacon and eggs had to be specially ordered from the kitchen, but you'd be hard-
pressed to find anyone in this crowd to admit they ate
such cholesterol-laden no-no's.

Glancing through the Miami paper, Regan read about
the usual assortment of crimes that you'd find in almost
any big city's newspaper. Robberies, murders, drug
deals gone bad, arson. A new favorite in Miami was to
bump the car in front of you at a stoplight. When the
driver gets out to check for damage, someone else comes

out of nowhere, reaches in the window and grabs purses, briefcases, whatever he can get his hands on. In really bad neighborhoods you were encouraged to hand over your wallet by the barrel of a gun. Regan folded the paper. Thank God there wasn't an article about a successful hit-and-run on Ocean Drive last night.

On the way home Richie had told her the name of the real estate agency that was handling the option on the Fourth Quarter. It was called the Golden Sun. Regan had looked up its address and was happy to discover that it was only a few blocks away. She planned on making a little visit there this morning.

I should have taken Nadine's number, Regan thought. But hopefully she'd find Nadine's Joey at the Golden Sun and get some information out of him. Dolly Twiggs's suspicious death and the near accident last night, both around the times of real estate transactions, were a little coincidental for her taste. Transactions having to do with valuable waterfront property in a booming area.

The big clock on the wall read ten-fifteen.

At ten-thirty Regan walked up the steps to the Golden Sun. It was actually a small white house off Washington Avenue. Inside Regan found a pleasant-looking guy with a baby face sitting behind the receptionist's desk.

"Hot enough for you?" he joked.

"Yes, actually it is getting a little warm out there, isn't it?" Regan agreed.

"Unusual for November. But I say it beats the cold. That's why we're always so busy. People realizing that they want to throw away their snow shovels and enjoy nice weather year round. Is that why you're here?''

"Actually, I was looking for someone named Joey."

"That's me."

"Oh, are you Nadine's boyfriend?" Regan asked.

"The only one, I hope. How did you know? No, don't tell me. You're the one who sat next to her on the plane yesterday."

"That's right," Regan laughed. "By the way, thanks for the ride into town."

"No problem. Nadine's got me trained. She told me all about you, that you're here for a wedding and that you're a detective." His eyes sparkled.

The phone rang and Joey held up his finger. "Just a sec, Regan."

Boy, Regan thought, he even knows my name. She turned to glance out the window and saw Nadine teetering up the block in stiletto heels and chewing on a piece of gum. As Joey finished up his conversation, Regan watched Nadine spit her gum into a tissue and shove it into the side pocket of her purse.

"Here comes Nadine," Regan announced.

"Oh, good, she was coming down to join me for my coffee break. She'll be real glad to see you."

"Hi, Regan," Nadine said breathlessly as she came through the door. "I was going to stop by your hotel after coffee." She went over and gave Joey a kiss.

"Nadine, I smell spearmint."

"Breath candy, Joey, breath candy." Nadine turned and winked at Regan. "I always carry it around but am afraid to offer it to people because they always think it's because they need it I'm offering. Sometimes that's the case, but mostly it's just to be polite." She pulled them out of her purse. "Want one, Regan?"

Regan blinked. "Sure."

"Are you coming with us for coffee?" Nadine asked.

"I was just about to ask her, dollface," Joey said quickly. "How about it, Regan? We never got around to talking about why you stopped by in the first place. Or how you even found out where I work."

"She's a detective, Sherlock." Nadine pinched his cheek.

Regan laughed. "I'd love to join you, as long as I'm not intruding."

"No way," Nadine insisted.

Good, Regan thought. I really want to talk to this guy, and what better way than over coffee?

In the coffee shop down the street Regan sat across the booth from Nadine and Joey. They were served immediately, and as Regan stirred her third cup of the day, she commented that she and Joey know someone in common.

"Who?" Joey asked.

"Richie Blossom. He lives at the Fourth Quarter."

"Oh, yeah. He's a nice fellow."

Regan took a sip and placed her cup back on its saucer. "He said that you saved the people who live there from losing the place last year."

Joey shrugged his shoulders. "The owner lived there but couldn't keep up with paying all the repairs. But she didn't want her friends to be kicked out. So she decided to option the place to them and give them a year to come up with the money. We drew up the agreement and she was supposed to come over here the next day to sign it. I decided to just take it with me when I left work and stop there on the way home. I guess you heard she died the next morning.''

"Yes, I did,'' Regan said.

Nadine had become very quiet, her eyes darting back and forth as they talked.

"Dolly Twiggs was a decent woman,'' Joey said matter-of-factly. "She could have gotten a lot more money for that place than she was going to sell it to them for. But she said one point one million dollars was all she would ever need and these people were like family to her. If those papers hadn't been signed, then chances are that place would have been scooped up immediately. I'm sure you know what's happening with real estate around here, especially beachfront property.''

"I've heard,'' Regan said. "Did you spend much time with her when you went over there that day?''

Joey leaned back in the booth and played with his spoon. "I went up to her apartment. Her sister was there. They both collected seashells. They were all over the place. I sat on one and it broke. They said not to worry because they always took a six A.M. walk together every morning and that was the best time to find more.''

"Her sister?'' Regan asked. "I didn't know she had a sister.''

"She was in town for a visit. They both were going

to take off on a three-month cruise. A lot of cruise ships leave out of the Port of Miami."

"I thought Dolly was by herself when she died."

"She was. Her sister wasn't feeling well that morning and decided to sleep in. Needless to say, she was devastated."

Regan shifted in her seat. "Where is her sister now?"

"She ended up going on that cruise by herself and then went home to Dallas. Said she felt too sad being around here, although I understand she's coming into town this weekend for a memorial service."

"So when the place is sold, the money will go to her?" Regan asked.

"She's not looking to get rid of the people there, but she can't afford to keep up the place either. The taxes around here have gone crazy. From what everybody says, the residents of the Fourth Quarter can't come up with the money, so it's going to end up going to somebody else."

"Your office is handling it?"

"We handled the option and we also have people who are willing to put up a lot of money for it as soon as it's free. We even have somebody who's willing to pay them a bonus if they give it up before the weekend. But if Twiggs's sister has somebody else who wants to buy it, she doesn't necessarily have to go through us. So we could make a killing, or we could lose everything. But let me tell you something," Joey said as he looked directly into Regan's eyes. "I was happy I brought over that option when I did. My boss wasn't too thrilled because we probably could have made a sale right away so they could settle the estate. I want to make a lot of money just as much as everybody else does. But all I could think about was what if it was my own grandmother in the same situation? I wouldn't want her to lose her home."

Nadine kissed him on the cheek. "See why I love this guy?"

"I sure do," Regan said as Joey checked his watch.

"I've got to get back to work."

"I'm going to the beach," Nadine pronounced. "Want to come, Regan?"

"I've got a few things to do, Nadine, but give me your number and maybe we can get together later." Regan was very anxious to head back to the Fourth Quarter and find out about Dolly Twiggs's sister.

IRVING FRANKLIN LOVED his mini laboratory in the basement of his home. Not only did it allow him to continue his experiments away from work but it also provided an escape for him from the annoyances of family life. Not that he didn't love his family, but with his mother-in-law living under the same roof, his nerves were much more easily frayed.

It was Friday morning and he had just come down the steps to check on the panty hose that he had left steeping overnight in a Crockpot full of harsh chemicals. He pulled off the lid and with a large set of tongs extricated a lump of hose from the bubbling container. In awe he watched them dry off almost immediately and look as good as new.

"Damn," he muttered. "These can't be for real. There's got to be something wrong with them."

With that the basement door was flung open and his mother-in-law yelled down, "Let's go, Irving. Did you forget you're supposed to drop me off at the doctor on your way to work?"

Irving shuddered. He felt as if his day had been ruined.

"IRVING! Did you hear me?"

"Get in the car!" he yelled back as he dropped the hose in a plastic bag and set off for what was usually a pleasant commute to work.

I NSIDE DOLLY TWIGGS'S apartment, her sister Lucille Coyle turned on the gas jet underneath the kettle. She jumped back as the flame leapt upward, igniting with a miniature boom. Oh, my, I forgot about that, she thought. She adjusted the pilot and looked around. Everything felt a little dusty. Neglected-looking. Well, it has been just a year since Dolly breathed her last, Lucille thought.

A wave of sadness passed through Lucille, almost freezing her in place. Tears stung her eyes. I've got to get busy, she thought. It's the only thing that makes you feel better at a time like this.

She ran water over a shriveled orange sponge and smiled as it puffed up before her. Humming to herself one of her favorite hymns from church, she wiped the counters in the cozy kitchen. Poor Dolly, she thought as she straightened the decorative jars labeled FLOUR, SUGAR, COFFEE, TEA. I always tried to get her to put these on the other counter and have the toaster over here. It would have made so much more sense. And the glasses should have been right over the sink, where you can reach them if . . .

The doorbell rang. Lucille muttered, "Wonder who that could be," put down the newly vitalized sponge, and futzed with her hair as she walked across the living room to the front door. She pulled it open and gushed when she saw who was standing in front of her.

"Richie, how are you? You look wonderful. Please come in. And who do you have here?"

"Hello, Lucille," Richie said quickly, kissing her on the forehead. "I'm so glad you made it here for the memorial service. This is my friend Regan Reilly. She's in Miami for my niece's wedding."

"How nice. Would you two like a cup of tea? I'm just making a pot. I also picked up some lovely jelly doughnuts on the way in from the airport."

"That sounds great," Regan said, smiling at the thought of all the people who thought you had to eat alfalfa sprouts and yogurt to live a long life. Lucille had to be in her eighties and she obviously relished junk food. It just goes to show that being uptight about eating all the right foods is worse for your health than munching a jelly doughnut and enjoying every minute of it.

Lucille fluttered into the kitchen as Richie and Regan

made themselves comfortable. Regan looked around at the seashell decor and smiled. "When I was little and we went to the beach, I'd collect a whole bunch of shells and bring them home. Maura and I used to sit in the backyard and hold them up to our ears to see if we could hear the sounds of the ocean."

"The surf crashing . . ." Richie agreed.

"Well, actually I think we picked up a little interference from the Jersey Turnpike. But then we'd paint them with watercolors and douse them with some godawful glitter and give them away as presents. Talk about destroying the natural beauty of this planet. We were an ecologist's worst nightmare."

"They were cute," Richie insisted. "You sent one to me and Birdie for our anniversary. I still have it."

Lucille reappeared, carefully carrying a tray of jiggling teacups, a matching flowered teapot, a creamer and sugar bowl, and a plate of doughnuts. She ceremoniously placed it on the coffee table with the lace doilies. "Here we go." She poured two cups and handed them to Regan and Richie.

Richie helped himself to a doughnut. "Do you know what kind of jelly is in here?"

"Raspberry."

"That's my favorite."

"Mine, too," Regan said as she settled back with her first jelly doughnut in about eight years.

"Regan is a detective," Richie began.

"Oh, my," Lucille said as she sipped her tea.

Regan took a deep breath. "I'm not in Miami on

business, but last night Richie and I were almost run down by a car outside here—''

''You were what?'' Lucille interrupted, her expression aghast.

''We were on our way to Richie's niece's house when I think a car intentionally tried to hit us. I understand your sister was mugged on the beach right across the street from here. I couldn't help but wonder if there was any connection. Richie thought it would be all right to talk with you.''

Lucille's eyes clouded. It was still so hard for her to talk about Dolly without getting a lump in her throat. But she didn't want anyone else to get hurt, so she'd do her best.

''I understand it was quite a shock when she died,'' Regan gently prodded.

''Oh, Lord, yes. Whenever I visited, I used to love to walk the beach with her in the early morning. We were all set to go on a cruise together. I had flown in the day before to stay for a few days before our trip. She had made chow mein for dinner. Well, it's not really chow mein, but she loved to call it that. What you do is take a cup of Minute Rice, two tablespoons of soy sauce—''

''I remember Dolly used to make that,'' Richie interrupted.

''Right,'' Lucille continued. ''Now normally Dolly was a good cook, but the next morning I wasn't feeling quite up to par. I had just flown in from Dallas and flying is a little dehydrating and I had had a few glasses of wine, so maybe that's why I didn't feel like getting up for our walk, but I wasn't up to it, you know what I mean.''

"Of course," Regan answered.

"Anyway, she was gone for what seemed like a long time to me, and I got up and went downstairs and there was a commotion across the street, and oh, my God . . .'' Tears filled Lucille's eyes. "Dolly was dead on the beach. Her little diamond earrings were ripped out of her ears and her wedding ring, which she never took off, was gone, and so was her birthstone ring. The seashells from her tote bag were scattered around her and her change purse was missing. She always brought it with her so she could pick up some nice hot rolls from the bakery on the way back." Lucille paused. Her voice quivered as she said, "Dolly was face-down in the sand. Her forehead had blood all over it.''

"I understand she had a heart attack," Regan said quietly.

"Who wouldn't have a heart attack when somebody tries to attack you?" Lucille asked, exasperated.

"She had never had dizzy spells or a problem with her heart before?"

"Not at all," Lucille said firmly. "She was like an ox. Right, Richie?"

Richie swallowed the last bite of his jelly doughnut. "Right. She used to haul out all the folding chairs for our meetings herself. She was always doing, doing, doing.''

"So she'd never been sick?" Regan asked.

Lucille shook her head. "No . . . well, except for the time she got a piece of glass in her hand when she was washing the dishes at my place. We were using Mama's delicate china and glassware and Dolly insisted on doing it all herself because one time one of our guests tried to help and dropped a glass and we were heartbroken because it broke up the set of eight. Well, Dolly was there washing the dishes and one of the glasses broke and she got a little sliver of glass in her hand that didn't all come out, but she didn't feel it for so long, and then, when she came back to Miami, she had to have an operation to get it out and I had to fly back from Dallas to take care of her, and oy vay.''

"Hmmmm,'' Regan said, then tried to steer the subject back to the incident on the beach. ''Was there any sign of anything that could have been used to hit her on the head?'' Regan asked.

"She had landed headfirst on a rock. They don't know whether that's what made her bleed or if the mugger had hit her with it and dropped it. But the funny thing was it was a big rock and not the kind you usually see on the beach. But to murder her for a little bit of jewelry and small change? Why?'' Dolly asked and looked upward, shaking her head. ''Maybe it was somebody who was crazed and on drugs.''

Or maybe, Regan thought, it was somebody who wanted to make it look like a robbery when the motivation was something else. ''Was there ever any talk of the possibility that she had a heart attack and fell over and someone came by and stole her jewelry? That type of thing happens a lot with car-accident victims.''

"Not really. I would like to think that that's what

happened, that she died of natural causes. But in my heart I don't think that's what happened."

I don't either, Regan thought. "It must be hard for you," she said.

"She was all I had left. I haven't been here since she died because it's just too painful. Everything here is a reminder of her. That's why I'm hoping that Richie here can pull off his sale of the panty hose this weekend. I would love for the residents to buy this place, but if they can't, I have to sell it to someone else. I can't afford to keep it up and I just want to be finished with it. I want to get back to Dallas, where my friends are." Lucille blushed. "I also have a lovely gentleman friend back there waiting for me. Arthur Zipp. We met on a bus trip to the Alamo six months ago and have been keeping company ever since."

"Oh, that's nice," Regan said gently.

Lucille smiled. "And if I don't hurry back, I know that some of the other gals from our church group are going to start making casseroles for him. Moving in on Arthur, you know what I mean, Regan?"

"I know what you mean," Regan laughed, thinking of all the times she'd been to cocktail parties, ended up next to some guy, so you introduced yourselves to each other, and before you could say "Beam me up, Scottie," his wife or girlfriend materialized at his side, like a homesteader with a shotgun. Protecting her territory even though no attack had been planned. I can only imagine what would have happened if I were holding a casserole, Regan thought.

"When Birdie died I got a lot of casseroles and home-made cakes," Richie offered. "The only trouble was I didn't feel like eating. Regan, I've got to get over to the agency. Are you still interested in coming?"

"Yes, Richie; but Lucille, one more thing. Were there any newspaper accounts of her death?"

"A few in the drawer, including an obituary."

"May I borrow them? I'd just like to look them over."

"Of course. I'd be only too happy to find out who did that to Dolly." Lucille went over to the antique desk, pulled an envelope with the clippings out of a drawer, and handed it over to Regan. "Like the Lord says, the truth shall set us free."

"I'll get these back to you right away."

"Don't worry. I'll be here all weekend. God willing."

THE CALLA-LILY Hosiery Company had taken a suite at the Watergreen Hotel, setting up its world headquarters there for the duration of the panty-hose convention. Since their home base was Miami, the powers that be at Calla-Lily, namely Ruth Craddock, felt it was not necessary to pay for rooms for their employees to stay overnight. This even though these same employees were expected at all functions ranging from early-morning breakfast meetings to late-night powwows on how to improve sales in tropical countries.

But things were not going smoothly this Friday morning. Ruth, known as Ruthless by her long-suffering underlings, was on a rampage trying to locate the missing board members whose presence was necessary for the vote on Saturday. Somewhere amid the swirls of gray smoke, she was screaming into a telephone.

"What do you mean, he's bushwhacking his way through mountainous terrain on a mule in the wilderness! Track him and his backpack down and get him onto a plane! Let him bring the mule with him if he wants!" Ruth steadied herself and took a deep drag from her cigarette. "I don't care if he's pursuing a lifelong dream! If he wanted to find himself, he should have started looking before his eighty-third birthday!" She slammed down the phone.

"Ruth," her assistant, Ethel, said nervously, "you are due to give a speech in ten minutes."

"Which speech was that?" Ruth asked impatiently.

" 'Knee-highs as a fashion statement. Fact or fantasy?' "

"Where are my notes?"

"Right here."

"Have we heard from Irving?"

"Not a word."

"Ethel, you knew Grandpa," Ruth said.

"Of course; I was his secretary for many years."

"Don't you think I know that?" Ruth screamed. "You know, Ethel, the trouble is people just don't care anymore. They don't care that Grandpa built this business up from stitching together socks at the dining-room table. They don't care. They just collect their paychecks every week and let Calla-Lily be damned. But if we go out of business, with this run-proof panty hose coming out, they'll be sorry."

Ethel shook her head mournfully, tsk-tsking as Ruth

extinguished her cigarette and applied a fresh coat of lipstick.

"Your grandpa was very proud of you, Ruth, the way you took over the business. He was a very good man. He could get a little pushy at times—"

"Ethel," Ruth interrupted as she snapped her purse shut, "I'll be back in an hour, and hopefully there will be some happy messages for me."

If not, Ethel thought, I'll make some up myself.

NICK FARGUS WAS not in a very good mood. Last night he had barely sat down at one of the cafés on Ocean Drive when a waiter came by and lost his balance, spilling a bowl of capellini pomodoro onto his new shirt. In English, Nick thought, that means red spaghetti sauce that produces a very stubborn stain. The worst part of it was that Nick was sure that a girl sitting a few tables away had been eyeing him. She looked like she could be one of the models. By the time he had hurried home, changed and raced back, she was gone. Only later did it occur to him that he should have just gone next door and treated himself to another shirt. Those boutiques were open all night.

Sighing, Nick sat down at his desk. It was going to

be a very busy weekend with the two conventions. They had already had problems with overbooking. Too many fires to put out, and he had to be on twenty-four-hour duty. Now he wouldn't get back down to South Beach until next week.

Already that morning he had been awakened from a sound sleep by a panicked phone call from the front desk. Coffins were being wheeled through the lobby to the display room for the funeral convention, upsetting some of the guests. Told to use the service entrance, the offenders argued that they had seen mannequins wearing nothing but panty hose being traipsed through the day before, and no one had seemed to mind.

Nick's intercom buzzed.

What now? he thought as he picked up his phone.

"Mr. Fargus?"

"Yes, Maria." Nick rubbed his head.

"One of our guests would like to see you." Maria sounded excited.

Another problem, he thought. It's too early for this. "Tell them I'm tied up right now, but I'll see them later."

"Mr. Fargus, she's right here. It's rather important."

"Okay, send her in." Nick knew that he could trust Maria's judgment. He was lucky to have a secretary like her. She only bothered him with big things, taking care of minor problems herself.

An instant later the door opened and Maria walked in and beamingly introduced Nora Regan Reilly. ". . . And, Mrs. Reilly, this is Nick Fargus."

Nick shook Nora's hand. "Nice to meet you, Nora Regan Reilly. Say, your name sounds familiar."

Maria shot a reproachful glance at him. "Mrs. Reilly writes suspense novels." She turned to Nora. "I love your books. I have all of them."

"Thank you."

Nick jumped in. "Oh, of course. That's why your name sounded familiar. You see, I don't read much. Well, because I don't get a chance. But I really like books. I'm sure I'd like your books." Nick realized he was digging himself into a hole. "But come to think of it, my mother's a big fan of yours. She loves to read. Reading is important."

"That's what my publisher says," Nora said with a smile.

"Can I get you a cup of tea or coffee?" Maria asked Nora.

"No, thank you. This should just take a minute."

"Please sit down," Nick urged as Maria exited the room shaking her head.

"You have a lovely hotel," Nora began.

"Oh, thank you. We aim to please. Is everything okay with your room?"

"Oh, yes," Nora answered. "My husband and I are down here for the funeral convention."

"Really?" Nick tried to sound excited. "With his line of work, he must be able to give you a lot of plots for your books."

"He's got some good stories," Nora agreed.

"You know," Nick continued with enthusiasm,

"I've often wondered what it would be like to wake up in the funeral parlor, you know, before they started working on you." Nick laughed. "Would your family get their deposit back?"

Nora looked at him. "Well, I don't know. Everybody who's come through my husband's place has been dead on arrival."

"Right, right, right," Nick chuckled. "Maybe they'd just hit you with a pickup charge. Like I said, that had just occurred to me once or twice. I don't know why. Something to think about, I guess . . ." My God, he thought, I'm babbling, and it's only nine-fifteen in the morning.

"Well, what I'd like to talk about . . ." Nora began.

"Shoot," Nick laughed. "Of course I don't want you to really shoot me, it's just an expression I use . . ."

"I wouldn't dream of shooting you," Nora assured him, "except maybe in a book."

"That'd be great! Name one of your characters Nick and make him a handsome devil and I'll be sure to buy it."

"You've got a deal. Now what I wanted to ask you is about the availability of rooms for a cocktail party tomorrow afternoon."

Nick whistled and tried to look stern. He liked to do that when something big was happening. It made him feel important.

"I know it's late notice, but something has come up and it's rather important . . ."

Nick assumed the role of captain of the ship as he

pulled out his room chart and spread it out on the desk. "You know we have a lot going on this weekend and all my conference rooms and party rooms are booked, booked, booked. I don't know what to say . . ."

"That is a shame," Nora sighed. "And to think that Richie has all the models lined up . . ."

Nick's ears perked up faster than a dog's at the first sound of a howling coyote. He almost leaned his head against his shoulder and whimpered. He tried to sound calm as he asked, "What is the occasion for your party?"

"A friend of ours has a special panty hose he wants to show off. As a matter of fact, I'm wearing a pair right now . . ."

"They're lovely."

"Thank you. Oh—his niece is having her wedding reception here on Sunday. Maura Durkin."

"Of course. That's going to be a big one. They've ordered everything from soup to nuts. Now getting back to your party . . ."

"Oh, yes. Well, this friend, Richie Blossom, has this panty hose and he's asked several of the models from South Beach to be in an informal fashion show. We wanted to have a cocktail party for the panty-hose executives and the models beforehand, but I guess we'll have to figure something else out."

"Hmmmm." Nick didn't want to seem too anxious, but he could barely contain himself. "I hate to let you down, seeing as the family is having the wedding here. Now I've never done this before, but I'd really like to help you out. I live in a big penthouse suite upstairs, which is just perfect for parties. I'd be happy to let you use it. Of course I'll be on hand to help out.''

"That sounds like the best place of all to have a party!'' Nora enthused.

"Oh, it is, it is! I've had some great parties myself up there. You'll love it. You know, you could have the fashion show up there too. We could build a little runway running the length of my living room, against the windows, looking out at the sea. It will enhance and glamorize your product, I'm sure of it.''

Nora seized the opportunity to take advantage of his zeal. "I was wondering . . . do you have a list of the panty-hose executives and which rooms they're staying in? I want to send them personal invitations.''

"Right here. Aren't you going to send the models invitations?''

"I don't think we have to,'' Nora said, "since they'll be in the fashion show.''

"Of course,'' Nick agreed heartily. With trembling hands he pulled out the computer printout of the panty-hose people with their names, titles and room numbers.

"This is wonderful,'' Nora said.

"Now what we can do,'' Nick pronounced, "is set up a bar in the dining room . . .''

In the next few minutes they agreed on an open bar and hors d'oeuvres with waiters serving.

"I'll give you a head count tomorrow morning,'' Nora concluded. "Thanks for all your help.''

As soon as she was out the door, Nick picked up

the phone to housekeeping. ''Make sure my flowered print shirt is back from the valet by tomorrow morning.'' As he replaced the phone in its cradle, Nick's face settled into a frown. He knew he had a big decision to make.

REGAN AND RICHIE walked over to the Models Models Modeling Agency, located just a few blocks from the Fourth Quarter.

"Everything is so close to everything else around here," Regan commented.

"South Beach only takes up one square mile. That's why it's great for us old-timers. We can walk everywhere and we don't have to worry about the upkeep of a car," Richie replied.

As they climbed the stairs to the third-floor office, Regan's mind kept jumping in three different directions. I must call Maura, she thought. She said she was going to be out doing some errands this morning, but I bet she's home by now. I should see if she needs help with anything. I'd like to read over these articles about Dolly

Twiggs, even though it doesn't look like there's much there. But I don't want to leave Richie alone. Something told her trouble was brewing, and until the sale of the Fourth Quarter was settled, Regan had the uneasy feeling that he was not safe.

Inside the agency, two models sat on a bench and both greeted Richie by name. Elaine Bass sat behind a large metal desk. Pictures of models posing, running and frolicking covered every wall of the small office. Elaine's assistant, a young man named Scott, was stationed at a counter in the corner where he was sorting through pictures and answering phone calls. Bright sunlight streamed through the open windows.

As introductions were made, Regan took in Elaine's gruff yet appealing manner. She had a no-nonsense air about her that was necessary for her business. You couldn't be ultrasensitive when you had to turn away countless hopefuls—hopefuls who just didn't have the look that happened to be in style.

"Richie, you're doing great, honey," Elaine said. "We're really pleased about this commercial. And the client loves you." She turned to Regan. "We had every guy over sixty in Miami trying out for this part. Your friend here beat them all hands down."

"A couple of the guys at the Fourth Quarter tried out too," Richie said. "I was afraid to tell them I'd gotten the part."

"That's show biz, baby," Elaine said matter-of-factly. "Scott, get out Richie's check. Now, Richie, both Willow and Annabelle here are coming over to your place today for the rehearsal."

The girls smiled at Richie.

Elaine continued. "They can only stay for an hour. No overtime. Now that's a laugh, they're not even getting paid." She turned to Regan. "I don't know how he talked me into this." She did not wait for a response. "My models usually get paid from the minute they set foot on a shoot."

"Richie's got that way about him," Regan laughed.

"Yeah, right. Well, if he hadn't given me a pair of these panty hose,"—Elaine pulled out her leg from behind the desk—"I wouldn't have known how great they are. Listen, we're ordering up some sandwiches. You two want to join us for lunch? There's a photographer coming up in about an hour and I want him to take a look at you, Richie. I think you'd be right for a project he's got going."

Regan looked at her watch. It was just about noon. "Richie, I'd like to go back to my hotel to make a few phone calls. How about if I come back and get you at about one-thirty?"

"You don't have to come back and get me, Regan," Richie protested. "Don't you want to go to the beach?"

"She knows it's not a good idea to sit in the hot sun at this time of day," Elaine interjected. "I tell all my girls that. That doesn't mean they always listen."

Regan laughed. "I've never been to a rehearsal for a fashion show before. I don't want to miss it. I'll come get you and we'll head back to your place."

"Good enough," Richie said. "Elaine, I'll have a pastrami on rye . . ."

BACK IN HER hotel room, Regan immediately turned on the air conditioner. It was definitely getting hot and muggy. She poured herself a glass of water, plopped down on the bed, and called Maura.

"How's it going?" Regan asked when Maura answered.

"Well, I had a trial run this morning with a hairdresser to see what he'd do. I thought banana curls went out twenty years ago."

"I didn't know they were ever in."

"I think I'm going to go out back and jump in the pool. John's coming over in a little while and I don't want him to see me looking like this. It's not too late for him to back out."

"Maybe he has a fondness for banana curls," Regan

said. "They might remind him of a girl he had a crush on in the first grade."

"This is not the time to remind him of old girl-friends," Maura said dryly. "How are things with you?"

"I was with Richie this morning," Regan said. "I was a little bit concerned about him."

"I don't like what happened last night either," Maura said. "And he's so worried about losing that place. Your mother's so nice to help him out with the cocktail party tomorrow."

"I have to call her to see how that's going. I wanted to help Richie with his fashion-show rehearsal this afternoon if you didn't need me for anything."

"That'd be great, Regan. I'd appreciate it if you stayed with Richie. We'll all be getting together tonight, anyway. This afternoon I'll be bringing my tresses to a new salon to see what style they dream up. Maybe I'll end up with a Mohawk."

"Have them dye half of it purple," Regan suggested.

"To match my mother's dress," Maura replied. "Anyway, I'll see you guys tonight at the Watergreen." Maura paused. "Watch out for Richie."

"I will," Regan said, trying to keep her tone light. When she hung up the phone, she felt uneasy as she opened the file on her bed. "And now for a look at Dolly Twiggs."

NEARLY AN HOUR had passed since Nora had sat down at the desk in her room and started writing out the envelopes with the names of the panty-hose executives who were being invited to the cocktail party. There wasn't time for fancy invitations. Nora had drafted an invitation which Maria had offered to type up and run off on her computer. "I'll even fool around with the graphics and see what I can do to make it look special," she had said. As soon as they were ready, Maria was going to send them up to the room.

Nora took a sip of the cranberry juice she'd taken from the minibar. It was nearly noon. As soon as I finish this last envelope, I wouldn't mind having lunch by the pool, she thought.

Behind her, the door opened and Nora whirled around. Luke smiled at her.

"How did it go, dear?" Nora asked.

"There was a little mixup with which room the coffins go in, but once we got that squared away, everything was fine. We're all registered and now I'm free for a couple of hours." He took off his jacket. "Have you had a relaxing morning?"

"Relaxing, not really. Fruitful, yes. I've spent the whole time arranging Richie's cocktail party. All the party rooms in the hotel were booked, so the manager offered to have it in his penthouse suite. He's an awfully nice young fellow. Maybe Regan would like him . . ."

"She'll kill you," Luke said matter-of-factly.

"Oh, I know. It's just that he's being so nice and helpful. I really hope this party helps Richie out with the panty hose. It would be such a shame if Richie and his friends lost their place."

Luke nodded. "Stick to worthy causes like that. Not matchmaking, it never works."

"Are you forgetting, dear, that we met on a blind date?"

"That was different. First of all, it wasn't arranged by your mother . . ."

The doorbell rang.

Luke looked at Nora quizzically. "Did you order room service?"

"Are you kidding? I want to go down and eat poolside if you don't mind."

"I'll be your date," Luke said as he went over and opened the door.

Nick Fargus stood in front of him with a stack of folded papers in his hand. "Are you Mr. Reilly?"

"Yes, I am."

"Nick Fargus." He shook Luke's hand. "I'm the manager of the Watergreen and we're just trying to help your wife arrange a little party for tomorrow."

"Come in, Nick," Nora called.

"I've got the invitations here. They're all ready to go."

"How sweet of you," Nora said. "I just have to stuff them into the envelopes and stick them under the doors."

"Oh, no, we'll take care of that," Nick said firmly, assuming his captain's tone. He handed Nora an invitation. "Does this look satisfactory to you?"

Nora looked at it and smiled at the sketches of pantyhose-clad legs surrounding the border. "Luke, listen to this:

> "Don't be kept in suspense any longer. Nora Regan Reilly invites you to join her for cocktails, hors d'oeuvres, and the unveiling of panty hose you could die for.
> Don't hit a snag!
> Run to Penthouse A at three o'clock Saturday afternoon and you'll never have to get a run in your stockings again."

Nora took off her reading glasses and looked up. "What do you think, Luke?"

"I'd come."

"I appreciate your vote of confidence."

Nick laughed. "Well, I guess we're all set, then. I'll get these right out. Mr. Reilly, I know you're here for the funeral convention. Has everything met with your satisfaction?"

"Oh, sure. We had a little problem this morning with getting the coffins in and where they were to be displayed, but it's all straightened out now. I guess there was a mixup with the rooms."

Nick laughed nervously. "Oh, yes, I got a call about that this morning. We almost ended up with mannequins in their panty hose in the same room as the coffins. Now that would have been interesting. If we had laid them down in the coffins, it would have given new meaning to the term 'good-looking stiff.' " Beads of sweat broke out on his brow. Oh, my God, Nick thought, I can't believe I said that.

Luke looked at him. "I suppose it would have."

"Well, I guess I'd better get going. We want to get these out." Nora handed him the envelopes. Nick shook the invitations in the air and hurried out of the room.

Luke looked at Nora incredulously. "So that's what you're looking for in a son-in-law?"

Nora looked squeamish. "He means well."

Luke smiled. "Famous last words." He stretched out his arms. "I'm going to get changed. Then let's go downstairs, grab seats at the floating bar in the pool, and try one of the piña coladas this place is so famous for."

NADINE LAY SPRAWLED on the beach, covered head to toe with suntan lotion. This is great, she thought. But it's getting a little hot.

She got up from her towel and walked to the water's edge where the surf lapped up against her feet as they sank in the sand. It wasn't too cold, but Nadine, never one to endure unnecessary discomfort, didn't like the slow torture of getting used to water that was any cooler than the air. Impulsively she ran and dived in, enjoying the sensation of spiraling underwater, being cut off from all sound except for the muffled hum you hear on those boring shows about marine life they film underwater.

When Nadine surfaced, she threw back her hair and dived again in an attempt to catch a wave. She slowly rode it in and got up and dived again. Her hands hit the bottom, her fingers scraping the tiny shells and pebbles.

"Damn it!" Nadine said and swallowed a gulp of water. She got on her feet and examined the damage. Three of her precious nails broken. "This gets me really aggravated," she muttered as she walked out of the water and up to her towel. "It's a gorgeous day and I gotta go get my nails done."

Nadine picked up her belongings and headed back to Joey's house. She stopped at the faucet at the edge of the beach and got in line to rinse off her feet. While she stood there waiting for some kid who obviously felt he had to remove every grain of sand from his lower limbs, Nadine watched a model a few feet away posing for a photographer as an assistant held up a reflector. The model was wearing a winter coat. You'd have to pay me a lot of money to stand around and sweat, Nadine thought. And even more to put up with a photographer who sounds like he has PMS. What language was he barking at her in anyway? Swedish?

Finally getting her turn, Nadine rinsed off and slipped on her sandals. Crossing the street, Nadine tried to figure where she should go for her nail repair. Maybe I'll get in Joey's car and go for a little ride, she thought. There has to be a mall around here somewhere.

DISGUSTED, REGAN THREW down the papers on her bed. There was nothing in them that would help. Dolly Twiggs was a well-liked woman. She and her husband had bought the apartment building for a song forty years ago. When her husband died, Dolly took over the care of the place, but toward the end of her life she'd been anxious to sell it. She had no children. She was survived by her sister, Lucille Coyle, who also had no children.

Her body had been discovered by a group of early risers who made a ritual of their morning swim. One of them, Sid Bernstein, was quoted as saying, "We were all shocked when we came down to the beach and saw her there. I just wish we could have caught the guy who did this. I had been to some of the socials at the Fourth

Quarter. Dolly was a very giving person. She had told me that as soon as an apartment became available there, she'd get me in.''

An unidentified woman had said, ''This place has become a crazy combination of haves and have-nots. On the one hand you've got the people with all their money and glitz. And on the other you have the homeless and the transients who have nothing. You've got the drug-taking going on in the clubs and the whiskey-drinking in the alleys. And Dolly Twiggs, a decent, churchgoing woman who lived here for years before anybody even heard of this place, can't even walk the beach. I wouldn't put it past anybody I see around here to have done this.''

Great, Regan thought. The entire population is suspect. If it weren't for the fact we were almost run down last night, I could probably accept this as being another crime motivated by the desire for instant money. But something tells me there's more to the story.

Regan picked up her phone and dialed her parents. She let it ring four times before the operator came back on and asked if she'd like to leave a message.

''Yes,'' Regan said. ''Tell them their daughter is calling and I'll see them tonight.''

''Your name?'' the operator asked efficiently.

I think they know it, Regan thought, but said, ''Nancy Drew.''

''Thank you, Nancy. Have a good day.''

''You too.'' The second Regan hung up the phone, it started to ring. She picked it up.

''Hello.''

"Is this Regan Reilly?" the male voice at the other end said.

"Yes, it is. Who is this?"

"My name is Henry. I'm the waiter from the café where you nearly got run over last night."

"Oh, yes, hi."

"I thought you might be interested in knowing that I was over on Collins Avenue today. A tow-truck driver was hitching a car up that reminded me of the one that went by so fast last night. Well, I'll admit it, I'm nosy, so I went over and asked him why he was taking it away."

"What did he say?" Regan asked quickly.

"Are you ready for this?" Henry asked rhetorically.

"I'm ready." More than ready, she thought.

"It was a stolen vehicle."

A SCREAM PIERCED the air in the Calla-Lily suite. "I can't believe this! What did I tell you?" Ruth shouted.

Ethel stood dutifully by her side as Ruth read the invitation from Nora Regan Reilly.

"Now everybody will go to this cocktail party and take a closer look at the panty hose; won't they, Ethel?"

Ethel shook her head mournfully for the umpteenth time that day, then asked hesitantly, "Well, if you go, would you mind getting her to sign a book for me?"

"SHUT UP!" Ruth charged over to the desk and plunked down her purse. "Have we heard from the mule trek?"

"No. But we did get some good news," Ethel offered cheerfully. "Bradford Stempler the Third was sighted in the Canary Islands and is on his way back. They're still trying to locate Preston Landers."

"I'm glad everybody else has time for vacations. I don't suppose Irving has checked in."

"No, ma'am."

Ruth picked up the phone and dialed the lab. After six rings, Irving finally answered.

"Yes."

"What's going on?" Ruth demanded.

"Hello, Ruth."

"Is there anything new to tell me?"

Irving sighed. "This stuff is like kryptonite. It just won't destruct. These panty hose could bring down the whole industry. Just like computers have practically made typewriters obsolete—"

"Don't rub it in! How many more tests do you have to do?"

"A few. I gave another pair to my mother-in-law this morning. She will be running all over town today and is also in a bad mood, so maybe she'll manage to wear them down."

"Irving, we have got to get the patent on this."

"What about when the patent expires?"

"That wouldn't be for another seventeen years!"

"What then, Ruth?" Irving asked mildly. "But I guess you won't have to worry. By then you'll be able to park yourself on that hammock in your backyard without feeling too guilty."

"Not so, Irving! Grandpa stayed involved right until the end and I intend to do the same. Right before this patent expires we'll release these panty hose on the market. At least we'll get a jump on everybody else. And hopefully by then the fashion industry will have deemed it stylish to wear panty hose in twenty-two different colors."

"In the next seventeen years I'm sure you'll have figured out a way to make that happen. You always manage to keep in control, Ruthie." Irving smiled at the other end of the phone. "Well, not always."

Ruth squirmed in her chair. "I've got to go. Keep me posted." Ruth hung up the phone and called out, "Ethel, we have to hire more helicopters. We're going to find that Davy Crockett Wannabe if it kills me!"

NADINE GOT IN Joey's car and flinched when her bare legs hit the burning-hot seat. "Let's get some air-conditioning going here," she mumbled as she started the car and flipped the temperature control to full blast. As even hotter air came spewing out, Nadine cupped her hands underneath her thighs to keep them from sticking to the vinyl interior. "Hurry up, cold air, hurry up."

When she came back to the house she had showered and changed into a pair of shorts and a T-shirt. It was so nice to be in Joey's house, around his things, even though he and his roommates kept it a mess. There was something endearing about all the guy stuff all over the place. Barbells and a rowing machine in the living room surrounded by mismatched furniture that looked as if it had been picked off the streets after three days of rain. Faded curtains with uneven hemlines that were probably already old when Ponce de León discovered Florida. Sneakers and sweatshirts and gym bags and golf balls left wherever they happened to land on the once-yellow carpeting, and it didn't seem to bother them one bit. She had been tempted to start cleaning up but decided to forget it, remembering the earthy wisdom of her grandmother, "If a guy has a messy apartment, he's just your typical bachelor. But if a girl has a messy apartment, she's branded a slob."

Backing out of the driveway, Nadine thought that she could really get used to Miami. Now we just have to get Joey used to the idea of together forever. This cross-country commuting was getting to be too much, not to mention the effect flying was having on her sinuses. She hated the empty unsettled feeling she got when she headed back after these long weekends. Joseph, she thought, when are you going to buy me just a one-way ticket here?

Nadine drove along the busy two-lane road, lost in her thoughts. Suddenly she came upon a huge sign that said: GRAND OPENING—NAIL SALON. Quickly she glanced in the rearview mirror and decided she had time to make a quick turn into the driveway. She pulled into a parking space right in front. If it's a grand opening, she thought, then they'll want to do a decent job and make sure people come back. They don't have to know I'm not a resident of Miami. At least, not yet.

AFTER REGAN HAD picked up Richie at the agency, they sauntered up Ocean Drive, back to the Fourth Quarter. Once inside, they headed upstairs to Richie's apartment to gather the panty hose for the rehearsal. The message light on Richie's answering machine was blinking.

"It's always nice to come home and see that someone has left a message, isn't it, Regan?"

"Yeah, except when you play it back and it's a hang-up."

Richie pushed the playback button and an electronic voice that always sounded flat, no matter how many people had called, said, "Number of messages received—one." Somehow Regan thought the voice should sound more and more excited the higher the number got. Or maybe it should say something like: "Congratulations—you had eight people call." Or: "You must be *really* popular—twelve messages." Or: "Do you have a lot of overdue bills?—twenty-three messages."

A moment later, Nora Regan Reilly's message began. "Richie, this is Nora. I've got great news. We have a suite upstairs that we can use for the cocktail party and the fashion show. Give me a call."

"Your mother's a saint," Richie said breathlessly as he hurriedly dialed the Watergreen, "an absolute saint."

"Saint Nora," Regan said. "It has a nice ring to it. Maybe they should put her books in the religious section."

"Hello, Nora," Richie's voice boomed. "How are you, love?"

Regan watched Richie's face light up as her mother started to give him the details about the party. "Wait a minute, Nora, let me put you on the speakerphone. Regan's right here."

"Hi, Mom," Regan called out.

"Hi, Nancy," Nora said.

Regan smiled. "You got my message."

"Yes, dear. The clerk at the front desk asked me if I liked to carry the mystery theme through everything in life."

"Tell 'em you have a son at home named Edgar Allan Poe Reilly."

"Hey, Nora," Richie said excitedly, "tell Regan about what you told me about the arrangements . . ."

NADINE STEPPED INSIDE the red-, white- and blue-streamered doorway of the Hard As Nails nail salon and shivered. Ice-cold air was spewing from an air conditioner in the corner as a workman stood on a ladder trying to fix it. She was immediately greeted by a zealous aesthetician with jet-black hair and lots of makeup, whom Nadine guessed to be in her late forties.

"You'd like a manicure and a pedicure?"

Nadine rubbed her arms. "It's cold in here."

"We're fixing it right away. You'd like a manicure and a pedicure?" she repeated hopefully.

"Do you sterilize your instruments?" Nadine asked prudently.

"Yes, of course. We have the special sterilizing machine. It cooks the germs real good."

"Okay then." Nadine agreed to stay even though she was the only customer in sight, always a cause for wonder. But, Nadine reasoned, it was the grand opening and maybe they needed a little time to get cooking on all four burners. Everything certainly looked ready to go. Six manicure stations were set up in the tiny storefront. Magazines were piled on a bamboo table in the reception area, which presumably on busy days would be filled with clients with ragged cuticles and chipped polish, awaiting their turn side by side with others sporting tissue paper between their splayed toes, impatiently waiting for that magic moment when their nails were pronounced dry and it was safe to put their shoes back on.

"I'm Sophia," the woman said to Nadine. "Come sit down. I'll get a nice tub of hot water for your feet."

"I don't want a pedicure," Nadine said firmly. "I just need to have new tips put on these fingernails."

"We specialize in tips," Sophia enthused, masking her disappointment. "Next time you'll have a pedicure." It sounded like an order.

Nadine sat down at Sophia's station, listening to her explanation that a couple of her girls weren't starting until tomorrow, one had called in sick on her first day—can you believe it?—and she still had to hire a few more, but only the best.

Hurry up, Nadine thought. Get to work.

Sophia took Nadine's afflicted hand in hers and studied it. "You did some good job breaking these nails. They look awful." Then she added reassuringly, "Don't worry, I fix."

As Sophia diligently worked, interrupted by an occasional "Ow, be careful" from Nadine, Nadine watched the air-conditioning guy go up and down the ladder several times to rummage through his toolbox. He's cute, Nadine thought. But not as cute as Joey.

Suddenly the door to the salon was flung open.

"Can I get a manicure?" a robust elderly woman shouted. "I got one of your coupons in the mail."

Sophia dropped Nadine's hand and rushed over. "Of course, of course. One more minute."

The woman turned and yelled to someone waiting in a car. "You can go now. They'll take me. Come back soon, though. I don't want to sit around here all day."

"Come in, come in," Sophia twittered. "One more minute."

You said that a minute ago, Nadine thought.

Sophia's newest customer unloaded herself into the seat next to Nadine. "It's cold in here," she complained.

Nadine noticed the repairman throwing her a dirty look.

"The air conditioner is working too hard," Sophia joked. "We're fixing it right away, right away."

The woman looked at Nadine's bare legs. "Aren't you cold?"

"Freezing," Nadine said.

"Thank God I have my panty hose on. Otherwise I'd leave right now."

Nadine wrinkled her nose. "Isn't it a hot day to wear panty hose?"

"These are different," the woman announced with

authority. She lifted up her long housedress to reveal a beautiful pair of pink hose. "They breathe. They keep you cool when you want to be cool and warm when you want to be warm. And the best part is they don't run or snag."

"You've got to be kidding me," Nadine said as she stared at the woman's legs.

"Not at all. I didn't believe it either until I tried them myself."

"Where did you get them?" Nadine asked incredulously.

The woman let go of her dress and lowered her voice. "They're not out yet. My son-in-law is an engineer. He's testing them for his company to make sure they're for real. They want to buy the rights to them. It's some big hush-hush thing. He doesn't say much about it. As a matter of fact, he doesn't say much at all."

"All done!" Sophia blurted as she screwed the cap onto the nail polish bottle. "Be careful."

"I know," Nadine said. She leaned down for her purse at the same moment the panty-hose-clad woman started to get up from her seat.

"Oh, no!" Nadine wailed as her wet nails grazed the woman's legs and smeared. "My nails are ruined." After a pause she added, "And so are your panty hose."

"No problem with them," the woman said and wiped the bright-red polish off her leg.

Nadine was awed. "That's incredible," she said. "Nail polish is what you use to stop a run. It never comes off."

"I told you," the woman said, "these panty hose are

different. My only question is why did they have to wait until I'm this old before they discovered them?''

As Sophia reapplied polish to Nadine's twice-damaged nails, Nadine and the older woman exchanged addresses.

''As soon as those panty hose go on sale you've got to let me know,'' Nadine said. ''Have you ever tried to buy sheer black panty hose late on a Saturday afternoon during the holidays? The hosiery counter is a nightmare. I'll buy these in every color and never have to shop for them again!''

''Me too,'' Sophia insisted as she plopped down a bowl of hot soapy water into which she plunged the septuagenarian's unsuspecting fingertips.

REGAN AND RICHIE hurried as they set up the
folding chairs in the Dolly Twiggs Memorial Room.
It was a quarter of three and the models, young and old,
were expected at three o'clock.

"This works out great," Richie said as he unfolded
the last chair. "We'll be all ready for the memorial
service at four."

"Why didn't you just leave the chairs set up after
your meeting yesterday?" Regan asked.

"House rules," Richie said. "Or should I say, Flo
rules. She thinks the place looks like a church basement
when these things are set up. Takes away the homey
look. She said if we didn't make a strict policy, then
they'd never get put away."

Regan looked around. The spacious room was furnished with three floral couches and several armchairs, all arranged so they had a good view of the television set.

"Do people come down here at night to watch TV?" Regan asked.

"Day and night," Richie answered. "Most of the time you'll find someone in here watching something. The only time it gets real crowded and we have to haul out the folding chairs is when there's a program on that no one likes to watch alone, you know, like disaster reports, or the Super Bowl, or"—Richie chuckled— "when the President decides to talk to the nation. We get everyone in here heckling and shouting at the TV on those nights. Yeah, that's one tough job. Must be hard to live knowing there's always somebody out to get you."

"Hi, Richie." The two young models whom Regan had met at the agency appeared in the doorway.

"Hi ya, hi ya, how you doing, come on in," Richie urged.

By five past three, all the other models had filtered in. Fifteen residents of the Fourth Quarter, along with the five models sent over by Elaine at the agency, made up the cast.

Greetings were exchanged, and finally Richie said, "Ladies, ladies, please sit down. We have a lot to do and not that much time."

As they settled themselves in, Richie waited for absolute silence. He cleared his throat. "Tomorrow is going to be a very important and exciting day, not only for those of us who call the Fourth Quarter our home, but also in the history of panty hose.''

''We hope,'' Bessie Tibbens, who lived down the hall from Richie, yelled.

''You said it!'' shouted another.

''Your lips to God's ear,'' Flo pronounced as she circled the room with her tray of cookies, offering one to a young model sitting there crunching on a carrot stick.

''No, thank you. I never touch sweets,'' she purred.

''I'm sure glad I got old before they started pushing that rabbit food on us. A couple of cookies a day never hurt anybody.'' Flo moved along with her tray, only to have the next young model decline her offer with a shake of her head and a wave of her Evian bottle. ''Land's sakes,'' Flo mumbled.

''Flo, please sit down,'' Richie pleaded.

''I am, I am.''

''Tomorrow,'' Richie continued, ''is a day I liken to the day when man walked on the moon. Instead of 'One small step for man, one giant leap for mankind,' it will be 'One small step in the Birdie Panty Hose, one giant leap for womankind.' ''

''July 20, 1969,'' Pearl Schwartz recalled, uninvited. ''My little grandkids had just gotten halfway through lighting the candles on my birthday cake when that guy finally decided to come out of his spaceship. So they blew them out and then, after he'd bounced around for a few minutes up there, they relit them. The cake turned out to be a waxy mess. By the time I peeled all the wax off my piece, half the icing was gone.''

"You should have had a cheesecake in honor of the occasion," Flo offered.

"Pearl, Flo, please, we'll have time for chatting later," Richie moaned. "Now, as I was saying, tomorrow could be the beginning of a new era for women. To wear comfortable, flattering panty hose that doesn't run or snag, that dries in about thirty seconds, that doesn't bag around your ankles in embarrassing folds. This is what we will be revealing to the world tomorrow. I need you to help create the excitement." Richie looked to the young models seated together. "That's what fashion shows are all about, right, girls?"

They nodded their heads almost imperceptibly.

"Right," Richie said as if to answer himself. "What we have here is a great product, so it shouldn't be too difficult to get people interested in it. I hope. Hell's bells, when you think of some of the stuff they try to pass off at those fancy-schmancy fashion shows—those clothes look like they were designed by someone on Pluto. But people buy them even though their price tag is in outer orbit too. So why shouldn't a panty-hose company want to buy my invention?"

"Don't say hell, Richie," Flo admonished.

"Sorry. Now before I get started, I want to thank the models from the agency who came out to lend us a hand. They're donating their time to help us save our home." Richie started to clap and was soon joined by the rest of the group in a round of polite applause.

"And right next to me here . . ."

Oh God, Regan thought.

". . . is my friend Regan Reilly. She's here to help me out. Stand up, Regan."

Regan stood up, smiled, waved, then sat back down. Quickly. That has to be one of the more awkward rituals that human beings subject themselves to, she thought. The introduction to a big group. And having to wave. It made her feel sorry for the Queen and beauty-pageant winners, who probably wave in their sleep.

"Regan's going to arrange for us to have some nice music during the show tomorrow."

Feeble applause started in the back of the room, and before Regan knew it, she was smiling and waving again.

"Regan's mother, Nora Regan Reilly, has arranged a cocktail party in one of the penthouse suites at the Watergreen. That's where we'll have the show, too. They're setting up a runway for us."

One of the women in the front row smiled sweetly at Regan. Regan smiled back.

The woman leaned forward in her chair. "Are you married, dear?"

"No."

"I have a grandson who has a nice little business going for himself . . ."

"Minnie, please," Richie said with frustration. "We've got a lot to get done."

Regan found herself propelled out of her chair by the force of her nerve endings. "Richie, why don't we distribute the panty hose?"

"Good thinking."

The twenty pairs of different-colored panty hose were handed out after much discussion about who should wear which color, who had a dress to match a certain shade of peach, violet, ivory, rust, et cetera.

"Remember," Richie said, "you have to wear dresses short enough so we can see your legs at least up to the knees. Some of you might want to go shorter."

"Oh, sure," Minnie mumbled.

Respectfully, Richie left the room as they all struggled into their assigned hose, amid murmurs of "These really do feel nice," and "How pretty."

Finally Regan called Richie back in.

"Birdie would be proud of you, Richie," Bessie called out. "These make my legs feel good."

"Thanks, Bessie."

Regan and Richie placed all twenty models in a line, with lovely Annabelle from the agency leading the pack.

"Annabelle," Richie said, "let's see how you walk across the room and back, like you do when you're in a show."

With a self-assured attitude, Annabelle strode the length of the Dolly Twiggs room, turned from side to side, paused, and then sauntered back with one hand on her hip and the other flowing at her side.

"That was great," Richie exulted. "Now, did you see what she did, everybody? That strut, that look in her eye, that pause at the end of the imaginary runway. You all do that and we'll have the audience eating out of the palms of your hands."

"I feel ridiculous trying that at my age," Pearl kvetched.

"Do you want to go back to living with your daughter-in-law?" Flo asked her.

"Of course not."

"Then get out there and strut."

"Oh, all right. I'll imagine I'm at one of the USO dances during the war."

Pearl started to shuffle across the floor.

"You have to look happy, Pearl," Richie advised.

"I'm trying, I'm trying."

"Well, pick up your head and stretch out your torso like Annabelle did."

"Like Annabelle! She's two feet taller than me to start with!"

"It's all in your attitude," Richie insisted. "I want to show that women at any age will look great in and will love Birdie Panty Hose."

They rehearsed with Pearl several times and before too long they had her swinging her arms and cracking a smile. "This is good exercise," she said.

"Tomorrow, when we have music, you can really get into the rhythm," Richie declared.

The other models each took their turns at parading across the room, listening to Richie's instructions to "be natural," and "flirt with the audience."

"Now that wasn't so bad," Richie said when they were all finished.

"The show really won't last that long, will it, Richie?" Regan asked.

"No, but that's good. People's attention spans are getting shorter by the minute. Your mother is going to narrate a little script she's writing. We just want to grab them, hook them, and let the bidding begin!"

One of the old girls raised her fist. "Let's do it!"

"What about some sort of finale?" Regan asked. "Something to pull it all together at the end."

"Like the Rockettes!" Richie exclaimed.

"Well, something like that."

The models lined up side by side with their arms around each other's waists, and at Richie's repeated urgings, kicked up their heels. Slightly.

"Come on, a little more, a little more. Just look like you're having fun. At the end of the song you'll all file off the runway, snapping your fingertips. We want to bring the house down with this number."

"You're going to end up bringing me down," Pearl said. "If I kick too high, I'll lose my balance."

"Do what you can, Pearl," Richie advised. He turned to Regan. "Can you think of anything else we should cover before the group breaks up?"

"Richie, we want to get started with the memorial service," a voice said. Regan turned to see Elmer Pickett standing in the doorway.

"Have a chocolate cookie, Elmer," Flo snapped. "I can assure you, there are plenty left."

He's such a disagreeable soul, Regan thought.

"A couple more minutes, Elmer," Richie said and turned to the young models, who were now anxious to hurry off to other appointments. "If everyone could just leave their panty hose in one of the plastic bags and mark your name on it, I'd appreciate it. We'll have a changing room in the suite. Get there early tomorrow, everyone, and we'll knock 'em dead!''

If someone doesn't get to us first, Regan thought.

HE SAT IN the phone booth and sighed, twirling his finger around the cord. The crackling noise in his ear was finally joined by the sound of a foreign ring. The long-distance connection to South America was finally going through.

The phone was answered by a man with a heavily accented voice.

He let go of the cord and nervously identified himself.

"Well, what's going on?" the voice asked.

"We haven't been able to get him yet."

"Why not?" the man with the accent asked angrily.

"All day today he's been with that girl."

"So, get rid of her too! Don't you realize that we're running out of time?"

"I know. Don't worry. One way or another it'll get done."

"It better get done. There's a lot at stake here. I knew we should have started this sooner, but you . . ." The man took a deep breath. "You said there wouldn't be a problem."

"I didn't think there would be. And there still might not be."

"I don't want to hear any excuses or explanations. Get it done!" The phone clicked.

He sat there holding the receiver in his hand. "It will be," he said after a moment, slamming the phone back down and pulling open the door. "You can be sure it will be."

F I SHALL walk through the valley of death, I shall have no fear. I know that my sister, Dolly, will be there to greet me and we can go on that walk on the beach in heaven together." Lucille, with tear-filled eyes, looked around the congregation gathered in the Dolly Twiggs Memorial Room. "My sister was so fond of you all. I feel she's looking down right now and sending a spiritual greeting. But I know she would have wanted you all to have something physical to remember her by, something that was important to her. There's a box of her seashells by the door. Please take one on your way out."

A hum of gratitude rippled through the audience.

"I know that she also would have wanted you to raise the money to buy the Fourth Quarter and live here for the duration of your earthly lives. I want that too. More than anything. So let us join hands and pray silently, in the religion of our choice, for the sale of Richie's panty hose."

Regan and Richie joined hands. Regan turned to Elmer Pickett, who was sitting on her other side. He was sitting there with his arms folded. Clearly he did not intend to hold hands with anybody.

For someone who wanted to get this service started on time, Regan thought, he certainly doesn't seem to be fully participating in the tribute. Or was it the sale of the panty hose that he didn't want to pray for?

Regan looked around at the rest of the group. Everyone else's eyes were closed, some shut so tightly it looked as though they were squinting in the desert sun, as if the harder they squeezed, the more likely the panty hose would generate some cash.

"Amen," Lucille finally said.

"Amen."

"Amen."

"Amen."

Up and down the rows of folding chairs the word was heard.

Lucille quietly took her seat in the front row.

Flo, who Regan figured must have been president of the pep club in high school, got up and addressed the group.

"When Dolly died, with the way she died, on the beach, alone, we were all in shock. We had a funeral but we never really came together to talk about Dolly and honor her until now. Time is a healer, thank God, and today we want to celebrate her life with joy. This was a woman who kept our rents low all through the years. She wanted to keep us together as long as possible. When she could no longer afford to keep up this place, she promised us the chance to try and buy it for ourselves. This at a time when the prices around here started to skyrocket and she could have gotten way more than she was asking us. And now her sister, Lucille, who never really knew any of us before, has been so patient and is praying with us here so that we can raise the money to buy the Fourth Quarter. She isn't looking for a fortune, either. She just wants to get back to her gentleman friend in Texas.''

Lucille blushed. ''Flo, hush.''

''It's all right, Lucille. Now I invite anyone who would like to come up here and share. Share with us a story about Dolly, anything you'd like, about how she touched your life in some way.''

To Regan's surprise, Elmer Pickett got out of his seat and walked to the front of the room.

''I only moved in here shortly before Dolly died, but she was very welcoming to me,'' Elmer said almost accusingly to the other residents of the Fourth Quarter. ''My wife had just died and I didn't want to live all alone in our house. So I sold it and got an apartment here. Dolly was always there to talk to me when I was just moping around. One day we took a walk down the street outside here and saw all of those models getting their picture taken. They asked us to stop and be in the background. After that, Dolly encouraged me to try and get involved in the modeling. That's when I got an

agent. I used to report back to Dolly about all the goings-
on at the agency. She told me I should stop by there
every day to see, maybe a call would come in when I
was there and they'd need an old guy. It got me back
on my feet again. Heck, I'm not a star, but it gave me
a reason to get out of bed in the morning.''

Regan thought he directed his attention to Richie.

"I haven't gotten as much work lately, but whatever
I do get, I have Dolly to thank for it."

He's mad at Richie, Regan thought, for getting that
commercial.

Next up was Pearl. "Every year on my birthday,
which was the day the men landed on the moon, Dolly
always baked me a special cake and stuck an American
flag in it." Her voice quivered. "I'll always remember
that."

Minnie Kimble ambled out of her chair and recounted
how she and Dolly used to love to walk on the beach
together.

"Dolly was always picking up every seashell she
passed and inspecting it to see if it was worth keeping.
I used to say to her, 'Dolly, when are you going to stop
collecting those shells? Haven't you got enough?' And
she said her favorite tongue twister was 'She sells seashells by the seashore.' Try saying that three times
fast."

How about "The big black bug bled black blood,"
Regan thought.

Next up was Charlie Doonsday with his harmonica.
"Before this area got busy with people wandering by
all the time, Dolly and I used to sit outside on our beach

chairs and I'd play my harmonica for her. Dolly, I hope you can hear this in heaven.'' He held the instrument up to his mouth and started to blow ''Home on the Range.''

The sea of humanity that passes outside on the sidewalk of South Beach doesn't leave much room for the deer and the antelope, Regan thought.

The duration of the hour-long service was filled with more personal stories, a few songs, and a tear-soaked rendition of ''Good-bye, Dolly.''

As they filed out, Regan checked her watch. It was ten past five.

''Richie, I'm going to go back and get changed for tonight. I'll pick you up at six-thirty. You'll be here, won't you?''

''Oh sure, Regan. I'll be here.''

I hope so, Regan thought as she hurried out the door.

REGAN STEPPED INTO the late-afternoon sun and glanced across the street at the ocean with its mildly breaking waves. At this time of day the beach looked peaceful. The setting sun's rays were reflecting off the water and most of the sunbathers had headed home.

Regan breathed in the salt air, turned and moseyed down the sidewalk, observing the cafés on the way to her hotel. It might be peaceful on the beach, she thought, but these joints are already getting crowded. Another night of mixing and mingling about to take off.

She reached a side street and waited at the curb for a spurt of traffic to pass before crossing. After last night, she wasn't about to take any chances. She had just stepped down into the street when she saw another car coming. In a reflex action she jumped back onto the curb and crashed into a rollerblader, who was knocked to the ground with her.

She felt a sharp pain as her elbow smashed into the ground. As she fell she saw his hand scrape along the sidewalk.

She heard him curse under his breath. "Watch it, would ya, lady?" he mumbled as he pulled himself up.

Anger flared in Regan as pain darted through her body. "Watch it yourself," she snapped as she struggled to her feet. "You shouldn't have been so close behind me."

He did not respond. He was already halfway down the side street, skating like lightning in his sunglasses and wide-brimmed straw hat.

Jerk, Regan thought. Her body felt sore all over. The jolt had shaken her badly. He was a solid guy. It was like hitting a brick wall.

She rubbed her elbow and looked around.

A middle-aged couple approached her. "Are you all right?" the man asked solicitously.

"Yes, thank you."

I backed into him, she thought. And he was moving forward. If he wanted to turn right down the side street, then he shouldn't have been so close to the curb where I was waiting. He would have just rounded the corner at the high speed he was traveling. Unless of course he *wanted* to be right behind me.

Once again Regan waited to cross the street and continued on to her hotel. Did he hurry off because he didn't want me to get a good look at him? she wondered. He looked like a geek with that hat. Was that a disguise? Was this related to last night?

Back in the hotel room, which more and more felt like her escape from the outside world, Regan kicked off her shoes and flopped on the bed. The ceiling fan was doing its thing and it made Regan think of New Orleans, even though she'd never been there. But her mind came back to the rollerblader. Who was he, and would he have pushed her into the street?

I need a bath, she thought. My bod could use a good soak. With the sore knee from last night and the bruise that was developing at that very moment, it was a good thing she was not in Richie's fashion show. Panty hose for the injured. Next thing you know I'll be wearing Ace bandages.

Two mishaps or accidents, or whatever one would call them, in twenty-four hours. And they say they come in threes. What's going to happen next? I'll probably slip in the tub, she decided. It would almost be a relief. Get it over with. She hadn't noticed any foot-shaped appliqués stuck on the bottom of the tub, the kind that were supposed to prevent you from a nasty spill. They were very tacky but practical. Whenever Regan saw them in a tub she imagined that they were the final footsteps of the Roto Rooter man who got lost in the drainpipes.

She went into the bathroom and turned on the faucets full blast. It sounded like Niagara Falls. Regan turned. Did she hear a sound in the bedroom? She always thought she was hearing things when the water was running.

Regan went back into the bedroom to check it out. Nothing. Everything was fine. Let's not get paranoid, she thought. She returned to the bathroom and shut the door. Peeling off her clothes, she gingerly stepped into the tub, feeling herself relax as the warm water enveloped her injuries. Using a towel as a pillow behind her, she lay back and closed her eyes. Within minutes she felt herself being drawn into a semiconscious state, that never-never land between sleep and wakefulness.

A few feet away the doorknob to the bathroom turned.

Regan's eyes sprang open and she jumped up and screamed. Dripping wet, she ran over and with her body barricaded the door. "Who's there? WHO'S THERE?" she screeched, her heart beating furiously.

"I'm sorry, miss," a meek woman's voice said. "Would you like some fresh towels?"

Regan exhaled sharply. "No, thank you, I'm fine."

"Would you like me to turn down your bed?"

"No, thank you, it's okay." Regan was starting to shiver.

"Would you like some chocolates for your pillow?"

Regan wanted to say "Yes, a box of Milk Duds," but resisted the urge. "No, thank you, I'm fine."

"Okay, miss, have a good evening then."

"Thank you, you too." So much for this place making me feel laid-back, Regan thought as she stepped back into the tub and slipped, grabbing the shower curtain. Two of the hooks snapped and the curtain went awry.

Three strikes, you're out, Regan thought miserably.

RICHIE PULLED ON his jacket and adjusted his tie. It was six-thirty. He picked up a bottle of the cologne from his dresser that he'd gotten from the holiday grab bag at the Fourth Quarter and sprayed it on. Normally he didn't like to wear cologne, but the ads for White Knight showed the guy who wore it to be a powerhouse driving a sexy car, with all the girls swooning over him. I wonder if it works with selling panty hose, Richie thought. He looked over at one of the many pictures of Birdie that adorned his apartment. "I don't want any swooners, honey. I just want to give off an aura in case I run into any of those panty-hose types at the hotel tonight."

In the mirror Richie studied his reflection and practiced a "Hello, I'm Richard Blossom. Yes, I am the inventor of the Birdie Panty Hose. I'd love to take a meeting." He paused. "My agent?" Richie frowned. He'd have to ask Regan about that one. He peered closer at himself. Is this the guy who's going to be a hero tomorrow? he wondered. Or is this the guy who's going to let down his friends?

Richie shrugged. Hey, fella, he thought, what happened to the power of positive thinking? That and a dollar might buy you an ice cream. They were getting so close. This was it. Either he made money on the panty hose this weekend, or the old gang was going to have to break up.

"Birdie," he said and picked up the picture of her wearing a French beret and standing in front of the Eiffel Tower under a drizzly sky. "I need your help, honey." Briefly he got mad at her. "If you hadn't died, I would never have moved in here and gotten so attached. And now we might lose it and I'll end up alone again." As Birdie stared back at him with her crooked smile, Richie felt ashamed. "I'm sorry," he whispered. "I guess our joke that we'd both keel over at the same old age from driving each other nuts was just a dream." He carefully replaced her picture on the antique oak dresser.

I've got to get moving, he thought. Regan's going to be here in a few minutes. He gathered up his wallet and ran a comb through the hair on the sides of his head. This'll be fun tonight. Little Maura getting married and I've hardly given it a thought. Well, if everything turns out, I'll get them an extra-special present.

The box of panty hose was by the front door. He glanced at it as he got out his keys and locked the door behind him. He'd wait outside on a bench chair for Regan. He just wished that she'd stop being such a worrywart.

L UKE AND NORA had the news on in their room as
they dressed for dinner. But every two minutes Nora
pressed the mute button on the remote control and answered the phone. It was obviously the hour when people had gone back to their rooms to get ready for the
evening and they had found their invitations to the cocktail party and fashion show waiting for them.

The acceptances were rolling in.

Nora kept a list by the phone and checked off the
names as they called.

"Honey," Luke said, "why don't you finish getting
dressed? I'm all ready. I'll answer the phone."

"Thanks, dear," Nora said, "but you've been busy
all day. Just sit and watch the news."

"I haven't heard one story all the way through anyway," he said wryly as the phone rang and Nora pressed the mute button again.

"Well, okay," Nora said as she handed him her pen and the remote control and disappeared into the bathroom.

"Hello," Luke's deep voice boomed. "Yes, this is Nora Regan Reilly's room. No, we won't be selling books at the party tomorrow. I believe there are some on sale in the lobby store . . . they're all sold out? I'm sorry. Maybe in town you could pick one up . . . no, I don't know the name of the nearest bookstore . . . your name? Thank you. See you tomorrow." He hung up the phone as Nora came out of the bathroom.

"This party is doing wonders for your royalty statements."

"It's supposed to sell panty hose, not books," Nora said as she slipped into her heels.

The phone rang again.

"You can get it if you want," Luke sighed. "There's a commercial on that looks very interesting."

Nora laughed. "Hello . . . yes, this is the place to call about the party . . . Ruth Craddock . . . I'm happy you can make it, Ruth . . . yes, lots of people are coming . . . hello? . . . hello?" Nora hung up the phone. "She was in an awful hurry to get off the phone."

"She's got the right idea," Luke mumbled. "Before it rings again, let's get out of here."

"I just have to check my face," Nora said.

"It's still there," Luke assured her.

"Oh, I almost forgot! I've got to wear Richie's panty

hose!'' Nora quickly pulled them out of the drawer. ''Do you want to start downstairs?''

''No, I'll wait for you,'' Luke said as he settled back on the bed. ''*Gone With the Wind* is just starting on The Movie Channel, and I've never seen it all the way through.''

RUTH SAT TWITCHING at the desk in the Calla-Lily suite. She was right, as usual. She had just hung up after being told that lots of people were going to the cocktail party tomorrow. Great. Just great.

"Ethel!" she screamed.

Ethel peered around the corner of the kitchenette where she was making a cup of tea for herself. Today had been such a bad day that she'd only had time for a couple of cups. She hadn't dared ask for her afternoon break. That was always when she liked to sip her tea, have a brownie, and read the paper. And now they were into the dinner hour and Ethel knew better than to ask if she could go home. "Yes, Ruth," she said.

"Ethel, I'm out of cigarettes!"

"Right here, Ruth." Ethel pulled open the refrigerator, which she had stocked with cartons of Ruth's brand. If there was anything worse than Ruth in a bad mood, it was Ruth in a bad mood and going through nicotine withdrawal. If I don't have a heart attack working for her, Ethel thought as she opened the carton and retrieved a pack, her secondhand smoke will definitely kill me.

Ethel threw the cellophane in the garbage. It's not hard to figure out why they pay me so well, she thought. But if I won the lottery this minute, I'd be out of here so fast her head would spin, and Ruthless would be on her hands and knees picking up these cigarettes off the floor. And then, Ethel thought, I'd have lots of free time to spend with my grandchildren.

With a longing look at her cup of tea, she went into the living room. "Here you go, Ruth," Ethel said, trying to sound gracious.

"Thank you, Ethel," Ruth rasped. As she lit her cigarette, Ruth's mouth movements reminded Ethel of a baby getting a good hold on its pacifier after it had been lost.

"From now on, Ethel," Ruth pronounced as she exhaled, "whenever anyone from Calla-Lily goes on vacation, they have to wear a beeper."

"Umm-hmmmm. Good idea, Ruth," Ethel said.

"That way we'll never run into this trouble again. If, of course, we're still in business!" Ruth started to shake. "I would just be so happy if Irving found something wrong with those panty hose. It'd be such a relief, I'd feel like a new person."

I doubt I'd mistake you for Mother Teresa, Ethel thought.

"Now," Ruth said, "all the board members know that they're to meet here early tomorrow morning, do they not?"

Ethel nodded vehemently. "Everyone knows, except, of course," she hesitated, "the one we haven't been able to locate."

A low growl emanated from Ruth's throat. "Jungle Jim. They're still working on finding him, aren't they?"

"Yes. They're going to call as soon as there's any news."

"We have the cashier's check ready just in case?"

"It's all taken care of. Five million dollars."

Ruth grimaced. "And the papers have been drawn up so we can make a deal with this Blossom guy?"

"They're all ready to be signed. If the board agrees to it, you're all set to hand over the five million dollars and—"

"ALL RIGHT, Ethel." Ruth paused to collect herself. "Irving is in the lab, where I trust he will remain for the rest of the night, testing and retesting these indestructible panty hose, these pieces of fabric that could ruin my life. If he finds a way to snag them, my prayers will be answered."

Who do you pray to? Ethel wondered.

"And if he doesn't, we have to be the ones to take control of them. I've got to get downstairs to the rubber-chicken dinner. Just what I really feel like having. A lot of small talk when I have other things to think about. I trust you will remain here awaiting word as to the whereabouts of our overgrown Boy Scout."

Ethel managed a smile. "I'll be here."

"Good. I know it's late. You can turn on the television if you'd like."

"Thank you, Ruth."

"No problem, Ethel." Ruth started to leave when Ethel suddenly remembered.

"Oh, Ruth. One more thing. While you were on the other line, Barney Freize called. He's looking for his money."

Ruth swung around, her eyes bulging. "You call Barney and tell him we'll have his commission check of forty-five thousand dollars as soon as we know if the panty hose is good. He's already gotten five thousand dollars for letting us have first crack at it."

"But—" Ethel protested.

"No buts! Just do it!" Ruth slammed the door behind her.

In my own sweet time, Ethel thought indignantly as she picked up the hotel television guide.

AT FIVE MINUTES past seven, Regan and Richie's taxi pulled up in front of the Watergreen Hotel. A doorman rushed over to let them out.

"Welcome to the Watergreen."

"Thank you," Regan said as she got out behind Richie. Two well-dressed couples were waiting to hop in.

"Where are you going to?" the doorman asked them.

"Joe's Stone Crab," one of the women said excitedly.

"I hope you've got a reservation," he replied and leaned over to tell the cabbie.

"We're not a bunch of hicks," Regan heard one of the men mumble.

Regan pushed through the revolving doors of the hotel, with Richie following. They stepped into a dazzling lobby with bright green-and-white-checked carpeting, numerous plants, and a miniature waterfall on a side wall. The registration desk was to the left. Across the way was a sunken area with a large circular bar, and tables and chairs that had a great view of the pools outside and the beach that lay beyond. The whole effect was festive.

Regan spotted Maura and John seated by themselves. She and Richie hurried over.

"How's the blushing bride?" Regan asked as they all kissed hello.

"On my third nervous breakdown," Maura replied.

"Fourth," John corrected. "Here, have a seat. No one else has shown up yet."

Regan and Richie sat down and the waiter hurried over. Richie ordered an old-fashioned and Regan decided to have a mai-tai.

"Yours looks so good," she said to Maura.

"It's so good I'm already on my second."

"Your hair looks nice," Regan said.

"You think so? It's a wig."

"It is not," Regan said flatly with a half-smile.

"I know. But I'm beginning to think that's the way to go."

"Don't laugh," Richie said. "Poor Birdie tried one of those home permanents a few days before we got married. It looked like someone came up behind her and scared her real bad. She couldn't stop crying. God love her. I told her not to worry, it'd all be okay. But I must say I was relieved when it grew out about a year later."

"Uncle Richie, did she wear a wig at your wedding?" Maura asked.

"She wanted to, but her mother thought it was sacrilegious. I know. Go figure." Richie helped himself to peanuts.

"So, John," Regan said, "do you have any cute single friends who are going to be at the wedding?"

John's face, handsome with its sparkling Irish eyes and strong features framed by curly blond hair, settled into a frown. "Now, let me think . . ."

"That means no," Maura pronounced.

"What about Kyle?" John protested.

"Kyle?" Maura gasped. "I'm not setting up one of my oldest and best friends with Kyle. He's a pathological liar."

John nodded his head. "That's true. But other than that, he's a really nice guy."

Maura turned to Regan. "We used to double-date with him until I couldn't take it anymore. One night we'd be with one girl who'd be telling me all about her and Kyle's plans for the future. The next night there'd be someone else he was leading on. I couldn't stand it because I wanted to tell them, but John would have killed me."

"Gee, I can't wait to meet him," Regan retorted. "Oh, look, here come my parents."

Nora and Luke hurried over from the elevator bank and greeted everyone.

"Good news, Richie," Nora said as they sat down. "We're getting lots of responses for the party."

"Oh, that's great, Nora. A lot of people, huh?"

"Believe me, a lot of people," Luke testified.

Nora patted Maura's hand. "And the big day is almost here."

"That it is. You're coming to the luncheon tomorrow, aren't you?"

"Absolutely. The fashion show isn't until three o'clock. What time does the rehearsal dinner start?"

"Drinks at seven."

Regan laughed. "I've got some good stories for the toasts."

"That's what I'm afraid of," Maura groaned.

"Spring break in college. I came down to visit you. What was that guy's name again? The one who gave you his college ring five minutes after you met him at that bar in Fort Lauderdale?"

"REGAN!"

"Their whole relationship lasted about an hour and a half. Irreconcilable differences."

"I didn't hear about this one," John observed.

"That's because no one counted until I met you," Maura said, her voice dripping with sweetness.

"Thank God you broke off the engagement to that other guy a few years ago," Richie pronounced as he munched on more peanuts. "He was all wrong for you."

"I knew we should have eloped. Let's change the subject," Maura pleaded.

John put his arm around her. "We have no secrets, honey." He turned to Regan. "What else can you tell me?"

"Did she ever mention the guy who gave her a set of

jumper cables for Christmas? The worst part was that they weren't even wrapped.''

"He also gave her a set of windshield wipers," Richie offered.

"Oh yes," Regan chuckled, "he was a hopeless romantic.''

Maura hit John's knee. "I can't wait to get a couple of your friends contributing to the storytelling.''

"Now, now," Nora said. "Let's not pick on Maura.''

"We'll have plenty of time for that tomorrow night," Regan agreed.

The waiter came by and Luke and Nora ordered their drinks.

"Maura, what kind of music are you going to have at the reception?" Nora asked.

"Elevator music, if my mother has her way.''

"At least nobody will start to sweat when they dance," Regan offered.

"Actually," Maura began, "we've hired a band that plays all kinds of music. Or so they say. My mother's afraid that when they start playing rock and roll they'll blast the place out, so she's begging them to leave their amplifiers at home.''

"Speaking of amplifiers," Regan said, "we need to figure out what we're going to use for a sound system for the fashion show.''

"We just got a set of pots and pans you can borrow," Maura offered.

"We'll have to save those for New Year's Eve," Regan said.

The waiter appeared and deposited Luke's and Nora's drinks on the table. "Excuse me," Nora said, "do you know if the manager, Mr. Fargus, is still here?"

"I'll check for you, ma'am."

"Nick Fargus?" Maura said. "He helped us plan the reception. He's definitely a little weird."

Luke chuckled.

Nora looked at him.

"I know, Dad," Regan said. "Mom was looking to fix me up with him, right?"

"I didn't say a word," Luke said as he put up his hands.

"He is a lovely young man," Nora insisted.

Within minutes, Nick was scurrying over to the table, checking for dust buildup on the brass railings along his way.

"Hello, hello, hello, everyone. Hello, Maura. Hello, John. Hello, Mrs. Reilly. Hello, Mr. Reilly."

"Hello, Nick," Nora said. "I'd like you to meet my daughter, Regan—"

"Oh, nice to meet you, Regan. I thought you were one of the models for the fashion show tomorrow."

"No, no. I'm just helping Richie get the show organized. This is Richie Blossom."

"Regan is one of my bridesmaids," Maura said gleefully as Nick and Richie shook hands. "And we were just saying that there aren't enough eligible guys to dance with at the wedding. I do hope you'll stop by and take Regan for a spin on the floor."

"Hey, that's my job! Make everybody happy."

"Thank you," Regan said. "Yes, thank you very

much.'' I'll get you for this, Maura, she thought. "Do you have a stereo system?"

"A what?"

"A stereo system. We need music for the fashion show."

Nick snapped his fingers. "You know something? I don't. I've been meaning to buy a CD player, but I've been so darn busy. I knew I should have just gone out and gotten one. I wanted to read *Consumers Digest* to find out which was the best one to get, and now it's tomorrow—" His voice trailed off mournfully.

"Don't worry," Regan said as she unconsciously patted his shoulder.

"You still want to have the fashion show, don't you?" Nick asked.

"Of course," Regan said. "If I can get ahold of a friend of mine who is a stereo salesman and knows all about which one to buy, would you be interested in making a quick purchase tomorrow morning?"

Nick nodded. "You bet."

"Good." Now, I hope I have Nadine's number with me, Regan thought.

NADINE AND JOEY were enjoying a cold beer on the patio in his backyard when the phone rang.

"Why don't you let the machine pick it up?" Nadine asked as she curled her toes around the braiding of the chaise longue.

"It might be the office." Joey hurried into the kitchen.

A minute later he was yelling out the kitchen window, "Nay, it's for you."

"For me?"

"It's Regan."

"Regan?"

"Do I hear an echo?" Joey asked.

"Wiseass," Nadine said as she pulled herself out of the chair. "I don't know why they don't get a cordless phone for this house," she mumbled, "a little static in your ear never hurt anybody."

The screen door slammed behind her as she took the phone from Joey. "Hey, Regan, what's up?"

Nadine listened as Regan explained to her about the fashion show and the urgent need for a compact disc player.

"You're not going to believe this, Regan, but today I met a woman who claims she was wearing this run-proof panty hose. It was really nice."

"Where did she get it?" Regan asked.

"Her son is an engineer and he's testing it for his company to possibly buy. Oh, hi."

"What?" Regan said.

"Sorry, one of Joey's roommates just walked in. Anyway, we were both getting a manicure and I knocked into this woman's leg with my wet nails. The polish wiped right off. Your friend Richie could make a lot of money on those stockings if they're as good as they seem. I'd buy ten pairs."

"That's what we're hoping," Regan said, "which of course comes back to the need for the compact disc player. Can you recommend a particular kind? This guy Nick wants to run out and buy one tomorrow morning."

"It depends on how much he wants to spend," Nadine said. "Some people drive me crazy coming in and out of the store a hundred times, checking every last detail of every system, down to the color of the plug. I know they're really running around wasting gas comparing prices all over town. What's this guy like, anyway?"

"Ohhhhh, he's nice," Regan said haltingly.

"Nice means uh-oh," Nadine said as she sat down on one of the vinyl kitchen chairs whose stuffing was popping out in the back. "Before I met Joey, when someone tried to fix me up, if they started out by saying 'Well, he's nice,' you knew that was the kiss of death."

Regan laughed. "My mother thinks he's a lovely young man."

"Enough said. Wait a minute, how did your mother meet him?"

"She and my father are down here for a convention and for the wedding. She's hosting the cocktail party before the fashion show."

"Cool. Regan, I can tell you a lot of things to look for in a CD system, but it's probably better if I go shopping with him. Hold on. Joey, are you going to work in the morning?"

"For a couple of hours."

"Regan, if he wants, I can go with him in the morning."

"Nadine, that would be really nice of you. Are you sure?"

"Yeah. Besides, Joey and I can go to the beach tomorrow afternoon."

"You're certainly welcome to come to the cocktail party and fashion show."

"That might be fun. Old Nick'll probably need help setting up the CD player in his apartment anyway."

"I'm sure. I'd come shopping with you, but the bridesmaids are getting together at eleven A.M. for a luncheon. But I can meet you here at the hotel afterward."

"That's fine. Why don't you come over for a beer later? We're just going to cook some food and hang out with some of Joey's friends and his roommates."

"I probably won't get finished here until ten," Regan said. "Is that too late?"

"Are you kidding? In this part of town, the night hasn't even started yet."

"True. Give me your address."

After Nadine gave Regan the address, they agreed that Regan would have Nick call Nadine directly to set up their shopping date for the next morning.

"He's with our group right now," Regan said, "we're about to go in for dinner. I'll have him call you right away."

"I'll be here. By the way, Regan, do you have a boyfriend?"

"Why are you asking me that, Nadine?"

"Because I've got a guy here who you should meet."

"Only if he's really nice. Bye, Nadine."

"Bye, Regan."

BARNEY FREIZE WAS more than a little annoyed that Ruth Craddock didn't have the decency to call him back after he had been good enough to introduce her to the Birdie Panty Hose and very possibly save her company's ass. Barney paced around his little den. "It takes nerve, that's what it takes, it takes nerve," he said to the air. He pulled open the sliding glass doors that opened onto his tiny backyard and breathed in the pungent scent of the citrus trees. "Be calm, Barn, be calm," he said to himself but felt his anger rising.

Here he was hanging, waiting for a callback from the queen of the cotton crotch. Three times today the secretary had told him, "Sorry, sir, but she's in a meeting." Yeah, and I'm the Tooth Fairy, he thought.

I didn't have to go to Calla-Lily with the Birdie Panty Hose. I could just as easily have hopped a plane to North Carolina, where so many of the other panty-hose companies are located, and let one of them in on the big secret. He'd worked back there years ago and could have gotten in to see the big shots. If they had seen it, felt it, worn it, they would have known it was good. You can't believe what you read in a letter, especially from some dodo like Richie.

The other day over at Calla-Lily Ruth had told him that the tests were all positive, but they still weren't sure. For God's sake, the panty-hose convention is going on right now. Was she going to try and stiff him out of his big fee? She'd better not.

Barney walked into the kitchen and pulled open the refrigerator. This is all thanks to my nephew Danny, he thought. Danny had volunteered to get him in to see Ruth when Barney had told him, in deepest confidence, about the panty hose. It had all been so easy, it was almost surprising.

But Danny was doing the yard work for her at Casa Panty Hose. He dealt directly with Ruth. She was just getting rid of another husband. Maybe Danny had talked to her today and knew what was going on.

I'll call him, Barney thought. He shut the refrigerator door, picked up the phone and dialed his nephew's number. Danny's machine picked up. "Hi, this is Danny. I'm not home right now but if you leave your name and number . . ." It figures, Barney thought. What twenty-five-year-old kid is going to be home on a Friday night? Especially a good-looking kid like Danny.

"Danny, this is Uncle Barney. Give me a call, would you? It's important."

Barney hung up the phone. I'll probably hear back from him in another three days, he thought.

Now what am I going to do about dinner? I'll light a cigar first, that's what I'll do.

Barney went back to his cozy little den and sat down in his favorite place, a recliner chair that went back just far enough so that he could comfortably doze off watching television without waking up with a stiff neck. He opened the cigar box he had situated within arm's reach of this perch and pulled out a brand-new White Owl, sniffing it appreciatively. This would relax him. Alone and free with his cigar, and no one around to chase him outside to smoke it, like his ex-wife used to do. Of course she never minded the smell of cigar smoke when they were dating, but once they got married, boom, that was it. No cigar smoking in the house. He'd had about all he was going to take of that. This little room stank of cigar smoke, and he loved every whiff.

Barney held the lighter he had found on the beach under his cigar and watched it flicker as he inhaled. The whole ritual had a religious feel to it. When the cigar was finally lit, he pushed back in his seat, stretching out his legs on the footrest attached to his La-Z-Boy, which obediently appeared and disappeared at Barney's will. Whoever said a man's home was his castle was no idiot, Barney thought.

As he puffed, he listened to the sounds of the night in his backyard. The insects, an occasional plane flying by, the rustle of the breeze.

I could use the money, he thought. Another $45,000 if those panty hose are the real thing. And it looks like they are.

I'll enjoy my cigar for a little while, I'll make myself some dinner, and I'll wait for my callback. If I don't get it, he thought, I'll just have to figure out how to handle that Ruth Craddock.

JUDD GREEN SAT at a table in one of the dining rooms of the Watergreen Hotel. The group he'd been watching had just settled at a large table nearby. He'd made sure his table was close enough to theirs for good viewing and eavesdropping.

Regan Reilly, the girl who was Richie Blossom's shadow, was making an announcement. He strained to listen.

"Good news, Richie," Regan said as the waiter ceremoniously fluffed her napkin and placed it on her lap. She nodded her thanks as she continued. "I just talked to my friend Nadine. She bumped into someone today at a nail salon who was wearing what sounds like your Birdie Panty Hose. She says they're great. Her son-in-law is an engineer for a panty hose company that might be interested in buying them. He's in charge of testing them.''

"All right, Richie," Ed Durkin cheered. "We'll have a double celebration this weekend."

Richie jumped up. "What company does this guy work for? How did he get my panty hose?"

"Richie, you have given a lot of pairs away," Regan said.

"But just to my friends," Richie told her.

"You do have patent protection, don't you?" Regan asked, alarmed.

"Oh, sure."

"Then you don't have to worry. I'm going to see Nadine later. I'll find out what she knows, if anything, about the company testing it."

"Oh, God, I don't believe it!" Richie said exuberantly. He held up his water glass. "I propose a toast to Birdie's legs and Birdie's legacy."

Regan felt a sudden worry. "Richie," she warned, "we better not count our chickens before they're hatched. This is a good sign, but until you've received and accepted an offer, anything can go wrong."

"Regan, you're a worrywart. If this company doesn't come through, another one will." Richie's smile faded. A concerned frown creased his forehead. "Of course if they don't come through this weekend, it'll be too late for the Fourth Quarter."

"Don't think about that, Richie," Nora said soothingly. "We're going to give the best cocktail party this place has ever seen. We'll end up with a bidding war." She held out her leg and gave it a quick swing. "I love your panty hose."

Maura's mother, Bridget, agreed. "I love them too. I'm wearing them now. And Richie gave me a pair that perfectly matches my mother-of-the bride dress."

"Is that the same dress you were going to wear to Maura's wedding two years ago?" Regan asked sweetly.

"No. She put it in long-term storage for your mother, Regan," Maura said.

"Touché," Regan grinned.

"Seriously, Richie," Nora said, "they are lovely. If I owned a hosiery company, I wouldn't want to be competing in the marketplace with the Birdie Panty Hose. These are so good they could easily put everyone else out of business. If some company is testing them and realizes how good they are, and knows you're going to be showing them off tomorrow, you might get an offer before the fashion show."

"Provided it's Richie's panty hose they're testing," Luke warned.

"Of course," Nora agreed.

"At least we don't have to worry about *our* business, right, Luke?" Ed asked. "The only things you can be sure of in this world are—"

"Death and taxes," the whole group said aloud, having heard this proverb from Ed at least a hundred times before.

Maura and Regan exchanged looks before Maura turned to John. "Now you know why my brother's an accountant."

They ordered drinks and while they were sipping, the captain appeared to announce the specials.

"My favorite for tonight," he began as he kissed his fingers, "is"—he kissed them again—"frogs' legs!"

"That's a sign from Birdie," Richie announced, beaming.

A few tables away the solitary diner, Judd Green, ordered his dinner mechanically. From the sounds of it, things were coming to a head sooner than they had expected. There wasn't much time left.

When the conversation at the large table turned to talk about a wedding, he no longer paid close attention.

Regan Reilly was going to visit a friend tonight. It sounded as though she or someone else would drop Richie Blossom off at the Fourth Quarter. He'd tipped the valet to leave his car right out on the street in front of the hotel. He had to be ready to move as soon as he saw which car Richie Blossom got into.

Hurriedly he picked at his dinner and ordered coffee. It might be a long night.

When the coffee came, he asked for his check.

"Certainly," the waiter said cheerfully as he poured the steaming brew into his cup and was bumped from behind by a busboy. A few drops of coffee spattered onto Green's scraped hand. He yanked his hand back, cursing.

"I'm so sorry, Mr. Evans," the waiter stammered.

With difficulty Green calmed himself. The waiter had raised his voice and he sensed other diners were glancing at them. He did not want to attract attention.

"That hand looks nasty," the waiter continued. "That's some scrape you've got there."

"It's all right," he said testily. "Just get me my check, please."

"How about a drink on the house?" The waiter was determined to make amends.

For the third time Judd Green, aka Lowell Evans, requested his check.

"Right away, right away." The waiter hurried off.

When Judd Green finally signed his check, he noticed that Richie Blossom and his group were ordering dessert. He was outside waiting in his car when they emerged half an hour later.

A MILD BURP escaped from Ethel's lips as she folded up her napkin. That was mighty good, she thought. Nibbling on a bread crumb that had escaped previous detection, she surveyed the table that room service had wheeled in with her dinner. A single rose in a crystal vase was surrounded by the remains of shrimp cocktail, steak au poivre, pommes frites, and zucchini squash. Her salad plate contained microscopic traces of arugula and endive. A half bottle of wine had been emptied and the tricolor sherbet was a memory. Ethel made one final attempt to shake more liquid from the coffee pot and was rewarded with a few precious drops.

Maybe Ruth is eating rubber chicken, she gloated, but not me. If I have to stay and mind the store, then the store has to buy me dinner. Ruth knew I had to eat but, sorry, boss, McDonald's doesn't deliver.

Ethel stood up. No use flaunting it. I better get this table out of here before Ruth figures out what I ordered. And I'll open the window so she doesn't smell the steak.

Ethel glanced at her watch. They should be on the banquet speeches by now, she thought happily, knowing how much Ruth hated them. Ethel hoped the president of the National Panty-Hose Association dragged out that same old speech about the history of limb coverings. That was a real snore. She giggled to herself. Is it because I'm getting older that I'm having these nasty thoughts and feel free to enjoy them? Is it that all these torturous years of working for Ruth have finally hit me? Or, Ethel thought naughtily, could it be this delicious bottle of expensive wine?

As she opened the window, the phone began to ring. "Cominggg," she sang.

"Hello. Calla-Lily."

A male voice spoke from what sounded like a black hole. "This is the search party for Preston Landers. Is Ruth Craddock there?"

"No, this is Ethel."

"Oh, hi, Ethel."

"Well, how's it going?" she asked.

"We've got good news and bad news."

Ethel sat on the couch, wishing it had all been bad news. "Well, what's the bad news?"

"Most people want to hear the good news first."

"Suit yourself."

"Okay. The good news is that we're closing in on him. He's still in Colorado somewhere. His team picked up supplies at the outpost we're at now just a few hours ago. The bad news is we've got to call off the search until the crack of dawn."

"It all sounds so exciting," Ethel remarked.

"You betcha. Pass the word along that we intend to get him back there in time for Ms. Craddock's important meeting."

"The meeting starts at seven A.M. tomorrow morning."

"I didn't say he'd be on time. But we'll get him there."

"I'll let her know. Good luck." He should be wishing me good luck, Ethel thought.

"You betcha. Have a good night now." The line was disconnected.

"Over and out," Ethel said as she hung up the phone. After a moment she picked it up again and dialed room service. "Could you please come and collect my dinner cart as soon as possible? . . . Yes, everything was more than satisfactory. I can't wait to order breakfast . . . no, I'm just kidding, I'm not staying here . . . thank you."

Ethel suddenly jumped up. I never called that Freize guy. She hurried over to the desk where she had jotted down his number. Quickly she dialed. He answered almost immediately.

"Mr. Freize, this is Ruth Craddock's secretary, Ethel . . . Yes, I know it's taken a while to get back to you, but Ms. Craddock asked me to call you and tell you that you can come by tomorrow morning. That's when we'll finally know if the panty hose will be purchased. If so, we'll give you the check.''

At the other end of the phone, Barney sighed. ''To tell you the truth, I didn't think she was going to pay me.''

''Ohhh,'' Ethel clucked, ''she's been rather preoccupied.''

The doorbell to the suite rang. ''Hold on, Mr. Freize.''

Ethel opened the door to the smiling room-service attendant, who hurried in and efficiently disassembled the sides of the table. ''Looks as if you enjoyed your meal, ma'am.''

''No use feeding the garbage can,'' Ethel replied.

''That's certainly right. Now, if you'd like anything else, just give us a call. We're open twenty-four hours.''

''I need my job.''

''Excuse me?''

''Never mind. Good night.''

''Good night, now.'' He opened the door and Ethel watched the last vestiges of her dinner disappear around the corner.

''Mr. Freize . . .''

''I'm here.''

The phone in the bedroom where Ruth was staying began to ring. Oh, dear, Ethel thought. That might be the search party calling back on the other line because this one is busy. ''Mr. Freize, could you please hold on?''

''Why not?''

"Thank you." Ethel hurried into Ruth's bedroom, where the phone was insistently ringing. She dived for it before voice mail picked it up. "Hello," she gasped.

"Ruthy Wuthy," a young male voice cooed, "you sound sooo tiiii-ruddd."

Ethel sat up on the bed. "This isn't Ruthy—ahh—I mean Ruth. This is Ethel. Who may I ask is calling?"

The caller hung up so fast, Ethel blinked. Well, Ethel thought wickedly, what shall I tell Ruthy Wuthy when she asks if there were any calls? She shrugged and hurried back to Barney.

"Mr. Freize?"

"I'm here."

"I'm so sorry. Things are so hectic around here."

Barney hesitated and then decided to go for it. She had kept him waiting several times now. "Ethel," he began, "do you get any intimation as to whether the sale of the panty-hose patent to Calla-Lily will go through? I mean, you're right there in the thick of things."

You're not kidding, Ethel thought, but she straightened up and said, "I'm sorry, Mr. Freize, but I am not at liberty to discuss the matter. I was just told to tell you that we'll know tomorrow."

"You'll be seeing me then."

For the third time in ten minutes, Ethel wasn't given the chance to bid adieu to her gentlemen callers.

IRVING FRANKLIN SAT at the head of his dining-room table sipping his after-dinner tea as he listened to his mother-in-law's incessant chatter.

"Fern," she was saying as she held out her manicured hands to her daughter, "do you like this color? I don't know . . . I think there might be too much brown in it. When I had my colors done last year, they said I should stay away from brown."

"They look nice, Mother," Fern said wearily.

"Yeah, well, I'm not sure. Tammy's not here, so I can't ask her. What do you think, Irving?"

Irving put down his teacup. Deep down he wanted to say that he couldn't care less, but he caught the pleading look in his wife's eyes. "I think it's a very flattering shade, Mom."

He hated to call her Mom. It made him feel disloyal to his own dear departed mother, but it had started years ago when Fern's sister's husband decided to call her Mom. Easy for him. He didn't have to live with her. But most of the time Irving avoided the problem by not addressing her at all. He threw it in now to please Fern, who smiled back at him gratefully.

"Maybe next week I'll try a different shade. I don't know. Are you two going to a movie tonight?"

"Irving still has work to do," Fern answered softly.

"More work? You're always poking around downstairs in that lab of yours. It's Friday night."

"The panty-hose tests must be completed by tomorrow morning," Irving said with a steely grin.

"I was telling the girls at the nail salon about them today. I said how wonderful they are."

"We're not supposed to talk about them, remember?" Irving asked, his voice going up ever so slightly.

"Mom" looked at him sourly. "Well, I can tell you another test they passed, if it'll make you happy. The girl next to me smeared her polish on them accidentally and it wiped right off."

"It did?"

"That's right," she said smugly. "I bet you never thought of that test in that dungeon of yours."

Irving pushed back his chair. "All my *laboratory* tests are not complete. I'm still trying to break down the ingredients of the fabric. I personally believe there's got to be something wrong with those panty hose and," he paused, "I intend to find out just what it is." He kissed his wife on the top of her head. "Fern darling, let me know if you need me."

As he closed the basement door behind him he happily shut out the sound of "There was another color that had a little more red in it that I think would have been better, but . . ."

"THAT WAS REALLY fun, wasn't it, hon?" Nora asked as she and Luke stepped off the elevator.

"We always have a good time with the Durkins, don't we?" Luke agreed. "I'm looking forward to the wedding on Sunday. By then we'll be through with the fashion show and all my meetings . . . we can really let loose." He put his arm around Nora, grabbed her hand, and danced with her down the hallway.

"One-two-three, one-two-three, one-two-three," Luke sang.

"Oh, my," Nora laughed as they reached the door. "When Regan gets married, we'll have to—"

"Nora!" Luke admonished.

"I'm sorry. I couldn't help it but I was just thinking . . ."

Luke opened the door. "One wedding at a time. This one is Maura's." He pointed to the room. "After you, my dear."

Nora sighed. "Okay. Let's see if we got any more messages about the fashion show."

"I can't wait," Luke drawled.

Nora went over and picked up the phone. An electronic voice told her that they had received ten messages. She sat down and started to write them down as they played back. The first nine were from people RSVP-ing to the cocktail party. They'd all be happy to come. The tenth message started to play in Nora's ear.

A well-modulated voice said, "Hello, Mrs. Reilly; my name is Dayton Rotter. I met some of the models who will be in your fashion show tomorrow. Technically I'm down here from New York City for a few days' vacation, but I'm a venture capitalist and we're never really off." He laughed. "This panty hose sounds intriguing, and I was wondering if I could come by your cocktail party tomorrow." Nora scribbled down his number.

"Luke, you're not going to believe this!" she exclaimed.

"What?" Luke asked as he hung up his jacket and loosened his tie.

"Dayton Rotter wants to come to the cocktail party!"

"*The* Dayton Rotter?"

"It sounds like him. It must be him. He met some of the models and wants to check out the panty hose."

Luke whistled. "He's big. That could be just what Richie needs. Did he leave a number?"

"Yes."

"Well, call him back."

"I am, I am."

Nora dialed the number and sat tapping the desk with her pen. When a man's voice answered the phone, it sounded as though he was in a crowded bar.

"This is Nora Regan Reilly. Is Dayton Rotter there?"

"It's me," he said. "Sorry about the noise. I'm at a club right now. I've got my cellular phone with me."

Surprise, surprise, Nora thought.

"I got your message," she said, "and we'd be delighted if you came to the party tomorrow. We really think that this panty hose is something special."

Luke smiled at her and raised his eyebrows.

Nora strained to hear Dayton's voice and separate it from the blare of the music in the background.

"That's great," Dayton almost yelled. "I'd very much like to be there. Quite frankly, if the product is as good as the young ladies say it is, I'd be very interested in developing it. After all, my business is to find good ideas and run with them. By the way, I like your books."

Nora smiled broadly. "Oh, thank you. We'll see you tomorrow then."

"He likes your books?" Luke asked when Nora hung up.

"You do know me, don't you?"

"After thirty-five years, I would hope so. We'll have to spread the word that he's coming. The sight of that guy will get people bidding." Luke sat on the bed and untied his shoes.

"I'll call Nick in the morning. And Richie and Regan. Oh, Luke, I really hope this works out. It would make for such a perfect weekend."

Luke got up and walked toward the bathroom. "That and if Regan catches the bouquet on Sunday," he said as he closed the door just in time to avoid being hit by his wife's airborne terry-cloth slipper.

L UCILLE LEANED BACK on the pillows of her sister Dolly's bed as she talked on the rotary phone to her friend Arthur. She had just come upstairs after having a potluck dinner in the Dolly Twiggs Memorial Room.

"The service was so, so lovely, Arthur. I wish you could have been there. Everyone here just loved Dolly. We all broke bread together afterward." She paused. "What did you have for dinner, dear?"

A second later Lucille bolted upright on the bed. "What do you mean, Mildred brought over a tuna casserole? I left you plenty of frozen food you could have heated in the microwave . . . She says fresh food is better, does she? . . ."

Lucille felt herself begin to hyperventilate as she listened to Arthur tell her how delicious Mildred's casserole really was; not too fishy, just right. But when he started to suggest that she should give the folks at the Fourth Quarter an extension, she really began to have an out-of-body experience.

She swallowed hard. "Arthur, I can't afford to give them an extension. I get so depressed when I'm here." Tears filled her eyes. "I just want to get back home."

As she listened, the tears spilled down her cheeks. "Oh, I love you too, sweetness. I know you were just trying to be helpful. I miss you too." She covered the mouthpiece and sniffled. "I'll be home in time for your birthday next week. I already know what kind of cake I'm going to make you . . . Mildred's offered to have a party for you?! You didn't say yes, did you? . . . You told her you'd check with me? Tell her the answer is no, you've already got plans."

Five minutes later, when she hung up the phone, Lucille stuck out her jaw. Business is business, she thought. If I don't get home soon, Arthur will slip through my fingers. In their retirement village there must be ten women for every man, and he was the most handsome man left, not to mention the healthiest.

Lucille stood up. I need some air, she thought. After that conversation, I certainly don't feel sleepy. I'll go downstairs and watch the weirdos wander by.

Outside, Lucille flipped open a beach chair and sat down. No one else from the Fourth Quarter was around. But it was a Friday night and the street was buzzing.

Singles, couples, groups passed by. One outfit is

skimpier than the next, Lucille thought. Don't they ever catch a cold?

A taxi pulled up and stopped. The door opened. Richie got out and Lucille heard him say, "Yes, I'm going to stay home. I'll talk to you in the morning." He turned around and waved to Lucille as he walked up the sidewalk.

"You're out here by yourself? Where is everybody?"

"I think there's a program they wanted to watch tonight."

"Mind if I join you?" Richie asked.

"Of course not. This is your place."

"Let's hope so," Richie joked, but the remark hung in the air. "Are you okay, Lucille?"

Her lip quivered. "I suppose. Being here is hard for me. I miss Dolly so much. And now I have this boyfriend Arthur, and I'm missing him too."

Richie sat down.

"Someone made him a casserole tonight," Lucille sputtered.

"Oh, God," Richie said. "Oh, God."

"Mildred is a pest and I know it shouldn't get me upset because Arthur's not interested in her." Lucille wiped her eyes. "But I'm still scared. I'm hurting from losing Dolly a year ago, and now Arthur has just started to fill that void in my heart that I've had since my husband died."

"You were married before?" Richie asked gently.

"For forty-five wonderful years."

"Birdie and I were married forty-eight years. A lot of people would say that makes us pretty lucky."

"I know that. But statistics don't help when you get lonesome."

Richie paused. "You're right. Sometimes I get tired of people telling me how lucky I was to have been happy for so long. I say, what about now?" His voice grew tight. "I wish Birdie were here right this minute; that's what counts."

"Don't I know it," Lucille declared.

"Lucille . . ."

"Yes, Richie."

"Wasn't it hard to start dating after your husband died?"

"Are you kidding me? Of course it was. I never thought I'd look at another man. But one day it just happens. You realize that your spouse would want you to be happy. And then I was lucky enough to meet Arthur."

They sat in silence for a few minutes. Finally Lucille stood up. "I'm going to try and get some rest. Tomorrow is a big day, Richie; you should get some sleep too."

"I'll just sit out here for a few more minutes."

As Lucille walked slowly inside, Richie realized that if tomorrow didn't work out, they could never ask her for an extension. She's got her own life to worry about, he thought.

The screen door swung open and Elmer Pickett stepped outside.

"Hi, Elmer," Richie said.

Elmer stood there staring down at Richie. "You know, Richie, everyone could have used the bonus money the real estate agency was willing to pay us if we gave up the option early. Of course now that you're making the commercials, you don't have to worry."

"I made one commercial, Elmer."

"Whatever. I think you're leading the people in this home down the garden path with this crazy scheme of yours. Some of them are going to end up in the street, when they could have at least left here with a few dollars."

Richie stood up and stared into Elmer's eyes. Through clenched teeth he raised his voice. "It's not a crazy scheme! And we took a vote!"

His heart beating wildly, Richie hurried down the sidewalk and hailed a taxi. I've got to get out to the panty-hose factory, he thought. I want to be around the machines and make sure I have the names of everyone in the business I wrote to. There might even be more panty hose there. Just stepping inside the cab and giving the address made him feel better.

He didn't notice that a car nearby had just pulled out of its parking space and was following him.

REGAN RANG THE bell of Joey's house. As she stood there on the porch she rubbed her neck and rolled her head from side to side. Someone had told her the exercise releases tension. She had never figured out whether that was really true, but it was a good way to pass the time.

The door was pulled open.

"Hi!"

The guy who worked at Richie's modeling agency was standing in front of her.

"Hi!" Regan said back as he let her in. "What are you doing here?"

"I live here."

"You live here?"

"Do I hear an echo?" Joey yelled from the living room.

"I'm dating a comedian," Nadine pronounced as she got up to greet Regan. "You know Scott?"

"We met today at the agency." Regan glanced at him. He seemed so much more alive than when she had met him in the office. He certainly was handsome with his wavy dark hair, warm brown eyes, and ingratiating smile.

"Yes," Scott agreed and put his arm around Regan. He explained to Nadine, "She's using some of our models tomorrow in her panty-hose fashion show."

"Small world," Nadine said as she led Regan inside. "Walking through here can be hazardous to your health. Please do so at your own risk."

Regan stepped over a set of barbells and was reminded of the fraternities at her college, especially the one they'd dubbed P.U. Sometimes it felt as though that was another lifetime ago. Being here tonight brought it back in a rush. She laughed. The whole scene made her feel ten years younger. After all, people had got along just fine before vacuums were invented.

"Scott, I didn't know you knew Regan," Nadine commented.

"I didn't know that you knew her. Regan happened to come in with one of our clients today—Richie Blossom."

"Well, I'll have you know she's working hard to save your client from losing his home. You know, the Fourth Quarter."

"I know. Richie's a great guy."

"I'm going to help them get a CD player for the fashion show. And I met someone today wearing those panty hose. They're terrific."

Scott crossed his fingers. "We're all hoping it goes well, Regan."

"Thanks."

"And I hope I'm the one who hands him the papers to sign when he buys the Fourth Quarter," Joey said.

"Nadine," Regan asked, "do you know what company that woman's son-in-law works for?"

"No. But I can call her tomorrow if you want."

The phone rang.

"You get it, Scott. It's always for you," Nadine ordered. "Regan, what would you like to drink?"

"What do you have?"

"Beer, wine, soda. We've got a whole refrigerator full of stuff in the garage."

"I'll take a quick look," Regan offered.

"I'll get it," Nadine protested.

"No, no," Regan said. "I'm not sure what I feel like having."

"Okay, right through the door there."

Regan went through the kitchen and down the two steps to the garage door. She opened it and found, if possible, a bigger mess than in the house.

Stepping outside, she nearly tripped over a pile of newspapers. She kicked them out of her way and almost knocked over a can of gas. Oh, great, she thought. I'll just move it into the corner for safety. From the looks of things, no one in this house has an anal personality that will be disturbed by this rearrangement.

From the refrigerator Regan picked out a can of club soda and walked back inside. She sat down in the living room with Nadine, Joey and Scott.

"How many people live here?" Regan asked.

"Four of us and Nadine," Joey answered.

"Since when am I not a person?" Nadine queried.

"Excuse me. Four most of the time. Five every other weekend."

"That's better. The other guys just went out to hit the clubs. And some of Joey's other friends who were supposed to come over got waylaid by some action over at a café."

"There's plenty of action out there," Regan said. She turned to Scott. "So how do you like the modeling business?"

"Huh," Nadine chortled.

Scott laughed.

"He's in hog heaven," Joey said as he twirled a pillow in the air.

"It's pretty good," Scott replied, ignoring the comments. "What kind of work do you do?"

Regan sipped her drink. "I'm a detective."

"Really?"

"Really."

"Does this room have an echo, or what?" Joey asked again.

The phone rang once more. Quickly Scott escaped to answer it.

"He gets more phone calls," Nadine confided. "All

the models are crazy about him. Can you see why, or what?''

Scott poked his head back into the room. ''That was my date. I've got to go meet her. Good luck tomorrow with the fashion show, Regan.''

''Thanks.''

Nadine looked at Joey. ''I wonder who the lucky one is tonight.''

''Who knows.''

After he was safely gone, Nadine volunteered, ''His family used to be really wealthy, but then they lost it.''

''Nadiiiine,'' Joey whined.

''That's what you told me, Joseph.''

''You're not supposed to go telling people that.''

''Regan's not going to say anything.''

''Don't worry, Joey,'' Regan said. ''Does he have any interest in modeling himself? He would probably do well.''

''Nah,'' Joey said. ''He just wants to learn the business end of it.''

Through the garage door Joey's two other roommates appeared, fresh beers in hand.

''Back so soon?'' Nadine asked.

Matt and Dennis were introduced to Regan.

''We couldn't get a parking space, so we figured forget it,'' Dennis explained. ''I'm tired anyway.''

''Well, sit down and talk to us,'' Nadine urged.

Regan drained her can of club soda.

''Would you like something else?'' Nadine asked as Matt and Dennis made themselves comfortable.

''I must be thirsty. But I'll get it.'' Regan went back

out to the garage, careful not to trip over anything this time. She pulled out another can of club soda and noticed that the red gas can was not where she had left it. I don't give these guys enough credit, she thought. One of them must have an anal personality.

RICHIE LET HIMSELF into the factory with the key he always carried with him. He turned on the one dim light that was still working. With a sense of relief he shut the door behind him and stood there in the absolute silence, staring at his machines. It was comforting just to be here, alone, away from everything.

On the cab ride over he had done nothing but go over and over in his mind the possibility that something could go wrong tomorrow. Was Elmer right? Was he a fool to try and pull this off? Would they have been smarter to have taken the incentive money and run with it?

No, Richie decided as he stood there, gaining back his sense of self. I worked too hard on this to let the good that it could bring slip away. Birdie and he had always stuck to the projects they started together, however disastrous the results. "It ain't over till it's over, right Richie?" he could hear her saying.

Richie walked over to his workbench. A couple of pairs of panty hose were draped over the side. I sure did make a lot of these, didn't I? he thought. He gathered them in his arms and held them against his cheek. A vast aching swept through him and he felt as empty and isolated as the factory. Tears stung his eyes and he made no attempt to stop them as they ran down his face. Birdie, he thought, I feel overwhelmed. He sat down and gently sobbed, feeling a release from all the pressure buildup and worry. All the work he'd done, and it would all be decided tomorrow. Even if everything turned out well, he knew it would be a letdown of sorts.

Listening to Lucille talk about getting home to her boyfriend had been especially poignant for him. I have a lot of friends, he thought as his chest heaved up and down, but I wish I had someone special who would be there all the time for me. Someone who I could take turns with getting out of bed in the morning to make the coffee, like I used to do with Birdie. Someone who would listen to my stories, however boring they got. Someone I could take care of.

Finally Richie wiped his eyes. Boy, am I a sad sack, he thought. I've come this far, I shouldn't fall down right before the finish line. I'll go over the list of names of the companies I wrote to. I want to recognize the people's names if they come to the cocktail party. He stood up and felt better. Maybe it

was one of the big companies testing the panty hose.
That would be great.

But as he walked over to the picnic table with his
paperwork, he frowned, deep in thought. What was it
that he hadn't tested these things for?

B ARNEY FREIZE WAS back in his den, smoking his cigar, too excited to try to sleep. Ruth's secretary had finally called back and promised him he'd get the check tomorrow if everything worked out. Barney puffed. Tomorrow night I'll go out for a nice dinner, he thought. An occasional splurge was good for the soul. And if I get the big money, then it'll be time to make an appointment with my trusty travel agent. Europe, make room for Barney Freize.

I feel antsy, he thought. I can't just sit here, no matter how good this cigar is. He laughed aloud. If I'm going out for a big dinner tomorrow night, then I'd better work up my appetite. He went into the bedroom and got out his jogging suit. As he kicked off his Hush Puppies, he decided he'd run down by the beach. It would be soothing. After that he'd come home and sleep like a baby.

Judd Green watched Richie enter the front door of the factory. He pulled his car over to the side of the road where there were no streetlights. The area was deserted, which was a real bonus. He got out his phone and made a call.

Richie felt he had gone over his list long enough. We're going to have name tags anyway, he thought, but people like it when you know who they are.

As he gathered up the papers, the bench creaked. Boy, this place sure is making funny noises tonight, he thought. Either that or I have some imagination. But a few seconds later the sickening reality that he had not been imagining the noises hit him when the smell of smoke hit his nostrils and the sound of timber crackling filled his ears.

Out in the night air, Barney felt good. He ran along the beach and enjoyed the sounds of the waves breaking against the shore. When he looped around and started to head back toward his house, he decided he wasn't ready to go in yet. But what about a nice bath? he thought. These muscles are going to ache.

Wavering for a few minutes, he decided to stay out. It was a beautiful night. The bathtub would always be there. Before he knew it, his feet were taking him on the route he'd chosen that night, the route that led past the panty-hose factory. How appropriate, he thought. Maybe it'll be good luck. This is what started the whole adventure.

Barney turned down the long winding road that led to the factory. He thought he saw an orange glow in the distance, so he picked up his pace. What the hell is going on? he wondered.

With frightening speed, smoke filled the factory. Flames leapt up the walls and Richie ran with his panty hose to the front door. He tried to push it open but it wouldn't budge. This doesn't make sense, he thought frantically, there should be nothing blocking the door. He tried to run to the back, but flames had overtaken the rear of the building. Richie looked up and all the windows were barred.

I'm going to be fried, Richie thought. This is it. The smoke was getting thicker. He started to cough and ran for the front door again. It's my only chance, he thought. Through the barred window next to the door he could see out onto the dark street. I've got to get there. He screamed as he pounded and pushed on the door. "HELP ME! HELP!" But it was no use. The smoke was beginning to overcome him. He started to feel weak and thought that maybe he should just lie down.

With the panty hose in his hand, he started to slide down the door. Birdie's face filled his mind. "Get up, Richie," she seemed to be yelling. "It ain't over till it's over."

"But . . ."

"No buts, you've got a job to finish. Get up!"

Richie struggled to his feet and moved in front of the barred window. The flames leapt up behind him. He saw a lone figure standing out in the street watching the building. When the figure saw Richie, it ran up. To Richie, it was the most beautiful sight since he had first laid eyes on Birdie.

"Richie!" Barney Freize yelled. "What the hell are you doing in there?"

"Roasting marshmallows. What the hell do you think I'm doing? I can't get the front door open!"

Barney looked at the door. A Dumpster had been moved in front to block it. "Jesus Christ!" he yelled. "There's a Dumpster here. You push on the door and I'll try to pull it out of the way."

With all the strength Richie could muster, he threw his weight against the door, time after time, as Barney moved the Dumpster, inch by inch.

"Keep going, Richie," he could hear Barney yell through the roar of the fire behind him. Finally making enough progress to pry open the door a crack, Richie squeezed himself through and fell into the waiting arms of his former fellow maintenance worker, Barnard Thomas Freize.

"That's the punch line?" Joey asked Nadine incredulously.

"Wait a minute," she said. "I think I might have told it wrong."

"Helllllo, Nadine," he teased.

Regan laughed and looked at her watch. It was getting

late. "I hate to leave, but I'd better. I've got to get up early in the morning."

"You're not going on the stereo-shopping spree, are you?" Joey asked.

"No, I can't. We're leaving Nadine in charge of that one."

"I hope this guy has unlimited credit," Joey mumbled.

"Stop," Nadine protested. "Don't you worry, Regan. We'll get him the best buy in the Miami area."

"Nadine picked out the CD player for my car," Dennis said. "She did a great job."

"Thank you, Dennis."

"She fixed the one in my bedroom just this afternoon," Matt offered. "It took her about two minutes, and it had been broken for weeks. She stuck a wad of gum back there to keep the wire from coming out."

Joey looked at her. "Where'd you get the gum?"

"Found it."

He winked at Regan. "I wish they made a patch for gum chewers."

"I'll get Richie working on it," Regan said as she got up.

"We'll walk you home," Nadine said.

"That's okay," Regan replied.

"We insist," Joey pronounced. "This area is not the safest at night."

"Besides," Nadine said, "it's romantic to take a stroll in the evening, right, Joe?"

"You took the words right out of my mouth."

*　*　*

Regan climbed the stairs to her hotel room. Nadine and Joey are really nice, she thought. And they definitely belong together.

Inside the room Regan turned on the television. A long movie was just ending and the local news was coming up. She peeled off her clothes and threw them over the chair. Pulling an oversized T-shirt over her head, she went into the bathroom to wash her face and brush her teeth.

Five minutes later, she turned out the lights and got into bed. The sheets were crisp white cotton and felt fresh. She pushed the ''sleep'' button on the remote control so the television would automatically go off in thirty minutes. I just know I'll fall asleep with it on, she thought.

The news came on and there was the usual flurry of stories about local happenings. But when the announcer who looked like a surfer boy started to say, ''There was a fire tonight at a former panty-hose factory,'' Regan leaned forward and quickly turned up the volume.

Footage of the smoldering factory flashed on the screen as he reported, ''Arson is strongly suspected. It may even be a case of attempted murder, as a Dumpster had been used to block the front exit. Luckily no one was killed in the blaze, but a former factory worker, a Richard Blossom, is being treated at Miami General Hospital for smoke inhalation. Back to you, Barbara.''

''Richie!'' Regan wailed. She jumped out of bed and grabbed a pair of jeans. She stuffed her feet into her sneakers and pulled a light windbreaker off the hanger.

Within seconds she was out the door, hailing a cab, on her way to Miami General Hospital.

Richie lay stretched out on a bed in the emergency room of Miami General. Barney Freize was at his side.

"I feel much better now, Doctor," Richie was saying, "I really think you should let me go home."

Suddenly the doors swung open as a nurse tried to stop someone from charging in.

"Regan!" Richie called out happily. "I'm over here. It's all right," he said to the doctor, "she's my niece."

The doctor gave the nurse the signal to let her in.

"Richie, are you okay?" Regan said as she hurried over and bent down to kiss him.

"Good as new. Good as new. If this doctor would release me, I'd be even better."

"You shouldn't be alone tonight," the serious, young-looking doctor warned.

"I'll stay with him," Regan said.

"Isn't she a good niece?" Richie joked.

"He should be fine, but he needs to get some rest."

"I'll take care of it," Regan promised.

As Richie got out of bed he said, "By the way, Regan, meet Barney Freize. He saved my life tonight."

Regan and Richie had their taxi stop at Barney's house to drop him off.

"When I went out for a jog tonight," Barney joked, "I didn't know I was in for such an adventure."

"Thank God you like to exercise," Regan said. "Thank you so much."

"Yeah, thanks, Barn. I owe you one." Richie patted him on the back. "I've got a big weekend, but I'll call you and we'll have dinner next week." Barney started to get out of the cab. "Barn," Richie said.

Barney turned back. "Yeah, Rich."

Awkwardly Richie hugged him. "Thanks."

"You'd have done the same for me."

"That's true."

When they pulled away, Richie offered to stop at Regan's hotel to pick up a few things for her to spend the night.

"No way," Regan said. "I'm not letting you out of my sight tonight, not even to leave you waiting in the cab. I just want to get you home."

"Okay," Richie agreed. It was nice to be taken care of.

Barney Freize checked his answering machine. No messages. He opened the refrigerator and pulled out a beer. Sitting down at his kitchen table, the full effect of what had happened this evening began to dawn on him. Someone had tried to kill Richie. No two ways about it. But why? Did it have something to do with that panty hose? Am I responsible? he thought.

It was well after midnight, but he decided to call Danny. He needed to talk to him. As usual, he got his machine. But when the beep went off, Danny's tape must have started rewinding at high speed. It sounded like chipmunks on amphetamines.

Nothing could have prepared Barney for what he heard when Danny's messages started to play back. He

knew he should have hung up, but it was as if the phone
were Krazy-Glued to his ear.

"How's my Danny Wanny?" the familiar voice
started to say in a juvenile tone. "Oh, Danny Boy, my
scootchie-ootchie, we'll be together soon." Barney's
face whitened. The last line of the message confirmed
his worst fears. "Call back your wuving Ruthy Wuthy."

His nephew was involved with the Calla-Lily woman.
How deeply involved . . . ?

Back at the Fourth Quarter, Richie leaned on Regan
as they walked up the steps to the second floor. It was
late and everyone else had obviously gone to bed.

Inside the apartment, Regan asked, "Do you think a
cup of tea would be good before you went to sleep?"

"Great idea. I guess nobody knows what happened
yet, huh, Regan. There are no messages on the answering machine."

"I caught it on the Late News. I think everybody
must have already been in bed."

"Boy, are they going to be surprised."

"To say the least," Regan said as she filled the kettle
and turned on the gas.

"Someone's out to get me, do you think, Regan?"

"Unless that Dumpster moved itself in front of the
door."

"You know what this means, don't you?" Richie
asked happily. "Somebody must like my panty hose!
They think it's good enough to kill me for."

"Don't even joke about it, Richie," Regan said as

she brought the teacups, milk and sugar out to the coffee table in front of the couch, where Richie was sitting. The kettle started whistling angrily, a piercing, shrill sound that instantly set Regan's teeth on edge.

"That kettle would wake the dead," Richie remarked.

"Kettle? What kettle?" Regan asked as she hurried into the kitchen and yanked it off the stove.

"I like your sense of humor, Regan. It's important to have one."

"I agree, Richie," Regan said as she poured the hot water into the cups. "Life would be pretty tough without it."

Companionably they sat and sipped their tea. Regan noticed Richie's eyes grow heavy.

"We'd better get some rest. It's late. I'll just stretch out on the couch here."

"It pulls out," Richie enthused.

"It does?"

"It's a Castro Convertible. Birdie and I used to get such a kick watching that little Bernadette Castro pull apart those couches on the TV commercials. Come to think of it, we could have used her help tonight getting that Dumpster to budge."

"She's running the company now," Regan informed him. "And she does her own radio commercials on 'Imus in the Morning' in New York. Last time I was home I heard Imus yelling at her for dragging him to some boring luncheon."

Richie shook his head. "It's still hard to think of her

as all grown up. Boy, time does fly, huh, Regan?'' he asked as he got up and yawned.

"It sure does," Regan agreed. "And before you know it, it's going to be morning and that phone's going to start ringing, with everyone calling to make sure you're okay."

"That's nice," Richie said as he started for the bedroom.

Regan pulled the cushions off the couch. "Yes, it is," she said quietly.

AT DAYBREAK, A sliver of orange sun peeked over the horizon in the mountains of Colorado. The campsite of the Wild West Tour group was peaceful. All eight members of the posse, as they liked to call themselves, snuggled in their sleeping bags around the embers from last night's campfire. Preston Landers pulled his special-issue sleeping bag around his slight frame as he dreamed about the storytelling session that had taken place around the campfire just hours before.

As was their ritual each evening, one person led the group with stories about his boyhood. Last night had been Preston's turn.

He'd told them about his privileged life in New York City where his family's Fifth Avenue apartment overlooked Central Park. He'd hated it. All he wanted to be was a cowboy, out branding cattle, sleeping under the stars. A trip to a dude ranch when he was seven years old reinforced that ardent desire.

His family had tried to placate him by sending him out every Saturday, cowboy hat in place, into the wilds of Central Park with his nanny, who watched him go round and round riding a purple horse on the carousel, firing at her with his pop gun every 360 degrees. But somehow it just wasn't enough.

He had wanted to go to high school out in Wyoming on a special exchange program. Instead he was sent to a prep school in New Jersey. They didn't ride herd there, they rode to hounds. It had been a bitter disappointment.

Time slipped away, Preston recounted, and before he knew it he was caught up in the rat race, making money in business, his childhood dream buried but not forgotten. Until now.

He hoped he hadn't bored the group too much. He'd gone on a little longer than usual and a couple of the guys had lain back in their sleeping bags during his soliloquy, never regaining consciousness for the singing of "Taps," a ceremony that capped off each evening.

The air at this hour of the morning was fresh and crisp, with a slight nip to it. The occasional sounds of nature gently cut through the stillness, making it a perfect spot to film, say, a cornflakes commercial.

But in one brief moment it all ended. The mules started to bray wildly. Dust started to blow over the campsite. Preston Landers's peaceful slumber communing with nature in the great outdoors was rudely interrupted by the roar of a helicopter as it settled down in a nearby clearing. With a sinking heart he looked up and saw the Calla-Lily logo on its side and knew that, for whatever reason, his vacation was over.

With much grumbling, Preston pulled on his Levi's 501 jeans bought especially for the trip and packed up his vagabond stove, buddy burner, multipurpose pocket knife and video camera. He planned to put together a tape of the journey, set it to country music, and sell it to the other campers.

"Did everyone fill out their order forms for *High Noon Two*?" he asked his fellow ramblers as he rolled up his sleeping bag and tied it with a knot.

Most of them grunted, "Yeah, partner" as they rubbed the sleep from their eyes.

"You can send me your checks and self-addressed stamped envelopes when I've got it ready."

His gear in tow, Preston walked over and patted the heads of the mules. The one he had christened Ruth stared blankly at him and blinked.

"I wish I could take you with me," Preston whispered. "But where I'm going there's only room for one Ruth. And you wouldn't want to be there."

Preston boarded *Calla-Lily I*, strapped himself in, and waved good-bye to the Wild West Tour as the helicopter lifted him toward the heavens on his way back to the boardrooms of America.

REGAN WOKE UP to the delicious smell of fresh-brewed coffee. Surprisingly she'd fallen into a heavy sleep and had slept for a solid six hours. She heard Richie puttering around in the kitchen.

"Richie," she called out.

"Good morning, honey. I'll be right there."

Regan sat up in bed and watched as Richie carried in a tray with coffee, juice and bagels.

"What service!" Regan said as she gratefully accepted a cup of coffee. "I'm supposed to be looking after you."

"Eh," Richie muttered. "I heated up the bagels because they're from yesterday. You have to eat them quick before they get hard again."

Regan laughed. "Thanks. How do you feel this morning?"

"I have a little case of opening-night jitters, but other than that, I'm grateful to be alive."

The phone rang.

Regan raised an eyebrow. "Here we go." She sipped her coffee as Richie settled himself in the chair next to the phone.

"I'm fine, I'm fine," he said to the caller. "Regan, it's Bridget and Ed . . . huh . . . Regan heard it on the news last night and came to get me at the hospital . . . she stayed over . . . We don't know who tried to kill me . . . Don't worry about it . . . I'll see you later."

Richie hung up and smiled. "Everybody's a wreck."

The phone rang again. "Richie Blossom here," he answered. "Nora, love. I feel fine. Your daughter is here making sure I don't get into any more trouble . . . I'll put you on the speakerphone . . ."

"Regan?" Nora asked.

"Hi, Mom." Regan leaned back against her propped-up pillow.

"You both are okay?"

"Fine," they said in unison.

"Well, I've got some exciting news."

Richie leaned into the phone. "What's that, love?"

"Not only have we gotten a lot more responses from people who want to come to the party, but someone very important and influential and rich called to see if he would be welcome."

'WHO?" Richie yelled and spilled a few drops of coffee on his bathrobe. "Don't keep us in suspense!"

"She can't help it. That's her business," Regan remarked.

Nora paused and pronounced his name with emphasis. "Dayton Rotter."

"Dayton Rotter?" Richie repeated. "Dayton Rotter!"

"Wow!" Regan said. "He's really coming?"

"Yes," Nora said with satisfaction. "He heard about it from the models. Your father and I are doing our best to make sure the word spreads that he'll be there. I have to call the manager, Nick, and let him know."

"You better hurry up," Regan advised. "He's going out this morning on a hunt for a stereo."

"Dayton Rotter?" Richie said almost to himself. "I guess I'm in the big time now!"

There was a knock at the door.

"Excuse me, Nora, I have to answer the door."

"Sure, Richie. Regan," Nora asked, "do you want to come to the hotel this morning and we'll go over to the luncheon together?"

"Yes, but we can't stay too long," Regan said.

"We won't. Why don't you come by around ten forty-five?"

"Okay, Mom. I'll see you later."

Richie, followed by Lucille, hurried to turn off the speakerphone. "Lucille, sit down."

"Richie, I got so worried when I heard the news this morning. Hi, Regan. Sorry to barge in like this."

"Not at all. I've got to get going, anyway." Richie had lent her Birdie's old bathrobe. She went into the other room to get dressed. When she came back out, she folded up the Bernadette Castro Special and picked the cushions off the floor.

"Now, Richie, you do promise to stay here this morning and not go out alone."

"I promise, Regan."

"We're all going to bus up to the Watergreen together for the fashion show early this afternoon. Richie, you're going to come with us, aren't you?" Lucille asked.

"The Fourth Quarter contingent will proceed together," Richie said excitedly.

Regan looked at him. "There's not going to be a lot of time for me to come back and get you. If you go with them, Richie, please stay with them. I want to get you through today safely."

"No problem," Richie smiled.

"I'll keep my eye on him," Lucille assured her. "I'm very good at that."

IRVING FRANKLIN STIRRED at his work station. He lifted his head off the Formica countertop where he had been wrestling with the panty hose the night before. The big clock on the wall with the second hand he needed to time certain experiments precisely read eight-seventeen.

Fern should be coming down in a few minutes to check on me, he thought groggily. I can't believe I fell asleep. I just put my head down to rest my eyes an hour ago. Just before he fell asleep, as a final test he'd added dollops of the ridiculously expensive new cream that his daughter had insisted on buying just yesterday.

Uh, he thought. This place stinks. He walked over to the Crockpot that was really intended for the delicate slow cooking of meats and vegetables, not lingerie. He picked up the lid. Stew au hose. Good enough to drive Ruth crazy.

A quick examination of the specimen in question revealed that, indeed, it was as good as new.

Irving sighed. That's all, folks, he thought. I've done everything I can think of to make this stuff unravel, one way or the other. But it couldn't be done.

Disgusted, he dropped the hose back in the Crockpot, straightened up the counter, and started up the steps, ignoring the nagging little voice that told him to take one more look. He needed a shower and a change of clothes before he headed over to Ruthy Wuthy to break the bad news.

Thank God she can't take it out on me, he thought. What a shock it had been when he wandered down to his lab during the company Christmas party and found her experimenting with the gardener, who was calling her Ruthy Wuthy. Ruthy had looked up just as he snapped their picture.

BARNEY FREIZE HAD had a terrible night's sleep. He was still in shock over Ruth's message on Danny's answering machine. To think that those two were involved was bad enough, but what were they up to? Something told him he should not have brought those panty hose to Calla-Lily. And now Richie's life was in danger, probably thanks to him.

He paced around his little house. The best thing he could do was just to go and talk to Danny. That's it. Danny had never returned Barney's call but he probably got home late. The question was, from where? And God knew, that machine of his couldn't be depended upon to deliver the messages. At least not to Danny.

Barney grabbed his car keys and hurried out the door. It took him exactly eight minutes to reach Danny's neighborhood. He pulled his sedan into the driveway and turned off the car. It was still early, but he couldn't wait. Charging up to the door, he rang the bell and waited.

A few minutes later, a sleepy-looking Danny answered the door.

"Uncle Barney, what are you doing here?"

"We need to talk."

"Come on in."

Barney followed him into the kitchen. He cringed when he saw a can of turpentine on the counter.

"I tried to call you last night."

"I didn't get the message. My answering machine is screwing up a little bit."

"I know."

"How do you know?"

"Let's just say I thought I had reached the hallway outside a newborn nursery, scootchie-ootchie."

Danny's face reddened. "That's none of your business."

"What did you do last night?" Barney asked.

"I painted a friend's apartment. Why are you asking me these questions?" Danny asked, annoyed.

"What's the turpentine doing here?"

"To get the paint off my hands. What do you think?"

"You know, Danny, in Florida people can go to jail for a long time for attempted murder."

"What are you talking about?"

"You don't know?"

"Of course not."

"Then tell me about your wonderful plans to be with Ruthy Wuthy."

JOEY HONKED THE horn of his car. "Nadine, hurry up! I'm going to be late for work."

"Hold your horses, I'm coming," Nadine said as she struggled out the front door, her purse dangling in one hand, a cup of coffee in the other. She handed the cup to Joey to hold while she got in the car and buckled her seat belt. "Ready," she pronounced.

"Well, hallelujah," Joey said as they drove off.

Nadine raised her eyebrows. "That'd be a good CD to buy for the fashion show." She started to sing, "Hal-le-lu-jah, hal-le-lu-jah, hal-le-lu-jah, hal-le-lu-jah . . ."

Joey switched on the radio.

"Are you trying to give me some sort of message here?" Nadine asked.

"Who, me?"

"Yeah, you. Unless there's somebody in the backseat I don't know about."

"I love the sound of your voice, you know that." He patted her thigh. "But not your singing voice."

Nadine appeared nonplussed. "Nobody's perfect." She took a sip of the coffee that was sloshing around in the wide-brimmed cup.

"So, you know which stores you're going to take this clown to?" Joey asked.

"Uh-huh. Do you want to come over to the fashion show?"

"Sure. I hope that Richie guy can pull this off."

"Me too. I'll go back with Nick and help him set up the stereo, so why don't you come to the hotel when you're finished working?"

"Okay. That should be early afternoon." Joey paused. "If my boss only knew what the people from the Fourth Quarter are doing to hang on to that place . . ."

"Don't tell him. He wouldn't be too happy to find out that the commission check he's probably planning for the Golden Sun could be a lot skinnier."

"My lips are sealed."

They drove along, with Nadine flipping stations after every song.

"God forbid we should hear any news," Joey muttered.

"Buy a paper," Nadine suggested as she threw her drained coffee cup on the floor of the backseat. "It's got a big handle. It shouldn't roll around too much."

"Thank you for caring."

Finally, Joey pulled up the hill of the Watergreen's horseshoe-shaped driveway. He leaned over to kiss her. "Now don't run away with this guy."

"You never know." Nadine kissed him back. "He might like my singing."

She stepped inside the lobby of the Watergreen and was impressed by the beautiful view of the ocean from the huge windows on the opposite wall. The blue water sparkled under the brilliant sunshine. Not bad, she thought. I'll have to get Joey to take me here for a drink some night.

There was a bustle in the air. People with notebooks and pens were scurrying around. Nadine hurried over to the elevator. As she waited she studied the two signs, side by side, that listed the convention seminars for the day. The first one read: " 'Panty Hose in a Glass— Efforts to Make Our Packaging Recyclable,' Room 120A; 'The "INGS" of Panty Hose Production—Knitting, Weaving, Dyeing,' Room 124; 'Panty Hose for the Funky Crowd—Jeweled, Studded, Crazy—Cost of Production vs. Profit,' Room 126." Hmmm, Nadine thought. Things that I never lost sleep over.

The other sign read: " 'Ashes to Ashes—Cremation vs. Burial,' Room 112; 'Keeping Up Employee Morale Around the Home,' Room 116; 'The Latest Models of the Six-Foot Bungalow—Coffins on Display,' Banquet Room B." How cheerful, Nadine mused.

The elevator bell donged and the doors opened. Nadine pressed "PH" and was whisked up to the top floor of the Watergreen. Around the corner and down the hall were the double doors that opened into Nick Fargus's suite. One of them was partially ajar. Nadine knocked on it. "Hello."

Nick hurriedly opened the door. A valet stood next to him in the foyer, a hanger holding a flowered shirt in a dry cleaner's bag resting on his index finger. "Nadine?" Nick asked.

"Since birth."

"Come on in. I'm Nick." He turned to the valet. "Did you get out the stains?"

"We tried very hard, Mr. Fargus. There's still one little smidgen of tomato sauce, but I really think it blends in with the flowers."

Nick looked at him sternly. "Very well."

"Next time put some club soda on it right away," Nadine suggested.

The valet exited with a downcast look on his face. With all the stains they got out for all the people who only visited the Watergreen once, it was just such bad luck that they couldn't do it for the boss, he thought.

"Come on inside, Nadine. Take a look at the view," he said proudly, leading her to the windows.

"Nice place you got here," Nadine commented as she followed him in. "You've got a runway set up, I see?"

"A couple of the guys came up and built it last night. You like it?"

"Very professional. The view is great too. What a bachelor pad."

Nick's face lit up. "You think so?"

"Heck, yeah. I'm glad my boyfriend doesn't live in a place like this. As it is now, if he ever brought another girl home, she'd trip and break her neck right inside his front door. You don't have a girlfriend?"

"No. You really think this is a good place to have the party?"

"It's a great place. What are you worried about?"

"Nothing. Where should we put the stereo?"

Nadine looked around. "Now let's see. It depends on the system we get. How much do you want to spend?"

Nick shrugged his shoulders. "How much do you think I should spend?"

"You plan to live here for a while?"

He managed a little laugh. "Unless I get fired."

"That'd be a bummer." Nadine walked around the large room. "Let's see. Do you want to put speakers in the bedroom?"

Nick shook his head. "Uh-huh. The models are going to change in there."

"Lucky you."

Nick grinned. "I know."

"Ohhh, so you're looking forward to having the models here, huh?" Nadine teased.

He shuffled his feet, embarrassed. "It'll be fun. You think they'll like the runway?"

"They'll love the whole place," Nadine assured him.

The phone rang. His manner became efficient as he picked it up. "Nick Fargus."

Nadine sat down on the couch.

". . . more acceptances, that's fine. I'll let the banquet manager know . . . the more the merrier . . . who else? . . ."

Nadine watched as the expression on Nick's face clouded and he practically squealed.

". . . Dayton Rotter is coming? . . . No, of course, that's great . . . see you later." He hung up the phone looking dejected.

"The competition is coming?" Nadine asked.

"Huh? Oh. I don't care," Nick protested weakly.

"He's just another good-looking guy," Nadine said with forced cheerfulness.

"Who also happens to be rich and famous!" Nick blurted.

"Forget it, Nick. You're going to have a good time today. Just be yourself. You're the host! He's not going to tie up everyone's attention the whole time."

"I guess so."

"Let's get out of here and buy a stereo that's going to make this place rock!"

"Okay. Now, how much do you think I'm going to have to spend?" he asked as the door closed behind them.

JUDD GREEN SAT in the phone booth out by the pool bar. The bar was closed and there were only a couple of bathers sunning themselves at the other end of the pool. It was still early.

"You poured it! You saw the door was blocked! You saw him through the window! How was I supposed to know somebody was going to take a jog in the boonies late at night?"

He played with his mirror sunglasses as he listened. "I know how bad it is. I know you're getting the pressure. Believe me, I wish this job was finished. Although it should have been taken care of a long time ago . . . Listen, the funeral convention ends early this afternoon. I know what we can do. We'll need a legitimate-looking business van. Get two of the guys in workers' uniforms . . .''

Someone tapped on the window of the phone booth. ''Are you going to be finished soon?'' a woman in a skirted bathing suit asked.

Judd turned to her and opened the door. Trying to keep his tone civil, he said, ''I'll be out in a few minutes.''

Hurriedly he explained the rest of his plan as the bather wandered off. ''I tell you, it's going to work. We'll go straight to the dock. At the party, I'll concentrate on the old guy. You take care of Regan Reilly.''

I T WAS NOT just a gray haze of smoke that hung in the air of the Calla-Lily suite. The atmosphere was thick with the kind of tension you could cut with a knife.

"This waiting is killing me!" Ruth screamed as she puffed her twenty-seventh cigarette of the day.

The Calla-Lily board members sat on the couches looking glum. They had all arrived at 7 A.M., at the precise time that the cowpoke was spotted in the wilds of Colorado. While he was jetting back across the country, they were made to sit and discuss with Ruth, if "discuss" was the right word, Calla-Lily's final decision on purchasing the Birdie Panty Hose.

"To buy, or not to buy, that is the question," one of them had made the mistake of joking as he held up a glazed doughnut in the air for emphasis. The force of

Ruth's reaction had startled him so much that he dropped the doughnut in his cup of coffee.

The doorbell rang. Ethel, back in the salt mines, answered the door.

It was Irving Franklin. Late as usual.

"I don't know how he gets away with it," one of the board members muttered as he bit into a crumb bun that broke apart, dusting his suit with confectioners sugar.

"Good morning, everyone."

"Would you like some coffee?" Ethel asked.

"Thank you, Ethel. Yes, I would. Black."

Like Ruth's mood, Ethel thought. Easy to remember.

Irving sat down. He looked over at Ruth and smiled. "Good morning, Ruth."

"What's the deal, Irving?" she responded.

Ethel placed a coffee cup in front of Irving. "Ruth?" she asked.

"Is it important, Ethel?" Ruth demanded to know.

"I was just thinking that I'd run downstairs and get those papers you wanted photocopied . . ." Her voice trailed off. *Before this place explodes*, she wanted to add.

"Go."

"Thank you."

Irving sipped his drink. "Good coffee." He cleared his throat. "I guess you can tell that I did not come in here jumping with joy. I was up all night determined to find something wrong with that panty hose. I cooked it, beat it, washed it, stomped on it. I'm sorry. It *seems* to be just perfect."

An animal-like moan emanated from Ruth's throat.

"We've got to buy it! That idiot better get back here soon and sign his consent!"

The board members shook their heads, agreeing that indeed the best thing was to fork over the money.

Three minutes later the door to the suite flung open. Ethel was back, the papers in her hand yet to be copied. She could tell that the news from Irving had not been good. And now she had more bad news that she couldn't wait to tell Ruth.

"I thought you'd want to know . . . I was just down in the manager's office. The buzz is that Dayton Rotter is coming to the cocktail party. He's very interested in buying the Birdie Panty Hose . . ."

The last thing Ruth saw before she fainted was the vision of Grandpa pointing his finger at her, shouting, "You ruined my company!"

AT TABLES SET around the poolside in the backyard of the home of the Durkin family's good friends, Dina and Sean Clancy, fourteen women had gathered for Maura's bridesmaids' brunch. Regan and Nora joined the five other bridesmaids, Maura, Bridget, Dina, and a handful of other female relatives of Maura's and John's for the traditional hen party.

Colorful floral centerpieces adorned the tables, which were shaded by large yellow umbrellas. Small boxes with pale-pink wrapping and gold bows were waiting at the places assigned to the bridesmaids. A bouquet of balloons was tied to the buffet table, which would soon be filled with quiches and salads.

"What's John doing today?" Regan asked Maura as she sipped a tall glass of fresh-squeezed orange juice.

"Golfing. He figured he could get in eighteen holes before he took care of some minor last-minute errands like picking up the rings, the marriage license, and his tux."

"At least he's not the nervous type."

"He said I've been doing enough worrying for both of us lately."

"Just think, Maura, tomorrow night you'll be on your way, and everything will be all behind you."

"I hope so, Regan." Maura's look turned serious. "After what happened last night with Richie, I feel so sure that something else bad is going to happen."

Regan tried to conceal her worry. "If Richie manages to sell his panty hose this afternoon, he'll be the happiest guy in Florida."

"I hope so. He's had so many of these inventions before that have never worked out. We thought it was more a hobby for him than anything. But now everyone seems to think he's come across something that will really fly. Which could be dangerous. Do you know how many people have been paid to keep their inventions off the market?"

"I've heard of a few."

"Well, could it be that whoever blocked Richie in that factory last night didn't want to have to write the check?"

"I don't know, Maura. But we're keeping an eye on Richie today, and hopefully after the fashion show the panty hose will be someone else's worry."

"I wish I could come to that, Regan, but I'm not

completely packed and we have the rehearsal dinner tonight . . .''

"Don't worry about it. We're going to see you later anyway."

"Will everyone please help themselves?" Dina urged the group as she carried out two large dishes of quiche, fresh from the oven.

After dessert and coffee, Regan thanked Maura again for the pearl-and-sapphire earrings the bridesmaids would all be wearing the next day, and she and Nora hurried back to the Watergreen.

L IKE AN OLD pro, Nadine wandered up and down the aisles of Dobb's Stereo Store studying the CD players. Nick was close at her heels, looking slightly baffled.

"I want one that looks really good," he insisted.

Nadine held her finger to her lip and tapped it. "Right. Now, the woofers and the tweeters . . ."

"The what?" Nick asked.

"The woofers and the tweeters. Don't you know what they are?"

"Oh, sure, yeah, the woofers and the tweeters. Of course."

Nadine stopped and smiled at him. "What are they then?"

Nick gestured with his hand. "Parts of the stereo."

"The loudspeakers, Nick." Nadine started to move on. "You know, you don't have to pretend so much."

"Do you think I do that?" Nick asked quickly.

"Uh-huh," Nadine said as she checked a price tag. "You're too anxious, too worried about what people think. And people are going to think what they're going to think, so there's no use trying to control it."

"I don't do that," Nick protested.

"Yes, you do. Why else would you be agonizing about whether or not to wear that flowered shirt today?"

"I just asked your opinion."

"Three times. Wear what you want to wear and forget everybody else if they can't take a joke."

Nick followed her into the next aisle. "You think there's something wrong with me?"

"No. But I wish you would chill out and just let things happen. I get the feeling that impressing the models today is the most important thing in the world to you."

"I'm proud of the Watergreen Hotel and want to restore it to its former glory as the spot to be in Miami."

"No, you don't. You just want to date the models. Here we go," Nadine said. "For what you want to spend, this stereo here is the best buy. It looks good, has great sound, has an AM/FM radio and a tape deck besides a CD player, and it's in your price range. What do you say?"

"Fine."

"And we'll get you some of those woofers and tweeters for your bedroom too."

"Sounds kinky."

"There you go. Now let's find someone who can get this order moving."

After they had packed the car with the stereo boxes, Nick and Nadine hurried into the music store to pick up the CDs Regan had requested for the fashion show. Nadine bought a few extra ones for Joey and, after less deliberation than usual, Nick made a purchase that was the official start of his CD collection.

"Well, what do you know," Nadine said as they got back into the car and pulled out of the parking lot. "It's almost show time."

WHEN REGAN AND Nora got to Nick Fargus's suite, they stepped into a flurry of activity. Room-service waiters were setting up the bar and the hors d'oeuvres. A maid was retouching the windows, making sure that they sparkled. Flowers were being delivered.

Nadine stepped out of the bedroom, holding a hammer. "Hi, Regan!"

"Hi, Nadine. This is my mother—"

"Mrs. Reilly, I love your books. Regan, you didn't tell me your mother was the one who wrote those books that keep me up all night."

Nora laughed. "As long as they don't put you to sleep."

"No way. When I was reading the last one I got so scared that I got out of bed to make double sure the door was locked. The next day at work I had to go out to my car at lunchtime to take a nap.''

"Hi, everybody," Nick said, emerging from the bathroom in his flowered shirt. He was feeling proud of himself, having left out for the models everything he thought they might need, including his new skin cream.

"All set?" Regan asked.

"Nadine's in charge. She's got the stereo all set up. We were just going to put in our first CD." He laughed. "She also told me to put a sign on the bathroom door telling people that there's another bathroom one flight down in the health club."

Nadine said matter-of-factly, "You've got over a hundred people in here drinking and one bathroom? The one in your bedroom will be off limits because the models will be in and out of there. People come for one drink and they stay for another and before you know it you've got a line."

"I'll get out my Magic Marker," Nick promised.

"Speaking of that, Regan, we'd better write up the rest of the name tags for the people who just called in," Nora said.

"Hello, hello, hello," Richie called as he led the Fourth Quarter contingent into the suite.

"This is a good place for a party," Flo remarked.

"Beautiful," Lucille murmured.

Nick went over and shook Richie's hand. "Good to see you, Richie. And who do we have here?"

"The models!"

When Nick tried to speak, his voice had a croaky quality. "The models?"

"Yes. Say hello to Flo and Bessie and Pearl and—"

"We've been doing nothing but practicing our strut," Pearl reported.

"Great," Nick forced himself to say. "I thought you were from South Beach."

"We are, honey," Flo said as she walked past him to check out the view.

Nick hoped his disappointment didn't show, then realized Nadine was watching him. *You're too anxious. Just let things happen.* "Well, you all look terrific," he said heartily.

Nadine winked at him.

"We do have a few spring chickens coming up from one of the agencies," Richie explained. "They should be here in a few minutes."

Nick's spirits brightened. I don't have to feel guilty that I'm glad, he thought.

L UKE RUBBED HIS eyes. It had been a long morning, but the business end of the convention was coming to a close. All in all, it had been worthwhile. He had met with suppliers, gone to some of the seminars, hooked up with old friends from the business, and given a successful speech.

Now it was past noon and people were heading to lunch dates or out to the pool to take advantage of the beautiful weather. But Luke wanted to take one more look at the coffin display. He'd seen a few models that were interesting. They cost less and he could pass on those savings to his customers.

He walked down the carpeted hallway toward the display room. Everything was quiet. The large room was off the beaten path, away from the hubbub of the hotel lobby. He pulled open the door and stepped inside, alone in the room with rows of coffins. No matter how long I last in this business, he thought, I don't think I'll ever get totally immune to the sight of these things.

After jotting down the information he needed about several different makes, he put his pen away and looked around one final time. They'll be coming sometime this afternoon to haul these out of here, he thought. But after the problems of bringing them in the other day, the only way the management was going to let them be carried out was via the rear exit.

Back in the hotel lobby he headed toward the main bar. He was meeting Ed for a quick sandwich and then they were going upstairs to meet Nora and Bridget at the fashion show. And after that, he thought, who knows? Hopefully a little time to relax.

THE CALLA-LILY private jet touched down at Miami International Airport. When it finally came to a stop, the door was opened and Preston Landers was greeted with a blast of hot, sticky air.

"Now damn it!" he mumbled. "Where I just came from, the air was nice and cool." The flight attendant looked at him sympathetically.

"Have a good day, sir," she said as he stepped off the plane.

"I doubt it," he replied.

Down on the tarmac a limousine was waiting to whisk him to the Watergreen Hotel.

"We have to hurry, sir," the driver said as he held the door open for him. "They're waiting for you at the hotel. They've called several times to see if you'd landed yet.''

Preston kicked some mud off his cowboy boots. ''I guess they'll just have to wait a little longer.''

''Yes, sir.'' The driver shut the door behind Preston, ran around the side of the car, jumped in and screeched off.

Ruth was propped on a couch in the Calla-Lily suite. She was furious at herself for fainting in front of this bunch. It was just that the news about Dayton Rotter had been such a mortal blow. It made her all the more convinced that they had to get the check into that Richie Blossom's hands, and get it there soon. Thanks to Nora Regan Reilly, the cocktail party and fashion show had become a hot topic. See if I ever buy another one of her books, Ruth thought.

''WHERE IS THAT IDIOT?'' she screamed.

''Ruth, calm yourself,'' Ethel urged.

''Calm myself? How can I calm myself? My whole life is passing before my eyes and you tell me to calm myself!''

''He's on his way.''

''What is he doing, riding a pony in from the airport?''

There was a knock at the door.

''Thank God!'' Ruth screamed and ran to answer it. She yanked it open to find Barney Freize staring her in the face.

"I've come to pick up my check."

Ruth turned away, dismissing him. "I can't worry about that right now!"

"Well, Ruthy Wuthy, I think you'd better."

Irving fired a glance at Ruth before she flung back around.

"I think I'd like to come in and perhaps have a cup of tea," Barney said.

Irving jumped up. "I'm Irving Franklin, the engineer." He gestured for Barney to sit next to him as the other board members watched in astonishment. "Please join us. Won't you?" He smiled at Ruth, who for the first time in her life was left speechless.

Nora stood at the doorway greeting members of the National Panty-Hose Association. Some of them had indeed brought books for her to sign, and as she was busy writing "Happy Birthday" or "Best Wishes," she was aware of Richie pacing around nervously.

"You ought to write a book about a panty-hose convention," one of the guests told her.

"Maybe I will," Nora laughed.

"We've got some good stories," the woman chuckled. "Give me a call if you ever need any material."

As the guests floated in they accepted drinks and hors d'oeuvres from the passing waiters. A few wandered out on the terrace to appreciate the view fully.

All the models were waiting in the bedroom, dressed in their panty hose, ready to go. Nick was busy playing host, running in and out with drink orders. Nadine had the stereo going, playing lively energetic music, but at Nora's request kept it at a low-enough level so that people could hear each other talk.

Judd Green came up in the elevator with several other people, and when they stopped to get their name tags, he was happy to see that there were some blank tags left on the table for guests to fill in. For us bad guys, he thought as he wrote LOWELL EVANS in block letters.

Slipping past Nora without saying hello he went over to the bar and ordered a Bloody Mary. He looked around and saw the Blossom guy talking to a girl at the stereo. I'm going to have to get him out of here during the fashion show, he thought. He had a plan that he thought would work. It had to.

The traffic coming from the airport was terrible. Preston rested his head back against the seat and was philosophical.

"This morning when I woke up, my head was pressed to Mother Earth. The cawing of whatever bird it was up in the sky was music to my ears. I realized on this trip that the pursuit of money is something I should have given up a long time ago."

"Oh, someone broke down in the middle lane, that's our problem," the driver said nervously, concentrating on the road.

"Yup. My happiness was out on the trails with a mule I called Ruth."

The driver looked in the rearview mirror. "You want to call Ruth?" he asked quickly.

"I'd like to," Preston said with a tear in his eye,

"but I'm afraid she'd be a little hard to reach. The poor thing is probably struggling right now without me there on her back, my legs wrapped around her, patting her, tickling her, giving her encouragement."

The driver's eyes nearly popped out of his head. *I was told it was company policy not to date anyone else at Calla-Lily,* he thought.

Regan stood in the corner talking to Nadine, Joey and Scott. The guys had come over together after Joey finished work.

"I've got to see how my girls do," Scott smiled. "I want to find out if you're paying them too much."

"Ha-ha," Nadine said. "This is for a good cause."

Outside in the hallway Nora surveyed the few name tags left unclaimed.

"How are you doing, Richie?" she asked when he stepped out the door.

"The place is crowded, isn't it, Nora?"

"It sure is. Are you nervous?"

"Yes."

Nora smiled at him. "Keep the faith. Oh, good. Here come Luke and Ed and Bridget."

"We met in the elevator," Bridget said exuberantly. When she stepped in the doorway she added, "It looks like you have a sold-out show."

"Let's hope they're the right audience!" Richie exclaimed. "Nora, when do you think we should start?"

"Dayton Rotter hasn't gotten here yet."

"Then by all means let's wait."

Ruth deliberately kept a general discussion going, not wanting people to break into private conversations. The last thing she needed was to have Irving and Barney talk. Irving was a troublemaker and she couldn't stand the thought of him having any more power over her. It was bad enough he had those pictures of her and Danny from the Christmas party. When the doorbell rang, Ruth practically ejected from her seat. This time she found Preston Landers standing there clad in his boots and spurs, cowboy hat, plaid shirt, and fringed vest. He was twirling a lasso and was munching chewing tobacco.

"Howdy, partner," was his greeting.

"YOU!" Ruth practically lunged at him. "Get in here!"

"Whoa. Down girl, down girl," he said as he swaggered into the boardroom to the total astonishment of his colleagues. He tipped his hat. "Howdy."

"Howdy," they all mumbled self-consciously.

Ruth threw a piece of paper at him. "SIGN THIS!"

"I've got to look over the fine print here, ma'am . . ." he said, but Ethel interrupted, covering the mouthpiece of the phone with her hand.

"Excuse me, Ruth,"—Ethel braced herself—"but Dayton Rotter just pulled in downstairs."

"SIGN! SIGN! SIGN!" By now Ruth was jumping up and down.

Preston submitted, scrawling his name, and before he could finish saying "Here's my John Hancock," Ruth had flown out the door, with Ethel, Irving, Barney and the Calla-Lily board members in hot pursuit.

NORA GLANCED AT her watch. It was five past three. "It looks like everybody's having a good time, but we shouldn't keep them waiting too much longer," she told Richie. "Dayton Rotter might not even show up."

"You're right, Nora."

"If he's not here by three-fifteen, I'll give them a little welcoming speech to try and stall for a few more minutes . . ."

"She's got the gift of gab, Richie," Luke said soothingly. "Dayton Rotter will get here before she finishes telling everybody how thrilled she is to see them."

Richie watched Nora thread her way through the crowd to whisper something in Nadine's ear. He could tell Nora was telling Nadine when to lower the music so she could start her speech. Then Nora joined a cluster of people on the terrace.

"I'm too nervous to stay here," Richie moaned. "I might get sick or something. I'll give the girls a pep talk and then I'm gonna stand by the door. I don't want to faint or anything."

Luke watched sympathetically as Richie bolted down the hall to the bedroom door, followed by the young fellow who'd been introduced as Scott. He had something to do with the modeling agency, Luke thought.

Richie was about to tap on the bedroom door when he felt a hand on his arm. He jumped. "What?" Then he said sheepishly, "Gee-whiz, Scott, I'm a bundle of nerves, I guess. I didn't realize you were there."

"Richie, I finally get you alone. I have to talk to you."

"Gee, Scott. Can't it wait?"

"I wish it could. Richie, one of the biggest movie producers saw your commercial. He thought it was great. He's casting a movie that he thinks you might be perfect for. But he needs a special picture of you right away. His photographer is standing by at the elevator."

"Me in a movie? You need a picture? What about the stack of pictures you already got of me? I paid plenty to have those done."

"Richie, they're not right for this." Scott's face was inches from his. "Richie, trust me. Why do you think I'm in this business? It's because I get a gut feeling. It'll only take five minutes."

"Five minutes?"

"Absolutely."

"I can't miss the fashion show. I make a speech at the end of it."

"Richie, you'll be back. I swear. But don't mention it to anybody. If Elmer finds out, he'll want his picture taken too, and they're just not interested in him. You'll only be gone a couple of minutes."

"Okay. Okay. Sure. Why not? It's kind of fun doing commercials. I can just imagine doing a movie." He hesitated. "The only thing is maybe it's fair for Elmer to have his picture taken too. You know he's always been mad that I got the commercial he was up for."

"Forget Elmer. He's always hanging around the office moaning. See what I mean about not letting this get around? It may not even come off, so keep it under your hat."

Richie put his thumb and forefinger together. Gee-whiz, he thought, maybe this could really turn out to be my lucky day. Somebody might buy my Birdie Panty Hose, and I may become a movie star. The thought should have been reassuring. Instead it made him more nervous as he tapped on the bedroom door.

"Come in," someone yelled. When he opened the door, Annabelle said, "Oh, it's you, Richie. We're all set."

"You girls look great," he said fervently.

They were starting to line up in the order in which they'd appear on the runway. Annabelle was holding a copy of Nora's script. She explained, "Richie, we were doing a run-through," then turned back to the models. "Bessie, when Mrs. Reilly says, 'They come in all colors . . .' "

Richie interrupted, "Girls, I just wanted to wish you luck. I'm gonna ask you to do what I know you're gonna do. Your best. Your very best. For the Fourth Quarter. For home. For country." He swallowed, choked up.

"Get out of here, Richie," Flo ordered. "We know what to do. Bettina," she bellowed, "what's holding you up in there?"

"I must have gotten a sunburn yesterday," a voice called from the bathroom, "all of a sudden my legs itch."

WHEEZING AND GASPING, Ruth raced up the stairwell, threw open the door and stormed down the hallway, her entourage half a flight behind her. This almost makes me want to give up cigarettes, she thought as she aimed for the open door of the manager's penthouse.

Sounds of voices, laughter and music did not reassure her. There was a crowd in there. A crowd of sharks ready to devour the Calla-Lily Company profits, destroy her grandpa's lifework, all because some schlemiel had nothing better to do than invent unsnaggable panty hose.

A horrifying thought hit her. She didn't even know what that schlemiel looked like. She braked long enough to let Barney Freize catch up with her. "What does this jerk look like?" she snarled.

"I'll point him out to you," Barney panted. He knew that Richie might wonder why he was showing up with the people who were trying to buy his patent. Barney didn't care. He didn't trust Ruthy Wuthy as far as you could throw her, which wasn't very far. If she didn't hand over his check at the same minute she tried to get Richie to sign on the dotted line, he'd tell Richie that Ruth wanted his patent at any price.

And she did. But this way, Richie would come out with plenty of big bucks and Barney would have a little nest egg.

They were almost at the door of the suite when Richie stepped into the hallway. "There he is," Barney exclaimed.

In a final burst of speed, Ruth materialized like an apparition in front of Richie. "Five million," she gasped. She waved a paper in front of his face, thrust a pen in his hand. "Sign here. One-time-only offer."

"What?" Richie blinked. From behind he could hear the music fade into the background as Nora began to speak.

"Hello, everyone, and welcome. I'm Nora Regan Reilley, and I'm delighted to have you with us for what I think is one of the most exciting half hours any of you in the panty-hose business will ever experience."

"Sign!" Ruth snarled.

Richie's eyes became unfocused as he saw the check. RICHARD BORIS BLOSSOM . . . FIVE MILLION DOLLARS.

And it was a cashier's check. Not like the ones he and Birdie used to write to each other as a joke on their birthdays. The biggest one they had ever written was for one million dollars. They're kidding, he thought. It's a gag. He spotted Barney.

"Hey, you saved my life last night. What are you trying to do, Barney?" he asked. "Give me a heart attack now? What's this all about?"

He glanced down the hall. Barney was a real card but Richie didn't want to miss the chance to be in a movie.

"It's for real, you dodo," Ruth growled. "And ten percent of the Birdie Panty Hose line of the Calla-Lily Hosiery Company, Inc."

Something hit Richie. This might be on the level. "Wait a minute," he asked, "does your engineer have a mother-in-law who got a manicure yesterday?"

"What the hell does that have to do with anything?" Ruth screamed. "Irving?"

"Yes, Ruthy."

The Calla-Lily contingent was now gathered behind Ruth.

"Did your mother-in-law have her nails done yesterday?" Ruth demanded.

"Yes. And since you ask, she isn't happy about the shade. She thinks it might have a little too much brown in it, Wuthy."

"I'll get you," she hissed between clenched teeth.

This is for real, Richie thought. They've checked out my panty hose. They know it works.

Nora's modulated voice was clear on the loudspeaker. "Our first model is Annabelle. She is wearing a luscious shade of twilight-peach panty hose. Notice how it hugs her legs, how it shimmers in the light, how it flatters the ankle. That's it, Annabelle . . . Let everyone see how beautiful they are . . ." Ruth heard the genuine applause as the bile rose in her throat.

Down the hall, there was a flurry at the elevator. A bunch of people were getting off.

Ruth looked wild-eyed over her shoulder. Head and shoulders above his entourage and the photographers clustered around him, the familiar face of Dayton Rotter approached like a nightmare come true. Fish or cut bait. That's what Grandpa had always taught her. She forced herself to stand straight, act calm.

"Unless you sign this agreement immediately and accept this check, I officially withdraw my offer," she announced.

With unwilling admiration, Irving thought, Ruthy, I've got to hand it to you. You have guts. He knew if Blossom turned her down, she would kill herself.

Richie wavered. Maybe I'll get more, he thought, his eyes glued on the check. And maybe I won't. Like Ed said, there's nothing you can be sure of except death and taxes. And suppose the other companies like the Birdies a lot but want to take an option till they check them out. That won't buy the Fourth Quarter. This will.

"It's a pleasure to do business with you," he said grandly as he reached for the pen. He started to sign the agreement "Richard Blossom," then hesitated.

Dayton Rotter was footsteps away.

"Sign," Ruth whined.

"Just want to make sure I use my full name so the whole thing is legal," Richie assured her benevolently as, in clear Palmer Method penmanship, he wrote "Richard Boris Blossom."

He put the check in his breast pocket and exchanged a vigorous handshake with Ruth. Still not believing his good fortune, he said, "I never wanted to leave a spot less, but I promised to see someone for just a minute. Why don't you folks go on inside and watch your panty hose being shown off?"

"You bet we will," Ruth gloated as she locked her fingers around the contract. Triumph in her eyes, she smiled viciously as the Rotter entourage entered the foyer and began to watch the fashion show.

"I'll take my check now, too," Barney said to Ruth.

"Give it to him, Ethel," Ruth ordered.

"I have it right here."

ETHEL COULDN'T BELIEVE it. The contract was signed. Now they could all start to breathe again, she hoped. Like Snow White and the Seven Dwarfs, Ruth and the others swept past her to crowd into the room where the fashion show was taking place.

Ethel knew exactly what Ruth was doing. Making up the speech she'd deliver to announce to her rivals that Calla-Lily had struck a deal for Birdie Panty Hose. In a way it was a shame. That panty hose was really pretty and she knew that Ruth wouldn't bring it onto the market until the patent expired. That was in seventeen years. I probably won't be around to get any on discount, Ethel thought.

She realized she needed a couple of aspirins. She'd just take a minute to run down to the suite and get some. Sitting with Ruth since dawn waiting for Preston Landers had been a nerve-racking experience. Ethel thought she'd rather have a full-time job walking pit bulls.

She started down the hall and turned the corner. Mr. Blossom was stepping into the elevator with a tall man. "Hold it, please," she bellowed as she sprinted forward.

Richie smiled benevolently as he held the door, ignoring the photographer who told him to let her wait. "This lady and I just took care of some important business together," he said as Ethel hopped past him into the elevator.

Regan stood nervously in the corner of the room. She didn't want to obstruct anyone's view of the runway. It was going so well she couldn't believe it. She watched the way people were huddling and whispering. She could tell how impressed they were. Even so, it was a long shot that a valid contract could be signed as fast as Richie needed the money.

"It's looking good," Luke whispered in her ear.

Regan glanced up at him. "Dad, where's Richie?"

"He's okay. He's by the door. Said he can't stand to be in here."

"I don't blame him. What the heck was that noise outside?"

"Some latecomers arrived. Over there." He pointed at Ruth and the Calla-Lily group. "Look at the expression on her face. She looks like the cat who ate the canary."

"Never mind them," Regan said. "There's Dayton Rotter. He did get here in time. Keep your fingers crossed."

Six of the models were now clustered beside Nora. Three more were on the runway. They were all in great form, Regan thought. The Fourth Quarter residents were thoroughly in the spirit of the occasion. Bessie lifted her skirt to do a peekaboo of her knee as she coquettishly turned, stopped and posed. Their legs looked great. Regan could see the intense interest on Dayton Rotter's face.

Regan looked over at Nadine, who winked at her as a new CD came on. "Hal-le-lu-jah" started to play. The models near Nora began to sway, building up to the grand finale.

"Rotter missed the beginning," Regan told Luke. "I'm going to talk to him." She slipped through the crowd.

"Stunning!" Regan heard a thin, sharp-featured woman say as she passed. "The whole collection is absolutely stunning."

Dayton Rotter was whispering to Scott, who was shaking his head vigorously. "You've got me wrong," he was saying as Regan approached.

"I don't get things wrong too much," Rotter said. "But I'm sure *you* know who you are. I'm telling you, you're a dead ringer for him."

"Mr. Rotter," Regan began in a low voice. "I'm Regan Reilly. We're so pleased you're able to be here."

Rotter turned from Scott. "I thought I knew this guy," he said in a low voice. "Thought I met him with his uncle in South America last year."

"You didn't," Scott said shortly.

"Well, it wouldn't have been the worst thing if I was right," Rotter told him. "The man I thought was your uncle is one of the few who ever beat me out of a real estate deal."

Regan looked at Scott, who raised his eyebrows and shrugged.

"I've heard a lot about this panty hose," Rotter said quietly. "I'd like to talk to Mr. Blossom afterward."

"That would be wonderful," Regan whispered. "I just wish you had a better view."

"I've got good eyes."

Richie was not standing at the door. He's probably stepped out in the hall, Regan thought. It was almost the finale of the show. He should start moving up toward the microphone to make his speech. I'd better get him.

Before she could take a step toward the door she heard her mother say, "And now Bettina is wearing cameo ivory, the delicate shade that enhances the most enchanting summer frock. Bettina . . . Bettina, we're waiting."

Regan whirled around. Why wasn't Bettina coming out? Someone was obviously signaling. Nora's head was bent. She was looking in the direction of the bedroom.

"Oh, I'm sorry to say that Bettina's extreme case of sunburn has caught up with her. I'm afraid that she can't join us on the runway. So we'll go into our closing number. Ladies . . ."

Regan heard the sound of stifled laughter begin to

ripple through the audience. Bessie was scratching her legs vigorously. Annabelle was poking her to make her stop.

What's the matter with her? Regan wondered. She's ruining the show. And what's the matter with Bettina? Oh, my God, she thought. Is Bessie having an allergic reaction to the panty hose? This would kill Richie. And where the heck was he? She stepped out into the hall. With a sinking feeling she saw that it was empty.

"Bessie," Annabelle whispered. "Cut it out. Everybody's looking at you."

"I can't help it. I feel as though I fell into a patch of poison ivy."

A dismayed Nora heard the whispers around her. "I knew nothing could be that good" was the tone of the remarks. The atmosphere of the room was changing rapidly. People were starting to laugh, many with relief.

Irving leaned forward. The old itch test, he thought. A problem that can pop up no matter how many times you test something. What had brought on the reaction now? He'd bet his bottom dollar that in a few minutes they'd all be clawing themselves. Why is it happening to so many of them at once? He'd have to find out.

"What the hell is going on?" Ruth snarled.

The models were valiantly doing their well-rehearsed version of the Rockettes' famous kick. That only served to give everyone a better view of Bessie's legs, which were now beet-red. But a scream went up in the room

when the worst possible disaster of all unfolded. Everyone watched transfixed as a run crept its relentless path
up willowy Annabelle's nine-mile legs. "Get him,"
Ruth shrieked. "Get that lying, cheating schmuck."

She mowed people down as she raced from the room.
"Where is he? Where's Blossom?"

ENJOY YOUR PICTURE taking," Ethel said brightly as she left the elevator.

"That is one nice lady," Richie said heartily as the elevator door closed behind her.

Judd Green did not answer.

"I appreciate the chance to try out for the movie. Who did you say the producer is?"

"I didn't. I'm not supposed to say."

Richie's spirits refused to be dampened by the attitude of the man who had introduced himself as the photographer. Richie had protested going downstairs but Green had brusquely explained that his photography equipment was set up in a seminar room off the lobby.

The check in his breast pocket electrified Richie. He was so excited that he hoped he'd be able to concentrate on however they wanted him to pose. He was thinking of the party he had planned to throw if the contract was signed.

"Come on," Judd urged, taking his arm.

Richie hadn't even noticed the elevator had stopped at the lobby. "Oh, sure. Sorry." Dutifully he allowed himself to be hustled from the elevator bank down the deserted hallway to the cluster of abandoned seminar rooms.

The last door was closed. Green knocked on it three times, a staccato rapping.

It was opened instantly. "All set?" Green asked, his voice suddenly genial.

"All set," a burly man in a mover's uniform agreed.

"All set," an equally hefty guy in the same uniform confirmed.

"Holy cow," Richie said as the door closed behind him and he got a look at the room. At least two dozen caskets were lined up. "What is this gonna be, a horror movie?" he asked, laughing.

"You got it," Judd said. "Now we have kind of a funny request for you. You have to climb in this casket for the picture." He indicated one that was open.

"Climb in a casket? Holy smoke. Okay, I've come this far. I thought I was up for a speaking part."

"There's a flashback scene," Judd assured him.

"The crazy things actors will do to get a job," Richie joked as, supported by the two men in uniform, he climbed the little stepladder. " 'Can you jump out of an airplane? Sure. No problem . . . Do you ski with one foot? Every weekend . . . Can you walk a tightrope? Watch me.' "

He thrust his left leg over the edge. "Hope I don't get this nice satin lining dirty. Want me to take off my shoes?"

"Just get in."

Richie obediently hoisted himself into the coffin and asked, "Sitting up or lying down?"

"Lie down," Judd directed. "Have a smile on your face. I'll take your picture like that. Then, when I say, 'Now,' I want you to sit up straight with a great big grin."

"It's a comedy, not a horror movie. I like that better," Richie confided as he sank his head into the soft ruffles and shut his eyes. "My wife loved funny movies. She should see me in this one."

As the coffin lid snapped shut, Richie had the horrifying thought that he hadn't noticed a camera anywhere.

ETHEL TOOK THE elevator back to the penthouse floor. She knew she'd better be there for Ruth's victory speech. Already she was sure the aspirin was doing some good. Her headache was fading. As she turned the corner of the hallway, she ran smack into a young woman.

"Sorry," Regan said, then added quickly, "Are you going to the panty-hose fashion show?"

"Yes." Why on earth did the poor girl look so worried? Ethel wondered.

"Do you by any chance know Richie Blossom?"

"Oh, yes. I just met him."

"Do you know where he is?"

"He went down in the elevator a few minutes ago to have his picture taken."

"His picture taken!" Regan exclaimed. "Where?"

"I'm not sure. Something about a seminar room."

"Was he alone?"

"No. I think the man he was with was a photographer."

Regan experienced a moment of pure despair. "What did that man look like?"

Ethel knew this was serious. She frowned. "Tall," she said quickly. "Thin face. Wearing a light jacket. Wait a minute. When he pressed the elevator button I noticed he had a really mean scrape on the back of his hand."

Oh, my God, Regan thought. With total clarity she could see the hand of the rollerblader scraping along the sidewalk. She raced past Ethel and pressed her finger on the elevator button, holding it there.

Ethel followed her. "Is that nice Mr. Blossom in trouble?"

"Big trouble. My mother is Nora Regan Reilly. Tell her and my father it's an emergency. Send them down to the seminar rooms. They all have to be searched." The elevator door opened. Regan rushed into the car.

Ethel hurried around the corner and flattened herself against the wall as a herd of Calla-Lily directors charged behind Ruth toward the elevator bank. Preston Landers was swinging his lariat, yelling, "This is fun. I never thought I'd say it, but I'm glad to be back."

REGAN RUSHED OFF the elevator and didn't know which way to go. The hallway to the left led to the seminar rooms where the panty-hose convention had been held. She remembered that the funeral convention was down the hallway to the right.

The panty-hose area. That would be a logical place for someone to tell Richie he wanted to take his picture. Not caring that people stared as she passed, she rushed to that section.

The whine of vacuums greeted her. Discarded posters were being bundled into trash cans. There seemed to be an army of maids cleaning up. She could see that all the doors of the rooms were open.

Regan rushed up to a woman with a clipboard who

was supervising the activity. "Is anyone using any of these rooms?" she demanded.

"Nope, they've all cleared out."

"By any chance have you seen two men around here? One is in his seventies, wearing a blue jacket. The other is tall and thin and has a badly scraped hand."

"Haven't seen them." The housekeeper looked pointedly at her clipboard.

Regan turned and raced in the opposite direction. For all she knew, Richie was miles away by now. But she knew he wouldn't leave the building willingly. He had to think his picture was being taken somewhere in here. The woman upstairs who'd been on the elevator with him did say she heard the word "seminar." She'd try the funeral-seminar rooms now. She only prayed that her father had alerted the hotel security to look for Richie.

The moment she reached the corridor of quiet, empty rooms, Regan thought, this is the kind of place Richie might have been taken. She rushed down the hallway, glancing into every room, sweeping her eyes back and forth. Silence. No one.

Her footsteps echoed. The lights were dim in this area, and there were dark shadows along the interior corridor.

She was almost at the end of the hallway. Only one room left. This door was closed. She heard voices inside. She turned the handle. The door was locked.

Something pressed against her back. She whirled her head. Scott was standing behind her. "Need help, Regan?'' he asked as he rapped sharply three times on the door.

Scott! The gasoline can in the garage last night. Dayton Rotter's comments about real estate deals with Scott's uncle. Richie being led off to have his picture taken.

"You!'' Regan breathed. She knew better than to cry out. Scott didn't have to tell her it was the barrel of a gun she was feeling. From inside the room she could hear a thud like a door closing.

Scott rapped again. In that moment, she turned and with all her strength jammed her palm under his nose. His head snapped back and she twisted the gun from his hand. It went off, the bullet hitting the ceiling.

Preston heard the shot as the Calla-Lily group stepped off the elevator. "Enemy fire,'' he howled. Twirling his lariat, he raced past even Ruth, following the direction of the sound.

"Where did you tell my daughter to go?'' Luke asked Ethel urgently.

"I told her that the photographer said something about a seminar room.''

The panty-hose fashion show had come to a tragic end. The special cream Nick had left in his room for them to use on their legs had reacted badly with Richie's new fabric. It had just hit the stores in South Beach a few days before. And if *that* cream could do in the panty hose, others could as well.

The guests were happily ordering more Bloody Marys in unabashed celebration that the threat to their business had been permanently snagged.

Nadine had just received a request for a replay of "Hal-le-lujah" from H. Mason Hicks, Junior, a beaming panty-hose executive.

"Drop dead," she told him.

Nick hurried over to Luke. "What else is wrong?"

On his way out the door, Nora at his side, Luke stopped long enough to snap, "We think Richie's in trouble and Regan is trying to find him."

"I'll put out an alert."

"She was going to the seminar rooms first," Ethel cried as she ran behind Luke and Nora.

"Something's up, Nadine," Joey said.

From across the room Nadine had seen the distress in Luke's face. "Let's go find out, Joey," she said.

RICHIE TRIED TO bang his arms against the lid of the casket. The thick satin lining muffled the sound. He felt the casket being wheeled and heard a door opening. Those guys weren't actors, he thought. He tried to shout and knew that it was no use.

The casket was picked up, bumped into the side of something, then Richie felt himself being slid, as if they were pushing the casket into a van. Oh, Birdie, he thought, what do I do now?

Take it easy, he thought. Breathe slowly. There can't be much air in this thing.

He heard the sound of an engine, then whatever vehicle he was in began to move.

* * *

Regan aimed the gun at Scott. Someone must have heard the shot, she thought frantically. There was no longer any sound inside the room. This had to be where they'd taken Richie. What were they doing to him?

Scott was trying to come nearer. Wiping the blood from his nose, edging toward her, his eyes calculating.

"Don't take another step," she said.

"You wouldn't shoot me, Regan." His hand shot up; he lunged toward her. She aimed the gun down at his foot. She'd stop him if she had to.

An ear-splitting whoop made Scott jump.

"Need any help, ma'am?" Preston Landers hollered, hurling his lasso, which to Regan's astonishment settled around Scott's shoulders. "Want me to hog-tie this pup? My posse's on the way."

Regan was frantic to find Richie. She saw the crowd of people approaching. "This man is dangerous, hold on to him," she called.

Irving was a step behind Ruth. "We'll take care of him."

"Where's Blossom?" Ruth screamed.

Regan tried to open the door. It was locked.

"Stand aside, everybody," she commanded. "I've got to fire this gun to get the door open."

With the exception of Ruth, they scattered like leaves in the wind. Preston held one end of the rope as Irving herded the lassoed Scott into a nearby room.

Regan took aim. One bullet was enough to shatter the lock. She rushed into the room and gasped as she saw the rows of coffins. The room was completely still. She raced for the door at the far end of the room.

As she shoved it open, she saw a nondescript van pulling away. Taking aim, she fired at the back tires.

From behind her she could hear shouting voices—her father's, Nick's, Joey's.

Her first shot had barely missed the farther rear tire. Steadying the gun on her left wrist, she aimed again. This time she was rewarded by the sound of a blowout. The van careened. Once again she aimed. Got you, she thought as the other back tire blew. If only I'm not too late.

Three men jumped from the van. Luke, Joey and Nick appeared from behind Regan and began to chase them.

"Be careful," Regan shouted. "They may be armed."

Nick caught up with the tallest and jumped on his back, tackling him to the ground as security guards poured into the area and subdued the other two.

Regan raced to the van and yanked open the doors. The coffin. Richie had to be in it. She jumped up, crouched beside it, fumbled, desperate to open the lid.

She hear the click as the lock released, uttered a fervent prayer and raised the lid. A pale Richie smiled up at her. "Boy, are you a sight for sore eyes!" he said.

"Oh, Richie, I'm so glad you're all right," Regan said.

"So how'd the show go?" he asked.

"Richie, I have bad news. There is something wrong with the panty hose after all. You won't be able to sell it."

"You're right, Regan, I won't." Richie reached in

his breast pocket and pulled out the cashier's check for five million dollars. "I already did. Let's get to one of the quick-deposit machines."

Ruth was trying to climb into the van. "Thief. Impostor. Liar. Cheat. Scoundrel."

Richie whispered. "Regan, quick, put the lid down."

A CHEER WENT up in the Dolly Twiggs Memorial Room Monday afternoon as Richie ceremoniously received the deed for the Fourth Quarter from Dolly's sister, Lucille. A delighted Joey represented the real estate agency in the transaction.

"Speaking for my sister, Dolly, I am thrilled that you will all be able to stay in the house that she so loved," Lucille gushed. She was so happy she almost couldn't speak. Arthur had surprised her by flying in that morning. "I love Lucy," he'd said, "and I missed her more every day. I couldn't wait any longer to see her." Lucille gazed at him across the room. He winked back at her and threw a kiss.

"Thank you, Lucille. Bless your memory, Dolly.

Long live the residents of this home," Richie declared. "For it is ours and ours forever."

Flo put down her tray of Gatorade and cookies to lead the vigorous applause.

"And now, everybody," Richie concluded, "the caterers should be ready for us out back. They've got champagne and anything you can think of to eat. Enjoy."

He stepped from the podium and hugged a beaming Ethel. She was so special. And she'd played a part in his rescue by telling Regan where he'd disappeared to.

"I feel a little guilty about Ruth," he whispered to her, but looking into Ethel's smiling eyes made him forget. It was almost like when he had looked at Birdie.

"Don't feel guilty, Richie. They have her in therapy now." Ethel and Richie both laughed.

"You're bad," he said. "I love it."

"Richie."

Richie turned and Elaine was standing there. "From now on," she said, "I'm the only one who sends you on auditions, okay?"

"Okay, boss."

"Of course now I've got to hire a replacement for that ne'er-do-well."

"I'm available," Ethel piped up. "Believe me, I'm available."

Barney Freize came up and shook Richie's hand. "I've got to hand it to you, Richie. I was thinking that I wouldn't mind getting an apartment in this place. That is, if you're allowed to smoke cigars!"

"We'd love to have you living here, Barney. We'd

light up out on the front porch and watch the world go by.'' Richie looked around the room and got a lump in his throat. He was with all his friends. Everyone looked so happy. Even Elmer.

Regan leaned against the back wall and smiled. All's well that ends well, she thought. When Scott had been promised that the prosecutor wouldn't press for the death penalty if he came clean, he'd sung his heart out. His uncle had quietly bought up the property adjacent to the Fourth Quarter and had wanted to build a luxury resort building, which would have included space for a modeling agency for Scott. Judd Green was their hit man. Scott admitted that Green had been paid to kill Dolly last year. Elmer had unwittingly kept Scott abreast of the Fourth Quarter's attempts to raise money to save their home. They hadn't worried about the pot-holder sales, but when Elmer started talking about Richie's snag-proof panty hose, they got nervous and thought they might not get to buy the Fourth Quarter.

Nick was nearby holding the hand of one of the models who'd fallen in love when she'd witnessed his bravery on Saturday. They followed Luke and Nora and Ed and Bridget out to where the party was starting.

John and Maura were standing next to Regan. Their luggage was in the car. Everyone had had a great time at their wedding yesterday and had partied at the hotel until the wee hours.

''We couldn't miss this,'' Maura said to Regan. ''We're going to grab a glass of that champagne and be off.''

"I think our parents are back there popping the corks right now," Regan laughed.

Nadine and Joey came over to Regan.

"You know, Regan, now that Scott's in the pokey, I'm going to need a new roommate," Joey said and paused. "I asked Nadine to marry me."

"What a Romeo," Nadine beamed. "And I want to ask you, Regan, if you'll put on another one of those awful dresses in a few months and be a bridesmaid for me."

"I'd love to. Let's get a drink so we can toast you."

They started out the door when Richie called Regan's name. Regan turned and found him standing in front of her with Ethel at his side. There was a flicker in his eyes she hadn't seen for a long time.

"I'm so proud of you, Richie," Regan said.

"Proud of me? You're the one who saved my life. I don't know how to repay you. But what I was thinking of doing was dedicating this new invention I'm working on to you . . ." He put one arm around Regan, the other around Ethel as he led them to the back patio of the Fourth Quarter. "What I did was take this little gizmo and fiddle around with it and before you knew it . . ."

THUNDER MOUNTAIN

A clap of thunder sounded, and they all turned and stared. Dark smoke issued in a column from the mountainside two miles distant. "What the hell?" an agent muttered, his voice awe filled. Watching bits of flotsam float earthward in the distance.

A new sound emerged from the truck's console.

Link picked out the squealing dosimeter, then quickly switched on the rad meter.

"Ninety milli-roentgens," he said grimly.

"What's that mean?"

"I think someone just blew up the radioactive material at the site and scattered it all to hell."

"Ansel Turpin again," muttered the agent-in-charge.

Ansel Turpin, once the most talented agent, now the most deadly enemy.

DESERT FURY

DESERT FURY

Tom Wilson

A SIGNET BOOK

SIGNET
Published by the Penguin Group
Penguin Putnam Inc., 375 Hudson Street,
New York, New York 10014, U.S.A.
Penguin Books Ltd, 27 Wrights Lane,
London W8 5TZ, England
Penguin Books Australia Ltd, Ringwood,
Victoria, Australia
Penguin Books Canada Ltd, 10 Alcorn Avenue,
Toronto, Ontario, Canada M4V 3B2
Penguin Books (N.Z.) Ltd, 182–190 Wairau Road,
Auckland 10, New Zealand

Penguin Books Ltd, Registered Offices:
Harmondsworth, Middlesex, England

First published by Signet, an imprint of Dutton Signet,
a member of Penguin Putnam Inc.

First Printing, March, 1998
10 9 8 7 6 5 4 3 2 1

PUBLISHER'S NOTE
This is a work of fiction. Names, characters, places, and incidents either are
the product of the author's imagination or are used fictitiously, and any resemblance to actual persons, living or dead, events, or locales is entirely
coincidental.

Here's to those soldiers, sailors, airmen and agents of the free world who dared to serve in the long and often bloody cold war, and who had the moral fortitude and determination to say "no further." They knew heartrending anguish and tolerated craven dissent, but stood toe to toe with their enemies until they broke the back of a truly Evil Empire. If they had not persevered, it would be a different, much darker world.

ACKNOWLEDGMENTS

As always I thank those indispensable persons who make the production of a new novel possible. The agents, editors, artists, publishers, sales representatives, printers, book buyers, drivers, booksellers, and most essentially, the readers.

I'd also like to recognize those residents of northern Nevada who provided such a rich and colorful background, and offered their unique hospitality to a writer they hardly knew. The Carson City to Fallon section of U.S. Highway 50 has to be one of the most interesting sixty-mile drives in America. The Pony Express operated there, as did key stage and rail lines. Mark Twain's older brother was secretary (like our modern lieutenant governor) of the territory, and the great author spent his formative early writing years there. Great fortunes were made, sometimes in the finding and digging or huckstering of mineral ore, at others by the turn of a card or flash of a pretty ankle. Fifty years ago glitzy divorce palaces sprang up around the desert, and done-wrong ladies came for six weeks to rid themselves of inattentive husbands. The names of the establishments were fanciful. One was Break-a-Heart Ranch, and I used both name and location in the novel. The movie *The Misfits* was filmed at a nearby dry lakebed, and Clark Gable and Marilyn Monroe spent a few evenings in the winters of their careers hanging out at a saloon in Dayton.

I changed the names of some communities, businesses and organizations, so I could alter descriptions and nudge locations about to fit the tale. Most geographical and historical details are fact. Some, like setting off nukes underground, were done at different times and locations.

More than a few thank-yous are in order. Like for Rich and Bonnie; Mike and Vickie; Mac and Sallee; Elton Admire—thanks for the loan of your last name, Colonel; Fred—seventy plus, married thirteen times and still looking; Bob and Jan—who display my books in their Break-a-Heart Saloon; Pat—pistol-packing grandma who entertains with tales of how wild the West *really* was, and how it ain't all been won yet, pardner. There are a lot more great gals and guys, and a few scoundrels and no-goods, who helped form my impression of that feisty cross-section of the American West.

Prologue

The white Gulfstream IV with the Weyland Foundation
logo on its side taxied behind a green Gaz tug—a utili-
tarian vehicle that served the same purpose as "follow
me" trucks at western airports—to a location at the far
end of the field, out of the eye of casual observation. As
the Rolls-Royce engines whined to a halt, a dark sedan
pulled in beside the aircraft. A serious-faced Caucasian
male in a tan suit emerged and strode up as the hatch
swung open.

"Mr. Dubois?" he addressed the man in the doorway in
a respectful tone. He followed him into the airplane, and
when the hatch was closed, shook hands. "I'm Special
Agent Albee," he said. "Deputy agent-in-charge of the
Nuc-Safe unit." That was FBI jargon for the number-
two American in the joint Bureau/Criminal Unit group
assigned to prevent the plunder of radioactive material
and expertise from Russia. President Boris Yeltsin, during a rare moment of sensible sobriety, had asked the
Americans for help with the problem.

"First, does anyone from your office know you're
here?" Frank Dubois asked.

"No, sir. I was told to maintain secrecy, even from my
own people."

Frank Dubois glanced at the security officer who had
accompanied him. The man looked up from an audio
spectrum analyzer and nodded. The agent's voice pattern
checked. But they had to be certain. "Would you be
embarrassed if we took prints?"

When the agent agreed, the security officer had him press all four fingers of his left hand against a sensing screen. Ten seconds later he nodded again. "He's real."

Frank Dubois motioned the agent into a seat. "I apologize for our caution, but you'll understand when you realize what—or rather who—it's about."

"I was told to exclude our people. Surely you don't think they could be involved in anything illegal."

"Four of the Russians in your office are dirty. Only one of your Americans, but I'm afraid he's *deeply* involved. In fact he's our real concern."

Special Agent Albee formed an expression of disbelief. A few minutes later, when he'd heard the rest of it, who the American was and what he'd done, his jaw sagged in amazement. "It's not possible!" he blurted, and a birthmark high on his forehead became vivid as he flushed.

As they were being driven to the prosecutor's office— it was, after all, basically a Russian matter—Frank Dubois explained more. How the Weyland Foundation had been asked by the Russians to help with a nuclear weapons dismantling program—how three goons had roughed up a foundation project leader demanding access to the nuclear material, and the subsequent investigation pointed not only to the Russian mafia but also to the Nuc-Safe field office. Then to four of the Russians assigned to Nuc-Safe. Then to the brains of the outfit.

Not only was he an American, he was the top FBI agent in northwestern Russia. Special Agent Albee's superior, his reporting official, was a crook. He knew his nuclear physics and was an extraordinary impersonator. He'd taught it at the FBI academy. It was said that he could pose as your brother so convincingly you'd never suspect. Also your father. Your mother, maybe.

The rogue agent's name was Ansel Turpin.

When they arrived at the prosecutor's office, a stark, imposing granite edifice to justice, a dozen trench-coated policemen—armed, scowling, and looking precisely like what they were—waited. The prosecutor himself met them and treated Frank Dubois with the fawning respect due an executive of the Weyland Foundation, the organization that had been active in the rebuilding of Russia from the moment the statues of Lenin and KGB founder Dzerzhinsky were toppled. After five years of western-style mobsterism, a lot of people wished they had Vladimir and Feliks back, but they trusted and liked the foundation.

The prosecutor told them Special Agent Turpin was under observation. Not closely followed, since that might alert him, but surreptitiously. The prosecutor seemed proud that they were able to do that to a member of Washington's finest without being detected. He introduced them to a stern-faced woman from the Russian ministry of justice and an equally somber man from the American embassy, both just arrived from Moscow.

Special Agent Albee was still arguing there was no way it could be his supervisor, aware that the development might mark the end of his own career. But the prosecutor, the woman from the ministry of justice, and even the American diplomat ignored him. The air was increasingly charged with excitement. There would be no immunity involved. If he resisted the slightest bit, Special Agent-in-Charge Turpin was fair game. He was a plague upon the Russians and an embarrassment to the Americans.

Ansel Turpin had taken the day off—he was at home in one of several apartments he and his criminal group kept, and although he was alone, the prosecutor did not like the odds of his men facing a professional on his own familiar ground. He preferred a more neutral location and waited, ignoring the impatience of his detectives.

The prosecutor took a call from the people observing Turpin's apartment. A slight Russian woman, one of two on the Nuc-Safe project known to spend the night periodically with Turpin, had arrived. A short while later a tall, blond-haired male went inside.

"He's especially dangerous," Frank Dubois cautioned the already nervous prosecutor. The Weyland Foundation investigation had been thorough. The tall man had served as an officer in the Soviet special forces—was now a known criminal and Ansel Turpin's primary connection to the so-called Russian mafia.

A member of the plainclothes detail gave a macho
shrug, and said: "They all bleed." The prosecutor pursed
his lips, eyes narrowed, waiting.

Another call. All three had left the apartment. They'd
gotten into a Mercedes sedan. The blond was driving.
Ansel Turpin was not in disguise, as he normally was
when he ventured out of the apartments at night. All
three were talking animatedly.

The dour woman from the ministry of justice said they
might be celebrating. Her office had learned about a
transaction that had been consummated. The Iranians
had paid top price, a hundred million dollars in cash and
bullion, for delivery of a shipment of uranium 235.

Contact with the Mercedes was maintained. After
twenty minutes a tail confirmed they'd parked in front
of a popular American-style club. They could hear loud
rock-and-roll music from inside.

The prosecutor wanted to wait until they emerged to
take them, but the senior detective argued that they
could achieve surprise if they pounced immediately. The
prosecutor reluctantly approved. The FBI deputy and
the two from Moscow were asked to remain behind.
Frank Dubois was free to go along if he wished, part of
the esteem Russian authorities reserved for the Weyland
Foundation. After all, it had been the foundation that
had investigated and learned about the rogue FBI agent.

Frank took them up on the offer.

Just stay out of our line of fire, said the senior
detective.

When they arrived at the club they were told that the
three were inside, seated somewhere near the front. The
blond man had just been seen going toward the rear
alone. Likely to the rest room, the observers believed.

"Good." The senior cop decided that four would enter
immediately and take them while they were separated.
The rest would wait at front and rear entrances to catch
anyone who fled.

The policemen disdained subtlety, walked in, and
stood near the entrance in full view, intimidating, hands
in overcoat pockets and looking hard at customers.
Frank followed, unarmed.

The senior detective was in front, peering about with a hard look, when the room exploded with gunfire. Two of the policemen went down, one killed instantly, the other squealing with agony. Frank dropped with them, grasping for a free pistol that had clattered onto the floor.

Their quarry was off to the side in a booth, calm, big automatic pistol held in both hands as if he were on a firing range, ignoring his female companion who was sucking air through a bloody chest wound. His weapon bucked as he took out the police supervisor with a head shot. The fourth Russian policeman was bolting for the door as Turpin calmly switched his aim.

Frank found the pistol, a Tokarev 7.62 police issue, and hurried his fire. Got in an off-center but bloody knee shot. Ansel Turpin crumpled, leg twisting under him. He screamed—it seemed more from rage than pain—hit the floor and twisted, and was trying to bring the automatic up when Frank reached him and twisted it from his grasp.

The fourth policeman returned cautiously, face pale and pistol held before himself, and tensed angrily as he approached Turpin.

"Don't," Frank said, and placed a restraining hand on the Russian's arm. Someone was shouting that the blond man had escaped, and there were questions.

As they clamped his arms behind him, using heavy steel Russian handcuffs, Turpin turned his gaze upon Frank. Even when the policeman gave the cuffs a yank and jostled his shattered knee so violently he screamed in agony, Ansel stared. Hard. Until something passed between them. Nothing nice—more like pure hatred.

Frank should have let the policeman shoot him. Two days later, a heavily armed group broke into the hospital, executed a nurse and the three men guarding him, and carried Ansel Turpin away. The leader of the rescuers was a tall blond man.

An unsigned message was delivered to Frank Dubois, by then back in New York City attending to the affairs of his huge organization. It read: *We are not done. Now it is my turn.*

For the following month there was a bloody spree in and around St. Petersburg, and nineteen employees of the Weyland Foundation were stalked and killed as savagely as animals. When the renegade FBI agent died in a spectacular explosion, there was a collective sigh of relief. You probably read about it, maybe saw the coverage on CNN and didn't realize that an American was involved. It would have been an embarrassment for the administration, coming in the middle of a presidential election. Like so many other things at the time, it was withheld from the public eye.

The following year, Frank Dubois was severely injured in an aircraft accident, and upon his return to the Weyland Foundation, headquartered in New York City, he was confined to a wheelchair with poor prospects of walking again. But his crisp mind was not affected, and he was named chairman of the huge organization his grandfather had founded. Yet even after the passage of another year, he could not forget the hatred that had poured from the eyes of the man named Ansel Turpin.

May 1998—Misfits Saloon, Stagecoach Valley, Nevada

Trudy Schmidt had just come in the back door and was headed for the ladies room when Bob, the owner and present bartender, spotted her. "Gary's buying a round. You in?"

"Never turned down a drink yet," she called, and waved jauntily to the writer. She entered the rest room, squeezed a smidgen of Colgate onto a finger and ran it over her teeth, tidied her hair and face as best she could in her inebriated state, and went out. Her client was back, seated as far down the bar as possible and trying to act as if nothing had happened. Funny how guys changed so quickly. Snort and paw the dirt when they wanted it, then act like innocent babes the second it was over, like they'd got religion. Trudy knew a lot about the oddities of men.

She took her stool beside the grill cook and made a survey. There were no new arrivals, only the same barhounds, and the writer—who had never shown that sort of interest in her. Except for an occasional smile and leaning forward so more titty could show, Trudy didn't push herself on customers, lest Bob get upset and toss her out on her ass. She just made sure they knew what she was there for, and gave them their money's worth if they gave her the nod. Thankfully, in Stagecoach Valley there was no professional competition, and the amateurs required dinner and dancing on a first date.

When Bob placed a double rum-and-Coke in front of her, Trudy lifted the glass and thanked the writer again.

Forty-four years old and counting, Trudy liked to say she was "semi-retired," for she worked her own hours and could pick or refuse clients. She was still nice enough looking, even if she was so thin some clients called her Chicken Legs. In the summer, those who went out back at an inopportune time might see her crouched in the shadows in front of a client, head bobbing diligently—or in the winter notice her skinny legs pawing the air in the back of her station wagon. Trudy would make house calls if anyone was so inclined and timed the engagement before she'd imbibed too much to remember where to go, but she preferred working out of the bar so she could step back inside and sip a drink while she chatted up another client. Anyway, it just seemed more professional to be able to say she worked somewhere.

For twenty years she'd been employed at one or another of the brothels in Moundhouse, the suburb of Carson City where such establishments were legal. She didn't regret her life as a whore—it was what she did, the only thing she felt qualified to do—but a age forty she'd looked about at younger, prettier women joining the profession and had known it was time to change her life. She'd quit her bordello job and gone searching, looking at places like Elko, Eureka, and Battle Mountain, but nothing had seemed right. Then she'd headed back, and as she'd driven into the crazy-quilt community of Stagecoach, which she'd passed through a thousand times, something clicked. She'd walked into the office of the local entrepreneur who owned most of the valley and agreed to make $270 monthly payments toward the purchase of a mobile home on a barren acre, and the next day bought enough secondhand furniture to fill it.

Bob returned from his drink-pouring task and resumed talking to the writer, who always seemed interested in the history of the valley.

"Back in the forties there wasn't anything here except an army post up in the hills testin' jeeps and such, and an occasional desert rat passing through. Then came the big rumble of nineteen forty-nine, causing a bunch of slides in the mountains, and a covey of prospectors showed up to search through the debris for mineral."

"Rumble?"

"Earthquake. There's a fault line over by Minden that acts up every ten, twenty years. That time there was a couple little ones and then a real shaker."

"We're fifty miles from Minden. It's way over next to the California line."

"Yeah, but it caused those slides here, and there was gold-diggers all over these hills for a while. First civilians to live here since the pony express station shut down back in the eighteen sixties."

Neither Bob nor the writer nor Trudy Schmidt nor any of the others in the saloon knew she was being watched—and carefully evaluated.

When the grill cook—as close to a friend as Trudy Schmidt had—left for the night, Trudy felt it was time to get on home. *Her* home. While it was doubtful she'd actually pay it off, she treasured her acre of desert, and made payments promptly on the first day of each month.

Trudy's needs were not great—four hundred a month for home, auto, and utilities, two hundred more for booze, food, and smokes—so she got by on what she earned working out of the saloon. While her tax-exempt practice was illegal, no one complained. People in Stagecoach Valley weren't like that. Trudy was well enough liked by those who knew her, even if she had no close friends and her family consisted of a mother in Modesto whom she hadn't seen in thirty years, three ex-husbands, all of whom she was still legally married to, and a twenty-six-year-old son she'd given up for adoption but talked about often.

She tired of listening to Bob's historical ramblings, and moved over next to Lester, who had once been a cowboy over near the Ruby Mountains and sometimes liked to go out back for a quickie. He wasn't interested, though. Likely broke, since he lived on a government pension and it had been too long since the eagle had shit, which was how the Social Security bunch referred to payday. She'd turned only the single trick, that one done on credit, and doubted there'd be any others since it was getting so late.

"On my way," she announced cheerfully, as she did every night, and slid off the stool.

As she left she did not know that she was still being observed with particular interest.

The station wagon started with its odd growl, which was growing worse, and she prayed the engine would last until she'd built up enough funds to have it repaired. She drove home cautiously, even though the cops seldom patroled the back roads of Stagecoach Valley. Several policemen lived here and they had to get along with their neighbors.

As Trudy opened the front door she had the feeling that someone had been inside. Since the door had been locked and nothing seemed to be missing, she shrugged it off. Her pudgy, calico-colored cat also seemed skittish, but that was nothing particularly new.

In the bathroom Trudy douched and swished Listerine in her mouth, as she did faithfully every night. She'd learned to take care of the tools of her trade. Her monthly medical checkups—another occupational necessity—showed her to be in good health.

She scrubbed off pancake makeup and spent five full minutes stroking a brush firmly through her tinted brown hair, worn long because a customer had once given her a rare compliment. Finally she pulled on slippers and a cotton shift adorned with tiny rosebuds, checked the house to make sure all was secure, and padded down the hall to her bedroom.

And again came into the scrutiny of the unseen observers.

The cat was already in place on the second pillow, but it was not purring as usual, and stared somberly toward the doorway. Trudy stroked it for a while to turn on its purr machine, then switched off the light and curled up to sleep. Before she dropped off, she heard a faint whir, then a low humming sound from down the hall, and reminded herself to check the refrigerator in the morning to make sure it was operating properly. She was quickly asleep.

The nightmare began soon after. In it Trudy felt a tingling sensation, at first not unpleasant, accompanied by a sense of warmth that engulfed her entire body. It became more and more intense, until she grew so hot she could hardly stand it. Like she was in a microwave oven, being cooked from the inside out. She tried to open her eyes, to rouse herself from the dream, but the effort was too difficult and she only dropped deeper into the awful, pained slumber.

An hour later Trudy was awakened by a plaintive, guttural noise that rose from her own lips. This time she forced her eyes open, and moaned from the piercing sensation that lanced through them. It was as if her eyes had shriveled like prunes. Her body began to shudder, not of her accord, and the involuntary moan continued.

She was sick to her stomach. *Call for help!* her mind cried as the cat too began to thrash and make pitiful noises. The telephone was on the bedside table. With effort she managed to turn on the lamp, but light did little good for her vision was marred by flashing, waving lines that danced wildly and only made her more nauseous. The tingling in her scalp intensified, and when she felt there, hair came out effortlessly and fell about her in swatches.

She could hardly manage to lift the phone from the cradle, dropped it once and weakly retrieved it, then held it to her face and tried to decipher the numbers. She managed to punch in what she believed was 9-1-1 and pulled the receiver closer to her ear. The telephone was dead! Trudy jiggled the cradle lever and listened again—there was no dial tone.

Beside her the cat convulsed and yowled. It was something in the house, affecting the cat too! She had to get out, notify a neighbor. Get them to drive her to the clinic or to the volunteer fire hall where the emergency phones and the paramedic vehicles were located.

Trudy made it out of bed, started for the door, then stumbled and fell. She was too weak to regain her feet, so she began to crawl. She'd made it halfway to the hallway when her stomach was seized in a painful knot and, with a great heaving of her abdomen, she began to vomit. First came liquid and food, then only water issue with strings of blood. She couldn't stop. Each time a spasm subsided, another would follow. It seemed to go on for an eternity. She'd urinated and her bowels had released, but she did not care.

The constrictions continued, and Trudy Schmidt curled into a tight ball, wanting to scream but managing only low whimpers. She sensed that death was near and prayed it would hurry, seeking release from the awful thing that tortured her.

The viewers looked at the woman on the video screen with professional interest, yet their individual reactions were varied. The old man wore a smug look for the death had been precisely as he had predicted. The soft-spoken man was without expression. The corners of the woman's lips were curled downward as if she found the scene distasteful.

Trudy Schmidt was their first, referred to as subject number one. That part of the experiments, gathering information about human reactions, would become easier as they continued. It was an insignificant part of something much grander.

Retribution.

PART I

Break-a-Heart

1

Marie was gone. The person he cherished more than any other was irretrievably taken. That she'd died of a lingering and terribly debilitating disease no longer mattered. The how was in the past, and there remained only the why. When she'd been alive he'd worried about her welfare, done everything possible to reduce her suffering. Only afterward had he, Abraham Lincoln Anderson, dared to suffer the anguish of the survivor. When his fiancée was laid to rest after many months of dying, he went alone to the mountains and brooded with the wind and the soaring eagles, and questioned the judgment of Jehovah for allowing it. It seemed more the doing of *Na'pi,* Old Man, the capricious earthly representative of the creator, who erred often and caught the fury of his wife, *Ko ko mik' e is,* the Moon. "Don't take her, Old Man," he'd once cried out.

After his first month, Joseph Spotted Horse, Marie LeBecque's great uncle, found him in the mountains and joined him. They had not talked of the dead, but instead Joseph had told him about the ways of the Blackfeet in the heady years before the coming of the French traders who gave them whiskey and guns and blankets in exchange for the furs of endlessly plentiful animals.

Some of the full-bloods said that Joseph could dream of the future and speak with animals. Lincoln saw none of that during their stay, except for that last day, when Joseph had arisen and boiled his coffee and proclaimed that Lincoln was needed by his people. And sure enough, when he'd returned to his cabin in Boudie Springs, a messenger had been waiting.

Monday, June 22, 9:15 A.M.—New York City

As the helicopter pilot made his approach, Link Anderson studied the massive Weyland Building, and tried to remember what he'd learned during his brief visit the previous year. The eighth largest structure in the metropolis contained not only the headquarters for the Weyland Foundation but also a complete ecosystem for its inhabitants. There were offices, day care centers, gymnasiums, restaurants, and even fashion outlets on the street floor. Humans had to leave only to sleep and prepare for another work day.

The foundation was the largest and richest such organization in America, and the world was better because of its existence and good works. But for their newest employee there was still much to be understood. There were many tentacles to the organization, and he did not yet comprehend how they worked together, or even *if* they worked together. There were seventy-eight floors, the lower two dozen taken up by the foundation's most visible divisions: Cultural Earth (the arts), Habitat Earth (world ecology), and Mankind Earth (social betterment). But there was more to the Weyland Foundation. For instance, few were aware that parts of the upper building were leased to the various clandestine services of the federal government. And fewer still knew about three special floors where Weyland Foundation project leaders worked quietly, often with the American government, to maintain the world on a peaceful course.

It was that secretive side of the foundation that would make use of Link's skills. He had not sought the position—it was unlikely that he would have accepted it if conditions were different. But the organization's chairman, Frank Dubois, had asked him to return and run the covert operation—take the job he had held before he'd been crippled and promoted into the chairmanship—and Lincoln Anderson would do so.

They'd met as roommates in Saudi Arabia, fighter pilots waiting for the Persian Gulf air war to begin. From different backgrounds: Link raised as a military brat, Frank in great wealth. Dissimilar: Link matter-of-fact, quiet, and trusting, Frank brilliant, gregarious, and quick to suspect Machiavellian ploys. Yet a bond of friendship had formed, and a pledge had been made the night the combat flying had begun to come to one another's assistance without question or hesitation, whenever required. If either man asked for support, it would be given. And it *was* given. During the days of furious combat that followed, both men had found the opportunity to save the other's life. The pledge of support had continued when the flying and fighting had stopped.

The aircraft settled onto one of the rooftop helipads. As the main rotor blade slowed to an idle, Link unbuckled and dismounted. He wore a Western-cut suit, a bolo tie with heavy silver slide, Western boots, and a ten-star quality John B. Stetson hat with cattleman's crease.

A distinguished-looking man—a vice-president who acted as Frank Dubois' aide—approached from a rooftop island that bristled with so many antennae it looked like the superstructure of an aircraft carrier. Some, he remembered, were used by government agencies, others by the Weyland Foundation's worldwide communications network.

"Lawrence," Link said in greeting, and gripped the proffered hand.

"My condolences about your fiancée, Lincoln."

Link responded with only a nod. He did not want to dredge up the hurt.

"Mr. Dubois wanted to be here to greet you, but the Secretary of Energy arrived only a few minutes ago. Frank will join you as soon as he's turned him over to the Habitat Earth people. In the meanwhile I'll show you to your office."

He followed Lawrence into the superstructure, then into an obviously waiting, oak-paneled elevator. The aide depressed button 27 and the car descended.

"Was your lodging adequate?" Lawrence asked.

"Fine." He'd used a townhouse the Weyland Foundation maintained for their executives near Teterboro Airport, where their private jets operated. After depositing his bag there, he'd spent an hour walking and thinking. Reviewing the past year and the mental snapshots of

Marie's terrible affliction, of himself marching in still-time. The time in the wilderness had been necessary salve. Marie's memory no longer preoccupied his every waking thought—now she dwelled in a hidden, secretive recess of his mind.

The elevator door slid open soundlessly, revealing a counter and a perky young woman wearing a skirt, crisply starched blouse, and a blazer with the Weyland Foundation logo embroidered on the pocket.

"Welcome to the foundation, Mr. Anderson." She handed him a badge with color photograph and explained that he was to wear it on this and the other restricted-access floors. It was serious security. A video monitor showed the interior of the elevator they'd just left, and she controlled the door. A pistol-gripped twelve gauge shotgun was snapped into a rack beneath the counter, a snub-nose Ruger SP-10 revolver worn in an unobtrusive belt holster.

Link's image on the badge was current. When he'd returned from the walk the previous day, a trio of security people had been waiting to take photographs, palm and fingerprints, a cornea image, a voiceprint, a blood sample, and precise measurements of his body. His unique identity had been duly recorded and could be verified in several ways.

He followed Lawrence down a thickly carpeted hallway adorned with elegant paintings and rich paneling, their footsteps so muted he could hear the soft rasp of the aide's breathing.

Lawrence pointed out a recessed area with receptionist and heavy double doors. "The summit room," he reminded Link, his voice dropped to a whisper. Link had been inside during his previous visit, and had met the all-powerful financial board, called "the handful."

They passed another guarded elevator, one of only three used by financial board members and the personnel assigned to the secure floors. The other elevators in the building did not show floors 25 through 27 on their panels.

The aide led the way past a series of numbered but

otherwise unmarked offices, and stopped at 2775. When he opened the door, a woman looked up from her desk.

"Mrs. Frechette has been assigned as your personal assistant," Lawrence explained as she rose. She was short, thirtyish, with rust-colored hair, a shower of freckles, and tiny smile wrinkles that pleasantly marred the corners of her lips. Her clothing was modestly layered so there was only a hint of the form beneath.

Lawrence explained that he had to attend to urgent duties, that Mr. Dubois shouldn't be much longer, and in the interim Mrs. Frechette would show him about the office. He regarded her somberly. "Perhaps you should explain certain of our guidelines to Mr. Anderson. Section three of the handbook might be of particular interest." A smile twitched at his lips as he departed.

"Handbook?" Link asked her.

"A guide for foundation executives. Section three contains the dress codes. Vice-presidents and department directors are encouraged to wear business suits. Blue, brown, or gray, single or double-breasted. Low-cut shoes, preferably laced. White shirts and *appropriate* tie."

"He didn't seem worried about my clothes the last time I was here."

"You weren't employed by the foundation then. Anyway, Lawrence doesn't have the hang-up. It's his boss."

"Sounds like Frank." His friend had his stuffy side. He nodded at the door. "On our way down I was trying to recall Lawrence's last name," he said.

"I've always assumed Lawrence *was* his surname. Lawrence the aide, sort of like Jeeves the butler in an English play."

"Or Lawrence of Arabia?"

"Yeah." She thumbed through an organizational phone book. "Here it is. L. L. Lawrence, vice-president for protocol."

Link smiled. "Maybe it's Lawrence Lawrence."

"Or even Lawrence Lawrence Lawrence?" She exercised the smile crinkles. "Some coffee or tea before we begin the grand tour?"

"Coffee, please."

She opened an obscure door, displaying a kitchenette. "Let's see if I've got it right. You take a light breakfast. Orange juice, a cup of yogurt with wheat germ, or a small pastry. You like your coffee black, strong, and very hot. You drink tea periodically, the hearty Irish mixtures. No alcohol until after work, and then usually only a beer. Preferably Heineken or Samuel Adams, sometimes with tomato juice. Johnnie Walker scotch if there's only hard stuff. Black Label if they have it. Hennessey cognac after dinner. You don't smoke cigarettes but don't mind if others do in your presence—which I'll try not to let you catch me at since it's *verboten* in this building—and you have an occasional cigar." She smiled brightly. "How am I doing?"

He was impressed. "Where did you get all that? From Frank?"

She smiled, said, "We women have our ways," and handed over a steaming cup. "I was showing off so you'd know the kind of information I can gather. That took me twenty-eight minutes to scrounge up, and I restricted myself from using family or friends."

"They keep that sort of thing on file here?"

"Just the opposite. Since you first accepted the position last year, security's been digging up everything available on Abraham Lincoln Anderson and removing it from public access. If someone wants to learn about you, they'll find only what security wants them to. Some corporations hire publicists. The Weyland Foundation hires people to keep us out of the news."

"But you were able to learn all that?"

"I'm very good at that sort of thing." She was not boasting but stating a fact.

Link sipped coffee so hot it scalded his throat and ordered him to wake up—which was the way he liked it. He examined the room. Old Master art. Dark persian rugs and a matching gloomy tapestry. Floor plants so big they could be scaled and topped by lumberjacks.

"Ready to look over your domain, Mr. Anderson?"

He turned to face her. "I'd feel easier if you called me Link," he said.

She formed the easy smile. "And I'm Erin. Actually,

I'm assigned to you on a conditional basis. You'll be able to hand-pick your entire staff, including your personal assistant. Mr. Dubois felt you'd want to wait, but he ordered the adjacent suites cleared in case."

"Staff?" He chuckled. "I didn't even know they'd settled on my title."

"Executive Vice-President for Special Projects. It was Mr. Dubois's position, before he became chairman." She led him through a heavy oaken door. The inner office was sixty feet in length, with a massive desk at the near end. At the middle was a discussion area with couches, stuffed chairs, and another jungle of gargantuan plants, and at the distant end a glistening rosewood table, with padded leather chairs. Along the length of one side of the room were bookshelves, on the other a panoramic view, the glass so transparent it seemed he should be able to feel the breeze. He stared out over the skyline, searching for familiar landmarks, thinking how incongruous it was to spend one morning in the forest, the next in this mob of humans.

Erin misinterpreted. "It's natural to feel overwhelmed by the city. I certainly was at first."

He started to tell her he was seldom overwhelmed, but did not.

"Have you spent much time in New York?" she asked.

"Very little. I visited last year before I accepted this job, but then I was . . . delayed before I could report for work."

"I know." Her voice softened. "The hurt really does go away, Link."

He almost visibly bristled—what did *she* know of it?— but stopped himself and changed the subject. "Do you like it here?"

"Surprisingly, I do. I was raised in the Southwest, and my impressions of New York were trash heaps and muggings on every street corner. Of course that's as false as the I Love the Big Apple propaganda, but in ways this is the true capital of America. New York City is our financial hub, and also the theatrical, publishing, and arguably, the cultural center. There's a lot of diversity to enjoy."

Erin demonstrated how to operate the indirect lighting, then how to polarize the windows electronically to eliminate glare and UV rays. A door opened to a conference room, which would be for his staff meetings, when he had a staff, and another to a private bathroom with shower, walk-in closet, and marble vanity. She operated a sliding wall panel and displayed a wet bar with sink, ice machine, and stocked liquor cabinet.

"Impressed?" she asked with a grin.

"It's large." Link thought of offices as workplaces. If he wanted a drink he'd find a bar.

She explained the telephone system. He could tell at a glance where the calls originated—and even the identity of the caller if the voiceprint was in their database—and could switch on any of three different scrambling devices.

"Will I need them?"

"Most of what you do will be classified," Erin said. "Your clearance level is unlimited, recognized by all departments and branches of the government. There are only five others here with that kind of access, the members of the financial board."

"You've got a security clearance, I assume."

"Top secret. I worked for Grumman, up Long Island a few miles. My specialty was writing programs for imbedded processors in missile guidance systems. It was interesting, but when Mr. Dubois called and explained what we'd be doing here, I was intrigued." Erin revealed that she'd moved into the city from up-island and was the single parent of a seven-year-old named Johnny. Although she paused for Link's response, he didn't press for explanation.

"So you'll be gathering information?" he asked instead.

"Anything you need or want to know, it's my job to get or find out. Say you're in South Asia and need to find out about striped dung beetles, because one just bit you. You use your flip-top cell phone—which is next to impossible to compromise because it's low wattage, scrambled, and uses a network of satellites—and call me. If I'm in my car or watching my kid play soccer, doesn't matter. I ask you to stand by, transfer to a voice recognition circuit here, and give the computer a description of the beetle. Since we've got all those Habitat Earth people downstairs, some of whom run around South Asia to do their tree hugging, the computers contain everything worth knowing about South Asian animals, plants and insects, including dung beetles. Because you're concerned about being bitten, I preempt other work in the computer and *bingo*—I tell you you might as well cancel all your subscriptions because there's no antidote."

"Can I call the computer myself?"

"Are you good with them?"

"I had an Apple II when I was young."

"Well, I'm *damned* good with them, I've got a fancy degree in the stuff, and since it's my job, let's keep me in the loop. And remember, this works day and night, no matter where I am. The satellites and master computers belong to the foundation, and they're ours to use."

"Don't argue with her." Frank Dubois, wingman, friend, and most importantly, chairman of the financial board of the Weyland Foundation, rolled into the room with only a low humming sound from the wheelchair motor. He'd been badly injured in an aircraft accident and would likely spend the remainder of his life mending.

Link motioned about. "Hell, Frank, I don't need to worry about finding an apartment. I can pitch camp in a corner and have room left over for tennis courts."

"It's my old office."

"*You* picked out the decor." Link pointed out a painting showing a trio of nude, cavorting pansies. "What in God's name are *those*?"

Frank peered. "Cherubs. It's a Rubens. Not an original, of course, but . . ."

"That *goes*."

"I rather like it. Of course you've got to have a glimmering of appreciation for art."

"Send it to Mr. Dubois's office, Erin."

"I think I hear my telephone," she said with a grin, and left them.

Frank looked as the door closed in her wake. "She tell you who she was?"

"Computer analyst? We were still in the process of cautious introductions."

"Remember Lieutenant Frechette, the junior pilot in our squadron over in Saudi? Erin was his wife."

Link felt doltish for not putting the names together. John Frechette had been shot down by a track-mounted quad-23 anti-aircraft gun. Erin had said her son's name was Johnny, had even waited for him to pick up on it.

"When John was killed, Erin went back to school. She's more than an analyst, Link, she's got a master's in computer sciences. In fact she was in charge of a twenty-man software engineering team at Grumman when I talked her into coming here."

Link exercised his normally prodigious memory and wondered why it had failed him. He remembered John Frechette in the squadron day room, showing photos of the Southwest Rodeo Association's beauty queen, an *extremely* well-endowed girl in fringed dress and Western hat. As the photo circulated there'd been whistles, comments about brick shithouses and the girl with a pair of forty-fours, and quiet periods as others paused to admire the spectacular assets of a girl-back-home. They'd been married for only a year and had just learned she was pregnant. John Frechette had not lived to see the son bearing his name.

"When I explained this opening, she was only mildly interested until I told her who she'd be working with. Her husband had written great things about you, and she felt she knew you."

"I'm honored." *And thoughtless,* Link silently added.

"Erin will be your intelligence source." Frank cocked his head, a question on his face. "But how are you, Link? I worried when you took off so abruptly after Marie's funeral."

"It was what I needed." He did not wish to elaborate. "What's the rush, Frank? When I got back to the cabin, your guy couldn't wait to get me here. What was it that couldn't wait a couple of days while I paid bills and answered the mail?"

Frank looked uneasy, which made Link wonder. "Have Erin give you the background brief, then we'll discuss it."

"I've got to go back to Montana for a few days, Frank. Wrap up loose ends."

"Sooner's better than later. We need your help, but not as urgently as they let on." They talked it over and decided he would return the following afternoon, after his orientation briefings.

Erin announced on intercom that Lawrence had called for Mr. Dubois. The Secretary of Energy was waiting in the Habitat Earth conference room.

Frank made a face. "He's trying to get us to fund one of his pet projects, a research project on nuclear waste disposal that we refused last year."

"As I recall, the Secretary's not regarded as especially honest."

"Not many in this administration are. See you a little later, Link." Frank left the room, his wheelchair humming quietly and efficiently.

Erin came in toting the coffee jug and a classified document, and placed both on his desktop. "You've got a loose schedule today, with only a few briefings. So *between* meetings." She tapped the document. "It's important."

As he thumbed through the pages, Erin looked around. "I don't like the decor either. While you're reading, why don't I make a few calls. How about Southwest style? Light walls? Outdoors scenes? Get rid of the rubber plantation and bring in a few cacti?"

He nodded abstractly. "Do it."

"I love *anything* Navajo or Hopi."

"Fine with me. I'm half Piegan Blackfoot."

"I heard, so I read up on 'em. Bloodthirsty bunch. Want a few scalps strung from your door?"

Link laughed. She was not hung up about political correctness.

Erin stared. "Normally wear your hair that long?" She was no wilting flower.

"I've been a long way from barber shops lately."

"Hmmm, and you've got a meeting with the handful."
As she left the room, he opened the first page of the document:

Subject: Ansel Martin Turpin
Data Compiled by Erin Frechette, May-June 1998
Personal: Ht 5'11, Wt 175, Hair Brn, Eyes Brn, Born
    03/25/50, Died 08/03/96
GS–15, Special Agent, Federal Bureau of Investiga-
    tion, Terminated: 07/07/96
Specialties: Radioactive Substance Investigation;
    Electronic Eavesdropping and Surveillance; Per-
    sonal Disguise . . .

While at first Link wondered why anyone who had been
dead for two years could be important, he was soon engrossed. Ansel Turpin had been a fascinating individual.

He was halfway through the document when Erin
called on intercom. "The supply folks are on their way
up with catalogues. While I'm sorting through them, go
down to the second floor. Room 296. And remember
your meeting with the VP of personnel at eleven-thirty."

He glanced at his watch. "That's forty minutes from
now."

"296A is an empty office. I had security open it and
take in a chair, and a hairstylist's on her way. Get your
haircut, drop a fifty into her hot little hand, and walk
down the hall to Room 288, where you'll find the VP of
personnel waiting.

"Fifty bucks for a haircut?"

"You're not in Montana any more, Toto." As he left,
Erin was stalking about the offices with the calculating
look women use whenever they get a chance to remodel.

After the haircut, the vice president for personnel issued
Link three charge cards, all with unlimited cash and
credit lines, and a packet showing his employee number
and the official particulars of his position—which were
simply to assist the financial board as requested.

He was struck silent when he observed the salary. The benefits were equally generous.

He was told that nine thousand employees worked in the Weyland Foundation building, and several thousand more at project locations around the globe. There were fifteen levels for workers and supervisors, five for project leaders and department directors, and three more for vice presidents. Link's position was not shown as any of those.

"Where do I fall?" Link asked.

"You don't. You report to the financial board," explained the vice-president for personnel. "Since they're the only ones who can overrule you, that makes you sixth in the foundation's hierarchy." As he explained the structure, twice the man stopped and commented how *different* Link's heavy silver tie slide—a wolf's head—appeared.

Link took lunch in a staff dining room on the eighteenth floor (Erin had explained that there was one on every fourth floor, twenty of them in all), returned to the office, and continued reading about Ansel Turpin. At 2:00, Frank Dubois summoned him, saying he'd like to discuss the dress code, and Erin rolled her eyes in mock horror as Link placed his Stetson squarely upon his head and strode from the room.

The chairman's suite on the uppermost floor was so immense that Link's assigned digs were meager in comparison, and he was reminded that luxury was a relative commodity.

"*Now* I can see some familiar landmarks," Link exclaimed, looking out the window.

"You can't have my office," Frank said, fish-eyeing him as he settled on a couch. "I hear Erin's got the supply people hopping. Something about, 'Out with the Raphaels and in with the Remingtons'?"

"Do you hear everything?"

"Just where you two are concerned. She's rejected my art, and you're assaulting the image of this fine old establishment. My grandfather set the dress code in the forties, and we're one of the few bastions of civilized taste

in the city. Now I'm being besieged by junior executives
eagerly asking if the rules have been changed."

"And what's your button-down, Ivy League response?"

"I explain that you're a savage only a few years from
the loincloth and scalping knife, and to indulge but don't
copy you. Nice hat, by the way. You round up cattle
in it?"

"Nope. As we say in Montana, I'm all hat and no
cattle. I have a decent mare, but I haven't ridden her in
months. Did you call me up here to admire my
Stetson?"

Frank pushed the button on his wheelchair, and
hummed across the carpet. "Time to meet the financial
board," he called back.

"Slow down, damn it. I didn't bring a golf cart."

The summit room was a world of rosewood, brushed
velvet, and fine leather. Portraits of the five founders
were on one wall, facing a gallery of U.S. presidents. A
small conference table was centered at the near end,
with a raised dais and large video screen nearby. At the
far end was a more casually furnished conversation area
and a bar where the handful could take beverages.

Frank pointed out the visitor's gallery—a grouping of
comfortable leather chairs, each with its own side table—
and explained that over the years three different presidents had come to present requests that were important
to them. More often they'd send a representative, normally their Secretary of State or chief of staff. There had
been problems of trust with two administrations. Unfortunately, the current presidency was one of those.

At 2:20, a woman and three men—the remainder of
the handful—filed in. Only one was from the original
1944 group. The rest were, like Frank Dubois, heirs.
Frank took his place at the head of the table and reintro-
duced Link, whom they'd met the previous year. One
by one the board members welcomed him aboard, and
the nonagenarian offered a soliloquy about the importance of periodic relaxation and vacationing.

Frank waited patiently until he'd finished, then
switched on the video monitor. "I'll present a brief over-

view of some of our past and current projects for
Link's benefit."

"One moment," said the woman. She smiled at Link.
"I am from Wyoming, sir, and I applaud your style of
dress. Please do not allow this stodgy young curmudgeon
to change it."

"I don't intend to, ma'am."

She gave Frank an impish smile. "You may continue."

The large screen displayed a map of the world with a
profusion of red dots. During the next hour, Frank and
the others spoke of what had been and what was being
done by the Weyland Foundation. Massive industries
had been funded, huge projects constructed, and despicable tyrants toppled. Over the years some of the de-
mocracies they'd succored had failed, but others had
flourished. The names of corporations were provided,
along with the shares retained by the foundation. No
totals were shown, but Link estimated their present
worth was in excess of a hundred billion dollars, more
than the wealth of a number of developed nations.

Frank described several projects that Link might become involved in. Finally he asked him to leave the
room, for the handful were about to enter into private
discussions. It was no insult. Presidents had been asked
to do the same.

It was four o'clock by the time Link returned to his
suite, where Frank had said they'd meet later, and
watched as Erin thumbed through catalogs of artwork
and furnishings.

"Are we still employed?" she asked, looking up and
flashing a smile.

"Yeah."

"Link, I was the one that suggested you be called in
and if you weren't available that they assign someone
else. I felt it was urgent. I still do."

"Is something wrong?"

"I believe Frank Dubois is in jeopardy, and that something terrible may be about to happen to the Weyland
Foundation. It involves the man you've been reading
about."

"Ansel Turpin? Your report says he's dead."

"It's important that we know for certain. After he was broken out of the hospital, nineteen deaths were attributed to him. All cold-blooded and terrible, and all employees of the Weyland Foundation."

"I just read that the murders stopped when he was killed."

"That's true." Erin paused. "But I've got information that convinces me there's at least a possibility that he's alive. No smoking gun evidence yet, but . . ."

She stopped as Frank Dubois's wheelchair hummed into the room.

"Interrupting anything?" Frank asked.

"We were wrapping up," Erin said. "It can wait until morning."

"Good. Working late causes warts and acne. I just got a phone call from home. Dinner tonight at my place?"

"I'll be there," said Link. It would be good to see Frank's wife and daughter.

"Erin?"

She begged off. Something to do with spending quality time with her son before he left on a field trip. Frank invited Johnny too—and she accepted.

When the two men started into Link's office, Erin grabbed for her purse. "I'd better run if I'm going to get ready for a dinner that's only two hours from now." As she turned to leave, her form beneath the folds was framed in the light—and both men stared too long. Erin Frechette was still trim and well endowed.

Link took a seat on the couch, and Frank rolled up nearby. They looked out at the city, and for a while talked about Link's first day.

He finally brought it up. "Erin believes Ansel Turpin's alive. You?"

"I agree with the bureau that he's dead. But Erin's a bright lady, and I can't ignore a warning that he's planning something terrible."

"Perhaps I shouldn't go to Montana."

"It's been two years since we've heard from Turpin. A few more days won't hurt." Frank grinned. "Bring your clubs back, and I'll set up a game."

"You can *golf*?"

"I have a contraption that helps me stand up so I can swing. Hell, it's cured my slice."

Link hadn't touched a driver in eight years but didn't want his friend thinking he was whining prematurely. Especially with him having to be strapped upright to play.

Frank wore a look of amusement, "Remember the time Gary got us on the course in Riyadh?"

"Mostly I remember being thrown out," he said.

Frank and Link had been fighter pilots, and Gary Runyon the information officer for their unit. They'd hitched a C-130 ride to Riyadh, shown fake diplomatic passes somehow obtained by Runyon, and played a few rounds at the Royal Course before being discovered and booted off.

"You're probably invited there all the time now," Link said.

"I could have gotten us on then, too, but it wouldn't have been the same."

"Any idea where Gary's living?" Link asked. He'd lost track after the Persian Gulf War, knew only that their old buddy had authored a couple of successful books about air power.

"Some little desert town in Nevada. He called a few days ago asking about you. I was out, but he's on my good-guys list, so Lawrence gave him your number. You didn't get the message?"

"My recorder was shut off. Turned it back on before your guy drug me to the airplane."

"I doubt it's anything important. Gary's the least dependable person I've ever met. Can you remember him ever making a meeting on time?"

Gary Runyon was not the kind to enjoy discipline—neither the self-type nor the kind imposed by the military system. "I'll give him a call when I get home."

"Say hi for me." Frank reached for the lever on the arm of his racing wheelchair. "Come on, cowpoke. Let's not be late for dinner."

As they went out, Frank told him that he wasn't only golfing, he was also flying both fixed-wing airplanes and helicopters. All sorts of things were possible with modern inventions.

2

As Lincoln Anderson had his first lunch at the Weyland Building, across the continent Gary Runyon was jolted from slumber by a raucous sound. He bolted upright, hastily rubbed sleep-grit from his eyes, and looked about. He'd been dreaming of wizened features and eyes shriveled like prunes. Of a terrified expression frozen on a blistered face, skin darkened as if the victim had lain in the sun for weeks.

The bedside telephone rang again and Gary blinked, then slowly relaxed as the vision faded. He squinted through shafts of sunlight glaring in from about the frame of curtains, picked up on the fourth ring, and muttered a greeting.

Shelby's voice was cheerful. "Get up, sleepyhead. Half the day's gone."

He ran a hand through an unruly shock of red hair, and croaked: "It's Sunday?"

"No, it's Monday. And a beautiful one."

"I was up late." He sat up, yawning. "Gotta get the manuscript off pretty soon."

"Okay, mystery man. What's the book *really* about?" She'd brimmed with curiosity since he'd confided he was writing a blockbuster that would make his career.

"Nuclear waste, like I told you."

"But that's not all. I've got this theory you're a spy. Dad says you've got a mysterious instrument in your car. What is it? A long-range radio so you can contact your motherland?"

Gary grinned. After the somber vision, the bantering

felt good. "How about a Walkman because the Bronco's radio's broken. Part of my poverty act."

"Hmm. How's Aristotle doing with you keeping him up all hours?"

"Keeping *him* up? You're joking." He glanced at the corner the big mutt had claimed the day they'd moved into the Barn. The pleasant-natured beast was comatose, as was normal when he wasn't eating, defecating, or exploring the field for critters.

"Reason I called was you promised to take me flying, remember? The weather's perfect, and I can take the morning off."

"Mathilda's sickly," he told her. "Yesterday I flew her out for repairs, and it took forever to get off the ground." He'd named the temperamental pre-World War II Piper Cub after his mother's sister, who had a reputation as the most contrary woman in the Philadelphia area.

Shelby sounded disappointed. "Anything serious?"

"Maybe. Engine's not developing power, and Mathilda didn't have much to start with. Sixty-five horses, to be exact. If I'm lucky it's an adjustment. The mechanic's going to look tomorrow." He paused. "Where are you?"

"My folks'."

She owned a condo in Carson City but visited her parents in Stagecoach often. Since she was close, he considered inviting her over to lounge on the cedar deck built onto the side of the Barn while they sipped Bloody Mary's. Maybe tell her to bring a swimsuit so they could use the hot tub. Wondered if she'd consider skinnydipping, and grinned.

"Still there?" she asked.

"Yeah." He rejected his ideas. They both had work to do and needed no distractions. Their relationship remained platonic, which was the way he wanted it, even if Shelby had a face and body that could make a Buddhist monk forget his vows. Everything about her was sexy. Her name was something a movie starlet might conjure up, and the rest of her was better. Gary had seen men stare slack-jawed as she passed. The state should declare her a hazard to driving.

Shelby conducted a conversation off-phone, and came back on. "You missed breakfast, so Mom says to come by for lunch."

"I'll be there." Gary hung up, slipped on eyeglasses, and swung his feet over the side of the bed. He was average-American-male size—five-nine and twenty pounds overweight—with wild and unruly red hair and a pug face that could frighten a gorilla. He was also nearsighted, with corrective lenses so thick they were bulletproof.

Aristotle got to his feet, stretched, and followed him into the front room. Gary slid open the door, and the animal strolled out to a cottonwood to relieve himself.

"Get the coyote!" Gary yelled, and the animal immediately found new energy and lumbered into the alfalfa field. There was forty acres of it, planted in absentia by the man from out of state who had owned it before him. Gary had purchased home and property and each day switched on a big industrial pump that supplied a rolling irrigator. That was the extent of his agricultural ability. Soon he'd hire a firm to harvest it and both make a few bucks and start with his tax credits. Farmer Gary. Any extra income would be welcome.

He lit his first Marlboro of the day and watched as the field swallowed Aristotle. The hundred-and-thirty-pound dog was of mixed parentage, his mom a golden retriever of championship quality who had gotten loose and mated with a Great Dane or airedale, or *something* damned big and friendly. The disgruntled owners had turned the unsightly pups over to the local pound the day Gary had gone looking for a cat to replace the questionable companionship of his ex-wife—who had taken him for everything and left him for a more exciting life with a mousy accountant whose hobby was watching old Gary Cooper films on video.

It had been like at first sight. Both human and mutt were rejects and ugly as sin.

Gary's life was filled with endless stints at the computer, and a prerequisite for such a person's mate was an ability to either find sources of entertainment or endure long periods of boredom. Aristotle was content with the arrangement. He was somewhat obedient, stoically enduring, and so amicable that—as far as Gary was aware—he'd never once in his two years of existence uttered a growl. The dog disdained barking. Burglars could come and go at will as long as they didn't disturb his tub-sized food dish.

Gary noted a stirring in the alfalfa field a hundred yards distant, then a flash of Aristotle's mottled fur as he chased something. A terrified coyote or field rat, most likely. The big dog never caught them, just loped happily after them and got his exercise.

He smoked the cigarette down to the filter. He'd quit a number of times but found his concentration wandering and his writing gone to hell. Now he limited himself to one per hour, outside only, and tried hard not to cheat.

The Barn and acreage had been a find. Someone—Charles Boyer, it was locally rumored, although no proof of that was offered and the actor's name didn't appear on any of the titles or paperwork—had built it as a getaway thirty years ago. It had been one of the first structures in the valley, and the owner had come and gone so surreptitiously that no one knew if anyone really visited at all. A few years later it had been purchased sight unseen by an out-of-state investor, the rugged acreage cleared and planted with alfalfa to obtain lucrative government subsidies and the house rented to a series of tenants who let it go to hell.

Gary had not been impressed when he'd first eyed the wind-faded structure that looked like a decrepit New England barn with sagging-shuttered windows. The protective shield of elms and cottonwoods were parched and on their last legs, and hip-high grass on all sides had been watered just enough to keep it alive. Inside were accumulations of filth, discolored wallpaper, inoperative and ancient appliances, and carpeting that was rotted and threadbare. But he'd lifted the wallpaper enough to discover genuine wood paneling, and dug up threadbare cheap carpet to expose the original hardwood parquet.

The place had been on the market for years when he'd made his lowball offer. A local entrepreneur named Cal Admire—who was also Shelby's father—handled the sale. Gary had used the G.I. Bill to secure the loan, spent every loose cent on the minimal closing costs, swamped out the place enough to make it marginally livable, and set up camp. He'd started out living in the loft, sleeping in a bag pitched beside the table where he kept his computer. Gary had stripped away wallpaper and cruddy carpeting, refinished floors and walls, and completed four rooms. One a month. Five to go. Part of his rehab program, and the new, dependable Gary. Make a commitment and stick to it. Build and write. Rebuilding the Barn . . . and his career.

The deck had been falling down, so he'd plied hammer and paint and—on a whim—purchased the hot tub on credit, no payments until the first of the year. He spent evenings in the spa after long days of work, sipping California brandy and puffing on a cheap cigar, staring up at stars that glittered like diamonds, stoically enduring his state of poverty. Sometimes thinking it would be nice to have a sexy hardbody join him. Backing off when he remembered how sweet his ex-wife had seemed—and how her lawyers were making sounds like they wanted even more.

Screw you, he thought, meaning his ex-wife, but it rang hollow. God, he missed her. Same way he missed his old friends, and didn't *really* want to throw Frank Dubois to the wolves. It was as if his life was spinning and twisting in ways that were beyond his control.

Three years earlier Gary had been in different circumstances—owned a nice flat in Philadelphia and a weekend retreat in the Poconos, and been on his way to a semi-comfortable life as a productive writer. He'd done well with his first two books, and was pursued by first-line publishers. Then it had all been taken. His ex-wife and her greedy lawyer had scalped him and in the process planted an unreasonable feeling of failure. There'd no longer been savings, a nicely furnished flat, or wooded retreat. No pretty wife at the dinner table.

He'd gone into a writing slump. The garbled trash

he'd submitted for his next book—seven months late—was rejected, and the word went out that he was undependable. For months it had gone like that. Outlines for new books hardly considered. Magazine editors turning down ideas for feature articles. He'd tried submitting a manuscript under a pseudonym, but it hadn't helped. His work was simply *bad*.

His agent had convinced him to back off and start over. First as a freelance copy editor, working with various publishers, correcting prose of other authors. Next he'd sold a couple of two-bit articles to newspapers, and a small one to *Aerospace Weekly*. Finally, after a Herculean sales act by his agent, he'd been queried by his old publisher to write about a subject that had been only a single chapter in his second book. It was to be called *Nuclear Legacy* and be released on the hundredth anniversary of Marie and Pierre Curie's discovery of radium, and he'd been damned happy to get it. The advance had been paltry, but it was work, and he was doing what he'd been educated to do, and what he'd always wanted to do. Write.

"You're on your way again," his agent often said, but Gary Runyon no longer took anything for granted. The initial research had been grueling, and organizing the details was difficult—but Gary knew he must do a good job or it was over. The profession was brutal. Few second chances were offered, and a third one . . . ? He'd buried himself in work, imposed his own deadlines and met them, gone online with his computer to seek information beyond his rudimentary comprehension. Toured Yucca Mountain and other planned storage sites. Visited the companies doing the government studies. Nurtured friendships with Shelby Admire and other experts for scientific insight. Dug deep into his subject, trying to find meat and controversy.

That had been the rub, trying to make it interesting. It wasn't that the situation was not grave. America had worked itself into a corner by relying so heavily on nuclear-generated power. The plant sites and storage depots would soon be filled, and the toxic overflow would be disastrous. The government was *studying* the problem. But Americans had been told those things for the past twenty years and had not become excited. *Someone* would handle it, was the prevailing attitude, and delve as he might, Gary had found nothing new to arouse public emotion.

They would remain apathetic until their kids started glowing in the dark.

But a visitor had phoned him, then dropped in at the Barn to talk, and Gary had his very own whistle-blowing, government-bashing informant offering proof of a tremendous scandal involving corrupt politicians, avaricious businessmen, and staggering sums of money.

The hundred test pages Gary sent the publisher were proof he was on track. *Nightmare in Nuclear America* would create a furor, perhaps even bring down prestigious institutions and political leaders. The publishing house was moving him to front burner. A publicist had been assigned and the release date moved up. He would receive a hefty bonus upon acceptance. He needed it. He'd been living off credit cards, money received for writing a magazine article every month or two, and dwindling royalties from his books.

You'd think he'd be exuberant. He wasn't *really* betraying a friend.

The Barn was isolated. Beyond the alfalfa field to the south was high desert that stretched to State 50, aptly called "the loneliest road in America," and then to the dry lake bed and mountains beyond. Two miles west was a secluded property supposedly built by the Bing Crosby family after Boyer had erected the Barn. Off to the east were the clusters of small houses and mobile homes that made up Stagecoach Valley proper. The structure closest to the Barn was half a mile north, where the ground rose toward the mountains; a shanty owned by a reticent loner the locals called the hermit. The white-bearded man disappeared daily in a World War II-vintage military weapons carrier—a squared-off three-quarter-ton pickup built for the U.S. Army—to prospect for gold and silver, like a specter from the hurdy-gurdy days when young Mark Twain had been a reporter in nearby Virginia City.

Gary returned to the bedroom, pulled on jeans, a knit shirt, and loafers, then, as he was on his way to the kitchen, thought again about the gruesome dream.

Ray Watt, the local deputy sheriff, had told him about finding Trudy Schmidt's body, but he'd not believed the horror until he'd seen photographs. Terrible! Two more bodies had been found in the next ten days, in that same grisly condition, and their deaths had been attributed to the same virulent influenza. A flu virus? he'd asked, rolling his eyes. Come *on*. But that had been the local coroner's official finding, and who was he to argue?

Ray had said he'd give him a call if he came across another body like that, and Gary had mumbled agreement, hoping it wouldn't happen since he was sure he'd embarrass himself. But he'd asked a member of the local EMT, a medic with extensive training, if it wasn't odd about the victims' hair loss and sores and the skin turning dark, and the woman agreed. Then Gary had dropped the subject. The locals already thought him eccentric, and he didn't want to be branded a complete nut over something like the symptoms of a virus.

With the book's deadline staring him in the face he didn't have time to worry about it. Later, after the manuscript was submitted, he might delve some. His present concern was confirmation. Shelby would check his technical details—she'd agreed to that—but then there were the blockbuster revelations that would destroy the reputation of someone who had been a close friend. To check them out, Gary needed someone sophisticated enough to help without tuning out. Someone unafraid to tell him it was or was not possible and, most of all, someone he trusted. He'd decided upon Lincoln Anderson, although they'd not seen one another since Saudi Arabia. Not only did Link know both Gary and Frank, he was technically aware, scrupulous, and unafraid.

Gary had called around and gotten Link's phone number in Montana. So far there'd been no response, but he was still convinced Link was the right choice. Gary would sleep much better if he had Link's nod before he sent in the manuscript. He lifted the kitchen phone and again started to punch in the number scrawled on the pad beside it, then stopped and scowled, for the line was filled with static. The local service was erratic at best, and he'd have to get the telephone people out. He grumbled to himself as he toasted and ate a couple of tasteless frozen waffles, made marginally palatable by a liberal drenching of syrup, checked on Aristotle—still in the field—and was about to go up to the loft when he heard vehicular noise. A Nevada Bell panel truck pulled into the pea-gravel driveway and parked, and a tall, muscular man with a blond pony-tail emerged and approached the porch bearing a toolbox. Gary had seen him around the valley and considered him rude and unlikeable.

"Power surge last night screwed op phones," the repairman yelled in his Slavic accent.

Op? He let him in, told him about the hissing sound on the line.

"Gotta replace a distribution box opstairs."

Gary led the way down the hall, then up to the loft. The telephone repairman paused at the top of the stairs, then homed in on a plastic box on the wall behind the computer.

There were two lines installed: one for the computer modem, the other for the phones. The blond disconnected both and unscrewed the box from the wall. He cast him a look. "I'll be while," he said. Like he'd prefer if Gary went elsewhere.

"I'll watch." Gary would leave no one alone with his computer; his work was stored on the hard drive. The blond grunted and continued.

The replacement box was larger than the original, with a glass-covered aperture at top.

"This one got impedance matching and isolation circuit," he was told. "Reception should be better, an' if lightning hits line, you computer won't burn op."

"That's reassuring."

The blond man worked in front of the miraculous box, shielding it from view, then stepped back and plugged in a handset carried on his belt. He dialed, identified himself to someone on the other end, and informed them that he'd finished with the installation at Gary's number.

He grunted in acknowledgment of something said, and hung up.

After connecting the phone plugs and gathering his tools, the repairman walked to the stairs. "I let myself out." Gary followed him down anyway. "Jesus," he heard the man mutter.

Aristotle emerged from the field as the panel truck was departing. The big animal watched with interest, then meandered to the house, where Gary let him inside.

"So what poor animals did you terrorize?" he asked as Aristotle lapped water from a bucket. Getting no response, he returned to the loft.

Gary sat at the computer, switched it on, and as he waited for it to power up, dialed the number he'd been given for Link Anderson in Montana. A machine picked up on the fourth ring, and he listened through a short litany. Link's voice had changed very little.

"Gary Runyon here," he said. "I've been trying to contact you." He said he really needed to talk with him, and gave his phone number. After he hung up, Gary brooded for a moment, thinking at least he'd gotten through to something. Also thinking that Link had obviously been home to switch on the answering machine.

He went back to the computer, and opened the Nightmare file, where he kept his book. A small shudder swept through him, the sort that his ex-wife liked to say came when someone stepped on your grave. He looked slowly about. There was only Aristotle, asleep near the stairs, yet the feeling persisted that someone was watching.

After a moment the sensation went away, and he smiled at his own silliness.

The small group observing the writer were pleased, for both the mini-cam and audio connections were working well. They talked among themselves, wondering whom he'd been trying to contact.

3

Link arrived first—not surprising since Erin had to see son Johnny off to a five-day soccer clinic in Utica. He put coffee on, ambled to his office, and looked out over the morning city. Finally he sat at his desk and leafed halfheartedly through a summation of policies. After ten minutes he put it aside, deciding it was the sort of thing that could be stretched out over months, maybe years. He opened the safe and withdrew the document on Ansel Turpin. This time he read with certain things in mind, like dates and specifics.

Frank had encountered Ansel Turpin the year before the accident that had crippled him, and from Erin's account, he'd handled himself well. He'd grabbed a loose weapon, wounded Turpin, then disarmed him before he could do more harm. But during the month following Turpin's rescue from the St. Petersburg hospital, someone had methodically stalked and killed foundation personnel at two large construction projects in western Russia. They'd been murdered horribly, differently. Seven in the first week, all left alive long enough for discovery and a lingering death.

The Russian mafia had been involved, but the killings were obviously directed by Turpin.

Frank Dubois had returned to America, but every time another Weyland Foundation employee was killed, he'd felt responsible. After all, he had saved Turpin's life.

As the manhunt continued, CNN was first to get wind

that something was happening in St. Petersburg, but no one heard the name Turpin, whom the Russian president privately called "the terrorist sent to *help* us." Yeltsin explained privately to friends how America hadn't stopped the Russian mafia from stealing and selling nuclear material, they'd turned it's activities into a booming business. But he had not said any of that publicly. Instead, a shroud of secrecy was invoked that would have made the old Soviet Union leaders proud. A foundation investigation estimated that the payoffs—it was an election year—were massive. Promises of government-to-government cooperation, meaning plentiful aid for Russia. Political support from the U.S. government for Yeltsin regardless. Murkier, a lump sum cash payment from an untraceable source.

More Weyland Foundation personnel were murdered before the prosecutor's office finally pleaded for help, and Moscow had called in the military. But on day twenty-six after Turpin's rescue, when the army—in full battle gear—swept through the city, there was no trace of Turpin or the mafia leaders. Also missing were six truck loads of stolen weapons-grade uranium, shoulder-fired Strela missiles, and a hundred million dollars.

On day twenty-eight a Russian air force MiG-23 photo reconnaissance aircraft discovered a small, mixed convoy of military vehicles and expensive civilian Mercedes several hundred kilometers south of St. Petersburg, approaching the Belarus republic's border. They were confident that they'd discovered Turpin and his mafiosi friends fleeing with their loot.

A spotter team was transported by helicopters to observe the convoy. As the two rotary wing aircraft approached the vehicles, Strelas were fired. One evaded, the other disintegrated.

The Russian air force commander did not hesitate. Two flights of SU-27 Fitter ground attack aircraft attacked the convoy. The area was well-populated, so they prudently did not use bombs. Instead they employed more accurate forward-firing ordnance. The criminals fired more shoulder-fired Strela missiles, but the agile jet fighters spewed decoy flares and operated with impunity.

As the attack continued, a ground force was inserted for mop-up.

The aircraft were on their eighth strafe attack, and the defenses had already been neutralized, when a truck in the very middle of the convoy exploded with unexpected ferocity, sending spectacular arms of fire groping skyward. One of the fighters had been caught in the flash, and the damage was so extensive the pilot was forced to eject before reaching his base.

Since it was impossible for anyone in the convoy to have survived, the army sent in the ground team. They did not get far—their dosimeters showed the area was dangerously contaminated with radioactivity. Estimates placed the amount of plastique explosive at four hundred kilograms, and both large and small chunks of U-235 had been spread for hundreds of meters. No one could enter the cordon until the "hot" matter was removed, which would take days. That forecast had been optimistic. Robotic vehicles used at the Chernobyl meltdown were brought in to gather the uranium, but cleanup took six and a half weeks.

The prosecutor's office unearthed more about Ansel Turpin's time in St. Petersburg. He'd taken over four reactors and a centrifuge, and the nuclear material they'd produced, and had directly employed nuclear program managers, bankers, and weapons brokers. His subordinates had marketed beryllium and plutonium to Iraq and North Korea, and Turpin had masterminded the uranium deal with Iran. They'd also peddled weapons—including anti-tank and anti-aircraft missiles—to drug barons in Colombia, Peru, and Mexico.

Turpin had deserved a fiery death, and as Link read more he decided it was improbable that he could be alive. No one else in the convoy had survived the explosion, and a bloody and twisted dental appliance had been located five hundred meters from the epicenter. While his body was not identified, both dental x-ray and DNA records proved the bridge was Turpin's.

Why, he wondered, did Erin doubt? They'd not pursued it the previous night. It had been a social evening, and he'd been cajoled into relating episodes in Plains

Indian mythology. The Dubois daughter had become hooked the previous year, and Johnny too was soon listening raptly to tales—all quite tall—about Scarface the hero being chased by evil land and water spirits, and being pulled out of trouble by Coyote, Bear, and Swan.

Erin Frechette came into his office carrying a pair of steaming cups. "So far you're not bad at boss, but you're sure awful at making coffee," she said. "This stuff's for wimps."

"I didn't expect you until later."

"The kids were in a hurry to get away from us moms." She sipped coffee. "Ugh."

Link tasted, found it weak-kneed but not *that* bad.

"You've got your security briefing this morning. That's where you sign all the forms so they can tell you things like where O. J.'s money's buried and how Elvis is doing in Tahiti. Then there's a project briefing Frank wants you up to speed on. If you don't mind, I'll sit in."

"Good idea."

"Next comes lunch at the Governor's Club with the Secretary of Energy, Frank Dubois, and the VP's from Habitat Earth. That one I'll skip, thank you. When you're done you come back for a sit-down with Frank, then head for Teterboro Field, board a Learjet, and wing your way out to the land of Geronimo."

"Geronimo was Apache. These are Blackfeet."

"I don't recall any famous Blackfeet Indians."

"How about Lame Bull?"

"Never heard of him."

"He was a big man—chief of chiefs. Signed a treaty with the white man in 1855."

"What happened to him?"

"Mmmm. I think he was killed falling off a horse."

"And he's your hero?"

"Hey, Genghis Khan died after he fell off a horse. Those things are dangerous. Ask my mare when she's in a foul mood."

Erin snorted. "You Blackfeet ought to adopt somebody like Geronimo. Great name."

He sipped weak coffee. "Question. Why do you believe Ansel Turpin's still alive?"

"Because one, the guy's a great actor, and two, I know where he went after St. Pete."

"Frank says the FBI thinks he's dead."

"Not just them. The Russians, the CIA, and the task force on terrorism all agree."

"But not you."

"Nope. You want it with or without background?"

"With. I've got time."

"When I arrived, I spent a lot of time digging around and straightening up archives, and noticed there wasn't much on Ansel Turpin, even though he'd likely killed all those foundation people. So since I like tidy records, I added everything from his FBI files, talking with old acquaintances, the prosecutor's office in St. Pete, a foundation investigation, all of it. That's what you're reading there. Then I briefed what I had to Frank Dubois to add his recollections and learned he has a problem with it. He doesn't even like talking about him."

Link agreed. "When I asked him about Turpin yesterday, he said to talk to you and changed the subject."

"There's real emotion there on both sides. Ansel Turpin had never been known to torture anyone, but after he escaped from the hospital, he sent a note to Frank reading: *We are not done. Now it is my turn.* For the next month our people were hunted down and treated like animals in a slaughterhouse. They were all bad, but the last two were worst. They captured a man and woman employee together and sliced off noses and ears, the breasts and buttocks from the woman and the man's penis. Cut them open and tied them belly to belly, a caricature of lovemaking, and left them to be found— alive."

Link was disturbed by the awful vision.

"Thankfully that was just before Turpin left St. Pete." Erin eyed Link. "*That's* why Frank doesn't like talking about him. He feels responsibility. He saved Turpin's life, and Ansel responded with atrocities against his people."

"I can understand."

"You read the brief. How much do you recall about Turpin?"

"He was good at electronic eavesdropping and changing his appearance. Also he was a near-genius—certainly the FBI's smartest—when it came to physics and technology."

"That's a fair synopsis. Another important point: he's extremely vain." She lifted her cup and made a face. "This coffee is seriously bad, Link."

He got to his feet. "I'll make some more."

"Erin's rule number one. You're not to touch the coffeepot. It is not a division-of-labor argument, just that some are more equal than others when it comes to making coffee."

He followed her to the kitchenette, where she talked as she poured out the watery brew. "A few years back a man lived in an apartment not far from Ansel's townhouse in Arlington. Mousy guy with glasses and a lisp. Had a nerdy girlfriend and a cat. Played a clarinet on weekends, but never loud enough to upset neighbors. The week Turpin was reassigned, the guy dropped pussycat off with girlfriend and disappeared from the face of the earth."

She dumped out grounds, put in a fresh filter, then combined four scoops of coffee, a healthy pinch of hazelnut shavings, and a few grains of salt—carefully, not unlike a chemist.

"It wasn't another person, Link. Everywhere Ansel lived, he created personas. Some were discovered later, most were probably not."

She added water to the reservoir, switched on the coffeemaker, and they waited.

"Turpin is also obsessed with watching people unaware, using mini-cams and video. The two obsessions—living secret lives and watching others—are related. He's an orderly psychopath who creates private worlds. Of course he has no remorse. Why should he? Nothing's real."

"Which explains how he could mutilate people and not feel anything."

"That's how, but there's still the why. He'd never

done anything like that before, and he's not so stupid he would do it for no reason."

"Perhaps simple hatred, as we were saying?"

"That's part of it. I think it may have also been to draw Frank. Anyway, I kept digging. I found he had interests like classical music and medieval history, but except for the fact that they're somewhat escapist, I concluded they're irrelevant to his profile. I felt a key to knowing him might be found in the secret lives he's lived, so I opened a web page on the Internet and played it like a game, promising prizes for information about possible aliases at the different places he was stationed. People who showed up when he did and disappeared like smoke when he left. I didn't give his name, just his profile."

"Get anything?"

"Almost five thousand info inputs, most of them implausible, but some about people he'd probably been. There were two more aliases in St. Petersburg, the one I told you about in Arlington and eleven others I'm sure of. After a few weeks I was about to shut down the effort. Then, ten days ago, I got e-mail from a net-head in Aalborg, Denmark, who asked if I was certain about the final date—and whether he might have gone to her area. If I stretched the timeline, she'd known a likely candidate in late 1996. The nursing service she worked for had assigned her to a homebound patient who had fit all the profile criteria except . . . he'd had a gunshot wound."

Link stared at her.

"The patient claimed it was self-inflicted in a hunting accident." The coffeemaker began to growl as it completed its task. Erin immediately pulled the pot free and refilled their cups.

"Where was his wound?"

"His left knee," she said. "Interesting?"

"The time frame?"

"The nursing service was engaged on August third, a week before the explosion in Russia. He left Aalborg on September first."

"Description?" he asked, wondering.

"Older, but does it matter? He was the right size and spoke Danish with an Anglo accent. Said he was Canadian. Enjoyed Mozart—chamber music. Watched VCR tapes constantly. She walked in on him one day when he was on the phone. His voice was so different she wondered if it was the same person. He hung up and reverted back to the man she'd been caring for."

Could it be? Or had the nurse applied the description on the Internet to a patient she remembered only vaguely from the previous year?

"Three days after initial contact, while I was trying to verify the nurse's identity, she dropped offline. Next I started getting ridiculous garbage, all kinds of inputs like someone was trying to cloud the issue and make me look elsewhere."

"Who were those from?"

"There was no way to check, but they obviously came from someone trying to discredit her. After another day with no contact with the nurse, I explained it all to our FBI liaison. They weren't interested. To them Turpin is dead, period, and case closed. He was an embarrassment, and they're worried that someone's going to learn about the cover-up in St. Petersburg and implicate them. So I went to Frank Dubois, and he asked the Danish authorities to check on her."

"And?"

"I'm talking to the police officer in Copenhagen who's assigned to it. He's promised to investigate. In the meantime, I feel we should start looking *real* hard for Ansel Turpin."

Link was thoughtful.

"Great stuff, huh?"

He looked at her.

"The coffee."

"Superb. If it was Ansel, that would mean he wasn't in the explosion."

She nodded. "Just his Russian mafia buddies, who by then were *extremely* expendable. And if you buy that thinking, it was a handy diversion, scattering the radioactive stuff like that and slowing down the authorities long enough for his trail to get ice cold."

"How could he have done it?" he asked.

"How about if the truck carrying the explosives and radioactive material was wired before it left St. Petersburg, unbeknownst to the mafia guys, and set off by one of Ansel's subordinates following from a distance? Maybe the blond Russian special forces guy."

"How about the false teeth, the bridge they found?"

"The nurse said he had a sore mouth and claimed he'd recently had dental work."

Link pursed his lips, wondering. Begrudgingly agreed it all *could* be done.

"One last thing. If Ansel Turpin's alive, he hates Frank Dubois. Maybe all of us here, but especially Frank. Ansel prided himself on his intellect and not making mistakes, but that day in St. Petersburg he screwed up royal. Caught with his mob buddies. Didn't notice when he was being followed. That was bad enough, but then Frank, an amateur in his eyes, shot him, disarmed him, and stomped all over his ego. If he's alive, Turpin will keep trying to get to Frank until he either succeeds or he's neutralized."

"Interesting," was all Link said. It was a lot to swallow, but it was definitely interesting.

"Time for your security briefing," she said.

At eleven forty, the intercom buzzed. "Don't forget lunch," said Erin's voice.

Link pulled on his jacket and went to the door. "How do I find this Governor's Club?"

"You don't. A car's waiting at the main entrance. I told the driver to look for a tall guy wearing boots, a hat, and a confused look."

The limo chauffeur opened the rear passenger's door as he came out of the building, hurried around to the driver's seat, and deftly cut off a cab as he pulled out into traffic. Twelve minutes later they arrived at the club. "Good job," Link told him, still clutching the strap.

The driver gave him a grin and said he'd be waiting.

The Governor's Club was dark and stodgy, and the maitre d' frowned until Link gave his name. The man's

demeanor abruptly changed, and he was escorted to a
room at the rear. There a group of thirty correctly clad
Weyland Foundation executives looked on with interest
as he made his way to the head table.

"Lincoln Anderson is our newest executive vice-
president," Frank announced, "as well as my close friend."

There was a chorus of welcomes. The Secretary of
Energy, a graying middle-aged man with bulbous nose
and a calculating look, was seated beside Frank. His sole
qualification for the post was that during the last election
he'd raised several millions of dollars for the party from
his home state of Kentucky. Another couple million, it
was rumored, and he'd have gotten the coveted Com-
merce post where *real* fortunes were made.

As Link took a seat down the table, the Secretary
gave him a curious smile, then leaned closer to Frank
and spoke rapidly, not trying to disguise the sound of
sales patter. Frank caught Link's eye. "The Secretary's
telling me about the need for a universally accepted disposal method for nuclear waste."

"Oh?" was all Link said before turning his rapt attention to the wine list, the only available prop. The waiter
came. Link ordered tea but kept the list handy.

Since Frank was monopolized by the Secretary, whose
jowls were aquiver with excitement about someone pos-
sessing the initials N.E.L., Link turned his attention to
the chatter among the foundation's vice-presidents. He
joined in the small talk—not much, for it would have
been a complete departure for him, and formed a periodic on-cue smile. But the entrée was superb—alternat-
ing slices of melt-in-your-mouth tenderloin and smoked
salmon—and Link ate voraciously, his appetite whetted
after the lean time he'd spent in the wilderness.

When he returned to the building, Link wended his
way through the maze and on only his third try located
an elevator that could take him to the twenty-seventh
floor. In 2775, he found Erin standing in the middle of
the room, supervising the placement of a new forest of
cacti.

"Good lunch?" she asked.

"Great." As he went to his office he did not point out

that they were receiving as many plants as had been removed. Erin liked them.

It wasn't long before Frank Dubois rolled in wearing a scowl. "Politicians!"

"I don't envy you."

Frank sighed. "I'll deal with them. You just watch my back and make sure they don't leave cleat marks when they try to walk over us. Are you ready to leave?"

"The airplane's waiting. You wanted to talk first?"

"When I told the Secretary about you, he felt you'd be a good choice to check out NEL." The Secretary of Energy had used initials, but Frank pronounced it like the woman's name.

"Great. What does she look like?"

"Nucleonic Engineering, Limited. They do research and studies about ways to deal with nuclear waste. Last year they came to us looking for funding for a research effort in northern Nevada, up near Carson City, so we sent a team to look them over. Our experts felt they were breaking every safety rule on the books and recommended that we have no part of them. Now the Secretary says they've cleaned up their act, and they're on the verge of a breakthrough. That's the other catch. Our experts felt their premise was full of baloney."

"I didn't know you were involved with nuke."

"We're helping with a weapons dismantling project, but this is different. Nuclear waste disposal's a worldwide problem, and it's getting worse. There are a hundred and ten reactors in America and several hundred more worldwide. Together they're generating hundreds of tons of deadly garbage every week. Our government's spending good money trying to find answers."

"Ways to store the stuff?"

"That's the obvious one, but there've been other proposals. Dig a chute to the fiery bowels of the earth. Shoot it into the sun or deep space. Develop a breeder reactor that turns waste into fuel. The one NEL's talking about seems unlikely—except the government people want to give it a look."

Link had been the nuclear safety officer for their flying unit, and while he understood it well enough, he was seldom excited by nitty-gritty particulars of nuclear physics.

"Is this something I'll be working on regularly?" he asked.

"Not unless you're interested, but I'm going to ask you to check this one out. Our smart guys in Habitat Earth thought they were unsafe, but the supervisor at NEL says they were nit-picking and wants someone more objective."

"You want me to go there now, before Montana?"

Frank considered, then decided against it. "Go home and get everything wrapped up. When you're back, we'll talk about it again. Maybe they'll have found another sugar daddy."

4

Gary parked behind the police cruiser and pushed the scrap of paper with the address into his shirt pocket. The single-wide trailer had an established flower garden on one side, and patches of lawn battled hardpack alkaline desert between the front door and street. The acre had been cleared of sagebrush and manmade debris— tidy for this part of Stagecoach, where a number of homes had decrepit vehicles littering their yards. Whoever lived here had what real estate agents called pride of ownership.

He crawled out, took a courage-bolstering breath, and motioned for Aristotle to stay put. Deputy Watt had called, saying another body had been found. Gary was queasy at the thought of viewing a corpse, and wished he'd come up with an excuse. Sure his curiosity was piqued that a flu bug could wreak such devastation. Maybe Ebola or typhus, but a rather common flu that had run its course elsewhere? Yet he was not keen at all to view a corpse so unsightly that even medics had been sickened by the first ones.

Three days ago he'd been at the University of Nevada library in Reno, wrapping up the research for his book, when he'd remembered what the deputy had told him about Trudy Schmidt—the blisters, dark skin, and swatches of loose hair—and others found in similar condition. He'd not spent a lot of effort on it, but tried to match the symptoms with those of known diseases. After a half hour he'd stopped. The only easy matches, for a layman at least, had been those of the black death that killed off three-quarters of all Europeans in the year 1350, and victims of the Chernobyl meltdown and Hiroshima bomb. Since there'd been no nuke attacks or reports of bubonic plague, he'd given up.

Gary eyed the trailer, thinking he shouldn't be wasting time like this. He needed to finish polishing the book—in writer's parlance, making sure all the loops were closed. At the same time, he should keep trying to get hold of Link Anderson so he could talk him into coming out. He'd just decided to turn around and head back to the Bronco when the deputy came out, still in rubber gloves and surgical mask, carrying his Polaroid camera. He saw Gary and nodded his greeting.

If the corpse was in the same condition as the others, it would be the fourth such in the past month. There'd also been a burned-out trailer with a body inside. And a couple of people had disappeared, although that was not so odd. Folks in Stagecoach had a way of wandering off—some going on alcoholic hootenannies, others evading debts, most just wanting to get away for a while—then showing up after a couple of weeks.

Ray Watt pulled down his mask, exposing a grimace.

"Who is it?" Gary asked.

"Broken-down old cowboy named Lester Dunlap," said the deputy. He glanced back at the door and shook his head. "Damn, but it smells in there."

Gary remembered Lester from the saloon. A regular there, like the others. He started to ask his next question, but Ray spoke first. "Old Lester put the barrel of his six-shooter in his mouth and ate the bullet. Blew off the back of his head and splattered the walls with his smarts."

That surprised him. He'd thought it was another flu case. "When did it happen?"

"Neighbor heard a gun go off early Friday morning. Woke her up and made her mad."

"No one phoned it in?"

"People called ever time a shot's fired, I'd be chasing my tail day and night." Ray looked at the door. "Most of him's on the kitchen floor in there. Before he killed

hisself looks like he was in the same shape as those
others. You know, hair falling out, sick to the stomach,
skin all dark like he was in a toaster—which was why
I called."

Now Gary *knew* it had been a mistake to come.

"Puked and peed and shit his pants," Ray Watt added,
"but some of that might of been when he shot hisself.
Happens with people, same as animals. Couple years ago
I hadda crawl in a car where three kids had got killed
in a head-on. Piss and shit all over the seats. Went home
and washed my clothes and took a shower, but I smelled
for a week."

Gary let him ramble about his experiences with the
dead, as he girded himself. When the deputy paused he
motioned at the door. "Mind if I look?"

"Better not go all the way inside. You can see enough
from out here."

Gary eased the door open, and waited as his eyes
adjusted.

"Might be quick about it. Medics oughta be here
any time."

The body was in view a few feet away on the kitchen
floor. The stench that permeated the place was as awful
as Deputy Watt had said, causing his gorge to rise, but
Gary forced himself to continue observing. Lester was
turned toward him, skin dark, lips curled in a grimace.
Wisps of white hair in the dried vomit and blood surrounding him—and on the wall where brain matter still
clung. There were dried blisters on the exposed flesh.

His stomach began to lurch.

"The ambulance is here."

Gary gratefully closed the door, but his stomach continued somersaulting.

The deputy assumed his grim-faced official-business
look, and nodded brusquely to the medical attendants
getting out of their emergency vehicle.

"He was obviously sick before he died," Gary tried.

"Probably that bad flu. Still a matter of suicide. Likely
won't be *any* investigation, which is the way I like it."

Gary thanked Watt, and walked to the Bronco, where
Aristotle stretched out a window, trying to con a pet

from the attendants who were hauling a body bag and litter from the back of the ambulance. As he crawled into the Bronco and started up, his stomach did another flip-flop at the lingering awful image and odor. He drove slowly, not at his normal mach three speed, for what he'd seen was sobering. The sickness was horrific—bad enough that he believed Lester Dunlap had killed himself to end his suffering—yet he was underqualified to dispute the doctor, or whoever was telling the dumb-as-a-post coroner in Winchester that it was a virus.

Drop it, he decided, and felt good about the decision. Next time he saw Deputy Watt he'd tell him he didn't want to hear about it and sure didn't want to view another foul-smelling corpse.

Gary was thinking of that, and feeling pleased that he hadn't gotten sick, when his stomach lurched mightily. He braked hard, and the Bronco was still sliding to a stop as he threw open the door and released a gusher of vomit onto the dirt street. He spat and snorted, took his time coming upright, then sat gripping the wheel, breathing through his gaping mouth, thinking about it all again, no matter what he'd decided.

Like about the inept county coroner. Gary had met the current officeholder, an insurance salesman who had bested a store clerk in the polls by fifty-three votes and whose training consisted of reading pamphlets and attending a seminar in Carson City. His salary was paltry, and if money was squandered on unnecessary autopsies, his meager budget would be drained.

He wondered if the coroner would even open the body bag to look at Lester. If he didn't lose the blood sample, as he'd done with Trudy Schmidt's, he *might* remember to have a local doctor examine it. The last times he'd done that, Deputy Watt told Gary the doctor said the samples had been useless.

Useless? Gary wondered. Not contaminated or substituted. Useless. Maybe he should pursue it, at least get enough information to interest someone at the Carson City Appeal.

As far as he knew, not much was known about the old cowboy named Lester Dunlap, and it was just that, the dearth of information, that was a common string among the victims. All of them had lived alone, with no close friends or family in the area. No one to check on them. No one to give a damn whether they lived or died.

No one would claim Lester's body, for no one would want to pay for the burial. After the prescribed week in the morgue, located at the rear of the county's only funeral home, the once-cowboy would be cremated. It was doubtful anyone would miss him or mention his name.

He resumed driving, wondering if anyone had seen him puke, and again decided to drop the matter and let someone else worry about it. Then his mind came back at him with "Oh yeah? Who?" But he knew it was time to get back to business, meaning his book.

Gary parked at the Barn, left Aristotle to do his business in the field, and went up to the loft. He switched on the computer as the telephone rang. Expecting a call from his literary agent, he answered: "Sadie's House of Ill Repute. You got the cash, we'll haul your ash."

A man's voice laughed. "That you, Gary?"

It was not his agent. "Yes?"

"Link Anderson. I got in last night and found your message on the machine."

Gary formed a grin. "Been a long time, buddy."

"Yes, it has."

"I heard about your fiancée." They spoke for a while about Link's bereavement—he seemed to have his act together about it—then Gary started his sales pitch. "I've got a problem."

"Something I can help with?"

"Yes, but I'd appreciate it if you didn't mention it to anyone else."

"I'll keep it between us," Link said. "You sounded anxious on the answering machine. Are you in some kind of trouble?"

"Not me. But a mutual friend of ours may be." It shouldn't be a heavy dilemma. They had only one mutual friend.

"I just came from seeing Frank," Link said. "We

shared a laugh about the three of us getting kicked off the golf course in Saudi. He said to pass on his greeting."

Gary felt a twinge of guilt and wished he'd called Link four months ago, when the informant had first approached him with the information. "How much do you know about the Weyland Foundation?" he asked.

Link hesitated. "Quite a lot."

"Then I *know* you're the one I need. When can we get together?"

"I'm busy for the next few days. Look, why don't you call Frank? Hell, he *runs* the foundation, and if he's involved like you say—"

Gary interrupted: "I can't."

Link didn't fill in the awkward moment of silence.

Gary sighed. "I'd like to talk with Frank, but there's no way. Not yet. There are allegations that he's involved in something damned serious. Since he's a friend, I'd like to make sure the information's correct before it goes to print. That's why I need your help."

"Frank Dubois is one of the most honorable men I know."

"Fine. Come out and read what I have, check it out, and then tell me that."

"And if I can't make it?"

"It goes to the publisher, I get paid a bag of money, and Frank and the foundation get stung. Badly."

"Damn it, Gary. Frank should know about this."

"Once you've read what I've got and seen my evidence and decide its bullshit, be my guest and go ahead and tell him. But if you feel there's anything to it, I want to know that too."

Link released a painful breath. "Gary, we're talking about my closest friend."

"Friendship's the only reason I'm making this call. For a while I was just too excited about getting a big story like this laid at my feet. Then a few weeks back I started thinking about it being Frank, for Christ's sake, and I got a feeling like I was *betraying* him, although I've got hard evidence. My publisher feels it's enough. I didn't have to bring you into it, Link."

He was answered by silence.

"I'll pay for your plane ticket," he said, trying to recall the balance on his Visa card.

Link's voice was flat. "That's not necessary. I'll drive."

Gary's spirits buoyed. "You'll come?"

"Yeah. I'll finish here tomorrow. Take off Friday and make it to Winnemucca, and be there Saturday. How do I find you?" His tone was not joyous.

Gary gave directions, then, before they hung up, tried to smooth it over. "This is an interesting place, Link. Bags of history and fascinating people, and an Arnie Palmer golf course ten miles up the road. Bring your sticks and we'll play a few rounds while we check it out."

After the connection was broken, Gary brooded as he brought the computer screen to life with a movement of the mouse, and entered his password. He'd go through the manuscript and check for errors, also put in page numbers and make up headers and footers—an easy three-day task. When Link arrived he would print out a copy and they could concentrate on the revelations of his whistle-blower.

But first—since he would be dropping the matter for a while—he entered computer notes on the deaths in the valley, using his own notes and the information Deputy Watt had provided. When he was done he copied it onto a floppy disk, pulled out a plot map of Stagecoach, and circled the homes of Lester, Trudy Schmidt, and the others, and put it all into the folder he marked Dilemma.

Before putting away the folder, he reached into the jumble on the tabletop to pull out another note, delved through the stack, and paused. And then frowned—for things were not as he'd left them. The mess there, as well as on other work surfaces, appeared to be a haphazard collection of books, notepads, and scribbled-on sheets of paper. But there was a chronological and subjective organization to it, understood only by Gary.

He checked again and was sure. Someone had gotten in, come upstairs and rifled through his notes, then replaced them in almost the proper order. Without hesitation he opened the leather portfolio and frantically leafed through a collection of loose pages tucked under a flap. He heaved a sigh, for they were in place. The two memoranda were his smoking gun. Without them there would be no proof, no exposé, no book. He carried the portfolio everywhere he went, never let it out of his sight.

Was he wrong about the intrusion?

Gary started to relax, then abruptly caught himself. Had someone also tried to delve into the computer? With the left mouse button he selected START, then the DOCU-MENTS icon, to show the list of recently opened files. He stared with disbelief, and this time cursed loudly. Some-one had gotten past his password, examined several manuscript chapters and his reference notes.

When? Last night when he'd gone to the local saloon for a beer? This morning?

Gary popped the hood of the laser printer and felt the drum. It was warm. Something—his notes, likely—had been printed while he was viewing Lester's body. He clicked on MY COMPUTER, then the letter for the hard drive, then WRITING, and examined. The MODIFIED times matched with his last work sessions. There'd been no changes or deletions. His work was intact.

He blew out a sigh of relief, then forced himself to think through an appropriate response. The book must be protected. He would change the password, copy his work to a floppy diskette. Erase the information from the computer's hard drive and work with diskettes.

Paranoid? You bet. Mama Runyon didn't raise a com-plete fool. Then a chilling thought struck. No one had been pulling away when he'd returned. Was the intruder still in the Barn?

He went down cautiously, pulled his pistol from the nightstand, then checked the place from one end to the other—the weapon trembling in his grip, heart thumping a tango beat—overlooking nothing. As he peered into closets, he thought about the way everything had *almost* been right upstairs. Only that single stack of research work had been mixed up—the others were as he'd left them, as if the intruder had been taking his time, then hurried to finish and leave. How had he known to hurry? Had someone called to tell him Gary was returning?

It was frightening, but the more Gary thought of it,

the angrier he became. He did not let anyone, not even colleagues or friends, read his work before it was in final form. To have someone do so without his knowledge was outrageous enough. But this time the manuscript contained revelations that could cause serious harm.

He had a fleeting thought that the intruder might have been sent by his ex-wife. The previous morning he'd picked up a letter from the Philadelphia law firm with seven names. Another love note from his wife's attorney, trying to coax him into signing over royalties.

No, this intrusion was different, probably to do with the manuscript, since that was what had been opened. He considered calling Link, to get him here before someone tried something bolder. After mulling it over, he decided to wait, but he'd take the pistol—a Beretta model 92 with a pre-Clinton 15-shot clip—wherever he went. Nevadans were allowed, even expected, to defend themselves.

Gary went back upstairs, methodically transferred the manuscript onto a floppy diskette, then made a second copy. He entitled the two diskettes in such a way that someone who knew him might have an idea where he'd placed them. Finally, with deft clicks of the mouse button, he deleted the book from the hard drive, changed his password, and shut off the computer.

The telephone jangled. Gary hesitated, picked up on the second ring. "Hello?"

"You sound grumpy," Shelby chided. "I'm flying to Vegas this afternoon, remember?"

"Sure." Shelby was a geologist for the state, and the water board was issuing new guidelines. Water rights were a very big thing in Nevada.

"I'll be back Friday," she was saying, "so how about I make dinner reservations for Saturday evening? Maybe the Cabin in the Sky?"

"How about Chez Greasy Spoon?" It was Gary's turn to pay.

"Not good enough for a world-famous author. We'll split the tab, okay?"

He started to assert his masculine right to pay, then—remembering his state of poverty—thought better. Instead he said: "I got a call from Link Anderson. He'll be here this weekend."

"That's *wonderful.*" He noted the trill in her voice. It was one of those coincidences where they'd known someone through entirely different avenues and not realized it. Shelby had worked on a project about prehistoric Native Americans with Link's fiancée. She'd even attended her funeral and, when she returned, talked about Link's tragedy over dinner one night—until he'd realized she was speaking about his old friend. She hadn't known Link as well as he had, but it was an odd coincidence nonetheless.

"He can join us for dinner," Gary said. He looked about the room. The feeling that he was being watched seemed stronger. He started to tell her about someone breaking in but decided to wait. There was no reason to spoil her trip.

"I'll reserve a corner table for three so we can talk," she said. "Gotta go. *Ciao,* Gary."

As they broke the connection, his mind reverted to the intrusion. After lunch he would take one of the diskettes to a hiding place and keep the other locked in the Bronco where it would be handier. Whenever he needed it he'd load it into the computer, and when he was finished he'd make two copies. It would be a pain, running back and forth, but his work would be secure.

He picked up the Dilemma manila folder and placed one of the copies inside. The influenza deaths were a different project, but since he wouldn't be working on it for a while, he might as well hide it too.

As Gary stood, he could not shake the feeling of being observed. Aristotle plodded behind him as he searched the loft, peered into the storage room, even swung open cabinet doors. Nothing, just as there'd been no one downstairs. He stared out the window at the hermit's shanty on the hillside. The decrepit truck was gone. The bewhiskered old man was away on another prospecting trip, searching for whatever he looked for. The next time Gary saw him, he'd ask if he'd noticed anyone hanging around.

*　　*　　*

A few miles away three people watched closely as the writer left the loft. The minicam in the terminal box had captured every word and frown. The soft-spoken man looked on, his lips pursed in a prissy muse, an expression used by a man he'd replaced and whom he now emulated so perfectly that no one suspected, regardless of how well they'd known the other. While his countenance did not reflect it, his mind was awhirl with what he'd just overheard.

Another of the watchers—the woman who hated so bitterly—had identified the caller from Boudie Springs, Montana, and was going online to gather more information. The person in the soft-spoken man's façade needed none of it. He knew about Lincoln Anderson, who was Frank Dubois's closest friend. He'd studied Anderson's childhood, his adoption, his exploits in the military, his fiancée, and his grieving. The last time he'd checked him, Anderson had disappeared into the mountains, so he had believed it would take Gary Runyon several more days than it had to contact him. Anderson was coming *now*. The end game must not be rushed. Could they discourage him? Delay him somehow so they'd have those last critical few days to prepare?

The anxiety continued to grow until he felt like a ball player with pregame jitters. There was no reason for it, he told himself. He could adjust for the minor glitch. The plan was sound, and all possible contingencies were covered, weren't they? There'd never been doubts before the confrontation with Frank Dubois in St. Petersburg. Now there were times when his hand was unsure, and the foul taste of nervousness filled his palate.

Then, as quickly as the trepidation had descended, it evaporated, and he was the man he had been. He was master of his fate. Aware, because he was the one with the plan, and the plan was good. All that was required were a few fine tuning adjustments.

He looked down at the pages before him—the book notes he'd pulled up on the writer's computer and printed out. There were too many suspicions. Gary Runyon had contributed his part, and now he could only cause trouble.

Another thought. Frank Dubois had few vulnerabilities. But what if he held his closest friend? Use Gary Runyon to draw Link Anderson, and Anderson to draw Dubois? It wasn't a bad option, and regardless it would be smart to neutralize as many of Dubois's friends as possible.

When Anderson arrived he could visit him—in another guise, of course—and, if conditions were right, take him prisoner before he realized what it was all about.

But all of that was simply food for thought. First there was Mr. Runyon to deal with. He smiled in anticipation of bringing grief to someone who had been close to Frank Dubois.

5

Link brought the duffel bag from the rear bedroom and opened it near the washing machine. Started tossing dirty clothes into the washer. When it was close to full he added soap, shut the lid, and started it.

Joseph Spotted Horse came in the back door and deposited a load of wood beside the fireplace. In the high country, even in temperate June, a fire was needed to knock off the evening chill. Joseph was not one to mince words. "You walk like a white man," had been one of the things he'd observed when he'd joined Link in the wilderness, and he'd refused to listen to excuses, such as the fact that Link was only half Piegan and had been raised by a white family. It was a long while until Joseph felt he walked properly. Now he looked on gravely and said: "In all of my years I have not smelled anything like that, and I will soon be seventy."

Link did not remind Joseph that he was much closer to eighty. The odor was indeed strong. The clothing had ripened in the duffel bag, forgotten during the months Link had been away, dealing with Marie's passing and then healing in the mountain wilderness. As he opened the duffel so it could air out, Joseph frowned and coughed, came over, and gingerly picked it up.

"I think it should be put out, although it will frighten many animals." Joseph held it at arm's length as he went through the door. When he came back inside he sighed dramatically, as he'd done for the past hour since Link had received the call from Gary Runyan.

"I won't be away long," Link said.

"I would like to see this New York before I die," Joseph complained. Link had once offered to show him the great city. He'd arrived at the cabin from the reservation that morning and announced that he wished to accompany Link on the drive. The phone call from Gary had bollixed the plan, and Joseph did not appreciate it.

Now the telephone rang again, and Joseph glared grumpily as he picked up his suitcase and took it into the spare bedroom. He'd agreed to watch after the place until Link returned, and displayed proprietary interest in such things as the odiferous duffel bag.

"Anderson," Link answered.

"I just spoke with Erin," said Frank Dubois. "What's this about you going to Nevada to see Gary Runyon?"

"Only for a few days," Link said.

When he didn't explain, Frank sighed impatiently. "Okay, Link, *why* are you going?"

"I told Gary I wouldn't talk about it."

"Hey, this is Frank. Your friend, remember?"

"From what he told me, the trip's necessary. Beyond that, don't ask, okay?"

Frank made an irritated sound. Then, "Gary isn't far from Carson City, so while you're there, check out the nucleonics firm we talked about. The Secretary of Energy called back. Maybe we can get him off my back."

"No problem."

Frank gave him a contact's name and phone numbers. "Lawrence will tell him you're coming. Take a hard look at their safety practices and make your decision. And stay in touch with Erin. Did you take a secure phone?"

"I didn't think I'd be doing company business," he said.

"From now on, take it everywhere you go. If you're going to be long, we'll send one out."

"I'm not."

As the connection was severed, Link heard Joseph Spotted Horse in the other room, muttering about telephones and New York City and the bedroom. "In all of my days," Joseph was grumbling, "I have never seen a bed with so many lumps."

6

**7:35 P.M.—Highway 50,
Near Stagecoach Valley, Nevada**

For a while that afternoon, Gary had felt upbeat despite
the intrusion, since Link would be there by the weekend
and they'd decide about the book. Then things had
steadily become bleaker.

He'd nuked a frozen burrito for lunch, stopped by
and chatted with Shelby's father about setting up a golf
foursome when Link arrived, and driven to the airfield
suffering from severe heartburn. Then he'd spent the
afternoon talking with the mechanic about his ancient
Piper Cub—once fondly called Mathilda. No more
fondly though, because he'd been told that greedy Mathilda needed a replacement engine, and even for an old
J-4 model Cub, those were expensive. The heartburn got
worse and his mood had just sunk past glum when he'd
asked the mechanic to hold off while he scrounged up
some cash. He'd left the folder and diskettes in Mathilda, and on the drive back worried about how he'd jug-
gle paying for the engine, house payments, and the
renovations on the Barn. Food? Forget it.

If Link agreed there was truth to it, the publisher
would give Gary his bonus on acceptance of the manuscript. But like all publishing houses, they were incredibly slow, so book or no book, he wondered if it was
possible to return a slightly used hot tub. Then there
was the possibility—growing in his mind as he realized
how all the things he'd gotten from his informant
seemed just too good to be true—that he and Link
would discover that the exposé was screwed up and Gary

would have to call the publisher and let them know he'd been scammed. He had ideas about how to salvage his work, but regardless, it would be lean times for a while.

The evening sky was as dark as his mood by the time he entered Stagecoach. He turned off on the very first street, delaying his return to the Barn as he drove slowly down the streets and peered at the homes. As he passed Trudy Schmidt's place he glumly noticed the For Sale sign.

Aristotle placed his heavy canine nose on his shoulder, and Gary reached back. "You'll have to cut back on dog food, old buddy. Maybe catch some of those critters in the field for dinner. I'll just stop eating altogether." He scratched Aristotle's furry muzzle, then turned onto a side street. He thought about the break-in and tried to conjure a mental picture of the intruder. Write it down, he decided, and as he drove he switched on the overhead lamp, opened the portfolio on the seat, found the notepad and poised his pen.

Someone with the ability to break in without leaving obvious signs, he thought. A burglar? No, there'd been too many valuables around and nothing taken. But it had been a slick job nonetheless.

B&E Expert, he wrote.

Gary ran a hand through his shock of red hair, trying to wipe away cobwebs.

Someone who knew computers. That eliminated most inhabitants of the valley, where few were computer literate. There was a new IBM in Cal Admire's office—he'd helped Shelby's father set it up for his real estate business—but Cal wasn't savvy enough to get past a password, and wouldn't give a hoot about what Gary was writing about. *Computer wise,* he wrote.

Which led to the next point. Not only was the intruder knowledgeable about computers, he or she had been interested in what he was writing—which likely meant he or she had known it was an exposé—and no one knew that except his publisher and agent. He'd told Shelby it was special, nothing more. The idea of a break-in artist who was not interested in thievery—only in his writing—

was somehow unnerving. There was no one who knew . . .

Yes, there was. He sat back, amazed by his foolishness. Thinking of a person who could break in without leaving a trace, who knew computers *and* the importance of what he was writing. He printed the initials. A dangerous man, he'd decided during one of their meetings.

But why would his own informant break into his computer? They had work sessions. Why not just ask Gary for a look at the manuscript, or even a copy of his notes? Then he remembered how strained the air had become during the final visit, when Gary had voiced his concern that Frank Dubois was a friend and had never seemed deceitful.

"Have a third party check it out," the informant had snapped, as if he was irritated about having to spell out something so obvious. "There's got to be someone you trust. Somebody who knows both you and Dubois."

Upon reflection, it was as if he was *leading* him to Link Anderson. And how would he know that Gary knew Link, and Link knew Frank? Because the informant's business was checking people out. *That's* how. Damn and double damn!

The thought was disturbing that he might have been tricked into betraying not one but two friends—yet Gary knew something like that was happening.

If he let it happen.

No way.

Gary ripped the page off the pad and stuffed it into his shirt pocket with the dead ex-cowboy's address, then reached under the seat and touched the handle of the Beretta to reassure himself. A round was chambered. All he had to do was grab it, thumb off the safety, and pull the trigger. But could he shoot a man? It was a valid question. He was no warrior—not like his friends Frank Dubois and Link Anderson. Not a pro like the informant.

He turned onto Iroquois Trail and headed toward the Barn, heart pounding as he drew closer, wondering if he shouldn't drive on past. An inner voice reasoned that there was nothing concrete about his trepidation; except for the break-in there was no reason to suspect the informant, and even then no reason to believe the intruder meant him grief.

Aristotle sensed that something was afoot, and placed his muzzle on his shoulder again.

"I was ready to turn on my friend just to make a buck," Gary complained to the mutt. The big dog whined, which was not his nature. Leave! his mind suddenly shouted, and Gary decided to honor his fears and stop at the Barn only long enough to get a few essentials. He'd drop Aristotle off at Shelby's folks, drive to Reno and get a room, and call Link. Meet him in Winnemucca when he was driving down and explain it all. See if he had any ideas on a good next step. Call the publisher and tell them there'd be a delay, that the real story wasn't anything like they thought but would still be juicy.

The outside of the Barn was well illuminated. Floodlights automatically switched on at nightfall, and Gary could see no vehicles or sign of activity. He pulled into the driveway and parked beneath the bright glare of the lights, and pulled the Beretta up into his lap.

And waited. Wondered if he was doing the right thing by fleeing.

Yes. The more he thought of him, the more the informant scared the hell out of him. That last time he'd looked into the guy's eyes, he'd noted something intense and frightening.

He looked at the house, worried that someone might be waiting for him, and considered leaving immediately. Chewed on his lip and brooded as he stared. Finally decided to keep the engine running, get a change of clothes and toiletries, and *go*. If there was nothing to worry about, he'd still feel better when he was a few miles away. Gary gripped the pistol and climbed out cautiously, eyes fixed on the dark doorway.

He staggered as he was rudely nudged, and almost pulled the trigger in his panic. Then he laughed nervously. Aristotle had jarred him as he'd jumped out behind him. The dog trotted over to a cottonwood to relieve himself.

Gary unlocked the front door and went inside, holding his breath, the pistol extended before himself as he'd seen in movies. No one waited in ambush. He flipped on lights, hurried into the bedroom, and stuffed clothes and shave gear into an athletic bag, trotted out to deposit them in the Bronco. Aristotle was gone, likely chasing something in the field, but thinking of the mutt jogged his memory. Gary returned inside, shoved the pistol into his waistband, and hefted an unopened forty-pound sack of Dog Chow. He emerged, glanced out at the field, then lugged the bag toward the idling Bronco.

"Going somewhere?" asked a shadow in his informant's deep voice.

Gary was numbed with fear. "I shouldn't be away long," he managed, mind churning as he lugged the sack to the back of the Bronco, balanced it as he swung the tailgate open, and dropped it inside. His hands were unencumbered. He prepared to reach for the pistol—hesitated at the thought of confrontation as the man came closer, now in half-light.

Gary gathered nerve as he edged the hand toward the Beretta. "Just need to get away for a couple of days." He peered at the Barn as if wondering if he'd forgotten anything. Wanting to snatch the weapon free, warn the man back as he crawled into the Bronco, but his hand was frozen into place, still inches from the pistol. If he fumbled it . . .

His visitor stepped into the illumination and Gary's heart plummeted. A heavy pistol was already aimed at Gary's chest, and while he swore the voice had been that of his informant, the man before him was a stranger with a prissy but amused expression. He wore leather gloves.

"Please," Gary whispered, his voice so low the word was hardly audible.

The man took a single step. His gun hand swept forward in a fluid motion, and metal smacked hard into Gary's head. He groaned and began to reel, but the stranger put his weapon away and restrained him, holding up a mini-tape recorder to capture his agony. As Gary sank to one knee, the Beretta was yanked from his belt, the recorder held close to his lips. The man hit him a couple more times, hard, and kept the microphone poised as Gary cried out.

His tormentor signaled, and a dark-colored pickup backed into view. A figure dismounted and emerged into the light. Tall, with long blond hair tied back.

The telephone repairman came closer, looked down.

"Good. I don' like him," he said as he knelt, and pulled Gary's wallet from his hip pocket.

"It's yours," Gary whispered, unreasonably hoping that was what they were after.

There was an ominous growl. "Watch out for the dog!" the blond yelled as Aristotle came galloping from the field. The first man raised Gary's weapon, casually aimed, and fired. Aristotle woofed in surprise, stumbled, and fell against the Bronco.

"Now no more shooting," said the prissy man. "Cut its throat," he ordered. The blond pulled a lockblade knife from a leather belt-case, and started forward.

"Get the coyote!" Gary managed in a hoarse voice, hoping Aristotle wasn't so badly injured he couldn't respond.

The prissy one hit him with his own gun and this time let him fall.

Time warped, moved in spasms—Gary on all fours, drooling into the pea gravel, blood dribbling from his nose and right ear, hearing himself moaning from pain so intense it was dulled, as if he were watching from some detached view, and all of his sounds captured on tape.

The prissy man switched off the floodlights, then came back and—in a soft voice—gave instructions to the blond. "I'm going in," the new voice said.

The repairman extended Gary's wrists and wrapped them with wire. Tightly and expertly, as if he'd done it before. He secured his ankles with a few deft wraps, like a rodeo calf-roper, grasped a handful of hair, and dragged him to his feet. With wire connecting wrists and ankles, Gary crouched. The world was fuzzy, for at some point he'd lost his glasses.

The blond hoisted him into the pickup bed, where he

fell against a barrel. "Stand op!" the repairman said, crawling into the bed with him. Gary reached up and grasped the rim of the open barrel and tried to raise himself, but the effort was gargantuan.

"Get op." He was dragged to his feet and shoved nose-first into the dark maw. It was then that Gary realized what the man wanted—to enclose him in the barrel! He found a vestige of strength and desperately gripped the rim. The repairman smashed his fingers with savage blows. Gary let go and released painful sobs as his bound ankles were lifted. He fell into the barrel, collapsed onto neck and shoulders, and was instantly numbed . . . as if he'd been stabbed with a giant shot of Novocain.

"Oh, dear God," Gary whimpered, but the words were heard only by himself as the lid was placed over the top. He heard the man pounding, tamping it in place . . . and drifted into unconsciousness.

The repairman rifled through the Bronco, found and removed the diskette and the portfolio, then settled down to wait. Twenty more minutes passed before the soft-spoken man emerged from the house carrying a half-filled cardboard box, which he placed into the pickup cab.

"Everything ready?"

"Yes." The repairman placed the diskette and portfolio into the cardboard box, and squinted at the dark alfalfa field. "What about the dog?"

"Probably crawled off to die. I'll go now. You know what to do?"

The repairman stared at the field for another moment, then walked to the still-idling Bronco. They drove the vehicles from the yard and turned in separate directions.

A large shape emerged from the field and trotted painfully behind the pickup, head drooping and eyes glued to the dark barrel, blood bubbling delicately from its nostrils on each breath. Periodically Aristotle would stumble, but each time he would rise and go on. The pickup soon left his view, but by then the big dog had stored its peculiar scent, and he continued toward the highway, and then across, and beyond into the desert. Finally the animal fell.

Gary Runyon regained a spark of consciousness as a hard jolt and shift of position restored blood circulation to his brain. He was so paralyzed he could not even utter a moan from the intensity of his torment. The barrel was bouncing and shuddering, the vehicle obviously being driven over rough terrain, and bolts of fiery pain swept through his neck and torso.

The agony continued until the barrel slammed sideward, tipped, and teetered—then fell over with a crash. His head slammed into metal, but as the barrel rolled about his neck no longer bore his full weight. As more blood drained from his brain, Gary was able to think better—but the thoughts were not reassuring. They would kill him in the desert. He prayed as the endless bouncing continued, remembering litanies he hadn't uttered since childhood. He implored God to make death come swiftly. To have charity and remember that he had not *always* ignored His will.

As the confused rolling and bruising crashes continued, idle thoughts arose. There could not be much air. Fifty-five gallons of it, minus body displacement. How long would it take him to consume it? Perhaps he'd be dead when they removed him. If not, would he feel the kill shot?

Gary was on a new prayer when the rolling and bouncing ceased. He waited for them to open the top. Tried to make up pleas for his life, like promising not to tell what he'd learned. That he would cooperate. That they could have the diskettes. Anything.

He heard a faint, high-pitched sound, then a metallic clank as something contacted the barrel. He sensed motion. A forklift? The machine trundled across an uneven surface. Then the thing stopped, tilted, and the barrel rolled off the forks. He tumbled, braced for impact, but instead the barrel smacked against something, and then he felt the sensation that he was accelerating, plunging downward in a fast elevator ride. He was thrown to one side, then the other, as the barrel careened down some sort of chute, slamming against the sides and slowing, picking up speed again. A hard clang, then free fall for two long seconds before . . .

The impact was tremendous. Gary shrieked as a lightening bolt of pain shot through him. The barrel bounced, rolled for a way, then became still.

"Oh, dear God," Gary moaned aloud, then pulled in a breath and became quiet, for his words were no longer muffled. He bent slightly and felt with his bound hands—then reached farther. His battered fingers contacted the barrel's rim.

The lid had been dislodged by the force of the final impact. He extended his feet part way out and moaned as raw pain shuddered through his right leg.

Were they waiting for him?

Gary Runyon gingerly pushed himself out, then slowly and carefully looked about. There was no sign of the men—or of anything else. The silence and darkness were absolute.

7

Two of the watchers sat about the modest-sized room, waiting on the soft-spoken man, the one who had once frightened the woman more than anyone before and convinced her to come to this place. That had been only eight months ago, but it seemed like a lifetime.

She'd certainly not expected him; in fact he had come to her in the bedroom of her apartment in the middle of the night. She still did not know how he had gotten in, only that she'd been awakened by his whispering, "Do you know what he's saying?"

When she'd started to cry out, he'd ordered her to remain still. He had not told her the consequence, but the soft voice had somehow relayed the fact that he was deadly serious.

"Do you know what he's saying?" The words spoken so low she could hardly hear them. She'd always been prudish, but that night when the soft-spoken man had whispered for her to remove her clothes, she had done so without hesitation. Nor had she fought as he'd strapped her into a leather halter and placed a collar about her neck and shackles on her limbs.

"He says you enjoy exhibiting yourself," he'd explained, and switched on the lamp, exposing her nudity under its harsh glare. "I *don't*," she cried, and he'd told her to not be so loud. She'd lowered her voice, and whispered much as he did. "Those were all filthy lies."

"Oh?" As he'd opened and spread her, then tied her in that manner, she'd finally begun to cry, not from pain but from the mortification of his words, for he'd repeatedly whispered: "He told the faculty board and your students. He's *still* telling them, you know." Of course she'd known. It had been three months since her dismissal, and she'd prayed for the board's reversal but knew it would not come. They'd believed him and rejected her denials.

"Do you know what he's saying?"

Her body had been wracked by sobs as the soft-spoken man prodded and examined her.

Then: "He said you especially enjoy pain."

"Please," she'd blubbered, but quietly as he'd wanted.

He'd brandished a knotted strap. "Especially this," he'd said in the soft voice, and the strap made a swishing sound as it cut through the air, followed by her shrill squeak.

The leather knot didn't cut into the most sensitive area of her body, but instead thudded into fabric at her side. He'd whipped the sheet—*swish*—a lash at a time—*swish*—relentlessly—*swish*—and while there was no pain, she'd felt the knots cutting into her bared genitalia as plainly as if they'd become bleeding and swollen.

He'd shown her a tremendous strap-on penile device, which the liar said she preferred, and explained how it could be used to delve into and stretch her orifices.

"What were you working on when they dismissed you?" he'd asked.

"The isolation of leptons," she'd whispered. She'd dedicated her life to their study.

"He's prepared a paper for presentation at the convention next month. Do you know the subject?" He'd told her how her work had been stolen. The final disgrace.

"I've also been humiliated," he'd whispered, and explained how things would be made right. She had listened. She had agreed to join them.

When the soft-spoken man—who spent his time in his office, the door locked so no one knew whether he was in or out—finally joined them, the woman was observing her computer screen, the old man reading a journal. It was the first time they'd seen him since the previous night, when they'd observed him savaging Gary Runyon outside his own home. He'd suggested that she and the old man watch. She felt it was to remind them that he was not always placid.

"You should have left the writer alone," she offered as he was taking his seat. "He isn't like the subjects we use for the experiments. He has family and friends, a literary agent and a publisher. He'll be missed."

"He had no choice," the old man said, raising his brittle voice. "You heard him. The writer was beginning to suspect something was wrong." There was little that the soft-spoken man could do that was wrong in the old man's eyes since he'd provided funding for the experiment.

After a moment of silence, she asked, "What did you do with him?"

"Mr. Runyon took a trip," he said, obviously pleased with his ingenuity.

"Where?"

"Remember our agreement?" he reminded her in a chiding tone.

"Look," she reasoned. "I don't care who you send away, or where, or how, so long as we succeed. I don't even care to know why you were so determined to eliminate Runyon. But last night I noticed that the repairman found only one diskette in the vehicle. Runyon made *two* copies of his manuscript and took them as well as a manila folder."

"There were two diskettes?" he asked with a frown. Good. She'd captured the soft-spoken man's interest.

"Yes," she said. "You'll need to ask Runyon where he put them."

"It's too late," said the soft-spoken man. He looked at them both. "From now on we'll remove the corpses after each experiment. We should have done that before."

"I agree," said the woman. She'd felt there was the possibility that someone might perform a real autopsy, regardless of how the soft-spoken man told them there was no interest in the subjects. Even more than the others, she felt they *must* not fail.

She decided upon one more question. "The man in Montana who's coming to visit Runyon. Won't he be suspicious when his friend's not here?"

"Perhaps. I certainly don't *want* him here," the soft-spoken man said primly, and she wondered if he was going to make Anderson disappear too. But she'd nudged the line of rebellion enough for one day, and did not question further.

She worked the computer keyboard, bringing up the information she'd previously gained from an Internet investigative service that guaranteed anonymity.

Individual profile, Level 5 (all available sources)
Name: Abraham Lincoln Anderson Desc: Unk.
SSAN: 503-43-5114 DOB: 07/04/64 POB: Peshan, MT
Education: BS, Aero Engineer, USAF Academy, June 1985
Military Service: USAF, RegAF Captain, Hon Discharge: 03/12/92
Last Known Address: 128 Evergreen Tr., Boudie Springs, MT
Marital Status: Unk.
Present Employment: Unk.
Last Known Employment: Charter Airline Pilot, terminated July 1997
Credit Rating: A2, Homeowner, No Outstanding Obligations, Need current employment information
Note: No physical description available.
Note: No inputs since July 1997.

She read from the screen. "He has a technical degree."

"An *engineer*," scoffed the old man. "A glorified mechanic. He could never understand what we're doing."

The woman mused: "Perhaps when he shows up and his friend's gone, he'll leave."

The soft-spoken man seemed uninterested. "Time to work," he said, concentrating on one of the video monitors on the wall, and the image of a middle-aged female seated at a saloon bar beside a movie poster of Marilyn Monroe. She was plump, red-faced, and obviously intoxicated.

"Please bring up the data for subject seven?" he asked politely.

The woman worked the keyboard, then sat back so the others could view the screen.

Individual profile, Level 2
Name: Heidi (NMN) Gage Desc: 5'4"–170 lbs–blonde–blue
SSAN: 413-28-8006 DOB: 05/12/45 POB: Enid, OK
Education: 9 Yrs
Current Address: 11009 Apache Trail, Stagecoach Valley, NV 89430
Rent: $300 Mo. Avg Util–Gas: $32.27 Elec: $46.25 Tel: $15.15
Marital Status: Divorced–01/20/66; 11/09/77; 07/30/83
Children: 1, Female: Edna Stowe, Born: 02/16/65– Current Address: Unk.
Court Record: 10/12/68–Theft, Petty–30 days, Mariposa County Facility (CA) in lieu of $500 fine; 02/13/78–Possession stolen property–Dismissed; 07/15/88–DUI–$300 fine.
Present Employment: Waitress, Break-a-Heart Cafe–$5.15/hr
Credit Rating: D5, Unloanable Outstanding Obligations: $1,800+
Observed: Distraught abt daughter/boyfriend; fair health; hvy smoker; mod hvy drinker; few friends; no current sexual involvement

The Observed data had been added by the soft-spoken man, who often knew more about the subjects than the investigative service did.

The woman motioned at the monitor screen. "So far she's had six drinks."

"She'll do," said the soft-spoken man.

They tried to agree on the adequacy of subjects before proceeding with the lethality experiments.

"I concur," said the old man.

"Yes," the woman said and felt a trill of excitement as she activated another monitor—showing the exterior of a mobile home on a barren lot—and slued the camera until she found the white van parked just down the graveled street. "The repairman's in position."

The soft-spoken man had found and hired the repairman. He'd proven useful.

"Background reading in the subject's bedroom?" asked the old man.

She pressed a switch, activating a sensor. On one side of the monitor appeared a digital readout. "Seven milliroentgens per hour," she said, and typed the information into the computer. It was a normal background reading, to be found anywhere.

After viewing the street for activity—there was none—she looked about at the others. "Ready?" The old man nodded curtly, so she lifted a hand-held radio to her lips.

"Take the device inside," she ordered. A few seconds later they watched the tall figure emerge from the van carrying a cylindrical object. He disappeared around the back of the home.

She observed the bar. Heidi Gage was listing on her stool, speaking to a man who had moved in beside her. He rested a hand on her plump thigh, squeezed lightly, and Heidi did nothing to remove it.

"Damn," she muttered. "Is she going take him home?"

It was a concern. Each experiment considered a subject's height, weight, and body mass. Control data for subject seven had been entered, and if a second subject was introduced, the results would be distorted. And since they were to remove future corpses, there would be two to dispose of.

"She won't leave with him," said the soft-spoken man. He twisted a knob. As the audio increased, the bar scene came to life. Besides the subject and her suitor, there was a bartender, four customers at the bar, and four at the pool table. All spoke in loud voices. They'd noted that the volume in the saloon increased in proportion with the amount of alcohol consumed.

He zoomed in on the subject. The directional microphone focused, and other sounds were muted. The man beside Heidi listened dutifully as she complained about her back hurting from the day's work, and how no one at the café appreciated her. He started to comment, but she cut him off, "No one gives a shit about me," she muttered, began cursing a man's name, and then to cry, oblivious of the hand sliding higher on her thigh. The man studied her angry, beet-red face, and came to a decision. He removed his hand and struck up a conversation with the bartender. A moment later he moved down the bar, leaving Heidi to stare wet-eyed at a seventh drink.

The soft-spoken man observed. "She's upset about her boyfriend leaving last week."

"He's not going to show up unannounced?" the woman asked.

"He's in Reno living it up with Heidi's daughter. This place is like daytime television."

On the other monitor the tall shadowy figure came from the back of the dark home, and walked briskly toward the van. "It's on the hot water heater," came the repairman's call a few seconds later.

"Fourteen point six feet from the subject's bed," the woman said aloud. The distance had been measured on an earlier visit. She made the entry in the computer. "Background has increased to seventy milliroentgens," she said, and entered 10:41:40—70 mr/h. The reading was ten times stronger. Human tissue would be harmed if exposed for an extended period.

They settled back to wait.

At 11:07, Heidi Gage left the bar. She arrived home at 11:21, parked haphazardly, unlocked, and went inside. They switched to another monitor. A low light camera showed an unkempt bedroom with clothing piled in a corner, bed covers left in disarray. Heidi stumbled into view, sat heavily on the bed, and began to cry.

They waited. After several minutes the subject lay down, still clothed. Her sobs diminished, and her breathing evened. At 11:44 they heard her first snores.

At 11:49 the old man nodded. "She's asleep."

"Agreed." The woman spoke into the radio: "Shut down the telephone line."

They did not want an incoming phone call to interrupt the subject's sleep, and after the experiment began, didn't want her to be able to call out for help.

A short pause. "It's off," came the reply.

The old man looked at the table before himself, going over everything again in his mind. He was trying new amounts of substances. "We're ready," he finally said. "Proceed."

The woman lifted her radio. "Press button one."

"One pressed." The repairman liked to play it as if it were a military operation.

From the monitor showing Heidi Gage came a momentary whirring sound. Numbers flashed as the digital readout dramatically increased, then stabilized.

The woman watched with interest, entered a reading of 112 r/h. "Press button two," she said into the radio.

"Two pressed."

After ten seconds they heard a low hum. The woman muttered, "Device activated at 11:50 and seven seconds," and entered the time into the databank.

The soft-spoken man stared at the subject—Heidi had begun to snore louder—then at the digital readout as it rapidly increased, captivated by what he saw. Suddenly the reading sprang from five hundred to more than two thousand. The image captured by the low light camera became obscured, as if they were viewing the subject through a veil of blue plasma.

"We have critical mass," said the old man in his tremulous tone.

"Critical mass at eleven fifty and twenty-one seconds," she intoned.

The digital readout was still climbing: 3,000 then 4,000, and higher yet. The device had never given a reading that high.

"Unbelievable," the soft-spoken man whispered.

"It's working!" she trilled excitedly. "We're about to break through the barrier."

The old man said nothing, just sat with narrowed eyes. The numbers slowed, flickered back and forth, and then stabilized. The woman drew a sharp breath, held it, waiting, then remembered to enter the data: 11:51:42—5,429 r/h.

"It's very strong," the soft-spoken man warned.

She radioed for the repairman to move the van another hundred meters down the street from the home, using an even voice that did not betray concern.

The old man watched for another moment, eyes glued on the reading, which now remained steady at 5,431. Then he sighed. The phenomenon had not occurred.

"We're closer each time," she said, not wanting either of them discouraged.

The old man nodded. "Yes. Closer."

The subject had begun to move restlessly on the bed.

The soft-spoken man stood. "I must get some sleep. Wake me, please. I'll have to help the repairman remove the body."

It was her turn to remain at the console and ensure that everything was properly recorded. "I'll call when there's a development," she told him.

As he left the subject was already making low, groaning noises. A few minutes later the old man also departed, and she was left alone. For an idle moment she thought of the deaths. Initially she'd wondered if they shouldn't use baboons, since the tissue was so similar. But the soft-spoken man had insisted, and she had to admit she had little regard for the elimination of such . . . flotsam.

She blanked her mind of extraneous thoughts, and returned her attention to the readout.

At 01:49:02, the humming sound ceased, and the reading decreased. At 01:51:34 she radioed for the man in the van to shut the device down.

The reading diminished even faster, until at 1:55 there was no longer a threat to human life. But by then Heidi Gage had long before been stricken beyond any chance of recovery.

At 4:32 A.M., she called the dormitory and told the soft-spoken man it was time.

"Did she try to call anyone?"

"No," she said. "The receiver's still on the hook."

Heidi Gage had weakened so quickly that she'd hardly made it off the bed. Her skin had darkened, and she lay with a leg propped obscenely on the mattress, the remainder of her on the floor in a pool of vomit, loose hair, and expelled blood. The seventh subject was now in the terminal stage. The woman had the audio up— the sounds of breathing were wet and faint.

She radioed the man in the van. "Switch the telephone line back on and drive closer."

The repairman sounded sleepy. "It's back on."

She slued the outside camera, and waited as the van approached. "You can go inside and remove the device and monitoring equipment."

There was a moment of hesitation. "Is it safe?"

"Of course." Foolish man, she thought. He'd already accumulated enough radiation to develop lymphatic cancer soon. "Help's on the way," she added.

She wondered if the soft-spoken man would dispose of the subject in the same place he'd taken the writer, and where that was. There were many places in the desert. "Respiration of subject terminated," the woman said aloud to herself, glancing at the time as she made the entry. At 4:51:20, she noted a reading of only forty milliroentgens.

When Gary had emerged from the barrel into inky darkness and utter silence, head throbbing almost beyond endurance, he'd soon succumbed to the combination of exertion and emotion, curled up beside the barrel, and slept.

Not restful sleep, more like delayed unconsciousness from the terrible blows that had bruised his tortured brain. Periodically he whimpered himself into semi-awareness; drifting, dreaming he was trapped alive in a pitch-black tomb. He had no idea how long the slumber lasted but knew it was more than a few hours. When he had awakened there was no single place on his skull that was not tender, and when he touched it, it was so puffed he imagined his head looked rather like a watermelon.

Pain encompassed him, had no beginning or end, just a continuing agony. But Gary Runyon was pleased to be alive, and made his first assumptions.

One, he was in a mine. The barrel had fallen through a long, chutelike shaft. There were numerous mines in the area, and he'd obviously been dumped into one and left for dead. Two, mines had timbers. Find them. Climb out. When he reached the top, make his way back. He could not be that far from civilization.

Despite the suffering, those simplistic thoughts had provided hope as he'd begun struggling with the wire that cut viciously into wrists and ankles. Then a wave of claustrophobia had swept through him, and set him to work frantically with teeth and aching fingers.

The repairman had made only a few simple wraps, yet as he'd tried to free himself, the wire seemed only to become tighter. Wetness flowed onto his hands. Sticky stuff. He'd tried biting through the thin wire. The result was a chipped tooth. He'd tried twisting the wire back and forth, hoping it would break. It was resilient. He'd released a cry of frustration and felt increasingly helpless. That did not work either.

He'd forced himself to stop, to wait as his chest heaved with effort and emotion, willing himself to calm down and think it out. To be logical. Then Gary had tried to remember each detail of how the repairman had bound him—how he'd started with his wrists, made a final tight loop, then wrapped his ankles and finished the same way. He thought it through and decided it was the final loops—half-hitches, they called them—that foiled his efforts. He'd concentrated first on his ankles, found the end and worked with it, using fingers that were boil-sore and swollen as sausages. Made himself take his time. He'd freed the ankles, then the wrists, but by then there was a lot more of the sticky liquid.

Gary Runyon had clenched his eyes and given solemn thanks.

He was dog weary but drove himself to remain alert as he checked his injuries. The old headbone was concussed, maybe cracked, but all he could do about that was refrain from making sudden movements. He successfully wiggled toes, tried to stand, and grew dizzy with pain and vertigo. His right leg wasn't broken, just bruised. Except for his head, it was his fingers that hurt most. Those on his right hand throbbed with each heartbeat.

Again he'd lain down, curled up, and slept for a long time.

Gary came awake, disturbed by a distant clatter. Without thinking he rubbed at his eyes, then groaned and cradled puffed fingers. The rattling sound came from above, grew ever louder.

He sat up, wondering . . .

A projectile crashed onto the floor nearby. He cringed as a barrel-shape bounced, rolled noisily about, then came to rest. He stared, then was jolted into action by the thought that a human might be inside, struggling to free him or herself as he had done. He crawled to it, and felt. The top was secured. He yelled that he was trying to get it open, went to his own barrel and found the lid, then returned and pried and battered frantically.

It finally loosened, and he released a painful cry as he prized the top free with crushed and sore fingers. He reached in, felt cloth, then a bare leg—and using all his remaining energy, dragged out a human form. A woman clad in a thin dress. The stench of feces, urine, and vomit was strong as he held his face close to hers. There was no stir of air. He felt no pulse.

He sighed and shook his head in dismay.

Then, as he looked at the woman's dark form, Gary realized that his world had been transformed as he'd slept. The light was dim, and without his eyeglasses everything was indistinct, but he could distinguish the shapes of barrels lying about.

If he was in a mine deep in the bowels of the earth, how could he possibly see? How long had he slept? Why hadn't the glow been there before?

He turned slowly about, and stared in wonder at a beautiful green glow that radiated from a distant wall. Then his happiness was replaced by the horror of what he observed, for the glow was very like that of a radium-painted watch face. He uttered a tortured cry. There could be no escape. The only question was how long it would take the source of the glow to kill him.

8

Saturday, June 27, 10:25 A.M.
—Friendly, Nevada

Link turned off I–80 at the desert town thirty miles east of Reno. For the next twelve miles the only signs of habitation were a school, a gravel airstrip with a gaudy yellow hangar daubed with the letters FLYING TIGER FIELD, and road signs warning of the wind that wailed like a banshee and threatened to blow the pickup off the steadily ascending highway. A few miles beyond the airfield he crested the long hill and descended toward the scattered community of Silver Creek. According to Gary's directions he was now eight miles from Stagecoach Valley.

The sameness of the countryside since Winnemucca had made the distance seem even farther than it was, but the old Dodge was running well. The iron beast had odd idiosyncrasies, like an ominous rumble at sixty-eight miles per hour, and a shudder from some undiscoverable resonance at seventy-two. But it had carried Link and its preceding owners—and untold numbers of heavy loads—for two hundred thousand miles, and showed no sign of quitting. He'd considered trading it, lured by the spate of sporty new utility vehicles made popular by baby-boomers searching for lost youth, but he was pleased that he'd kept it. It was tough, sure-footed, and would take him almost anywhere. A dependable constant in a life of tumult.

He turned at a four-way stop sign, turned west on U.S. 50—called the loneliest road in America—and accelerated until the rumble began. The sagebrush was still green, not yet withered by the sun. It was warm, already eighty degrees, but not scorching like the low deserts he remembered around Las Vegas, Yuma, and Phoenix. Stark mountains rose in the distance. Beyond were the picturesque Sierras, called the mothers of mountains by their Spanish discoverers, unaware that the Indians called them the same in their own tongues. His fiancée had once told him that. He'd thought of Marie during the drive—even spoken to her, sharing landscapes and a spectacular sunset as he'd driven from Idaho Falls toward Winnemucca. Twice he'd read her letter—the words were memorized, but he enjoyed looking at the script written in her still-familiar hand—which she'd composed before her lucidity had slipped away. Her aunt had not given it to him until after Marie had died, but now it was dog-eared and worn.

My dearest Lincoln,
  It is not the length, but the quality of life that is important. Mine was wonderful, and if I were to do it again and could choose my path, I would change nothing. I was blessed with opportunity, colleagues who respected my accomplishments, friends who cared, and a great love.
  I will soon be gone. Please don't continue to grieve. Find good purposes and a good woman. Raise beautiful children. Live! I would ask you to do these things for me, but you might misconstrue that as being more than it is. Do them for yourself. Accomplish what I wanted for you most of all. Make your life meaningful and happy.

Love,
Your Marie

Link touched his shirt pocket to make sure it was there. He'd carried the note since first receiving it and could not force himself to leave it in a place of safekeeping.
Last night he'd tried to phone Gary Runyon before he'd slept. Getting no answer, he'd left a message: "I'll be there mid-morning," and before dropping off had

wondered again about Gary's request, and how Frank Dubois and the Weyland Foundation could possibly be involved.

Link drove over a rise and had a vista of Stagecoach Valley, ten miles of colorful desert surrounded by modest-sized mountains. A dry lake bed to his left, south of the highway. Most of the population gathered to the right, at the northeastern end. He continued for four miles and was well past the last clusters of mobile homes when he turned onto a paved street. He noted green vegetation in the distance; the alfalfa field Gary had told him about. The Barn should be on its far side. After a mile and a half he turned right at a T-intersection.

It looked like a New England-style barn, with canted roof and a myraid of shuttered windows, surrounded by trees and lawn. He pulled into the driveway that led around to a cedar deck where he'd been told to park, and was surprised that there were no other vehicles.

He climbed out and stretched, looking forward to seeing his friend, wondering how much he'd changed. Greeted by quiet, he stepped up onto the newly refinished cedar, knocked, waited, and knocked again. There was no response. After trying twice more, he walked completely around the home. The wood siding was faded and thirsty for paint, and the shutters needed repair. Gary had told him he was renovating an ungainly dinosaur. The description was apt.

When Link arrived back at the pickup, he picked up a folded scrap, opened it and found two three-by-two-inch pages from a notepad. Both contained what looked to be formulae. On the outer page was written: *B&E Expert + Computerwise + Aware of Book = D.A.* The second, inner page showed an apparent address: *9505 Cherokee.* Notes Gary had taken for his writing?

As he pocketed them, a glint caught his eye. He knelt and picked a thick eyeglass lens out of the pea gravel. After turning it over in his fingers, he dropped it into the same pocket, crawled into the pickup, settled comfortably, and tilted his hat over his face to wait.

He napped lightly, once heard a faint noise, and looked out into the alfalfa field, but whatever it was was not visible. A coyote or desert varmint? Twice he heard the clip-clopping of helicopter blades and observed industrial choppers a few miles to the south, carrying slings filled with barrels. He idly wondered what was there. When he'd been stationed at a base in Arizona, he remembered someone philosophizing that helicopters were the burros of the modern west.

An hour had passed when a dusty silver-and-blue Suburban pulled into the drive and parked beside him. A weathered face topped by a curled-brim straw hat nodded from the driver's seat. "Lookin' for someone?" the man asked.

"Fellow named Gary Runyon. I think he lives here."

"Your name Anderson?"

"Link Anderson." He climbed out as the man dismounted and came around.

"Cal Admire." He was in his sixties, slight in stature but with a confident air. The last name clicked in Link's mind, but he couldn't remember where he'd heard it. Cal measured him as they shook hands. "Gary said you were coming to visit."

"Any idea where he went?"

"I was about to ask the same thing." Cal motioned toward the highway. "Wednesday about noon he stopped by my office and told me about you. Wanted to set up a golf foursome for tomorrow. Then he said he was going to check on his airplane and drove off, and we haven't seen him since. My daughter tried calling last night and this morning, but couldn't raise him."

Link remembered Gary's reputation. It was not the first time the redhead hadn't been where he'd agreed to be.

Cal added: "My daughter says she's met you."

The name association came to him. A professional friend of Marie's, close enough to have attended the funeral, came from around here. "Shelby?" he asked.

"Yep." Cal nodded at Link's truck. "Might as well put your things inside. Gary said you'd be staying with him."

As he retrieved his bags from the metal toolbin behind the cab, Cal sorted through a batch of keys and unlocked the sliding deck door. "I check on things whenever Gary's away."

Link followed him inside. "I suppose he'll be back shortly," he said.

"I'd say so." Cal led the way into the front room, which, in contrast with the exterior, seemed sparkling new. "He just got through with this one. He's also finished the kitchen, his bedroom, and the loft. Doing a good job of it too." He explained how the home had been built by a movie star as a getaway but was a disaster by the time Gary bought it.

"He got it for next to nothing," Admire said, and explained how the property was zoned for agricultural use and couldn't be subdivided. Link listened and followed him through the rooms. "There's two empty bedrooms, so take your pick," Cal told him.

The one they were in had faded wallpaper and threadbare carpeting. The only furniture was a battered footlocker and a bed, unmade but with fresh bedding laid out on top. Link put a hangup bag in the closet, dropped his B-4 bag into a corner, and asked his first question. "How does Gary get on with the locals?"

"Folks like him. His books are on display in the saloon. Bob—he's the owner—has 'em set up next to the Clark Gable poster, which is a place of honor."

Link let that one go unquestioned.

"Gary says you were a fighter pilot. Still fly?"

"When I can, but it's been a while."

"Gary's airplane's older'n he is. Said it had engine problems someone's lookin' into." When Link just nodded, Cal filled in the silence, explaining he was in real estate "and such." He'd arrived thirty years ago with two hundred dollars and a license, and had since bought and sold most of the valley. He added, unsolicited, that he was a constitutional fundamentalist, wary of both Washington and local rednecks who were burying weapons in the desert and preparing for the Armageddon that would come when the government tried to take their guns.

As Cal rambled on, Link followed him through the Barn, admiring renovations. Then he picked up on something Cal was saying. "It's not like him to take off and not leave Aristotle—that's his moose-sized dog—with us. We've got a brindle boxer that's been in love with Aristotle since she first saw him. She's spayed, but she's still got an eye for big dogs."

When they came to stairs, Cal led the way up.

"Gary calls this his loft—where he does his writing." He switched on a window air conditioner unit. Three metal tables formed a U at one side of a freshly painted room, with a computer set up on the middle one. Stacks of books and papers cluttered work surfaces. A telephone and answering machine—light blinking furiously—were within reach from the chair.

Cal examined his watch and said he had to meet with some people from Silicon Valley. They wanted acreage in Silver Creek to build a circuit-board-manufacturing plant.

"Half the state of California's moving here, bringing all the problems they're trying to get away from." He handed over a doorkey. "Good to meet you, Link. When Gary shows up, have him call. Shelby's concerned, and I'm getting that way."

Cal touched the brim of his straw hat and started downstairs.

Link stayed to nose about some more. Across from the computer and littered tables was a counter with sink and coffeemaker. At the far end was a bathroom and a closet stuffed with manuscripts, boxes of paper, and outdated computer paraphernalia.

He heard engine noise and stepped to the window as Cal Admire drove from the yard. His eyes rose then, drawn by a flash of yellow-brown fur across the alfalfa field. Moving slow. Too big to be a coyote. He continued scanning for the next few minutes, but it didn't reappear.

His attention turned to the blinking light. The answering machine readout showed seven messages, and he wondered. He pressed the PLAY button, heard a voice telling Gary he should submit his manuscript the moment he had verification. How close was he? A synthesized voice said the call had been made at 12:10 on Wednesday. Next came two hang-ups on Thursday. On

Friday a feminine voice said she'd just gotten in and asked Gary to phone, and Link said he was in Winnemucca and would arrive in the morning. The same female voice again, saying it was Saturday morning and fussing because he hadn't called. Another hang-up.

That was all. There were no explanations about Gary's absence. Link punched the SAVE MESSAGES button, and stood brooding. Gary hadn't monitored his calls since Wednesday noon, after Link had phoned and he'd talked with Cal Admire on his way to check his airplane.

Beside the answering machine was an opened and very obvious—almost as if laid out for examination—business letter. Across the typewritten body the words *DAMN LEECHES!* had been boldly printed using a felt tip marker. At the bottom of the page was scrawled an 800 telephone number. Beside it was a postal receipt for a registered letter, signed for by Gary on June 23. Tuesday, the day before Cal had last seen him.

He picked up the letter, at first feeling he was prying into personal business, then remembering he'd just driven all that distance to arrive at an empty house. It was from a Philadelphia law firm acting in behalf of Gary's ex-wife, and contained a threat to attach half the royalties from his published books. They demanded Gary's immediate response.

DAMN LEECHES! glared at him from the page as he lifted the phone and punched in the 800 number.

"Reno Air. May I help you?"

He hesitated. "Do you fly to Philadelphia?"

"Daily, sir."

He thanked her, hung up, and frowned. Had Gary flown to Philadelphia to handle the matter, hoping to return before Link arrived? If so, why hadn't he taken the letter? And what about Aristotle? He looked out at the field, wondering if it had been Gary's dog he'd seen. It all seemed wrong, but the letter was the only clue he'd found to explain his friend's absence.

The telephone rang. Link hesitantly picked up and said hello.

"Link?" The voice was the same as he'd heard on the answering machine. "Shelby Admire. I worked with

Marie." As soon as he confirmed that he remembered her, she hurried on. "I just spoke with Dad on the phone, and he said you were there. Has Gary shown up?"

"Not yet."

"That rat. It's a good thing he can write, because he'd never hold down a regular job." Her words came in energetic bursts. "When you two talked, did he mention dinner?"

"I don't believe so."

"I've got reservations for tonight. Have you been to Virginia City?"

"I'm new to the area, but I don't—"

"Takes about twenty minutes to drive there. Head west on Highway Fifty for a few miles, and turn right when you see a sign reading Six Mile Canyon. Keep going until you get to town. I'll meet you at the Bucket of Blood. Sixish?"

"Shelby, I don't—"

"Gotta run, Link. Looking forward to seeing you again."

He found himself listening to a dial tone, remembering that Shelby Admire was one of the most attractive women he'd ever met. Blonde and beautiful. Not the kind you'd normally associate with scientific skills, although he recalled Marie saying she was some sort of whiz.

It was now past eleven o'clock, moving toward noon. Where the hell was Gary?

He was about to go downstairs to unpack his clothes, something mundane and understandable, when he heard tire on gravel sounds. He looked out, ready to open the window and call out some kind of caustic greeting, but it was not Gary.

A man emerged from a sedan, looked over at Link's old Dodge, then at the house, wearing a brooding expression. Salt and pepper hair. About six feet and solid-looking, unsmiling and displaying an officious air that matched his light gray suit. He took a couple of steps, then paused. Reached up and touched his lapel, as if for assurance of something, then walked resolutely toward the sliding door to the front room. He pressed the buzzer, stepped back. Still acting just a bit nervous. He turned slightly and his eyes were drawn to the window through which Link observed him. He gave a slight start, and they locked eyes.

Link watched for a few seconds longer, then went down. Slid the door open as the visitor was about to ring again, and stepped out onto the deck. He was about to explain that the owner of the home was away when the man spoke in a deep voice. "Abraham L. Anderson?"

Link nodded, trying not to show surprise that he'd known his full name.

"I'm Special Agent Albee. FBI."

"Maybe." Link noted discoloration on the man's forehead, unsuccessfully masked by skin toner. A birthmark? "Perhaps you should show identification," he said.

The agent gave him a fish-eye as he pulled out a leather case. Link observed the number on the badge with the eagle and scales of justice. The I.D. read "Albee, Destin C.", and although it was pulled away before Link had a good look, the photo appeared to be of the same man.

"Can I help you?"

"Let's go inside." As the agent put the I.D. away, Link noted the pistol bulge on his right side. Meaning he was left-handed.

"I don't think so." Link did not like rudeness, especially from people he didn't know, and anyway, it was not his home.

The agent's face flushed. His eyes were gray in color, and their intensity betrayed heat of rising emotion.

"Can I help you?" Link repeated.

The deep voice became more reasonable. "This discussion would best be held inside, out of view of others. It concerns a sensitive matter."

"It's not my house. We'll have to talk out here. Would you like a seat?" Link motioned toward a pair of deck chairs beside the covered tub, but the agent shook his head. Preferring to stand. Meaning he wanted to play the power angle and not be looked down upon?

"How well do you know a man named Gary L. Runyon?" The question was asked curtly. Albee was still seething, unaccustomed to not getting his way.

"Well enough. Why?"

The man shook his head. He was there to ask, not answer. "Have you seen him recently?"

"Why?" Link prodded.

"Spoken to him?"

"Why?"

The deep voice dropped to a snarl. "You don't cooperate with authorities, do you?"

"I prefer to call them public servants. Why are you asking about Gary?"

"He's under investigation." The voice and gray eyes remained hard.

"What for?"

An impatient, angry sigh.

"Why are you investigating Gary?"

There was something going on with the agent that was entirely separate from their conversation. Some kind of inner struggle that caused a tic to pinch at the corner of his eye. Perhaps it was confusion about Link's refusal to roll over, but he thought it was more. Something that alerted Link not to let down his guard.

When the agent stepped slightly back, Link followed, determined to stay up close in case the man actually succumbed to temptation and pulled the weapon.

The man's voice deepened even more, to a low rumble. "It would be best if this visit and this conversation aren't mentioned to others."

"Why?"

Did he hesitate? "He's writing about illegal subject matter. That's all I can tell you, except revealing it could be harmful to the national interest."

"He's a writer," Link said. "It's his job to look into things."

"We're talking about weapons data that not only shouldn't be released, it's damn illegal to do so. He took an oath of secrecy in the military, where he picked up the information."

Link felt the agent was making it up. Mouthing words. Searching for something.

"Military secrets?" Link asked incredulously. He started to tell him that Gary had been a PR officer, not a pilot, and had received no classified briefings—but he held his tongue, waiting for more. Waiting for the agent either to get to the point or to make a more obvious error.

"Mr. Runyon will be in grave trouble if we can't convince him to desist. So would those who assist him. It might be in your interest if you . . . left for the present."

"What makes you think I'm considering staying?"

"We know a lot of things."

Link regarded the man, observed the sheen of perspiration that had formed on his upper lip, knew something was amiss and stored the words he uttered.

"I'll think it over," Link said, still watching.

The voice became an angry hiss. "Stay away from Runyon, and don't tell *anyone* about this conversation. *Period!*"

Link disliked the imperious tone. "I said I'd think about it." He nodded toward the sedan. "Now why don't you leave?"

The FBI agent flushed brighter, and again his left hand raised very slightly. Threateningly? Link waited, thinking the agent had definitely made the movement, Intemperance was a definite shortcoming in a federal law enforcement officer. But there was something less to this visit than was being touted—as if it were a probing effort to check Link out. From first glance, Link had disliked the agent, and somehow he knew the feeling was mutual. Very bad chemistry at work.

Albee confirmed it. "Don't fuck with me, Anderson. People get hurt that way. Go *away*." The agent turned abruptly, and almost stumbled as he stepped off the cedar deck.

Link watched him stalk to his vehicle and noted a slight limp. The unmarked car was still crunching driveway pea gravel when Link found a telephone in Gary's kitchen.

"You've reached extension 2775," Erin answered pleasantly.

"It's Link," he said, then remembered it was Saturday. "You're at work?"

"At home. That's just the way I answer this line. You're in Nevada?"

"I made it to Gary's, but he's not here. Mind looking something up for me?"

"Not at all. Let me grab a pen." After a pause she told him, "Shoot."

Link had a superb memory. "Albee, Destin C. FBI badge number 75–4145–03. Six feet. Salt and pepper hair. Either a scar or birthmark high on his forehead. Gray eyes—maybe light blue. He has a slight limp, but I don't know if it's permanent or which leg. Driving a slate-colored Lincoln with California plates: 1–MMF–301. I think it's a rental."

"Got it," she said.

"He said he was FBI, but something doesn't ring true. He was also nervous and made a couple of not-so-subtle threats about wanting me to leave. Can someone there check him out?"

"I'm sure we can, but we may have to wait until Monday unless you want a priority on it."

Link thought about it. "Not really."

"Also, Mr. Dubois wanted to know when you called in, so I'll leave your number on his e-mail. Anything else you want passed on?"

"Just tell him I shouldn't be long. I'll check out the company we talked about, and if Gary doesn't show up in a couple days I'll head back."

As he hung up, Link noticed a list of numbers written on a stickum note beside the kitchen wall phone. One was his own, and he remembered having seen one of the others.

He dialed his telephone in Boudie Springs, Montana. There was no answer, so he left a message for Joseph Spotted Horse to check with friends who were boarding his mare and make sure she was okay. Joseph was good with animals, and it would give him something to do.

Link returned to his chosen bedroom and pulled boots, slacks, and a fresh shirt from the USAF-issue canvas B–4 bag, and hung them. Satisfied that they'd be adequate, he went outside and opened the tool bin bolted behind the pickup cab, hauled the golf clubs into the Barn, and set them near the door. All that remained in the bin were tools and rifle case. He thought about the veiled threat from the agent, but decided the rifle should remain inside the metal bin.

As he went back inside, the telephone rang. Frank Dubois was on the line.

"I just read Erin's message. She doesn't have to check Destin Albee. I know him. He was deputy SAC of the St. Petersburg field office when I went there two years ago."

Link put it together. "He worked for Ansel Turpin in Russia?"

"That's him. Destin was eligible for promotion when the incident happened. He was cleared of wrongdoing, but the embarrassment stalled his career for a while. Now he's trying to work his way back. They've put him in charge of the Las Vegas bureau office, but no promotion."

"And you think that's what made him so bitter when he was here?"

"I'd say so. What did he say?"

"He tried to tell me Gary's writing about classified information. That he's about to release unauthorized weapons information. That's crazy, Frank."

"I don't know. We get awfully good cooperation from the bureau."

"Albee threw his weight around and ordered me to stay away. Most senior agents are law school grads, and it's hard to believe one would willingly put his weenie in a wringer like that."

"They're human, and Gary's obviously giving him problems. Admit it. Runyon can be damned maddening when he wants to be."

"This was something more. Albee implied I could get hurt. I'm concerned about Gary."

"He brings on his own troubles. Maybe you *should* get out of there."

"Gary's a friend, and he asked for help." He didn't mention Gary telling him that Frank and the foundation were involved. Maybe later, if Gary didn't show up.

Frank released a weary breath. "If you insist. By the way, security says a query was made regarding you. One of the major Internet investigative services asked for information. They didn't get much. Our security sees to it there's minimal available."

"That's good." But Link wondered.

"Services like that are mainly used for credit checks. Buying anything big?"

"No." Link remembered something. "I'll give the manager at NEL a call."

"Good. Might as well get something out of this. Anything you want passed on to Erin?"

"I'm still interested in this Albee fellow."

"Drop it. He's real, Link, and it sounds like he wants you to stay away from Gary. If you insist on staying, at least get along with him. One more thing. If Gary's doing anything even remotely illegal, get out of there and let it be." Frank's voice was firm. It was not a request.

When he hung up, Link pulled out his wallet and fished out the scrap of paper showing the NEL supervisor's name and phone numbers.

He glanced again at the stickum note. It was the supervisor's work number. Gary had been in contact with the company Link was going to check out. Another coincidence? Since it was Saturday he dialed the home number. Dr. Fred Jameson's wife answered, then a man's gruffer voice took over. "Help you?"

"Sorry about calling on a Saturday. My name's Link Anderson, and I—"

"I got the foundation's warning call," Jameson growled. "Where the hell are you?"

Link paused.

Dr. Jameson's voice changed to a chuckle. "Seriously, why don't you drop by? We don't work on weekends, and there's a revolving outdoor get-together every Saturday afternoon. Today's my turn to cook, I'm afraid. Several of our people will be here, and they can meet you and complain about my leadership and deplorable cooking skills."

Fred Jameson was the ebullient sort.

"Some other time," Link said. "I've made arrangements for dinner."

"Then we'll see you Monday morning. By then I'll have our briefings doctored enough to impress you with our brilliance."

And improved safety? Link wondered. "Monday's fine. Where are you?"

Jameson gave directions to the Carson City airport, then told him to be at the general aviation terminal at eight. They kept a helicopter company on contract for their transportation, and the pilots had the nasty habit of liking to depart on time.

"Look for a tall, handsome James Bond-type," said Jameson. "That's the pilot. I'll be the short, fat, bald guy with him. Since I'll still be getting over my chili, I'll be belching a lot."

"Gotcha," Link said, smiling.

"Looking forward to meeting you, Mr. Anderson. We're anticipating working with the foundation, and from what I was told, you're the right man to talk to."

Link remembered the number on the stickum note. "Before we hang up, do you know Gary Runyon?"

"The redheaded writer? Sure. My people gave him a briefing a few months ago, and he's called me for information a couple of times."

"I'm trying to locate him."

"If I remember correctly, he's buying a home out in the desert."

"I've found it, but he's not here. Any ideas where he could have gone?"

"None offhand. I'll ask my people when they arrive, but I doubt any of them know him that well. What's your number?"

Link read it off the telephone, and Jameson said he'd call if anyone knew anything.

After they'd disconnected, Link went upstairs and re-read the lawyers' letter, feeling as vexed as before. He fished the scraps of paper and the eyeglass lens from his pocket, placed them beside the letter—his meager collection of clues—and went downstairs and outside.

He stood at the edge of the field, again wondering if it was Gary's dog he'd seen.

Another helicopter clip-clopped in the distance and began its descent into the mountains. It seemed busy there, and he wondered about that much activity on a Saturday afternoon. He stood there for ten minutes, vainly scanning the field for the dog—or whatever he'd seen—but the only sign of life was a telephone repairman on a nearby pole, working on a junction box of some kind. Just down the street was a white van, with Nevada Bell painted on its side.

Link left at five-thirty and drove west on the highway. Five minutes after descending into the next valley, he saw the sign reading Six Mile Canyon. He slowed and turned, passed through a small subdivision, and continued toward the high mountains on a hard-pack road. It soon entered a canyon that followed a trickling creek and began to wind skyward. Cottonwoods and wild flowers flourished in the stream bed, adding delicate colors to the desert ravine.

A pair of bicyclists passed, a couple coasting down the steep incline—the only traffic he'd seen. He glanced into his rearview mirror for another look at the pair and noted a dark pickup following at a distance. On the next straight stretch he glimpsed it again and felt it odd that it hadn't drawn closer. Likely hanging back to avoid his dust, he decided, so he sped up a bit.

He passed a prominent boulder that towered two hundred feet into the air, looking like a tremendous forefinger, and shortly afterward emerged from the canyon and entered nineteenth-century civilization—staunchly squared brick buildings, immaculate churches, Victorian homes with gingerbread trim. The dirt road became a graveled street and angled sharply upward.

Far behind the dark pickup emerged from the canyon and followed.

9

The man in the FBI agent's façade gripped the steering wheel tightly, staring ahead as Anderson turned onto the main street of the old city. Twice as he'd followed, tears of anger had come to his eyes, bleeding down his cheeks so profusely that he'd had to slow down and wipe them away to see. And then, a moment ago, he'd done the unpardonable and lost control, slamming his fist into the steering wheel so violently that it had been knocked askew and was no longer concentric. If there'd been an airbag, it would have inflated.

He'd gone to see Anderson as planned, and had had his chance to take him—the repairman had waited down the street with the pickup and barrel, and even if it had been outside in the daylight, as he'd rationalized, there'd been no one around to see except the old man and the bitter woman. He'd told them to watch on the video monitors, wanting an audience for the way he was going to maim Lincoln Anderson before he dumped him into the barrel so he could join the redheaded writer. But all they'd likely seen was a guy they didn't know—he'd never let them see him before in this disguise—drive up, talk to Anderson, and leave. It was natural that he hadn't liked being there, or liked Anderson, but it wasn't natural that he hadn't pulled the pistol and beat the hell out of him as he'd gone there to do, but instead just kept on thinking. Mostly about the time with Frank Dubois, and how Anderson might somehow get the jump on him as Dubois had done. Then he'd tensed up and done screw-all except babble nonsense.

He'd driven to Reno like a robot and turned in the car, driven away in the pickup, and found a place to change into the soft-spoken man. Drove back to the valley and then changed his mind and himself back into the FBI agent, deciding to go back and not screw around this time. Forget about shoving him into a barrel and just kill Anderson. Beat him up and shoot him and get on with things. When he'd driven toward the Barn he passed Anderson leaving, and now he'd followed him to fucking Virginia City and was on treacherous roads with a warped fucking steering wheel.

Only one thing was going to make him feel better. Wait for dark and then take him. Hurt him. Kill him and forget the rest. The bastard. He hated him almost as badly as he did Frank Dubois. He raised his fist and slammed it into the padded dashboard, causing the sun-hardened vinyl to crumple and crack.

Then he realized what he'd done—and thought how unprofessional it was to explode like that. He reached the top of the hill and turned onto the main street, into a dense mob of tourists, chest heaving as he crept along, trying to keep Anderson's truck in view, wanting to calm down but still seething with hate.

Twice the wall had come to life, slowly gaining in intensity until much of that side of the enclosure glowed in a dim and eerie fluorescence. Gary did not know how long the green glow remained before it faded. Like his eyeglasses, his wristwatch had been lost during the struggle.

The first time he'd seen the ghostly glow, he'd crouched behind the barrel, trying to avoid its deadly rays. But then he'd emerged, knowing it was futile to hide. And oddly, although he'd not been able to subdue the melancholy thought that he would soon die from one cause or another, he'd become intrigued. He'd even used the dim glow to assist in his investigation of the vast enclosure, searching vainly for timbers or anything else to climb.

Two barrels had been dropped in before his arrival, and he'd used his battered lid to pry and pound them open. The larger contained a man's body and, when opened, exuded an awful odor. The smaller one was empty.

Gary had stuffed the man's corpse back into its container, as he'd done with the woman's, and closed it. The smaller one he'd lugged over by his own barrel, then sat on it for a while, eyeing the dim glow. The exertions had left him parched and even hungrier, and he craved a cigarette. He'd explored during the period of the first glow, alternately crawled and hobbled at a steady and leisurely pace, and felt that escape was unlikely. There were minor dips, ridges, and irregularities here and there, but in all directions the floor angled gently upward, until the walls became too steep to climb. There was a deposit of grit on the floor, a trace of it at the perimeter increasing to several inches in the middle. Beneath was a hard, smooth, and impenetrable surface.

Although he couldn't see the ceiling, he'd determined the location of the opening to the overhead shaft by returning to where the barrels had struck, leaving chips and gouges in the floor. The opening was directly above, high enough to cause the terrible jolt yet not enough to kill him.

Gary had examined the chips, and found one to be long and sharp. He'd stored the dagger-sliver beside his barrel. If he began to suffer unbearably, the sliver could penetrate the veins of his wrists, or perhaps his aorta. He did not dwell on it, tried to remain positive lest he lose the fragile remainder of his sanity, even though he could not find a single timber to climb.

During that initial glow-period he'd made a first measurement, inaccurate for he carefully avoided the glow-wall. He believed the circular enclosure to be more than three hundred feet in diameter. The ceiling could not be nearly that high, though, or he could not have survived the drop. The image of the sphere he'd formed in his mind's eye became flattened at top and bottom.

After a while the glow on the wall had diminished and the absolute darkness had returned, and he'd fallen asleep. Again the transformation had come as he'd slept—he'd reawakened as the fluorescence returned to the wall.

His right hand was puffed, the swollen fingers more sensitive than he'd imagined possible. He also discovered that his leg would not completely straighten.

He made his Oliver Hardy face. "A fine kettle of fish you've got us into, Stanley."

"Then let's find them and *eat* them, Ollie."

Gary laughed at his wit, then tried to exercise his leg. He huffed a painful breath. "Screw 'em, Stanley." And bent more energetically. "Damn!" he yelled.

As he continued working with the leg, he decided no longer to avoid the glow-wall. If it killed him a little sooner, so what? Perhaps sooner was better.

He began his next trek by hobbling directly toward the glow-wall. It seemed to pulse and shimmer as if it were alive, welcoming him. His eyes were fixed on the dim light when he heard the sound, so slight that he stopped and held his breath for utter silence so he might hear it again. *Ping*—a very long pause—*ping.*

Gary ran his tongue over parched lips. *Ping.* He smelled a musty, moist odor, and shuffled forward. *Ping.* He hurried faster. His foot splashed into liquid. He gingerly stepped back. *Ping.* Then he walked around it, wondering.

In the lowest depression of the floor, not far from the glow-wall, was a pond of indefinable liquid, measuring some twenty feet across and several inches deep. The slow drip—each droplet taking a count of fifty to form and fall—was seepage from above.

Water? He mentally girded himself, knelt painfully, and scooped it into cupped hands.

It was odiferous, giving off a slightly unpleasant smell.

He sipped. It was bitter and alkaline. He drank more, then sat back and waited, eyeing the glow-wall as it changed to a lighter shade. When a long period passed and there were no cramps or suffering, he knelt and drank greedily, until he was sated and could not possibly hold more. So much he realized he was about to be sick, like a child who'd consumed too much forbidden soda pop. He stumbled toward his barrel, holding it in until he got there, quickly opened and bent over the small barrel, liquid streaming from nose and mouth.

He took a breath. "Thank you, God," he whispered, and decided henceforth to use the small barrel to relieve himself, so he would not foul the wonderful life-sustaining pool.

Even at its brightest, the glow-wall provided little light, and without his eyeglasses he was hardly able to discern the dark shapes of the barrels unless he was right on top of them. But as far as he could tell, those and the ebony-dark pool were all there was to see.

The temperature was cool but not unbearably so, and was constant. He had water and would not die of thirst. It was more likely he would succumb either from the substance that made the wall glow, or from starvation.

But of course there was also the sharp sliver.

10

5:50 P.M.—Virginia City

The old town was perched precariously on a tall and steep-sided mountaintop. Pedestrians swarmed on wooden plank sidewalks. Automobiles crawled bumper-to-bumper along the narrow street, drivers searching vainly for vacant parking places. Pressed by time, Link drove out of town, pulled onto the roadside, and hiked half a mile back.

Tourists' license plates were from disparate states and Canadian provinces—yet there was a smiling but rude, shorts-and-halter sameness about them. He passed stores with gunslinger names selling artwork, cheap Western clothing, curios, gold nuggets and semi-precious stones. There were tours of the graveyard, churches, and a mine built into the back of a saloon. A museum featured artifacts of the city's notorious shady ladies, another the newspaper office where Mark Twain had worked as a reporter when his brother was lieutenant governor, then called secretary, of the territory. In the 1860s, Virginia City had vied with San Francisco for the title of the West's most cosmopolitan metropolis.

The Original Bucket of Blood Saloon was on the main street. He entered only five minutes late, looking for Shelby and remembering Gary's awful history with women.

In Saudi a reporter for A.P. with prominent nipples and thin T-shirt had suckered him for an early news release. A USO dancer had given him a sad story about losing her money and borrowed his credit card to pay a hotel bill in Riyadh. She'd departed without warning, and he'd paid for a shopping spree in Paris before he was able to contact the Visa people from their forward location and shut down the card. Women had lined up to take the unpredictable redhead, but he'd jumped into each relationship gleefully. Then he'd returned to the States to marry his hometown sweetheart. The lawyers' letter showed how that one had ended.

Had he learned anything? Perhaps. Link remembered Shelby only vaguely but recalled that besides a rather luscious appearance she'd been pleasant, and Marie had thought highly of her work—whatever her work had been. Something sciency and technical.

A massive bar extended along one entire side of the room, and at its end was a twenty-by-twenty-foot window with an eagle's-view of mountains and valleys. Old mines sprawled haphazardly below. There'd been no easy commutes up here, so the miners had built the town where the color had been found, perched at 6,500 feet on the side of the mountain.

Link examined the people near the window. A couple with matching blue-gray hair glared unhappily at people coming in. A brunette with fat pigtails, cherry-red eyeglasses, nails and lipstick was snapping chewing gum and sipping a margarita. She wore sandals, miniskirt and bandanna top, and smiled invitingly.

Shelby Admire, with her honey-colored hair and startling blue eyes, was seated alone. "Link?" She got to her feet. Five-ten. Mid to late twenties, and flawlessly gorgeous. A modest sun dress covered from neck to calf, daring only because of the way she filled it.

"Welcome to Virginia City." She smiled and took his hand in a delicate grasp. He handled her chair as she sat back down, and took the one beside her.

"Still no sign of Gary?" she asked.

"No." A waiter came by. He ordered a beer, she an iced tea. "Any ideas?" Link asked.

"Nothing that makes sense." She observed him for a moment, measuring, then turned to look out the window.

"Spectacular view," he said. The road through the canyon was visible below. In the distance were successions of desert valleys and high, stark mountains.

"It's arid now, but once it was covered with water," she said in her soft voice. "At the end of the glacial period there were tremendous rainstorms, and the runoff from the ice fields formed a series of freshwater seas that extended across the continent. Lahontan's the name we give our local one. It stretched from Nevada into Oregon and California, but it's most apparent here. See the discolored area around the bases of the mountains?"

He squinted, nodded.

"That's the old shoreline. Visualize vast pine forests around the water's edge. Great dire wolves, giant bear-like sloths, and miniature horses and camels gathering to drink the fresh water. Then, a few hundred years later, they were all gone."

"Like the dinosaurs?"

"That extinction happened sixty myrs ago."

"Myrs?"

"Scientist jargon for *million years*. These were quite recent. Thirty-five kyrs—that's thousands of years—ago, give or take a few millennia. An eyeblink in the geological sense."

"You know a lot about it."

"That's what I do. I'm a geologist."

He tried to recall what Marie had told him about Shelby. *Smart, capable,* and *a pleasure to work with* were quick to surface.

"Did Marie tell you how we met?" she asked.

"I don't believe so."

"Two years ago she spoke at a symposium in Reno sponsored by the state. The subject was Lake Lahontan and its impact on the region, and one day was devoted to various Lahontan life forms, when they arrived or became extinct. I spoke with her after her talk—after she'd created the uproar."

"Uproar?" He remembered Marie's announcement that she was attending a Reno symposium, but she hadn't mentioned the outcome.

"She stepped on toes by questioning prevailing wisdom. There's seldom consensus among scientists without incontrovertible proof and often not even then, but the conventional view was that there'd been no coexistence of humans and most of the extinct animals. That there'd been a considerable gap between the disappearances and man's arrival."

"And Marie thought differently?"

"She felt it was at least *possible* that they'd over-lapped. Every few years there's another discovery that suggests humans arrived earlier than we'd formerly believed. For instance, there are signs that man dwelled in South America twenty kyrs ago, which suggests they passed through here long before. She felt there was not only the possibility that they'd coexisted but that humans may have had a hand in their extinction, like they did with the mastodons and woolly mammoths up north, and a lot of others since. A number of the attendees were upset. One called her amateurish. Another suggested she was an opportunist trying to attract attention from the press. Most ignored her—academic snobbery because she didn't have her doctorate yet."

Link found himself bristling. "How did Marie take it?"

"She was embarrassed. The scientific community is often cruel. Many gifted scientists are myopic. They spend half a lifetime developing a thought and the other half defending it. If you suggest an approach other than theirs, they feel threatened. You need a thick skin if you're going to disagree with prevailing wisdom."

"And what did you think?"

"I was upset because they treated her shabbily. Since then I've investigated every scrap of evidence regarding our early inhabitants. That's what we were collaborating on."

"And—?"

"The jury's out. No one's sure when the first humans arrived. They were nomadic and left very little sign, so there's no proof positive. But that's what Marie was trying to get across, that there was the *possibility* of coexistence, and it should be investigated. After her talk I became interested in the complete picture of what once existed. I'm still enchanted by the earth's structure, but there's so much more." She pointed again. "See the oddly shaped mountain?"

It was elongated, with peaks at both ends and a bowl gouged into its middle.

"After Lahontan disappeared, pockets of forest remained. One was in that mountain hollow. The earliest trace of human inhabitation in this area came from petroglyphs—rock carvings—found in a cave on the mountainside. About twelve centuries ago—and perhaps long before—a group of nomadic desert dwellers discovered that the trees in the bowl produced an especially tasty variety of pine nuts, so it became a regular camping place. For the next few hundred years children were born, people lived, and oldsters died there. Then they left on their annual pilgrimage and simply didn't return."

"What happened to them?"

"We don't know. Yet another mystery for anthropologists. For a long while no one lived there, then two hundred years ago Paiutes arrived from the east and rediscovered the glen. The trees were still flourishing. The ghost of Lahontan had become a vast aquifer just beneath the desert surface, and there was a spring and a creek that flowed through a crevasse to the Carson River on the other side of the mountain. The forest glen became special for the Paiutes, as it had been for the ancients, and they made frequent visits to gather the pine nuts."

He was beginning to envision it. "I like the place."

"If it were around today, people would be *fighting* to live there."

"What happened?"

"Miners. By 1859, when the Comstock Lode was discovered here in Virginia City, prospectors were swarming around the mountains. Mining towns sprang up wherever they found color, and the pines were harvested to construct Dayton." She pointed out a community not far west of the oddly shaped mountain. "Without the trees the heat became intense and the grass withered, and since there was no longer a source of food, the Indians stopped visiting."

"Progress," Link said sadly.

"If they'd left it at that, we'd still have the treasure of information about the ancient ones. There are such places in Utah, you know. But in 1863 a promoter announced he'd found color there, named it Millionaire Mountain, and showed off a glory hole—unfortunately the cave where the ancients had carved their petroglyphs—and pried chunks of pure gold from the walls. He sold his claim to the highest bidders and left on the next stage. During the next year the miners dug three deep shafts into the mountain before they realized they'd been swindled. By then they'd dynamited the spring to improve water flow, and both it and the creek dried up. Finally they tore down the buildings and carted the lumber off to the next mine."

"And the gold?"

"It's suspected the promoter planted melted down gold pieces. The owners had other names for the mines on Millionaire Mountain, but the miners called them the Break-a-Hearts."

"And the ancient rock carvings?"

"All blasted away. Our only knowledge comes from drawings made by a young reporter named Sam Clemens, who was mildly interested in such things. Also, all sign of the ancient campground was trampled over. In the twenties the University of Washington established a dig at Millionaire Mountain, but they didn't find much. We'd lost *centuries* of early Nevada history."

Link watched as Shelby stared moodily out the window. She seemed not at all the type he would associate with the ebullient redheaded writer. "How did you and Gary meet?" he asked.

She came around with difficulty, as if pulled bodily from the distant past. "He was getting a tour of the place where I worked, and I knew a lot about the subject of his book. He kept pestering me for answers and we started to talk."

"What *is* the subject of his book?"

"Nuclear waste disposal."

It made sense that Gary would befriend a geologist. "You work on the NEL project?"

Shelby looked surprised. "Gary told you?"

"I'm with a group they're trying to get to fund their research."

"The Weyland Foundation?"

He nodded. "This afternoon I spoke with Dr. Jameson. I'll be going out Monday morning to look things over."

"Fred was sure he'd get funding from the foundation last year, and when he didn't, it really upset him. But then I heard the Weyland Foundation provided interim funding."

"That wasn't us. Must have been someone else."

"That's odd. I'm sure he said the foundation came through. They were on the verge of cutting back when the money appeared. Not as much as he wanted, but Fred was pleased."

Link mulled it over more. "What's Jameson like?"

"Ambitious." She stopped herself then and looked out.

He picked up on her discomfort. "Is there something I should know?"

"Not really. It's just . . . I don't work there any longer, and I want to be fair."

"You quit?"

"There was a difference of opinion."

"I didn't mean to pry."

"There's more brain power at NEL than you can imagine, and they're trying to solve terribly difficult problems. It was interesting, but now I've got a good job with the state of Nevada." She smiled. "I'm still learning to speak bureaucratese, but I'm happy."

"You work in Carson City?" he asked.

"I've got an office there, and field offices in Stagecoach and Winchester to check on water tables, radon levels, things like that." She observed her watch. "I've *also* got reservations at a great place for dinner, and we'd better get moving."

Link followed in his pickup as Shelby led the way in a twelve-year-old, cherry red Corvette, which she'd explained was her college graduation gift. Unless she'd been a child genius, she was older than he'd guessed. He revised her age to early thirties, a year or two younger than himself.

The Cabin in the Sky was a couple of miles down the road toward Carson City, built on a promontory that overlooked another panorama. As they pulled into the lot and parked, he made up his mind. He liked Shelby. She was off-limits—her friendship with Marie was inhibiting, and she was involved with a friend—but he liked her.

It was a nice restaurant, and again they were seated near a window with a spectacular view. As evening settled, ebony mountains were outlined against a purple sky. When the hostess departed, Shelby pointed out the twinkling necklace of lights of Stagecoach, two valleys distant.

"You obviously like it here," he said.

"I thought it was *awful* when I was growing up. Everything so stark and windblown, and the people all ignorant hicks. When I was accepted at Stanford, I became a *real* snob. My parents footed the bill without a single complaint, and I responded by coming home as seldom as possible. Whenever they visited my dorm, I was terribly ashamed."

"But you came back."

She stared at the dark mountains. "Yes, and you can't imagine how good those looked."

"There's an old saying about the desert: You'll always come home to the dry."

"The dry. I like the description." Shelby smiled as the waitress came to the table.

When he offered to buy wine, she declined. "I'm allergic to alcohol. One drink and I do silly things." He asked for iced tea, as she was having, and they both ordered the prime rib special. His well done, hers medium rare.

"You're like Gary," she said. "He likes his burned too."

"You learn that when you're in foreign countries where cleanliness isn't a virtue and meat's aged by hanging it until it rots. Burning it kills some of the bugs."

"I'll live on the wild side and enjoy the taste."

He chuckled, then asked, "Are you and Gary serious?"

"Seriously good friends. You should hear our conversations. I gripe about my time in California, and he complains about his divorce, and we get it all off our chests." She rolled her eyes. "He gave his ex-wife everything—money, home, car—and now she wants the royalties from the books he wrote when they were married."

He remembered the letter in the loft. "Is he concerned?"

"Not since Dad had him talk to his attorney. Her lawyers don't have a chance of getting anything more unless they reopen the property settlement issue, and they'd be *crazy* to do that. All Gary has to do is sit tight, ignore them, and not make a dumb statement."

When their food arrived, he found he was hungrier than he'd believed. Shelby too pitched in, not at all hesitant about the way she wolfed down her meal. Halfway through, she said almost forlornly, "I sure wonder where Gary chased off to. This just isn't *like* him."

"But he's done it before?"

"Little irritating things like being late for dinner, but never anything like this. He was bursting with excitement about your visit, and I can't imagine him purposely missing it."

As she went on, Link's attention was drawn by a shadowy movement outside the window. Without staring he made out an irregularity, then a vague shape standing no more than a dozen yards distant, observing them. If he'd not thought so much about the encounter with the FBI agent, he might not have noted similarities in shape and stance.

He took a couple more bites, thinking he was likely wrong as Shelby told him how her father had said Link was a "likable sort."

"That's as much compliment as he'll give *anyone* the first time they meet," she said.

The shadow-shape moved, and he was sure. "Be right back," Link said, and rose, keeping his eyes averted from the figure. He walked toward the bar, where the rest rooms were located.

A couple was entering the front door. He slipped out behind them, trying to organize his thoughts about how to handle Special Agent Destin C. Albee. *Cooperate,*

Frank had advised, and by the time he reached the corner of the building he'd decided to avoid any semblance of confrontation. He'd be open, walk up and identify himself. Tell him he was with the Weyland Foundation, and that they often worked with the bureau. Ask about Gary and see if the FBI had any ideas where he might have gone. If they had Gary under surveillance, surely they'd know.

Link approached the deep shadow where he'd seen the man, and slowed. "Special Agent Albee?" he called out to make certain he didn't surprise him, and went closer.

No one was there.

Inside he saw Shelby Admire staring toward the bar where he'd disappeared. The waitress came over and the two women talked.

He saw movement near the corner of the building. "Special Agent Albee," he repeated in a louder voice, and started there. "We need to talk." The agent was good. He'd not seen him move away. As he hurried, Link forced a smile, determined to be friendly.

The attack was unexpected. Albee whirled about, swinging a glinting pistol around in an arc. Without thinking Link swept his own arm upward, made contact, and the weapon flew from the agent's hand.

Before Link could reposition, a sledgehammer blow slammed into his med-section. He grunted with pain, and as the breath was forced out of him, he instinctively tucked, dropped to the ground, and rolled away, desperately trying to regain his breath. The shadow-figure kicked out again and missed. Link rolled further, now out of easy reach, still unable to speak.

Albee stooped, retrieved the pistol, and Link barely heard a hoarse emotion-laden whisper as the agent's shadow came closer. "It's time to die, Anderson. It's *time!*"

The dark shape of Destin Albee raised his hand, and Link dared not wait. He grasped a stone and hurled it, heard a painful yelp as he ducked down and rolled again—and this time dropped off an unseen precipice. He fell four feet, and landed on his side. Hmmphed and lost more wind. Then he waited, huddling against the earth, trying to make little sound, and also to inhale a precious breath.

There was no gunshot from above, only the sound of cautious movement.

"Anderson." The deep voice was pained. "Get away while you can."

Link took in a small gasp of wind. He crouched, crabbed forward on elbows and knees until he could peer over the earthen ledge, prepared to grab an armful of legs. Nothing. Link remained on all fours, slowly recovering his breath, watching carefully, making sure the man didn't attack unseen. He waited until he'd pulled in several more breaths before rising and following— warily, his anger growing hotter with each step.

There was no sign of the agent in the parking lot, no automobile like the one he'd seen at the Barn. A van full of customers departed as Link waited and watched. When he had his full wind back, he brushed the worst of the dirt off and returned inside, sore where the agent had kicked him, and where he'd fallen. Anger pulsed in his chest. He spent ten minutes in the rest room on clean-up and repair, and calming himself.

"Had to make a phone call," he explained to Shelby, who did not examine closely enough to pick up on the damage. After fifteen minutes of small talk—and insisting on paying the tab—he walked Shelby to her car. She climbed into the low-slung Corvette and powered down the window.

"Thanks," she said in her soft voice.

"It was enjoyable." Except for the part about being kicked, he didn't add.

As he walked away, the Corvette's engine came to life with a resonating growl. Link started the Dodge and waited, then followed her out of the lot. Shelby was spending the night with her parents in Stagecoach Valley, and led the way.

As they passed through Virginia City, then turned down the incline toward the canyon road, he fastidiously watched the rearview mirror. Thinking it had been Special Agent Destin C. Albee who had followed him up the mountain in the dark pickup. Wondering where he'd hit him with the stone that he'd thrown. Feeling pleased that he'd heard pain in the man's voice.

11

Link rolled out of bed at his normal hour and had finished his warm-up exercises before he'd completely awakened. He pulled on sleeveless and cut-off sweats, running shoes and headband, stepped outside and savored the air, locked the door, and set up a loping pace. Out the drive and onto the lane, not hurrying but not dogging it, feeling the long strap-muscles coming to life. Taking in pleasant mixed odors of sagebrush, alfalfa, scrub grass, and dry air.

Two pickups and a battered Honda passed him on the lane, none bothering to slow. As he came into view of the highway, the traffic flow was substantial—all of it headed toward Carson City—and by the time he'd reached it and turned back, it was heavy.

He thought about his missing friend some as he ran, but mostly he concentrated on the world about him. Gary had been so impressed with the area that he'd stayed and purchased the Barn. Link understood. He too had once sought solitude, and Boudie Springs had beckoned.

Link estimated the distance at three miles, and by the time he'd returned to Gary's driveway knew he mustn't stop too abruptly or his calves might knot up. He slowed to a jog, then to a walk, breathing deeply to provide additional oxygen. Then, as he approached the old Dodge, he forgot all that and stopped cold.

Blood and hair were matted on the hood, and FED GO HOME! was daubed in crimson on the windshield. The driver's-side window was smashed and a gutted coyote's carcass had been stuffed inside, blood draining onto the seat, purple-gray entrails coiled on the floor.

He went to the street and observed. No one was in sight.

Fed? he wondered. Had someone confused him with Albee or one of his people?

Who knew he was here, beside Cal and Shelby Admire—and the FBI agent?

An hour later the telephone's shrill ring pulled Link from the shower.

"Anderson," he answered gruffly.

"Didn't wake you, did I?" It was Cal's country-boy drawl.

"No." He held the phone in the crook of his neck and began to towel off. He'd hosed down the pickup inside and out, found a shovel in the workshop and buried the bloody carcass in soft earth at the edge of the field. Then he'd stood on the deck for a while, waiting to see if the vandal might return. Wondering who had left the unwelcome present, what made them think he was a federal agent—and why that angered them.

"Any word from Gary?" Cal asked.

"Nothing."

"Well, I hope you haven't eaten. Both my daughter and the wife just gave strict orders that you're to be here for breakfast."

Link accepted. There were too many unanswered questions, of which the butchered coyote was only one.

The Admire Real Estate sign was impossible to miss—four ancient sheets of plywood placed side by side, painted yellow with green lettering, all of it sun-fading together. Link parked by the office, then walked to the rear as Cal had said to do. The flora was lush, the home all but hidden in dense foliage.

Cal Admire emerged from the house wearing a purple jogging suit and his trademark curled-brim straw hat.

"You're a runner?" Link asked.

"Hell, no," Cal said, as if disgusted by the thought.

"Sally heads for Reno ever' time there's a sale in the paper, an' saves so much money she'll drive us broke. Bought a dozen of these suits. I thought they were a waste, but now I eat, sleep, and relax in the things. They're sort of a flag. People see me in regular clothes, they know I'm working. When I'm in these, they don't even bother to stop." He motioned at the office. "No one except Ray, that is. Poor soul's so hard over in love with Shelby, he's lost all objectivity."

A brown police cruiser had pulled up beside Link's pickup, and a uniformed officer with a pencil-line mustache emerged. As he approached he offered an easy smile. "Dispatcher said you wanted to talk, Cal."

"Link, meet Deputy Sheriff Ray Watt, our local law enforcement." Watt wore a Smokey hat, tan uniform shirt and trousers with razor-edge creases, a glittering badge and metal nameplate. Everything about him seemed official except for a silver belt buckle with raised gold letters.

"Didn't waste any time," Cal told him. "Usually takes you half a day to respond. You must've heard Shelby's home."

The deputy gave him an aw-shucks grin. "What can I do for you?"

"This is Lincoln Anderson, Ray."

The deputy started to offer his hand, then stiffened and pulled back. It was obvious he connected something unsavory to Link's name.

Cal hardly noticed. "He drove all the way from Montana to visit Gary Runyon," Cal said, "but when he got here, Gary'd taken off. No one's seen him since last Wednesday. Any ideas?"

Watt fastidiously avoided looking at Link. "Maybe he had business somewhere. Or just didn't want to be here when his guest arrived."

"He invited him, Ray. They're old friends."

The deputy didn't answer.

"How about you put out the word to keep an eye out for Gary's Bronco?"

Watt took out a pen and pad. "Any of our deputies see him, we'll give you a call."

"Make it statewide. Parking lots, airports, everything."

"That might be hard without him being suspected of breaking any laws."

"I'd like it done, Ray."

Watt gave Link a sideward look, obviously disliking taking orders from Cal in front of him. "We'd have to get the state troopers involved. This doesn't—uh—maybe . . ."

Cal sighed. "I'd better call the sheriff. See if he'll help."

"No need," the deputy rushed, deflating. "I'll put out the bulletin."

"Put a priority on it, Ray."

Deputy Watt nodded.

"Do you know Gary?" Link asked.

The deputy's mouth calcified in a thin line.

"Link is Gary's friend," Cal repeated. "Damn it, give him an answer."

"I've heard of Mr. Runyon," Watt said evenly, not meeting Link's eyes.

"Link's *my* friend too, Ray. Why can't you give him a civil answer?"

The deputy drew an unhappy breath. "I know Runyon better than most. Help him get information for his writing when I can."

"What kind of information?" Link asked.

"We've been talking about some people died of a flu bug that went around. He looked at photos, and once he took a peek at a body."

Link digested that, then asked: "Know anything about an FBI surveillance on Gary?"

The deputy spat out his next words. "Try keepin' track of your own fuckin' people." Watt turned on his heel and stalked toward his cruiser.

"What do you mean?" Link called after him, but the deputy didn't respond.

Cal Admire was frowning. "Wonder what kind of burr got in his drawers?"

"I don't think he's a fan of mine," Link said, as Watt slammed the door of his cruiser so hard the vehicle

rocked. The reaction was puzzling. Had he thought Link
was FBI?

"I'll give his boss a call," Cal grumbled. "We can't
have our law enforcement people being rude."

"I'd rather you just forget it."

Cal looked at him. "This time. Next time I'll take it
personal. I told him you were my friend."

"You obviously have leverage with the sheriff."

"Been here a while and know the politicians from top
to bottom, local, state, and federal. When I put a candidate's sign up, some here take notice." Cal nodded at
the desert. "This county's the same size as New Hamp-
shire, but we only have twelve thousand people. Be surprised how politicians try to keep you happy when you
can bring 'em a dozen votes."

"I noticed the deputy's belt buckle. What does
AODM mean?"

"Ancient Order of Dirt Muckers. Been around a long
time. Back in the Comstock days the mine bosses had
their fine Masonic lodges, and kept out the lowly diggers
workin' down in the shafts. So the muckers started taking over a bar ever' week and holding their own meetings. Began as a joke, a drinking and carousing society.
Then they started collecting dues and helping miners'
widows and children, and generally doing good work.
Up 'til ten years ago, you wouldn't of had a chance at
senator or governor unless you were a Mucker. Now
there's so many outsiders pouring into Vegas it doesn't
matter much. More than two thirds of Nevadans live
there. And lately the Muckers been changing for the
worse."

"White supremacists?"

"My God, no. Those guys don't like the law, and most
of our cops and prison guards are members. They just
don't put emphasis on trying to help people like they
used to."

"And they don't like federal officers?"

"Not many around here do. The government's been
awfully heavy-handed about the way they handle state
and private property like it belongs to them."

FED GO HOME, the blood message had read, and Ray

Watt had acted as if Link had the plague. Had they confused him with Special Agent Destin Albee?

"I'll show you around. Can't take long, though. Sally's in a dither about breakfast, and Shelby's full of herself this morning." As they walked, Cal explained the Admire oasis. The home had begun as a modest, flat-roofed cottage. Then this bedroom was added one year, and that bathroom or hobby shop another, until there were so many some became semi-forgotten and were used as repositories of junk. The result was a large, oddly shaped, meandering structure, around which a wide screened porch had been built. Mostly—except during harsh weather—they lived on the porches. In back were ducks, geese and peacocks, a pond, and more than two hundred trees—mostly cottonwoods, red maples and Mormon willows—planted by Cal's wife over the years. A handyman used a rider mower to manicure two acres of lawn.

As they entered the porch through a screen door, a brindled boxer greeted them, wriggling in happy anticipation. Cal scratched her ears and called her Maggie.

"Hi, there." Shelby came from the interior carrying tall glasses of orange juice. She'd transformed herself into the girl-next-door—walking shorts and blouse, no makeup, hair drawn into a ponytail—but there was no way to mask her sensuality, and Link felt a long-suppressed stirring as she guided him to a large table and seated him at the end opposite Cal. The tabletop was Formica, the chairs fifties-vintage tube chromium, the padding covered with plastic. Down the porch was an elderly television set and a pair of comfortable-looking stuffed chairs. While the Admires had amassed wealth, they remained unpretentious.

An older, plumper image of Shelby burst from inside, balancing a platter of biscuits and a boat of gravy. "I'm Sally," she announced as she deposited her load. Next were eggs, ham slabs, plump sausages, wedges of cheese, potatoes O'Brien, and a steaming pitcher of coffee. Last came freshly cut cantaloupes and honeydews. "Those are grown in Fallon, forty miles east," Sally said as she joined them and took her seat. "They claim to be the melon capital of something or other."

"Used to be the West," Cal said. "Now it's the world."

Link tried one, pronounced it delicious, and Sally beamed. They talked as they ate, about the weather and the area. Small talk, but the Admires refused to let him feel ill at ease.

"What did Gary tell you about our valley?" Sally asked.

"Not much," he admitted.

"I told him about Millionaire Mountain and the Break-a-Heart mines," said Shelby.

Cal nodded toward the mountain beyond the dry lake bed. "Back in nineteen forty-nine, before there was anything here, the U.S. Army built a small post there. Then came the big rumble."

"Earthquake," Sally explained, but Link noted that Shelby held her tongue. Odd, since that was an area of her expertise.

"The post was abandoned the next year," Cal said. "Probably damaged by the quake. I'd take you over for a look, but its fenced off. Shelby worked there for a while."

"That's where NEL's located?" Link asked her.

She nodded, and Link stared at the mountain only five miles distant, wondering about having to drive thirty miles to Carson City tomorrow, then taking the helicopter back.

"You know what they're doing there?" Cal asked, casting a look at Link.

"Some of it."

"Then you know more than the rest of us. Shelby won't talk about it."

"I told you, Dad. The employees sign forms promising not to discuss the project."

Cal wasn't finished with grumbling. "People of Nevada oughta be used to the federal government using our land. Almost ninety percent of the state's claimed by Washington. Makes me damned mad they won't even discuss what they're *doing* with it."

Sally rolled her eyes and told Cal to stop rambling

and monopolizing. She motioned to Shelby. "Did you tell Link about *The Misfits*?"

"I don't believe so."

"Biggest thing that's ever happened here, and you didn't tell him?"

"I wasn't even *born* then, mother."

Sally regarded their guest. "Remember a movie called *The Misfits,* with Clark Gable, Marilyn Monroe, and Montgomery Clift? 1961. It was Monroe and Gable's last film."

"I've heard of it," Link tried, not saying it was before his time too.

"Not much of a story," Cal groused. "About a couple losers and a tired hooker trying to round up mustangs. Wild horses running everywhere here, but they brought in fakes."

"It's considered a *classic,*" Sally said, giving Cal a dangerous glare.

"Only good thing about it was they went back and told their Hollywood friends about this place out in the middle of nowhere where you could get away and listen to the quiet. That's when the movie stars built those places over where you are."

"No one's sure of that, Dad," Shelby said.

"Well, *someone* built 'em, and saying it was them helps sell homes." He daubed butter and honey on another biscuit. "Everything here's named for either the mines or the movie. Break-a-Heart Café, hair salon and general store. Misfits saloon and auto repair. Except for my business, that's all there is."

"I'll take you to lunch at the saloon," Shelby told Link. "You haven't lived until you've had a Misfits Burger."

Link decided to pass. Even without makeup she was stunning, and his renegade body reacted in very natural ways when he viewed her, or when she just spoke in her husky voice.

They sat back from the table, stuffed.

"I haven't had a breakfast that good for a long while," Link said in appreciation.

Sally beamed happily. "Gary eats here regularly, and I'll expect you to do the same."

"How long are you going to stay?" Cal asked.

"Two or three days. I was in the middle of moving to New York when Gary called," he said. "I've just taken a job there, so I've got to get back."

"What was that you asked Ray about? Something about the FBI?"

"I was just fishing for anything I could get," Link said. He'd told Frank he would cooperate with the bureau, and decided that still included Albee, although his charity had dwindled considerably.

"Gary's been gone for four days," said Shelby. "I'd like to go to the Barn and look around, see if there's anything to tell us where he went. Do you mind, Link?"

"Of course not." He did mind, but not for a reason he wished to explain.

Sally waved them away. "I'll clean up here. You two go on."

Shelby followed him in her Corvette, clean two days before but now so dust-caked the color was indefinable, wondering where in the world Gary might be. Thinking she was attracted to the dark-haired man in the pickup. There was a chemistry taking place, and it had been long enough since Marie's passing for Shelby not to feel guilty. Yet there was an almost feral presence about Link Anderson, and she wondered if it would be wiser to keep her distance.

How long has it been since he'd been with a woman? she wondered, then chastised herself. Shelby had not been to bed with a man in more than three years, since before she'd broken up with her boss-boyfriend in San Diego. They'd worked for an off shore oil drilling company. She'd gone out on a seismology effort to the Berents Sea—and returned to find herself replaced by a wannabe fashion model. Until Link's arrival she'd reverted to abstinence, but she'd caught him staring a couple of times and her resolve was slipping. He was quiet-spoken, and she wondered if he wasn't shy with women. The idea made him more appealing.

Marie LeBecque was your friend, part of her mind argued, and she sobered some and made herself think of other things, like where in the world Gary might be off to.

When they arrived at the Barn, she parked beside his sturdy old pickup, killed the engine, and looked out at the alfalfa field where he'd seen a large animal. It was doubtful it had been Aristotle. Gary doted on the dog and wouldn't have left it to fend for itself.

Link opened her car door, and gave her a hand out. She spoke as he hauled her upright. "Ready to level about the FBI thing?"

"Just fishing for information from the deputy."

"You're a *terrible* liar. Dad didn't buy it either, by the way."

He didn't answer.

"Share with me, Link. I'm concerned about Gary. Maybe together we can come closer to finding out where he went."

"There's nothing more."

But there was, and Shelby felt he was purposely withholding it. She wondered if she wasn't being pushy, although she'd seldom been accused of that since the break-up and accompanying loss of pride. Then, following an awkward silence, she realized the truth. Link Anderson did not trust her.

She spoke normally, as if her heart hadn't turned to lead. "The manuscript's called *Nightmare in Nuclear America,* and he said it's almost done. It's probably in his computer."

Damn you, Link Anderson.

He unlocked then slid the door back and waited for her go in.

Shelby led the way up to the loft, feeling his distrust poison the air. She told herself to worry only about Gary's disappearance, and to hell with sharing anything with Link Anderson.

She looked about. "The tables are so messy I don't know how he finds anything."

Yet the last time she'd seen it, it had seemed even more cluttered.

As he nosed about, looking for the manuscript, Shelby took her seat at the computer. A typed letter beside the answering machine caught her eye. DAMN LEECHES! was printed across the body. After she'd scanned it, she caught Link frowning as he searched for something near the telephone. Something was amiss and again he wasn't telling her.

Shelby replaced the letter. "It's another demand from his ex-wife's lawyers, like the ones I told you about last night. They're just scare tactics. Even Gary jokes about them now."

"Then why did he print that across it?"

She switched on the computer and, as she waited for it to boot, examined the scrawled words. "I don't think it's Gary's hand. He uses bold strokes and those look too tentative."

"You think someone else was in here?"

"How would I know," Shelby said too curtly, then: "Let's see what's in his computer."

The screen came to life. ENTER PASSWORD_____

"Damn," she muttered helplessly.

"Any way to get around it?"

"Not that I know of. I can run programs, but that's the limit of my expertise."

Link picked up the phone. A moment later he was talking to someone named Erin, explaining that Gary was still missing and they needed help getting into his computer. Without further word, he handed her the phone.

"Hi, Shelby," said a pleasant voice. "I'm Erin, and I work with Link. He says you've got a computer problem. What is it you're after?"

Shelby told her.

"Is it equipped with a modem?"

"There's a phone line hooked into the back."

"Great. Is the telephone number shown?"

Shelby read off a number taped onto the side of the computer.

"Super. Now hang up and stand by for a couple of minutes, okay?"

"Hang up?"

"Yeah. You'll see why."

As they waited Link remained close, peering at the screen, and she could hear the sounds of his breathing. Yes, she decided. A feral presence. She idly wondered who Erin was, and a pang of unreasonable emotion trilled through her. Jealousy? Ridiculous.

Almost magically the screen came to life and began to flash through various functions and displays. After thirty seconds it went dark, and then words began to scroll.

Hi Link & Shelby,

1. If you need access to the computer in the future, the password is REDHED. I found a folder called WRITING on the hard drive, but there are *no* books or notes stored there. However, a sub-folder with numerous files and titled N-MARE was recently (June 24) opened, copied onto floppy diskettes (2 copies), then *deleted* from the computer. Unfortunately I can't recreate it. One copy was relabeled "N-MARE PONY," the other "N-MARE BIG CAT."

2. Also, the telephone *voice* line you just used showed heavy impedance loading, which *may* indicate an online shunt. That means that it's either being monitored, or you have a terrible line. *This* line is secure.

3. If you use that location in the future, I suggest that you *not* use the voice line for sensitive discussions. Leave the computer turned on, and periodically check the screen for my HELLO. Then just type OK, and we can exchange secure messages. I will now stand by for instructions. Whenever you wish to terminate, type END, and press ENTER.

Cheers, Erin

p.s. Link. Last Thursday three senior employees showed up wearing boots.

"Wow," Shelby said. "She's good. Your secretary?"

"My assistant," Link said, rereading the words.

An asterisk blinked on the screen, awaiting their input. "Do you want to ask her anything else?"

"Not that I can think of. *Are* the phone lines bad here?"

"Atrocious. Anyway, I can't believe anyone would want to bug Gary's conversations."

"Tell her."

At the asterisk Shelby typed:

*Hi Erin,
   Phone service here is awful, which is likely the problem with the voice line. Link has no more questions, so we'll terminate.
   Nice talking with you, and thanks for the info. Shelby. END

Link leaned forward, squinting at the screen, close enough that Shelby enjoyed the masculine scent of him. Then she remembered. Distrust? How dare he!

"Why would Gary delete his book?" Link wondered aloud.

"I suppose he was worried that someone might break into his computer."

"Like we just did?"

She snorted. "If he can run off and worry us like this, he can expect us to be nosy. I don't want to read his damned manuscript, just find out where he went."

"June twenty-fourth," he muttered, which had been the date the files had been deleted.

"Yeah. Wednesday, the day he took off, something made him suspicious."

"So what do we look for? The diskettes? He probably took them with him."

"Erin said he made two copies. N-Mare Big Cat, and N-Mare Pony."

"Does either of those mean anything to you?"

"I assume they're code names for where Mr. Mysterious put them." She opened a diskette container. "I'll check through these."

The exchange with Erin was still sinking in. Link's assistant had somehow been able to check the telephone lines for security, switch on Gary's modem, learn his password, and search through his computer. Some assistant, she thought.

One by one Shelby loaded and examined diskettes. Some were software programs, others empty, and yet others contained old notes and correspondence.

"Damn it. I miss the redheaded nut," she said as she worked.

Link remained quiet.

"Gary's my touchstone," she said, and checked the last of the diskettes—keeping her eyes on the screen, dwelling again on the fact that Link refused to tell her what he knew.

"I didn't find any diskettes under the stacks of paper," Link said.

Shelby had angrily pushed back from the computer, suddenly needing to get away from Link Anderson, when he abruptly stepped to the window. "Damn!" he exploded.

He went downstairs quickly, taking them two at a time, and she followed.

"What is it?" she called, but he didn't respond. Link was out the door like a shot, with Shelby close behind, then he stood, staring. All four of the pickup's tires had been slashed.

He walked to the corner of the Barn and disappeared from her sight.

Shelby examined her Corvette. There was no damage.

Link returned. "No one's around."

"Who could have done it?"

He spoke through clenched teeth. "Obviously someone who doesn't want me here."

12

Unless she was a consummate actress, Link decided that Shelby was just as outraged as he was. Now she was on the phone with her father, explaining, and held the receiver away from her ear as Cal exploded. "Let me talk to Link," they finally heard, and he took the telephone.

"What the hell's going on?" Cal asked. "If it happened to me I could understand, but you haven't been here long enough to *make* enemies."

"That's what I thought when I got up." When he explained the coyote carcass left in his truck, Cal was first struck silent, then voiced more oaths.

"Any ideas how I can get tires on a Sunday?"

"Don't worry about that part. I'm just damned mad it happened. You're a guest, and by God, our guests aren't treated this way." He huffed a curse. "Now, what size tires do you need?"

When Link hung up, Shelby was outside, staring at his truck and wearing a hurt look. She glared as he joined her. "Why didn't you tell us about the coyote this morning?"

"I try not to saddle others with my problems."

She thought that over, then nodded at her car. "You'd think a self-respecting vandal would rather get his hands on a Corvette than a scruffy old pickup."

"The messages aren't meant for you. Did Gary go through this sort of reception?"

"Not at all. The people here like him. People move here all the time, and they're made to feel at home. The locals aren't sophisticated, but they've always been friendly."

"When I asked Deputy Watt about the FBI, he acted as if I were one of them. Since I'd just read 'Fed go home' written in blood on my windshield, it got my attention."

"Ray wouldn't have any part of that sort of thing. He takes his job seriously. He's not mean-spirited either, just gullible. I'll ask where he heard you were FBI."

"I'd appreciate it." So far nothing made sense to Link.

"The surveillance?" she asked. "What's that about, Link?"

"It's sort of involved," he tried. He was still evasive, but his conviction was waning.

"When did Dad say your tires'll be delivered?"

"Early this afternoon."

"We've got plenty of time. Let me take you for a ride, so I can show you our sinister little valley. Then we'll talk." She looked at him. "Or not."

As they pulled out of the driveway, Shelby pointed out a shanty on the hillside, nondescript amid the sagebrush and hardscrabble rock. "An old prospector lives there. Wears a Santa Claus beard and mumbles a lot. Drifted in more than a year back, hardly able to get around from some kind of fall he'd taken. Goes out prospecting in a World War Two army truck. They call him the hermit."

"He stays to himself?"

"Every few nights he'll show up at the saloon and sit in a corner. Once in a while he'll say a few words, but not often. Gary enjoys characters like him, and we've got our share."

"Does he actually find gold?"

"Who knows? It's around. Last year a big new mine went in just seven miles north of here." Shelby explained that the valley was ten by twelve miles, inhabited mostly on the northeast and northwest elevations. Two thousand people, and more arriving every month.

She began at the westernmost end, and drove him past "ranchettes" with large homes on twenty-acre lots, and explained the explosion of retirees pouring in from California. She proceeded eastward, pointing out a sod farm, and several sprawling oases on the hillside said once to have been inhabited by film stars, and finally idled through the heavier populated east side, with single- and double-wide mobile homes on one- and five-acre lots, some well maintained, others not. Mostly working people lived there, where housing was affordable, and commuted to work in Carson City or Reno.

"All kinds," she said, waving cheerfully at a middle-aged woman tending a small yard. "That's Irene Staples. Very bright but she's suffered terrible luck. Born near Sacramento. When she was young her father died and didn't leave much. Since she was determined to go to college, she knuckled down and won a full scholarship to the University of California in microbiology, which is not mundane stuff. She was sixteen when she was enrolled, and made the president's list for the next two years. In her junior year, her mother was diagnosed with multiple sclerosis and she had to drop out. There was no money. In the early seventies they moved here and Dad sold her the trailer for a promise of small payments. By then her mother needed full-time care, so Irene did telephone work. You know the kind. Cold calls to sell shares in vacation property."

"The sort of phone calls I hang up on."

"Me too. Two weeks ago her mother died after thirty years of suffering, and Irene was set adrift. She's bright, but she's also middle-aged and unskilled."

As she finished, he recalled the address he'd found. "Know where 9505 Cherokee is?"

"Sure," Shelby said, and turned left. She turned again, onto a street named Cherokee Trail and pointed out a trailer. "Lester Dunlap lived there. A real no-kidding cowboy from the Ruby Mountain country. They found him dead last—what was it . . . oh yeah . . . Tuesday morning."

Link craned his neck, remembering that Ray Watt said Gary had been interested in recent deaths in the valley. Shelby slowed as they passed a park where children played. A mother hovered as her toddler crawled up a slide. Younger kids had a merry-go-round spinning, and older ones were tossing a baseball back and forth. "Dad donated it to the community," Shelby said. "He feels responsible for what he's created."

She crossed the highway and drove onto a dirt road and after half a mile stopped at an isolated and small, crumbling stone structure.

"The old pony express station," she explained as they climbed out of the Corvette. "We used to come here when I was little, and Dad would explain what it was like when it was in operation. There were corrals then, and a Mexican couple lived here and looked after the horses. Every day they'd wait until they could see the rider's dust coming across the valley. From the time they saw it, they had twenty minutes to prepare a replacement mount. When he reached the dry lake bed he was two miles out, so they'd cinch up. The change of horses was done in seconds. The riders were young, and some became famous, like Buffalo Bill Cody."

Shelby led him into the musty interior, with its crumbling adobe and fallen rafters. "No one's inhabited it for the past hundred and thirty years. Most don't realize that the pony express was in business for less than a year. 1860 to 1861. It was a financial disaster, and the owners were ruined." She observed a collection of debris and dusty pop bottles.

As they emerged from the building, a weather-savaged, once-military truck rattled by, headed toward the community across the highway.

"The hermit," Shelby explained. "You don't often see him during the day."

Link turned to see where the vehicle had come from.

"He was obviously looking near Millionaire Mountain," Shelby said. "Prospectors still nose around there, like they don't believe the old Break-a-Heart mines were as barren as they were."

"I thought access was restricted."

"Only on the north side and in the hollow where the mines and the army post were located. Now there's just NEL, but they still keep out intruders."

A moment of silence passed during which they stared

toward the mountain, and he felt increasingly uneasy. He glanced at her, and she chose that moment to do the same. Their eyes locked and the stirring became pronounced.

"I'd better get back," he said.

"Not until you level with me about Gary's disappearance."

"I doubt I know much more than you."

"You *still* don't trust me?"

"It isn't that. I told Gary I wouldn't tell anyone." He didn't add that his reluctance to share had also been for another reason—that while his brain might still grieve, his glands were reacting as if they hadn't received the briefing. After a moment he folded. "You've got a right to know, considering your relationship with Gary . . ."

"We're just friends, Link. When we met, Gary was gun-shy of women because of his ex-wife, and I was bitter about men. The nice part was we could go out to dinner or just talk and feel normal, without entanglements. I also gave him technical information for his book. End of story, except I cherish the guy like a brother."

They really weren't lovers. The fact was inexplicably pleasing.

"I still guess that gives you the right to know what I do, which, as I said, isn't much." He told her about the telephone conversation. "He said there are parts of his manuscript that aren't complimentary to my employer, who is also a close friend. Did he tell you about it?"

"Only that what he was writing was interesting and revealing, and he needed our help. He wanted me to look through it from a technical angle, and you to verify something."

"Nothing else?"

"Nope." She formed a smile that fell somewhere between pleased and smug. "He asked you to keep quiet about it? That's why you wouldn't tell me?"

"If it can hurt my friend, I don't want anything getting out until I know what it's about."

"Mum's the word, but we share everything, okay?" She raised an eyebrow. "Like the fact that Gary said he had an informant giving what he called dynamite information."

"An informant? Any idea who it could have been?"

"Not until you mentioned the FBI. Gary called his informant—he mentioned a him, so it was a man—an agent, and said he was a world-class whistle-blower."

Could Destin Albee, SAC of the Las Vegas bureau office, be Gary's source? Thinking back on the man's visit, it seemed improbable. Someone who worked for Albee? Maybe Albee was the bad guy being ratted on. But what would that have to do with nuclear waste?

"Tell me about Deputy Watt again," he said. "Why is he so hostile."

"I have no idea. I've known Ray for a long time. He tries to be a ladies' man, but there's nothing sinister about him. He likes Gary and brags around that he's friends with a *real* author."

"Gary didn't believe he was in trouble. He said my friend was the one in trouble."

"Sure makes you wonder now."

"Yeah." He paused for a moment, trying to sort it out.

"You still haven't told me how the FBI's involved," she prodded.

The final crumb of charity for Destin Albee evaporated. "I was visited at the Barn yesterday," he started, and told her about the FBI agent's visit, omitting his subsequent discussions with Erin Frechette and Frank Dubois.

"Giving away military secrets? Gary would never do anything like that."

"He was our unit public information officer. I doubt he even *knew* any secrets."

"And the FBI agent said that? Was he real?"

"According to an unimpeachable source, Destin Albee's all he claimed to be. I met him again last night, by the way." He explained what had happened outside the restaurant.

"You were attacked?" she asked incredulously.

"He caught me off guard," Link said defensively. He described Albee—including the masked birthmark and graying hair. She said she hadn't noticed him around Stagecoach.

"Could he be responsible for this morning's vandalism?" she asked.

"Maybe. He made it clear that he doesn't like me being here."

"We should go to the authorities with all this, Link."

"As far as I know, Destin Albee is presently one of the highest ranking law enforcement officers in the area. And Deputy Watt?" He shook his head. "I've got to go to NEL for the briefings tomorrow. Would this Dr. Jameson have any ideas about what Gary was writing?"

"Probably not. Unless it's something to do with his project, or his cooking—it really is atrocious, by the way—I doubt Fred could help. He's very focused."

"Perhaps Gary was writing about NEL?"

"No way. He didn't have the slightest idea about the real project out there. They gave him an unclassified, very general look at the problem in America, but nothing concrete."

"How about the project people? Were any of them Gary's friends?"

"Not that I know." A frown crossed her face.

"Something wrong?"

"The original people there have been replaced. I feel uneasy around the new ones."

"Are they the ones you had your differences with?"

"Primarily. Did you notice all the helicopters coming and going yesterday?"

He nodded. "Big ones."

"They're hauling in radioactive material, everything from plutonium, which is still the most toxic substance known to man, to californium and more exotic stuff."

"Why?"

"Some kind of future experimentation. I wasn't involved in that part of the research. But I felt they should at least level with the locals and the state about the stuff being there, and brought it up with Fred Jameson. He and several others pitched a fit, and said everything had to be done in secrecy because another company might steal their procedure."

"I don't understand."

"I didn't either, since I wasn't part of the real research effort. But I can tell you this. America's running out of electrical energy. The demand is growing at a far greater rate than the supply. We're getting it where we can. Windmills, buying it from Canada and so forth. We figured nuclear power might provide a quick fix. But now eleven reactors are idle and more will have to shut down.

"What's the problem."

"There's so much waste stacked up around the country—fifty thousand tons of it by next year, and growing—that if the public knew how dangerous it really is, right now, there would be a rebellion. Forget about reactor meltdown hazards. It's the waste that's dangerous."

"What does that have to do with all the secrecy at NEL?"

"Just that the problem of what to do with nuclear waste is very big business, with lots of money at stake. Many millions of dollars have been spent on studies, but there'll be a lot more for the company that comes up with a solution. *Hundreds* of millions. Even more."

With that much money involved, Link felt the likelihood of skullduggery had just gone up considerably. "*Is* there a solution?" he asked her.

"Fred Jameson thinks so. I heard him tell that to the Secretary of Energy when he requested more plutonium for his research."

"Did he get it?"

"Yes. And I had the temerity to suggest they tell the local officials about it. So much pressure was put on me, a mere geologist with only a master's degree—remember what I told you about academic snobbery?—to shut up about it that I felt it would be better if I left."

Link wondered about the academicians he'd meet tomorrow.

"Let's talk about Gary," she said. "I think we should try to find Mathilda."

He gave her a perplexed look, then remembered Gary telling him about an ancient Piper Cub he'd named after an aunt. The airplane Cal Admire had talked about.

"He may have flown it somewhere," she said, "or even have crashed."

"I doubt he moved it if it had a bad engine. Where was he going to have it repaired?"

"Carson City and Reno are the biggest airports in the local area. I'll call around and see if he left it at either one." She pursed her lips thoughtfully. "I think we should tell Dad about the FBI involvement. He knows a lot of people."

"Not yet." Link still felt uneasy about sharing with Shelby, and Cal talked entirely too freely. "Let's keep it between the two of us for the present."

She nodded back toward the highway. "We still have an hour to kill. How about we order a couple of Misfits Burgers, and have a Bloody Mary while we wait."

"I thought you didn't drink?"

"Only when I'm not prepared to be wild and crazy," she joked. Then she glanced at him and smiled, and Lincoln Anderson wondered what she was thinking.

At 12:30, when they were back at the Barn, finishing off a pair of the best char-broiled burgers in Link's memory, two service trucks arrived from Reno. The crew from the first mounted four new tires, and a repairman in the second replaced the side window. Cal Admire was a friend of the owner and had told them he'd handle it, but Link insisted on using his corporate credit card.

"Dad won't like that," Shelby observed as the trucks pulled away.

"He didn't do the damage."

"Yeah, but he feels responsible. He also likes you, and there's not much you can do about it." She crawled into her Corvette and started the engine. "I've got to get back to Carson City and go over some reports for tomorrow. Thanks for lunch."

"I enjoyed the company."

"I'll be back tomorrow afternoon. If you're free after you're done at NEL, maybe we can get together."

"Let's see what develops."

"Yes," she said in the low voice, smiled pleasantly, and drove away.

Just friends. Link repeated to himself.

As the guttural engine sounds receded, he went inside and directly to the loft.

The computer screen showed: Hello. Standing By, E. but it was not that that he looked at, rather the area beside the answering machine where he'd placed the items—the scraps of paper and the eyeglass lens found in the driveway—when he'd first arrived.

The lens was there but the notepad pages were missing, as he'd noted when Shelby was reading the Damn Leeches letter.

He took his seat, peered at the screen, and laboriously typed: *Ready for some work?

Twenty seconds later the screen came to life: Who's there?

*Link. I'm alone.

Confirm your mother's maiden name.

*Linda Lopes, he typed.

The image fluttered, and a moment afterward words scrolled:

Link, since we last talked this connection was *also* corrupted. It's likely just poor line maintenance as Shelby explained, but I've temporarily loaded a encrypt/decrypt program on the computer you're using, and will do so each time we communicate so no one can listen in.

An asterisk blinked, and she awaited his input.

*I need information on 4 people. Anything out of the ordinary, like a criminal record or affiliation with some nut group.

Shoot, Erin replied.

He typed:

*1. Ray Watt, Deputy sheriff for Line County, NV.

2. Shelby Admire, geologist for State of NV.

3. Cal [??] Admire, realtor, Stagecoach Velley, NV.

4. Destin C. Albee, FBI SAC, Las Vegas field office.

There was a slight pause from Erin, then: Frank may not like the last one.

*Frank wasn't jumped by him like I was last night. Do you have the description I gave before?

Yes. You were jumped?

*He kicked me and threatened to kill me, and I did not like it. See what you can find out. If Frank has a problem with it, have him give me a call.

Will do. Anything else?

*Check out a group called the Ancient Order of Dirt Muckers.

You've got to be kidding me.

*No. END.

The screen underwent a few flashes, likely Erin removing the encryption program, then went blank. Link was pleased with his newly acquired computer skills. Then he huffed a grumpy breath and stared where he'd left the scraps of paper, wondering who had taken them. He picked up the lone eyeglass lens and turned it in his fingers. It was a quarter of an inch thick, as he remembered Gary's spectacles had been. He wondered if he could have removed the notes himself, but knew he wasn't that forgetful. His recollection of placing them with the lens beside the Philadelphia lawyers' letter, of thinking about his sparse trove of clues, was too distinct.

Had Shelby taken them? Maybe, but he believed he would have seen her do it. He knew about the address now, but brought up the other one in his mind.

B & E EXPERT + COMPUTER WISE + AWARE OF BOOK = D. A.

Written in a bold hand like Shelby said Gary used. Was D. A. Destin Albee?

He went down and sat on the porch, thinking about all he'd learned, wondering where the floppy diskettes might be, and what Gary had meant when he'd labeled them. Since Gary drove a Bronco, N-Mare Pony might mean he was keeping a set there, close at hand. N-Mare Big Cat seemed more elusive.

How did the FBI fit into the picture?

Each time he searched for answers, there were more questions.

PART II

Collegium of Death

13

Link had hurried through his exercises and finished his run—two laps on the primitive road around the perimeter of the alfalfa, keeping the pickup in sight. When he returned he trotted up the stairs to the loft, still huffing in his cut-off sweats.

Hello. Standing By. E. showed on the screen. He sat and typed: *Link here.

Erin was obviously in the office, for she immediately responded with: My son's game?

He'd talked to the seven-year-old at the Dubois dinner. *Soccer, he replied.

The screen flashed and altered as the encryption program loaded. Good morning. I have information. Any word about your friend?

*No. Go ahead with info, he typed.

There's nothing bad on record about any of the names you gave me.

Of note, Deputy Sheriff Raymond Charles Watt was on the NHP for five years, but could not pass the written test for promotion to senior patrolman. Six years ago he talked the county sheriff (his uncle) into letting him come aboard to add "professionalism" to the department. His co-workers find him self-centered, lazy, but also honest and (slow but) reliable.

Shelby Ann Admire is *very* bright. A four-oh average at Stanford, and all sorts of honors. I'm looking at her photograph on the screen and understand why you like having her around, you sly dog you.

Link smiled, but Erin's next entry wiped it away.

James Calvin Admire, her father, was once the "High Muckety Muck"—meaning the supreme leader—of the Ancient Order of Dirt Muckers. Seven years ago he vocally disagreed with the direction the group was taking, away from good works and toward secrecy, and dropped out.

Why hadn't Cal told him? Was he hiding something?

Deputy Raymond C. Watt is currently sergeant at arms of the local AODM chapter there.

Interesting, he thought.

The Bureau of Alcohol, Tobacco and Firearms have infiltrated with at least one paid agent as a member, and are monitoring the AODM. ATF does *not* presently consider them a threat, more of a nuisance. The Muckers are more of an old-buddy drinking society than anything, but collectively and generally do not like interference in local matters by federal officers and politicians, and spend much of their time complaining about it.

A blinking asterisk showed she was awaiting his input.

*What about Special Agent Destin Albee? he hunt-and-peck typed.

Frank learned I opened the query and was upset until I told him about the attack on you. I then had to request that he *not* take action to have him reprimanded until we learn more. SA Albee is out of pocket, but will contact me from his Las Vegas office in the morning. My contact there, a female agent, said he is a dedicated, well-regarded agent. I went over your description and found some items of interest. I'll have more tomorrow.

*Good work, Link typed.

By the way, you'll love what they did to our offices. They're bright and cheerful, and today I'm wearing my squash blossom necklace, pardner.

Link smiled, then typed: *I'm going out for a look at a company here for Frank and will not be available until later. END.

The machine went through its gyrations as the encryption program was downloaded, then the screen went blank. He was getting to be a regular computer whiz.

Link trotted downstairs, stripped off his running clothes, and prepared to shower, his mind filling with what else he might do to find Gary. First, though, he had to endure the briefings at the study site. He resigned himself to spending the day buried in an avalanche of academic minutia understood only by people of science.

7:55 A.M.—Carson City Airport

Link walked into the general aviation terminal in open-neck shirt, slacks, boots, and hat, and found a small group of chattering men and women gathered at one end, waiting to board the passenger helicopter parked just outside.

Dr. Fred Jameson's self-description was apt. He was rotund, bald, and pleasant-faced, and spoke at a rapid Yankee clip. As he shook Link's hand with too much sincerity and welcomed him to the NEL project, the others took little heed. Some seemed to be staring vaguely into the distance, as if their minds were filled with important things. He was willing to bet that more than a few often lost eyeglasses that were perched on their foreheads.

"My esteemed crew," Jameson said, "and I'm lucky to have them. We employ one of the most prestigious groups in the nuclear physics field." He mentioned universities and research centers he'd recruited them from, and whispered the name of a Nobel prize winner Link had never heard of.

"Is this all of them?" Link asked, counting seven in addition to the doctor and himself.

"No, there are twenty-six in all. Some were on the early bird flight, and a small number stay in dormitories onsite." Jameson regarded him. "Your people said you'd only be able to spend a short while. How much of your time do I have?"

"Could we wrap it up today? Then if things work out, I'll fly back out in a month or two for another look."

"We'll take what we can get," the doctor said. "I'll

have you stuffed with knowledge and back here by three. Headed straight back to New York?"

"Soon. I'm still looking for my friend."

"Mmm. I asked at the barbecue and no one knew anything about your Mr. Runyon."

The pilot announced it was time to load. Jameson shepherded the group out and, once aboard, loudly reminded them to fasten their seat belts. "We do this twice a day," he explained to Link, his expression serious, "but some are already so engrossed in their work that they forget."

The helicopter took off, canted over, and headed east. The half-empty craft was light and maneuverable, and Link found the soundproofed interior surprisingly quiet.

"What did they tell you about the project before you left New York?" Jameson asked.

"Very little, except there was a problem with safety."

Fred waved dismissively. "But you understand our objective?"

"To determine the best ways to store nuclear waste."

"Or render it safe," Jameson added. He handed Link a green plastic tube the size of a ball-point pen, with a clip to hold it in place and the NEL logo on its side. "Please wear that while you're on the site. There's no danger, but there *is* radioactive material present, and DOE requires that everyone carry them."

Link was familiar with dosimeters, and automatically peered through the end. The pointer was in the green. If it rose to the yellow range, you were to remove yourself from the source of radiation. Red meant danger, and on this advanced model a buzzer would sound.

"Keep it for when you return," Jameson told him as he clipped it into his shirt pocket.

Link examined the countryside as they passed over the town of Dayton and the golf course Gary had told him about. The flight took a total of nine minutes before the pilot made his approach arc and Link got a closer look at Millionaire Mountain. From their overhead vantage, the hollow appeared larger, perhaps a half-mile in diameter. Inside were a dozen buildings, elongated and painted white like those in other old military camps he'd seen.

Fred Jameson pointed out the mountainside wooden structures that masked the openings of the three Break-a-Heart mines.

"The buildings are in better condition than I'd imagined," Link said.

Jameson looked surprised. "You know about them?"

"Just a little history from the locals. I was told the mines were dug in the eighteen hundreds."

"Eighteen sixty-three. The army rebuilt the structures in nineteen forty-nine, when they put in the post."

"Why fly all the way out here? Wouldn't it be better to do your brainstorming in a lab?"

"We've got a modern laboratory here," said Jameson. "The rest will have to wait until we deplane. We keep quiet about what we're doing, and I'll ask for your discretion as well."

"Certainly." He wondered why secrecy was required.

After they'd landed, the passengers dutifully waited until the rotors had come to a complete stop before leaving their seats. Outside, a modest-sized white-on-dark-green sign read NUCLEONIC ENGINEERING, LTD. and beneath it, A DEPARTMENT OF ENERGY RESEARCH PROJECT, both printed in precise lettering.

Dr. Jameson regarded the scientists as they filed off in different directions. "Our personnel are divided into five collegia and work in different parts of the campus."

A fortyish, uniformed woman drove up in a Yamaha motorized golf cart, nodded curtly to Jameson, and immediately began to walk back toward a building a hundred yards distant.

Fred Jameson watched her. "Our security was quite slipshod until a few months ago, when we put in sensors and surveillance cameras. It's proven efficient, and I was able to cut our personnel by half." As the helicopter departed for Carson City, he crawled onto the golf cart. "Get aboard. We'll start with a tour and I'll explain what's so special about the place."

When Link joined him, Dr. Jameson put the cart into gear. "The miners named it Millionaire Mountain, and sank three shafts. All they found was sandstone, gypsum, and clay—no gold and nothing to show for their efforts. But there's a lot more to the story."

He started up a paved roadway that coursed up the mountainside, explaining how for the four years following the end of World War II, the United States had sole possession of atomic weapons. Then, under the supervision of Andrei Sakharov and Gustav Hertz, and using information gleaned from the Manhattan Project by such superspies as Klaus Fuchs and Harry Gold, the USSR detonated one of their own.

When President Truman was told about it, he brooded for a week, for he'd been presented with a new option. Dr. Edward Teller of Columbia University felt that a new family of weapons could be devised in which the process of fusing hydrogen isotopes into common helium would produce a thousand times more energy than the Hiroshima Fat Man. The H-bomb would not be easy to build. Its development was dependent upon a nuclear source being subjected to superheat—temperatures approaching those at the sun's surface—and massive neutron bombardment, both at the precise microsecond of maximum "supercritcality."

Dr. Jameson looked at Link. "Do you understand what I mean by the term *critical*?"

"A critical mass," Link recited, "is the smallest amount of fissionable material—such as uranium or plutonium—that will sustain a nuclear reaction."

"Yes. You need a critical mass for a nuclear reactor, and get it by removing buffers from between rods of uranium. That creates heat, which circulates water, which drives a turbine and so forth. To explode a fission weapon, you don't sustain a reaction, but multiply it to get maximum energy release. To get that, the mass must become so dense we call it *super*critical."

"Give 'em hell, Harry" Truman was concerned about whether to proceed with the superbomb. No one had tried showering plutonium with so many neutrons, or superheated it at the instant of supercriticality. J. Robert Oppenheimer, who had directed the Manhattan Project, felt a stupendous burst of uncontrollable radioactivity might be unleashed. Others predicted mankind might be devastated by a disaster similar to the one that brought about the extinction of the dinosaur.

Those things made the president pause.

America's nuclear programs were controlled by two agencies: the Atomic Energy Commission, responsible for general research, and the Armed Forces Special Weapons Project, established for military applications. AFSWP's scientists offered to disprove the concerns— using weapons only a tenth of the size of Fat Man and for the first time conducting the tests underground. The military had found the right places, three deep, isolated, long-abandoned mineshafts in Nevada.

President Harry told them to proceed but to take no chances.

The army post was hastily built. Prototype MB–1 Genie air defense missile warheads were flown in to the dry lake bed and prepared to be lowered into the mine shafts, each accompanied by a Jergen neutron gun and a chemical-oxygen flash generator. Radiometry equipment was placed at key locations above ground. Test animals were caged near the entrance to the first mine to determine the effect on living tissue. Two warheads would be exploded. A third was available in the event a test was invalidated. Security was absolute.

The week of the first test, the Nevada state governor was given a briefing that in the interest of national security a number of devices would be detonated somewhere in the state, sometime in November. They would pose no hazard to human or animal life.

They were several hundred feet above the desert floor when Jameson halted the golf cart in front of the first sturdy wooden building. It sported large double doors, and a forklift was parked nearby. On a small, nondescript sign was stenciled *B–1*.

"Welcome to Break-a-Heart One," Jameson said. "On the twentieth of November, 1949, a Genie warhead was set off seven hundred and nineteen feet below us. The results were unusable because of late activation of both the neutron and heat generators. There was minimal radiation leakage. The monkeys were upset by the rattling of their cages, but they were otherwise fine."

As the cart was set into motion, Link observed the sprawling community of Stagecoach five miles distant. Nearer was the dry lake bed and, east of it, the tiny pony express station.

They stopped before a second building on the mountainside. This sign read *B–2*.

"They readjusted timing circuits and detonated the second device on November twenty-ninth. The test went as advertised, except one instrument showed the neutron gun had fired a few microseconds early, so the third test was called for." He released the brake, and as they drove forward, explained that the test had produced a slight increase in instantaneous radioactivity but not enough to affect the monkeys' health.

When they stopped, Dr. Jameson stared at a small building, identical to the others. "Break-a-Heart Three," he said. "I've spent most of my adult life trying to reveal her secrets."

Without warning a sense of foreboding swept over Link. Only with considerable effort did he manage to ask: "That . . . third blast . . . was different?"

"Yes." Jameson stared at the closed door. "All preparations were carefully made, taking into consideration everything learned on the first two. Nels and Piers Jergen, two brothers from Denmark who had invented the neutron gun, made miniscule timing adjustments. Then, at four a.m. on December ninth, the warhead was detonated in precise harmony with the gun and the heat generator." He pointed at the building. "All test animals in the mine shack died within minutes from a burst of radiation so powerful that the ionization chambers of the radiometry instruments were destroyed. Nine military personnel and three scientists were nauseated from atomic poisoning, and they'd been in bunkers fully a mile distant. A bulge had formed on the south side of the mountain. From seismic measurement, they learned that the explosion's force had been seven times the predicted yield. We can be thankful the mountain contained it."

"How did—" Link stopped cold, for the uneasy sensation became stronger.

Fred Jameson noted his discomfort. "It happened a long time ago, Mr. Anderson."

Link brought a hand to his face, shook his head to clear it. "I'm sorry. Go on."

Jameson looked at him longer to confirm he was okay, then continued. "The project manager, an army brigadier general named Spearman, ordered a fourth Genie warhead to be detonated concurrently with heat and neutrons—but at the Pacific test range, with personnel in a battle cruiser thirty miles distant. He also directed that the three mineshafts be rebored."

Link was recovering from the strange bout of anxiety, but slowly.

"One by one the shafts were opened, and the radiation measured. At B–One and B-Two they found residual levels within normal bounds. But here at B-Three it was quite different." Jameson's voice lowered to an almost reverential awe. "There was absolutely *no* trace of radiation, not a single milliroentgen. Nothing. Nil. As if something had eaten it up."

"But there'd been so much. That seems impossible."

Dr. Fred Jameson nodded, staring at the small building with its nondescript sign. "*Something* negated the radioactivity, Mr. Anderson. Even the natural radiation found in the rock strata was reduced to zero."

"Still?"

"A very small background reading has returned. Not much."

"So what did General Spearman do about it?"

"AFSWP went on with their development of the H-bomb. AEC took over this site. When they went out of business they passed it on to the Department of Energy."

"And now you're trying to duplicate the phenomenon?"

Jameson smiled. "Precisely. Not the explosion, of course, but the rest of it. Learn what caused the effect that day in 1949, and use it to treat the dangerous garbage from our reactors, render obsolete nuclear weapons harmless, neutralize sludge pools at Hanford that are so radioactive humans don't dare even approach. Eliminate the nightmare mankind has built in the last hundred years, and make the world safe for our grandchildren."

"It sounds terribly difficult." Link did not add that it also sounded fishy and in violation of several laws of nature.

"If we were to start from the beginning it might be impossible in our lifetime, but we're standing on the shoulders of physicists who have investigated it for the past half-century. Scientists like myself, and others who contributed and suffered so much."

"Suffered?"

"Last year we engaged Dr. Piers Jergen, one of the brothers who perfected the original neutron gun. He'd had the misfortune to be born abroad, and during the McCarthy years, when America feared communists were lurking behind every rock, he lost his security clearance, then the esteem of his fellow scientists. His brother killed himself, and Piers took demeaning jobs to feed himself. Three decades passed before he was accepted again and able to return to work at Lawrence Laboratory, trying to explain the phenomenon. In 1994, he presented a classified paper about his hypotheses at a symposium attended by our country's foremost scientists."

"Vindication at last?"

"I'm sure he felt some of that. His paper concerning the effects of low and medium speed neutron bombardment of actinide metals—including uranium and plutonium—was received with skepticism. There'd been other theories about accelerated depletion, but . . ."

He noted Link's bewildered expression. "One explanation of what happened in 1949 is called accelerated depletion, often referred to as A.D. It involves decreasing the half-life of radioactive material from thousands of years to a much shorter period. Pierre Curie mentioned it in 1898, and Einstein again in 1921."

Link nodded for him to continue, although he did not understand.

"While Dr. Jergen's paper wasn't seriously considered, it generated interest. I was intrigued, because I'd been coming to the same conclusions, that A.D. was the only explanation of what had happened here. But when Jergen's new reaction device—his invention to prove his work—was tested the following year, an assistant received a lethal dose of radioactivity."

"He died?"

"Unfortunately, yes. Dr. Jergen tried to explain that he'd failed to follow established procedure, but all backing for his experiment was withdrawn and he was terminated. A ridiculous response, considering the importance of what he was doing."

Link pondered that. "And you're testing his theory?"

"We've looked at various theories and hypotheses surrounding accelerated depletion, but no, we're not quite ready to test. Dr. Jergen was *close* in his assumptions and so was I, but our work needs refinement." Jameson paused. "But of course, there's no way his name can appear on published results, or even be officially associated with either NEL or the Weyland Foundation."

"If it works, he won't receive credit?"

"Too many remember his background. Some believe he actually *was* some sort of spy, and *everyone* recalls the Berkeley disaster. If we included his name, we could expect delays and questions that could impact what we're trying to do. In the longer term, he'll be rewarded, of course. I'll see to it."

"But in the meantime, whose name *will* go on the project?"

Jameson lifted his shoulders in a helpless shrug, sighed. "Mine, I suppose."

"Does he understand that?"

"Certainly. It's not as if I'm going behind his back. Dr. Jergen came to *me* last year, shortly after the Weyland Foundation inspectors left, and said he wanted to bring himself and his two colleagues aboard. He wanted his hypothesis proven using his reaction device, but although he'd found initial funding, he required our facilities . . . and my expertise, of course."

"He had found the funding?"

Jameson raised an eye. "When you return to New York, I suggest you ask your people about it. The left and right hands of an organization really *should* know what the other is doing."

Link recalled what Shelby had said. "You think the Weyland Foundation provided it?"

"I'm quite sure of it. One of his associates said a proviso was that the source not be identified, and that's understandable, considering Jergen's reputation. But Piers himself confirmed it was from your foundation, and he had no reason to lie."

"I'll check it out," Link said. Today, as soon as he got back to the Barn. He did not like being blindsided. "If you have the funding, what do you need from us now?"

"That money's almost exhausted. Twelve million-five doesn't go far on an intensive project like this." Jameson brightened, smiled. "But just think of the discovery. For years Dr. Jergen and I worked on parallel paths. Competitors, so to speak. Now together we're refining the formulae for the divisions of slow and medium-speed subatomic particles."

It was way over Link's head. "And you're close to a breakthrough?" he asked.

"We'll begin testing in six months. This afternoon you'll receive a talk-through of what we'll be doing. I think you'll be impressed." Dr. Jameson smiled. "Perhaps even impressed enough to recommend renewed funding for next year's experimentation."

Link didn't comment. As they started down the mountain, Jameson explained they were using the same structures, renovated of course, erected by the Corps of Engineers in 1949. Five were inhabited by the study groups, another contained a radiometry laboratory, two warehoused radioactive substances to be used in the experiments, and two more were used as dormitories for those who slept over. The security people, the woman he'd seen and three others, did necessary cooking and housekeeping, since with the automation they had so much idle time on their hands.

"Our technical personnel are organized into five collegia, groups of equals who share common goals. Each collegium has a spokesman, but there's no team captain or leader."

It seemed an odd arrangement, Link thought. He was accustomed to a disciplined approach to management that was likely disdained by the scientific community.

"Collegia Beta and Gamma examine the suitability of various short and mid-term storage locations. Delta investigates extraterrestrial concepts, like using old ICBMs to fire waste into the sun. Those three briefed your Mr. Runyon four months ago."

"And the other two?"

"Our work is classified. Alpha consists of myself and three colleagues. Epsilon has Piers Jergen and two associates. They're working on test preparations. In January all but Alpha will be removed from the site so we can concentrate solely on A.D. experimentation."

"What about Epsilon? Dr. Jergen and his people?"

"The Department of Energy will bring in observers, so they'll be . . . ah . . . relocated."

"The pariahs."

"Only those with problematic backgrounds would work with Dr. Jergen after the accident." He paused. "I'm being frank, Mr. Anderson. Others might hide unsavory details, but I want you to understand us. Dr. Jergen and his associates may be pariahs, but they're brilliant. Dr. Juliette LaCoste, for instance, was considered the most gifted nuclear physics scientist at Berkeley. After a scandal she was removed from her teaching post, but her brilliance is undiminished." Jameson nodded at the buildings below. "Are you ready to go down?"

"First a question. Have you corrected the safety violations our people found?"

"Mr. Anderson, we've had two years of research experimentation without a blemish. No accidents and no incidents. We're extremely proud of our safety record."

"Aren't hazard signs required wherever radioactive material is contained or stored?"

"You'll find them in the warehouses and laboratory."

"But not on the building exteriors, or on the fences and grounds, or even on the barrels of material being flown in? Also, aren't double fencing and roving patrols required at nuclear storage facilities?"

Dr. Jameson's expression turned almost unfriendly. "We're not classified as a storage facility. Anyway, the same government that requires those also demands that we keep everything secret. That's a proviso to our being able to use the site. According to their records there were no underground nuclear detonations in 1949."

"Only earthquakes," Link said. "The big rumble, the locals call it."

"Yes. I concur with the government, by the way. We mustn't release *any* of this prematurely." He turned the cart around, and they started down.

1:05 P.M.

Link, Dr. Jameson, and two others were gathered in the main laboratory, watching and listening as Dr. Adam Russo, assistant to Dr. Piers Jergen and member of the Epsilon collegium, explained the Jergen Reaction Device. Russo was fiftyish, prissy and correct, with sagging shoulders, protruding belly and dark, slicked-back hair. He spoke in a whispering tone that was difficult to hear, and for no good reason, Link found himself disliking the man.

Russo hefted a metal cylinder, ten inches in diameter and thirty in height, turned it so they could see it was precisely machined, and placed it on the table. "Please note its resemblance to a beverage dispenser," he said, "which is why—no slight meant to Dr. Jergen's brilliant work—we call them coffeepots." He made an irritating *heh-heh* sound. "Unloaded, the titanium shell and internal electronics weigh only twenty-nine pounds, meaning it is easily transported."

As he droned on, Link noted that Piers Jergen, a drawn and quite elderly man, looked on from the rear of the room, neither smiling nor reacting.

Dr. Russo held up a remote control and ceremoniously pressed a side button. Two plates slid back, one at the top, the other at the bottom. "We call the reservoirs R-One and R-Two, and in those we place the radioactive substance. Our calculations conclude that four kilograms of Pu–239 placed in each will be minimally sufficient, so we'll start with that amount." He placed a gray bar, marked *Inert,* into each reservoir, and pressed the button again. The covers slid over the fake plutonium.

He displayed a six-inch cube. "A miniaturized descendent of the Jergen neutron gun. The first units used tritium, a hydrogen isotope. Today we use californium, a man-made metallic element created in 1952 that literally spews neutrons when properly excited." Russo pushed and the square snapped into place. "The loaded coffeepot weighs sixty-one pounds." He pressed button one on front of the remote control. A whirring sound emanated.

"R-One and R-Two are moving," he said, "bringing the plutonium together in the eye of the gun." The sound stopped. "When the mass density achieves a critical state, the air glows with a blue iridescence." He pressed button two on the remote. "You would hear a humming sound as the neutron gun activates, flooding the critical mass with slow and medium-speed neutrons."

Russo stepped back then as Dr. Jergen came forward, reached out, and touched the top of the metallic device. His voice was old, brittle. "When the critical mass is bombarded by the perfect mix of subatomic particles, there is a sudden, dramatic change. The glow becomes vivid, and the radiation surges—rises, rises, poises like a young woman about to reveal her beauty—and then dramatically begins to drop as the plutonium depletes at a thousand, fifty thousand, then two hundred thousand times its normal rate." His voice was aquiver with emotion. "The radiometric readings free-fall. Down to a thousand roentgens, to five hundred, to one hundred and then past even normal background . . . to absolute *zero!*"

Dr. Jergen's tensed body relaxed, as if he were returning to the mundaneness of normal life. His voice lowered. "All of that will happen when we achieve accelerated depletion."

He pressed another button, labeled *safe.* After another, longer whirring sound, the covers opened. "Once we've achieved A.D., the previously deadly plutonium will be no more toxic than common lead." He held up the two bars of fake material. "And mankind will benefit."

Link regarded Jergen, and asked casually, "Do you really think it can work?"

Jergen glared, as if dealing with a student who had not listened. But to Link, it was all smoke and mirrors using a neat prop. "What you explained was conceptual. Can it work?"

"You *fool*," Jergen exploded. "You *heard* about Break-a-Heart Three, and now—"

"Piers!" Jameson exclaimed. He rose, waited as the older man stalked to the rear of the room, and turned to Link. "We believe very sincerely that it will work. In fact we're staking our reputations on the fact that the tests will succeed, and reputations, Mr. Anderson, are the lifeblood of a scientist's world."

He inserted a VCR tape into a player. "But can they be done safely, you ask?" He pressed PLAY. There was no preamble, no credits or title. The screen was dark, then bright lights illuminated, and the camera slowly panned in a 360–degree sweep. The walls were curved and smooth, colored a milky white hue that glittered eerily in the camera's light.

"This is the bottom of Break-a-Heart One, where the first underground explosion occurred. We're setting up a robotic laboratory there. There's no human access, only a thirty-inch diameter, almost vertical borehole. The lab will be expensive and difficult to construct— robots setting up other robots. But the A.D. experiments will entail extremely high surges in radioactivity, and we refuse to compromise safety.

"You'll note that it's a flattened sphere, a distorted bubble in the natural silica melted by the heat of the nuclear detonation. B-One and B-Two are small. B-Three is much larger, because of the greater intensity of the blast. All three are wired for video and control. The first experiments will be in B-One, the final ones in B-Three so radiation measurements can be precise."

The camera focused on a coffeepot like the one on the table. A robotic arm hovered over two gray bars of metal that looked much like the ones they'd seen but bore yellow-on-white radioactive-material symbols.

"Only you, the Secretary of Energy, and a very few others know about this," said Jameson. "With appropriate funding, we'll be ready for the first experiments in January when we'll have the calculations done, and the formulae are perfected for the coffeepot."

"Six months? What about all the plutonium I just saw in your warehouse?"

"That's coming from an ongoing weapons dismantling program. There's a concern that we may not be able to get our hands on it later," said Jameson.

"We're talking about eight kilos of plutonium per experiment, but you've got several hundred kilos stockpiled. Why so much?"

Jameson sighed with exasperation. "We've had no incidents, no accidents, nothing of that nature. Why are you so concerned about safety?"

"Because," said Link, "you can't *get* too safe when you're handling nuclear material."

"Of course," Jameson hastily agreed. "I'll look into it."

Dr. Jergen snorted at the back of the room. Link glanced over and watched as the elderly man made a production of walking from the room.

Jameson shook his head. "Please don't take offense. The members of the Epsilon collegium have been working night and day, sleeping and eating here and hardly leaving."

"Yes," said soft-spoken Adam Russo, also rising to leave. "There's much to do."

Jergen's other associate, Dr. Juliette LaCoste, was a severe-looking woman in her early forties. She took her feet. "I must go too. We're working on a troublesome algorithm."

Link regarded her, remembering that Jameson had said she was particularly brilliant. "Dr. LaCoste, do you truly believe you can reduce radioactivity?"

"It was done during the 1949 test. All we have to do is recreate the phenomenon."

"But we must have proper funding," Jameson reminded Link.

The two Epsilon scientists departed, and Link was left alone with Fred Jameson. He examined the device they'd called a coffeepot. "How many of these do you have?"

"Five," said Jameson. "The old prototype and four new, improved ones."

"The cost?"

"About three hundred fifty thousand each."

Link's eyes widened.

"A bargain," said Jameson. "Then there are the neutron guns—subatomic particle emitters, to be accurate. Those can be used only once. They run about one-seventy."

"Thousand?" Link asked incredulously. "Each?"

At three o'clock, Link was in a helicopter, looking out the window as it lifted off, trying to digest what he'd seen and heard. Jameson had said there would still be critical questions after they achieved the A.D. phenomenon, which might take years of testing, such as how the coffeepots could be enlarged to take greater quantities of nuclear trash. American reactors alone generated eight tons of it per day. The one thing that did not waver was his certitude that it could be done.

Link was surprised—it had definitely not been boring—and pleased that he'd been able to understand most of it. Yet he also remembered the intense feeling that something was terribly amiss. That had been at Break-a-Heart Three, the site of the phenomenon.

He decided that after Gary was found and he'd talked all of this over with the experts at the foundation, he must come back for a deeper look at what was going on at NEL.

14

Lincoln Anderson drove to the Barn thinking of the NEL project and if it worked how it could serve as a sort of broom, cleaning up after man's century of tinkering with the atom.

Without a waste problem, nuclear reactors presented a great solution for an electricity-hungry planet. He also envisioned the neutralization of weapons stockpiles—perhaps an end to the capability. The thought of a safer planet made funding by the Weyland Foundation seem appropriate. It was the sort of benevolent research that *should* be done.

Especially since it seemed they'd already funded part of it. Or had they? It seemed odd that Frank hadn't mentioned it. Other things about the NEL project troubled Link. The lack of proper warning signs was bothersome, as was the fact that no one was leveling with the local citizenry. People had a right to know what was happening in their backyard.

Another concern had been brought up as Fred Jameson had taken him to the helipad. The formulae—algorithms for the computers imbedded in the coffeepots—that Alpha and Epsilon were perfecting were extremely complex. In January, prior to each test, they would be entered into a computer that converted them to numerical settings, and the settings would then be electronically uploaded into the coffeepots. The NEL manager was so concerned that their secrets might be leaked to another company that he kept only a single copy of the latest formulae, and that was locked in his safe. Only he knew the combination. Security maintained a vigil on Jameson's office, but Link had suggested that copies be maintained at other locations.

His recommendation had not been well received.

As he pulled into Gary's driveway, he felt rivulets of sweat—the only air conditioning the pickup possessed was a pair of opened windows—coursing down his chest. The temperature was holding in the high nineties. Tomorrow it was to be hotter yet, creeping past the hundred mark.

It was a good time to consider moving on.

Link arranged a towel over the seat to ward off the sun's rays and went inside, where the swamp cooler blasted moist air into the living room. He then trotted upstairs. The computer screen showed Erin's hello, and the blinking display on the telephone answering machine showed that two messages had been received.

He pressed the PLAY MESSAGES button. "Link, Cal Admire. I got a call from Ray Watt. The Reno police found Gary's Bronco at the airport long-term parking lot at one this afternoon. Since it's not exactly a crime to leave your vehicle there, I guess all we can do is wait until he shows up. If you think of anything, give me a call."

So Gary had gone to the airport. Link glanced at the lawyers' letter. The phone number written on its margin was for Reno Air, which had a daily flight to Philadelphia. If two plus two equaled four, Gary was in Philadelphia.

The second message was from Gary's publisher, asking when the manuscript would be ready. They were anxious to receive it. Again Link wondered about Gary's sense of responsibility. He stared out the window, thinking about leaving.

Motion drew his attention. Across the field two shapes merged, a large, lumbering animal and a small gray one. The coyote whirled and yelped so loud it was audible at the distance, then dashed away. The huge dog trotted after it for a few steps, then stopped, panting, head hanging. It stared where the coyote had disappeared, then settled clumsily into the green alfalfa.

Aristotle?

The telephone rang shrilly, and he picked up. "Link Anderson."

"It's Shelby. How did your visit go?"

"It was revealing. Where are you?"

"About two miles away. I spent the afternoon setting up the office here. Actually it's just a room off a water-table measurement shack, but its going to do just fine."

"Can you come over? There's something I'd like you to see."

"Five minutes," she said cheerfully, and hung up. No questions. Just like that.

There was nothing more to see in the field, and he wondered at the wisdom of approaching a hungry animal, regardless of how domesticated it had been.

He sat at the computer, with its blinking asterisk, and typed: *Link here.

This time he waited a full minute before words scrolled down.

What was on the painting you didn't like?

*A couple of sissies, he typed.

The computer went through its blinking as the encryption program loaded.

Actually they were cherubs, but that's close. Whatcha need?

*Find out if anyone in Habitat Earth or elsewhere in the foundation funded a research grant for a scientist named Piers Jergen. Frank might be a good source.

Will do. Anything else?

*Yes. How are you getting along with the FBI?

Great.

*The police found Gary's car at the Reno airport parking lot. I'd like it checked. See if there's any sign of foul play. Look for computer disks. Also like to know where he flew to last Thursday.

The bureau can do the first part and I'll do the last. Gary *Runyan*, right? Give a description.

*It's spelled *Runyon*. Bright red hair, pug nose, med. height & build, talks a lot, thick glasses. Link heard the roar of the Corvette's engine, and added: END

The screen fluttered and went dark.

Link glanced where he'd left the notepad pages, as if

they might have magically reappeared. They had not. He started downstairs, wondering why anyone would go to the effort to break in and take them, perhaps when he'd gone to Virginia City or while he'd gone to the Admires' for breakfast. He'd come to the decision to trust Shelby. Part of his rationale was the favorable report, and part because Marie had been a good judge of character and the two women had been friends. Then there was the more whimsical fact that he *wanted* to trust her.

Link opened the sliding door as she emerged from her car, clad in a cotton blouse, jeans, and hiking boots.

"I just saw a large dog out in the field trying to run down a coyote."

"Aristotle?"

"Maybe." He described the animal. Mottled brown. Big. Slow.

"That's him, Link."

"I'm not sure we should go out there. He didn't look well, and he's obviously hungry."

"Aristotle wouldn't harm a fly."

"He was sure as hell trying to harm that coyote."

"The poor guy's probably starving. Take me to him."

Link walked toward the perimeter road, and she fell in beside him.

"He looked sick?" she asked.

"Or injured."

They circled the field to a point closest to where he'd last seen the animal, then walked into the green and still-moist-from-watering alfalfa.

Link saw movement, heard a whine, then a convincing growl. "Stay back," he warned.

"Aristotle?" Shelby called out.

The growling stopped. She called him again, and they heard a thumping sound. When they cautiously approached, Link eyed a massive animal so bedraggled it could hardly be classified as canine, tail thumping weakly against the ground.

"Oh, God!" Shelby cried. She rushed forward and had her arms about the huge dog's muzzle before Link could warn her away.

Dried blood was matted in the dense hair of the animal's chest.

"He's hurt," he cautioned.

"Poor Aristotle," she said sadly, tears streaking her cheeks.

Link knelt, and the big dog eyed him warily. Shelby touched Link's arm. "He's a friend, Aristotle." The dog visibly relaxed and thumped its tail again.

"We've got to get him to the vet," she said.

"Yeah." Link stood. "I'll bring the pickup."

"While you're at the Barn call Dad," she said, and recited the number. "Ask him to get hold of the vet in Dayton, and tell him its an emergency."

As he strode away, Link decided that Shelby was good in emergencies.

On the phone, Cal was quick to respond. "Just bring him here. We'll do the rest."

Link went into Gary's bathroom, scooped up an armful of towels and deposited them into the truck bed for padding, then drove around the perimeter road. When he was abeam of Shelby, he turned directly into the tall grass and proceeded to make his own trail.

As he crawled out, Shelby was still sitting, holding Aristotle's massive head and talking to him. "He's breathing in gasps," she said. "I don't know if he's going to make it, Link."

Link lowered the tailgate, then went back and cautiously knelt. When he picked him up, Aristotle grunted in obvious pain, then licked his arm.

"Just a little longer, Aristotle," Shelby pleaded as Link laid him in place. She crawled in back and soothed the animal as he latched the tailgate and walked around to the cab.

At the Admires', Link carried Aristotle inside and deposited him onto a pile of blankets Sally had prepared on the screened porch. The dog had hardly settled when Cal came in, leading a youthful man with a medical bag.

"I'll need a pail of water," the vet said. He knelt and went to work cleansing the wound. "He was shot," he announced a bit later. "The bullet came out under his front leg. A lung's collapsed."

"Will you take him to the clinic?" Sally asked.

"I'd rather not move him again. If he makes it through the next few days, which is very iffy, I'll bring him in for x-rays."

"Good," Sally said firmly. "I want him right here where I can keep an eye on him."

The brindled boxer hovered nearby, looking on.

"Where Maggie and I can keep an eye on him," Sally corrected.

By the time the vet left, Aristotle had been sutured, pumped full of antibiotics, fed nutrients and watered, and was sleeping. Sally brought in a battered rocking chair and her needlepoint, a mat for Maggie the boxer, and settled nearby.

"Let's go over to the saloon for a burger," Cal said. "I could use a drink."

Sally shushed him, and made a motion for them to leave.

Link and Shelby followed Cal to the Misfits Saloon, which was abustle with happy-hour customers. Inside they found seats at the bar near a life-sized poster of Marilyn Monroe. Clark Gable grinned at them from nearby.

Cal introduced a man named Bob as owner and light-fingered bartender. He had a head of white hair, a matching goatee, and a wide grin. "Gary back?" he asked.

"Not yet." Cal pointed to a video camera mounted at the far corner. "That's new."

"Not really. The local Nevada Bell repairman came by a couple months back. He moonlights and sells the things. I got it secondhand and dirt cheap. First week I caught one of the barmaids with her fingers in the till, so it's already paid for itself."

"How about a beer?" Cal asked. "And let me see you open it, so I'll know you didn't water it down."

"We got a policy about serving grouches. Costs 'em double."

Two men several seats down the bar stared at Link

with open hostility. He idly observed their glares, then turned back to Cal and Shelby.

Bob left to fetch beers for Cal and Link, a vodka tonic for Shelby.

"Aristotle was shot," Shelby repeated with disbelief. "He's so friendly, I can't believe anyone could have been frightened by him."

"It's also hard to believe Gary would leave him." Cal told her about the Reno police finding Gary's Bronco at the airport.

"That's not the Gary I know," she said. "Something's bad wrong."

The two men down the bar whispered together, then one of them, a large, barrel-chested man with a Copenhagen cap perched back on his head, grinned and nodded. The other one, skinny and lanky, looked at Link, then quickly averted his eyes.

Deputy Ray Watt came into the room—fancy-dressed in a pristine black hat with a silver band, gaudy shirt, and shiny boots—saw them, and sauntered over.

"The vet waved me down and told me about Aristotle."

"Then you ought to be out looking for who did it," Cal groused.

"Soon as I'm back on duty." Watt beamed a smile at Shelby. "Saw your car down at the water-table station this afternoon."

"I'm setting up a field office there," she said.

"I'll tell the other deputies, so we can keep an eye on it."

"Thanks, Ray."

He grinned as if he'd done something of note, and walked down the bar. The two men greeted Watt, then pushed back from the bar and started outside. Link followed them with his eyes. The big one was six-four, lantern-jawed, and generally mean-looking, the other weasel-like. They stopped at the door, cast him another glance, and departed.

Shelby hadn't noticed. "I still can't believe anyone would shoot Aristotle."

"Someone shot Gary's dog?" Bob asked as he returned with their drinks.

"Yeah," Cal said with an angry scowl, and Shelby started to tell Bob about it.

"I'll be right back," Link said in a low voice.

Shelby nodded, and went on.

Link paused at the old-fashioned swinging doors and scanned. The men were beside his pickup, which he'd parked by Cal's Suburban in the row of vehicles at the back of the lot. When they knelt down out of his view, he went out and walked rapidly across the gravel.

The two were crouched by the front fender, the skinny one removing a clasp knife from a belt holster. The larger man held a pry bar.

"It's not for sale," Link said.

The big man looked up, squinted, then let a smile form. He stabbed the forked end of the bar violently into the door, penetrating the heavy metal. "Damn. Sorry about that," he said, then levered the bar to enlarge the tear. "Damn," he said. "Slipped again."

Link's eyes were fixed on the bar. "You're a clumsy fellow."

"Yeah." The big man jerked the bar out, grinned, and poised for another jab.

"I don't want you to do that," Link said softly.

"Fuck you." The muscles on the forearm bunched.

Link struck quickly, his full weight behind the fist that smashed squarely into the forehead. The big man's jaw went slack and his eyes crossed. Link grasped his shirt front and with effort hauled him to his feet, and pushed him up against the pickup.

"Now you are on my truck," he said, and again thumped him between the eyes.

The big man sagged, so he pulled him upright.

"You are still on my truck," Link said conversationally, and thumped him yet again.

He released him. The big man slid off and lay in a crumpled heap as Link turned to the skinny one, who bleated in terror and scrambled away.

"Dropped your knife," Link called after him, scooped it up and hurled it. The still-folded clasp knife struck the fleeing man on the shoulder. He let out a squeal and ran faster.

Ray Watt had emerged from the saloon with several others, and looked on without comment as the skinny man scrambled into a battered Honda, started up, and fishtailed out of the lot spewing gravel.

Link picked up the crowbar, grasped the big man by the collar, and dragged him toward the still-growing crowd. He released the dead weight at their feet, dropped the bar beside him, and stared down. Finally he raised his eyes and regarded Deputy Watt.

"I don't like people fooling with my truck," he explained, and went inside.

At the bar Cal and Bob were talking, and Shelby was staring moodily at the door.

"What's happening out there?" she asked as he took his seat.

"Not much." Link gingerly lifted and sipped his Heineken. His hand hurt.

The crowd drifted back in, muttering among themselves and looking at Link with a mixture of suspicion and respect. A few minutes later Ray Watt came inside and settled at the bar, took a single drink, and regarded Link with a puzzled frown, as if something did not add up.

"I ordered us Misfit Burgers," Shelby told Link. "You wanted one, didn't you?"

"Sure."

Cal grinned. "I was telling Bob about you being a fighter pilot, in combat and all."

Bob motioned at Link's beer. "It's on the house. I'm a retired army master sergeant."

"Then I should buy you the drink."

A very short, inebriated fellow seated by Cal peered at Link through bleary eyes. "You in Vietnam?"

"Before my time," Link told him.

The man looked puzzled. "Thought he said you was in combat."

"Desert Storm."

"Wasn't much of a war. I was in Vietnam," he said with pride. He began to ramble, explaining how he'd spent his time on river patrols, machine-gunning VC water buffalo.

Link looked past him at a man who had taken a seat in the corner. His gray hair and beard were bushy and unkempt, and he motioned at Bob for a drink in a tired gesture. The eyes that peered from the wrinkled face were milky blue but alive and constantly moving.

"The hermit," Shelby said in a low voice.

The rheumy but alert eyes swept the room, rested briefly on Link, then Shelby, and proceeded on. Bob approached him and he mumbled his order, yet it seemed the eyes hardly registered the bar owner's presence.

A neatly dressed middle-aged woman seated by him spoke, but he didn't reply.

Link remembered Shelby saying he lived in the small shanty on the hillside behind the Barn. From his vantage he could see the place clearly, and Link wondered if he might have noticed something out of the ordinary the previous week.

The woman spoke to the hermit again, but he continued ignoring her. He was a strange one, and Link wondered if the oddness was because of his lonesome life or if eccentricity drove him to solitude. Chicken-or-egg stuff.

The drunk beside Cal realized they weren't listening to his stories about his three Vietnam tours, so he turned to a fellow on his other side and began all over.

Shelby nudged Link. "The woman beside the hermit's Irene Staples. I told you about her, remember?"

"The lady who looked after her mother while the world passed her by."

"Yes, but I talked with her this morning, and she's really pulled her act together. She's taken a job at a doctor's clinic in Carson City, and wants to save enough to go back to school. Forty-nine years old, but she's determined. I wouldn't bet against her."

Link studied the bad-luck lady. Beside her the hermit finished his drink and got to his feet. He avoided others as he walked from the room, carefully favoring a hip.

Bob came down the bar at the same time their charbroiled burgers arrived.

"Fellow down there told me what happened outside, Link. Sorry about that. People here don't usually fool with other folks' vehicles."

"What happened?" Shelby asked, and Bob gave her a generally accurate account.

"You did that to Mike Bragg?" she asked incredulously.

"I'm tired of people trying to destroy my truck," Link said.

Cal was grinning. "Couldn't have happened to a better guy."

"Yeah, but Mike's *big*," Shelby said in awe. "Everyone's afraid of him."

"Mike had a girlfriend named Heidi Gage who rents from me," Cal explained. "Used to beat her up all the time, then he went to Reno to live with her daughter. Showed back up last week, but Heidi had took off someplace, so he came to me and tried to get a key to her place." Cal hmphed. "Fat chance."

Link wondered if he shouldn't have thumped him one more time.

A voice spoke evenly from behind Link. "I saw the damage done to your truck."

It was Ray Watt. Others in the bar watched with mixed expressions. A number wore frowns. Consorting with the enemy?

Watt took a breath. "I'll get him to pay for repairs."

"I'll handle it," Link said.

The deputy cocked his head. "Someone passed a note around at a Muckers meeting the other night saying you were a federal agent coming to make trouble for us."

Link didn't respond.

"That true? You work for the government?"

"I've got friends there. Working stiffs like the rest of us."

Watt went fishing. "How about you? DEA or ATF? You mentioned the FBI. That it?"

When it was apparent that Link was ignoring him, Cal spoke. "Ray, instead of hassling my friend, you ought to be out looking for whoever shot Aristotle."

"I talked to Mike Bragg when he woke up. Said he hadn't shot a dog or cut anyone's tires. Said this was the first time he'd seen Anderson, and when he heard he was a troublemaking fed, he got upset. I believe him."

Cal snorted. "Mike's dumb as dirt and mean as a snake."

"Mentally disadvantaged," Shelby interjected from the sidelines.

Both Cal and Ray turned to her with puzzled looks.

"That's government talk for dumb as dirt," she explained, smiling.

Cal glared at Ray Watt. "*Somebody* cut Link's tires and shoved a gutted coyote in his truck, and that sounds like something your damned Muckers might do."

"Come on. You really believe we'd do things like that?"

"I got out, didn't I? Didn't want anything to do with a bunch who sneak around to hold their meetings and rant about somebody's about to take away their toys."

"We stand up for our Second Amendment rights. It's a citizen's right to bear arms, long as he doesn't do anything illegal."

"Then come out and say it, and quit sneaking around. People'd listen a lot better if you went back to helping kids and stopped burying guns all over the desert."

Shelby gave Link's arm a tug. "I like that song. Let's dance." She led him out to the open area near the pool table where other couples were two-stepping.

"This is not my strong point," Link said as she moved into his arms.

"Humor me. You've got to admit it's better than listening to grown men arguing about an organization so shameless they call themselves Muckers."

Link gave it his best. He was no Travolta, but when the song ended, Shelby held fast. "One more." He glanced at the bar, where Ray Watt was watching, wearing a doleful look.

"I'll leave tomorrow," Link told her.

"So soon?"

"There's still no sign of Gary, and I'm finished at NEL."

"I wish you'd stay longer," she murmured in the husky voice that made him think of pleasant alternatives. *Just friends,* the inner voice reminded him.

The watchers periodically viewed the scene in the crowded bar, but most of their attention was given to reviewing data from their last experiment. The reading had reached 6,329 roentgens per hour, an astronomical figure, and all were convinced they were about to achieve their goal.

The eighth subject's death had come at four hours, twenty minutes. Also impressive.

Adam Russo entered the room and took his seat. After observing Anderson and the blonde geologist for a few quiet moments, he spoke to Juliette LaCoste. "Were you able to break the code they're using with the computer?"

"No," she replied.

He leaned back in his seat, staring at the scene in the saloon. Lincoln Anderson and the geologist were seated, legs touching, she with her hand on his arm. Getting cozy.

"He found the dog," he said, mostly to himself.

The woman also watched. "If we do nothing, he'll leave. I doubt he'll call for help. His type likes to work alone. Anyway, Anderson's too important to deal with the way you did Runyon."

He was starting moodily, feeling his hatred simmer. Thinking she was wrong, that he was definitely going to deal with Anderson. Put him with Runyon, where both of them could rot together. He just could not allow himself to lose control again.

"The Weyland Foundation would send investigators," she said.

"There's too little time for them to do much. We're almost done here," he said. "You'll soon get everything you want."

Dr. LaCoste's demeanor brightened at the thought. "It would be nice if we achieved the A.D. phenomenon first."

"Nice but not necessary," said Russo. "The important

thing is that the device is already deadly enough for our purposes."

"We *must* succeed with A.D.," the old man interjected in his crackling voice.

The soft-spoken man didn't respond, just continued staring at the image of Lincoln Anderson until he was convinced his temper and disposition were well in control. The plan would be difficult enough to achieve, and the next phase would begin very shortly. All that remained here was to improve the formulae, using two more subjects, and deal with Lincoln Anderson.

15

Link was halfway around the alfalfa field for the second time when Cal Admire's Suburban pulled up at the Barn. Shelby emerged from the right seat, looked out and waved, and ducked into the Corvette, which she'd left the previous day. By the time he approached the house she'd driven out of sight, and Cal Admire was leaning on the fender of his Suburban, waiting.

He was huffing and reaching for the towel he'd left on the porch, when Cal nodded sociably. "You do that every morning?" Link nodded, breathless and still not ready to talk. "Shelby had to go into Carson. Some kind of meeting. Still thinking about taking off today?"

He pulled in a deep breath and exhaled it. "Yes." There was no change in his rationale. He would wait for Erin's report, leave a note for Gary, and try to make it as far as Idaho Falls.

"I figured we should go to breakfast over at Dayton. There's a place there that fills a man up, and we can talk."

"I'll have to shower."

"I'll wait."

The Roadrunner Diner served gargantuan omelets and melt-in-your-mouth biscuits that would reduce a dietician to tears. Cal filled him in about Dayton's history— it had been a boisterous mining town, even the territorial capital for a short while before they'd settled on Carson City—then grew silent as they devoured the last morsels.

Cal doused his final biscuit with honey. "Some odd things going on here, Link."

Link waited.

"Ray Watt says Gary was interested in the people dying off, and come to think of it, there have been a few more than normal. County coroner said most of 'em died of a flu bug, but he's not exactly a medical whiz."

"Where could I find out about them?"

"Winchester's the county seat. Ask for Debra and tell her you're my friend."

"I'm out of time here, Cal. I promised the guy I work for I wouldn't be long."

Cal observed him. "How about leveling with me? It's sort of hard to believe you'd interrupt a move and gettin' started at a new job to drive all the way from Montana so you could play a round of golf. Gary told you there was some kind of trouble here, right?"

"No. He just asked for help with something he'd written."

Cal sighed. "I was hoping you might have some ideas."

"Just a lot of questions." Link told him about the encounters with the FBI agent—Cal said he hadn't seen anyone around matching the description—then the diskettes he and Shelby were searching for at locations Gary had called Pony and Big Cat.

"Pony?" Cal muttered, and came to the same conclusion as Link. "His Bronco?"

"Maybe."

"Big Cat?" Cal cocked his head. "I'll think on it."

"I'll leave you my phone numbers in New York. Give me a call if you come up with anything." Link paused, then added, "and when Gary shows up."

"I don't think Gary's *going* to show up."

Link's eyes narrowed.

"You don't understand how much he cared about that dog. Aristotle was his best friend. He said he fell apart after his divorce, and the only thing that perked him up was the pup. Something he didn't say, but you could tell, was that he was still in love with his ex-wife, no matter she'd left him and took everything. Shelby knew, which was one reason she could have him for a friend. She wasn't ready for anything else, and he kept hoping that some way, somehow his ex-wife would take him back."

"You think Gary's dead?"

"There's no way he'd have just left Aristotle while he flew off somewhere. He had a pistol he showed me. Kept it in a drawer next to his bed. I looked for it the other day when I was there, and it was gone. Since he was grieving so hard about his ex-wife, I figured he might have gone out in the desert, shot the dog, and then himself."

"But they found his Bronco at the airport. Someone had to drive it there."

"That's the part that doesn't percolate—which means I'm wrong about it being suicide. Somebody else was involved. Maybe someone who shot Gary and the dog in Stagecoach Valley, since you found Aristotle there, then drove the car to Reno."

"Have you told any of that to Deputy Watt?"

Cal snorted. "He'd screw it up and we'd *never* learn what happened. Reason I'm telling you is so you can add it to your pot when you're thinking of reasons to stay."

Link nodded, wondering if he shouldn't delay until things made more sense, as nothing was doing at the present.

Cal rose to his feet. "And in case you're blind and can't figure it out, Shelby doesn't want you to go." Link started to assure him that they were only friends, drawn together because of Marie, but Cal had already walked to the counter to pay.

They'd driven his pickup because Cal hadn't believed it a good idea to leave it untended with all the rancor against Link still festering. As they descended into his valley, Cal pointed out a network of corrals near the highway.

"Fellow used to raise camels there. Wasn't much of a market for 'em, so he went broke."

There was no end to the novelties to be found around Stagecoach Valley.

As they approached the turnoff, Cal idly picked up

the radiation dosimeter Link had left on the console between the seats and looked at the NEL logo. He muttered that it was a "nice lookin' pen," and put it back.

Back at the Barn, when Cal had departed, Link went
up to the loft.

Hello. Standing By. E. showed on the screen. Erin
wanted to make contact.

*Link here, he typed.

After a short pause: Lawrence's first name?

*Lawrence, he typed, smiling.

The screen convoluted as the program loaded. Then:

Actually it's Leland, but he doesn't use it. I have
information regarding your requests. Last night certain of my "friends" examined the Bronco in the Reno
parking lot. Only prints found were Runyon's, but
steering wheel and handles had been wiped down—
looked like a pro job, they said. Found no diskettes,
but blood (canine, not human) was spattered on right
rear fender.

Vehicle entered parking lot at 9:49 p.m. Wednesday, June 23. I learned the following from Reno Air:
One-way ticket was issued to Mr. Gary L. Runyon for
10:20 a.m. *Thursday.* That was the next day. Tried
paying with his Visa card, but it was over the limit so
he used *cash.* Airliner (Boeing 727) departed at
10:50 a.m., dest. Philadelphia, PA, with someone
using the ticket. They don't remember a description
but he must have shown identification, now an FAA
requirement for all passengers. No luggage checked
through, but may have taken carry-on. I've learned
who sat with Runyon in row 14, and will talk to them.

Link read it through twice. Aristotle had been shot
near the Bronco on Wednesday, then it was driven to
the airport, where a one-way ticket had been purchased
and used Thursday morning. More questions, he
thought, like why one-way, and why had the steering
wheel been wiped off?

*Thanks, he typed, and was about to end the conver-
sation when Erin added more.

I asked Frank about a research grant for Piers Jergen. He says none was given. Habitat Earth people know of him & say his work is crackpot stuff.

Also, I'm supposed to talk with SA Albee in an hour, so stay tuned & be —

Wild lines scrolled across the screen. Then a message flashed:

!!MODEM DISCONNECT. ENCRYPTION PROGRAM AUTO-DOWNLOADING!!

The telephone at his elbow rang. He picked up and heard Erin's voice. "The modem line crashed."

"What was the last thing you were saying?"

"The next word I was going to use was *careful*. Let's drop it for now. Call in a couple of hours on another line at another location."

Be careful, she had wanted to tell him.

He made his decision. There were simply too many unanswered questions, and if Cal was right about Gary being dead or hurt . . . "I'm going to stay for another day or two," he said.

"Tell it to your old wingman. He'll be on with me when you call. Cheers." She hung up.

His "old wingman" was Frank Dubois. Erin hadn't liked talking on the unsecure line and wanted him to call back from elsewhere. Link punched in the numbers for Cal Admire's real estate office. The girl who worked there turned him over to Cal, who had just walked in. When Link made his request, explaining he was having trouble with the phones at the Barn, he was told that an empty office and telephone were available any time he needed them.

Cal was as good as his word. When Link showed up at ten-thirty, he was shown into a back room complete with a desk and phone. Wall plaques showed that it had last been used by a licensed agent named Robert Schilling— who, a photo showed, just happened to be Bob from the Misfits Saloon—in 1988. An inscription recognized Bob for his benevolent service to the Ancient Order of Dirt Muckers. The group's name kept popping up, Link thought as he took his seat and dialed the number of his New York office.

"Twenty-seven-seventy-five," came Erin's prompt reply.

"It's Link."

"Just a sec." He waited. "You're at a place called Admire Real Estate?" she asked.

"You said to call from another location."

"This line's just as dirty, Link. What's going on out there?"

"Shelby said the service is bad."

"I sure wish you'd taken a flip-top so we'd know it was secure."

"Next time. For now, let's assume this line's okay."

"You're the boss," she said, but her tone implied she was unhappy. "I'll hook up with Frank in a minute, but first let's talk about the agent who visited you and called himself Destin Albee. The height, weight, hair, the fact that he's left-handed, and even the birthmark were accurate. I also checked with Avis in Reno, and whoever rented the car also used that name."

"Then it was obviously him."

"Let me finish. The guy who rented the car paid cash, and the bureau issues American Express or Diners Club cards to their agents."

Interesting, he thought. Why cash? So he'd leave no credit card trail?

"And how about this? I just spoke with Destin Albee in Las Vegas. He's been out of the office on a case for the past week but he hasn't been anywhere near Reno or Carson City for the past couple of months."

Out on a case, Link's mind registered. Meaning he could have been anywhere.

"He's never heard of Gary Runyon, and neither has anyone else in either the Vegas or Reno offices. My bureau contacts here confirm that no surveillance has been authorized on him."

"And you believe them all?"

"Darn right. You didn't meet Destin Albee, Link. The man who came to see you was a ringer, like you first thought."

"If the description matches, and he's been away for the past week, I'm not so sure."

Erin sighed. "So now you think it *was* him?"

"Maybe. I'd like to meet him."

"Albee had to leave his office—he was wrapping something up—but he'd like a phone call from you tonight at his home. Around nine o'clock?" She gave him the number.

"I'll call." Perhaps hearing the real Albee would convince him, but a face-to-face meeting would be even better.

"Something else. Albee thinks he knows who your visitor might have been, but he wouldn't tell me. I have my own idea, but I want to hear it from him after you've talked. What he was positive about was that you should be careful. *Very* careful. He repeated that three times."

"Careful about what?"

"Your personal safety. Second subject. I talked with two people seated in the same row with Mr. Runyon on the flight to Philadelphia. Both said he's tall, blond, and unfriendly."

"That's not Gary," Link said, and his heartbeat rate stepped up a notch. Cal Admire was right. Something sinister was going on.

"Your old wingman's standing by in his office. I'll connect him." She went offline.

"Link?" Frank Dubois's voice.

"I'm here."

"Erin briefed me about what she learned. Still no sign of Gary?"

"No. I've decided to stay for a few more days."

"I think we should get the bureau involved."

"That would just slow things down. They're not in love with federal officers here."

"Then I'll send a couple of our people."

"Hold off at least until after I've talked with Albee. I do have a request, though. I'd like an airplane available, and that means I'll need a checkout."

"You name it."

"Something relatively small and slow, with good visibility." If Cal was right, Gary's body might be found in the desert nearby.

Frank was not stupid. His voice turned grim. "You think Gary's *dead*?"

"Maybe. In fact I'd say it's a good possibility."

"I'll have Lawrence call Executive Connections." EC was the charter service—the majority shareholder being Link's stepfather—that managed the aviation needs of the Weyland Foundation."

"One last thing, Frank. There's either a misunderstanding or someone at the foundation really has their wires crossed about this fellow Piers Jergen being funded by the Weyland Foundation. You guys didn't lose track of twelve million dollars, did you?"

"No way. The people downstairs say he's a wacko. If he's involved with NEL, they don't want any part of them either. Anything else?"

"Nothing I can think of," he said, thinking that Jergen and his group were pariahs at the foundation as well.

When Link left the office and told the female real estate agent he was finished, she asked about the clarity of the phone line. She said it had been scratchy, but the phone maintenance man had visited before Link had arrived and replaced a junction box.

Link didn't mention what Erin had said, and told her the line was just fine.

After lunch, Link drove to Winchester as Cal had suggested and found Debra. She remembered Gary Runyon, and gave Link the same plot maps she'd provided the redhead. She then looked up all deaths occurring in Stagecoach during the past month—there'd been six, three from the flu, one from a trailer fire, one from injuries suffered long ago in an automobile accident, and a suicide—and circled the locations.

She told him there were photos of each corpse taken by the officer on the scene. He was interested, but the files were in the office of the coroner, who was out on business.

Back in Stagecoach Valley, Link drove past each address and found them to be in scattered locations throughout the community. Debra had said all the victims had been single, all but one had no family in the area, and all but one was middle-aged. The older one with family nearby was Irene Staples's mother. If he dropped her from the list, the commonalties were significant. The thing that struck him was that the victims had been loners, people about whom no one likely cared. He disliked the cruelty of the thought.

As he pulled around the Barn and parked, Link's attention was riveted on the sliding door, the glass broken, the lawn hose snaked inside. He hurried in. The living room and kitchen were a shambles, with broken furniture tossed about haphazardly. The hose was gushing water that stood an inch deep on the newly renovated hardwood floors.

He dragged the hose out, jogged to the corner to see if anyone was about—he saw no one and no vehicle— and went back in. Damage was limited to the living room, kitchen, and Gary's master bedroom. On the dresser mirror a message was hastily scrawled: FED GO HOME.

As Link went to the utility room, pulled out mop, bucket, and rags, and began the cleanup, he was fast approaching the limit of his patience.

For the third time the soft-spoken man listened to the end of the audio tape. Stared hard at the recorder, wishing he could see them. Lincoln Anderson, Erin Frechette, and most importantly, Frank Dubois. A difficult remembrance, never far from the surface, played in his mind. He was another man, cornered in a St. Petersburg café—watching the third Ivan policeman drop like a stone, desperately swinging his pistol toward the last one. Inwardly screaming curses at himself for allowing it but realizing that after this one he would be able to escape.

New movement in the corner of his eye. Someone with a pistol? Before he could switch his aim point he felt the knee collapse. Heard a pistol's muzzle report. Fell hard and grunted when he hit the floor. Stunned, then slowly lifting the weapon in his hand. Rising up . . .

The same man who had shot him had his hand on the pistol and easily twisted it from his grasp. The Ivan policeman came back and wanted to kill him, but the man would not allow it. Saved his life, their eyes locked, emotion flowing like water in a closed loop pipeline. Emotions raging beyond hatred or love. Frank Dubois.

He knew of Erin—it had taken all of his computer skills to find her identity after she'd discovered his trail through Aalborg. Erin Frechette was dangerous. Too smart. He'd learned about Lincoln Anderson—the close friend of his tormentor—even earlier. Knew that Lincoln Anderson would be physically dangerous and that he must take special care when he dealt with him. The knowledge had made him hesitate when he had gone to see him. Erin and Lincoln. They were doubly dangerous working together and at some point would have to be dealt with.

Now, because of them, there was a threat to the plan. He had erred, shouldn't have used Destin Albee's identity when he'd gone to see Anderson. Now Albee's suspicions were aroused and a minor adjustment to the schedule was required.

You're getting better, Destin, he thought. Two years earlier the man had not noticed even those things going on under his nose. He'd not had a clue. Still wouldn't if it hadn't been for Frank Dubois and his Weyland Foundation.

He switched to the outside view of Runyon's house, where he'd seen the vandal an hour before. Anderson appeared on the porch and dumped a pail of water over the rail. Cleaning up.

"Should have taken the hint and left, Anderson," he said, but he was glad he had not. He telephoned the airport and reserved a seat on a flight. He was lucky, for there were few available.

8:20 P.M.—Las Vegas, Nevada

Destin Albee was moderately large, fit, with graying hair and an air of caution that had not hindered his eighteen-year career. He had trained as an attorney at Cornell University but had never practiced law. Instead he'd gone directly into the employment of the Federal Bureau of Investigation at age twenty-four. He was fastidiously honest, with a penchant for correctness.

Professionwise, his worst flaw had once been his faith in the bureau, and his trust of those appointed above him. No more. Now he took few chances and was suspicious of anyone who might be able to sully his career.

Two years ago he'd been stung when his supervising agent on the Nuc-Safe project in St. Petersburg had proven to be a bigger crook than the people they'd been sent to ferret out. As a result, Destin had undergone the indignities of multiple polygraph tests, questionings, and even mental fitness examinations. Thank God for the intervention of his rabbi and mentor, the Director, Southwestern Region, and thank God he'd needed a SAC at the Las Vegas office. Destin had jumped into the position with vigor, working fifteen-hour days as a norm and sending his wife back east to her parents whenever he took on a tough investigation so he wouldn't be distracted. The marriage was suffering, but he would make it up to her when he knew he was redeemed, which would be when he won his next promotion.

And damn you to hell, Ansel Turpin, for being the asshole monster you are. For Destin knew with every fiber of his being that Turpin had not died in the explosion south of St. Petersberg, with dangerous radioactive material strewn over a half-mile radius. Not only because of the lack of positive identification of the irradiated chunks of flesh they'd found, but also because Ansel Damn-you-to-hell Turpin, was the kind who simply did not die that easily.

And when the woman from the Weyland Foundation had called and told him about the fake agent showing up near Carson City, showing Albee's identification and looking precisely like Destin, he knew that Ansel Damn-you-to-hell Turpin was back to plague him.

Destin ran an angry hand through salt and pepper hair. Glanced at his watch. It was half past eight. Lincoln Anderson would call in thirty minutes. He wanted a drink—deserved one after a week of helping the DEA crew with their big cocaine bust in North Las Vegas that involved big-time crime—but decided to wait until after the call. He would play it smart, get everything possible

out of Anderson before revealing his suspicions about
who he was dealing with. Tell him to watch after his
butt, because Ansel Damn-you-to-hell Turpin took no
prisoners, and also because Destin knew it was smart to
cooperate with the Weyland Foundation.

The telephone buzzed. It was Anderson, who said he'd
flown down for a face-to-face meeting rather than call.
He asked for directions to Destin's home from McCar-
ran Airport.

Destin told him, thinking it was better this way. He'd
get to know him and offer his assistance. It could prove
rewarding to have a top Weyland Foundation executive
on his side, with easy access to directors and attorneys
general, and—he'd heard—even presidents.

Fifteen minutes later the doorbell rang, and Special
Agent Destin Albee set a correct but warm smile on his
face. He prudently looked through the peekhole. The
visitor who stood in the light had dark hair and was
dressed in Western hat and boots.

Destin opened the door and displayed the smile.
"Mr. Anderson?"

They shook hands, and Anderson followed him inside.
There was something . . .

"You're alone?" Anderson asked.

"My wife's in Connecticut. A drink?" He started for
the liquor cabinet.

"I don't drink when I work, Destin. You know that."
The voice had just changed.

Albee turned, paused. Looked at the pistol aimed at
his chest.

"Sloppy work, Destin. I thought you'd improved, with
the new job and all. Still the same dumb jerk, though.
Did you know that's why I wanted you to work for me
in St. Pete?"

Albee's eyes widened. "Ansel?" He breathed rather
than spoke the word.

His visitor lashed out viciously. The heavy pistol made
a cracking sound against the side of Albee's skull—he
cold *hear* the bone fracture—and he grunted and started
down. But Destin was held upright, patted down
thoroughly.

"Now the questions, old friend. Such as why you wanted to talk with a man from the Weyland Foundation? And what you said to Erin the bitch?"

Albee moaned, leaning against Ansel Turpin, knowing he would die.

Turpin shifted the gun to free his left hand. His voice was deep, flint-hard with hatred. "To show you I'm serious, I'm going to pluck out your eyes, Destin."

He tried to speak, but heard only a croaking noise as Turpin's forked fingers approached his vision, plunged and grasped. Albee could feel his eyeballs being wrenched and pried, the pain so unbearable it was numbing. There were wild flashes of light, and Albee heard the screaming almost abstractly, as if the sound came from someone else.

He wanted to fall and writhe about, but could not.

"Pluck's such an old-fashioned word." Ansel Turpin readjusted his grasp, still holding him upright. "You can't see it, but it's quite messy."

He took a breath, screamed again, now almost continuously.

"Stop that, or I'll cut you open now. You shouldn't have talked to the bitch from the foundation, Destin. Surely you guessed that I was alive. Didn't you realize what would happen?"

Stagecoach Valley, Nevada

Link called at precisely nine o'clock from the unused office at Cal's.

The receiver on the other end was picked up after the second ring. "Yes?"

"Special Agent Albee?" he asked.

"So we speak again, Mr. Anderson."

"Then it *was* you?"

"Certainly." The voice held the same rumble. Link remained silent, unprepared for the response. In the background he heard a steady thumping noise, and an occasional wet gurgle.

"You interfered, Mr. Anderson. Even after I told you not to." The voice was calm.

"Where is Gary Runyon?"

"In Philadelphia, perhaps? Actually I've been working on other projects, and your Mr. Runyon is of little interest to me."

"You wanted to speak with me?" Link asked.

"Just to tell you that I'm disappointed at your lack of cooperation. You shouldn't have involved others. I told you to keep the Runyon matter quiet. Now whatever has happened to Mr. Runyon, wherever he may be, rests squarely on your shoulders."

"What do you mean by—"

"Goodbye, Mr. Anderson." Irritation was heavy in the man's tone.

The connection was broken.

Link replaced the receiver, thoroughly vexed. It was as if he and Erin had spoken to two entirely different people.

16

Link had been up late swamping out the Barn. This morning he had arisen slowly, was slothful about his exercises, and made only a single lap of the field, all without remorse for he'd earned a respite. Still in running clothes, he settled agreeably into Gary's easy chair and switched on the television. It was turned to channel eight, Reno. He'd catch up on current events, then shower and maybe go to the Roadrunner for chow and a thinking session about what to do next.

The local news coverage began with a revelation that Reno had been declared one of America's top ten small cities for economic opportunity. Also, the city's largest casino was about to expand, which would impact growth. Next an announcement that a senior FBI agent had been viciously murdered in Las Vegas the previous evening. They showed his official photograph and said he was survived by a wife and both parents.

Destin C. Albee's face was similar to the one Link remembered. He sat stunned as the next picture displayed a ranch-style house festooned with yellow crime-scene ribbon, and a grim-faced FBI spokesman who mouthed a canned statement that the perpetrator would be brought to justice. The camera slued to a female reporter who said the agent had been slain so brutally that there was speculation that the death might be gang-related, possibly linked to a major FBI-DEA cocaine bust announced the previous day. A 911 call from an unknown source had brought the Las Vegas metropoli-

tan police to the home, where they'd found Albee cling-
ing to life, so mutilated he could not be moved.

The program switched to coverage of the commuter
traffic flow around Reno, which allowed Link to realize
he'd been holding his breath and to exhale.

Good Morning America took over the screen, and a
couple of minutes later the national newscaster mentioned the FBI SAC's murder. Link was still staring, trying to correlate what he had just heard with the previous
night's conversation, when the telephone rang.

He switched off the television and went to the kitchen
wall phone.

"Did you hear about Albee?" Erin's voice was
strained.

"Just now. I phoned him last night like you wanted."

She paused. "This line's still corrupted, Link."

"You said the other one wasn't any better."

Erin sighed. "It wasn't."

"Let's blame it on poor maintenance and not worry
about it. Anything more on Albee?"

"I just read the preliminary bureau report. It was horrible, Link. His eyes were removed and his tongue cut
out, then he was eviscerated, and his—his intestines
spread about. When the police arrived he was in *three*
different rooms, and still alive."

"The television reporter speculated it was a gang killing over a dope bust."

"I was told the same by the bureau. That's how some
of the gangs deal with informers so they can control
their turf."

Something plagued Link. "When did they get the
nine-one-one call?" He'd called at nine and Albee had
hung up on him less than a minute later.

She paused to look it up. "Nine-twelve."

Only ten minutes after the hang-up, he decided.

"The police arrived eight minutes later. They went in
at nine-twenty and found him more or less alive. It was
three more hours before a doctor pronounced him
dead."

Link remembered the thumping and gurgling. "I

spoke with the killer." He detailed the conversation. "It was the same voice I heard here. I'm sure of it."

"Ansel Turpin," Erin said in her quiet, sure voice.

He frowned. "Come on, Erin. That's *really* wild speculation."

"Turpin was Destin Albee's boss in the St. Petersburg bureau office. Yesterday when I told Albee someone was using his identity, he believed he knew who it was. I think he was going to warn you that his old boss was involved."

The idea seemed bizarre to Link. "Did he mention Turpin's name?"

"Just that he had an idea who it was, and for you to be careful. I've been looking at the description of your visitor and matching it with Turpin and Albee. Their height and weight were similar—Turpin's an inch shorter. He's ambidextrous and Albee was left-handed. But Albee didn't have a limp and Turpin couldn't fake that part. He was shot in the knee in St. Petersburg. Another identifier is his eyes. You call them intense. He changes the color, even alters the shape, wears thick glasses and corrects them with contacts, but he always uses a two-hundred-watt gaze, missing nothing. That's the observation technique he taught to others at the FBI academy, and I don't think he *can* change it."

"I understand him killing Albee, especially if he somehow learned he was cooperating with us. But why was he interested in Gary?"

"Something he was writing about? Or just the fact that he was once Frank's friend and he despises Frank Dubois?" She paused. "I just thought of something. If Turpin said he had no more interest in your friend Gary Runyon, that may not bode well for him."

Link was staring out at the truck, thinking about her words, when the windshield cracked and spider-webbed, followed by the booming report of a rifle.

"What was that?" Erin asked in soprano.

He forcibly calmed himself and made himself think clearly, as he'd learned to do in emergencies. His voice was cold. "Someone doesn't like me being here. Anything else?"

"That's all I've got, but Frank wants me to transfer you over."

A hole was punched in the hood, followed by another loud report.

"Link, what's happening?"

"Tell Frank I'll call back." He hung up, eyes fixed on the truck as yet another hole appeared in the hood, followed by the gunshot sound. Radiator water drained onto the ground.

Link slid the door partially open and went out, ran to the corner of the Barn, and squinted into the brightness, scanning the hillside. There were no vehicles, and the only building in sight was the hermit's shanty half a mile distant. The shots had come from somewhere closer.

He heard a *spang!* behind him as the pickup was hit again, then the report from somewhere on the hillside; saw movement from behind a cluster of sagebrush, then the barrel of a rifle being withdrawn. He judged the distance to be two hundred yards.

Link's rifle was in the toolbox behind the pickup's cab. He decided against trying to reach it, since it would take him into the shooter's view, and instead carefully memorized the terrain and landmarks surrounding the cluster of sagebrush. Unless he was totally stupid or suicidal, there had to be an avenue of escape for the shooter—he saw no vehicle, so it was likely hidden. He remembered a rough path through the desert off to his left that passed through a depression. It was the logical place to leave it.

He was still clad in olive drab T-shirt and sweatband, dark running shorts, and athletic shoes, which suited his purpose.

First build his confidence. Make him think he's dealing with a frightened klutz.

Link stepped into full view, looked about frantically as if he were anxious and had no clue, then hastily withdrew behind the cover of the house.

Now go for him. He won't expect it.

Out of the shooter's sight he trotted around the Barn, to the other side where he hoped he would not be anticipated. He calmed his breathing and tried to recall the lessons Joseph Spotted Horse had imparted about blending with your background, then bent low and went slowly to the wrought-iron fence near the road. He paused, took a breath, stepped into the open, and continued across to the ditch on the opposite side, careful to avoid abrupt movement.

There was no shot.

He lowered himself and wriggled forward on elbows and shins, staying flat, chest and belly an inch from the hard-crust earth, eyes searching as he continued up the hillside. Moving smoothly and with no sudden motions, trying to blend with stones and brush. Using the terrain and watching for any sign of activity from the shooter's position. Taking long minutes to travel the first hundred feet, then moving faster, still making no hasty movements, covering the next distance quickly as he flanked the shooter's position. The name Ansel Turpin came to mind, but he suppressed it. If he'd somehow survived, he would be cagey. This was a fool.

He was abeam of, then beyond the shooter's position, continued farther and then angled toward the crude path where a vehicle could be hidden. The shooter came into his view, and he stopped and watched him craning his neck, peering first at the Barn where he'd last seen Link, then at the road as if anticipating a vehicle. He turned and looked toward the hidden path, as if thinking of going there but unable to make up his mind, then turned back and continued scanning the Barn.

Link wondered if he shouldn't do as planned, find the vehicle and wait for the shooter to come to him, but decided on a bolder route. He began his approach, moving smoothly and silently, making no abrupt motions. As he came closer, he realized what Joseph Spotted Horse had meant when he'd said warriors had to "think like the earth" they used for masking. Do not make movements that threaten. Become one with the earth. Be a branch, a tree, in this case a stone or clump of sagebrush.

When he was ten feet distant, Link rose to his feet, staring at the back of the person who had caused him grief and done so much damage. He stepped close, reached forward, and clamped his hand down on the rifle in the man's grip.

The shooter turned with gaping mouth, eyes wide with fright. Young, no more than sixteen, skinny, with a scraggly beard and bloodshot eyes with pupils like pinpricks. Trembling, head moving in abrupt jerks. Cranked up. Probably spent the night mustering his courage.

Link clenched the boy's neck in an iron grasp, lifted him to his feet, hefted the rifle in his other hand, and started toward the hidden trial.

The youth tried to struggle, so he stopped and shook him—anger rose in his chest, and he shook harder yet. "Do . . . not . . . *do* . . . that!" he said through gritted teeth as the boy's head and body jolted from side to side.

"Ever hear of Blackfeet Indians?" he whispered in a loud hiss.

"S-sort of."

"Know what we do to people who fool with us?"

The boy whimpered.

"Remember the coyote you killed and put in my truck?" He tightened his grasp of the boy's neck. "Coyote is my friend. Should I do that to you?"

When he started walking again the youth was shaking with fright.

"They s-said you were a f-fed," he managed.

"Who?"

"Pa and s-some others."

Link stopped when they came to the rough path, turned the boy and stared hard into pinprick eyes. Pointed at a large anthill, his voice emerging in the ominous whisper. "In the old days, Blackfoot warriors skinned their enemies, pinned them to the ground by driving stakes through their muscles, and left them to die."

"I'm s-sorry," the youth wailed. "I thought you were . . ." He stopped, started to cry, and to tremble more violently.

He regrasped the skinny neck, dragged the boy along the rough path. A new Suzuki four-wheeled all-terrain vehicle was parked in a low area where it couldn't be observed.

Link dragged the boy around and tried to hand him the rifle, a J.C. Higgins bolt-action in 30–06 caliber with a three-power Weaver scope. The youth refused to take it, so he grasped his hands, forced them open, placed the rifle there, and closed them.

"You shot my pickup," he said with a hiss, and pointed.

"It's my *Pa's*." The youth sniffled, regarded him with fearful, hate-filled eyes, and Link knew what he was considering.

The boy was not imaginative. He sucked in a fortifying breath, trying to build the courage to swing the barrel toward his oppressor.

The rifle barrel moved. Link waited until it was almost trained, then slapped him so hard he stumbled, released a loud and terrified wail and dropped the rifle. He slapped him again and spittle flew, and then again, and he cowered and began to sob.

Link motioned at the firearm. The youth scrambled and grabbed it. He hardly aimed, but the first round went through the engine. He cried louder, worked the bolt with shaking hands, and shot the ATV twice more. Tried again but the weapon was empty.

"Not enough," Link said in the hard whisper. He pulled the rifle from his hands, turned it and handed it to him barrel first. The boy was still crying as he began to smash the rifle into the vehicle and destroy it.

When the rifle stock was splintered and the scope bent, and gasoline, coolant, and engine oil were draining from the ruined ATV, Link moved forward.

The boy dropped the weapon and held his hands up defensively. A moment later, Link had him in his grasp, asking questions and receiving plaintive answers as they made their way down the hillside. When they arrived at the road in front of the Barn, a police cruiser finally appeared in the distance, red and blue lights flashing.

"Do not come *near* me again."

The youth frantically shook his head.

"If you do I will find you."

"I won't."

Deputy Ray Watt stopped the cruiser beside them and

gawked first at Anderson, still painted with desert grime, then at the boy in his grasp.

Link's voice was quiet. "He likes to shoot people's vehicles."

Watt switched off the lights and crawled out, hesitantly and as if not sure how to proceed. "He's a juvenile. Better let him go."

When Link released his hold, the youth stumbled, then scrambled behind Watt.

"Did you do that, Danny?" Watt asked.

The boy was staring at Link. "Yeah."

"He also told me he cut my tires and did the trick with the coyote."

"Did you?"

"Yeah."

"You hit him?" Watt asked Link almost hopefully. "He's a juvenile. Touch him and you get the book thrown at you."

Link looked at the boy, let his eyes burn into his muddled brain.

The youth drew farther behind Watt. "He didn't do nothing," he whispered.

"I'm going to take you in to ask some questions, Danny." The youth did not resist, in fact appeared grateful as he was ushered into the back seat.

A few minutes later the two men examined the pickup, and Watt begrudgingly wrote down what Link told him. Then he paused. "You just went up there and *got* him?" he asked incredulously, looking at the doped-up youth in the cruiser.

"I was tired of cleaning up after him."

When the deputy had left, Link took a last look at the old truck, sighed as he decided it was likely terminal, and went inside. His first call was to the number Watt had given him for a tow service, the second to Frank Dubois at the Weyland Building.

"You're calling from Gary's?" Frank asked.

"Yes." He massaged an aching muscle.

"Erin doesn't trust that phone line *or* the other one you used. Now, what happened? She heard gunshots."

He explained, ending with ". . . just a kid cranked up on amphetamenes who thought I was a DEA narc about to take away his candy."

Frank wasn't buying. "A kid can kill you just as dead. Erin also told me who she thinks was involved in Destin Albee's murder. If you insist on staying, I'm sending backup."

"And scare him away?"

"If Turpin's there, he doesn't scare."

"I thought you were convinced that he's dead."

"Erin also heard from her police contact in Aalborg today. The Danish nurse was murdered two days after talking with Erin. She's right. Turpin may be alive."

"If he's done something with Gary, I'd like to know. I can handle myself."

"Is that what you want, for him to come for you?"

"Maybe." It was time for a change of subject. "What did they say about the airplane?"

"Just show up at the Silver Creek airport at first light, and someone will be there to give your recurrency rides."

When he hung up, Link went out, unloaded the remainder of his belongings from the old Dodge, then sat back to await the tow truck and adjust to the loss of a dependable friend.

The telephone buzzed inside. He picked up in the kitchen. "Anderson."

Deputy Watt opened by telling him he hoped he had a good lawyer, using a tone entirely too gloating. "Danny's pa's here, threatening to sue your pants off. He doesn't appreciate what happened to his four-wheeler and rifle."

"I've got someone he can call." Link gave him a phone number from memory—of the Vice-President for Personnel at the Weyland Foundation.

"That who you work for?" Watt asked in a surprised voice.

"Yeah, and they've got more attorneys than the State of Nevada." He hung up on Watt, felt a flush of satisfaction, then called the same number he'd just given the deputy. He gave his title and was put through, and told the vice-president to alert the foundation lawyers to fight it tooth and nail. As he put down the telephone, Link was smiling. He *wanted* the word out that he worked for the Weyland Foundation, wanted Ansel Turpin, or whoever it was, to come for him. He was tired of questions. He wanted answers.

At eleven-thirty the tow truck pulled into the driveway, followed by Shelby Admire's freshly washed Corvette. Shelby got out as he told the driver to haul the old pickup to the Dodge dealer in Carson City and leaned against her car, drawing rapt attention from the driver's assistant.

Link walked around the pickup with the driver, examining.

"Gonna cost you more'n the thing's worth to get 'em to look at it."

"Maybe."

As the driver hooked up, Shelby told Link the news was spreading about the morning confrontation. Opinion was mostly on Link's side because Danny's family were troublemakers. Some were asking if the Weyland Foundation wasn't part of the federal government.

"Ray said it was crazy for you to go after Danny," she added. "He's impressed, even if he doesn't like you much."

He didn't respond, just looked on sadly as the pickup was towed away.

"If you're real good to me, I'll give you a ride," she said coyly.

"I'll need to go into Carson City to rent something to drive."

"There'd be a better selection in Reno. That'll cost you dinner, mister."

Gary Runyon wondered if he was insane, or still just on his way there. How long had he been in the cave? An hour? A month? He was ravenous, growing steadily weaker from the lack of food. From that, it was likely he'd been there less than a week. Longer and there'd be no more hunger—he remembered being told that by pilots who had gone through survival training.

He remembered other things too, and had regrets. About having been so self-centered in the real world—which was how he thought of his life before being dropped into hell. About not being punctual for meetings and dinners. About burying himself in his writing and not spending more time with his wife. About telling everyone—after the divorce—that she was a bitch when that wasn't the way he felt, and never telling them he was the one at fault.

He wondered about Aristotle, and whether the mutt had survived, and about the Barn and whether the next owner would continue with the renovations or let it go back to rot.

How insignificant his life had been! An insect had as much impact upon planet earth as Gary Runyon, who had contributed nothing of substance. He'd rolled his barrel and his meager possessions closer to the pool, nearer the deadly glow-wall that never failed to intrigue him. Now he stared at it with rapt attention, as others might view a sunrise or sunset. Periodically it pulsed, especially while coming or going, and he wondered what caused the effect.

Lincoln Anderson was often on his mind. Had he come to the Barn, then left, angry that his old acquaintance had not been there to greet him? It seemed likely.

If Gary had it to do over, he would change things. Be more attentive to others, be there when they expected him, pause with his ex-wife to observe a fine painting, compliment her flower garden, no matter how scrawny the plants. He'd remember that friends were to be treasured, not betrayed as he had been about to do to Frank Dubois. But he'd listened to the informant telling him about vast sums being wasted on DOE backroom deals and corporate payoffs. So much money being taken by Frank Dubois and his Weyland Foundation. It was a journalist's dream to believe it was true, and he had not been able to resist it.

Gary went to the pool, slowly so he would not expend precious energy, knelt, and drank from cupped hands.

Stood slowly and surveyed the glow-wall, then returned to his nearby nest.

God, he was hungry. The emptiness in his gut was overpowering and continuous.

He had visions of someone finding the diskettes, not the ones in the Bronco—his abductors had undoubtedly destroyed those—but the others. He had thoughts of the discoverer reading his notes and putting it all together. Learning the truth. But of course that wouldn't help him, because no one knew where he was, not even Gary Runyon himself.

17

8:45 P.M.—Stagecoach Valley, Nevada

Link pulled up to the Misfits Saloon in the shiny new GMC Yukon 4X4, got out to admire the vehicle, and decided it was nice. There'd been no resonant growl or shudder during the drive, only an efficient hum as he'd sped along the highway. He missed his old friend, and went inside feeling gloomy.

He'd had dinner with Shelby in Carson City at the Ormsby House, called the grand old lady and one of the finest establishments in town by the locals. Afterward she'd invited him to her condo for a drink. He had almost accepted before something inside said it might not be wise.

When he'd replied that he was tired, that it had been a busy morning, Shelby had hastily agreed and hurried off. His inner voice—conscience, whatever—had been assuaged, but there was a competing feeling not unlike disgust. As he'd driven back to Stagecoach Valley in the alien and boring Yukon, the indefinable emotion had turned to melancholy. He went into the saloon, hoping a cold beer might help wash away dust and loneliness.

There were a dozen customers, mostly seated at the bar. Link paid them little attention, found a stool near the Clark Gable poster, and nodded to Bob.

"Heard you fixed your vandalism problem," Bob said with a smile.

"Yep." Link ordered a Heineken with tomato juice. The owner-bartender brought the green bottle and a large glass half filled with red. Link mixed beer and juice and sipped the concoction. Took a longer drink, thinking it was helping.

"Word's around you work for some big company back east."

"The Weyland Foundation," he confirmed.

"Yeah. That's the one. And I've been making sure everyone knows you were an air force pilot flying combat over Iraq. People here take to vets."

The short man Link remembered from two days before was listening from four stools away, and immediately started talking about how he'd been in Vietnam. Four tours, he said.

"Damn it, Tom. Quiet down some," Bob told the drunk. "We already know about it."

The drunk continued, trying to impress the woman seated beside him, who was squinting at a video poker game and attempting to rebuild a dwindling stack of quarters. When she didn't appear interested, he called out to the hermit, hunched over the end of the bar.

"Hey, hermit. You in Vietnam?" he called out in his loud voice.

The hermit ignored him and finished his drink, then pushed back and departed.

Bob waited until he went out the door, and laughed. "Hell, Tom. The hermit was around for the Civil War."

"Not very friendly," the drunk groused. "Not like my buddies from 'Nam. They call all the time. We talk about shootin' gooks and water buffalo. One time I remember . . ."

The woman lost the last of her quarters and stared at the video camera in the corner. "Big Brother's still watching us," she said, raising her voice so she could be heard over Tom the drunk.

"Best investment I ever made," Bob told Link. "Don't even have to keep a cassette in it, but people don't know, do they? Keeps 'em honest." He cocked his head. "Cal was in a while ago and said Aristotle got up and walked some. Sally took him out so he could lift his leg, and he tried to take off. She caught up and hauled him back."

"Where was he headed?" Link asked.

"Across the highway. Cal thinks there's a coyote bitch in heat over there."

Everyone liked the big dog.

Bob leaned on the bar, relaxing and eyeing customers. "Cal was asking about people who've died around here the past month. Said it was something you and him talked about."

"Come up with anything?" Link asked. The red beer was going down fast, and he contemplated ordering another.

"Maybe. We talked about the deaths, then about some just flat disappearing." Bob held up one finger after another and named three.

"I noticed," he said, "because they were good customers, like the ones who died."

"*All* were customers?"

"All except Irene Staples's mother. Eight of my regulars gone now. Five dead and three disappeared. Cal was interested."

So was Link. He wondered if any of the ones here would be next to die—or disappear. "I'll have another tomato beer," he said.

"Sure."

"And let me know if anyone else disappears."

The viewers were watching the bar, alternately focusing on Lincoln Anderson and the man named Tom, who was spouting about Vietnam to an equally inebriated man down the bar.

"Took us a while before we realized they were using water buffalo to blow up our boats. See, they'd stuff some kinda mines up their ass and—"

"Aw, you're full of shit."

"No, no. They did it, see, and after a while we caught on. That's why we'd shoot the water buffalo when the brass wasn't around." He got up from his stool and went closer, to gain the man's full attention. "Hit the fuckers just right and they'd blow all to hell. I *seen* it. Shit and blood and horns flyin' everywhere."

"Bring up his data," said old Piers Jergen, and Juliette did so.

Individual Profile, Level 3

Name: Tommy Lee Grundy Desc: 5'2"–125 lbs–gray–brn

SSAN: 506-21-7990 DOB: 02/11/47 POB: Caliente, NV

Education: 8 Yrs

Mil. Svc: Rejected by USA, USMC, USN in 1968, 69 due to height rqmt.

Current Address: 44101 Comanche Drive, Stagecoach Valley, NV 89430

Hse Pymt: $310/Mo. Avg Util–Gas: $34.17 Elec: $48.00 Tel: $15.35

Marital Status: Widowed 01/31/80; auto accident

Children: 1, Male: Tommy Lee Grundy, Jr. Born: 09/12/72–Died: 01/31/80

Court Record: 01/31/80–reckless driving under influence–$300 fine; 07/10/80–Public Drunkenness–Dismissed; 02/01/81–DUI–30 days in lieu of $500 fine; 07/13/97–Public Nuisance–$100 fine.

Present Employment: Laborer, SC Construction–$8.15/hr

Credit Rating: D5, Unloanable Outstanding Obligations: $4,100 +

Observed: No local friends or known family; fair-to-poor health; hvy smoker; hvy drinker; no current sexual involvement exc. occasional local prostitute.

"This one's not acceptable," said the woman, "because of his health." She had just come in and found the old man had already ordered the repairman to take the coffeepot device inside Grundy's trailer. It was irritating that he hadn't waited.

"Too late," said Jergen. "Everything's already set up." He was not interested in the mortality testing. Only in the device and achieving the A.D. phenomenon.

"I don't like using this subject," said Juliette LaCoste. She pointed. "Especially with Anderson suspecting that we're picking our subjects from the bar."

"He doesn't know *anything*," the old man snapped moodily. He'd particularly disliked Anderson since the briefing, called him "that damned mechanic."

The repairman's voice sounded over the radio. "The device is in the house. In the living room closet." Juliette switched to the scene outside Tom Grundy's small home. Slued to the street and saw the white van. "Did you hear me?" came the repairman's voice.

She took the hand-held radio from the old man. "We heard." She kept a stern expression as she entered initial data. The coffee pot was located 26.8 feet from the bed, with four thin walls separating them.

Piers Jergen studied the information on her computer screen. They'd changed the formula only slightly, but had loaded the coffee pot with nineteen kilos of Pu–239, the most to date. Jergen was so confident that this time they would succeed that he'd made a little joke about vacuuming the dust out of the valley along with the radiation.

Juliette had determined the changes, then made Piers think it had been the idea of both of them.

Death of the subject should come at four hours, but that mattered little when compared with the importance of achieving A.D. Perhaps that would happen tonight. If so, history would record that Piers Jergen was the father of accelerated depletion, and that Juliette LaCoste had been at his right hand. No one would doubt for there would be no living experts to dispute it.

She smiled. *Destroy thine enemies,* sayeth Juliette.

Adam Russo came in. "You're late again," the old man snapped irritably. The soft-spoken man glanced at Piers without expression, and took his seat beside Juliette.

"Background reading is now eighty-four milliroentgens," she droned. She looked at Russo. "We're waiting for the subject to come home. Piers picked Tom Grundy."

"The little drunk?" he asked with surprise.

"Yes. I would have disagreed, but the repairman had already taken the device inside."

Piers Jergen gave a dismissive shrug, then looked past her at Russo. "Today Jameson stopped me and questioned our funding. I told him it came from the Weyland Foundation like you wanted, but he says the foundation's been calling the NEL board of directors, threatening to sue and saying they'll have no part of anything involving us."

Russo shrugged. "It doesn't matter. We're almost finished here."

"What if they find out *you're* funding it?"

"We'll be gone before they can do anything."

"What if Jameson inventories and discovers that we've already used the material he's planned for January's tests?"

Russo gave him an amused look. "What if the earth stopped rotating and fell into the sun? That's more probable than Jameson suddenly becoming responsible."

"We mustn't have anything go wrong before we achieve the phenomenon."

"I told you from the beginning, Piers. You have ten chances before the next phase of my plan. There are two experiments remaining."

"I think we should stop the ridiculous lethality tests," said Piers. "Concentrate only on the A.D. phenomenon."

"No," said Russo. "We need the information."

"*You* do, you mean."

"Yes," said Russo, the voice even softer now. Becoming dangerous. "I do."

Juliette's mouth became a firm line. "Adam's right. We've gone this far. We'll continue with both experiments."

"Sometimes," the old man said, "I wonder who is the assistant here."

Juliette sighed audibly. She'd been carrying the experiments. Once she'd understood them, Piers had just been along for the ride. That was why Adam Russo had come to her. Why they still needed her. She was the one who would make the phenomenon happen.

Or not.

Piers Jergen knew that, and his voice changed to a near whine. "I still don't understand why the Weyland Foundation wants no part of A.D. experimenting."

"Possibly it's something Anderson is reporting to his bosses in New York," said Russo.

Jergen nodded, his eyes narrowed, his dislike for Anderson apparent.

Juliette interrupted, her voice businesslike. "Let's get ready. The subject is leaving the saloon."

18

Gary Runyon came abruptly awake and sat upright, listening, the clatter far above alerting him that another barrel was falling. He knew what to expect, waited as it rattled its way downward, then held hands over his ears as it free-fell. The newest arrival crashed into the hard floor, rolled a bit in the darkness, and came to rest.

The glow-wall was turned off and the darkness absolute, so he felt about, picked up his prising lid, and cautiously made his way toward the last sounds. He missed it on his first try, and established a zigzag search pattern. Stumbled into it and banged his knee.

"So who are you?" Gary asked, then he knelt and listened for movement. There was none apparent so he took his time prising off the top, now weakened to the point of dizziness when he expended the slightest effort.

The body was small, male—a boy?—and, like the others, smelled of vomit and feces. It was also clothed, so he searched the pockets. There were several coins, a wallet, and a Bic-shaped lighter and half-empty pack of *cigarettes*. The last discovery evoked mixed but strong emotions. One of the promises he'd made to God was to never smoke again, but of course that decision had been easy since there'd been no smokes or source of flame.

Do not backslide, the righteousness within him said in Charlton Heston's voice.

"I'll try," he answered.

Don't be a sap. What's wrong with having a cigarette? They even give 'em to prisoners about to be executed, for crap's sake. The other, caustic voice. He'd tried to recognize it and decided it was Jerry Seinfeld's.

Gary knelt at the man's head and flicked the lighter. The flame produced a brilliant light that half-blinded him. He released it almost immediately, having seen enough.

It was Tom—he'd forgotten the last name—a drunk who hung around the saloon, wearing the same awful grimace as the others.

He went through Tom's trousers again, more carefully, and was rewarded when he found a comb in a rear pocket and in the depths of a front one . . .

Gary stopped cold, hardly daring to believe.

. . . an almost full roll of Lifesavers or mints, or something in a cylindrical paper wrapper. His fingers trembled at the touch as he withdrew the tube, and he wanted to strip away the paper, shove the entire roll into his mouth, making pleasurable oinking sounds.

Gary laughed exuberantly, grasping the cylinder tightly. He placed it into his own pocket with the care he would have given to precious diamonds in the real world, stuffed Tom back into his barrel, and replaced and tamped the lid down. From experience he knew the stench would linger for an entire glow-period.

Don't wait. Eat them now! Seinfeld coaxed.

He fought valiantly, allowed Charlton Heston to admonish him. *Impetuosity has ruined your life. Cast away the cigarettes, offer thanks, and eat the Lifesavers one at a time.*

When the glow-wall came on, he would roll Tom's body over with the three others he'd collected at the far, dark end. Then Seinfeld said . . .

Damn it, eat the frigging Lifesavers!

Gary kept his right hand held against his trousers so he could not possibly lose them—he wondered if they were cherry-flavored, his favorite—and felt about the floor with his feet. He had memorized the swirls and ridges in the surface, knew where he was from their pattern. He walked slowly and surely to his home. Felt around and settled his bony rump on the small barrel.

Perhaps they were Tums or Rolaids.

A delectable thought.

Cherry-flavored Lifesavers, said the greedy Seinfeld voice.

He took out the lighter, then very carefully extracted the roll. Turned it in his fingers and decided it was too fat to be Tums or Rolaids.

They might be chocolate candies, or . . . Mentos. Wonderful, chewy Mentos.

Give thanks, said Heston.

Thanks, now find out what the hell they are, said Seinfeld.

Mentos, Lifesavers, Rolaids. Saliva drooled onto his jaw and trickled down his neck. Such dreams would likely not come twice.

He took in a deep breath and flicked the flame on, remembering to squint.

Lifesavers. Assorted Flavors.

The light flicked off. He put the Bic away, laughing again at his superb luck. An *assortment* of wonderful tastes. It was even better than he'd hoped.

He pulled out the first one—orange—and very carefully placed it into his mouth.

Gary ate half of them, one after the other. An orange, lime—he'd been wrong, lime tasted best—cherry and lemon. He determined there were eight, so he ate the four, then folded the end over, put the remainder back into his pants pocket, and sat crying on the small barrel.

Not from sadness, but from the joy of the moment, thinking about the flavored juices flowing down his throat. The lemony taste of the last one lingered.

He did not want a steak or lobster, no potatoes and gravy, no sumptuous salads. He craved the other Lifesavers in the roll. He could *feast* on them, savor them.

"Thank you, Tom," he said in a fervent voice. Then he sat back, watched the glow-wall as it began to pulse and come to life, lit one of the generic cigarettes from Tom's pack, and drew the smoke into his lungs.

He coughed, pulled in and released an unadulterated breath, and coughed again. Then he dragged deeply on the cigarette and decided it was not worth it. He would quit—as soon as he'd finished the pack.

Charlton Heston was quiet.

Thursday, July 2, 6:30 A.M.
—Silver Creek Airport, Nevada

Link was waiting at the end of the hard-pack gravel runway when the sleek, single-engine airplane appeared on the horizon and began a slow descent. The pilot made a turn over the field to ensure the runway was clear, then lowered flaps and landing gear as he continued around a closed-loop pattern and flared beautifully for landing.

The pilot made a long roll-out on the 6,000 foot runway—built in World War II to train bomber pilots, now an unsupervised strip where a dozen-odd airplanes were parked and the sheriff's department kept a watchful eye out—to get a feel for its entire length. The turn-around at the far end was done sharply, and the airplane's engine revved as it taxied back.

A perceptible sense of pleasure coursed through Link as he watched the sleek, royal blue bird approaching. He loved to fly and realized how much he'd missed it over the past months.

He could see the pilot's form. As he drew closer, Link began to smile.

The chief pilot for Executive Connections—and close friend of his stepfather—gave him a thumbs up from the cockpit. He shut down, was quick to dismount, then pumped Link's hand vigorously.

"Didn't think I'd let anyone else check you out, did you?"

"How's Dad?" Link was concerned about the heart condition.

"That last bypass scared the hell out of us all, but it did the trick. He'd be here, but your mom thought it was too soon. She put down the law on another matter, too. You're to get your young puppy butt home for a visit soon as you can."

"I will."

The chief pilot was a retired colonel in his mid-fifties named Bowes, had flown with and worked for Link's father in the air force, and loved him as dearly as any distinctly macho and heterosexual male could love another. He was also one of the finest pilots Link had ever met. He regarded the single engine bird, with its sleek lines and pointed silver nose.

"Piper Comanche 160 Turbo, built in 1971 and just refurbished. Think that'll do?"

"Yes, sir. Good choice."

"Our *only* choice. It's the smallest we had available out west."

"How's the company doing?" Link asked.

"Hell, we're gonna be rich no matter how hard we fight it. The Weyland Foundation keeps us flying day and night, and other business is picking up too. We're maintaining fifty-three birds for the foundation, and fifteen of our own. We've also got two new Learjet Sixties on the way and the general's thinking about another Gulfstream."

Bowes was one of four partners, all close friends from the days when they'd flown combat over North Vietnam. Link's stepfather was majority owner. The chief pilot had the fewest shares but earned a decent salary.

Link observed the bird.

"You gonna sit there and grin, or you want to fly? I figure to have you take it up a couple of times, get in a few stalls and panic turns, and put you under the hood. I also brought the written exam along, which should warm your heart."

Link's smile faded. "It's—ah—been a while."

"Just think of flying like riding a horse."

"You never forget?"

"Nope. Ignore it for long, and it'll kick you square in the butt."

Ten minutes later they were airborne, and Link was amazed at how rusty he'd become. For the first half hour he just soared and wheeled around the sky to get the feel of it. The Comanche was responsive, with sufficient horsepower to keep him out of trouble. Link flew over Stagecoach Valley and pointed out the Barn. Then they crossed to the other side of the highway.

"Odd-shaped mountain," observed the chief pilot. "Hollowed out, with buildings inside."

"Millionaire Mountain," Link said. A helicopter had just landed, and a forklift was carrying away and stacking a sling-load of olive drab barrels. A pickup and several golf carts were parked up on the mountainside near the Break-a-Heart One mine. Already preparing for the big test in January?

As he turned and descended, he saw something odd, and flew lower.

There had been a wind the previous night, and in an arroyo not far from the security fence, netting had been blown off one side of a parked vehicle. While he could not tell precisely, the sharp corner of a fender made him think of the hermit's old army truck.

Link pointed it out and explained how the old man spent his time prospecting.

"Why does he hide his truck like that?" the chief pilot asked.

"That's government property," Link responded. "Likely doesn't want 'em knowing he's nosing around that close. The hermit's an odd coot." He reminded himself to strike up a conversation. The man with the Santa Claus beard just might know a lot of things that were going on in the valley.

"That's enough playing around." The pilot pointed upward.

Link climbed to eight thousand feet, then was told to make hard turns and enter a series of stalls. When he'd responded properly, he was handed a hood—a device designed to restrict his vision from seeing anything outside the cockpit.

"Put that on and we'll go through some unusual attitude drills."

As soon as Link had the hood in place, the chief pilot took the controls, rolled the airplane over on its side, raised the nose, then pulled into a hard turn.

"You've got the airplane," Bowes said amiably as the Comanche began to shudder.

By the time the chief pilot had finished with him, and the hood was stowed, perspiration ran freely down Link's face.

"Not bad for a pup out of practice," he was told.

Link made two approaches to the Silver Creek airport,

the first too high and the second acceptable, then came around again and landed.

The pilot told him to shut down the engine, pulled out a thick packet of papers, got out, and stretched as he looked out at the mountains. Link knew what was next. He deplaned and watched him extract a pamphlet and answer sheet from the folder.

"I haven't had time to study," he tried.

"Hold your excuses for someone who sympathizes," the chief pilot said without charity.

Link filled out the instrument exam, using the Comanche's wing as a writing surface. Bowes graded it, grumbled that Link had missed four easy ones, and pulled out a local area chart.

"I thought we were done."

"Just started. We'll make some approaches and landings at airports in the area, head to Reno for some real instrument work, land and refuel, and come back."

"You're the boss."

"And you're damned rusty. Last year you were one of the best I ever flew with, and you're letting that talent go to waste." Bowes pored over the map, and said, "First take me to Tahoe for a couple of approaches, then over to some place called . . . Flying Tiger Field."

"It's on the way to Friendly," Link said, remembering. Then he became quiet.

"Something wrong, or you got a sudden case of fear of flying?"

A smile played at Link's lips. "I think something just went *right.*"

Three more hours had passed before they returned to the Silver Creek airport, and Link taxied up to a royal blue Learjet 60 now parked at the end of the field.

As Link shut down the engine, the chief pilot handed over the instrument card he'd just signed off. "That's good for single-engine recip. I'll need you back in Washington so we can get your other checks out of the way."

"I shouldn't be here much longer." At least he hoped that would be the case.

The chief pilot peered meaningfully at him. "Need anything, you know our number."

They crawled out of the cockpit and bedded the airplane down by tying it to stanchions driven into the concrete-hard earth and covering it. Done, they walked together toward the open hatch of the waiting Learjet.

As the right engine began to whine and come to life, Bowes reached inside and pulled out a metallic briefcase. "Stopped by New York on our way out, and a pretty girl there asked us to give you this. It's some kind of mobile telephone, and she said it's charged and ready. Also said to give her a call right away."

"Thanks for bringing it."

"Something else she felt you should know. This guy you're after likely got away with a hundred million dollars, *plus* a few shoulder-fired missiles. The kind the Russkies used to hand out to terrorists." He grinned. "*Awful* pretty girl. Said her name was Erin. Damn shame how the nice ones like you pups and forget us old dogs are the ones that know everything."

"She's my assistant," Link explained.

The chief pilot stared beyond him. "Another assistant?"

Shelby was leaning on the door of her Corvette. She smiled and waved.

Link almost explained she was just a friend, but Bowes's grin told him it would be for naught. After a hearty handshake, he boarded the airplane and pulled the hatch firmly into position. A moment later he could be seen crawling into the right pilot's seat in the cockpit.

Link stood watching, the case in his hand, until the Learjet lifted off and disappeared into the eastern sky.

Shelby had quietly approached as he'd watched the takeoff. "I saw the airplane over Stagecoach Valley. It's beautiful, Link."

"Busy?"

"This job runs hot and cold. Things are slow right now. Next week all the monthly readings have to be taken and the reports come due."

"Let's take a real short flight, and see if we can't find Gary's airplane."

She hurried to follow as he walked to the Comanche.

"I called the airports at both Carson and Reno. He didn't leave Mathilda at either one."

"I know. Let's check out Big Cat." He climbed up and opened the door for her.

Link made his best landing of the day, making the tires kiss the earth as they touched down at Flying Tiger Field. There were two hangars, one small, the other larger, and three makeshift airplane shelters across the strip.

"Keep your fingers crossed," he told her as he taxied up, then shut down before the smallest hangar. A fading sign read *Licensed A & E Mechanic* and showed a list of repairs available for ailing airplanes.

"You bet." Shelby said cheerfully as he shut down. She obviously enjoyed flying.

Link crawled out and went inside, Shelby following, and found a lanky man studiously picking a sandwich from a lunch pail. He wore smudged coveralls and had the proper look.

"You do the repairs?" Link asked amiably.

"Yep." He munched his sandwich and did a good interpretation of ignoring them.

"Do you want us to come back later?"

"Nope." He poured iced tea from a thermos and sipped it, staring beyond them.

"I have a friend who's trying to get his Piper Cub fixed. Brought it in last week."

A voice spoke from behind them. "He's eating." They turned and took in an angular woman dressed in short-sleeved coveralls that matched the man's, except they were cleaner and a heart with wings was sewn over her left breast. A shoulder patch showed a snarling tiger's head.

"Like I just said, I have a friend who—"

"Mr. Runyon owes us forty dollars for keeping his airplane in the hangarette."

Ten minutes later Link had paid the fee, added another forty for another week, and told the woman Gary still hadn't decided whether to replace the engine. He walked with Shelby across the grass stubble toward the closest shelter. The barely visible rounded tail was that of an old Cub.

Mathilda's engine had been removed, the open maw protected by a draped section of canvas. They found an unmarked manila folder in the space behind the pilot's seat. Inside were a marked-up street map, and two 3.5–inch floppy diskettes labeled *N-Mare Big Cat* and *Dilemma*.

19

Link was putting the Comanche to rest—covering it with a tarp and tying it down—when a passing deputy sheriff wheeled off the highway and asked what he was doing there, and remained until he'd shown his pilot's license and aircraft registration and explained his connection with the airplane. That's reassuring, Link thought as he walked Shelby to her Corvette.

"I can't wait to see what's on the diskettes," she said.

"See you back at the Barn." As he watched her pull out behind him, a feeling of concern began to prickle at his neck. When they passed the women's prison on the hillside to the south, it became more distinct. The bravado he'd voiced to Frank Dubois—that he *wanted* to attract Ansel Turpin—had come from his confidence that he could defend himself. That belief had not diminished, but he wondered if he might be endangering Shelby. The thought was dismaying, and as they descended into Stagecoach Valley, he worried even more. In fact, he cared . . .

Cared? The word echoed. The inner bickering began . . . she'd been Marie's friend, and did the attraction have something to do with that? There was no argument that she was exquisite, so sensuous that men, even women, tended to gawk. But he was made of nobler stuff—right? Yeah, sure.

The lie was obvious. He was attracted to her, had just admitted that he cared for her, and it had nothing to do with Marie, who had freed him, *told* him to find a good woman and live. Shelby might not be the one, but it wasn't wrong to feel for her. The inner dueling diminished, and he felt easier about himself . . . and the glandular activity as well.

Lighten up and chill out, he told himself. Why shouldn't he be attracted?

Because you're not going to be here long. Shelby's not the kind for a hit and run, and as she said, she's not ready for a heavy relationship.

He reluctantly accepted the rationale. Gee, thanks, he inwardly joked.

Which might allow them to become better friends.

He did like Shelby. Then he thought of Erin, and the metal case on the seat beside him . . . there were four miles to go, which should give him sufficient time.

Link opened the briefcase. The molded rubber interior contained a flip-top cellular phone, a charging stand, and two spare batteries. A stickum note on the telephone read: *Press SEND button, then MEM, then 1.*

He opened the cell phone and did as instructed. A light-emitting diode at the upper right on the phone illuminated. He listened.

"Two-seven-seven-five." Erin's voice.

It worked. "Link here," he said.

"Great." She paused. "You're on the satellite, I see."

"The connection's very clear."

"And secure. Keep the phone with you and turned on. It's no biggie to lose a charger, but they don't like having to destroy flip-tops."

"Destroy? You can do that from there?"

"It's nothing new. In World War I both sides had destruct circuits in their trench phones. Want a demonstration?"

"No, thanks." He had visions of the thing exploding in his hand.

Erin laughed. "It just disables the frequency chip and encryption circuits."

"Tell Frank the bird arrived safe and sound."

"I take it you passed your check ride?"

"By the skin of my teeth," Link said ruefully. "And the instructor was an old friend."

"Passing is better than the alternative," she observed. "Anything else to tell Frank?"

"We've located Gary Runyon's diskettes."

"Great!" She paused. "You're not alone?"

"Shelby's following in another car. We're going to the Barn to see what was so important about the diskettes that made Gary want to hide them."

"Make sure you disconnect the computer phone line before you use it."

"The line went dead, remember?"

"Humor me. If Ansel Turpin's involved, it's a technology game, Link. He knows computers, and he's good at surveillance."

He almost told her he was still unconvinced the rogue agent was involved. Instead he reasoned, "We're out in the country. Anyone seen sneaking around putting in bugs would be obvious."

"Not sneaking. Being obvious is usually best, Link. After you've had your look, find a computer somewhere away from that place, and I'll copy the diskettes."

"Using your modem?"

"You're getting the lingo down. Next thing I know you'll pop out a big word."

Link came up on the turnoff. "I'd better go."

" 'Bye. Just press the End button and you're done."

He dropped the flip-top into his shirt pocket, closed the metal case, and stowed it on the floor in the back of his seat, feeling a mental lift as he did whenever he spoke with Erin Frechette.

Shelby pulled into the Barn, parked beside Link, and crawled out, giddy with anticipation as he emerged from the Yukon with the envelope. Finally they might learn what was up with Gary.

They hurried inside, then up to the loft where she switched on the computer and waited for it to boot. She noted that Link disconnected the phone line from the back, and wondered but didn't ask.

He handed her the envelope and she peered inside, picked out the disk marked *N-Mare Big Cat*, and snapped it into the A-drive. She clicked on 3½ Floppy

(A). The folder was titled *Nuclear Nightmare in America.* In it were a Prologue, thirty-two chapters called Chap 01, Chap 02, and so forth, research notes called Nuke Data, and other notes called Personal Info and Scandalous Stuff.

"Which do you want to look at first?" she asked Link as he pulled up a folding chair and stared over her shoulder so close she could smell the soap he used. Irish Spring, she decided. There were earthier odors as well. Perspiration earned when he'd flown.

"Nuke Data?"

Shelby highlighted the icon and double-clicked. A word processing program auto-loaded, then text appeared. They read it together.

Gary had done a good job of reducing technical jargon into useful English. There were outlines of how different kinds of nuclear reactors worked. How graphite moderator rods and nuclear fuel rod assemblies—some 36,000 "hotrods" were used in a typical reactor—interacted to create heat, move water, operate the generators. The rods were very large and eventually deteriorated, creating a monthly total of 250 tons of radioactive waste from reactors in America alone. Something must soon be done about the dangerous stuff.

Trudging their way through the notes took half an hour. They sat back.

"Trust me," she grumbled, "there's nothing here you couldn't get from a textbook."

"Try looking in Personal Info."

She brought that one up. Found a list of key people in the nuke power business, starting with the Secretary of Energy, continuing through the Nuclear Regulatory Commission, on down to operators and workers Gary had met in his interviews and briefings.

"Here I am," Shelby said, pointing. Her name was listed under Nuclear Waste Management Studies, Ongoing. She scrolled down to the descriptions, unable to resist seeing what he'd written about her.

ADMIRE, Shelby A.–Formerly with NEL, MM Study. MS, Geology. Helpful source re: geological strata and radioactive substances.

"That's all?" she asked feeling put out.

"Looking at the others, I'd say it's complimentary. Try Fred Jameson."

JAMESON, Frederick L.–General Manager & Alpha Collegium spokesman, Millionaire Mtn. Study, NEL research project. Ph.D., physics. Held teaching post at Columbia U., then AEC & NRC. Married, no children. Colleague at (now defunct) AEC said: "Openly ambitious, a man in search of fame." Seemed like nice guy, but more going on than meets the eye.

Link nodded. "Now Dr. Jergen."

She raised a surprised eyebrow at him, then searched through the file.

"Did you know Jergen at NEL?" he asked her.

"He was with the Epsilon Collegium. Alpha and Epsilon kept to themselves. Especially Epsilon. The rest of us weren't allowed near their buildings."

JERGEN, Piers (NMN)–Epsilon Collegium, MM NEL study. Born 1922. Early Los Alamos work on neutron generation. Lost clearance, barred fm further gov't work in 1950 because deceased father was mbr of Danish Communist Party in 1932–34. Piers denied involvement. Wife (American) divorced & left him. Unable to find work in his field. Nothing more until 1992–95, worked at UC Berkeley research center. Presented paper to AFSE symposium on Accelerated Depletion in '94, but later discredited when lab accident killed assistant. Location unk. until Oct. last year when came to MM NEL project with 2 colleagues. DA said he brought 12.7 $M research grant from the Weyland Foundation.

There was D.A. again, like he'd seen on the missing scrap of paper.

"What's AFSE?" he asked Shelby.

"The American Federation of Scientist and Engineers. It's a professional organization."

"Are you a member?"

"You've got to have a doctorate before they'll even *consider* you. It's an elite group. Very clannish."

Link nodded at the screen "So far there's no surprises."

"How about the mention of the grant from the foundation?"

"I called New York about it. They haven't funded anything here. They have no connections with Piers Jergen, and his presence just squashed NEL's chances for a grant next year."

"Sounds odd that they'd lie about it, and Gary's informant too." She looked at the screen. "Who's next?"

"We'll come back later. Try the other notes file."

"Scandalous Stuff." She smiled at the title as she brought it up.

As they read the first paragraphs, he whistled. Her smile disappeared.

Again, Gary had converted complicated gobbledegook into plain English. Something called the Nuclear Waste Fund, established by act of Congress, had been loaded with nine billion dollars over the past decade, using large contributions from various American power companies. Except for a modest set-aside—not to exceed five percent for studies and research—it was sacrosanct, not to be used until solutions were approved by Congress. The fund was then to be used to clean up nuclear waste.

Gary's whistle-blower had provided an FBI memorandum to a deputy director in the criminal division. Half of the Nuclear Waste Fund had *already* been expended, provided to firms shown in the memo for highly questionable studies and research projects. Some of them were just titles. Others were useless make-work. More than four billion dollars had already been siphoned off.

The next paragraph was marked DO NOT RELEASE BEFORE VERIFICATION.

Seventeen companies were named. The top four shown, including Nucleonic Engineering, Ltd., were listed as subsidiaries of the Weyland Foundation. Altogether they'd received one third of the total pilferage.

"How did Gary learn all that?" Shelby asked.

"It's got to be all lies," Link said grimly, and she remembered that he worked for the Weyland Foundation.

The interoffice memorandum had been written in May 1996 by an agent assigned to an investigation of another matter—blatant misuse of Department of Energy travel

funds—when he'd come across a collection of notes and
sums, program element code numbers, and funds trans-
fers that at first had not made sense. With clarification,
they'd turned into dynamite; the giveaway theft of *four
thousand million dollars*. When he'd brought up the matter with various supervisors (names provided) he'd been
ordered to "forget everything about it," and was
abruptly transferred to an out-of-country project called
Nuke-Safe.

The enormity of his findings had plagued the agent
throughout his absence. When he was on his way home
he could live with it no longer, and decided to blow
the whistle.

Four months ago, Gary had felt he was getting nowhere, trying to put a real story together on nuclear
waste. Then the FBI agent had visited, shown his identity card to prove he was who he claimed to be, and
after a discussion and exacting a promise from Gary to
try to keep his name out of it, the agent had provided
a certified true photocopy of the memorandum. The
original had been conveniently misplaced somewhere in
the criminal division hierarchy at the Hoover Building
in Washington. The agent believed a number of upper
echelon personnel were involved, along with all five
members of the financial committee who controlled the
Weyland Foundation.

The agent's worst diatribes were reserved for the
foundation.

Gary had needed a story. He had a blockbuster. His
reservations had come later, when he remembered that
Frank Dubois, once a close friend, was chairman of the
Weyland Foundation. He'd agonized about it and told
the agent he needed more verification.

The agent said he would provide specific proof about
Dubois. Before he'd left the Barn he asked Gary Runyon never to call his Las Vegas office, where all calls
were monitored. He'd said he would stay in touch and
had been as good as his word, phoning every week to
give Gary more data, sending proof through the mail.

Gary disclosed the agent's name, Destin Albee, but

used only his initials, D.A., in the manuscript, and said that even those must be changed before final publication.

"It sounds awfully real, Link," Shelby said.

"Remember me telling you about the agent who visited me? He showed identification saying his name was Destin Albee, and since then I've learned he was a fake."

"Gary's source was an impostor?"

"Sure. Gary was thirsty for a story and the fake Destin Albee gave him a *big* one. Thank God Gary didn't send it in. With Albee dead, it would have been hard to disprove it all before a lot of heavy damage was done."

"You're *sure* he didn't send it?"

"Pretty sure. There are phone messages from his publisher telling him to hurry. But Gary was waiting for you to look over the technical part, and me to verify the foundation's role."

Shelby picked up on something. "Albee's dead?" She pulled in a sharp breath. "*That's* where I remembered the name. He was in charge of the FBI office in Las Vegas."

"Yeah."

"They said he was mutilated."

"So it would look like it was done by a drug gang. Erin believes he was killed by the impostor. After reading this, I think she's right."

Shelby recalled Erin—Link's assistant—and remembered she'd sounded intelligent on the phone, and was a whiz on the computer. A troublesome flutter of jealousy rose in her stomach.

She nodded at the screen. "If the informer was an impostor, then these are all lies?"

"Yeah. He refers to chapter four. Let's take a look."

She brought up Chap 04, and they read together.

Gary crucified the DOE as well as the companies that had received the illicit funds, reserving his worst criticism for the Weyland Foundation. He'd received his proof. According to another memo—this one carrying a Weyland Foundation, Habitat Earth banner and initialed by FD—the amount of the next NEL contract was to be increased. On the margin he wrote about the importance of supporting their hidden assets—such as Nucleonic Engineering, Ltd.

"It looks awfully convincing." Shelby shook her head. "You're right. Thank God Gary did submit this. Your company would have been publicly tarred and feathered, and when the truth was discovered Gary would never have published again."

Link did not respond, for he'd became thoughtful. She observed him, his face only inches from her own. Definitely feral, Shelby thought, and a delicious warmth crept over her. She wondered what he'd do if she kissed him.

His eyes returned to the present. "It's all malicious lies."

"Gary didn't know the agent was a fake."

"I'm not blaming Gary. The guy was up against a real professional." He nodded at the computer. "This answers some of my questions, such as why the imposter wanted me to leave."

"Was he responsible for Gary's disappearance?"

"Probably, but it doesn't track. You'd think he'd want him around until the book's finished." He reached for the folder containing the second diskette. "Let's see what Gary's Dilemma was about." His hand brushed her arm, and he pulled back as if burned.

Her voice emerged unnaturally low. "I'm famished. Let's go to the Misfits for lunch, then come back and check it out."

Touch me again, Shelby said with her eyes. She ejected the diskette, handed it to him, stood and stretched. Felt his eyes on her. *I like you watching me,* she wanted to say. Then she felt silly for acting such a tease.

She went downstairs first. Paused at the swamp cooler in the living room and let the breeze pass over her body. Felt her nipples stiffen and knew her clothing were molded to her body. Turned and watched him emerge from the stairwell. Waited as he came closer.

"Forget something?" he asked, his voice as thick as hers had been.

"Damn it, *kiss* me," she hissed.

He needed no more encouragement, bent slightly, and kissed her mouth, his lips gentle. She snaked her arms about his neck and grasped ferociously, made a sound from deep in her throat. They broke for air, but neither pulled away.

"I want you," she said, and felt surprised that she was so brazen. She raised her lips to his, closed her eyes. His sound came next, guttural and nice. Shelby moaned in response, holding on tight. It had been so long.

When she brought her hands down from his neck he tried to break, but she whimpered and kissed him more fervently, exploring with her tongue as she tugged her halter top out of her shorts. He took over, unbuttoned the front. She shrugged free, lips still open, tonguing and kissing him ardently, making odd sounds. Her fingers flew over his shirt, freeing buttons, then went to his jeans, where she pressed her hand into his trousers and felt the hard flesh that had pressed against her.

Time was forgotten, lost, and at some point her bikini panties were at her knees and she was tugging desperately at his undershorts. His voice was hoarse. Something about was she sure. Shelby answered with the involuntary sounds from down in her throat as she pressed herself to him—she afraid to stop the kiss lest he come to his senses, he going nowhere. She made another sound as he carried her to the couch, then as he knelt, kissing first her belly, then the fire-hot core of her. She thought she screamed, knew she shuddered and bucked her hips violently. He was over her, hovering as he sought, penetrated, slipped inside easily for she was moist.

They moved together happily, hungrily, making loud love sounds. Grasping and holding onto one another. He groaned, tensed, and his heat spread into her. This time she *knew* she screamed—and shuddered grandly.

She lurched upward with her hips, hungry for more. He did not stop, only slowed so she could join him, moving more languorously—now, she knew, doing it for her pleasure—pressing and giving as she arched and cried out. But after a moment, he did it not only for her. Link slowed, stopped, lifted slightly as she slowly writhed, pausing for her delight but not done with his task. She pulled free and moved to the end of the couch, stopped and looked back with a come-on blink of eyes and grin.

He started for her.

Shelby squealed and ran, peeked back again, and let him catch her in the kitchen. She leaned back against the heavy butcher-block table, grasping the edge with her hands, lifted herself slightly so he could enter her. He did so, then worked slowly but relentlessly. They whispered and conspired—he lifted her onto the heavy table, crawled onto her. They made love there, she writhing so fiercely they almost fell off at a critical moment.

He pulled her to the floor and they continued, whispering so low the wet sounds of their joining bodies seemed loud, then she squealing and he groaning fiercely, neither of them restraining their sounds of delight—giving everything, taking greedily. He flooded her with more warmth, slowed and stopped, panting.

She raised her lips and pecked his nose, felt him growing soft within her and became mushy with sentiment. He brushed her lips and rolled over. They lay side-by-side on the parquet floor, silent, listening to the loud hum of the cooler, communicating with warm thoughts.

After a few minutes he broke the spell, said, "The floor's hard," as if just discovering the fact. Shelby managed to stand, poised with hands on hips, looking down. "Come on."

"I'm an invalid."

She grasped his hand, tugged. He groaned and gained his feet, visibly spent in more ways than one. "I've been dreaming about us taking a shower together," she told him as she led him into the master bedroom. An idea half-formed, lingered, grew. She stopped and smiled. Then she turned him and pressed until he sat on the edge of the bed.

His eyes questioned. He started to speak.

Shelby stopped him with a finger to his lips, bent and kissed his forehead. "Lincoln Anderson," she whispered. "I like you, very much." She bent, kissed his lips, now touching his chest with light fingers, paused on a terrible scar there. His body was hard and muscular, with no trace of excess fat. She traced fingers lightly over his nipples, hers too began to respond, presented a breast to his lips. He caressed the tiny rosebud with his tongue—it instantly hardened. She felt the thrill beginning anew, tingled from it.

She knelt and ran her tongue over his chest, lingered on the scars, and continued down his belly, then lower. She cupped and stroked him, although he was not nearly ready, took him into her mouth and worked slowly, taking her time as he had done to ensure her pleasure. For a while there was nothing. Then she felt movement and took more.

Shelby heard him groan, and continued. A minute later he tried to escape, but she did not allow it. When she had finished, savored him as she'd done with no previous man, she rested her head against his legs and sighed deeply. My present to you, she thought but did not say. Periodically he'd stroke her hair, and she would nuzzle his skin with her lips. It was a quiet and private time.

"Ready to get something to eat?" he finally asked.

Shelby almost responded with something brazen. Kept it inside, and just smiled and felt enigmatic. "First I'm going to shower," she said. She sweet-talked him, and Link joined her.

It was as nice as she'd thought it would be.

They arrived at the Misfits Saloon at six-thirty and found the place so crowded they had to search for adjacent stools. Bob had once told her Thursdays were good business nights, late enough in the week that folks were tired of working, close enough to the weekend that they wanted a sample of the sinning that was to come.

Bob called socializing sinning—he felt everything that was enjoyable was either illegal or sinful so preachers and lawyers could stop them from having fun.

As the bar owner approached, Shelby wanted to announce that she'd just made love with the sexiest man in Nevada. Ray Watt was seated a couple of stools down, and she wondered how he'd take it. Probably pout even more than usual.

They ordered Cokes—there was the second diskette to look through—and Misfits Burgers. As Bob went to the grill to pass on their orders, Link made a face.

"What's wrong?"

"I just remembered something. Where are the memorandums?"

"Memoranda," she corrected. "We bureaucrats know our Latin."

"Gary wrote that he was given photocopies. He said the first one was three pages long."

"The one the FBI agent said his superiors tried to hide."

Link nodded. "And the second one supposedly from the Weyland Foundation. I don't remember seeing either one. He didn't send off the manuscript, did he?"

"Gary told me it still needed work. I'll look for the memoranda when we get back."

"We've gone over the loft too many times for it to be there. Anyway, I'd like to find another place with a computer and modem."

"My new field lab's just half a mile down the highway." She kissed her forefinger and put it to his lips. "And I refuse to be unhappy. That was very nice, Mr. Anderson."

Ray Watt gawked so hard he almost lost balance and fell from his stool.

Bob returned, wiping a glass and peering inside as if he'd likely missed something, and regarded Link. "Remember yesterday, when we were talking about people disappearing?"

Link nodded.

He handed over a list. "Last one on there's Tom Grundy."

"The short fellow who was here last night?"

"Yeah. He didn't show up for work in Silver Creek this morning. His boss came by this afternoon, saying he'd checked his house. His car's there, but no sign of him. Said the lock was broke, so he went in. Place smelled awful and he found vomit splattered on a wall and a mess someone had tried to mop up, but no Tom. Came here thinking he might be on a bender."

"If his car's there, he'll likely show."

"Hope so. I'm getting tired of losing customers." Bob's face lit up then as Irene Staples squeezed in beside Shelby, made up as she'd never seen her before.

"A Southern Comfort Manhattan?"

Bob was already at work on it. "Light on the ice and an extra cherry?"

Irene gave him a coy expression. "Please," she said demurely, then greeted Shelby.

"How's the job?" Shelby asked.

"I get my first raise Monday," Irene said, and for the first time Shelby realized that she was attractive. Nice hairdo, even features, new dress, a figure that was mature and full but firm enough, Irene was trying to look attractive, and she did. Her expression was intelligent and alert. No downcast eyes or hopelessness. Even her skin appeared more healthy.

"This one's on me," Bob said, then added, "because of the job."

"Still planning on going back to school?" Shelby asked her.

"I interviewed at the University of Reno yesterday. Fifteen credits and I'll have my B.S., and then I'm going for a master's degree. I suppose I'll have to move closer to campus."

"I dunno," said Bob. "It's not a bad commute from here, you know."

Irene smiled, showing even teeth, and he looked almost bashful, which was certainly out of character for the grumpy old Bob Shelby had known since she'd been fourteen years of age, when he'd retired from the army and gone to work for her father.

None of them noted that the video camera on the ceiling had moved and was aimed directly at them.

20

They'd brought Shelby's Corvette, and as she drove them to the field laboratory, Link knew he mustn't wait much longer to alert Frank Dubois. If the falsified memos got into the wrong hands, they could generate a major problem.

Another thought. If Ansel Turpin was indeed alive, Erin was likely correct in her assumption that the Barn was under surveillance. Minicam videotaping was one of the ex-agent's fortés. That alone was good reason not to return to the loft.

"Nice night," Link observed as they got out in front of a small, windowless blockhouse.

"It's a *wonderful* night," Shelby said, coming around and hugging his arm, then holding on as they went to the building. A lighted sign read State of Nevada Natural Resources Management Station. She found keys in her purse and unlocked the metal door. The interior was a single room, with networks of pipes behind a maze of shelves filled with fittings, gauges, and large wrenches. In a corner were several metal cabinets, a desk and computer, and two folding chairs.

"Welcome to my unglamorous world," Shelby said.

The computer had been left on. She took the folder from him; inserted the second diskette, and looked at the contents. It was entitled Dilemma, and on it were three documents: Suspicions, Log of Events, and Conclusions. She double-clicked on the first one.

Gary opened by explaining the night in late May when he'd seen a fortyish prostitute named Trudy Schmidt at the saloon bar. Later, Deputy Ray Watt had told him Trudy had died the next day—of Asian flu, the coroner had said—and had shown him a photograph. Gary had been shocked, for it was as if he were viewing an entirely different person than the lively one he'd seen at the bar. The old woman in the photo wore a grimace, her hair was falling out, she'd voided bowels and stomach, and had blistered, darkened skin. Medics had told him bodies deteriorated quickly in the heat, but Gary couldn't shake a feeling that something was amiss.

In the next weeks other corpses were found in that awful condition, all attributed to that same, virulent strain of influenza. He'd checked at the University of Nevada library but could find no ready explanation to fit the symptoms. He'd also borrowed file photographs of the first two corpses from Ray Watt and intended to show them to someone in Reno who could tell him more. Finally he had viewed the corpse of Lester Dunlap . . .

"But Lester shot himself," Shelby said.

Gary had noted the same symptoms plus the lethal gunshot wound, and concluded that Lester had committed suicide because of the agony.

Shelby reached for the manila folder, dug through it, and found a packet of Polaroid photos, individually wrapped and separated by tissue. "I *thought* we might find them. Mr. Forgetful probably forgot all about them."

She looked at each one, then passed them on. "These are *awful.*"

Link concurred. He'd seen gorier combat casualties, but nothing quite like the people in the photographs. The faces were worst, with their horrified grimaces, swatches of loose hair, and darkened skin splotched here and there with open sores.

"I've only seen one effect that comes close," Shelby said, observing the last ones. "The photographs of the worst victims of Chernobyl."

"Radioactivity?"

"*Intense* radioactivity. Like thousands of roentgens per hour."

"Could it be from the nuclear material at Millionaire Mountain?"

"Too far away. The readings here aren't affected at all by what's stored there."

"But you think the people in the photos are radiation victims?"

She sighed, shook her head from side to side. "That was just a first reaction, probably because I've worked with radioactive substances."

"Any other ideas?"

"No, but I'm not into medicine."

Link looked at the photo of the woman's darkened, awful face. "Do you think it *could* be influenza?"

"Like I said, I'm not into . . ." Shelby's voice tapered off. She took another quick look at a photograph, pulled a small book from her purse, and used a telephone at the desk. She spoke for the next fifteen minutes, describing the victims and explaining the situation.

When she hung up, Shelby stared at Link for a moment. "That was a doctor friend from Stanford. She took a lot of pathobiology, really enjoyed digging down to the causes and effects of afflictions, and there's no flu that produces those symptoms. A couple of the Ebola strains, maybe, but she says this entire valley would be filled with corpses. The Asian-style flu that went around was a pussycat, she says. When I described the corpses here, told her about the vomiting, sores, darkened skin, and hair falling out, she said to take a blood sample and see if there were any reds left, because they're classic symptoms of massive radioactivity poisoning."

Link felt a chill, recalling images he'd seen of victims at Hiroshima and Nagasaki.

Shelby was shaking her head. "But it *can't* be radiation. I've checked for hazards all over this part of the state. Radon, low-level electromagnetism, *all* that sort of thing. There are minor problems a hundred miles east of us, but I've never had anything but normal readings here."

They went to Gary's Suspicions. The only matches of symptoms to diseases Gary had been able to find were the plague from the Middle Ages called the black death, a couple of the fast-killing African viruses, and severe radiation sickness.

There. He'd said it too. In fact Gary had telephoned Fred Jameson at the NEL study site and asked what dosage would cause death in a human. The answer had been inconclusive. Radiation destroyed living cells. The effect on living tissue was accumulative, although a subject could develop healthy replacement cells. The swiftness of onset of nuclear sickness varied according to the condition of the subject and proximity to the source—it was often a long and lingering death, involving breakdown of immunity. Also, radioactivity was measured in various ways. The basic unit of radioactivity was the roentgen, and field strength was measured in roentgens per hour, per day, or per year. But the unit used in the medical world was called a rad, measuring the effect of radiation upon living tissue.

Roentgens or rads, which did he want?

Gary had had no clue.

Thirty milliroentgens per hour, if experienced long enough, might cause sickness.

Gary had asked what could cause death in a short period. The doctor said it would take hundreds of roentgens per hour, over a period of several days, and even then death might take a month or longer. A man had stood *beside* the Chernobyl reactor just after meltdown, received an estimated dose of ten thousand roentgens, and—painfully—survived. He'd not been exposed for long, of course. Jameson had recited cases involving x-ray technicians.

"And to cause death in only a few hours?" Gary asked again.

Thousands of roentgens? Since the only ways you could achieve those readings were to melt down a reactor or explode an especially dirty nuclear weapon, it might never be determined. And since no figures were available, a number of governments would covet such knowledge.

Using those inputs, Gary had dropped radiation as a potential cause of the deaths.

That was all there was in the Suspicions document.

Shelby opened the second document. Gary's entries were shown in date-time sequence.

Log of Events

5/28–2300: Trudy Schmidt seen alive, Misfits Saloon. Appeared healthy.

6/01–0830: Trudy found in her home (death certificate: flu).

6/04–2230: Doyle Baker seen alive, Misfits Saloon.

6/06–1050: Doyle found in home (death certificate: flu)

6/06–2030: Sam Holmes seen alive, Break-a-Heart Cafe.

And so forth, until:

6/11–2130: Becky Pearson seen alive, Misfits Saloon.

6/12–0130: Riding home from the bar my NEL dosimeter alarm sounded. I looked at the tube and saw the needle at 500 r/hr; I was about to flee when the reading dropped to normal! Call Jameson tomorrow!

"Five hundred roentgens? Isn't that awfully high," Link said.

"Definitely. He's obviously talking about milliroentgens, which is a thousand times less potential and *still* dangerous at that level.

"He says the dosimeter alarm sounded. They don't do that unless there's a real problem."

"You're right. Ten roentgens or higher. The dosimeters aren't meant to be accurate, but they shouldn't be that much in error." Shelby was frowning, trying to make sense of it.

6/12–0330: No more readings/Went to bed.

0530: Becky's trailer burned, her body found in rubble (death cert.: smoke/burns)

1200: I was told abt Becky Pearson by Cal. This is *scary*, because the *high rad readings had happened ¹/₂ block from her trailer*. Called Fred Jameson and told him about dosimeter alarm & readings. He was dubious. Asked me to send the dosimeter to him so he could check it for malfunction.

1400: Mailed dosimeter to NEL, attn. Dr. F. Jameson.

"I wonder why Jameson didn't tell me about that call." Link mused. "Could they be doing something fishy out at the research site to cause the deaths?"

"I wasn't part of the real research. My collegium studied the suitability of the various storage site candidates. But I doubt Fred would want to put his career in jeopardy."

Link mulled something over. "Did they tell you about the old underground nuke tests?"

"Yes. That was the government's deep, dark secret."

"And you know about the third explosion."

"That was the other secret. It may have been the only recorded instance of accelerated depletion, if you believe in such things."

"Do you?"

"Admitting it would be like saying I believe in reading entrails. However, we found abnormally low radiation in Break-a-Heart Three. That was eerie and extremely unusual."

"Here's a what if," he said. "What if they try to duplicate the phenomenon and in the process produce a very high level of radioactivity?"

"Is that what they're doing?"

"It's what they're planning starting in January." If they were spreading false stories about the foundation's funding, Link had no qualms about telling their secrets.

"How much radioactivity will they generate?" she asked.

"I heard seven thousand roentgens."

"My God, that's high. Surely they won't conduct experiments in those leaky old radiation labs."

"How about down in the mines, beginning with Break-a-Heart One?"

She considered. "That's a good idea, using the bubbles. The access shafts are very narrow and the earth provides a natural shield."

"Yeah. But it would be an even better idea if they told the locals."

"The Department of Energy is being deceitful," she said.

"You're assuming Jameson is keeping the DOE informed."

"I've seen the Secretary himself out there twice."

Link lifted a photograph. "From what you said, this has nothing to do with NEL or what they're doing there."

"What I meant was, I don't understand what's happening."

They returned their attention to the screen. Gary had written about viewing Lester's body, about Link calling, then about someone breaking into his computer. He ended with:

1145: On my way to Big Cat to check on Mathilda & leave diskettes, then get the ms. cleaned up so Link can have a look & verify before I ship it away.

I know this is important, the deaths of these people are involved, but I've got to get back to my manuscript. I'll take this dilemma up again after Shelby and Link have looked over the manuscript & I've sent it in.

Shelby shook her head sadly. "Those five people did die, and it certainly wasn't the flu."

Link fished out the note Bob had provided.

"Here are four more who disappeared. Bob wrote down the last times he saw them at the bar." He read the names.

"I know them all. Jack Tripp's been Dad's handyman since I was little."

"Anything else on the diskette?"

"One more document." She opened it. There were only two short paragraphs.

Conclusions

Cause of Death:

Asian Flu—Very Unlikely

African Virus (i.e., Ebola C)—Unlikely

Bubonic Plague—Unlikely

Radioactive Poisoning—Unlikely

Commonalties of Victims: It's as if they've been pre-selected. All are in fair to good health. All are customers of the Misfits Saloon. None have close friends or family in the area. No one cares about them.

"We've got to go to the authorities with this, Link."

"This time I agree. This stuff is all way over my head. Any more ideas?"

Shelby wagged her head in a negative response. "It was over Gary's head too."

Link looked at her. "Tell me more about the Ancient Order of Dirt Muckers."

"For what you're thinking I can do it in two words: no way."

"Like the folks who blew up kids in Oklahoma City?"

"That's cruel and absolutely wrong."

He wondered about Ansel Turpin. "Could an outsider steer them into doing something?"

"It's unlikely. They're too resistant to change, and that means they're politically incorrect. They're also patriotic, which isn't as popular as it once was. They don't trust the government in Washington—but don't take that to mean they'd bomb a federal building. A lot of them *work* in federal buildings in Carson City and Reno. They're playing armadillo. Rolled up in a protective ball, waiting for the government to stop their verbal attacks on people like them and stop sounding like they're going to make them turn in their guns so they can solve someone's problems in big inner cities."

"You trust them?"

"I'd turn to them if I needed help. That includes Ray Watt. He's just confused because you're here and I'm puppy-dogging around after you." She pecked his cheek.

Link was running out of ideas. "Bring Gary's log back up. Maybe we can make something of it."

She did so, pulled a Day Timer from her desk drawer, and opened it to June. "I want to try something," she said, and began entering names on the appropriate days when they were last seen alive.

"There doesn't seem to be a pattern," he said. "It's sort of helter-skelter."

Then Shelby saw something. "*Every* Thursday night since May twenty-eighth, someone was seen alive and later found dead, or went missing."

"Also on other days in between."

"Yes, but every Thursday."

Something about Thursdays niggled in his memory.

"This is Thursday night," she said darkly. She went to a cabinet and opened it, pulled out an instrument, and checked the calibration date shown on a card.

"A Geiger counter?" he asked.

"They call them rad meters now."

"And you want to ride around, checking the radiation levels?"

"Why not? Someone could be dying right now, Link. If we get a reading, we can at least wake everyone up and tell them. Most people don't know much about radioactivity, but they know enough to be scared of it."

He looked at his watch. It was ten o'clock. One in the morning back east.

"Load the first diskette," he told her, and took out the flip-top phone.

Erin's voice was sleepy. He gave her the phone number of the computer line and told her what he wanted. "Stand by," she said and went offline. This time five minutes passed before the computer screen began its convolutions, as the one at the Barn had done.

"Insert the second diskette," Erin told him, and he relayed the instruction to Shelby.

Again the computer did its trick.

"Both were successfully copied on the mainframe server in the building," Erin said. "And by the way, *that* one's a clean connection."

"Get someone at the building to take a look at this information right away. Make it someone with a heavy clearance. And when you get to work in the morning, tell Frank I'll take him up on his offer for backup."

Erin came awake and sounded concerned. "Bureau people or our own?"

"Whatever Frank decides. Just make it someone who's damned smart."

"Is she done with the computer?" Shelby asked, and he nodded. She shut down.

"Both of you be careful," Erin said. "I've got new information about Ansel Turpin."

"Tell me tomorrow. Gotta go."

Shelby had replaced the diskettes and photos into the manila folder, and now joined him at the door. When they were outside she locked up, and they hurried to her car. A moment later they were headed down the street, Link examining the rad meter.

"Darn it, I'm low on gas," she said. They decided to go to the Barn, transfer to the rented Yukon, then he'd drive while she monitored the meter.

Juliette was monitoring the screen, peering as the tenth and final subject drove up to her home.

The lethality part of the previous night's experiment had gone badly, as she'd warned. This one was in better health. She would not drop drunkenly onto her couch and immediately fall asleep, as Tom Grundy had done, and expire half an hour into the project, while the radiation level was still building. It was as if the little man had just given up.

Adam Russo had been switching between cameras, trying to locate Lincoln Anderson and the geologist, who hadn't returned to the Barn after leaving the saloon. They'd disappeared to some unmonitored location, and that seemed to trouble him.

Juliette shifted her attention to the subject's home. The coffeepot was in place, loaded with slightly altered amounts of plutonium and californium.

The previous night, after Grundy had breathed his last, the radiation level had climbed to a spectacular 9,400 roentgens per hour, hovered for only a few seconds, then entered the first stage of accelerated depletion. The counter had reeled from nine to seven to five thousand, still picking up speed, and old Piers Jergen had hardly breathed as Juliette had read off figures as they'd flashed downward. Then he had allowed a smile to creep over his face for the first time since she'd met him. But the readings had slowed and held at eight hundred roentgens.

They'd been on the threshold of discovery, and Piers and the woman had been unaware that they'd stood, mouths agape, not daring to laugh or congratulate one

another. Even when Russo had gone to help retrieve
Tom Grundy's body, they had not spoken about their
near success, as if discussing it might somehow keep it
from happening.

Only once had old Piers slipped. "We must tell the
world," he'd said that afternoon.

"The world will know of it soon enough," Juliette had
told him in a tone reflecting the return of bitterness.

Piers Jergen watched from his chair, bored and utterly
ignoring the subject as she undressed in her bedroom.
He was impatient for the test to begin and did not see
the smile lingering on the subject's lips as she examined
herself, then pulled a gown over her nakedness and left
the room. They heard water being turned on, and the
sounds of her brushing her teeth.

Juliette brought up the subject's profile, and confirmed
that she was in superb health. While this one had friends
in the area, they would not remain long enough for it
to matter—and she particularly wanted the experiment
to go well. To watch as the radiation soared, and claimed
and withered the subject, and was sucked into oblivion.

Then she would know they were ready for the final
experiment.

Adam Russo announced that he'd located Lincoln Anderson and the geologist, that they were changing to
another vehicle, but she scarcely heard him.

The radiometric counter was switched on. Even with
the coffeepot closed and at rest, the bedroom's background gave a higher than normal reading because of
the increased amounts of nuclear fuel.

"Where are they going?" Juliette heard Russo say,
but her attention remained fixed on the bedroom. The
subject came in, checked the alarm setting on the bedside clock, then lay back against the headboard. She'd
had only two cocktails but was unaccustomed to drinking
and they'd forecast that she would fall asleep quickly.

She glanced at the second monitor, of the exterior of
the home. The white van was in position, the repairman
inside with the remote control, ready to begin the
experiment.

The subject picked a paperback from the bedside table

and then a pair of half-glasses. She did not appear at all sleepy, and the fact made Juliette release a sigh of displeasure.

The subject was an insomniac.

Friday, July 3, 1:15 A.M.

"Six milliroentgens," Link heard Shelby intone. "That's normal background reading."

They'd driven all around this side of the valley where the majority of the people lived, and where the previous deaths had occurred. After an hour of it, they'd begun to park for fifteen minutes, watch and wait, then drive to another position. They'd also begun to doubt.

Shelby had talked him out of getting more people involved, saying she didn't want to take time away from their task to brief them. Tomorrow she wanted to flood the area with people driving and watching. She would brief her bosses in Carson City and try to get their approval. If not, she'd turn to friends. She also spoke about how the next body they found would be properly examined until plausible answers were found.

"Ready to drive some more?" she asked.

"Sure," Link responded, and started the engine. "Reading?"

"Eight. Up two from the last one, but still in the normal range." For the next few minutes she had him turn on various streets, but noted only small changes in the readings.

Link hunched over the wheel, peering out, letting the vehicle idle along and wishing Shelby wasn't with him. Should *it* happen, they were talking about massive amounts of dangerous radiation—if Gary had actually been talking about roentgens and not thousandths. Again Link wondered if Gary hadn't misread the dosimeter; certainly there was the possibility that the dosimeter had malfunctioned, as Jameson had believed.

Shelby broke into his thoughts. "Hmm. Up to eighteen milliroentgens. It's done that every time we passed through here. Not a really big deal, but higher than normal. I'll check the charts tomorrow and see what we've measured in the past."

Shelby started to chatter again. By the time ten more minutes had passed Link was becoming lulled, and looking for another parking place. She was facing him, still talking, when a faint, high-pitched squeal sounded from the console compartment between them.

"What's that?" she asked, then laughed nervously. "I jumped a foot!"

"Check the reading," he said, and opened the console lid.

"It's gone berserk!" she said in a quavering voice. She turned a wafer switch. "Link, it's going up—past a *hundred* roentgens and rising!"

Link picked the NEL dosimeter from the bottom of the compartment. "It's working as advertised," he said grimly as the squeal continued.

They passed the white van parked at the side of the road that they'd noticed before. Link believed he saw a figure hunched inside, but paid no further notice.

"The reading's *still* climbing," she announced, awe in her tone. "Past four hundred."

Link continued ahead on the street. "*Milli*roentgens?"

"No. We're reading hundreds of *roentgens* per hour, and that's potentially *lethal*. My *God*, Link. What could cause it?"

"I saw a device at Millionaire Mountain. It looked like a beverage dispenser, and . . ."

"Forget it. It couldn't create this kind of reading all the way over *here*. It just went through *seven hundred* roentgens per hour!"

Link stopped the vehicle. "What's it doing here?"

"Through nine hundred and *still rising*."

He looked about. "Damn it, where's the source?"

"I have no idea, but it's got to be close. It just topped a thousand roentgens!"

He swung the wheel, backed up and turned around. Crept back down the street.

"We've got to get the people out of these homes, Link."

He flashed the lights and leaned on the horn, setting

up a din that pierced the moonless and still night. "It's past twelve hundred!" She had to shout to be heard over the sound of the blaring horn. "Stop!"

He braked and let off the horn. She opened the door.

"Where are you going?" he shouted.

She started for the nearest house. "We've got to warn the people. You go the other way. Tell them to get in their cars and get the hell out of here."

The NEL dosimeter on the console stopped squealing. He leaned over, stared at the rad meter, observed the numbers. "It's dropped to fifty milliroentgens," he yelled to Shelby.

She continued running.

Link climbed out, ran to his side of the street to warn the people in the other direction.

"Have him press the Safe button," Juliette LaCoste said anxiously.

"That will shut the device *off*," said Piers Jergen. "We won't be able to restart it."

"We can*not* have them discover it." She jabbed a finger at the scene. "The woman's a geologist. She'll find it. Go to Safe."

Adam Russo agreed. "Tell him," he said but the old man was stubborn.

Juliette pulled the radio from Piers's hands.

"Don't," the old man pleaded.

"Press the Safe button," she said into the microphone.

A moment later the repairman's voice sounded. "The green light's on."

"Good. Now go inside and bring the device out."

"*Damn* Anderson!" Russo exploded as he hurried for the door.

"Forget Anderson for now," Juliette called after him. "It's the geologist who'll be onto us first."

21

Shelby spoke forcefully to the man who stood before her, blinking through groggy eyes. "Take your family and leave! There's intense radioactivity. You're in danger."

The man peered past her. "I don't understand."

"Nuclear radiation. Go right now!"

The man's wife showed up, holding her robe about herself. She grabbed his arm. "That's Cal Admire's girl. She knows about that sort of thing."

"Get your family out and get away!" Shelby repeated.

"Where?" He still did not comprehend.

"It doesn't matter. Just leave the valley until you hear it's safe to come back."

He mumbled something and closed the door.

"You heard her," Shelby heard from inside as she started for the next home. As she hurried, she noticed that the white van had been moved, was now parked before Irene Staples's place, just two doors down. She slowed near the front door of the next home, noted there were no vehicles, almost passed it by but decided that someone might be at home.

She stopped and banged hard. "Hello inside!" she shouted, as she'd been doing at the others. After the third pounding she backed off and looked. There were no lights coming on.

A car pulled away from one of the homes she'd alerted and drove past, headed toward the highway. At least someone had listened. She started for Irene's, then slowed as she saw a dark figure come from the back, lugging something. Irene? She wondered, then saw that it was a tall male, carrying a heavy load. He crossed the street, heading for the Nevada Bell van.

"It's dangerous here!" she shouted to him. He turned and paused, then continued. He pushed his load into the rear of the van, closed the doors, and loped toward the driver's door.

Shelby hurried onto Irene's porch, then pounded with both fists.

There was no response, yet Shelby noted that Irene's old car was in place. She pounded again, then stopped and turned. The van was pulling away. What had the man been carrying?

A device that looked like a beverage dispenser, she remembered Link saying.

Her heart pounded. The source?

She ran out onto the street, cupped her hands and yelled at the top of her lungs toward the distant Yukon. "Link! I've found it!"

She waited, called again. Finally saw a figure running down the street toward her. Headlights illuminated him. It was Link. The vehicle passed him, accelerated, and Shelby moved to let it by. A family of frightened faces peered out of a sedan.

As Link drew closer, Shelby pointed. "A man came from the back of Irene's house with it, and she's still inside. The front door's locked but it may be open back there!"

He angled toward the rear, still running.

"Get her out quickly! It's likely contaminated inside."

As Link disappeared a dark pickup squealed to a halt, but she ignored it. Waited and saw a light come on. He was inside! *Hurry!* she silently encouraged Link. If the powerful source had been in her home, Irene would need immediate care. She prayed it could come in time.

A figure walked up, crunching gravel. She turned, thought he looked vaguely familiar. "Find a telephone and call nine-one-one. Irene's inside. She's going to need—"

Shelby's head snapped back from the impact of his fist. She grunted and reeled. He struck again, then grabbed and dragged her. The attack had come too quickly, the blows too stunning in intensity, and she could only struggle weakly. He grasped and hoisted her, and tossed her into the truck bed. Shelby fell against a barrel, managed to rise up on hands and knees. Again his heavy fist thumped into her head, and this time she dropped like a felled ox.

Link found Irene Staples in the rearmost bedroom, unconscious and smelling of vomit. He'd carried her outside, deposited her in the back seat of her old sedan, and when he could not find Shelby, returned inside to call 911.

The telephone line was dead, and he remembered the Nevada Bell truck that had been parked outside. *Here to repair it?* he wondered. He went back out, pulled the flip-top from his shirt pocket, and found it worked well as a normal cellular telephone.

He was connected with a Line County Sheriff's Department operator, who asked the nature of the emergency. He gave Irene's name and address, said she was very ill.

"Describe her condition."

"Radiation sickness," Link told her twice, and when she didn't comprehend, said she was so ill she would die unless she received immediate help. The operator refused to send a med-evac helicopter—said the paramedics would have to make that determination when they arrived.

He punched the End button and peered about at the street, wondering if Shelby had gone for help. A dark-colored pickup had driven up just as he'd gone around back. A friend of hers? Someone she'd stopped and asked for assistance?"

A dark pickup? A chill shuddered through him as he remembered being followed to Virginia City the night the fake Albee had tried to attack him.

Shelby was only vaguely aware that the truck had crossed the highway, lights still turned off, and continued on the old pony express station road, but she instinctively knew that she had to escape. She tried to rise up, but at first her limbs refused to respond. When she was able to will them to react, she found that her hands were bound with wire that cut harshly into the flesh.

They struck an obstacle and she slid against the tailgate. The heavy barrel rolled wildly into her back, causing a new bolt of pain to shudder through her. Shelby held fiercely to the rim of the tailgate. *Get out!* her brain screamed. She inched forward, pulling desperately until her head was over the gate, then grunted and tugged again, harder.

Too difficult, too little energy left in her to crawl over it.

Got to get away!

She felt, found the tailgate release handle and grasped it with both tethered hands.

Don't make it obvious, she thought. *Lower it slowly. Quietly.*

Shelby pressed hard with her fingers, broke a nail, and winced with the sensation of the quick tearing. Continued pressing until she felt the latch come free. Her heart pounded wildly as she very slowly pushed—and the tailgate lowered very slightly. That's it. *Slowly.*

Her captor was still driving with the lights turned off. Going too fast for her to feel good about jumping—but she knew that she must. She took a fortifying breath, lowered the tailgate all the way, then slithered toward the lip, the dark earth rushing past just inches below her face.

Got to do it!

The truck struck another obstacle and she was flung onto the edge of the gate, clung there precariously. Another jolt brought the barrel—and it had rolled half over her before she was carried with it into the void. She landed on the packed desert surface on her stomach, tumbled and skidded, and came to rest. The wind had been knocked from her by the impact, and she tried desperately to pull in a breath, but could only make *eek*ing sounds.

She heard sounds of the pickup braking.

Get away! He'll come back. Got to breathe! She eeked

frantically, suffocating, frightened. The first small intake
was precious. She pulled in more, listening to the roar
of the engine as the pickup was turned around.

The lights came on, capturing her in the glare. He
accelerated, coming directly at her—*He was going to run
over her!* Shelby whimpered, tried to rise, slipped and
fell, then lay sobbing, knowing she was about to die.

The truck braked, missed her by mere inches as it
skidded to a halt. The lights were switched off. She
heard a door slam, the sound of his approach. Something
metallic trembling against the back of her head. A pistol? As the sounds of breathing grew more harsh, she
resigned herself. Then the metal was pulled away as his
breathing evened.

"You'll serve a purpose," he said. She'd heard the
distinctive soft voice before. One of the new physicists
at NEL. He had seemed a gentle man, and she wondered
if it wasn't some sort of terrible mistake.

He left her, found and rolled the empty barrel back
to the truck, then returned.

"Shelby," she managed. "I'm . . . Shelby, remember."

"Yes," he said in the prim voice. He placed a small
rectangular object on the ground near her face. "Shelby,
I'm about to introduce you to a person I don't believe
you'll like. Just remember one thing. If you fight him
too hard, it's likely he'll beat you to death." His tone
was quite conversational, but the words terrified her.

His voice changed, a remarkable feat, for it was instantly mean. "Take off yer damned clothes." When she
hesitated, he grasped and harshly felt her, and ripped
the thin clothing away.

In the growling voice he ordered her to think of Lincoln Anderson. As he lowered his trousers he said he'd
be doing that. Then he dropped upon her, and she was
still exhaling when he grunted loudly and attempted to
push himself into her. Making filthy utterances. Stopping
periodically to hit her or squeeze her breasts, each time
encouraging her to cry out—moving the dark object
closer when she sobbed or pleaded for him to stop hurting her.

Then she realized that it was not sex he was after but her utterances.

He did not penetrate her or come to orgasm, whether because he was unable or unaroused she didn't care to determine. But although he did neither of those he pressed himself upon her in the tempo of sex and she grunted in unison, which was what he wanted. At some point, after it seemed a lifetime had passed, he simply stood and calmly zippered his trousers. He recovered the dark object from beside her, then grasped her arm and lifted her to her feet.

"I won't tell anyone," she tried, hoping it might be enough.

He chuckled as he drew dark leather gloves from his pockets and pulled them on, then paused for a moment. "Damn right yer won't tell, bitch." He hit her squarely in the face, hard. Shelby blubbered, felt the numbing pain in her nose. He struck her again, squarely, and she slipped down, out of his grasp, bleeding profusely. He dragged her upright by her hair, poised his fist. She crying and pleading, he cursing her in the belligerent voice, hitting her. A front tooth splintered. Spots danced wildly in her vision.

She didn't struggle as he manhandled her toward the pickup. With the slightest movement, bolts of fire shot through her in a dozen places. He shoved her forward and kicked her in the bare buttocks. Shelby cried out and sprawled onto the ground, nude and uncaring.

"I do enjoy tormenting the friends of my enemy," he said happily. He kicked her again, then turned and grunted with effort as he lifted the heavy barrel, walked two steps to the pickup, and deposited it upright into the bed. A display of strength. He returned and stood over her. She'd not dared to move, and now managed only a single plaintive word. "Please . . . don't."

He held the dark object toward her, changed his voice again. "Don't what, Shelby?"

"Don't hurt me anymore!" she blubbered through swollen lips. "Please."

He asked questions. Shelby didn't hesitate or try sub-

terfuge; there was no shred of fight left in her. She
wanted only to get it over.

Finally he lifted and threw her violently into the truck
bed. Her knee smacked against the gate, and she landed
hard in the metal bed. She could not stop crying, even
as she realized he was climbing in behind her, and she
did not try to fend him off.

"See, I remember you quite well." Shelby only
vaguely noted that his voice had once again softened.
Then he stuffed her headfirst into the barrel.

A next-door couple had come out of their home to see
what the hubbub was about, so Link put them in charge
of watching over Irene, who was reduced to periodic
moans and occasional gushes of vomit, while he ran up
the street toward the Yukon.

Shelby was not there.

He called Cal Admire, thinking she might have been
driven home, told him some of the story, and said Shelby
was missing. "Did she come home?" he asked.

"Nope. Where are you?"

Link told him.

"I'm on my way."

Ray Watt pulled up in his cruiser, bleary-eyed. He'd
gotten a call from the sheriff's department asking the
reason for all those phone calls about atomic bombs or
whatever.

Link tried to explain. More blinks and yawns and no
comprehension.

"Shelby's missing," he finally said, and that got Watt
to sit up straighter and take notice.

Cal arrived in his Suburban. The wail of the ambulance's siren sounded, and more people gathered. It
seemed like something out of an old slapstick movie,
and might have been funny if Irene Staples were not on
the brink of death, and Shelby had not disappeared.

22

The barrel was falling, careened and bounced, slammed hard into the side of whatever she'd been dropped into, and fell again. She could feel it, although it came dimly through a painful veil. Another crash and a teetering sensation. Then another free fall, followed by a tremendous crash as the barrel fell onto something hard, then rolled . . . and became still. She was reduced to low moans. It seemed astounding that a human body could take such abuse and remain alive.

Now to expire from suffocation? The thought was punctuated by sharp paroxysms that coursed through her body. Get it over with, she prayed, and she would have taken in gulps to use up the remaining air if not for the pain each breath generated. Broken ribs, she decided, from the fall from the pickup, or being kicked.

Something clanked hard against the barrel, and a flush of terror shuddered through her. Then came a pounding at the end of the barrel where her feet rested.

Was her tormentor reopening it to finish his task?

"Kill me," she whispered, hoping it would be done quickly.

The lid came off, and she heard his breathing sounds. He touched her ankle. She waited as the hand grasped and tugged. But it was weakly done and she heard a grunt of exhaustion. The person paused, panting at the simple effort. It was not her tormentor, who could have easily dragged her out.

Shelby moved, cried out from the pain in her side, then tried again to extend her legs and push her way downward. Felt the hand on her ankle again as whoever it was tried to pull her free.

"Don't," she screamed as agony shot through her. Then she very slowly backed down, freeing her legs then her hips, paused, then pushed on out . . . into absolute darkness.

Had he blinded her?

She was on a hard surface covered with a thick layer of fine sediment, now perched on all fours, breathing tentatively, shallowly, smelling a sickly sweet odor.

She tried to speak but found that her mouth was filled with acrid liquid and matter.

"You're *alive*," said a high voice wonderingly. "The others were dead."

Shelby spat out an accumulation of vomit, blood, and fragments of the splintered tooth.

"No," the shrill voice chastised. "Use the waste barrel. Don't foul our nest."

Shelby let her head droop, breathed very gingerly to reduce the aching.

"Did you bring food like Tom did?"

Despite the sopranic register, she knew the voice. "Gary?"

He became still and quiet.

"It's Shelby, Gary."

She heard a whimper, then groaned herself as a wave of agony swept through her.

"Don't die." His sound was mournful.

"It's dark," she managed.

"That's because the glow-wall's turned off."

That didn't make sense. "Where are we?" she tried, wondering if he was mad.

He whispered. "Welcome to hell, Shelby."

Russo entered the room. "I got her," he told the watchers.

"Right in front of them," said old Dr. Jergen with obvious disapproval.

Adam Russo pulled off his gloves, picked his eyeglasses off of the table where he'd left them, and carefully polished the lenses with an immaculate handkerchief. Blinking primly and nodding to himself as he decided things had gone well enough, considering.

On the screen a crowd had gathered on the street.

"The subject's alive?" he asked, peering.

"They've taken her away in the ambulance," said Juliette LaCoste.

"She still may die," old Piers Jergen said. "The device was activated for only thirty-two minutes, but it was showing nine thousand roentgens."

On the monitor three men had gathered near the police cruiser. He identified them as Anderson, the deputy sheriff, and the missing geologist's father. They spoke somberly, the deputy periodically lifting a microphone to make a radio call. The look on his face showed that he had not an inkling of what it was about.

The geologist was neutralized.

Now the danger came from Anderson.

"We should leave quickly," Juliette said, staring.

If they left, it would be three days before he'd planned, and Adam Russo was busily running alternatives through his mind. He finally sighed. She was right. The chance of compromise was too great if they remained.

"We'll move up the departure date but continue with the plan." The soft-spoken man watched the monitor with pursed lips.

"It was going to work," the old man lamented. "If it hadn't been stopped, this time we would have seen it. I want to try once more before we go."

"No."

"Where's the device?" Piers Jergen asked in a petulant tone.

"The repairman should be bringing it through the side gate right now. We'll need you to prepare four of them. Nothing changes, Piers. We will follow the plan. You will show the entire world that you are the creator of the first controlled A.D. phenomenon."

The soft-spoken man turned to the woman. "Go with him. Remember your purpose, Juliette. It will be very soon now."

She nodded happily. "Come, Piers. These will be best of all."

He waited until they'd left for the laboratory—the woman by far the more important of the two, for she was making it work—then he walked outside into the inky darkness.

Waiting were the chief of security, a hulking and muscular man, and the telephone repairman. "There are changes?" asked the repairman, lighting a cigarette. He smoked incessantly, unfiltered, the stronger the weed the better.

"Yes," said the soft-spoken Russo, and briefed them. When he told the security chief what he wanted next from him, the big man balked.

"She doesn't deserve that," he cried.

"She was going to die anyway," Russo told him evenly. "You're being paid well. Now go and have your last fun with her. I'll want her ready in half an hour."

The repairman remained behind. "You want help with Anderson?" he asked.

4:25 A.M.

Link had not tried to calm Cal Admire's fears about his daughter, for it would have done no good. In back of both of their minds was the fact that Gary had also disappeared suddenly, and there was still no sign of him.

Deputy Watt had contacted the emergency preparedness office in Carson City about the radioactivity, using words Link fed him so he'd get it right. Although the rad meter now showed only a fraction of what Shelby had measured, the EPO had called for a military decontamination team to deploy from Indian Springs, two hundred miles to the south.

Watt had also called in help from other peace officers in the area.

Link had encouraged both actions.

After a fruitless circuit of the valley, Link returned to the Barn, intending to check for messages, make a thermos of coffee, and get back on the road. It was still dark, not yet five a.m., when he parked in front of Gary's home, wondering about the pickup and the telephone van he'd seen. He'd told Cal and the deputy about them. Watt said he would notify Nevada Bell and have them identify the driver so they could question him. As for the other, he guessed there were a hundred dark-colored pickups in the valley.

Link had also told them about Shelby shouting. "A man came out of Irene's with it!"—although he did not know what *it* was, and they were as perplexed as he was.

He went inside, stopped and listened for a prudent moment, then mounted the stairs. Thinking about the probability of surveillance if Ansel Turpin was involved.

The answering machine light blinked. A message had been recorded. He played it back, and was surprised to hear Joseph Spotted Horse's somber voice. "It is four in the morning here in Montana, and I am having trouble sleeping because my mind will not rest. I think you should call me, Lincoln, so I can know you are not dead." With that Joseph hung up.

"Not now," Link said aloud. He had no time for distractions, regardless of how prescient the old man was in sensing that something was amiss.

But there was another call to make. As he picked the flip-top out of his shirt pocket, his eyes were drawn to the oblong box behind the computer. Twice the size of other telephone terminals he'd seen in homes, with a small, clear glass eye near its top. It did not seem right— certainly it was different from any other he had ever noticed. Screws at top and bottom secured the box. He touched it, lips pursed, wondering, and then pulled out a small pocketknife. Slowly and carefully he unscrewed the thing, wondered if it wasn't some special unit used by Nevada Bell, since the line for the computer also ran from there. He lifted off the cover and drew out a small unit that was not connected to any of the four telephone wires. While he was no expert, the tiny device with a lens and gimbal-driven swivel did not appear appropriate. As he watched, it came to life and tried to rotate in his hand.

He raised it, stared into the fish-eye. "Give me a call,

Turpin. We need to talk." When he yanked the thing out of the box, wires dangled like loose spaghetti.

Images came to him. The long-haired telephone repairman working on telephone poles—Bob said he moonlighted installing video cameras. Like the one in the Misfits Saloon. To pick out victims like Tom Grundy, the wannabe veteran? Like Irene, and all the others?

When they'd noted the increase in radioactivity, he had turned their vehicle and started back, and whoever had been radiating Irene Staples had shut down what they were doing. The valley was wired for video. And Erin kept picking up dirty telephone lines.

Link looked about, saw no other units similar to the one he'd just liberated, opened the flip-top phone and punched MEM, then 1.

"Two-seven-seven-five." Erin sounded weary.

"It's Link," he said.

"I'm at the building, in Frank's office. We've got problems, Link."

"Here too." He told her what had transpired.

"Shelby's missing?" Erin's voice was horrified.

"Yeah. Tell Frank to send in the Marines. I need help."

"Talk to him."

Frank Dubois was on the phone. "Erin called me at three this morning, after she read the contents of the first diskette. We've been trying to get through to you for the past two hours."

"I had the cell phone turned off. There's big problems here, Frank. Erin's right. Either Ansel Turpin or someone with his talents is trying to take us down."

"Help's on the way. There's a Special Agent Gordon Tower on his way with backup. Just sit tight and wait for 'em."

"Erin said you have problems too?"

"Yeah. Gary sent the manuscript off after all, with copies to the world. The major networks are going to run excerpts on the morning news."

It took a moment for Link to comprehend. "Not Gary, Frank. Someone broke into his computer. They have the manuscript, and probably the memos as well."

"Well, the media certainly have copies of everything. The White House is involved so they're trying to plead security and get restraining orders, but they're only temporary measures. There'll be bad publicity and full-fledged investigations of the companies involved, with us up front. It's all lies, so we'll eventually be cleared, but it's going—"

The telephone beside the computer buzzed. "I'll get back to you, Frank. I've got a local call coming in." Hopefully from someone who had located Shelby.

Erin broke in. "This time keep the flip-top turned to standby, Link."

"Yeah." He collapsed the cell phone and lifted the receiver on the table. "Link Anderson," he answered.

"We've got your playmate," said the deep voice he'd once believed belonged to Special Agent Destin Albee.

"Let me talk to her," he said.

There was a low chuckle. "She's busy right now. You want her back, maybe we can work a trade. You've got something I want."

"Let me talk to her, Turpin."

"As I said, she's busy." He hadn't denied the name. "Here, listen to her."

He heard a series of groans made to the tempo of sex, then a sharp sound, like a slap. She cried out. It was Shelby. The carnal sounds continued.

"See. Told you she was busy."

A cold wind flowed over Link. "What do you want? The diskettes?"

"Damn, but you're smart. Have you shown them to anyone?"

"You're the surveillance king. You know I haven't." Link hoped that was true. Erin had said Shelby's field office hadn't been wired.

"Don't try to copy them or anything before you leave there."

"I don't even know how," he said truthfully, looking at the computer, pleased that Turpin didn't realize they'd already been sent. Horrified at the sounds he could still hear over the telephone. "Let her go, Turpin."

He heard Shelby release a pained sound. "Please . . .

don't." she pleaded. "Don't what, Shelby?" asked a mean voice. "Don't hurt me anymore," Shelby pleaded.

"Where do I go?" Link asked.

"Someplace you've been. Show up at the pony express station at six sharp. Unarmed, which means leave your rifle, and don't try to call *anyone* until we've made the swap."

"And you'll have Shelby with you?"

"A friend of mine. Same guy's been bangin' her. He's saying goodbye to her, if you know what I mean." He chuckled. "Now don't you wish you'd stayed in Montana? I'll bet she does."

"If he's hurt her . . ." Link stopped, realizing the futility of words as the line was disconnected and the dial tone buzzed in his ear. Link considered calling Frank to alert him to what was happening, but decided he couldn't take the chance that Turpin had activated another minicam.

The telephone buzzed again, and he picked up.

"Lincoln?" Joseph Spotted Horse's voice was tired.

"I don't have time to talk, Joseph."

"Lincoln, I am going to—" The telephone went dead, then crackled back to life.

"I shut him off so you wouldn't be tempted to say anything stupid," said the voice he now knew was Ansel Turpin's. "Concentrate on the trade, Anderson. One well-used woman for two diskettes. You have twenty-three minutes."

Again the phone went dead in his hand. Link replaced the receiver and tried to think of options, which were few for he did not dare delay. He went down and outside, picked the manila folder from where he'd left it beside the rad meter in the Yukon, took out the diskettes, and held them up in plain view in the growing morning light. The repairman had worked on a box located on a nearby telephone pole, so he supposed Ansel Turpin was watching.

Well-used woman, Turpin had said. As he crawled into the rented Yukon, Link vowed that when he'd retrieved Shelby he would hunt the man down.

He drove directly to the highway, not wishing to be

intercepted and have to explain to Deputy Ray Watt, and headed east. After five miles he turned onto the dirt road. Then, kicking up a rooster tail of dust in his wake, he accelerated toward the pony express station.

As Link pulled up to the old adobe building and shut off the engine, he read the odometer. The station was located four miles off the highway, another mile from the nearest homes. Well out of sight and earshot. He emerged and looked about but saw no sign of the kidnappers. The sun glared over the hill to the east, casting yellow light and morning shadows over the desert. The blanket of ground dust showed no recent tire tracks other than those he'd created.

He'd obviously arrived earlier than whoever was making the trade.

Saying goodbye to her, if you know what I mean.

A chill swept through him as he knelt, as if inspecting a rear tire, then rose and looked about. He went inside the old structure, and found it empty as he'd expected. Saw only the same collection of empty beer bottles and soda cans. Since there were no phone lines he assumed there were no minicams or audio transmitters—but assumptions were fodder for fools, and he did nothing that might arouse Turpin's suspicion.

A splintered and warped three-foot two-by-four lay by the corner of the old building. A discarded and rusted length of rolled barbed wire was not far beyond. Link retrieved the board, examined it idly, and aimlessly chucked it over by the rented four-by-four.

His attention was drawn then, as a dusty pickup emerged from a nearby gully where it had been parked, hidden from his view. Beneath the dust layer the color was forest green. As the vehicle came closer, then was parked ten yards distant, its nose pointed to his left, he read the neatly lettered logo: Nucleonic Engineering, Limited.

The engine was turned off. The driver was alone. He wore a sardonic grin, and sunglasses with reflective lenses masked his eyes. Link's mind boiled. *She's busy . . . he's saying goodbye to her . . . well-used woman.*

The man emerged. There was a smear of dried blood

on his trousers. It was not a wound, had likely come from another person. Link's rage simmered.

"Where is she?" he called out.

The man was solidly built and moved smoothly, with few wasted motions. "First the diskettes," he said, his voice as belligerent as his expression. Link remembered it from the background in the conversation with Ansel Turpin.

"Not yet," Link said.

"Oh, yeah?" A sneer. "What's that in your hand?"

"Blanks." He held them up for his view. Link had held no illusions. If the opportunity presented itself, he'd known there would be no trade, only the killing of one half-Blackfoot, former-air force fighter pilot named Lincoln Anderson. So he'd cheated. The diskettes he'd held up outside the Barn had been swapped for two others, blanks he'd palmed in the loft. The originals were now hidden.

He tossed the blank disks at the man's feet.

The rapist's eyes swept over them and slowly raised. A mocking expression came to his face as he unholstered his sidearm, a stainless steel Colt Python, and casually pointed it at a barrel in the truck bed. He thumbed back the hammer, aiming at the top portion.

"Guess who's in the barrel," he said, and before Link could respond, fired. The report echoed from the nearby foothills. The barrel rocked only slightly, but a faint squeal came from within.

Link's heart plummeted as the man thumbed back the hammer.

Shelby was in the barrel! "Wait," he shouted.

The man grinned maliciously. "I fucked her brains out and just shot her in the ass. You probably wouldn't want her anyway."

"I'll give you the diskettes."

"Well, I'll be damned," he said in the mocking voice as he took careful aim at the barrel. "Guess you better get 'em, don't you?"

23

Link had no option. The magnum's muzzle was pointed at the very middle of the barrel, and Shelby was obviously alive, for there were movements and faint screams. He walked to the rented four-by-four, wondering if the man would shoot him as soon as he knew the diskettes were genuine. He decided it was likely.

"Get the damn things," the shooter hissed impatiently, trigger finger taking up slack.

Link knelt and reached under the wheelwell to where he'd placed the disks on the tire.

"Bring 'em out where I can see them."

The fingers of Link's left hand closed on the diskettes, those of his right on the two-by-four behind him. He half-rose and nonchalantly tossed the diskettes—and as the man's eyes followed them, he swept the board around in a single fluid motion, hurling it with all of his strength. The missile spun end-over-end once before striking the shooter squarely in the chest. The man grunted, both from surprise and pain, but had the presence to stagger back and away. By then Link had launched himself. The pistol fired as he impacted, arms wrapped about the man's waist, the force driving him back and into the side of the NEL pickup.

The man grunted loudly as he bounced off the truck, and as they grappled desperately for the gun in his hand, Link found they were of equal strength.

The revolver discharged again—and Link felt a searing sensation in his back. The other man cursed, raised the revolver while Link held onto it, and brought it down hard, thumping into flesh. Again, and Link felt an explosion of pain as his ribs cracked. He could not withstand another assault. As the other man raised the heavy pistol for a third blow, Link twisted free, snatched up the two-by-four—and swung. The man yelped as the Colt flew from his grasp. Again Link swung, and this time the board impacted the side of the man's head.

The rapist dropped, mouth agape, eyes gone blank and already unconscious.

Link slowly rose, chest heaving, leaned against the truck for support as he watched him warily. Wanting to smash him to pulp for what he'd done to Shelby. Knowing he mustn't for he would have answers, and more than anything, he needed those.

His back wound shrieked with agony, but it was not especially debilitating and tending it would have to wait. Link grunted at the fiery sting as he bent to retrieve the revolver. A shrill but weak voice sounded from the barrel, and there were occasional shuddering movements. He cast a last look at the man—he was going nowhere— then unlatched the tailgate and painfully crawled onto the bed.

The top of the barrel had been tamped unevenly. He reversed the heavy revolver, grasped the muzzle and battered at the highest point with the butt, not wanting to see what was inside but knowing he must. He would rush her to the nearest facility—he remembered one on the way to Silver Creek not far from the airport—and pray she would live.

Link heard the man moving on the ground, then a moan. He continued with his task. With the fourth blow the lid came loose. He lifted it, got a glimpse of bare skin . . .

"Put the gun down!" Link froze at the sound of the accented male voice. He considered options, like plunging over the side of the truck bed as he reversed his grip on the revolver. Anything to . . .

Ch-ch-ch. The sound was muted, but three new bullets appeared in the uppermost part of the barrel by his elbow. It was a fully automatic weapon, so effectively silenced that only the sound of the blow-back slide was distinct.

"Next I kill her," said the voice. "Drop the gun."

Link released his grip. The revolver clattered onto the metal bed.

"Get down and stand by the building."

Pain shot through his back as he dismounted. A tall, blond man awaited him—the lanky, ponytailed telephone repairman he'd seen working around the valley—and motioned with the barrel of a silenced Skorpion machine pistol.

"We have to help her," Link tried.

Neither compassion nor patience were among the blond's virtues. "Get over there."

Link complied. There was no way to help anyone if he was dead.

"Face the building, then put your arms out wide and lean on the wall."

He displayed trouble raising his left arm, groaned theatrically. "My back's hurt." He complained, wanting to lull the blond into thinking he posed no threat.

"Do it!" ordered the blond.

Link moved hesitantly and made more pained sounds.

"You okay?" he heard from behind. The first man muttered a few incoherencies.

As he waited, Link tried to recall what he'd just seen. An inverted and nude woman's form exuding a musky scent of sex and perspiration. Slight movement—a bloody leg? He'd had no time to digest the image more—yet something about it seemed wrong.

"The disks are next to your foot. Don't step on them." The rapist's voice was halting.

"Want me to shoot him?" The blond's voice.

Another painful grunt, then, "I've got another use for him."

Link dropped his head enough to look back under his right arm and see the man he'd hurt sitting up, the blond hunkered beside him, awkwardly holding the Skorpion, the diskettes, and the revolver.

He recalled data on the Czech-manufactured Skorpion 61. With the wire stock folded back it was small enough to tuck and hide. Effectively silenced using a factory-supplied noise suppressor. Fired 7.65 mm shorts at 750 rounds per minute. Good gun, bad ammo. Underpowered. Misfires were common because of the lousy rounds.

"Where the hell have you been?" the first one grumbled. He did not look well.

"I hid the van and brought a golf cart."

A painful whimper sounded from the barrel.

The blond man saw Link staring. "Turn back around!"

"Let him look." The first one struggled to his feet, staggered once. "No use to make more noise than necessary," he said, and reached for the Skorpion. He turned to the barrel, and forced a smile to his pale face. "Watch this, Anderson."

"No!" Link yelled hoarsely.

Ch-ch-ch-ch-ch. New holes appeared, these at the base of the barrel. There was no way any could have missed. The barrel shuddered violently for a five-second count and became still. The mewling whimpers ceased.

Link was stunned into inactivity as the man turned his head and grinned. "Remember me?" His voice had changed midsentence, become that of Destin Albee. But Albee was dead, and there was only one man this could be.

Ansel Turpin's sunglasses had been knocked off in the struggle, and the eyes were intense. "Gotcha, Anderson. Live bait works wonderfully."

"You've killed her," he croaked.

"Likely. One more time and we'll dump her out and see. Then it'll be your turn in the barrel." He smiled at his wit, grimaced at a jolt of pain, and aimed. *Ch-ch-ch-ch-ch.* Bullets stitched higher on the barrel as blood drained from the lower holes.

An unexpected metallic *click.* Followed by pregnant silence. Either the round had not chambered or the firing pin had struck a dud.

Link immediately rolled hard to his left, heard the blond's warning yell as he reached for the roll of rusted wire. The repairman was crouching, the revolver coming around, when the barbed wire struck him in the face. He stumbled, blood streaking his nose and cheek, as Link dove behind the old adobe structure, scrambled upright, turned and ran directly away, using the building as a shield.

The blond yelled and the revolver roared. The bullet passed so close that Link felt the air disturbance by his ear. He sprinted faster.

"Don't kill him," he heard Turpin rasp in a pained voice. "Shoot his legs."

The Skorpion had been cleared. Dusty plumes stitched the earth in a neat row. A hornet stung Link's calf, and he tumbled headlong into a small arroyo.

"Got him," Turpin wheezed, still not sounding well.

Link lay flat. Took a couple of breaths as he slithered backward for a few feet, and raised his head just enough to view them through the veil of a small clump of sagebrush. They were forty yards distant, at the rear of the pony express station, looking intently at where he'd disappeared. Ansel Turpin was bent slightly, breathing through his opened mouth and holding his chest where the two-by-four had impacted. He pulled in a slight breath and grimaced, then handed the Skorpion to the blond and nodded toward the hillside. "Bring him in, but don't kill him."

The blond gave him a narrowed look of concern. Turpin was still holding his chest, and wore a pasty look that made Link wonder if the two-by-four hadn't done more damage than he'd first believed.

"Wait here." The blond disappeared toward the vehicles.

Link pulled off the T-shirt, found a six-inch bloody line where the .44 magnum round had dug a furrow down his back. The second bullet had penetrated his lower leg, and the puny Skorpion round—designed for quiet, close-in work—was lodged inside the muscle. Both wounds stung furiously, but except for the fact that they were draining blood, neither was life-threatening.

He wallowed on the ground, remaining out of Turpin's view as his skin and jeans assumed the color of the dusty earth. Then with one hand he patted dust onto neck, face and hair, and with the other grasped his calf and applied pressure to stop the bleeding.

But those were physical actions, and all the while he concentrated hard, thinking about how Piegan warriors had once masterfully blended with their surroundings.

The blond man returned to the adobe hut, and he too was preparing; tightening the laces of his boots, adjusting a floppy campaign hat. Strapping a sheath knife to his calf, clipping a canteen of water to his belt, loading a small pair of single-prism binoculars into a shirt pocket.

Link finished with his cosmetics and, still staring, backed down the shallow arroyo on elbows and shins, careful to erase all sign of blood and his passage.

Turpin was looking no better. "What are you waiting for?" he grumbled.

The blond nodded at the arroyo. "He's better than you think." He pulled on a pair of yellow-tinted shooting glasses.

Link determined the man's identity. He'd seen Russian special forces in photographs and video clips, been briefed on their intensive training. Of those Ansel Turpin had worked with in St. Petersburg, one had been a renegade officer, a Speznaz captain turned mafioso. He was said to be capable in the field and good with electronics. From observation Link decided he was also careful and had probably not forgotten all of his training.

He had backed some thirty yards when the indent became too observable. He stopped and watched as the blond reloaded the Skorpion, ratcheted a round into the chamber, slipped two more clips into side pockets of his utilities, and started forth. As he closed Link was momentarily masked by a small bramble, and backed away farther.

"I saw something!" Turpin yelled.

The blond stopped, head slowly scanning. "Where?"

"It was out of the corner of my eye. Over to your right somewhere."

Link was very still.

"Maybe not," Turpin said after a pause.

The blond man arrived where Link had first lain and studied the earth. "He's bleeding." He raised his gaze and looked carefully about, then began a slow zigzag course directly away from Link.

I've got a rifle in the pickup," Turpin called out, and pointed to a road below that paralleled the hillside. "I'll drive down there and make sure he doesn't get past." Turpin still did not sound well. He moved slowly. The thought that he was hurting was satisfying.

Link lost track of the ex-Speznaz officer as he continued his zigzag pattern. He took the chance, rose slightly and moved crab-fashion toward the next arroyo. As he did the blond came back into view, looking away, then sweeping his vision back.

Link froze, not daring to breath. *Become a stone or a bush,* Joseph Spotted Horse had instructed. *Become the earth.* He was in plain view but the blond continued to scan past him, stared at a discoloring of rock—it was different and captured his attention—then went on. He turned and began his zigzag search in the opposite direction, toward where Link had just been.

Link continued to the second arroyo. He heard the pickup, knelt, and observed as it stopped on the road below, then as Turpin leaned over and focused binoculars on the hillside.

It was not going to be easy getting past them. The men who pursued him were trained professionals. He was about to determine how well he'd listened to Joseph Spotted Horse.

He had on a pair of well-worn Western boots. They were comfortable, and—as with the old Dodge pickup— he regarded them as reliable friends. But they left heel prints that took too much of his time to smooth over. He pulled them off, hid them beneath the base of a large sagebrush, and went on in dusty stocking feet. The desert floor was harsh on them but not nearly as bad as wildernesses he'd trekked through in Idaho and Montana. He went on silently until he arrived at the end of the larger arroyo.

When the Speznaz renegade was searching intently, and Turpin was not watching from the pickup below, Link brazenly crept across an open area to a gathering of large rocks. There was a light flurry nearby, something that captured the blond's attention, for he stared at the rocks, then readied his weapon and began walking there. Directly toward Link, with no looks to either side. When he was twenty yards distant, Link went out the back, hidden by the outcropping.

The blond's radio cackled to life. "He's on the other side of the rocks."

Link forgot caution and began running, angling uphill. A moment later he heard the *spang, spang* of ricocheting bullets, but he continued ahead, finally diving into a thicket of sagebrush. More bullets thumped into the earth about him as he flattened to the ground, then slithered forward, snakelike.

Wondering what rabbit or ground squirrel or other small animal had betrayed him, he rolled into a new arroyo, knowing he was leaving a trail as he quickly went down it toward the road, then crept back and erased only most of those signs. Finally he backtracked farther up the hill—then froze into immobility as the sounds of pursuit became distinct.

The Speznaz officer came into view, doggedly following his sign, looked down the arroyo where Link had feinted. He lifted his radio. "Coming your way," he said, then added something in Russian.

"I *want* him to come." Turpin was back to using the soft voice, and sounded more alert. He was recovering, and came to a decision. "We're running out of time. Next time, shoot to kill."

It was definitely not going to be easy.

24

Ansel Turpin was impatient—watching the repairman move so cautiously on the slope only a football field's length away was irritating. For the hundredth time he wondered why the man was so slow about it. Anderson wasn't even armed, for Christ's sake.

But the ex-Speznaz officer was reliable, smart enough to pick up quickly on how to work with listen-ins, minicams, and relays, and once had been capable of taking out a company of enemy soldiers singlehandedly. Or at least that was the way he'd packaged himself when they'd met in Russia. But if he was so damned tough, why didn't he just stomp up there and *take* Anderson? Turpin would have done so, if it hadn't been for his chest, which felt as if it were filled with lead since Anderson had thrown the two-by-four.

He'd actually felt as if his heart had stopped when it hit, and he'd believed he was dying. It was better now, but he'd need more time before he went loping around the hills.

His radio sounded. "Adam, this is Juliette. How much longer will you be?"

Turpin answered in Adam Russo's soft voice. "Not long."

She seemed nervous. "The chief of security said you would be back by now."

"Are all of the devices ready?"

"Another hour. We can't rush it." Her voice cracked,

and Turpin was glad he would not have to depend on her much longer.

"Concentrate on your task," he told her, "and tell security to prepare for the helicopter's arrival. He knows what must be done."

"Yes." Juliette signed off.

The repairman's voice came over the second frequency. "Anderson is very good."

Turpin's eyes were drawn to vague movement high on the hillside. "While you're talking, he's up there running."

The repairman whirled about, saw the motion, and fired. The sound was muted but puffs of dust stitched a pattern on the desert surface. By the time Turpin looked through the rifle scope, there was nothing to see. "It's time to finish," he told the blond. "Find him and kill him."

Link was bellied into the dust, a stone. This time when he'd run the wounded calf muscle had sent forth a spike of pain so intense it had made him stumble and become visible. Much more abuse, he knew, and the leg would rebel even worse.

They'd gone seven miles in the hills paralleling the highway. Past the women's prison far below, where they'd made sure he didn't get past, then beyond the medical clinic near the highway. Ahead and to his left, on the near side of the highway, was the Silver Creek airport. The bad news was that after a hundred more yards there were no more arroyos, and the terrain became so flat and exposed that hiding would become impossible.

He'd overheard the Russian's side of the conversation again, this last time saying he would find Link very soon. The Speznaz officer was wrong. Link's confidence had grown. All he had to do was go over the hills, directly *away* from civilization, and he could evade them as long as he wished. He remembered a road ten miles in that direction. He'd considered it, and now it seemed the only route of prudent travel remaining. But there was a growing urgency about the men, and they were obviously on some kind of schedule. The trek to the north would take two hours, and it might take as long to get a ride back. He did not want to lose them.

"Sure," his mind sneered. "Got 'em right where you want 'em."

He looked north, wondered if it wasn't a good idea after all.

The Russian had known to be careful, and if he had not been, Link would have taken him. Turpin was increasingly impatient, and if he had been the one searching, the contest would be over. But that was if he'd done it right away. Twice now the leg wound had reopened and drained more blood, and Link had had to apply direct pressure to the wound for as long as he'd dared to stay in one position. He felt too dried out to pose a direct threat to either of the men, even Turpin, unless they did something particularly stupid.

Link remembered Turpin shooting the barrel, murdering Shelby—or whoever was inside, for he was still unsure of what he'd seen—and the cavalier way it had been done still outraged him.

He continued to observe, with only his eyes moving behind slitted, dust-laden lids. There were four aircraft parked on the gravel strip below. The Piper Comanche was closest, but to go there would mean first getting beyond the Speznaz officer, then past Turpin in the flat area. An impossible task.

Or at least impossible was what they would believe.

He began to slither soundlessly down the shallow arroyo. Five full minutes later he was only twenty paces from the Russian, another layer of desert grime applied to his body, utterly immobile and curled about the side of a medium large rock. The Speznaz officer came toward him, stopped and looked about, trying to take in everything, searching—Link knew—for the *exception* to his natural surroundings. Looking for a *human* form.

But none existed. Only rocks and sagebrush and dry grass. Some of it immobile like Link, some wafting in the slight morning breeze. The Russian began walking again—a boot came down inches from Link's leg—and he went up the hillside for a dozen paces.

Ten more minutes passed, and the man had moved twice more when Link began to crawl down the hill. His path would take him to the dirt road that Turpin traveled, some two hundred yards in front of the pickup. Link would cross there, in plain view, where he was least expected.

He went on, holding himself two inches above the ground, stopping often. Blended and waited. Slithered farther. There were no more arroyos or outcroppings, only small rocks and sagebrush. Link was in sight of both men when he came to the road and paused at its side. He eyed the pickup for a moment to make sure Turpin wasn't watching as he went across, then stopped cold. The engine had started, and Turpin was looking directly ahead—at Link!

He slowly lowered to the earth, and just as slowly readjusted himself about the base of the small—and *only*—sagebrush plant. Became immobile.

The engine sound came closer, closer, until the vehicle was abeam, then crept on past. Turpin parked and turned off the engine, the vehicle so near Link could rise and take a single step and be there. He stared at the back bumper, where blood from the riddled barrel had drained and congealed, and a new wave of anger came over him.

And with it a new plan. Link would go around the pickup. Surprise Turpin from the left as he looked to his right at the hillside. Then he would . . .

He forbade himself from thinking of revenge. Not yet. He must get answers. He judged the angle, could not see Turpin in the rearview mirror, and started to move.

The driver's door opened, and he heard footsteps going around the front of the vehicle. Turpin appeared, carrying the rifle, the pistol strapped to his side. Putting keys in his pocket. Looking up the hillside where the Russian searched. Raising the rifle so he could view through the scope. Taking a few more steps. He was no longer easy prey, was obviously recovered from the encounter with the two-by-four. Still, Link was tempted to try.

The radio crackled. A woman's voice encouraging them to return. Turpin walked farther up the hillside, now out of Link's reach for an attack. He was too weak anyway. If he tried, the ex-agent would overpower him.

Link waited until Turpin was turned away, then raised himself slightly and crabbed across the roadway until he was hidden from both men's view by the pickup.

There were homes within half a mile of the airfield, but he could not lead murderers to helpless families. He searched for alternative hiding places.

The Piper Comanche was four hundred yards distant, covered with the light tarpaulin under which he could conceal himself. Problem? The area around the strip had been graded and mowed, and he would be exposed during the entire approach.

There was nothing else.

"We've got to hurry!" he heard Turpin call out.

The Russian's voice was barely audible in the distance.

Link went on, moving faster as he hobbled directly for the Comanche. Bent low and moving forward, not pausing to check his trail until he felt a new stinging in the leg and looked—and found that the wound was bleeding again.

How long had it been draining? he wondered, and peered back to see a series of dark splotches in the earth. Like an arrow leading directly to him, and now he was in the open without terrain features to mask him. There was no time to apply pressure to stop the flow. No time to erase the trail. He rose higher and limped faster, wondering how long he had before discovery.

As he ran he looked at the highway, decided it would be foolish to go there on the odd chance he'd be able to stop a passing vehicle before Turpin reached him in the pickup.

Halfway to the airplane. Two hundred yards to go. He rose up the rest of the way and sprinted, felt the wounded leg weaken and give, tumbled, scrambled to his feet and ran again. Hobbling. Twenty yards from the airplane he heard Turpin's yell from far behind.

No time for niceties! Link pulled the pocketknife from his jeans and slashed the hold-down ropes.

Ping! A hole appeared in the side of the aircraft, followed by the sound of the rifle. Turpin was a good shot.

Link cut the ropes on the one side, hauled the tarp over the airplane.

Two more rifle reports, another round hitting the bird as Link pulled chocks from the wheels, then pulled the key from the fuel panel door where he'd hidden it, and opened the pilot's door. He swung it free and clambered into the cockpit.

Dared to look as he switched on power, then the fuel pump. Both men were at the pickup, crawling inside.

The fuel pump rattled away, then changed beats as it finally sucked more liquid than air. No time! He set the switches, waited another couple of seconds for the fuel pump to build pressure, and hit the starter.

It took four tries before the fuel pressure was sufficient and the engine caught.

Without warm-up there'd be reduced power—the engine would be damaged, perhaps permanently warped. He pulled the throttle to full, let the engine wind up for a count of five seconds, and released the brakes. Fishtailed slightly because it was hard to handle the brakes with the bad leg, and accelerated so slowly that he agonized.

The pickup was off the dirt road, coming cross-country toward him.

The Comanche picked up more speed, nosed directly down the runway, the pickup kicking up profuse dust on an intercept route. They'd arrive in time to block him!

Link kicked the right brake, turned so violently that the airplane almost teetered over, then accelerated in the opposite direction. Straightened the bird. Not much runway in this direction—just enough, he hoped, to build to takeoff speed.

Movement to his left drew his eyes—the pickup was pulling into view only slightly behind him, the blond Speznaz officer bringing the Skorpion up to bear.

Link held the airplane down, still accelerating, then pulling smoothly on the column, kept the pressure there, hoping—the wheels broke contact with the gravel. He jubilantly held the yoke back, climbing slowly, then faster.

He started to hit the lever to retract the landing gear, but decided against it.

Holes punched through the floorboard near his feet, smashing the console.

Climb faster!

Can't!

Pieces of cowling flew as the Russian found his mark. The engine skipped a beat, another, then shut down.

The silence seemed absolute. In front of him a house loomed. He was only three hundred feet above the ground, without power, headed for disaster.

Link eased in left rudder and tried to coordinate a turn, but the airplane responded too sluggishly. He worked to hold the nose up as he turned harder, gritting his teeth and shuddering at the painful effort of putting so much weight on the wounded calf.

The controls were stiff and unresponsive, but the aircraft was slowly coming about.

"Nose up!" he yelled aloud, working hard to keep it so. The airplane was traveling too slow *not* to stall, but he didn't want it to slam to earth nose first.

The shuddering worsened and the airplane tried to stop flying.

Keep the nose up! He struggled to do so. The turn had ceased and he was roughly aligned with the side of the highway, dropping to thirty, then twenty feet. Directly before him an oncoming sedan veered off the road and bounced through the tumbleweed.

The front wheel touched down, then the rear ones, and he porpoised back into the air.

Two more vehicles went off the road as he bounced again on the highway's surface, utterly out of control, then veered and headed for the side, smacked into the berm and sheared off the landing gear. Sliding on the airplane's belly now, snapping off the propeller, slowing.

I made it! Link exulted.

Another embankment loomed. *Damn!* he thought as he hit—and his head smacked forward onto the gauges. He groaned once, tried to move his head back, and lost consciousness.

He came semiawake, the world moving in half-time, and while he was aware that he must escape—that Turpin and the Russian were surely on their way—he was unable to do anything about it for his limbs would not respond.

Rough hands reached for him and someone was talking loudly, but nothing made sense and he could not move. He closed his eyes, feeling tired—and passed the rest of the way out.

"He needs blood and rest," said a woman's voice that cut through the veil.

"I need to talk to him." The voice was familiar.

"Has he committed some horrible crime?"

"Hell, I don't know. Maybe."

"You'll have to wait anyhow."

Link half-opened his eyes, blinked weakly. The woman was scrubbing his calf with a sponge.

"He's awake." Deputy Ray Watt's face loomed close. "Can you hear me, Anderson?"

"Yeah." Link moved his right hand, then his left. He was pleased. They worked.

"Man, you are *some* filthy," Watt observed, frowning.

"Could I have a drink of water?" Link asked in a croak, and the woman filled a paper cup and lifted it to his mouth. He was on a gurney. She was dressed in white. They were obviously at the dispensary.

"I've removed the bullet from your leg, and now I have to clean your wounds," she said impatiently. "The ambulance is on the way to take you to the hospital in Carson City."

"Cancel it," said Link.

"Yeah. I've got questions to ask him," the deputy said.

Link turned to Watt. "Shelby?"

"Nothing yet, but I've got fifty people looking." He looked unhappy. "A bunch of FBI agents showed up asking for you and acting like they want to take over. Now they're on their way here. What were you doing?"

"Two men from NEL had *someone* they said was Shelby. I think they killed her."

"Oh, Jesus." Then Watt's eyebrows furrowed. "Who's Nell?"

25

10:25 A.M.—Medical Dispensary, Highway 50

The nurse had finished with Link's calf and turned him onto his stomach. All the while Ray Watt kept asking questions, and Link went on ignoring them.

"It's my right to know what happened," Watt said in a sulky tone.

"Be still," the nurse said. She did not have to worry. Link had grown so stiff that the slightest movement was torture.

"If FBI agents are on their way," he explained to the deputy. "I don't want to have to tell it twice."

"Damn it, they're feds. This is *my* turf."

"Theirs too. It's mostly federal laws that are being broken."

"Which laws?" Watt cried, exasperated. "What the hell is going on?"

"There," the nurse said, having finished scrubbing the back wound. "Now the bandage. This one will be difficult so you'll have to lie very still. Then we start on your face." His face was battered from the crash, one eye swollen and plum-colored.

The door opened and a craggy black man wearing a fawn-colored business suit peered in. "Lincoln Anderson?"

"Yeah."

"Special Agent Gordon Tower." He showed identification, held in front of Link's eyes. "I was told to give you a hand. I brought a team."

"Jesus," Deputy Watt muttered.

"Do you *mind*?" the agent asked, and motioned for him to leave.

"Let him stay," Link said.

Watt's frown turned into a smug look.

"A woman disappeared last night," Link began.

"We heard about the radioactivity, and about the Admire woman," said the FBI agent. "There was a—uh—call from New York, and when we arrived," he glared at Ray, "and *after* I'd talked to the state attorney general who talked to the sheriff, Deputy Watt here briefed us about *his* perception of what's going on. First the radioactivity. Are my men in jeopardy?"

"How about the citizens here?" Watt asked. "Aren't you worried about them too?"

"What the hell's wrong with you? You got something against black law officers?"

"I don't know any black law officers, but I sure as hell don't like interfering feds."

The agent was glaring at the deputy with exasperation when Link broke into their tête-à-tête. "I don't think there's a problem with radioactivity any longer. The last reading we took was near normal. I've got a rad meter back in my vehicle, so we can check." Link moved slightly, grunted with pain. The nurse ordered him to remain still while she continued bandaging his back.

"This morning I got a phone call from a man saying he had Shelby," Link began, and told them about the meeting, the woman in the barrel, the chase, and the very short flight. He did not mention Ansel Turpin by name, or that the repairman was his Russian cohort.

The nurse continued with her work as if she heard such stories daily.

"You got away from them by hiding in the *desert*?" the agent asked incredulously.

"He can do it," Ray told him. He was now Link's buddy.

"Where's this NEL located?" the agent asked.

"I'll take you."

"You shouldn't walk," the nurse said. "And I *still* have to tend to your face."

He slid off the gurney, groaned as pain shrieked from back, leg, and forehead.

"I'm not finished," she snapped.

"I'll be back."

"Sure. And just who should I bill?"

"The Weyland Foundation." He limped toward the door.

"Tell him he can't leave until its paid, Ray," she said to the deputy as they filed out.

Four FBI agents milled in the waiting room, and fell into trail.

"We'll stop at my four-by-four for the rad meter," Link said when they were outside. "Then we'll have to find a way through the fence to the compound. I overheard them talking on the radio, and I think the NEL security people might be involved."

He and Special Agent Tower went with Ray Watt in his cruiser. The others followed in a too-plain dark sedan. As they turned onto the highway, the deputy reached for the siren switch. The FBI agent stopped him. "You want to *tell* them we're coming?"

Watt glowered as he pulled back. "Maybe I do," he muttered.

"Head for Stagecoach, then turn off toward the old pony express station," Link directed.

"You got it," Ray said, looking important as he accelerated.

"So you don't think much of federal officers," observed the FBI agent.

"Who would, after Ruby Ridge?" said Ray.

The agent sighed. "Look, half the bureau was canned over it and the other half's retired. That's ancient history, and for God's sake stop muttering about Waco."

Ray looked smug, having found a sore point. Another couple of miles and he slowed, then turned off onto the dirt road.

The rented Yukon was where Link had left it, but it would not be driven soon. The hood was riddled where the Russian had disabled it with the Skorpion. The same treatment had been given to a golf cart parked nearby.

When they dismounted, Ray dolefully observed the

plentiful amount of blood that had drained from where the pickup had been parked. "Is that Shelby's?"

"Maybe. I didn't get a good look." Link pointed for the agents' benefit. "That's Millionaire Mountain, where NEL's doing their research. A man named Ansel Turpin was driving one of their trucks."

"You're sure?" Tower asked in a brittle tone, squinting hard at the mountain.

"I'm sure. There's at least one other guy with him, and they're armed, so be careful."

"You think they're still there?" asked Special Agent Tower, looking.

"I don't know."

One of the big helicopters lifted off in the distance, turned west and clip-clopped away.

"Better have someone meet them at the Carson City airport," Link told the deputy. "A helicopter charter service there does their flying." He gave him the name he'd seen on the side of the chopper, and Ray didn't argue as he hurried to his cruiser.

The familiar old weapons carrier clattered up on the dirt road, the hermit peering out at the group. He halted and eyed them, as if wondering what was happening to draw all the visitors, then he too turned and stared at the mountain where the helicopter had lifted off.

"Better stay out of the way for a while," Ray called to him in his officious tone.

"Ready?" Tower asked Link as soon as the deputy had completed his radio call.

"Something to think about," Link said. "There'll be innocent people at the study site, and it could degenerate into a hostage situation. You may want to just contain the situation and send for backup." He crawled into the Yukon, opened the console compartment door, and emerged with the rad meter and tiny cellular phone Turpin had overlooked. "And we'd better—"

A clap of thunder sounded, and they all turned and stared. Dark smoke issued in a column from the mountainside two miles distant. "What the hell?" an agent muttered, his voice awe-filled. Watching bits of flotsam float earthward in the distance.

The old hermit's eyes grew saucer-wide and his mouth drooped. He ground transmission gears and sped away toward the highway, leaving a billow of choking dust in his wake.

"What's *that*?" asked Ray Watt as a new sound emerged from the Yukon's console.

Link picked out the squealing NEL dosimeter, then quickly switched on the rad meter.

"Ninety milliroentgens," he said grimly.

"What's that mean?"

"We'd better move back. I think someone just blew up the radioactive material at the site and scattered it all to hell."

11:10 A.M.—Stagecoach Valley

They did not have to call for a military decontamination team, since the emergency preparedness office had done so the previous night. They all moved back to the highway four miles distant, where the background reading was a semi-safe thirty milliroentgens. There Gordon Tower set up headquarters at Cal Admire's real estate office to await the team. He also left two agents in the sedan on a rocky hill to observe the site with binoculars.

Ray Watt called in the law enforcement people searching for Shelby, and they were contacting all residents and businesses, telling them about the radioactivity across the valley. Just don't cross the highway, they were telling them, and they'd be safe.

Cal Admire had listened grimly to Link's story about what might have happened to Shelby, and he and Sally refused to budge. "Not as long as there's the slightest chance that our daughter's out there," they said stubbornly.

The decon team was scheduled to arrive at noon to take over. A good thing, for Link had the distinct feeling that things were spinning faster and faster out of control.

The deputy and the FBI agent were in a corner of the office, talking.

"The helicopter," Link called out. "Did it land in Carson City?"

Ray Watt shook his head. "No show. Carson City police are talking to the company now."

The special agent spoke up. "I've got my office checking with the air traffic people to see if anyone knows where it went. We've also established the entire valley as a civilian no-fly zone."

"I was going to do all that," Watt said.

Link went to the back office he'd used before, called Erin on the flip-top, and told her about the explosion. She listened, then exclaimed, "It's Ansel Turpin's trick, Link. That's how he escaped in Russia. No one can go in until the material's removed."

"Yeah. I don't think this was done in the heat of the moment. Looking back to what I overheard them saying, it was all planned."

"Any ideas what he's up to?"

"More questions. No ideas. By the way, the FBI agent-in-charge here acted like he knew about Turpin."

"Gordon Tower is more or less the bureau's expert on Ansel Turpin. That's why they sent him to Las Vegas on the investigation, and why our liaison here felt he'd be our best bet to back you up. We're no longer the only ones thinking Ansel Turpin's back to making mischief."

Link heard a shout from the outer office, something about a survivor, and told Erin he had to terminate.

He hurried outside, where Gordon Tower was waiting. "The two men on the hill spotted someone running from the research site, so they took a chance and went in."

They waited and watched. Ten minutes later the unmarked FBI sedan bumped its way across the desert toward them, crossed the highway and pulled into the parking lot. A woman was in back—the middle-aged security guard Link had seen on his visit to the site—eyes wild and wide as hen's eggs. She refused to get out, just wanted to go home to Reno.

Special Agent Tower tried to sweet-talk her, which caused her to start to cry. "They killed them!" she sobbed.

"Who."

"Our security chief and the other male guard and

maybe some of the others. They had guns and herded everyone out of the buildings and up the mountain."

"But not you?"

"I hid when I saw them start acting crazy and waving guns." She shuddered. "I feel sick to my stomach."

"It may be the radiation," Link told Tower. "She'll need to be treated. Your men too."

"Radiation?" she asked in a trembling tone. "Oh God! My dosimeter was screaming so loud I left it and ran. I'm gonna die, aren't I?"

"You're safe here. Now start over and tell us what happened." the agent told her.

She drew a breath and closed her eyes. "The other female guard and I spent the night out there. Maylene was on duty and I was supposed to relieve her this morning. But she didn't wake me up, and when I got to the office she was gone. Then I heard someone in the food locker next door, getting something."

"You don't know what?"

She shook her head. "Next I saw the security chief and the male guard marching people out of the buildings and waving guns, and shouting "Get over there," "Get in line," that sort of thing. So I got a shotgun from the cabinet and crawled under the desk. After it got quiet I peeked and saw our chief marching them all up the mountainside, toward the old Break-a-Heart mines."

"There was only him and the other guard?"

She hesitated. "I'm not sure who had guns and how many were being forced. I wasn't at the window long."

"Were all the ones with guns going up the hill?"

"No, 'cause one of the helicopter pilots started running and someone shot him." She was talking ever faster, in obvious shock. "I wanted to go out to help, but I was scared. Then I wondered about getting in one of the pickups and trying to leave, but I chickened out, and after a while I saw our chief coming down the mountain."

"Alone?"

"There was others." She frowned. "Maybe two others."

"All men?"

"I don't remember."

"Who was watching the other helicopter pilot?"

She shook her head helplessly. "I'm ready to go home now."

"A blond man?" Link asked.

"I don't know. Maybe. Can I go?"

"Not yet. What happened next?" Gordon Tower was persistent.

"I saw our chief go toward the helicopter, then stop and look right at the security building, so I got back under the desk with the shotgun and stayed there until I heard 'em take off."

"How long was that?"

"Two, maybe three minutes. After the helicopter took off I went outside, *real* cautious, but everybody was gone."

"Did any of the hostages come down the mountain?"

She shook her head. "I was thinking of going up to see about them when the explosion came—right from Break-a-Heart Three, where he'd taken everyone—so powerful it knocked me flat on my butt. For a while I couldn't hear anything but a faint buzzing sound."

Her face wrinkled as she began crying again. "Then I realized it was my dosimeter, so I threw it away and started running. Oh, God! Am I going to die?"

"One more question," Link said. "What did your friend Maylene look like, and did you see her in the group being marched up the mountain?"

"She was thirty-seven, kinda short, brunette, and sorta skinny. I think the security chief was sweet on her. And come to think of it, I didn't see her goin' up the mountain."

"How did you get through the fence when you ran?" Gordon Tower asked.

"The side gate was locked, so I climbed over it. There's no electricity to it anymore."

"Maybe we should take her to the hospital," said Ray Watt.

"Where's the decon team?" Link asked the FBI agent.

"They just passed through Dayton," Tower said. "Should be here in a few minutes."

"Get her showered off good, your agents too. The decon team can take it from there." When the agent left with the security guard and his two men, Link stared across the highway at Millionaire Mountain, wondering if anyone else might be alive. He went inside the office and sat heavily at an empty desk, trying to think it out. It seemed odd that the security guard had been left alive. It was not like Ansel Turpin to make an error that blatant.

Unless he'd been rushed, as it seemed was happening when Link had overheard the radio conversations. If that was the case, had he made other mistakes? There were other questions, like how many had been killed, and how many escaped in the helicopter? And who?

Link was drained of energy and ideas, nodded forward and cupped his chin in both hands.

His eyelids became heavy and drooping as he was overcome by weariness, trying to think of everything that was happening. He slipped into an uneasy state somewhere between resting and precious sleep.

Images fluttered. Of Shelby laughing, and making love under the kitchen table. Of Turpin and the renegade Speznaz officer chasing him. Of observing the barrel with its slight movements and low sounds of agony. Of the glimpse of a bloody, nude woman.

Shelby was fair. Maylene the guard was brunette.

He woke up, a hand on his shoulder, Cal Admire peering into his face.

"It wasn't Shelby in the barrel," Link blurted in a strained voice. "The hair was too dark." He shook his head vigorously. "It wasn't Shelby."

"Then where is she?"

"I don't know."

Cal took a composing breath. "The decontamination team's arrived."

An army major was in charge of the convoy of HUM-Vs and two-and-a-half-ton trucks, all painted stark white, with CBR DECONTAMINATION COMPANY marked on their sides. He listened carefully to what had happened, had his men take rad measurements, and immediately set things into gear. They'd brought several six-wheeled robots with knobby tires, articulated arms, and built-in storage bins, and he said they were operating under a contingency plan drawn up to handle an attack by terrorists using explosives to spread chemical, biological, or nuclear material.

As had happened here.

"We were told to come prepared, so I brought military police," the major told Special Agent Tower. "Any bad guys in the area who might interfere?"

Gordon Tower nodded at Link. "Talk to him."

Link's face was battered. He was shoeless, wore only the dirt-encrusted jeans and a shirt loaned by Cal, and was filthy except for the cleansed wounds and bandages. The major looked at him no differently than he might a citizen in a three-piece suit, and repeated his question.

"I think they've all left."

"Do you know what kind of toxic material we're dealing with?" the major asked.

"They had plutonium, uranium, and californium that I know of."

"How much?"

"I saw several hundred kilograms. They were bringing it in barrels slung under cargo helicopters from some weapons dismantling project."

"Jesus," the major said. "We know about every nuclear storage site in North America, and this place sure isn't listed. What in hell were they *doing* with it?"

"At least some of them *thought* they were about to save the world from itself."

The major used a transmitter in a specially equipped communications HUM-V and called back to somewhere to order more robots. "The area's hot, and there may be a lot of it," he told someone. "We're about to go in and check."

A small person—it was impossible to tell if it was male or female—clopped up in heavy rubber boots and a bulky, white anti-exposure suit, carrying a portable ventilator.

"The reconnaissance team's ready to go in, sir." A woman's voice.

The major explained the area and the objective—the NEL research site—and gave a curt nod. "Go ahead and deploy, lieutenant. We'll talk you in on the radio. When you return, the decon tents will be set up on the lawn there. Go there first."

"Yes, sir." She went to a HUM-V pulling a trailer loaded with one of the robots, joining three others who were similarly clad.

"We like to get an idea of what we're up against right away," the major explained.

The vehicle was put into gear and driven across the highway. Every hundred meters it stopped, and the lieutenant's voice recited the radiation reading over the radio, then dropped off a remote radiometric station that could be monitored from the communications vehicle.

"A woman was radiated," Link told the major. "She was close to the explosion. We've got her inside with the two agents who went in for her, all taking showers."

"You did the right thing." He waved over three people wearing red crossed medic's armbands and told them. "Burn their clothes," he advised them before they left for the house.

Gordon Tower spoke up. "How long before we'll have access to the mountain?"

The major shrugged, as if to say who knows, and went back to running the effort. He asked Link about the layout of the site and how many people they might find, and said they had to get any survivors out as quickly as possible.

Two vans marked with call letters of local television stations pulled up on the road. The MPs briefed them to stay clear and not to go on the other side of the highway. They set up their dishes in a nearby field and began filming the white HUM-V working in the distance.

A sharp-looking lieutenant came over and spoke quietly with the major. Two representatives were being ushered over by a military policeman. "Handle it," said the major.

"What's happening?" one of the news people immediately asked.

The lieutenant flashed a ready smile. "There's been a

report of an incident involving explosives at a government facility over there. This is just a precautionary exercise."

"Nothing dangerous?"

Wider smile. "Probably not. We'll let you know."

"Anyone hurt in the explosion?"

"We don't know yet. I'll keep you informed. Please don't interfere with our people, and just keep your distance until we find out more."

Precautionary, Link wondered. *Exercise.* Why weren't they leveling with them? The spokesperson was walking with them, laughing at something one said. Again telling them to remain out of the way and let them do their jobs, and he'd keep them informed.

Link turned, found the major looking at him.

"We got a message to keep our mouths shut about the radioactivity and ensure there's no panic," he said. "We were also given your name and told you'd go along. If you have questions, you're to call your headquarters in New York."

Link pulled the flip-top from his pocket and called Erin.

Frank had just phoned her. Link was to cooperate fully, both with the bureau and the army. He would explain later.

As Link hung up, the major was talking with Special Agent Gordon Tower. They both turned and gave him a questioning look.

"What do you need?" Link asked. "My boss just told me to cooperate."

The major shrugged. "Just help keep the civilians back, and don't talk to the press. I don't understand either, but I assume there's a rationale behind it all. I was just told we're getting our orders from the top."

"Same here," said Gordon Tower, coming over from his sedan. "I was also told a chopper's on the way out from Reno, and there's someone aboard no one's going to see."

"They'll land here?" the major asked.

"Doesn't appear like it." Tower pointed. A large army HH–53 clip-clopped from the west, and descended toward a hilltop five miles behind them. It settled into place. A moment later the rotor blades stopped.

"No one sees it," said Tower. "And no one goes for a closer look."

"I get the distinct feeling," said the major, "that I have no earthly idea what's going on, and its doubtful they're going to tell me."

"I just got another call sir," said the lieutenant PR officer. "We're told to be especially watchful at 1300 hours. No other explanation, just to be watchful."

"Then we shall be." The major looked at his watch. "Twelve thirty-nine," he announced.

At 12:57 the reconnaissance team said they were approaching the research site's perimeter fence and encountering higher rad readings. "There's small chunks of material all around. All plutonium so far, and very hot. We're just marking them and moving on."

The major grunted in acknowledgment. "How much longer do you have?"

"The computer says we've got sixteen more minutes at this radiation level. We're at a gate, and there's a lock on it. The fence is not electrified."

"Good work, lieutenant. Use your bolt cutters, and as soon as the robot's deployed inside the compound and the camera's operating, prepare to withdraw."

"Yes, sir." She paused. "There's something odd just on the other side of the fence, major."

"What do you mean by *odd*?"

"It's a cylinder of some sort. Possibly a radioactive material container. It's not a normal birdcage or anything, and it is very strange-looking."

Link went closer to the radio, listening intently.

"A minute ago I heard a noise I think was coming from it. Sort of a whirring sound."

Cylindrical? A whirring sound? "Tell them to get out of there," Link said forcefully.

"Jesus!" they heard. Her voice was filled with awe. "There's a bright blue glow, and the rad meter just went berserk."

"Evacuate," said the major. "Now!"

"Should we drop off the robot?"

"Just get out of there!"

"We're on our way."

They did not breathe easier until they saw the HUM-V racing back across the desert, still dragging the loaded trailer. By then the rad meters at the temporary headquarters were reading three hundred roentgens per hour, and the major had ordered the team to move further back.

The headquarters was relocated to the Barn—fully eight miles from Millionaire Mountain—where the rad readings showed they were safe. Cal and Sally Admire had moved with them and were seated on Gary's porch, Aristotle tethered at their feet, all staring out at the mountain. The big dog had begun howling forlornly when the radiation had dramatically increased, as if he'd known something was amiss. Now he was whimpering and pacing.

Ray Watt was out with the other law enforcement officers, telling residents to get the hell out while they could. Link, the major, and special Agent Gordon Tower stood together in the driveway beside the command and control vehicle.

"What is it?" the major asked Link. "Some kind of weapon they haven't told us about?"

"Its called a Jergen Reaction Device. They also call it a coffeepot." He described the upcoming NEL experimentation to achieve accelerated depletion.

The major became thoughtful, then brightened. "Oh, yeah. In school they presented that one along with bullshit and magic. Were they serious?"

"Very."

"Well, all they've done so far is create one hell of a lot of radioactivity."

The lieutenant had noted a reading of a thousand roentgens as the team had fled. She and the others had shed their anti-exposure suits on Gary's lawn, and been hosed down thoroughly with a solution from a trailered tank.

"The blue glow's diminishing," called a sergeant who

was viewing the mountain through a telescope set up nearby.

The major shook his head. "I've never even heard of anything like it."

"The glow just turned off," said the sergeant.

Aristotle began to bark excitedly, trying to tell them something in his canine way.

"Radioactivity's decreasing," said a radiologist specialist, observing numbers transmitted from the various remote meters. The one dropped off at the fence had stopped functioning ten minutes after the glow began, its last reading in excess of five thousand roentgens and climbing.

The major was frowning, as if recalling something. "You called it a *Jergen* device?"

"Dr. Piers Jergen was one of the researchers. Have you heard of him?"

"The wacko who screwed up and killed his assistant at Berkeley."

People at the Weyland Foundation had called him the same. "Why do you say wacko?"

"They used bigger words, but wacko would be gentle in comparison to what they wrote about him in the AFSE journal."

"The American Federation of Scientists and Engineers?"

The major nodded. "They're a pretty strange group too."

Professional cruelty was the way Shelby had put it.

"The reading is still decreasing," came the radiology report. "The closest rad meter is back on the air."

"Reading at that one?" asked the major.

"Four thousand. Three thousand. *Wow.* It's going down like gangbusters. One thousand. Five hundred." He grew silent. "I've switched ranges. We're down to fifty milliroentgens. Thirty. Twenty." Silence again.

"Damn it," said the major. "What's the reading?"

"Zero."

"Switch to another remote."

"I just did. Zero. Here's another. Zero!"

"That's impossible."

"Yes, sir." Pause, then: "Here's a meter located three miles away. The reading is two milliroentgens."

"*Still* impossible," said the major. "A normal background is six to eight."

"Yes, sir, but unless every damned meter out there is broken, there's absolutely no radiation left at the site."

Like the others, Link Anderson stared out with disbelief. Someone had just shown the world that accelerated depletion was more than a hypothesis. The Jergen Device *worked*.

The press, who had been evacuated without explanation and had set up shop beside the alfalfa field, were told that the exercise was completed. The army team would now go to the government facility near the mountain to check out the explosives incident. The media people said it had certainly seemed realistic. They'd run clips of the exercise on the evening news.

"Who's in the helicopter?" one asked, peering at the big HH–53 lifting off from the hilltop behind them.

"What helicopter?" quipped a passing sergeant.

PART III

Retribution

26

Two days had passed since the deadly experiment in Stagecoach Valley. Frank had called for an emergency meeting of the financial board, and all members were present to hear Link Anderson describe what had happened.

"What we witnessed," he began, "was a spectacular demonstration. Plutonium, probably picked because it's the most toxic material known to man, was scattered by the explosion to create a hot zone that would take some twenty thousand years to deplete to half-life, another twenty thousand to half of that, and so forth. Just cleaning it up was going to be a dangerous task that would take weeks. Then the coffeepot was activated, surged up to a spectacular reading, and then, precisely as advertised, depleted all traces of the radiation."

Link had spoken for a full hour before he finished telling about his visit to NEL, the disappearances of Gary and Shelby, the deaths in the valley and the radiation at Irene's, the chase, and the A.D. phenomenon. Finally he turned to what the reconnaissance team had concluded when they'd gone back that afternoon.

The scientists had been marched up to the building at Break-a-Heart Three mine and locked inside. Several open barrels of plutonium and an estimated two hundred pounds of C–4 plastic explosive had been positioned outside. Approximately two minutes after the helicopter had departed, the explosive had been set off, likely by remote control.

They had no idea where the helicopter had gone, and except for the chief of security, a male guard, and one pilot, did not know who had been aboard.

"Is there no possibility that *any* of the NEL people survived the blast?" the woman asked.

"None. The people crowded into the mine shack were only twenty feet from the explosives out front. The building was obliterated, a ten-foot crater was blown into the hillside, and there were rockslides. The shaft was closed off by tons of debris."

"Were Mr. Jameson, Mr. Runyon, or Miss Admire among them?"

Link maintained a neutral face. "The decon team has been augmented by a morgue detail, searching for fragments of human remains, and so far they've found distinguishable parts of sixteen different bodies, none yet identified. The barrel I'd seen at the pony express station was still in the pickup with the corpse of the missing female security guard, Maylene Stubbs, inside."

He returned to his narrative. At twelve-thirty that morning the decon team commander had been alerted that *something* would happen at one o'clock, and the FBI team was ordered to look the other way when a helicopter landed on the mountain behind them.

"Advised and ordered by whom?" the woman asked.

"And who was in the helicopter?" Link added. "I think its important that we find out. No one out there knew, because it had been passed down through the system."

He explained that the coffeepot left by the gate had not been activated by remote control but by a timing device duct-taped to its side and set for one o'clock.

"Now I have a question," Link said quietly, looking directly at Frank Dubois. "I witnessed a world-class cover-up. Both the media and the public were repeatedly lied to. While the dust was still settling on dead people, the decon team was told if they spoke openly of any deaths they'd be court-martialed. The Admires were advised that the government would search diligently for their daughter as long as they didn't talk about it to anyone. When a deputy sheriff tried to tell his superiors that nuclear material had been involved, they'd already been briefed that he had interfered with a government exercise and no radioactivity had been involved, period. He wasn't sophisticated enough to know what he'd seen, so he shut up and went back on patrol with a lot of angry people wondering why he'd told them to leave if there was no hazard."

"We're aware of the cover-up," Frank said. "Our problem is our vulnerability. You know about Gary's manuscript. What you don't know is the Department of Energy's internal finding. They've located the original memoranda, the ones Gary—or whoever—sent copies of to the media, and they're saying the Weyland Foundation bribed two of their officials into giving out those contracts. Both officials committed suicide several months ago, and now, with the FBI agent who blew the whistle killed, who do you question?"

"You're saying we're being blackmailed into silence by our own government?"

"Let's just say that we're under intense scrutiny and being reminded that this is not a good time to be making accusations."

"If they've got the manuscript and copies of the memos, why isn't the media screaming?"

"Both the executive office and Department of Energy have been creating scandals for the last five years, and the media just makes excuses and acts as if that's Washington business as usual. Mention anything despicable the president or his people do, and they'll turn and point to the other party and say they did it too, even if it's a lie. The media have everyone so confused they don't know who to believe."

"Incredible," grumbled a board member.

"This administration has proven to be very good at hiding the truth," said Frank. "But as of last Friday the congressional investigations are underway and let's pray they get to the bottom of it all quickly."

"How about the Staples woman?" another member asked. "What's her condition?"

Erin had been listening from the side of the room, and got to her feet. "Improving. She was flown to the Mayo Clinic that same day."

"I'm impressed. The government did that?"

"We did," Link said. "I took the liberty of authorizing the funds."

There were no arguments. Link noted the fact that he could take such actions in the future, should it become necessary.

"All of that was bad news," Link said, "but now it gets worse. Three more coffeepots are missing."

"And you think they were loaded with plutonium?" Frank asked him.

"We've got to assume so. Which brings up the next point. Why is no one telling the public that a group of psycyhopaths are loose with three devices that can kill everyone within a quarter mile?"

"The order comes from the Oval Office," Frank said. "All government agencies have been told to keep their mouths closed. The Secretary of Energy feels it's essential that they find the formulae and at least one coffeepot intact. If the A.D. process works . . ."

"After what happened, I would say there's no doubt of that," Link said.

"That's what he's told the president," Frank said. "And if the scientists were all killed in the explosion, there's no hope of duplicating the process without an intact coffeepot."

"Perhaps that's what these—*terrorists*—are after," another member said. "To try to sell the coffeepots to countries with nuclear waste stacking up."

Erin differed with him. "We're now certain that Ansel Turpin is behind this, and it's doubtful that he's after money. In Russia, he disappeared along with almost a hundred million U.S. dollars."

"Are you *sure* he's involved?" asked the woman.

"I met him face to face," Link said, "and when he felt I wasn't about to escape, he let me know who he was. I've also identified the telephone repairman as the Russian special forces officer who worked with Turpin in St. Petersburg."

"That means we've identified two others on the helicopter," said. Frank. "Ansel Turpin and the Speznaz officer."

Erin agreed. "I'm sure of two things. Turpin orchestrated the disaster, and he escaped . . . again."

"Why were they so determined to capture Link?"

"Ansel Turpin knew Link worked for the Foundation," Erin said. "He despises us all."

Link was unsure that was the reason, but with no alternative in mind, he kept his counsel.

"Regardless of Mr. Turpin's rationale," said the woman on the handful, "Lincoln must remain especially watchful."

Link walked to the office with Erin, she explaining more about what had been going on regarding the charges leveled in Gary's manuscript.

"The memos were written on the proper forms and all signatures appear valid. Only the parts concerning the Weyland Foundation are lies. Over the past five years the Department of Energy really *did* pay out billions of dollars to at least some of the companies shown on their memo, and the two undersecretaries received massive kickbacks. DOE people are scrambling, but the scandal is unavoidable, and the congressional investigation is going to claim scalps. That's why Frank wants to move now to clear ourselves."

"So we won't go down with the DOE?"

"And possibly the administration, if it comes to impeachment. So far the president's tap-danced his way out of everything, but with another major scandal, who knows? We've got to avoid being painted with the same brush. We've proven that our finance and contracts offices received no funds from DOE, but a certain Massachusetts senator received an anonymous letter that the financial board members siphoned it all off to personal accounts."

"Can't they disprove it?"

"Sure, but that will take time, and now the congressional staffers are demanding access to every nook and cranny in this building, including those on the secure floors."

They entered the office, and Link went to the kitchenette, where he filled a mug for them both as Erin chattered on. The Foundation was being turned upside down. Subpoenas would be delivered in the morning, and Frank had ordered all departments to cooperate. New projects were on hold. Existing project offices had been told to sanitize any classified material that might endanger lives, but to keep *all* correspondence regarding domestic matters and dealings with government agencies. Next week a group of fifty congressional staffers and GAO inspectors would swarm into the place, and be given free access.

Erin trailed him into his office. "I retrieved more data on the Epsilon team."

"Collegium," Link murmured, for he'd been thinking about them.

"There's not much new about Piers Jergen," she said, "except his father really was a member of the Danish communist party, and his brother likely wasn't clean either. Some serious money appeared in his personal bank account that he couldn't explain, and he jumped off a pier in Oakland in the middle of the investigation."

"Oakland keeps popping up."

"Berkeley's right next door. That's where the Jergen brothers worked."

"Ansel Turpin was also raised nearby."

Erin leaned back against his desk, arms crossed under her bountiful breasts, looking thoughtful. "Different eras," she finally said, "but Turpin may have known something about Piers Jergen when he was growing up."

"What about the woman on the collegium?" Link asked.

"Juliette LaCoste was a full professor at the University of California, considered one of the most brilliant women in science in the country. A year and a half ago she was caught taking credit for a students' work and slapped with a sexual harassment charge. Masochism was involved and some really kinky rumors were circulated."

"So she too was humiliated?"

"Yep. Disgraced and removed her from her teaching post, and asked to withdraw her paper from the next AFSE symposium."

"I heard about it."

"The following month Jergen was fired too. Then they both showed up at NEL."

"How about the third member of Epsilon? Adam Russo?"

"No connection with the Berkeley area, but he was disgraced like the others. Dr. Russo was a visiting professor at the University of Chicago until nineteen ninety-four, when he presented a technical paper on cold fusion to an AFSE convention. Ten minutes into his presentation, several members stood up together and walked out. Then more and more left, until he was alone. All of that in front of the cameras. Talk about humiliating."

"What was their reason?"

"They said his work was stolen from a deceased scientist at MIT. Russo tried to argue, so the AFSE simply withdrew his membership and no university would hire him."

"How did he end up teamed with Piers Jergen?"

"Russo called Jergen and La Coste last year and suggested they collaborate and use the NEL research study as a vehicle to develop the A.D. hypothesis. They agreed."

"How did they know NEL would accept them?"

"I spoke with NEL's corporate headquarters. They didn't come to them hat in hand, Link. We'd just denied NEL funding because our inspectors felt they were unsafe. Epsilon brought twelve million dollars of private development money to the project."

"Twelve-five, I was told. They told Fred Jameson it was a grant from this building. So where did they really get the money?"

"I know a guy who was walking around with a hundred million burning a hole in his jeans."

"Yeah." So Ansel Turpin had found his instrument of death, but a lot of questions remained for them to talk about. Like where had Turpin been during all of that time? At NEL? In Stagecoach Valley? And more importantly, where was he now?

"Could Jameson have been Ansel Turpin, Link?"

"No way. Fred Jameson is five-four, and Turpin's nearly six feet."

"He's awfully good with disguise."

"You're telling me. He even changes his physical strength. I could have taken the guy who came to visit as Destin Albee. The character at the pony express station was as strong as I was. Turpin's fifteen years older than me, and I still had to use a two-by-four equalizer."

Frank Dubois wheeled into the room. "There you both are. How about lunch?"

"You two go ahead," Erin said. "There's something I want to look into."

As soon as the door closed behind them, Frank was quick to comment: "It should be a crime to have a body like that."

Link deadpanned. "I ought to tell you, Frank. You were staring again."

"I did *not* stare." Frank wheeled himself along. "Well, maybe a little."

"And you've got to watch the drooling."

"I don't think Erin realizes the impact she has on us poor males."

"I'm going back," he told Frank. "Tomorrow."

"This time don't try to tackle everything alone. The bureau people will work with you. Gordon Tower wants to keep track of everything, so keep him informed. He's not happy about the president's gag order either, by the way."

"I'll need another airplane."

"From what Erin said, you almost failed your checkout."

"The big mouth. I'll never confide in her again."

"We haven't even gotten the bill for cleaning the Comanche off the countryside, and you want *another* one?"

"Maybe a Learjet. Something I can get around fast in."

"Think you can handle it?" Frank's eyes turned capricious. "From what you said, you almost nosed in in a stall."

"Give me a break. They'd just shot up my engine. I had no airspeed and no power and had to turn so I wouldn't smack into a home. I should have gotten a medal."

They looked at one another and chuckled as they came to the elevator and waited for the car. "How are the wounds, Link?"

"I keep a headache, my back stings, and the leg's gimpy, but nothing vital's missing and I've felt worse. How about you? Making any progress on your therapy?"

"Another couple of months and I'll be out of the wheelchair for a couple hours a day."

Link noted something missing, and looked about. "Where are the security desks?"

"We're getting ready for the circus next week. All classified documents have been removed to the vaults."

The elevator door opened and they went inside.

"Sorry I didn't get the information to you sooner," Link said.

"Thank God we got it when we did so we could minimize *some* of the impact."

They got out at the lobby, and two of Frank's plainclothes bodyguards silently fell in behind them.

"Taking a limo?" Link asked hopefully as they arrived at the glass doors.

"There's a little café about a block away with a great brunch. Are you too sore to walk?"

"I'll keep up."

The two friends went slowly down the sidewalk, neither of them complaining, but not trying to break any speed records either."

Forty minutes later, Erin looked up. "How was lunch?"

"I'm surprised you're still here. It's Sunday."

"Johnny's out west with his grandparents. Eight years old and he travels like a jet-setter."

"Then go rest up for tomorrow. Frank says the investigators start coming in at noon."

"That's the advance team. The *real* mob doesn't get here until Wednesday when the auditors arrive and everyone has to be here to answer any questions they have."

She followed him into his office, where he immediately sat down, sighing with relief as weight was removed from the throbbing calf muscle. He picked a rectangular box from his desktop, and handed it over. "One of the minicams Turpin's Russian buddy planted around Stagecoach Valley. They're made in Slovakia. You may want to show it to security."

Erin examined it with interest. "While you two were at lunch, I queried Ansel Turpin's background sheet when he joined the FBI. The *first* one, not the later ones I'd been looking at."

"Something new?"

"You were right. A *lot* went on around Oakland, California. Now the bombshell. Guess Turpin's last name before his mother changed it to hers?"

"You tell me."

"How about Ansel Jergen? He put it on the original forms, and all the dates match. Dr. Piers Jergen is his father."

"I'll be damned," Link muttered, then realized it was yet another answer that asked more questions. "Was there contact between the two?"

"Probably not when he was a child. From what I learned, Ansel's mother despised Piers Jergen and undoubtedly let her son know what she thought of his father. She was also very strong-willed—demanded that he not play contact sports, that he take certain courses, things like that. Young Ansel may not have been so happy about his home life."

"And looked up Piers when he was older?"

"Possibly. I'm going to do some more digging, but here's a scenario. Ansel Turpin helped his father develop the A.D. phenomenon. Now they're together somewhere with three coffeepots loaded and ready, so they can prove to the world that Dr. Jergen was not a fraud."

"And his associates on the Epsilon Collegium?"

"Maybe them too, since they helped him. And if all *that's* true, whom would they target with the coffeepots?"

Link continued with her line of reasoning. "The people who humiliated them? There were three of them on the collegium, and they took three coffeepots."

"That's their most obvious motivation, Link. They were driven by revenge."

"So we should try to locate those people who humiliated them most."

"It's a believable scenario, and that poses a problem for me. Ansel Turpin seldom does the expected."

"You think we're wrong?"

She sighed. "No, just that it may be what Ansel Turpin *wants* us to think. He's a master manipulator."

"I'm flying back out there in the morning. Any ideas about where I should start?"

"Yeah. Your cabin in Montana. There's a man named Joseph Spotted Horse who keeps calling about you."

Link smiled. "Some of the pureblood Blackfeet say Joseph dreams truths about the future and can talk with animals. You believe that?"

"Maybe. We've gotten to be telephone pals. Three mornings ago Mr. Spotted Horse called to tell me the old people would cry, and that you would hear them."

Link smiled. "He says odd things like that. Any idea what he meant?"

"I don't know, but the next day the coffeepot was set off at Millionaire Mountain. Did you hear anything like old people crying?"

"Nope." His mind was on the Epsilon Collegium, and the briefing they'd given at NEL.

"He wants to help, Link."

"I don't want him in the way."

"It may be difficult to stop him. The last time we talked, Joseph said he just might drive to Nevada. He asked how he could get in touch with the Admires."

"You gave him Cal's number?"

"Why not? He sounded like he wanted to help."

He suppressed a flash of irritation that she'd not consulted him. "Let's get back to the problem. Epsilon has the coffeepots. Who's going to be their victims?"

"One other consideration first, Link. If you're going to be flying around the countryside, remember Ansel Turpin and his Russian buddy had a stockpile of smallish shoulder-fired missiles that are just great for shooting down smallish airplanes."

27

Monday, July 6, 7:00 A.M.—The Sphere

Shelby had been in constant pain since her arrival in the sphere, but with passage of time the hurting diminished. Now there were periods that it almost disappeared, but she didn't know if it was because she was healing or forming a new pain threshold.

Soon after her arrival she'd told Gary where they were, how the nuclear explosion had created the glass bubble, but he'd not been surprised. "I thought it was something like that." He'd pointed out the green glow coming to life on the farthest wall. "Radioactivity," he'd explained.

"No," she'd said, enduring a wave of agony from the broken tooth. "When I was at NEL we studied it in detail. There's hardly a trace of residual radioactivity."

"Then what causes the glow?"

"Sunlight. The bubble almost burst through the southern side of the mountain. It's morning, Gary."

"Glass," he'd muttered dumbly. Then almost hopefully, "Glass?"

"Yeah, but there's no way to break through. It's four feet thick." The shock, even the process of thinking had taken her reserves, and she'd curled up for an hour to endure the pain.

Although Gary had seemed almost mad from his eight days of hunger and solitude, the fact of her presence—of being able to relate with another—had revived him. He'd been solicitous of her condition and tried to do everything possible to alleviate her agony. Such magic was impossible. She needed painkillers, a dentist, surgery to repair a broken ribcage. While she'd huddled, occasionally rocking and moaning, Gary had told her about his exploration. The walkable perimeter of the sphere was a thousand feet. He'd found four cracks in the wall but none pronounced enough to allow him to gain a hand or foothold. There were possibly more, better suited for climbing, and he looked every day.

"It's a bubble," she'd said. "I doubt we could get very high before we fell off."

"It doesn't matter. I'm too weak to try."

"My clothes," Shelby had managed as the first glow had become brighter. She'd been nude when Russo had stuffed her into the barrel, but he'd tossed them in before sealing the top. Gary had retrieved them, and when she'd had trouble, helped her put them on.

He'd told her about the barrels periodically dropping in, and how they'd all—before Shelby—contained foul-smelling corpses. Tom Grundy's pockets had yielded treasures, but he'd quickly finished the Lifesavers and had only three cigarettes left.

Shelby still had her watch strapped to her wrist, and Gary had illuminated the face with the lighter. "Nine o'clock," he'd exulted. It was morning, for the wall was aglow.

He'd checked the watch face periodically after that, even when she huddled and rocked and whimpered, and he had just announced that it was ten forty-five when they'd heard faint metallic sounds from far above.

"Another barrel," he'd announced. "Move back. They bounce sometimes."

The sound of its falling had become louder until it crashed onto the floor, then rolled about. As soon as it had come to rest, Gary had scrambled to it, carrying a lid.

"I always try to hurry. There may be someone inside," he'd said as he'd begun to bang away. A moment later the second lid went clattering.

"Got it open," he'd said. A moment later his voice had crackled. "Another live one!"

She'd heard a painful groan, and gone to help. Joined Gary in helping pull a thin male from the barrel.

He'd clicked the lighter, but as soon as the flame flared, the man's hand swept it aside.

"Who are you?" she'd asked, but the man hadn't answered, just looked about, moving his head in small starts and jerks in the semidarkness.

Gary pulled something else from the barrel and illuminated it with the lighter.

"Oh, dear Jesus," he'd cried.

"What's wrong?" she'd managed.

It was a plastic trash bag containing two loaves of bread, a head of lettuce, four raw potatoes, two tomatoes, and ten pounds of frozen, uncooked hamburger. Gary had identified each in the glow of Tom Grundy's lighter, literally dancing about as he'd laughed joyously.

The new arrival had shown no interest, had just slowly made his way to the glow-wall, stood there with his arms outstretched, feeling the glass.

Shelby had been hurting too badly to help Gary roll the new barrel over to the others at their encampment beside the pool, but sat rocking nearby as he clutched the food bag as if it was filled with emeralds, and repeating over and over how Shelby had brought good luck.

"Who is he?" she'd managed to whisper, looking back at the new arrival.

"Don't know. Oh *God,* but I'm hungry, Shelby. Just thinking about the food's making me salivate like crazy."

Shelby had been holding her mouth again, enduring another shuddering toothache.

"Can I eat some of it?" Gary had asked her in a childish tone.

"Sure."

"My fingers don't work very good. They broke them," Gary had said.

She'd taken the bag closer to the glow-wall to examine it better.

"I've been dreaming of stuffed potato skins. I don't care if its raw, I'd like one."

She'd handed a potato over and he'd stared at the dark shape in his hand for a moment, then took a tentative bite.

"It's *wonderful,*" he'd whispered.

They were deafened then as a blast of air and dust erupted from the ceiling, pushing them from their feet and sending them sprawling toward the curvature of the wall where the newcomer was kneeling. A deluge of large stones and sandy earth followed, pouring from the hole high above, and they'd been stunned into mouth-gaping inactivity.

The downpour of stones and earth had paused, then was followed by a new torrent crashing onto the bottom. Shelby had glanced over—the new man's shadow was huddled by the wall, as if he'd *known* it would happen.

Gary had risen and stumbled toward the downpour. "Got to get the rest of the barrels," he'd screamed through their deafness. "They'll be covered up."

Shelby had scuttled to him and pulled frantically on his arm. "You'll be buried with them!" she'd managed, but it took more tugging before he followed her back.

A new torrent of stones had crashed down from above and rolled about. The pyramid had continued to grow, to crumble and spread at the base, then grow higher yet—until she'd believed it might completely fill the sphere. But the downpour had finally slackened, and then stopped.

"Oh God, the water!" Gary had cried out, and had hurried there.

While a few large rocks had splashed in to create small islands, the pool was intact.

They'd remained very still, listening for more rumbling. There was none. For the moment, at least, it was over.

"We have the food," Gary had finally said with wonder in his tone.

"It's mine." Those hissed words had been the new arrival's first.

"We'll share it," Gary said.

"He's been here for eight days without food," Shelby had told the new person.

The old man had released a sound of displeasure, but did not respond further.

"Who are you?" she asked him again.

He'd sat and stared wordlessly at the glass wall.

"It doesn't matter," Gary had said in the giddy voice, holding fast to the food bag.

But Shelby had not been as pleased. Even if the food was good, their deaths had only been prolonged. With the shaft closed, there was no possible way into or out of the sphere. And there was something about the new arrival that she did not like at all.

That had been her first day. On the second and third Shelby had felt the pain diminish some, and that made her feel better about everything. After all, they were alive. Gary had carefully avoided the glow-wall before, but they'd moved their barrels closer. But only their two, for the new arrival had rolled his own to the other side of the pool, farther back into the darkness. Gary had heard him urinating somewhere in the rock pile, and had called out for him to use the waste barrel, but he'd been ignored.

They looked at the glow-wall a lot, enjoyed it as a reminder that just four feet beyond it was some sort of crack in the mountain that let in sunlight, and beyond *that* was fresh air and animals and plants—and life.

When they talked it was in whispers, so the newcomer couldn't overhear.

They'd reminisced about their childhoods, and about their loves. Shelby told him that she and Link had become . . . close . . . in the five days they'd known one another, and he knew what she meant but didn't spoil it with questions. He told her he still missed his ex-wife, no matter what he'd said about her. When she said everyone already knew that, he was surprised.

Gary was pleased Aristotle had survived. "Crazy dog," he repeated several times.

Shelby parsimoniously rationed food each day, giving Gary the most to make up for his period of fasting. Beginning with the hamburger and lettuce, for it would spoil first. Saving the bread for last because it and the potatoes should keep longest. With her broken tooth she had trouble chewing, but they made each meal into a special and sacred ceremony and ate slowly, savoring each calorie.

The newcomer had taken his share silently, neither with a display of happiness nor of displeasure. Just a single, hardly audible grunt acknowledging that he'd received it.

The previous night Shelby and Gary had whispered a solemn promise not to give up hope, and sealed it with another—that if either was irretrievably terminal and in severe pain, the other would assist with the glass dagger-splinter Gary had discovered on his first day. Otherwise it was to be kept at a distance lest either of them become so melancholy they were tempted. They'd gone to hide it together, and both memorized the location.

When they'd come back, they found the newcomer opening the food bag, and Gary had screamed for him to get away. For the second time the man spoke, cursing them loudly as he'd returned to his dark place.

They'd agreed that he must not be told where the long sliver was hidden, and tried even harder to think of ways to escape.

While the air in the sphere seemed lifeless, Shelby was certain it was being replenished, for there were occasional pleasant odors that did not fit with their surroundings. Did that mean there might be a crack Gary hadn't found in his explorations—perhaps one large enough to slip through? They reexamined the periphery carefully, this time together, and could not find one, then tried again and found a rupture, but it was only an inch across and they were unable to widen it. They wondered about stacking a pyramid of rocks as high as possible, then crawling up to the hole at the top, but after they'd hefted a few they'd stopped. Most of the stones were far too heavy to lift and they were using up precious energy, and besides, they knew the top of the sphere was much too high to reach.

The most mundane of their plans was to gather the lids and the hardest stones and chip away at the thinnest section of glow-wall. After a day of it, their efforts had created a few new glass slivers—but those were the only signs of real progress they'd seen, and it finally seemed they were doing *something* about their situation, so they continued to take turns banging and chipping.

The new man remained in his dark hiding place and refused to help.

As they worked, Shelby would say "Don't give up," and Gary would reply, "Never!" When either of them periodically began to cry, the other would honor it with silence.

It was Shelby's third day in hell.

28

A nice, quiet neighborhood, Link noted as he walked from the home and climbed into the rented automobile. It had been an early flight out of Teterboro in the Lear-jet 60, and since they'd provided both pilot and copilot, he'd slept as they shuttled across the continent. The first stop had been O'Hare, then the drive to the Chicago suburb.

Adam Russo's wife had refused to answer Erin's questions on the phone. As soon as Link had opened the conversation, the reason for her reticence emerged. Link was one of *them,* and she'd told him precisely what she thought of men's inconstancies. Russo's wife harbored bitter resentment against her husband of twenty-plus years.

He put the car in gear, opened the flip-top phone, and punched MEM, then 1. Erin answered promptly.

"Russo's wife says he left without warning. One day he's here, writing to second-rate colleges trying to get an interview for any kind of a teaching post, the next night she gets a call from him saying he's out of the state, working on a research job, and for her to stay home."

"No explanation?"

"Not much, and hardly any phone calls afterward to her, and none to their daughter who'd just presented them with a grandson. His only contacts were the weekly checks that arrived like clockwork. Those she didn't complain about, since they'd been dipping at the bottom of their piggy bank. She says the checks are generous."

"I've got her bank account on the screen, and she's right."

Link did not question Erin's ability to pull up anything she wished. She probably chatted with Elvis on the World Wide Web. "I asked if her husband had been hostile after everyone at the convention walked out on him. She said he was dispirited, but he's a meek sort who could never even consider revenge. In fact, when it happened she *hoped* he'd get mad. She felt anger might have been better for him than moping about it."

"Has anyone contacted her about the fact that her husband may be dead?"

"Not a peep from anyone. She didn't even know who was employing him."

"One last question, Link. Is her description of him consistent with what you observed when he briefed you?"

"Yeah. He looked like a nerd and talked in a sort of whisper."

"Still waters run deep. Maybe she didn't really know him after all."

"Obviously, if he's considering wiping out people. Now give me directions on how to get to Russo's boss at the university. The one who fired him." He felt like they were racing with the devil, trying to find out where the members of Epsilon might use the coffeepots—whom they might be holding grudges against. In the light of the new day, it made less sense.

"He's not there, Link. He and his wife are off to a convention in Las Vegas."

"Anyone else here he might be after?"

"No one I've dredged up on the computer."

He sighed. "Then I'll head for Berkeley and try talking to Jergen's superiors."

"Soon as I get your arrival time, I'll set you up." She paused. "I received another phone call from Joseph Spotted Horse this morning. He said he's dreamed of the old people again last night. Now he's determined to drive to Nevada."

"Maybe that'll keep him occupied. I've got enough distractions." Link pulled onto the Interstate.

Erin handled something offline, then came back on. "I just alerted the flight crew at O'Hare that you were on your way. Keep driving and I'll call back."

He folded up the phone. Four minutes later it buzzed. Erin again.

"When you land at Oakland, head for the UC campus and find Building 500. You'll be asking for a Dr. Kenneth L. Thorsness, who's the regent of Lawrence Laboratories, which are a part of the University of California system. His secretary took the message."

"Did you tell her *why* I'm coming?"

"Just that you're with the foundation and we're considering giving some sizable research grants this fall. If that doesn't get you in, nothing will."

2:40 P.M.—Building 500, Lawrence Laboratories, Berkeley, California

Kenneth Thorsness was prematurely gray and distinguished in appearance, and approached the security desk with a smile, hand extended.

"Dr. Anderson? It's so good to see a representative from the Weyland Foundation. I have nothing but admiration for your organization, sir."

Link went along with the title and praise, nodded, and shook hands.

Thorsness motioned grandiosely. "Most of this building is limited access, since we have a number of sensitive government programs. On your next visit we'll have your security clearance information, and you'll be able to see just how impressive it all really is."

They went into a reception room, the regent's hand resting on his shoulder as if they were fast buddies. Link took a seat on a sofa, Thorsness a chair facing him. A coffee table was laid out with hors d'oeuvres and cold beverages, but Link declined.

"I'd like information about two of your former employees."

"Certainly," his host murmured.

"Dr. Piers Jergen?"

Thorsness's eyes became guarded, the smile faded.

"He *was* employed here, right?"

"For a period. Most of his work was done at our Livermore facility, however."

"And who hired him?"

"I was on the board that made the decision. I—uh—forget which way I voted."

"He researched the accelerated depletion phenomenon?"

"I believe so." Thorsness was not forthcoming with his responses.

"You don't know what your employees work on?" Link asked.

"Our scientists have a great degree of autonomy, especially those involved in investigatory research, but yes, he was involved with A.D. In fact he was rather singleminded, as if little else interested him."

"And Dr. Juliette LaCoste?" Link asked, feeling his way.

"She was Jergen's associate at the very end of his tenure." Thorsness canted his head, no longer as friendly. "Where are you going with this? Neither of these people is here any longer."

"Certain of our people at the Weyland Foundation are *very* interested in the potential of accelerated depletion, possibly as a means to treat nuclear waste."

"Ah," Thorsness said, warming again. "I just heard the same from the Department of Energy. I assure you we're doing some interesting work in that direction. *Very* interesting. In fact we're on the brink of an exciting breakthrough. With appropriate emphasis we believe—"

"You're improving on Dr. Jergen's hypothesis? Using his device?"

"Good God, no. The man's a fraud, and his device is a worthless contraption."

Thorsness had obviously not yet been briefed about the demonstration at Millionaire Mountain.

"Jergen's a fraud?" Link asked, pressing Thorsness.

"I assume, sir, that you didn't read the October 1995 issue of the *AFSE Journal*?"

"No."

"There was an article that reached that conclusion.

One statement was, and I quote: "Dr. Jergen continues to wander in a wasteland of misconception."

"And the author?"

"I wrote it." Thorsness smiled fondly, as if he particularly liked the sound of the words. "It was quite well received," he added.

Link regarded him incredulously. "You were Piers Jergen's superior here, and you wrote an article in a professional journal condemning him?"

Thorsness shrugged. "Truth is where you find it, Dr. Anderson. The man was pig-headed and simply would not listen. By then he'd killed an assistant with his contraption, and if we hadn't pulled the plug, there might have been more."

"And now the lab here is doing *new* work with A.D?"

"If you haven't received the AFSE convention agenda, tomorrow afternoon I present a briefing called the Truth About Accelerated Depletion. Are you attending?"

"Tomorrow? Where?"

"Why, in Las Vegas. The convention opens this afternoon. This year's theme is A Century of Nuclear Legacy. Precisely one hundred years ago, Marie and Pierre Curie discovered the first radioactive element, you know."

"And you'll be there?"

"Everyone who *matters* in the field will attend. There's a reception tonight, and the display booths at the convention hall open in the morning. The briefings begin at nine." Thorsness paused, frowned. "You're not a member of the AFSE?"

"No," Link said, considering what he'd just learned. All three members of the Epsilon Collegium had cause to feel victimized by the AFSE.

"Why are you *really* here?" Thorsness demanded.

Link abruptly stood. "Thank you for your time, doctor." He stood and hurried toward the door—leaving Thorsness agape at his rudeness, calling out more questions in his wake—and as soon as he was outside, he hurried to the waiting taxi.

He climbed in. "One more stop in the local area, then

we'll beat it back to the airport. Take me over to Oakland Hills."

"Long ways," said the Pakistani with a calculating look.

Link gave him the address, then brought out the cell phone and rang Erin.

"Two-seven-seven-five," she answered.

"Good, I caught you at work."

"Nope. I took off early. I'm in a bathtub filled with bubbly and a flotilla of my kid's rubber boats."

He ignored the distracting mental image. "I just saw Thorsness, and now I'm headed out to see the student who got Juliette LaCoste in trouble."

"Fred Vincent is on his seventh year as a grad student there at Cal Berkeley. You have the address?"

"Yeah. After I talk to him I'm heading for Las Vegas."

"The AFSE convention?"

"You know about it?"

"Sure, and I was going to bring it up. It's at the Hilton. Think it over. Do you *really* think Ansel Turpin might head that way?"

"Why not? Every member of Epsilon got a raw deal from AFSE."

"True." She ran water for a moment, then shut it off.

"You don't sound convinced."

"It's just too easy. Ansel Turpin is a maestro at deviousness, a student of Niccoló Machiavelli and his work called *The Prince*. Ever heard of it?"

"Yeah. The end justifies the means. Truth is only a weapon."

"That's the one."

He heard water slosh, could not help forming an image. He was troubled by a thought of floating cantaloupes. Found himself smiling and made himself stop.

"Another of Turpin's medieval heroes is Cesare Borgia, who lured his enemies to his pad and had them strangled. That's the one I've been thinking a lot about."

"You don't think it's logical that he'd take a coffeepot to Vegas?"

"I simply can't believe he'd do anything that obvious.

That's what's wrong with our whole premise, Link. I don't mean he's above revenge, just that he won't be that obvious."

"Unless you've got something better, I'm going there after I've seen Vincent."

"I guess I really don't. Anything I should set up?"

"I'll need an invitation to the convention."

"AFSE is a closed society, but I'll see what I can do."

Link found Fred Vincent at home and formed an immediate dislike for the simpering, self-centered scarecrow who had been Juliette LaCoste's student.

Vincent was not reticent, and seemed to linger longest on the most intimate details.

For a year he'd worked closely with Dr. LaCoste, and she'd guided and encouraged him to develop his ideas. He'd enjoyed the special attention, although she was *much* older, and he had not dared to complain as the relationship became physical. Then he'd discovered a research paper she'd prepared on the various ways to isolate leptons, meaning to separate electrons from their associated neutrinos. He had been writing a thesis at the time and asked if he might use it—reasoning that they discussed the subject often, so at least *some* of it was his work—but she'd said no. He had gone ballistic, and she'd shown him the door of her apartment.

This from the woman who liked him to strap her into a leather halter and lash her genitals with a leather thong until they were bright and rosy. He spoke with animation as he described their kinkiest sex acts. How she liked him to pierce her nipples with needles, and . . .

The following week he'd gotten a lawyer and gone to the department faculty board and charged that she'd seduced him and stolen his ideas.

A lawyer? An idea came to Link, and he stopped him. "Tell me something. Was it your idea to go to the faculty board?"

"Sure it was."

"You didn't get encouragement from anyone? No one came to see you and talk you into it? Maybe a guy with a bad limp, telling you he'd provide the attorney?"

Vincent frowned so hard that Link knew he was on the right track. He started to turn sullen. "You from the attorney's office?"

Link remained quiet.

"I thought the guy you just talked about already handled the expenses."

"I'm sure he did," Link said. "What else did he talk about?"

"Just that he knew all about Dr. LaCoste, and how she liked to show off and be strapped down and hurt and all."

"You didn't do any of those things with her though, right?"

Vincent looked nervous. "Sure I did. Like I told 'em, if I hadn't, she would have failed me."

"Have you seen the man with the limp lately?"

"Her old boyfriend? Not for months now."

"Did he tell you to keep his visit quiet?"

"No way. He said I should tell everyone about *all* the guys who'd had sex with her." Vincent grinned at Link. "The lawyer agreed, so I told everyone in sight, even showed off some of her toys that her old boyfriend gave me, and by the time I got to the faculty board they were all ready to cave in. I mean, it was pure sexual harassment. The university had hired this deviate and allowed it to happen."

Link told Erin about Fred Vincent on the way to Oakland International. "Kind of guy you really warm up to," he said. "He's about to become rich. The university settled for five million." Erin had finished her bath. "Interesting about Juliette LaCoste's old boyfriend. It was obviously Turpin. Good thinking, Link."

"The lady was set up."

"I'm putting some ideas together on my computer. And by the way, I've got a contact for you," she said. "When you get to the Vegas Hilton look up a Dr. Dan Roper so he can get you into the convention. I've also got a room reserved for you."

"Tough duty. You still think it's a mistake going there?"

"I just think Ansel Turpin's too smart for something

so obvious. By the way, I picked up a message from the army. The morgue team identified their first body parts at Millionaire Mountain. Four of them so far, and none from Epsilon. Looks more and more like Jergen, Russo, and LaCoste were on the helicopter."

"How about Gary and Shelby?"

"Nothing yet. I'll give you a call in an hour or so."

The Sphere

The previous day they'd found what appeared to be the brightest portion of the glow-wall and concluded it might also be the thinnest, and had moved their efforts to a seam there, taking turns at it. First one then the other banging, scraping and chipping with the barrel lids. Today they'd continued, from the first glimmering of light on the wall until now, when it was beginning to fade. Wondering if there was any possible way to get through the four feet of glass before their food and energy gave out. Not daring to doubt out loud.

The newcomer had not offered to help. In fact had once raised his voice to tell them they were stupid to try. Just wasting energy.

"Your turn," Shelby said. She pushed back and sat, chest heaving from the exertion. Blisters had formed early on the palms of both hands. Now there were blisters on blisters.

Gary took over. He had difficulty grasping the lid.

Each strike on the glow-wall created a dull thud. Periodically the lid would slip from his grasp, and there'd be a clang.

"I'm going to look for lava," she said. "It might work better."

Gary stopped, ran a hand over his sweaty brow, and grasped her arm. "Be careful," he whispered.

"What for?"

"He's sneaking around back there, and I don't trust him."

"Mmm." Neither of them liked the newcomer—or at least the little they'd heard from him—but she wondered if they weren't overreacting because of his refusal to cooperate. She went to the rockslide and nosed around in the darkness, sorting through what was mostly pieces of crumbly sandstone, picking out the occasional chunk of red lava spewed from a nearby cinder cone some forty thousand years ago. Most pieces were too small for their purpose, but a few seemed appropriate, and those she tossed toward the glow-wall.

A noise came to her from the darkness beyond the limit of her vision. A slight sound, as if the newcomer was trying to be stealthy.

"How're you doing over here?" Shelby asked him. As usual, there was no response.

She came across the niche where she and Gary had hidden the splinter-dagger, started to go on, but decided the newcomer was acting spooky enough to warrant protection.

Shelby reached into the cranny, felt around, and pulled her hand back out.

The dagger-splinter was gone.

A noise immediately behind her made her spin about. The newcomer's shadow was close.

"Scared me," she muttered.

He did not respond, just readjusted himself and—perhaps in her imagination—seemed to poise, as if preparing himself. He took a tentative step, coming closer.

Shelby panicked, made a squeaking sound and scuttled for the glow-wall.

Thud, thud, thud, clank. The lid was jolted from Gary's hand and rolled about. Settled onto the glass floor with a metallic click.

Gary cursed, and looked as she arrived at his side.

"The dagger's gone," she whispered as she retrieved the lid and handed it back.

They stared toward the shadows, where the newcomer had again disappeared.

4:10 P.M.—Airborne over Tonopah, Nevada

"Hi," came Erin's voice. "I'm putting pieces together. Got a few minutes to talk?"

"Sure."

"Keep in mind that Ansel Turpin is the son of Piers Jergen, and almost two years ago he escaped Russia with a hundred million smackeroos and a bad case of the hates for the Weyland Foundation."

"That would be hard to forget."

"Now jump forward a few months to when Piers Jergen's assistant dies in an experiment. The death seems odd, since the assistant is familiar with the device, and just perhaps Ansel is involved because everything to come hinges on that screw-up. The university very predictably decided they should part ways again, and a couple of months later old Piers is living on social security checks, and his only possession is a contraption that promises to build up lots of radiation—whether or not it then does a little magic."

"A killing machine," Link murmured.

"Yes. All it needs is someone who is utterly brilliant to help it along."

"Piers?"

"Nope. He's losing it. But the smartest gal at Berkeley, who is a female Einstein only smarter, is suddenly charged with sexual activities so loathsome that no one's going to talk to her except the sales clerk at a San Francisco chains-and-spikes shop. For a straight single female, the thing is sheer hell. Then Ansel pops up and talks about revenge. I've thought about it. In her place, I'd take him up on it."

"And now they've got their killing machine perfected."

"Give the man a cigar."

"So tell me about Adam Russo."

"What's to tell? The way I figure, the poor klutz is turning to fertilizer somewhere. So guess who gave you the briefing out at NEL and you didn't know?"

"Ansel Turpin."

"Keep it up and I'll run outta cigars."

29

Link was with the Learjet crew. The copilot was driving the rental car, and as they approached the Hilton, the captain pointed out the marquee.

WELCOME AMERICAN FEDERATION OF SCIENTISTS AND ENGINEERS.

"That the bunch you're here to see?"

"Yeah," said Link, staring. "Drop me off in front."

"You're not going to need us?" There was no more room at the Hilton, so the crew was billeted at the Mirage.

"No, but stay on call. If one of you wants a drink, fine. Both, no. And the sober one carries the cell phone." Link got out with his bag, gave a nod, and went inside.

Check-in went quickly. As soon as Link's identity was known, he was ushered away from the line and provided with a key card. He gave the bellboy his bag, received directions to the AFSE registration desk on the second floor, and went up.

A pinch-faced woman was at a table, crossing out names and handing out plastic-covered badges. Beyond her was a ballroom where people milled and sipped libations.

Link didn't feel out of place in casual shirt and boots. The man in front of him wore a formal tux, orange sneakers, and carried a handbag. He awaited his turn, and gave his name.

She didn't search the list, just looked up and glared at him. "Are you a member?"

"Mr. Anderson," exclaimed a florid-faced man of sixty-odd years. He took Link's elbow and led him to one side, out of the woman's earshot. "Lincoln?"

"Yeah?."

"Dan Roper from Habitat Earth at the Weyland Foundation. I got a call from your assistant saying you needed an entré, so I asked them to let you in as my guest. Unfortunately a member of the AFSE's board of directors had called and told them you were a trouble-maker and not to admit you—regardless."

"Dr. Ken Thorsness?"

"The same, from the Lawrence Labs. He's an ass, but they listen to him."

"Did Erin tell you why I wanted in?"

"Just asked me to provide support, and if I need veri-fication, to call Frank Dubois. That's unnecessary. We haven't met, but you're already a cult hero to my Habi-tat Earth bunch."

Dan Roper was wearing a pair of lizard-skin Justin boots.

"So how can I help?" he asked, smiling.

"How many people are here?"

"About three hundred and fifty members, and most bring spouses. I don't have one."

"Have you ever heard of the Jergen Reaction De-vice?" Link began.

"Sure. Jergen brought it to a symposium a few years ago. Most said it was a pipedream."

"It wasn't." The telling took half an hour, but Dan Roper listened intently.

When he finally spoke, his voice was filled with won-der. "It actually *worked*?"

"Yes."

"And you think this Turpin guy might bring one of the things *here*?"

"Maybe. All three members of the collegium were in-sulted by AFSE."

"Yeah? I don't usually attend the conventions because of all the infighting. AFSE's the worst of the professional science groups. With these guys the three rules are pub-lish or perish, discredit others to make room for your own ideas, and do unto others before they do unto you. The games start tomorrow morning with the technical presentations. They're bloodlettings."

"But you're a member."

Roper shrugged. "I received a Nobel five years ago. It makes membership in organizations like this sort of automatic."

Link was impressed.

"So how much plutonium would the device have loaded in it?"

"I don't know," Link said truthfully. "The demonstration I saw at NEL used four kilograms in both reservoirs, but the amount may have changed."

"Eight kilos is less than twenty pounds of the stuff. Plutonium's damned heavy, so that's not much. The device is lead-coated?"

"Mostly titanium and graphite, so it's portable."

Dr. Roper peered back at the half-filled reception room.

"I don't think it would be here," Link said, "*If* they use it, they'll pick a time when more of the members are present."

Roper nodded at an uniformed pair of women. "They use armed security guards to keep undesirables out. I'll try to find a rad meter and tell them to make sure no one gets past them with anything that faintly resembles a big coffeepot."

The cell phone buzzed in Link's pocket, and he extracted it.

It was Erin. The local FBI office was onto something, and Special Agent Gordon Tower had been told to pick him up in the lobby. Before Erin disconnected she said, "Maybe you're right about Epsilon, Link. They're close by after all."

"I'll go right down," he told her.

"Business?" Roper asked as he folded the phone.

Link nodded. "I'll see you in the morning."

Special Agent Gordon Tower was alone. He shook hands quickly and led Link toward the elevators. "The chopper's on the roof," he said as he pressed the top button.

"I heard you were told to pick me up."

"How about a call from the regional director, who got the word from a couple folks higher up? Nothing official, just heard you needed some more help and some looking out after."

"Thanks."

"They just found a helicopter in the desert, Link. Last time you and I saw it, we were standing at that old pony express station."

Link's adrenaline surged. "Was anyone inside?"

"One." A couple with suspicious stares shared their elevator. "Tell you more when we're airborne." Tower cocked his head and changed the subject. "It's a damned raw deal your bunch is getting. I've worked with the foundation before and they're straight-shooters. I sure as hell hope they make it out of this shit they're in. It's an obvious setup."

They arrived at the helipad at a trot, crawled inside the aircraft, and were still strapping in when the rotors surged and they were on their way.

"Where's the helicopter?" Link shouted.

"A few miles out of Pahrump, over by Death Valley. They found it two hours ago. The new SAC here asked the local cops to stand off and wait for the hostage rescue team."

"You've got one here."

"Have had since they first thought Ansel Turpin might be around. I know him, I take him damn serious. Anyway, the HRT guys should be landing there soon."

The left-seat pilot turned and gave him a thumbs up.

"Like right now," said Special Agent Gordon Tower.

"Does everyone know what they may be up against?"

"Same thing we saw a Stagecoach Valley. Everyone's carrying rad meters. We get a high reading, we get the hell out of Dodge."

"Have they told the civilians."

"You joking? They haven't even told the local authorities. We're told to give them the mushroom treatment. We hear all sorts of rationales, like not causing undue alarm and not impacting the local economy, but they're bullshit. Believe it or not, there's a government negotiating team set up to deal with Turpin. They *really* want to get their hands on a coffeepot."

They crested the mountains and flew on in the lengthening evening shadows.

Five minutes later they touched down beside two other rotary wing craft, where a man and woman in dark vests awaited them.

Tower got out, paused for Link to join him, then they strode together over to the others as the helicopter blades clattered to a halt. A rep from the Hostage Rescue Team was explaining the situation to the man obviously in charge. She pointed to a dark house two hundred yards distant. "The team's inside."

"Where's the helicopter?" Tower asked her.

The vested woman pointed out a shape partially covered by a sand-colored tarpaulin. "One dead in the right pilot's seat, shot in the head. It's been a few days, and he's ripe."

She took a radio call, spoke into her boom mike, then came closer. "Four bodies in the house. A couple and their two kids."

"Why would they do that?" Link blurted.

She motioned at the garage. "They needed ground transport. The locals say they had two vehicles. A late-model van and a pickup. The van's gone."

Link was introduced to the new SAC of the Las Vegas office. After they shook hands, the SAC asked Gordon Tower if he had any ideas.

Tower frowned thoughtfully. Shook his head.

The SAC turned to the HRT coordinator. "Where are the nearest neighbors?"

She pointed southward. "Half a mile toward town."

"Check around. Ask when they last saw the van and who was inside."

They waited as the directions were relayed.

"Remember when we talked about the possibility that Ansel Turpin might be involved?" Link asked Gordon Tower.

"I *know* he's involved," he was told. "Destin Albee

sent a priority message to the Hoover Building, saying
he was convinced Turpin had paid you a visit. The deputy director said bullshit, but the director called me in
and alerted me I might be traveling. That night Destin
was killed by someone who strolled right into his home,
and there's only one person who's good enough to do
that. There wasn't any gang or drugs involved. It was a
flat-out bad-ass killing. The old Turpin wouldn't have
done it like that, but he's turned animal. Maybe it's all
the radioactivity zapping his brain cells." Tower looked
at him. "You know Turpin?"

"Mainly what I've been told. You?"

"Like I told your sidekick Erin, I met him when we
were kids just out of college and new to the bureau.
Drank a lot of martinis with the guy and got to know
him as well as anyone. Then a few years later I attended
his course at Quantico. Brilliant! He stood right in front
of us and told us what he was going to do, turned
around, and when he turned back he'd changed his appearance so much you'd swear it was someone else—
with us watching. Sucked in his cheeks, narrowed his
eyes and dropped his shoulders, walked in a little shuffle
and talked funny, and you'd have sworn he was an old
guy you'd never seen before."

"Anything else you remember that I should know?"

"He taught us to operate in one of two places. Either
where there aren't any people and you know everything
and everyone around you, or in the middle of so many
people they'd never be able to find you. Turpin made
the rules, and he lives by them. That's why I don't think
he's in Vegas. It's too easy to stand out. Just doesn't
sound right, him going there."

Like it had not sounded right to Erin. "What if there's
someone he wants to kill there?"

"Look, Turpin knows we're looking for him, and one
thing he does not have is a death wish. He is the wiliest
survivor in the world. If he wanted to knock someone
in Vegas off, he'd get them to come to *his* turf and
do it."

"Live bait," Link remembered Turpin saying.

"Yep. That's what he prefers. Get someone near and dear, and draw them in."

Link mused about that for a moment. "It sounds like he was respected in the bureau. Why in the world did he turn like he did?"

"Ansel not only was good, he knew it. In fact there wasn't much in this world that he didn't think he wasn't the absolutely best at. Then one day he looks around. He's over forty and only has a few years to go until he'll have to retire, and he's not going to be director, or even deputy director, or even an assistant regional chief. But he knows he's the best, and ought to be able to cash in on it *some* way." Gordon sighed. "Well, he did."

Link looked at the house and the several police cruisers that were pulling up there. The SAC had told the locals they could go in. It was now their game. He turned back to Gordon Tower. "If not Las Vegas, where would he go?"

"How about Los Angeles? Think of what his radiation toys could do there"

Link could not be *that* wrong. He tried another tack, thinking of old Piers Jergen. "What if his own family's involved, and he was doing something to help them?"

"The only relative he ever gave a shit about's dead. He idolized his mother."

"His father's here with him. Piers Jergen."

"We don't know who's here, Link. We won't know until we get prints or a witness. But if his pop's with him I pity the poor shit, because Ansel hated his father with a passion."

Link grew silent, thinking that just maybe he *was* that wrong.

"Yeah," Gordon Tower was saying, "He told me once how he wished he could put his father in a cage and watch him slowly starve to death."

It was late even by Las Vegas standards by the time Link finally returned to the Hilton and went up to his room. There he sat looking out over the city, thinking about all he'd learned, and how there was so much he still did not know.

Erin felt it would be out of character for Ansel Turpin to attack the AFSE convention. The FBI SAC felt he'd be breaking his own rules. And if Turpin despised his father, the rationale that he was driven to avenge his honor was equally faulty. But Turpin was loose with three terrible machines of death, and he must be found before he used them.

Link went to bed, deciding to check out the convention hall the following morning, then fly to Los Angeles. Where should he search when he got there? he wondered. He did not even know where to begin.

30

The shrill warble did not fit with his dream. Marie turned to him with startled eyes, like a doe about to bolt. Since they'd been walking in a primeval forest his mind tried to fit a bird into the scenario, although all had been silent before the rude intrusion. Another raucous sound erupted. He reached out desperately, for Marie was fading and with her the peace they'd shared.

The cell phone on the bedside table buzzed again, and he came sufficiently awake to fumble and lift it from the charger base. The gentle realm was gone, and he was in the reality of another, this one a hotel room designed to provide lavish comforts.

"Anderson," he croaked into the flip-top.

"It's a beautiful day here in New York," Erin said brightly, "but I just saw a report that said it's already ninety-five degrees there in Vegas. Get ready for a hot one, pardner."

"Yeah." The heavy curtains were drawn and the air conditioning quietly and unobtrusively corrected any temperature abnormalities.

Her voice flattened. "I just read a summary from the morgue detail at Millionaire Mountain. Parts of eighteen bodies have been I.D.'ed using prints, records, and DNA match."

"So who's missing?"

"The ones we suspected. The pilot, two security officers, and the three in the Epsilon Collegium. For your info, neither Gary Runyon nor Shelby Admire were among the dead."

"Fred Jameson?"

"Positive identification."

"I sort of liked him."

"Too bad. By the way, the army's finished at the mountain."

"Aren't they going to reopen the mine shaft?"

"They're estimating that sixty tons of rock is blocking the passageway. Not only would it be difficult to remove, if they tried they'd just fill up the glass bubble."

"How much of all this has the government released to the public?"

"Only that a few people died in an explosives accident. Not how many, and they're not telling *how*."

"With that many deaths, surely they can't *hide* what happened."

"Well, they're certainly trying. The families have been flown separately to Washington, given an 'I feel your pain' speech and told there's been an accident. Then a counselor advises them to keep it quite because if there are questions their *extremely* generous life insurance and benefits claim just might be held up in red tape."

"That's blackmail . . . again."

"According to the eye of the beholder . . . again. A veil of silence has been invoked for all concerned. The administration is justifying it by saying it's a public safety matter, that they don't want the country unduly concerned because it might affect the economy, and finally, the future of the country depends on them getting their hands on A.D. The gag order includes all foundation employees holding security clearances, so hold your tongue."

"Who's briefing the president?"

"Lots of folks, including the Secretary of Energy."

Link recalled the middle-aged man who had been, and still reminded him of, a slick used car salesman. Her next words did not surprise him.

"We've learned that the Secretary observed the A.D. phenomenon first hand."

Link had seen the helicopter land on the mountain, stay until the A.D. phenomenon was finished, then depart. A question plagued him. "Who told him where to go, and when?"

"There was obviously some kind of communication."

Link wanted to cast that troublesome idea aside. He got up and padded to the window. "Are they even looking for Turpin?" he wondered aloud.

"Both the FBI and ATF have been ordered to locate and secure the coffeepots."

"Good."

"Maybe. Last night the director of the FBI asked the attorney general to authorize a large-scale search in Los Angeles. His agents feel Turpin might try to hold the city hostage with his three coffeepots. Maybe even conduct another demonstration. The A.G. took it to the National Security Council. They met all night and couldn't come up with anything except arguments. The FBI wanted to position explosives experts and hostage rescue teams in key areas. The NSC has agreed to negotiating teams only. Both sides are tearing their hair out. They're concerned about public safety, but they *really* want to get their hands on the devices."

"What do you think Turpin will do?" Link drew the drapes, and shielded his eyes from the brilliance. It *looked* hot out there.

Erin released a sigh. "Except for the humiliation and revenge angle, I'm stumped."

He told her what he'd learned from Special Agent Gordon Tower about Ansel Turpin the previous evening. Erin had known most of it but was surprised that he'd despised his father.

"I thought it was his domineering mother he disliked."

"Not according to Tower. Of course, that was twenty years ago."

"Ansel Turpin is a constant, Link. I doubt very much he's changed his mind."

"Then we were wrong. If he's not trying to redeem Piers Jergen's honor or helping him get revenge, he's not going to target the AFSE convention."

"Then why did they head for Vegas in the helicopter?"

"Probably bound for L.A. like Tower thought. Or maybe he was just trying to escape."

"No way. Regardless of what's happening, its part of a plan." She paused. "So he despises his father. I hate being *that* wrong. I've got to go plug all this into my computer. If I come up with anything, I'll call."

Link found a coffee shop without a line, took a seat at the counter, and ordered a cholesterol lover's delight with juice, three-egg bacon and cheddar omelette, and pancakes. As he waited for the food, he mulled through possible courses of action, but he could come up with only two. Ask Gordon Tower *where* in Los Angeles he thought Epsilon and Turpin might be headed, and go there and search, or return to Stagecoach Valley and learn what happened to Gary and Shelby.

Neither option sounded much better than one he'd rejected, which was just to wait for Ansel Turpin to make the next move, then try to react quickly enough to neutralize him.

The food came, and with it Dan Roper, the scientist he'd met the previous evening. "Mind if I join you?" Dr. Roper asked, then ordered a juice and bagel and balefully eyed Link's bounteous fare. "You don't know how long it's been since I've been able to eat. When I hit fifty it was like a switch was turned on so everything turns to fat. Low-cal, low-fat, low-saturates, doesn't matter. Five minutes after I eat it, it's suet."

"When do the morning festivities get underway?"

"Everything's moved to the convention center—the building next door. The exhibition hall opened at eight. Manufacturers, chemical and medical companies, computer hardware and software folks, all sorts of new gadgetry." Roper smeared a thin layer of low-calorie cream cheese on the bagel, took a bite, then pulled a paper from his inner coat pocket and perused. "There's a membership meeting at nine, thirty minutes from now. Old business, new business, resolutions, upbeat message from the president saying he sure wishes he could be here, that sort of thing."

"Then the presentations?"

Dr. Roper nodded. "First off the blocks is Ken Thorsness. One hour of speechifying, then another explaining something called the Thorsness Reactor."

"Which sounds suspiciously like Dr. Jergen's device."

Dan Roper make a mocking face. "You don't think he'd mimic someone he calls a fraud, do you?"

"You live in an odd world, Dan."

"Yep, but somehow we American scientists still make three quarters of all the world's breakthroughs." Roper mused. "You *really* think the terrorists might visit us?"

"I doubt it."

"I told security to look out for anything that faintly resembles a beverage dispenser, *and* to set up a rad meter at the entrance. They had trouble with that until one was offered by one of the exhibitors. By the way, I mentioned what you said about the disaster up north to a couple of the DOE folks, and they looked like I'd just revealed a big dark secret."

"Unfortunately that's the way they're treating it. Now they don't want to discuss it."

"That's crazy." He glanced at his watch. "I'm headed over to the hall. Care to join me?"

"I thought I was barred."

"Only from the meetings. It's the more the merrier at the exhibitions, which are just a bunch of marketers trying to peddle their wares. Once they find out you're a vice-president from the biggest and richest foundation in America, they'll *carry* you in."

The hotel's main floor was crowded with revelers, gamblers, and conventioneers, but Dan Roper steered the way surely through the maze, then down a long connecting hallway to the hall.

"Been here a few times," Roper told him. "Used to be my favorite convention center until the wimps at the Pentagon screwed our organization over a few years back."

Link was slow in putting it together. "You're a tailhooker?"

"Marine pilot during Korea. Seventy-two combat carrier landings, and one hairy one over the side. Got out after the war and got my doctorate, but I stay in touch."

Two security guards were at the entryway to the exhibition hall. Roper showed his plastic-covered pass and told them Link was with him. He motioned at a rad meter. "See you got it working. Any higher than normal readings?"

"None yet," said the female. "In a few minutes they're going to bring in something called a Thorsness Reactor, and we've been told to ignore the radiation readings."

"Do you have an objection?" came a chilled voice. Dr. Kenneth Thorsness stood just behind them, wearing a sour, irritated expression. "I assure you there's only enough uranium to jog the meters for my demonstration. Now, just *who* ordered the rad meter set up here?"

"I did," Dan Roper said, ignoring the glare. "Didn't want you characters from Berkeley zapping the rest of us with your weird gadgets."

Thorsness snorted and went inside. Dr. Roper and Link followed.

"I heard you were air force," Roper said cordially, and Link nodded. They walked past exhibits, talking about flying and how jets had changed in the forty years between their combat tours, and all the while Link studied the vulnerabilities of the place.

The exhibition hall was tremendous in size, able to accommodate multiple conventions through the use of movable walls and curtains. The AFSE used only a third of the building, set up in a large square. At the rear were rooms for meetings. In the vast, open front area were several rows of vendors' displays. Between each, and lining the walls at the back and sides, were narrow, three-foot wide alleyways created by dark blue curtains that moved on tracks attached to the ceiling. In those the vendors kept their wares, supplies, and collapsible displays, and occasionally went to rest, talk privately, or sneak a cigarette. Getting in would be small challenge for someone of Turpin's skill, and there were a thousand places to hide a coffeepot. Just as bothersome, the curtained alleys provided a maze for anyone who wished to remain unseen.

They stopped at several of the various displays, and listened to spiels about various products, most to support or enhance laboratory work and too specialized to gain Link's interest. Yet the gathered scientists stared in wonder, like kids at an electronic game store.

At the rear of the exhibition hall was a guarded doorway with a scrawled sign: *AFSE Membership Meeting at 9 o'clock. Show your I.D. cards and bring your ballots.*

Roper led Link over to an adjacent unmanned government exhibit, a mock-up of the nuclear waste storage facility going in at Yucca Mountain, a hundred fifty miles to the north.

"The project's on hold," said Dr. Roper. "Politics and the not-in-my-back-yard types are winning again, but something's got to give. No one likes the idea of building more dams to screw up the ecology, and no one likes nuclear reactors or the garbage they create. But sure as hell, no one's about to give up their electricity."

"What about the A.D. phenomenon?" Link asked. "It works, Dan. I saw it take the radiation right down to zero."

"Truthfully, it scares me to death." He started to explain, but was interrupted.

"Link?" Special Agent Gordon Tower approached them, accompanied by another agent.

"Busy night?" Link asked.

"You wouldn't believe." Tower shook his head. "Bad news last night, now this morning too. I got another phone call about you, Link. It's been reported that you and a friend have been talking out of school." He looked over. "Are you Dr. Daniel Roper?"

"Yes."

The agent introduced himself. "Sorry, but I've got to take you both in for a talk."

Dan Roper grew an outraged expression. "What's the subject?"

"Security. We won't keep you long, doc. Just sit you down, slap your wrist, tell you to shut your yap, and bring you back."

"You didn't answer my question. What's the subject?"

"We can't talk about it here."

"What's this about?" Roper said in a loud voice of outrage. "You don't want us discussing the fact that there's a group of nutty terrorists on the loose with nuke devices?"

"Keep your voice down," said the special agent.

Roper snorted. "We've got a right to talk about anything we want. And if anyone's in danger we damned well *should* be talking about it."

Gordon Tower looked as if he didn't like his orders but was damned well going to carry them out. As he leaned into Roper's face and quietly mentioned physical restraint, Link stared beyond them.

The woman was in the purple uniform worn by people at the hotel desk, with heavy makeup, tinted glasses, and frowsy hair, looking around with narrowed eyes and a heavy frown. Beside her a big, beefy man, also in a purple uniform, pushed a cart with something on it shrouded by canvas. A placard read *Thorsness Reactor.* Both were trying not to appear hurried. She looked directly at Link, and her stony expression altered just a bit as they disappeared behind a nearby curtain.

Alarm bells went off. The man was an unknown, but he'd seen her before—and not at the hotel desk. He made some mental adjustments—kept the horsy look, long aquiline nose, and high cheekbones but took off twenty pounds and changed the mop to severely swept back hair.

"There's one of them," he told the special agent.

Gordon Tower swiveled his neck, instinctively knowing what he'd meant. The second agent started to say something, but Tower held up a hand and shook his head, as if telling him to listen up. Link started for the curtain. They followed.

"Here's where they went into the curtains," Link told them in a low voice. "The LaCoste woman and a guy I haven't seen before, pushing a cart."

"You're sure it was her?"

"Absolutely." The inner warning continued to sound. If Erin were here she'd say they'd been obvious. Too easy. "Be careful," Link said. "You know what they have."

The senior FBI agent stopped at the curtain, took a breath, drew a pistol, and held it at his side, out of view of others in the room. The other agent did the same, then pushed the curtain aside. There was nothing, only a passage into the next room where AFSE members had begun to file in for the business meeting.

They entered hesitantly. People were gathering, starting to take seats.

Link nodded toward the front of the room. "There's the cart," he said, and started there. The canvas shroud had been removed, was folded neatly on top beside an odd-looking rectangular box fashioned of metal and polypropylene, adorned with a yellow radioactive hazard warning. *Thorsness Reactor,* the placard read. There'd been room for a coffeepot to be secreted with it under the shroud, and neither the woman nor the man were in view.

Where were they, and where was their device?

"What are you doing in *here*?" came an acid tone. Dr. Ken Thorsness strode toward them with a determined look. He cast a glare at Link, another at Special Agent Tower. "Please leave," he said. "Both of you."

Gordon Tower regarded the device on the cart, then looked at Link with an inquiring expression.

"That's not it." Where was the woman—and the man who'd been with her?

"Security," Thorsness called toward the door. "Please escort these gentlemen out."

"We're leaving," said Tower. His pistol had disappeared into its hidden holster. They started for the door, then Link turned back to slowly scan the hundred-odd members already seated. He was sure. Neither the man nor the woman was present.

"We'd better head downtown," said the agent, but he too was looking about.

"She's here somewhere," Link said.

"Like I told you last night. Turpin wouldn't pick Vegas. If he's running the operation—"

"Damn it, Gordon, I just saw Juliette LaCoste. She was with a man, and they looked like a couple of kids trying to get away with something. The coffeepot was probably hidden under the shroud. At least take a look around."

They'd stopped just outside the meeting room, and Gordon was chewing vigorously on his lip, considering what Link was saying. Finally he turned to the other agent. "You know what we're looking for. Start where they went behind the curtain and check all nooks and crannies."

Dr. Thorsness had followed them to the open doorway, stood with his hands on hips and regarded them coldly as AFSE members continued to trickle in for the membership meeting.

As the other agent disappeared into the curtained area to search, Tower motioned Thorsness over and quietly identified himself. The doctor was not impressed.

"Who delivered the box there?" Special Agent Tower asked.

"Thorsness *Reactor*, not *box*, and I have no idea who brought it. The hotel people guarded it last night, and were told to deliver it before nine o'clock. Now *please* leave. Our business meeting starts in precisely three minutes, and you are not a member."

Gordon Tower led Link and Dr. Roper farther from the door. "Asshole," he muttered.

Link heard a low *pop*. "What was that?" he asked, suspicious.

Neither of the others had heard it.

Juliette LaCoste peeked through the curtain only forty feet away, the wide-eyed chief of security from NEL standing nearby, shaken because of the dead FBI agent at her feet. They were about to irradiate hundreds of people, and the idiot was concerned about one man?

His voice was a strained whisper. "I told you to keep your head down out there."

"I wanted to see their faces." She was pleased that she'd observed them, and also took pleasure in what she was about to do. "I remember many of them. They're despicable."

"Maybe we should wait to set it off," he said. He'd had cold feet since they'd left the NEL site. It had been his job to kill the pilot, but Juliette had been forced to do it when he'd frozen. Same with the family. The only reason he and the other guard weren't running was greed. Juliette was in charge of the paycheck. Half a million for him, half of that for the other.

And she was about to receive the biggest payoff of her life: The deaths of the swine who had believed she was capable of repulsive acts and that she'd steal the work of a fool. They'd hastened to believe, and passed lies around like candy at a child's birthday party. Ignoring her achievements. Whispering, snickering at her expense, saying she was a sex-driven slut.

She felt no remorse for what she was about to do, only sweet vindication.

The two apes, this one and the other waiting in the van, were only along for muscle, and they were useless now that the coffeepot was planted.

"You can go ahead," she told him. Now it was just a matter of pushing a couple of buttons and leaving. She'd thought of dying here with the others, and had not made up her mind. It didn't matter. She'd died the day she had first heard of the rumors—again the night Adam Russo had come to her home and shown her so graphically. The same night he'd told her of her salvation.

"I'll wait," the burly man said, avoiding looking at the dead man.

Juliette stepped past the man with the extra eye in his forehead, opened her handbag, and removed the remote control. "We'll stay behind the curtain and go straight ahead to the corner. Then I'll start the device and we'll leave. Out the door, down the hall, and outside."

"They may see us," he said.

Juliette sighed. "Just bring up the rear and make sure they don't catch up." They carried pistols with silencers. The man she'd just killed had learned they worked.

Link had heard the metallic sound distinctly, but it had taken an argument before Special Agent Tower told them to stay put while he checked it out.

He poked his head into a curtain a few feet away.

"Farther down," Link told him.

"Look!" said Dan Roper, staring where a rivulet of

crimson liquid pushed its way out, then pooled on the tile floor.

Link did not wait. He ran past a startled Tower to the blood, yanked the curtain aside, then knelt over the agent's body. Obviously dead. He scooped up the man's pistol, a government-issue Beretta. The agent had switched off the safety but hadn't had time to fire.

Gordon Tower arrived, looked, and cursed loudly.

From behind Link heard a low whirring sound.

"They're close by," Link said, and trotted farther down and yanked another section of curtain aside. The man he'd seen pushing the cart was in the curtained alleyway, fifteen feet distant, hurrying. Link yelled out, but he lunged behind the next curtain.

"Oh my God!" Dan Roper's voice. Link turned. A brilliant blue aura glowed from the curtain at the doorway to the business meeting.

"Tell everyone to get out!" he yelled to Roper, then spun and ran faster, eyeing the curtain and praying he'd find the remote control, which was the only way he knew of to turn off the device.

The same hulking figure he'd just seen burst from the curtain at the end of the room. The man turned, saw Link coming, and pointed a silenced automatic sideways. He jabbed as if pushing the bullets, took three rapid shots. *Pop, pop, pop.*

Link crouched, brought up the Beretta, and aimed carefully. Target on leveled sights. He ignored three more wild rounds, then fired twice, hitting him high and low on the body trunk. The big man faltered. Stopped and regarded Link dumbly, mouth drooping. A gunshot boomed from behind Link. The big man lurched with the bullet's impact, dropped awkwardly to the floor, and curled up as if to sleep.

Special Agent Tower walked grimly past Link, Beretta clutched in both hands, face ashen.

The burly man looked up at the agent. The pistol was still in his right hand.

The SAC's face wrinkled with outrage.

"Don't kill him!" Link screamed. There were questions.

"Bastard's dead." But the agent vehemently kicked the pistol away.

Link looked back. Dan Roper was shouting for everyone to get out of the building. Beyond him the blue plasma had grown, was now pulsing and wafting as if it were a living thing.

The remote? Link ran to the farthest curtain, where the man had emerged, and hauled it back. Juliette La-Coste was on hands and knees, eyeglasses askew. A heavy purse was opened on the floor before her, contents scattered. The big man had run into her in his zeal to flee.

The remote control lay at Link's feet, two of the red LEDs illuminated. He stopped, reached down.

Her expression turned into a snarl. "Don't!"

Link grasped the remote, stepped back and pressed the button marked SAFE. The red lights winked off, and after a few seconds a green LED came on.

Juliette LaCoste looked mournful. "They deserved to die," she said.

The blue aura was gone. He released a pent breath. "Where are the others?"

"Stay back," she said in a hoarse monotone, then found and lifted an automatic pistol fitted with a noise suppressor.

Link aimed the 9mm. "Don't make me shoot," he said.

"You won't have to." She'd turned the muzzle so it was pointed at her own left eye. Placed her thumb on the trigger. "I did not do those horrible things they said."

"I know," he said. "Put down the gun, and we'll tell everyone." He took a single step.

"Come no closer," Juliette warned him.

"Where's Ansel Turpin?"

She blinked, looked at him. "I've never heard of him."

"Your leader, then. Who was in charge of the experiments?"

She contemplated him for a moment, and came to a decision. "Dr. Russo," she said.

Turpin had posed as Adam Russo. "Where is he?"

"I have no idea. He didn't come with us." She tensed. "Piers Jergen? The other coffeepots?"

"I don't know." She used her free hand to smooth her uniform jacket. "I'm such a mess."

"Talk to me, Juliette. My friends? Gary Runyon and Shelby Admire? Where are they? *Please.*"

"All I know is what Adam said that last day. He said they were test bunnies in a cage, and that he was going to drop in a rabid old fox and watch them all die."

"Where's Russo, Juliette? Who's next?"

"I truly don't know." Her voice softened. "Thank you for believing me."

As she began to apply pressure with her thumb, he lashed out. The automatic went off before his hand impacted and sent it flying. She slumped, body convulsing and shuddering, blood draining from her face onto the floor.

31

The coffeepot had been shut off after six minutes, and while there were a few cases of eye soreness and stomach sickness, no one was severely ill. The scientists were comparing notes and excitedly discussing what had happened, upset that no one had had the presence to measure the radiation level. For the first time members of AFSE seriously considered Piers Jergen's concepts and openly wondered whether, if the device had been left on, the A.D. phenomenon might have occurred.

This time secrecy was an impossibility. The episode at the exhibition hall had been witnessed—some of it even video taped—by too many credible people, among them a reporter from the Las Vegas *Review Journal* and a newswoman from Channel Five. The city's broadcasting media had broken into normal programming with zealous fear-mongering, warning about a radiation-spewing "nuclear device" that had been activated. A "knowledgeable source" confirmed that two other devices were missing and in the hands of terrorists. The first attack had failed due to the prompt action of the FBI (a video clip showing Link was indistinct), but there might be more.

After only two hours Las Vegas was fast emptying as frightened Los Angelenos and ship-jumping locals fled on Interstate 15 in a bumper-to-bumper crush. The traffic snarl near the California line was backed up for thirty miles. Then a radio talk show host quoted *another* source who said the terrorists were in the mob bound for L.A., and those who heard him began to veer off in other directions.

The McCarren air terminal and all train and bus stations were filled. Stores were closed, and there were sporadic reports of looting. Some of the hotels on the strip were operating with skeleton staffs, so floor managers told the remaining dealers and security guards to gather up the cash and close the tables. Those personnel who agreed to remain were paid double time.

The telephone system became clogged and citizens were implored to limit 911 calls to true emergencies. And over both radio and television stations, each fifteen minutes a recording was aired: a government spokesman speaking in a smooth voice, asking that the "persons with the Jergen Reaction Devices" call an 800 number to engage in *meaningful* discussions.

A field hospital was set up outside the convention center by chemical, biological and radiation decontamination teams from Indian Springs and Nellis AFB, and all who had been anywhere near the source were being examined.

Link Anderson was back in his room, listening to the radio and watching it all on television—CNN had continuous coverage—waiting for a call from Special Agent Gordon Tower on his cell phone and trying to understand what Juliette LaCoste had said.

He'd gotten through to the crew staying at the Mirage and told them to make sure the Learjet was fueled and ready. No, he didn't have a destination yet. Then he'd called Erin. After her initial shock, she'd recorded everything. She wasn't overly interested that Adam Russo—surely Ansel Turpin in disguise—had been the Epsilon leader, for Turpin had by now undoubtedly assumed another persona, exercising his chameleon abilities God-only-knew-where. What she was interested in were the nuances of what Juliette LaCoste had told him.

Link answered a knock on the hotel room door. Dan Roper came in and took a seat, and stared grimly at the wall for a long moment. Finally he hissed, "We're damned lucky."

"Yes."

"The A.D. concept is dangerous." His voice rose. "The thing went supercritical, Link. That's what caused the blue glow. You know what it takes to create an *uncontrolled* sustained fission reaction—which are just big words for a meltdown? A supercritical mass. Add a plentiful source of neutrons and you get an atomic explosion. That's *all* it takes, and it's also what it takes to make the A.D. phenomenon work. It's just a matter of how much fuel you use. The device downstairs was loaded with so damn much plutonium we're lucky it didn't blow half the city away."

"I suppose the government's happy now that they have an intact device."

"But they don't. When it's safed, the formulae set into the device's digital processors are erased and the neutron generator is disabled. Those are logical safeguards, but the Department of Energy and NRC people are acting as if they lost some kind of treasure."

"So that's why they're on the radio trying to make a deal."

Roper continued his ranting. "They're crazy. Jergen, Thorsness, the DOE and NRC people, all of them. Trying to take us back fifty years, to when we just had to be the first to get thermonuclear weapons." He exploded, "And all this A.D. talk is *bullshit!*"

"I saw it work at Millionaire Mountain, Dan. The radiation peaked, then it went down faster and faster, and *something* happened, because it decreased the radioactivity of everything else around it. The A.D. phenomenon or whatever took the rad count to *zero*. The government wants the secret. They think it will solve their problems with all the nuke waste."

"Don't be naïve. There may be a few noble impulses involved, but there are just as many idiotic ones. The A.D. phenomenon would give them a way to neutralize everyone *else's* weapons. Then they'd be the only kid on the block with nukes." Roper shook his head. "What the device also provides, and what they won't be able to resist fooling with, is a way to focus and send out a spike of radiation so lethal it could selectively take out the population of a city or a country and then go away and leave everything nice and safe for the mop-up crew. No one should have that kind of capability, Link. No one's that trustworthy. Then there's the Armageddon aspect. In 1949, Robert Oppenheimer warned us to quit fooling with neutron-fission combinations or we'd unbottle a genie we couldn't handle. I agree."

Dr. Dan Roper looked at him evenly for a long moment, then stalked to the door. "I'm going downstairs for a drink, if I can find a bartender. If not, I'll pour a few myself. See you next time you're back at the building. They're recalling me to New York for some kind of idiotic investigation. The GAO inspectors want to talk to all department heads."

"You may have trouble getting an airplane. The airport's jammed."

"Good. Maybe I won't get back in time. The inspectors are scheduled to show up at eight sharp tomorrow morning. I guess they feel anything happening out here is far enough away for them to operate business as usual."

"Thanks for all the help this morning," Link told him.

Roper nodded and left.

As the door closed the cell phone buzzed.

Special Agent Gordon Tower said they'd been operating on overload, trying to handle the convention crime scene, sorting out the various kinds of federal agents and officers pouring into nearby Nellis Air Force Base, and assist local authorities with their crowd and traffic control problems. In the past two hours he'd gone from being second in charge of bureau affairs in southern Nevada to number eight on the totem pole. The deputy director for terrorist activities was now on his way from Washington, which would drop Tower to number nine.

"Twenty minutes after it happened, the president called the director and ordered him to make sure this doesn't happen again," the agent said.

"I certainly feel a lot easier knowing he's involved." Link said acidly. He recalled Dr. Roper's warning. "And they still want an intact coffeepot?"

"That's the other top priority. Also the formulae. And

now the field office here is going berserk trying to find the missing remote control."

The control had been either lost or stolen in the frenzy at the exhibition hall.

"You don't have any ideas on that, do you?" the agent asked wearily.

"Maybe someone wanted a souvenir. Do you still want to chew my ass for talking too much?"

"Nope, talk all you want like everyone else. I'm just touching base, seeing if you've come up with anything new about where Ansel and the rest of the terrorists might be."

"You said L.A. before. Change your mind?"

"My guesses don't carry much weight. They located the stolen van in the Hilton parking lot, so the feeling is the others are here in Vegas. I keep telling 'em how Turpin prefers to operate differently, but no one's listening." He paused. "Have any new thoughts about what the LaCoste woman told you?"

"You were there."

"Most of what I got was gibberish, except the part about Adam Russo being their boss. What do you think? Turpin killed Russo and took his place?"

"Probably."

"And she said Russo hadn't come with them. But if the stolen vehicle's here, that doesn't make sense, because there's no other missing vehicles, and I can't see Turpin hitchhiking outta Pahrump with a coffeepot in each hand."

Link had just had the same thought. "Don't forget the Russian," he cautioned.

"Yeah. His name's I. G. Chernko and his photograph's being circulated with Turpin's, like that's going to do us any good."

Link too wondered what they looked like now.

The agent sighed. "Gotta go. Think of anything, give me a call at the office."

Erin was getting everything rearranged in her computer. The FBI was using expert help, their laboratory, flowcharts and storyboards, and their computers. Both had access to the same information. It would be interesting to see what they came up with.

Link sat at the table by the window and looked out at the heat waves shimmering over the city. The last temperature reading he'd heard had been 107 degrees. It might reach 110. A good time to stay inside, so long as there were enough maintenance people left to keep the air conditioners going.

Was Ansel Turpin holed up out there, waiting? Maybe holding a remote control and getting ready to press the first button to prove some point or other?

He began sorting and cordoning off information in his mind. A, B, C, and D. What did he know about Turpin? Where and how would the man attack next? What was the best way to handle it? Last, where were Gary and Shelby—the bunnies placed with the rabid old fox?

Start with A, the accumulation of what he'd learned about Ansel Turpin. His initial briefing, combined with what Erin, Gordon Tower, and then Juliette LaCoste had told him.

Turpin was brilliant, Machiavellian, psychopathic, complex, and conniving, doted on his stern, long-dead mother, a chameleon at disguises, preferred to operate in population centers or isolation. He despised his father and the Weyland Foundation. Erin felt he was driven but still always played by some kind of rules. He had a lot of money available to help achieve his goals.

Following that synopsis was B: What would Ansel Turpin do next?

First analyze what Turpin had done to set it up. Started by helping develop the coffeepot, killing helpless people for some odd reason, then blowing up the scientists—which was likely just a way to eliminate unnecessary folks who might know too much—and spreading nuclear material around so he could demonstrate to one and all what the coffeepot could do. Those things had accomplished several ends, one being that the government now lusted after the process and wanted very badly to capture an intact device. New thought. A coffeepot just might be Turpin's guarantee of safe passage at some point. *Smart.*

But Link was digressing. Turpin had done some dumb things. Like taking off in a helicopter for parts unknown and not having a landing site set up with wheels waiting. Killing a family for their vehicle. Then this morning's brouhaha, which could only be described as ill-conceived and poorly executed. Also, everything had been predictable and obvious, which was not Turpin's way. Picking Las Vegas for the attack. Not his way at all.

LaCoste had said Russo, a.k.a. Turpin, "didn't come with us."

He played with the idea that Ansel Turpin had not even been on the helicopter.

Which would mean the Las Vegas convention disaster was just a scam. Why go to the trouble to set it up?

Perhaps to attract the attention of hundreds of federal agents to the wrong place?

So where was the *right* place? What was his *real* target?

"Damn!" he exploded as he reached for the cell phone.

It buzzed in his hand before he could open it.

"Anderson," he answered.

"Link, I know where he's going to attack." Erin's voice was rock-sure.

"Yeah. I'm calling for the airplane. Tell Frank to get on the phone in half an hour. We've got a lot to talk about."

They filled out a flight plan on the way to the airport, filed it at operations in record time, and were "wheels in the well" at 12:45. Five minutes later, while they were still climbing, Link unstrapped himself from the jump seat behind the other pilots and made his way back to the passengers' compartment, picking up a couple of bottles of Perrier along the way since it might take a while.

Dr. Dan Roper waved from one of the rearmost seats, happily intoxicated and no longer angry at the world. He'd made good on his pledge to get a drink at the Hilton, stretching it into several by the time Link had latched onto him and offered the ride.

After settling into one of the plush leather seats, Link

opened the aluminum case and snapped a fresh battery into the cell phone. There'd be a lot to talk about. Ansel Turpin and his Russian buddy would attack the Weyland Building in Manhattan the next morning, when all of the foundation people were present, entering with the flood of government inspectors, bringing with them at least one of the remaining coffeepots. Or did they already have a device in place? Probably. Security had been downgraded for the past several days.

He pressed MEM, then 1, waited for Erin to answer.

"Two-seven-seven-five." Her tone was businesslike, more guarded than usual.

"I'll be landing at Teterboro in four hours-ten," Link told her. "What's happened so far?"

"Nothing." She spoke quickly, as if wanting to cut him off. "I tried to tell Frank you came up with the same thing I had, and he snapped my head off. He'd talked to the FBI liaison here and the bureau's convinced the terrorists are all in Las Vegas. Our chief of security agrees. He says there's been nothing to indicate a threat here. I tried to argue, but it did no good."

Link was stunned. "Frank won't take *any* preventative action?"

"Yeah. He gave me that much. When I reminded him about Turpin's fascination with surveillance, he ordered an electronic sweep of the building for bugs and minicams. That'll begin in half an hour. If they find nothing, they'll assume its a false alarm."

"Patch me through to Frank. Maybe he'll listen to me."

"I can't. He's in with the handful, briefing them about tomorrow's inspection. It's very important that everything goes well. The foundation will be paralyzed until we're cleared of all the charges in Gary Runyon's manuscript."

"Damn it, that's part of Turpin's setup." Link shook his head, feeling downright gloomy.

"I don't know." Her voice was uncertain. "Maybe they're right, Link."

Link could hardly believe she'd said that. Less than

an hour before she'd been as sure as he. She'd known *precisely* what Ansel Turpin wanted to do.

"Leave a message for Frank," he told her, still determined. "Tell him I'll give him a call as soon as we land. We'll need to talk."

"Link, he doesn't want to talk to you until after the inspection. I think he's still upset with you. He said it was time for you to remember your place, and for you to think about what happened to some guy back in your squadron when *he* got out of line."

Still upset? Out of line? Link frowned, wondering. "What was this guy's name?"

"I think he said Lieutenant Jester. Something like that."

Link nodded to himself, finally realizing what Erin was up to. He played along. "Tell him to go to hell. Come to think of it, *I'll* tell him after his damned inspection."

"As you wish. Now I've got something for you to pass on to the crew. They'll be staying at a new place tonight. The address is two-one-five Greenwich Avenue. That's Falcon Townhouses, a few blocks from Teterboro Airport."

When she disconnected, Link immediately went forward. The key words she'd spoken—taken from his tour in Desert Storm—were clear. Jester had been the code word used when the enemy was believed to be monitoring their transmissions. Falcon was the nickname of an air force fighter aircraft, and 0215 Greenwich Mean Time was the universal standard used by aviators.

He told the airplane captain what to look for, and when.

4:00 P.M.—New York, New York

The seven-room office suite was far too large for only two executives, and since there were so few furnishings and as of yet no receptionist or secretarial staff, it seemed barren. But the shorter of the two men, with his slicked black hair, tortoiseshell-rimmed glasses and pompous three-piece suit despite the summery weather, had for the second day walked around to visit their neighbors to get to know them, and he seemed outgoing and friendly enough.

They were there to establish a sales network for a Hungarian-based gypsum company that produced highly specialized reinforced concrete forms used in the foundations of multiple-story buildings. While the earth was well stocked with gypsum, only certain deposits were sufficiently pure for that purpose, and most were presently supplied by a Fort Worth, Texas, firm who'd had a corner on the market. Hungarian gypsum forms were just as structurally sound, and less expensive due to modern fabrication techniques.

One of their initial problems was the eight-hour disparity of working hours between Eastern Europe and New York, meaning they had to work very early and somewhat late hours. Ah well, perhaps they could adjust to a more civilized environment once they'd been underway for a few weeks and were properly manned. As for now? Gallic shrug. The men had French-sounding names and spoke with European accents. Their immediate neighbors, staffs of an advertising firm and a law office, were not very interested, but neither were they suspicious.

The availability of the fifth-floor suite, leased in advance two months before, had been fortunate. Former *Kapitan* I. G. Chernko, who had served in the Special Actions Group of the Russian Army, was seated at the only table in one of the inner offices, peering through a darkened window with a twenty-power spotting scope, observing the entrance of the massive building only a half block away. Three days earlier he'd placed reflective film on the window's surface and cut out a strip measuring four inches in height by twelve in width, too small for detection from outside, but through which he could see all who entered and exited the building.

He wore a headset. One of the flip-top cell phones had been carried home the previous evening by a senior Weyland Foundation project leader, whose death would not be reported for another day, when he was scheduled for duty. The circuitry had presented a challenge, but he'd found the proper key. The effort had been worthwhile. They'd intercepted transmissions between Erin Frechette and Lincoln Anderson, who was now on his way. They were onto them, had guessed the what and when, but no one else was listening and Erin too was beginning to doubt.

Behind Chernko was a video monitor, showing the massive roof of the building under observation. The camera they'd mounted eighty stories above was equipped with a transmitter to relay the video signal and a powerful battery that would last much longer than they required. There were other monitors connected to the minicams the Russian had planted atop and inside the Weyland Building, but they'd been alerted that an electronic sweep was underway and had shut them down. Soon they would turn them all on again.

Ansel came into the suite, using the mincing steps of the person he'd become.

"Nothing out of the ordinary," said Captain I. G. Chernko, "except there seem to be a lot of people leaving early. More than normal."

"The secretary next door's meeting a friend who works there. They were told to leave an hour earlier than usual so the cleaning crews can prepare for the inspection tomorrow." Ansel Turpin took the only other chair and leaned back against the wall. "She also spoke about this morning's tragedy in Las Vegas." He smiled. "Terrible."

"None of them were left alive?"

"One of the security guards fled on foot. It doesn't matter. He knows nothing."

While Chernko continued peering through his scope, Ansel lifted a telephone receiver from its base, punched in seven digits—an FBI cut-out number so no one in the city could tell where the agents called from—and waited for another dial tone, then punched in seven more. When there was a response he spoke jovially, in a voice utterly different from the one he'd just used.

"Joe, Bill Howland from the Bronx. We gotta situation here tryin' to cover the office with all the shit goin' on in Vegas. I just talked to John Rivers down at J. Edgar's palace and caught him before he left. Yeah, he's headed there too. Workin' like a white man now he's about to get the promotion. Who knows? De shadow do." He laughed shrilly, sounding precisely like Supervising Agent-in-Charge Bill Howland. "Anyway, Johnny said you have three guys you can loan me 'cause of some stupid inspection shuttin' you down. . . . Yeah, I know that leaves you bare, but I'm *hurtin',* buddy. Johnny says you help me, he'll sign the request for more travel funds. . . . Great! Tell 'em to check in at my office about eight-thirty in the morning, okay?"

Ansel hung up, smiling. I. G. Chernko never ceased to be amazed at his versatility. It had taken Turpin only four other calls, using two other voices, to learn everything that had happened in Las Vegas and set up the call he'd just made. Three FBI agents who would normally be in the Weyland Building tomorrow would be in the Bronx, trying to find out what was going on.

Chernko turned to him. "The woman just came out. Looks like she's going home."

"Erin Frechette," Ansel said. He moved Chernko aside and took the telescope, searched until he found her in the taxicab lineup in front of the building. "If there were more time I'd enjoy dealing with her more personally."

"As with Anderson?" Chernko watched him. "I don't like it, Ansel. You said you'd never break your own rules, but now you want to destroy him just before an operation."

"What I *wanted* was to capture or kill him earlier. He's too dangerous. When the device was set off in Las Vegas, I was told that everyone but Anderson began rushing around like lemmings. He was able to stop it in time. Now he's coming here and suspects the truth."

"The coffeepot's in place, and there are thousands of them inside. We could set it off right now, before Anderson arrives. We've confirmed that Frank Dubois is there. Set it off and destroy the helicopters that try to take him away, as you're planning for tomorrow."

"*That* would be changing the plan. Timing is everything. During a normal day, fifteen thousand people work in the building, nine thousand of them employed by the Weyland Foundation. The foundation has recalled several hundred from the field for tomorrow's inspection. The building will be *packed*. But if Anderson warned them and they stayed away . . . ?" He shook his head. "I can't take the chance. Do you see a problem with him?"

"Not really. I'll use two Strelas. If both miss, I'll shoot him as he gets out of the airplane." But again Chernko wondered why. They'd almost run late in Nevada trying to kill Anderson. Ansel was obsessed with killing him, yet now he refused to face him.

Ansel Turpin began looking at other faces through the scope. By this time tomorrow, the employees he observed would either be dead or very ill, and the foundation would be finished. Then Turpin would be free to return to Nevada and watch the slow demise of the man he despised more than any other.

Chernko decided he would not go with him. Ansel Turpin was no longer the man he'd met in Russia, whom he'd decided to follow. When the task here was done, he would return to Europe. To St. Petersburg, perhaps, where he'd relax for a while before resuming his old endeavors. He'd not felt well for the past month, since they'd begun the experiments.

7:10 P.M.—Over Cincinnati, Ohio

"How are you coming with it?" Link prodded Dan Roper, who was on his fourth cup of coffee.

"Too many martinis." The physicist blew out a tortured breath. "Something's inside my head, banging away with a hammer."

"Want more aspirin?"

"I've already taken too many." He finished opening the electronic appliance, peered at the jumble of components, and sighed. "I really should wait until later."

"There's no time. You've got to do it now."

"Then I'd better have another cup of coffee. I'm seeing double again."

Link brought him yet another steaming cup from the small galley, then went forward and looked at his watch as he took the jump seat. It was 7:14 local, 2:14 A.M. in Greenwich, England. One minute until the time Erin had called for.

"There it is," the airplane captain murmured on intercom, staring out to their left through the bright night sky at the lights of another aircraft.

At first there were only the running lights, then the formation lightstrips along the side of the fighter became visible. Finally the ghostly shape of an F–16C Fighting Falcon slid into position on their wing. The pilot turned his cockpit lights to full bright, then raised his right gloved hand into view. He held up fingers. Three. Two held sideways. One. One.

The airplane captain, a retired air force colonel, nodded curtly, then set 371.1 into the UHF radio.

The F–16 dropped down twenty feet, almost out of their view. "EC four four, this is Falcon One, transmitting on upper antenna, low power. How do you read me?"

"Loud and clear," the pilot answered. Yet the Falcon's transmission would not be heard at a distance of more than a quarter mile. Since they were flying much higher than that, it could not be overheard from the ground.

"EC four four, I have a message for Captain A. L. Anderson. Is he aboard?"

"Roger, Falcon One," Link responded. "I'm ready to copy."

"This is from your headquarters. Subject is in place, but his location remains unknown. He has obtained a secure telephone, and it's suspected that he's monitoring your conversations. It's also assumed that a coffeepot is already in place in the building. Copy?"

"I copy, Falcon One."

"Next item. Quote: The subject is believed to have at least four SA-Seven missiles, and we anticipate that he may attempt to neutralize you on approach to Teterboro. Suggest you take the following actions." The F–16 pilot told them what had been arranged.

"Roger, Falcon One. We copy. Anything else?"

"Just one thing. I understand Captain Anderson and you were both air force. Give 'em hell, gentlemen."

"You've got it," the airplane captain said with a smile.

32

The Strela—a Russian word meaning arrow—ground-to-air missile has been in the Soviet and their Russian heirs' military inventories for forty years. It is infra-red guided, uncooled—which makes it less sensitive—and simplistic, and is not known for its range or accuracy. But it is rugged and when used appropriately, fired at a low, subsonic target with a steady heat source such as a jet engine, it is somewhat reliable.

The standard military version has a range of only five thousand meters. Another, smaller version, the FP model, once distributed freely to communist guerrillas, measures only one and a half meters in length and has a range of a thousand meters—a bit more than three thousand feet. A problem is that the Strela FP must be turned on before the cross-hairs can illuminate and the seeker head can activate and acquire a target. Then the missile must be fired within seven minutes, after which the batteries become depleted and must be laboriously replaced.

As an officer of the Speznaz, Kapitan I. G. Chernko had been trained to operate all the various Strela models. The stubby, lightweight Strela FP, while no one's favorite, had been proven to work when he'd shot down a low-flying CIA spy drone over Afghanistan.

Chernko stood beside a parked sedan at the corner of a desolate airport employee's parking lot at the southern end of the runway, listening to the pilot chatter over the VHF radio scanner, eyes glued to the southern sky where six different sets of landing lights were visible.

The second of those, a Learjet, call sign EC 44, was on its final approach and should prove to be little challenge for the stubby missile.

"EC four four, Teterboro approach radar has you at nine miles on the glide slope."

"Roger, Teterboro."

Chernko had slipped the first of the Strelas from its outer tube, and now felt in the darkness and refamiliarized himself with its shape. He looked about again to ensure he was still alone, then placed it onto his shoulder, clicked an arm into position, and slid it back into position. The things were unisize—built to be handled by everyone from pygmies to giants, and not for comfort. When he fired it, it would gouge harshly into his shoulder unless he held it firmly.

"I have you at seven miles, EC four four," said the radar controller's voice.

Meaning that the target was less than three minutes away from I. G. Chernko.

He held up the missile tube and sighted. Reached forward on the side and felt, then switched on the battery. A bull's-eye reticle glowed. He centered the aircraft's landing light and waited. Touched his fingers on the lever he would depress after the airplane passed overhead and the seeker found the heat of the jet engine's exhaust.

The single bright headlight shuddered, then began to porpoise wildly in the dark sky.

Chernko frowned, had difficulty keeping the target centered.

"Teterboro, EC four four is declaring an emergency. We just hit something up here."

He felt disbelief, followed the airplane's running lights as it soared, dipped, and soared again. Then the lights disappeared and there was only darkness where the aircraft had been.

The pilot's voice was filled with terror. "Teterboro, we're out of control."

What was happening?

Chernko lowered the missile tube and searched visually, swiveling his head and wondering, listening hard for the sound of jet engines. Yes, there it was to his . . .

His eyes were drawn by a flash over on his left, at one side of the field. He gawked as the twin arms of a powerful explosion reached skyward.

"EC four four, this is Teterboro radar."

Silence.

"EC four four?"

No response.

Another voice, this one grave: "Teterboro's declaring runway zero-seven closed. All aircraft discontinue your approaches. We have a fire on the airfield. I repeat . . ."

I . G. Chernko looked out to where he'd last seen the aircraft's lights, then to where the explosion had erupted, wondering if it could have possibly gone that far in such a short time, craning his neck to see what was burning. He could make out an aircraft's skeletal shape in the flames. Blue beacons were converging there. Sirens wailed.

Chernko listened as the controllers hastily repositioned airplanes in the busy sky, stacking them at thousand-foot intervals.

After ten minutes the flames had diminished enough at the edge of the airfield to allow the first aircraft to land. He eyed each one carefully, but saw no Learjet with an EC call sign.

Eighth in line was a small jet of dark color, like the one he'd targeted, but the call sign was wrong. That one taxied to the other end and into a FedEx service hangar.

He again examined the wreckage and dwindling fire. It seemed inconceivable that there could have been survivors.

The battery of the Strela FP was depleted, so the thing was no longer useful. He discarded it in a dumpster and went to the sedan where he replaced the second Strela, still wondering.

He used the rental car's telephone.

"Yes?" Ansel's French-accented voice.

"No survivors," Chernko told him.

"I just heard on the radio that there's been a crash at Teterboro."

Chernko looked back at the fire. "I didn't do it. They ran into something."

A pause of silence, then: "It seems too convenient. You're sure it was them?"

"The call sign's the same. I saw the explosion when it hit the ground."

Turpin paused longer, then released a relenting sigh. "There's no reason for suspicion. They couldn't have known what we were doing. Start back now."

As the hangar doors rumbled into the closed position, Link swung open the Learjet's hatch and deplaned, wondering if there'd really been a reason for all the subterfuge and if an SA-7 Strela had actually been awaiting them or if he'd just been needlessly delayed.

He waited until Dan Roper joined him—unsteadily, for he had lost the contents of his stomach as they'd gyrated about the sky—and led him toward the entrance.

"Hold up," said a terse male voice, and they stopped. A man stood in the semi-darkness, a pistol loosely held at port arms. "Anderson?"

"Yes."

"Who's your friend?"

Roper was still hung over, felt awful, and had repeatedly told Link he was in dire need of sleep. He was certainly not prepared to acquiesce to authority, and stepped forward belligerently. "I'm Daniel Roper. Who the hell are you?"

"He's with me," Link said.

The man slipped his weapon into a belt holster, and identified himself as Detective Sergeant Thomas J. Hall, NYPD, on special detail with the mayor's office.

"Come with me, please."

"We've got to meet someone," Link said.

"I know. They've been in session for the past half hour."

They went out a side exit and entered an unmarked car, driven by a man introduced by Sergeant Hall as another of New York's Finest.

Flames still flickered half a mile distant where the airport fire department had dragged the training shape and doused it with flammables before torching it off.

The building and the street were nondescript and not memorable, located in an older but respectable enough neighborhood. Vehicle parking was conveniently located in the basement, out of casual view, and they were let out beside a group of limos and sedans watched over by a pair of squint-eyed men and a woman who stood at least six feet and looked even meaner.

Detective Sergeant Hall took them to the basement elevator, then up to the third floor, where he rapped on an unmarked door and waited.

"Either of you armed?" asked the one who answered, looking at Link and Roper.

"No," Link answered, but the greeter patted them down before leading the way into the adjacent large room. A group of two dozen men and women sat about on couches and chairs.

Frank Dubois saw him, waved, and wheeled his way over. "Welcome back, Link."

Erin was at Frank's side, stood on tiptoes, and pecked Link's cheek. "Hi, pardner."

"That was some greeting at Teterboro," Link said.

Frank motioned at a gaunt man who observed them from a stuffed chair. "That gentleman set it up, with a little assistance I pulled in from friends in the air force and the FAA."

The mayor of New York nodded in their direction, then returned to his conversation with the group seated about him. Link looked around for Dan Roper, but the scientist had found an empty couch at the side of the room and was settling, looking grumpy and utterly uncaring about who might be in the room.

"No fix on Turpin?" Link asked Frank.

"No, but he's here. This afternoon our security chief noticed a minicam in the reception hall of the lobby floor. If it hadn't been precisely like the model you brought from Nevada, he said he wouldn't have known what he was looking at. In fact he went back to his office to compare and make sure. He called me, and I called for Erin, and we decided to keep it in place."

"No reason to tell Ansel we were onto him," Erin said brightly.

"You knew he was here before we talked on the phone the first time?" Link asked her.

Frank answered. "We didn't know until you were on your way to the airport in Vegas. By then I'd ordered a check of key personnel and we learned one of the project leaders had been killed and his satellite phone taken. Since they're good with electronics, we felt they might be listening in on our conversations."

"So we confirmed it," Erin said. "Remember when I told you security was going to make an electronic sweep? Well, they'd *already* done that without being obvious, and located four more minicams. Frank told them to leave them all in place, still operating. Five minutes after out conversation they were shut off."

Frank added: "Which confirmed they'd been listening on the cell phone."

"Pretty cagey, huh?" Erin asked with a grin.

"Yeah. Are the cameras working now?"

"They turned them back on at five o'clock, but we know where they are and how to stay out of their fields of view."

"What made you think they'd try to attack the Learjet with missiles?"

"Erin again," Frank answered. "She told me about them having Strelas, and according to her computer profile that's what they'd do. Since Turpin seems so determined to kill you, we thought it might be a good idea to let him think you were dead."

"Frank?" the mayor called out, and Dubois wheeled back and joined him in conversation.

"It wasn't just the computer profile," Erin whispered. "I got a phone call from Joseph Spotted Horse telling me you were in danger from an arrow."

"I thought it sounded farfetched," Link said.

Erin frowned. "Joseph may have saved your life."

"And he talks with animals, right?"

She looked exasperated. "Don't be crass. Joseph's

concerned. He's driving all the way to Nevada to try to help."

Link looked about. "Who've they got here?"

"Everyone Frank and the mayor could think of who might be able to help. You met the Weyland Foundation chief of security, seated next to the mayor. The ones on his left are the fire and police commissioners, and several of their chiefs. On the mayor's right are the commander of the New York City Fire Department, the state disaster preparedness chairwoman, and the commanding general of the New York National Guard. They've been on the telephone with the governor and have his full support."

One omission was surprising. "No federal authorities?"

"The administration's still telling their people not just to find and neutralize Turpin but to take all necessary steps to get the formulae and an intact coffeepot. Frank feels that's unacceptable, and the governor and mayor agree. They want to stop him, period, and no deals or playing with lives."

"And the biggest problems they face?"

"How to do it."

Frank called to her. "Erin, the mayor has some more questions."

She went closer. "Yes, sir?"

"If this Turpin can get into the building, as he's obviously done, why doesn't he just blow up the place? Why set off this nuclear contraption?"

"Because he wants it to appear as if we're responsible for everything that's happened both here and out west. I'm sure there'll be an announcement of some sort saying we brought one of the devices we built back to the building, and there was a tragic accident."

"*We* built?" Frank exploded.

"Mr. Runyon's manuscript and the Department of Energy memoranda make it appear we've worked hand in glove with NEL perfecting the Jergen devices."

Frank hmphed. "We're the ones who refused to fund them because of safety violations."

"He's covered that base. When Piers Jergen went to NEL, he told them the twelve million he brought to the table had been provided by the Weyland Foundation. The NEL executives will testify he told them that we're about to buy NEL. We're set up as the patsies."

The police commissioner regarded the mayor. "How do you feel we should approach it, sir? Prevent the disaster, or minimize the damage and capture him?"

There was no hesitation. "Both. If we don't stop him, a lot of people may be killed. If we stop him but he gets away, he'll be loose to do it again."

"I agree that's best," the commissioner said, "but we may have to settle for one or the other." He regarded Erin. "You've said he has to be within a couple of blocks to set off the device with the remote control. If we took everyone out of that area and closed in, we'd have a chance of taking him, and if he set it off with no one in the building, so what?"

"There are problems with that," Erin said. "For one, he's a master at surveillance and would likely set it off well before you got to him. Two, you'd never know who he is."

"Take everyone in and sort 'em out later."

"Everyone? There's four thousand emergency, maintenance, and security people working the late shifts in the Weyland and surrounding buildings. And there are two coffeepots. He may have the other set up somewhere else, like Police Plaza, or the World Trade Center."

The commissioner looked thoughtfully troubled, unable to think of a logical response.

The mayor regarded Erin. "So what are we up against?"

"Worst case, if we did nothing: at eight a.m. there'd be sixteen thousand people in the building and twenty thousand more in the affected area." For the next few minutes she told them of the horror, estimating that from twelve to eighteen thousand humans would receive a dangerous dose of radiation poisoning if the device was activated in a lower floor of the building. The ugliest scenario, if the radiation levels were as high as had been measured at Millionaire Mountain, would leave two thousand dead or dying.

"And if we cordoned it off now like the commissioner suggests?"

"If Turpin caught on right away and set off the device there'd be three thousand radiated. Three hundred dead or dying."

"What if we went door to door and very quietly told the inhabitants to leave?"

"That *might* work for everyone except the ones in the Weyland Building. He's likely watching there more closely than the others."

The mayor turned to Frank. "How many are in your building?"

"We're at minimum manning, so it's one fifth of the normal numbers. Four hundred of our maintenance and security people, and a hundred tenants."

"And you can't get them out without Turpin seeing them?"

"Not if he's watching closely, as we assume he is." His eyes narrowed. "But if we had a diversion to attract his attention, we might be able to mask their departure."

Erin spoke. "Part of our problem is not knowing where the coffeepot's located. We believe it's on the first floor, but we're getting rad readings from several locations there. It's likely they've hidden small radioactive sources around the area to make our job more difficult, and now that he has his surveillance camera turned back on in the lobby, it's almost impossible."

"Five hundred people still inside," the mayor muttered. He looked at her. "If the coffeepots are down on the lobby floor, could we take them off the roof in helicopters?"

"Sure, if he doesn't have his missiles anywhere within a half mile."

"Excuse me, Mr. Mayor." Link walked to the forefront. "How many terrorists are we dealing with, Erin?"

"Probably just two. Ansel Turpin and I. G. Chernko. It's another of Turpin's rules to operate with a minimum of personnel."

"Then I have a couple of options to offer. Frank mentioned a diversion to capture their attention while everyone's being evacuated. I've got one in mind."

The others grew silent as Link outlined his first idea.

As he finished, the police commissioner interrupted. "Once they catch onto what you're doing, what are the chances they'll set off this damned coffeepot thing?"

"I'd guess very good."

The mayor wagged his head dolefully. "Frank just told us as many as five hundred people are still inside this building, and there are more in the others."

"The diversion should give us time to get most of them out. Then we'll put them out of business." Lincoln Anderson drew his ace in the hole. "Show them what we've got, Dan."

He drew a ragged snore from Dr. Dan Roper, who was curled up comfortably on a couch.

33

Dan Roper yawned, took in another sip of steaming coffee, and described the operation of the remote control. He began by explaining the functions of the four push buttons.

"One tells the coffeepot's battery to activate, and brings the nuclear material together. Two turns on the neutron generator. At that time everything's working, and the radioactivity level begins to climb. Three is like a pause control, temporarily shutting off the neutron generator to interrupt the process. The fourth switch is labeled safe, and that's precisely what it does—renders the device safe."

Link interjected. "And once in the safe position, the coffeepot can't be reactivated."

Dan Roper glared. "Do *you* want to handle this? If so, I would prefer to go home and sleep off this hangover."

Link held up his hands. "Sorry."

Roper nodded curtly, then turned to the audience. "As the different buttons are pressed a unique UHF frequency is generated. Switch One transmits on the base frequency, Two is next highest, Three higher yet, and Safe is the highest frequency of all."

He pulled off the outer shell and pointed out three tiny white switches. "These are called DIP toggles," he told them, "and they control the increase between frequencies. Each DIP toggle has two positions, which means there are only eight possible combinations."

"Can the base frequency be altered?" asked . the

woman in charge of the state's disaster preparedness program.

"Very good. Since this Russian fellow is an electronics specialist, and they know one of the remote controls is missing—this one, which Link lifted in Las Vegas—I would assume they'd do *just* that. It wouldn't be difficult to change a capacitor in both transmitter and receiver."

The woman sighed. "Then there's no way to determine the frequency they'll use. We—"

"Madam, are you interested in *listening*?"

She glared but held her tongue.

Roper held up the device. "Unless they've completely redesigned both the remote control and the receiver in the coffeepot, there are constraints. Foremost, they're confined by antenna circuitry to a forty megahertz spectrum in the lower UHF band. There are the four switches on the remote, each generating different frequencies, separated by the same amount, which as we've seen can *only* be one through eight megahertz."

"You have utterly lost me," said the mayor.

"Let me put it this way. Once the device is activated, we can neutralize it."

The mayor's face brightened.

"If we use a sensitive UHF receiver and detect a transmission, we'll know they've pressed button One. And since we'll then know the base frequency, there are a limited number of possibilities to activate the Safe circuit."

"And we could transmit on all of those and shut it down?"

"Yes, but we really wouldn't want to do that. What we would *want* to do is wait until we intercept the *second* signal, which would reveal the DIP toggle setting. Say we got a sequence of two hundred, then two-oh-four megahertz. We would immediately know that the DIPs were set to four, and if we transmitted on two-twelve it should activate the safe circuit and shut down."

"Should?" the Mayor's eyebrow elevated.

"There is always the possibility that they've redesigned the entire thing."

Erin asked, "Has Chernko had time to do that?"

"It's doubtful."

"Then you can neutralize the Jergen device?" the mayor asked Dan Roper.

"I believe so. I studied the coffeepot in Las Vegas after it was safetied and more or less dissected and biopsied the remote control while I was on the airplane."

The woman who ran disaster preparedness spoke again. "If the coffeepot's already in the building, why not just transmit on all of the possible frequencies right now to safe it?"

"Because instead of shutting it down, I would very likely activate it, and by the time I randomly found the safing frequency there would likely be casualties. More than any of you, I realize what we're facing. For a short period at Millionaire Mountain they radiated almost ten thousand roentgens per hour, the equivalent of the hottest part of Chernobyl. Put differently, it's the same radiation you'd receive from a medium-sized nuclear bomb."

"But there were no deaths from the coffeepot in Las Vegas."

"Link Anderson shut the device down before the radiation had a chance to build. If I can do that here, we'll have the same result."

The mayor stared at him. "And you're confident you can do it?"

"Quite, if I have the equipment I need. It's readily available."

"We need a decision, sir," Link said to the mayor of New York City.

"The decision's made about Dr. Roper and the remote control. We'll do it." He turned to an assistant. "Get him what he needs, and set him up where he thinks is best."

"On the ground floor of the Weyland Building," said Dan Roper.

The mayor's eyes narrowed. "Erin feels that's where they've planted the device."

"Yes, and I'll know I'm picking up the same signals as the Jergen device."

"It sounds damned dangerous."

Roper smiled. "I work best when properly motivated."

"Get him whatever he needs," the mayor repeated, and the assistant went off to the side of the room with the scientist.

The mayor turned to Link. "*Now* your diversionary tactic makes more sense, but why in God's name do you want to be dropped in *alone*?"

"Because that's the best way I know of to draw their attention while we get our people out, and Doc Roper sets up his equipment."

"Erin?" the mayor asked. It was obvious he'd grown to value her opinion.

"I don't think he should take the chance."

"Would it work?"

She hesitated for a long pause. "Ansel Turpin has a hate fixation for two people: Frank and Link. There's also some kind of fear factor involved. So yes, under the conditions Link just explained, there's a good chance he'd break his own rules, and that might draw out one or both terrorists."

"But you don't think Link should do it?"

"It's too dangerous. Turpin and Chernko are undoubtedly prepared for contingencies—they plan meticulously—and Link would be vulnerable."

A senior police official stood up and regarded Link. "I'm the SWAT commander. We've got two fully manned special weapons teams on call, and they can be ready within half an hour. That should cut down on the odds."

Link shook his head vigorously. "If we land more people up there, Turpin won't bite. I've got to appear vulnerable. Anyway, our intention is to take people *out* of the building, not put more inside."

The mayor raised an eyebrow. "You're saying you're expendable?"

"Not at all. I'm using one of Turpin's rules. Operate where there are so many people you can become lost, or so few you know where everyone is."

"And if he activates the Jergen device while you're in the building?"

"That's fine," Link said, "as long as he does it according to *our* plan."

"Explain it again?"

"As soon as we get Doc Roper inside with his gear, we'll broadcast the fact that I'm on my way, and a chopper will drop me off on the rooftop. While they're watching me—Erin says they've set up a camera on the rooftop—our employees start scooting out side and back doors. I'll take my time and go to the fiftieth floor, where they've planted another minicam, and put on a little act—tell Ansel Turpin how we're onto them, and how we've evacuated the building. Then I'll start for the bottom, staying in view of the minicams on the way, and hopefully have him so upset he'll come after me. But if he's going to activate the coffeepot instead, *that's* when we'd want it, with Doc Roper's set up to safe it and a minimum of people to radiate."

"What if *both* coffeepots are in the building? Neither of you would have a chance."

"There's only one coffeepot here."

"You sound awfully sure."

Link didn't wish to spend precious time explaining his rationale. The agent in Las Vegas, who had known him, said Ansel Turpin was the ultimate survivor and had no death wish. The third coffeepot was Ansel Turpin's ticket out of trouble.

"What if they say forget the coffeepot and both of them come after you?" the commissioner asked.

"All the better. Once our people are out, have your sharpshooters take out anyone who tries to get in, regardless if they look like Madonna or Groucho Marx."

The SWAT commander shook his head. "Our rules of engagement say we can't fire unless we have positive I.D."

"At least observe the entrances and let me know if you see someone force their way in."

"We can do that."

"One more thing before I decide," said the mayor. "You want to tip them off that you're being flown in. A few hours ago Erin and Frank convinced me they have portable ground-to-air missiles in their possession. Wouldn't a helicopter present a target for them?"

"I've considered that," Link said, but he wondered if he'd thought it through well enough.

10:55 P.M.—LaGuardia Airport

The Weyland Foundation helicopter pilot leaned toward Link and explained it all again—gave a quickie course in operation of collective, cyclic, throttle, trim, gyro and countergyro effects, as well as the unique cockpit instrumentation.

They were in a Jet Ranger IV, built by Bell, now stripped of rear doors and forward windows, turbojet engine whistling shrilly and blades clattering as they idled. The pilot—one of their most experienced—made a demonstration takeoff, and settled back onto the tarmac.

"Let me try," Link said. He'd insisted on the short course, even though the pilot had volunteered and would fly him in and drop him off.

He lifted off, immediately almost disastrously tipped over, and the pilot had to stabilize the bird. Link took the controls back, climbed, and descended. Rose a few more feet. Dropped and landed with a bump and ominous wobble.

"You're a hazard," his instructor announced. "Stick with fixed-wing birds and let me do the flying."

Link glanced heavenward. "After tonight, I promise. Now, let me have another go at it."

He did marginally better. When they'd bump-landed for the fourth time, the helicopter pilot stayed behind, wrestling a wheelchair into position in the rear, as Link went into the hangar, where Detective Sergeant Thomas J. Hall of the mayor's special detail, now assigned to watch after Link Anderson, had a portable television set tuned to a local channel.

"Twenty more seconds until air time. Was that you flying it out there?"

"Yeah. He says I'm a natural."

Hall chuckled, then nodded at the TV screen. "What

you'll see is being shown on our local channels and broadcast over the news radio station."

A break-in message announced an important bulletin. A talking head—black woman, pretty in a pristine way—gave an update on their earlier story about the aircraft accident at Teterboro Airport.

All aboard the airplane had survived. Photographs of faces were shown, all false except for that of A. Lincoln Anderson, an "executive for the Weyland Foundation" who'd been treated for minor injuries and released. Amazing how all had survived the accident that had destroyed the Learjet.

"They'll repeat it every five minutes for the next half hour," said Hall.

"Good." Link hoped Ansel Turpin and I. G. Chernko were listening.

The detective was observing his watch. "It's time to make your fakeroo phone call."

Link lifted his cell phone, which they knew Turpin was monitoring. He pressed MEM, then 1. Erin answered on the second buzz, sounding very concerned.

He told her he was fine, just shaken up by the crash, that the copilot was in serious condition. "I'm at Frank's apartment, and he's agreed to listen. We're about to take a helicopter to the Weyland Building so I can show him some of the reference material in our safe."

"Do you want me to come in?" she asked.

"No. Just get ready to start notifying people to stay away tomorrow, in case I'm able to change Frank's mind about Turpin." After a few words of chitchat, Link pressed the END button.

If Turpin was listening, everything was set.

"Lift your arms." Detective Sergeant Hall helped strap on a shoulder rig, secured a Colt .38 Special revolver into a holster, and snapped a miniaturized two-way radio into a pouch on the other side. He clipped a collar microphone into place, and handed Link the ear plug.

"The radio's courtesy of the SWAT commander. Our tactics teams use them," the detective said. "They operate on J-band so no one can listen in."

"Where's the mike button?"

Hall showed him a switch on the radio. "Once you turn it on, it's hot, active all the time until you shut it off."

"Testing," Link said, leaning his head into the microphone.

The detective nodded, and adjusted his own volume.

"Hi, pardner," came a response from Erin. "You sounded convincing on the cell phone. If that didn't get Ansel's attention, I'll be surprised." Her voice was scratchy, as if broadcasting from a long distance.

"Where are you?" he asked suspiciously.

"Tell him, Sergeant Hall," Erin said. "I've got work to do."

The detective switched off both his and Link's radios. "We put her and the others into the Weyland Building half an hour ago."

"She's in the building?" Link exploded.

"Her, Doc Roper, and a couple of female detectives from Queens. Put on uniforms and walked in like they were just another clean-up crew working the late shift. Pushed in two cleaning carts loaded with the electronic gear Roper's going to need."

"Get her *out* of there." He had already lost too many friends.

"Can't. She's running things in the building. Doc Roper's with her, and security and the detectives are using the back stairs, going from floor to floor and telling everyone to get ready to take the freight elevators in back and how to stay out of sight of the minicams."

"How much longer?"

Hall peered at his watch. "They'll start down in twenty-five minutes."

Link looked out at the idling helicopter.

"The SWAT commander sent something else for you." He pulled up a molded plastic case. "There's a rifle and a couple other specialized weapons."

"The revolver's all I need. I don't plan on spending much time on the roof, and a rifle's not much use inside." He took a bolstering breath. "I'd better go."

"Yeah." The detective hefted the weapons case. "See you." He went outside.

Link delayed longer, taking another look at an aerial chart of the city . . . and as he readjusted the radio mike on his collar, had his first second thoughts.

11:02 P.M.—New York, New York

"Get over there!" Ansel Turpin screamed, "and finish what you were supposed to do before."

I. G. Chernko shook his head. "The accident I saw could have *had* no survivors. It is a trick, Ansel. They *want* us to react."

"There's no trick," Turpin fumed. "Only your incompetence. Use the Strelas. Use your rifle. Use your *hands*! But do not let those two into that building."

"It will give everything away," Chernko said, trying to use reason.

"You heard Anderson. He's *already* aware of our plan." Turpin's eyes were so intense they seemed to burn into him. "Kill them both, and this time bring me proof. Then we'll set off the coffeepot and escape during the confusion."

Chernko rose slowly, wearing a disdainful look. "Again you send me to do your work. You say you hate Anderson and Dubois, but it's something else. You're *afraid* of them."

"I fear no man." Only a twitching nerve near Ansel's left eye betrayed the turmoil inside.

I. G. Chernko returned the stare. Turpin had been changed ever since he'd first met Frank Dubois and been so easily disarmed. Changed even more since the day he had visited Lincoln Anderson and failed to take him. He was obsessed, and obsessions were not a good thing on a dangerous operation.

The Russian stalked to the door, then turned and spoke evenly. "When I return I'll have their ears, like we did to prove kills in Afghanistan. Four ears for half the money, Ansel. Then you can set off the device and go back and play your game with your fox, but I'm leaving."

"Bring me their ears and you can have all of the money."

There was another vast source of funds developing. The Russian had overheard those conversations too. Chernko went out and down the hall to a private express elevator meant solely for top executives. He inserted his key and the door slid open. Stepped inside and pressed the button for the top floor. There was an exit to the roof, and on the roof a large container he'd planted near the video camera overlooking the Weyland Building. Inside there were several things he would need: a selection of firearms; a modified grenade launcher that could sling a wire cable four hundred meters; four nondescript-in-appearance, meter-and-a-half-long tubes containing more Strela FPs. He would need only one.

11:10 P.M.—LaGuardia Airport

Link walked briskly across the tarmac toward the idling helicopter, the chart in hand. He looked about for Detective Sergeant Hall, noted that he wasn't in sight—a good thing for now he had only one to deal with—and climbed into the chopper. In back was the strapped-down wheelchair with the dark shape of the dummy he'd told them to lash in place. It should appear realistic enough in the camera's view from a hundred yards' distance.

"I won't need that," the pilot said, nodding at the map in Link's hand. He looked nervous.

"I will," Link said, and slid into the empty copilot's seat. Another oddity of the world of whirlybirds was that the copilot sat on the left and the captain on the right, opposite the arrangement for fixed-wing birds.

Link slipped the revolver out of its holster. "See this?" he said.

"Yeah."

"I don't want to point it at a friendly, so just crawl on out and I'll be on my way."

The pilot's face became grim. "Link, you may be a super whiz at handling airplanes with pointy ends, but you can't fly helicopters worth a damn."

"I know, but I've gotta go anyway and there's no use for two of us to make the trip."

"They'll pull your pilot's license."

"I doubt it, long as I don't kill anyone but myself. Go on. I don't have much time."

It was not a good takeoff, but Link had decided that any liftoff he survived was acceptable. He climbed to a thousand feet, then dipped—awkwardly overcorrected, then corrected again—and accelerated. Gingerly and not at all like the hotshot fighter jock he'd once been.

A radio call came over the cockpit speaker. "Whiskey Foxtrot Seven-one, you're cleared from LaGuardia direct to the Weyland Building. Watch for other aircraft."

"Roger," he responded, wondering who had called for clearance, also if the person he was talking to realized it was his first time alone at the controls. Cool night wind blasted mercilessly through the windowless cockpit. A box just behind him was open, filled with fast-igniting railroad flares. His idea with the open windows and doors and flares had been to respond should an infrared missile be fired. He doubted that would be the case, and now wondered whether a lit flare wouldn't just be blown back inside the helicopter.

Might be a dumb idea, he thought.

"Hey there!" The cheerful voice came from behind, and Lincoln Anderson flinched so hard he tilted the bird over.

"What the hell are you doing here?" he asked, looking into the passenger area. It was not a dummy in the wheelchair.

Detective Sergeant Thomas J. Hall grinned broadly. "Used to be a crew chief and door gunner for the Yewnited States Marine Corps. Volunteered for combat in Desert Storm, and all I got to do was take prisoners. Thought this time it might be meaner and better. When you wheel me inside, I'll look more real than a dummy."

"You're crazy."

"Mayor said to keep an eye on you, and I can't do that from back there." He pointed. "Better turn right. The Weyland Building's way over there."

Link took his advice and horsed the bobbing helicopter back on course. "Strapped in?"

"Yep. and I'll take these." He hefted the box of flares. "Yell if you see anything, and I'll start chuckin' 'em out."

"You'll have to be quick. Missiles come on fast, like an eyeblink."

They continued toward the building looming in the distance. Not the tallest one in the cluster, but the most massive.

I. G. Chernko moved the ratchet handle with effort, drawing in the remaining slack on the cable that now connected the two buildings until it was taut as a drawn bowstring.

He neither liked nor disliked Dubois or Anderson, but it was bothersome that they had eluded them for so long. This time there could be no doubt. He would check the bodies personally, and Ansel Turpin would have his ears.

Chernko snapped the metal slide into place on the Teflon-coated cable, and tested the mechanism. It rolled smoothly, quietly, on small titanium wheels. Going across would be no challenge. It was a ten-degree incline down to the deserted and huge rooftop, and fortunately the slide mechanism had a built-in brake for such circumstance. Returning would be more difficult, laboriously pulling himself hand over hand for seventy meters. Once his task was complete, perhaps he should go inside the Weyland Building and use one of the elevators. There would be few people. Mainly a janitorial staff and a limited number of security guards, who shouldn't be difficult to avoid.

Chernko ensured that his harness was securely tethered to the slide, crawled onto the concrete lip, and purposefully stared at the street far below, wanting to feel the fear of being so high, his existence dependent upon the fragile-looking slide mechanism. Adrenaline flow honed and sharpened the senses. He pushed the machine pistol around to his back, grasped the Strela missile tube firmly to his side—and stepped into space.

The wheel made a slight squealing noise as I. G.

Chernko sped along the cable, using the brake sparingly for a helicopter was already approaching far to his right. Not flying smoothly, but bobbling as it came—obviously either with mechanical problems or a neophyte at the controls.

As they flew closer—half a mile, and thus far no missiles or gunfire—Link could make out dark shapes atop the mammoth building.

Sergeant Hall held his earpiece in place and yelled over the wind noise. "The Police commissioner just shut off all vehicle and foot traffic for two blocks around the building. Next they'll start sending special weapons teams through the buildings, looking for the terrorists."

The last of the workers in the building should be approaching the bottom floor, avoiding the minicams, watching warily for signs of Turpin or Chernko. They'd use the distraction caused by the helicopter's landing to mask their departure out the back doors.

A quarter mile away now, Link could make out the clusters of antennae and the superstructure. His defensive tactic was simple—to get over the building quickly, so someone with a rifle or Strela missile wouldn't have enough time for a shot from below.

It would be crazy for Ansel Turpin to try to take him—it would threaten his entire plan—but Link believed he would react just that way, and he even had an inkling why. The dislike he'd sensed when Turpin had visited him had been real. Sort of a hate-at-first-sight thing. Was there such a thing in humans as natural enemies? You bet. If only one of them came for him, he hoped it would be Turpin. They had scores to settle.

Focus your thoughts, Link chided himself. He dropped lower and swung out parallel to the building in a sort of landing pattern—not at all professionally like a helicopter pilot would do, but enough to eye the helipad he intended to use and—

"Watch out!" the sergeant's voice boomed, and Link reflexively hauled back on the cyclic, slipping the helicopter aft. He stabilized, and together they stared out at a thin and shimmering stainless steel cable strung between the two adjacent buildings.

"What the hell is that?" the sergeant asked. "It could have sliced us in two."

"Save the talk for later and prepare for landing. It's going to be quick." Link looked at the several helipads on the rooftop, quickly but awkwardly lifted the bird and headed for the nearest one, and blew out a sigh of relief that they were no longer visible from below.

He flared the bird too much like a fixed wing airplane, then carefully leveled as he started to descend. Hovering and shuddering at twenty feet above the concrete, then just ten more feet and they'd be down, and then there was only . . .

"Oh, *shit!*" The sergeant ignited and threw out a flare, then another. Chucking them as far as possible across the concrete roof.

34

The missile rocketed across the expanse, exploding just overhead and spewing a deadly fireball that rolled across the rooftop behind them, taking engine and rotor blade with it. The fuselage tumbled hard onto the concrete, rolled completely over, and came to rest on its side.

Link moved mechanically, pawed at the seat harness, hit the right levers on his second try and pushed out of the seat. A moan came from behind. He twisted, grasped for and found the sergeant, felt and released his tether belt.

"Watch my leg," the detective cried hoarsely, but he held desperately to the molded-plastic rifle carrier. Link hauled Thomas J. Hall around and pushed him, along with the plastic case, out the shattered windscreen onto the concrete. He quickly followed.

Fuel was draining from the wrecked fuselage, pooling and spreading, and he had to get them both clear. Link grasped Hall beneath the armpits and began to drag him, and heard a low rattle followed by the *thock-thock-thock* sound of a silenced automatic weapon's bullets impacting. There was a bright flash and shower of sparks from a transformer on the side of the superstructure. The floodlights on the rooftop blinked twice, then went out.

Without illumination Link could not see well enough to know if they were out of the pool of fuel, so he laboriously continued dragging the detective, ignoring his grunts and pained groans, all the way to the superstructure—which was the opposite direction from where the missile had come—and stowed him there.

"Sit tight," he told Hall. "I'm going back. How many did you see?"

The sergeant's voice was a painful whisper. "Just the one guy holding a tube to his shoulder, getting ready to fire the missile."

Link stared into the darkness beyond the helicopter. "Description?"

"Tall, long hair, dark clothes, and wearing some kind of harness. I think he might have used it to come from the other building on the cable."

It seemed illogical to Link that anyone would dangle from a wire suspended eight hundred feet above the ground. But why else the cable? It was certainly not a normal thing, couldn't be because it would be a hazard for the helicopters flying in and out daily. The detective sergeant was right. Someone—I. G. Chernko?—had come across.

He made sure the earplug was in place, felt his shoulder rig, found the radio switch and turned it on. "Link here," he said in a low voice. "How's it going down there?"

Erin's voice was now crystal clear, and betrayed concern. "What was the explosion?"

"Bad landing." He'd explain later.

"Dan Roper's all set up down here, and the employees are leaving through the back entrance. No problems so far."

Link didn't answer, just bent low in the darkness and started back toward the helicopter's shape, and beyond that the end of the roof where the thin cable connected the buildings. He came to an open expanse and paused. The fifty feet ahead was barren. There was a quarter moon, but it's light was made murky by the city smog. That part was good, he decided.

Go carefully.

Time to turn Blackfoot. Snippets from Joseph Spotted Horse's tutoring surfaced. Walk smoothly. Stay low. Don't let yourself be outlined against the sky's light.

Move like a ghost.

Link stopped again, making no sound, looking and listening hard. His adversary would have to pass him to get to the superstructure. Ansel Turpin had taught his students to operate in barren areas where you knew everything about you. Good advice. There were no friendlies except the police sergeant and himself, and he knew where he'd left the sergeant.

His patience was rewarded by the crunch of a footstep, and he moved his eyes toward the source. Nothing *but* his eyes. Staring at the ebony shape of the helicopter's carcass. It was the first noise his adversary had made. He too was stealthy.

Link waited, motionless and in silence. Saw subtle movement near the fuselage. Someone was crouched there, visually checking the wreckage for bodies.

Field of fire is open.

The shadow straightened, slowly scanned the rooftop. Link confirmed it was the Russian's shadow. Tall and lithe. Same careful moves. Carrying the weapon as if he knew what he was doing. Yeah. It was I. G. Chernko, once-captain, Russian special forces. Now crook. Thorough, but too slow. Screwing around with radioactivity for too long?

Dan Roper was right. Shouldn't fool with the stuff. Awful for your health.

He must take the Russian alive. Hopefully he'd be a better source of information and make more sense than had Juliette LaCoste.

Link moved fluidly, easily, cautiously feeling his way as he placed each step, hid in the shadow of the fuselage and went closer, until Chernko's silhouette was just on the other side. Link was lower, invisible, watching.

There was a sound of movement from the superstructure—the sergeant? The Russian stared, attention attuned. Link took cautious steps, coming around and behind Chernko.

The Russian sensed him! Half turned and began to bring his weapon around. Link lashed out with a stiffened arm and sent the firearm clattering across the rooftop, but when he grasped for Chernko there was only air.

The Russian had evaded him, now stepped inside and lashed out with a rock-hard hand that caught Link above his ear and made him stumble.

Metal glittered as Chernko pulled a thin-bladed knife from a sheath on his calf. Link evaded just in time, felt the razor's edge slice through the fabric of his shirt.

"Your ears," the Russian muttered, still coming. "I need your ears, Anderson."

Link took another backstep, pulled and brandished the revolver from the shoulder holster. "No ears. This is a pistol, Dumbo."

"Lights!" The shout came from Detective Sergeant Hall at the superstructure, and with unfortunate timing, the emergency floodlights behind Chernko illuminated the rooftop.

Blinding light! Link took two quick steps back, hand held up to shield his vision from the glare. The Russian's knife-hand lashed out—almost too late, Link parried with the revolver. The knife blade snapped off cleanly, but the blow was so forceful the pistol flew from Link's grasp.

Chernko scrambled toward the weapon he'd dropped, a Skorpion machine pistol like the one he'd used in the desert.

"Raise your hands!" Sergeant Hall called in a commanding voice. He was crouched, weight removed from the broken leg, aiming an M–16 rifle.

"Don't kill him!" Link yelled, and began running for the Russian.

Ansel Turpin stared at the video monitor with disbelief, watching the dark comedy of errors being playing out atop the adjacent building. I. G. Chernko had always been tough and reliable, yet now Ansel wondered. The man had made basic errors, like not showering the wreckage with a hail of bullets before Anderson and the other man, too bulky to be Frank Dubois, had had a chance to get out.

He also felt self-reproach. Chernko had gotten one thing right, and it plagued him. Ansel had become spooked, convinced that Frank Dubois had been more than lucky when he'd disarmed him, that Lincoln Anderson was somehow possessed of superhuman qualities.

But no more, he told himself, staring at the screen. It was time to finish things between Anderson and himself. Then he would deal with Dubois. If not tonight, later.

Movement on another video monitor caught his attention, this one showing the lobby floor of the Weyland Building. A security guard had surreptitiously emerged into view, now looked directly past the camera and motioned. A dozen night workers came from an office and hurried for the rear, all passing quickly out of the camera's eye.

What was happening? Ansel wondered. His focus had been riveted on the rooftop battle. It came to him then that for the last several minutes he'd been hearing sounds of motor vehicles, but had ignored them for none had been in sight on the street below.

They were taking people from the rear of the building.

Again Chernko had been right. Anderson's arrival had been a distraction, meant to capture their attention while the night employees in the Weyland Building escaped.

Ansel hastily switched the view to another camera, this one in the bottom floor hallway of the building he was currently in, and saw dark-clad figures darting from door to door. Fool! he thought in angry reproach. They'd used his hatred of Anderson and Dubois to try to capture him, and had almost succeeded.

They would soon arrive at the fifth floor.

He scooped up the remote control for the coffeepot and dashed out the door. As always there was a escape route, but first there was a task to complete.

"Don't kill him!" Link repeated as he ran toward Chernko.

The Russian froze, glanced back at both the crouched policeman and Link Anderson, then made his decision and dove toward the machine pistol.

Sergeant Hall fired the M–16, and sparks flashed as the steel-jacketed bullet impacted gunmetal. As the Skorpion skittered away on the concrete, a flame flickered to life. The kerosene-based jet fuel had been ignited.

Chernko fled across the rooftop as the flame crept tenaciously toward the helicopter fuselage. "Stop!" came the detective sergeant's voice. He held the M–16 to his shoulder, sighting.

Link was running hard, in hot pursuit. "Stop!" Hall cried again, as the two men merged in his vision. Sounds of harsh breathing and running feet marred the silence. Chernko was desperately trying to escape, Link steadily gaining.

Erin's voice spoke in Link's ear. "Doc Roper says there's no signal so far, and the last of the people just left the building. Are you on your way down?"

"We're still on the roof," he heard the sergeant reply.

Link was only two paces behind Chernko as they neared the edge of the building. He launched himself in a semblance of a flying tackle, got a grasp of Chernko's right ankle, held fast long enough to twist and trip him. The Russian sprawled, grunting as his torso struck the concrete. He rolled, reaching for a clip attached to the body harness, then, almost with the same motion, clambered over the waist-high chain-link fence that protected humans from the precipice, and jumped—eaglelike, with arms spread wide.

Sickness rose in Link's throat, but there was no scream of terror from the man falling seventy-eight floors to his death. He pushed to his feet, chest rising and falling dramatically from the effort of the run, and tottered to the fence.

I. G. Chernko's face was only three feet below, twisted into a snarl, long spider legs clawing at the air, dangling over the avenue so distant it appeared like a ribbon strand bejeweled with tiny headlights. The Russian's hands grasped the thin cable connecting the buildings, blood running freely from cut flesh. Periodically he'd lurch and try to attach the clip-fastener to the slide mechanism, but he was too drained of energy, about to fall to his death.

Link grasped the Russian by long hair and forearm, and with strength stoked by anger, hauled the man upward. Chernko squealed at the pressure on his scalp, but Link did not pause until his foe was over the lip and held fast against the chain-link fence.

The Russian must live. There were questions to be answered.

He paused for a breath and moment of respite, but Chernko would not go meekly. He grasped desperately at Link's shirt, clutched and tugged mightily, and Link felt himself being pulled over the fence toward the dark void.

"Let go," the Russian gasped, "or we both fall."

Link kicked, wedging the toe of his boot into the chain link to anchor it, released his grip on the man's hair, and reached under Chernko's arms. He poised both stiffened thumbs into the soft and vulnerable flesh of his armpits, and yanked fiercely upward.

It was an old firefighter's trick to remove hysterical pilots quickly from burning cockpits. No human could willingly ignore or withstand the agony, and the tendency was to scramble in the direction of relief. Link pulled with all his strength, his thumbs gouging deeper and deeper into the pliant flesh, and I. G. Chernko was screaming at the top of his lungs as he came clawing up and over the fence.

Only when the Russian was on the concrete surface did Link release his tenacious hold. Chernko sank to his haunches, shuddering at the blissful release from pain, clutching his underarms. Behind them, flames were crackling more vigorously about the helicopter's carcass.

Anderson crawled onto Chernko, sat astraddle him and grasped two handfuls of hair, lifted. The Russian's head made a hollow sound as it thumped into the concrete.

"Hurry," the detective sergeant yelled from the superstructure, two hundred yards distant.

Link dragged the dazed Russian to his feet, grasped him about the torso, and began to stagger forth. Despite his weariness, Link was pleased. More than anyone except Ansel Turpin, I. G. Chernko would know truths. For the past two years they'd been together. The early reports said Turpin had taken the Russian Speznaz officer into his confidence.

It was likely Chernko knew what had become of Gary and Shelby.

Link hefted him, stumbled, and went on. The Russian recovered slightly, raised his head some, and took the next step on his own.

Good. He was getting damned heavy.

They were skirting the sheet of flames that reached out from the helicopter's skeleton and were still doggedly stumbling toward the superstructure when I. G. Chernko showed a burst of strength and twisted free.

Link staggered, and as he turned to follow, the stiffened knuckles of the Russian's hand slammed into the bridge of his nose. The cartilage made a cracking sound as it gave way, and a sick-sweet sensation swept through Link's face. He reached out to clutch Chernko's shirt and they grappled, leaned forward face to bloody face, each using the respite to regain strength, circling and holding on, both trying to get inside the other's grasp.

The Russian drew his head back to butt Link's broken nose, but Link was able to twist away in time. He pulled his right hand away and slammed his fist into Chernko's abdomen. The Russian's breath left him and he became compliant once again.

Fifty paces distant, Link could see Sergeant Hall crouching, the rifle again raised as if he was aiming, but it was no longer Chernko he targeted.

"Watch your back!" Hall shouted, and began to fire in full automatic mode. Kept on until all twenty rounds in the clip were expended. "There's a shooter on the other roof," he cried as he reached for another clip.

Link swung Chernko about, placing him between himself and Hall's target, and began to backpedal toward the superstructure. He heard the *spang*ing sound of silenced rounds striking metal, then a *thump, thump*. The Russian twisted and grunted in his grasp.

Sergeant Hall had the second clip inserted, and resumed the crouch position. Again the sounds of his shots were loud as Link backed toward him, still dragging Chernko, who had become dead weight.

Damn! he raged inwardly. Live, damn you!

Still twenty yards distant, the detective sergeant rose painfully and leaned against the superstructure, wearing a determined look as he scanned the opposite rooftop.

"There was a man with a rifle," he said. "I don't see him now."

Ansel Turpin? Link wondered. "Did you hit him?"

"I don't know. Maybe. I sent a lot of lead his way."

"We've intercepted the first signal!" came Erin's excited voice over the radio.

Too bad. Turpin was still alive.

"There's the second signal. The coffeepot's activated!"

Link lowered Chernko's body and examined. One round had struck the Russian mid-back, the other high on his right buttock, and both wounds were bleeding profusely. He raised his eyes. Flames had reached the helicopter's fuselage and were licking along its side, working their way toward the second, still-filled fuel tank.

Link lifted the bleeding Russian in a fireman's carry, one arm looped around a leg, another holding an arm, stood, and staggered under the heavy weight toward the superstructure.

"There's the blue glow. It's coming from the elevators," Erin said on the radio.

"Get out of the building," Link told her, continuing toward the superstructure.

"Doc Roper's determined the frequency and he's transmitting."

Link arrived at the superstructure, where the detective sergeant waited.

"It's still glowing, Link." Erin's voice had gained an octave.

"Oh, shit," said Sergeant Hall, listening over his own radio.

"Let's get inside," Link said. "The fuel tank's about to blow."

Sergeant Hall managed to open the door of the superstructure, and hopped on his good leg to follow him in. Link deposited Chernko, and quickly knelt to check his condition. The detective sergeant leaned against the wall by a large window, looking out at the burning fuselage, then down at Link. His eyes widened at the sight of his bloody and battered face.

"You look like you lost," Hall said.

"Doc Roper says he must have misread it. He's trying a transmission at two-three-zero point five." Pause. "Didn't work."

"Damn it, Erin, get out of the building," Link told her.

Chernko was breathing in shallow gasps, still bleeding profusely. Link applied direct pressure to the back wound, since that one appeared to be leaking most.

"He's trying another transmission at two-three-zero point three."

"C'mon, c'mon," Hall was saying, looking out the window and trying to encourage Dr. Dan Roper from a distance.

The helicopter exploded in a brilliant fireball. A metal fragment smacked into the thick safety glass window and cracked it, wedged there with part of it extending inside.

"What was that?" Erin's voice cried out.

"The helicopter blew up. We're okay." Link pressed down hard, and the Russian's bleeding was slowed to seepage between his fingers.

Sergeant Hall's mouth dropped as he regarded the metal shard. If it had come through it would have skewered him.

"It worked," Erin exulted from far below. "The glow's decreasing."

"Yeah," the detective sergeant whispered, wanting to be exuberant, staring at the fragment as if just now realizing his mortality.

The Russian's body shuddered in convulsions.

"Damn you, don't die!" A moment later Link rose to his feet, blood bright on his hands.

Ten minutes later, as the fire dwindled to a few residual flames licking here and there about the rooftop, Lincoln Anderson walked outside. Helicopters were on their way. The sounds of sirens came from the streets below. The situation would soon be in hand.

He could see policemen arriving on the opposite rooftop.

"Any sign of Ansel Turpin?" he asked Erin.

"Not yet, but half the city's looking for him. How're you doing up there, pardner?"

He wiped blood from his own face, still dribbling from the broken nose. Waves of dull pain coursed with each heartbeat. "I. G. Chernko is dead," he finally said.

"That's no loss."

"Maybe," he said, thinking of Gary Runyon and Shelby Admire, wondering if he would ever know of their fate. Link looked out at the million lights of the city, trying to guess where Turpin could have gone. About anywhere he wants, his mind decided.

35

The Secretary of Energy was wide awake in the rear of the twelve-passenger government jet, despite the hour. Who would not be, if they'd just received the worst phone call a man could get?

He had been in Las Vegas with his people from the Nuclear Regulatory Commission, using sensitive radiometry to vainly try to track down the last two coffeepots. The showgirl provided with the room by the hotel had heard his phone's buzz and shaken him to life.

"I do not give a diddly hum-shit what time it is." The reedy, cracker voice had steadily risen in tone and loudness. "Your asshole friend just set off another one of his toys. This time it was smack in the middle of New York, and the mayor there didn't even trust us enough to tell us what was happening, and then one of Frank Dubois's people, not ours, defused it. I do not *need*"—he'd screamed the word and paused—"this kind of shit!"

"I'll get on it," the Secretary had said, thinking it was unfair because he was hardly awake and had no idea what was happening.

"You bet your sorry ass you will. You and the attorney general and the director of every bureau I've got. And you'll find that last toy, and it had better do everything you said. And if your asshole friend sets *it* off, you might as well be sitting on it, learnin' to glow in the dark."

"He's not really my friend, Mr. Pres—"

Click. The dial tone had sounded ominous. He'd

called for the airplane and told them he wanted to fly to New York right away.

Now his cell phone rang again, and he picked up warily, for very few people knew his unlisted number. "Yeah?" he answered, not at all exuberant like he normally was.

"This is your friend," came the distinctively soft voice of the scientist.

"You lied to me," the Secretary blurted.

"There's one more coffeepot," the voice said. "Do you still want it?"

Four minutes later the small jet banked and began to turn to a new heading.

9:45 A.M.—Stagecoach Valley, Nevada

Link had left New York in the midst of the furor. Hurrying across the bridge to Teterboro, then sprinting westward in the Learjet. Half an hour out, approaching Cleveland, he'd telephoned Erin, who was still at the building. Too much excitement to sleep, she'd said, but he'd cajoled her into going home and to bed, since he would need her help the next morning and wanted her alert. Then he'd taken a handful of Advil to subdue the screeching ache from the hastily repaired broken nose, settled into the plush aircraft seat, and slept fitfully, mind churning with questions all the way to Reno-Tahoe International.

He'd rented another GMC Yukon from the same Hertz agency, which seemed not at all reluctant to trust him regardless of the fact that their last vehicle had been riddled with bullets, and drove south to Carson City, then eastward.

As he descended into the familiar terrain of Stagecoach Valley, the flip-top phone buzzed. A new one, with different encryption circuits and programs so no one could be listening.

Erin was working at home, for there were crime-scene ribbons and a flood of law enforcement people—everyone from remotely associated federal agencies to local precinct cops wearing NYPD blue—searching the Weyland Building for clues. She said it was almost noon there, and she'd just crawled out of bed. "Johnny wasn't here to jump on me and wake me up," she groused. He was still visiting grandparents.

"What's the latest on the search for Ansel Turpin?"

"*Nada.* He did it again, Link. Got away when he was completely surrounded. There was no blood, so they don't think Sergeant Hall hit him, if it was him he saw over there. The mayor's concerned, considering the other coffeepot's unaccounted for."

"He doesn't have to worry."

"You keep saying that as if you know where it is."

"I don't know where it is, but Turpin's not going to use it. How was the mayor's speech received?" Before he'd departed the mayor's assistants had already been preparing for morning broadcasts, when he'd explain to his city what they'd unknowingly endured.

"Really well, considering everyone's still so concerned."

"I was impressed with the way he handled it last night."

"He's impressed with you too, and he's *very* upset that Frank wants your name kept out of it. He wanted some photo ops with a real hero."

"You and Doc Roper are the heroes. All I did was wreck another bird."

She chuckled. "Frank says they're going to make a new form for your expense allowance, with a block so you can enter the number of airplanes and vehicles destroyed."

He slowed as he approached the turn off to the Barn. "What's happening with the GAO's investigation?"

"Postponed. The congressional committee's in emergency session, reconsidering everything in light of what happened last night. After all the mayor included in his speech, we're the good guys again, and this morning Frank flew down to Washington to answer questions. It finally looks like they're listening when we say it was all a plot."

"And what do you hear from the president on your secret lines?"

"Not much, except early this morning we're picked up that the White House was preparing for a big media blitz about how wonderful it would be if they could get their hands on the A.D. phenomenon. How America could use it not only to neutralize nuclear waste but also to get rid of atomic weapons, disarm bad guys, stuff like that."

Link was not surprised. It was as Dr. Dan Roper had warned. If the government had A.D., only the good guys would have nukes. They'd talk about wonderful intentions while they reopened Pandora's box and initiated a new arms race. The rumors meant they were about to deal with Ansel Turpin. Which was why Turpin was saving the last coffeepot.

"Next question," he said. "What are you hearing from the FBI about Turpin?"

"Nothing. Were you expecting something?"

"Turpin's in contact with *someone* in the government, and he knows the bureau best. It might be someone else, though. See if you can find out quickly, because he's probably dealing with them right now. It may also be difficult for you because it'll be done in very dark secrecy and involve only those in top echelons."

"Why would he talk with the government? They're trying to find him."

"He's got something they want. That's why he's not going to use the last device. It's his last-ditch ticket to freedom."

"But he's responsible for all those deaths."

"Are you sure?"

"Of course I am."

"Think it over. If Ansel Turpin was standing in front of you, could you recognize him?"

"Probably not in disguise."

"Next question. What's the present official status of Special Agent Turpin?"

"He was declared dead."

"Gordon Tower once told me that might be a problem, because a death certificate's been issued. Dead people can't commit crimes. Who was responsible for the deaths in Stagecoach Valley? Who killed Special Agent

Destin Albee? Who blew up the NEL scientists at Millionaire Mountain? Who kidnapped—probably killed—Gary Runyon and Shelby Admire?"

"Ansel Turpin."

"Show me a witness, anything at all, that proves he's alive."

"If we find him, there are fingerprints."

"And if he's working a deal with the FBI, or with people who can leverage the bureau?"

"I don't understand."

"Where are fingerprint records maintained?"

"At the National Crime Information Center. But the archives are now digitized and kept on computer tapes in a facility in West Virginia, about two hours from Washington."

"Whose name's on the front door?"

"The FBI's. But this time you're wrong, Link. They're terribly embarrassed by all of this. If someone's involved, I really don't think its them."

"Try to get that information for me, would you? Any indication that a senior government official's talking with someone about the last coffeepot."

"I'll try."

"I'm also worried that we're running out of time with Gary and Shelby. The only way I know to find them is to get their location from Ansel Turpin." He pulled into Gary Runyon's driveway and parked beside a dust-laden Suburban. Cal Admire was obviously here.

"You think Turpin will show up out there?"

"Yeah. I've been thinking about what Juliette LaCoste said. That Gary and Shelby are test bunnies, and Turpin's dropped in a fox. I think he'll show up somewhere here so he can watch them die, like she said."

"Maybe that's also where he's keeping the last coffeepot."

"It makes sense. See what you can find?" he asked.

"You bet," she said.

He got out and walked toward the porch. Halfway there the door opened and Cal Admire looked out. "Good to see you, Lincoln." He'd not smiled much since Shelby's disappearance.

Link nodded. "Anything new?"

"Nope. Came over to look around, see if we overlooked anything." Cal observed his bandage-swathed face. "Looks like you came in second in an argument with a lawnmower."

"Feels like it too." A doctor in New York had inserted splints into the nasal passages, which had proven to be more agonizing than when Link had acquired the damage. The mound of bandages on his proboscis made Link appear distinctively like a Disney cartoon character.

Cal stepped outside, glanced back and shook his head. "Just got here a few minutes ago, and the swamp cooler's still trying to cool it down in there." The outside thermometer registered ninety. A few degrees cooler than Las Vegas, but it was still climbing.

"Joseph Spotted Horse show up?"

"Yesterday afternoon. I talked to your assistant and told her to give him our address. Smart lady that Erin. Joseph says she must have some Piegan Blackfoot in her blood."

"She's a light-skinned redhead."

"Maybe way back. Anyway, Joseph's at the house talking to Sally. I told him he could stay here. I don't think Gary would mind."

They sat in a shaded area of the porch, looking out over the heat-shimmering valley. Link rubbed the bandage on his nose, trying to get to an itch. "Joseph's been dreaming about me?"

"That's what he says." Cal pointed across the valley toward Millionaire Mountain. "He's never been here, but he told me the old people once lived there. I think he means the ancient tribe Shelby used to talk about."

"Who knows, Cal? Just because Joseph has dreams doesn't make them true."

"You and I know that. Like the saying goes, "We been to school." But I sincerely like him, and he's serious about his dreams."

"I've heard some of his tales. He taught me about the old ways of warriors."

"He said he likes you because you listen."

"Have you tried not listening to him? Doesn't work. Joseph was an uncanny hunter in his day. They used to say he could talk with animals, but I'd think it odd if an elk told him where he'd be so he could have the honor of being shot."

Cal chuckled.

They were quiet for a while before Link spoke again. "I'm going to be looking for Gary and Shelby. I know who took them."

He told Cal about Ansel Turpin, and what Juliette LaCoste had said before she'd died. Cal explained the relentless search for Shelby. Deputy Ray Watt and the local members of the Ancient Order of Dirt Muckers had examined every square foot of desert for the surrounding ten miles. It was as if she'd been swallowed up.

The two men looked out at the shimmering desert and tried to make sense of it.

At noon Link followed Cal home, where he greeted Joseph Spotted Horse and looked over his badly rusted stakebed truck that had somehow made it all of that distance. Then Sally Admire came out, gave him a warm hug, and ordered everyone inside for lunch.

Joseph declined, saying that in all of his years he had never met a woman who tried to feed him so much. After eating Link looked out the window to where the old Indian was hunkering beside Aristotle, talking and looking very solemn.

"He's got a way with animals," Sally said. "He's taking Aristotle for another long walk."

The cell phone buzzed in Link's shirt pocket.

"Anderson," he responded.

"I may be onto something," Erin said. "But just like you said, it's awfully deep and dark."

"Go on."

"Two senior FBI agents are headed in your direction from Las Vegas, They'll meet someone unnamed—from the secrecy it's obviously a government official—in Reno."

"Where'd you learn all that?"

"From Gordon Tower. I called him to share insights.

He's not a happy camper. He thinks some kind of deal's going down that could hurt the bureau."

"With Turpin? For the coffeepot?"

"He didn't say, and I'm not sure he knows any more than I just told you. He got that far and decided he'd said enough, but I think he wanted us to know it's not the bureau's idea and they're being ordered to go along. He's one of the senior agents going up there, by the way."

"I'll need more, Erin. Like who, when, where, what? Anything you can get."

"I realize that, but now Gordon Tower is out of pocket and I keep butting up against dead ends." She exhaled a heavy breath. "Something dumb keeps running through my mind."

He waited for her to continue.

"We operate the satellites that provide covert communications nets for the government. We also provide the encrypting circuits for the satellites, and those on the other end here in the building. That's what goes on with all those agencies up on the top floors, *including* the bureau."

"What does that mean in plain English?"

"We have the ability to listen in on their secrets."

"Can you get Frank's approval?"

"Frank isn't back from Washington. He had to brief the congressional committee, remember. Oh, hell, Link. It's a terrible idea. It's the same system that provides presidential and State Department links. Also for the Department of Defense and CIA. Anyone who did something like that would be facing serious jail time."

"Yeah." He thought about the trouble she could get into. "Unless you get Frank's approval, let's forget about that one."

"Frank may be a while. He called two hours ago from Washington and asked some questions about Turpin. Like what his temperament would be with all that's going on, and a real odd one. Years ago Turpin was a rotary wing pilot, and Frank wanted to know what kind of helicopters he'd checked out in."

"Unless he gets back and approves it, forget about the secret comm, Erin. Like you said, it's a bad idea."

"Here's another tidbit out of Washington. The Nuclear Regulatory Commission's gathering all possible information on the A.D. phenomenon and labeling it top secret. The rumors weren't wrong. Accelerated depletion has become a top priority."

Link watched as Joseph Spotted Horse walked toward the highway, Aristotle at his side.

"I'm going for a drive," he said. "Keep digging, Erin. Find out where they're going. I have to locate Ansel Turpin before the government does."

She was downbeat. "We may already be too late."

Link drove around Stagecoach Valley as he'd done with Shelby. This time with no rad meter, only the hunting rifle in back, still in its case.

Gary and Shelby were here *somewhere.* He knew it. Juliette LaCoste had said they were together. Test bunnies, with a rabid fox.

In a cage, such as test animals were kept in? Where?

Who was the fox? He thought he knew. Someone Ansel Turpin despised. Someone he'd once said he wanted to watch die.

Link drove back to Highway 50, saw Joseph Spotted Horse walking across the desert in the distance with Aristotle, not far from the dry lake bed. He pulled off the highway, bounced along the hardpack surface, and drove up close.

"Going anywhere in particular?" he asked.

"Sally said there's a little river a few miles this way. I think this big dog wants to go there." Joseph looked at Millionaire Mountain. "The old people lived there a long time ago."

"I heard. I guess it was really pretty until miners came along and cut down all the trees."

"Is that right?" Joseph regarded the mountain with solemn interest, then turned and pointed beyond the pony express station. "Better get your boots. Good ones are hard to replace." He made a clicking sound with his tongue, and continued walking with Aristotle.

Link observed where Joseph had pointed, and remembered leaving the boots on the hillside. Then he looked back at the old man and wondered how much more he was aware of.

Joseph Spotted Horse continued walking, the big dog at his side, not moving fast but steadily and as if he had purpose.

Link returned to his dilemma about Gary and Shelby. If his idea was right, Ansel Turpin would return to observe the bunnies and the fox. Perhaps then he'd meet with the government official Erin had learned was on his way.

The White House was touting the accelerated depletion phenomenon, as if preparing the public for the fact that they had the secret. No one would know they'd dealt with a terrorist to obtain it. He dropped that chain of thinking, since he did not know it to be true.

A thought surfaced. Turpin had a fixation about watching people who were unaware. Did he have a video camera in the cage with Gary and Shelby—and the rabid fox?

36

Shelby lifted the chunk of lava and thumped it solidly into the glass. Lifted again, struck again. For three days they'd worked and made little progress.

The food was gone, stolen.

Gary made a whimpering sound, and she put down the stone. Reached out and touched his face. Not long and he'd be dead. There had been too much bleeding.

The newcomer had made his move during the night, after the glow-period had ended. They'd been working in the darkness, continuing to chip away relentlessly at the glass wall, and due to the noise they hadn't heard his approach.

It had been Gary's turn with the rock.

"The food's gone!" she'd cried.

Then there had only been the sounds of Gary's breathing, heavy because of his weariness.

He had tried the cigarette lighter, and found no one was about them. The food had been in the bag beside her, so the newcomer had come close.

"I'll go for it," Gary had finally said.

Shelby had been unable to subdue her fright. "He's got the sliver," she'd warned, panicky that he was leaving her side, but knowing that without the food they would weaken and die much sooner. He'd taken a barrel lid, thinking he might be able to fend off the newcomer, and, trying to make as little noise as possible, slipped into the darkness.

Poor brave, wonderful Gary.

She'd seen the flash of the lighter as he searched. At the edge of the huge pile of rubble that had fallen from above, then farther around. Gary had called out in a reasonable tone, saying they had to share the food or they would soon perish. He had been reminding the newcomer of how fair they'd been, and how they should all work together when, in the middle of an utterance, he'd screamed. Just once.

"Gary?" she'd tried in a trembling voice. She'd crept toward the sounds of Gary's whimpering, closer and ever closer, feeling the choking trepidation of the unknown surround and invade her. She'd finally found him, drawn by the pitiful sounds, and tried to comfort him. Felt the life leaking from his side where the sliver still impaled him. Pulled it free and used the remnants of his already-blood-soaked shirt to bind him. Then she'd laboriously dragged him back to the glow-wall and huddled with him and comforted as best she could. Stanching the blood with pressure and the bandage, knowing he'd already lost far too much life-fluid.

The newcomer had the cigarette lighter, and twice during the dark period he had flashed it on the other side of the rubble. She'd also heard the sounds of him eating.

Shelby lifted the lava rock and thumped it into the glass, as she'd done all night and all day. Fingers and hands battered and numb, but not so senseless she couldn't feel the awful pain firing through them with each blow of the rock.

"Made another big chip," she said airily to Gary. "We're making progress."

He didn't, couldn't respond.

She choked back a sob, raised the rock and smacked it hard into the glass.

There'd been only the small crack when they'd begun, and they'd chipped first on one side until there was a quarter inch of progress, then on the other. If the glass had been four feet in thickness to begin with, it was now only three.

"Don't give up, Gary."

Silence. *Thump.*

"Never give up."

Thump.

She had a vision of Aristotle, wagging his tail and barking like he did.

Thump.

She raised the rock and paused.

Then Shelby Admire held her breath.

It was very faint, but she could hear it. A dog's barking.

"Oh, God," she cried out.

Again she heard the barking, now more strident.

She banged lava against the glass. *Thump-thump-thump.* Pause. *Thump-thump-thump.*

Tick-tick-tick. That one was not hers! Someone had tapped on the glass from outside.

She laughed exuberantly.

"Hello!" came a very faint voice.

"Help!" Shelby screamed. "Oh, God. Help us!"

She began to cry, and patted Gary's arm. "We're going to be saved!"

Her words muffled a vague rustle of movement as the newcomer came toward her.

Ansel Turpin watched with amusement as the woman beat on the glass sphere. It was far too thick to ever get through—at least not before they all died of hunger.

While he'd been away old Piers had done as Ansel had expected: bided his time, then stabbed the writer and made off with the food. A fox placed with helpless, conscience-ridden bunnies. Too bad he'd missed so much, but he'd be able to watch him kill Shelby Admire. For the past few minutes he'd followed as the old man had crept ever closer to her, wielding a barrel lid as if it were a weapon.

Ansel adjusted the low light enhancement and zoomed in to observe their silent images. Only two of the four cameras in the sphere had withstood the rockslide, and the audio circuitry had been destroyed, but he'd be able to view part of the endgame. Basic animal survival instincts were emerging. It would be a fitting death for the man and woman, who should have killed old Piers when he'd first been dropped in. Now they would perish, then a slower, crueller fate for Jergen. Lingering starvation after he was reduced to skin and bone. A pity he'd not be here to see his father breathe his last, but this was almost as good. The confrontation was imminent, for Piers Jensen had crept up upon Shelby with the lid raised, a snarl fixed on his old features.

The barrel lid flashed downward.

Amusing, Ansel thought, for the woman had moved aside in time and the lid glanced harmlessly against the glass. Turpin pursed his lips and nodded in admiration. The woman held up the glass sliver he'd last seen when Gary Runyon had first collected it.

"Go away!" she silently mouthed, and the old man took a step back.

"Don't *trust* him," Ansel said in a sing-song tone, as if observing a game.

The old man had turned away from her, was removing something from his pocket.

"Poor stupid girl," Ansel said.

Piers Jergen turned back, surprisingly quickly for a man of his age, and dropped onto her, swinging the jagged rock in his hand.

Too slow, though, for his eyes widened and his mouth drooped in surprise.

The glass sliver protruded from Piers' abdomen, dark liquid draining.

Ansel clapped enthusiastically. "Bravo!" One of the bunnies had done away with the rabid fox. Not dead yet, the old man writhed, but soon enough.

He frowned then, for the woman was obviously calling out, now facing the glass sphere where she'd been laboring. Was someone on the outside?

A hint of a shadow moved on the glass. Then again.

Ansel got to his feet. He could not allow it. He'd crowed to Piers Jergen entirely too much while he'd stuffed him into the barrel, before they'd herded the others up. Cursed him for bringing shame to his mother. Told him how he would periodically think of him rotting and dying as he sipped mai tais on the lavish estate he'd purchased on Kauai.

The old man had not been as surprised as Ansel had believed he'd be. After all, he'd thought, they had worked hand in glove, killing people in the valley together. A father and son operation. But Piers Jergen had acted as if he'd expected Ansel to turn on him.

Were distrust and treachery in the genes the old man had passed on?

Piers had to die in the sphere. It was a part of it all. And what of the other two, trapped with him? Had he told them about Ansel and where he was going? They all must die.

Ansel went to the door, where he picked up a rifle, an aged and well-scarred Winchester model 92 that fit perfectly with the role he played. He hurried out, knowing that he could not be too long about it. He had guests to greet before he embarked on a well-deserved vacation.

With no better purpose, Link had done as Joseph Spotted Horse had said, gone into the foothills and searched for the boots. When he dug them out he decided it hadn't been worth the effort expended—they were dried and curled at the toes—but he had exercised his mind as he'd looked, trying to think of the delegation that was coming. Where they'd go and who they were coming to see? Ansel Turpin, of course, but in what disguise?

Link had parked near the old pony express station, and was returning there when the cell phone buzzed in his denim shirt pocket.

Erin was uncharacteristically short, as if frightened. "I've got news about the FBI trip."

"Shoot."

"I intercepted three different cut-out messages. Those are phone calls that go through a number that supposedly can't be traced, but I did that too."

"Damn it, Erin. I told you to leave the system alone."

"Just *listen*, would you?"

He wondered if he'd be able to pull her out of trouble if she was caught. "Go ahead."

"They were using a sort of verbal code. Dragon— Ansel Turpin, I assume—has provided the first item to show his good faith. Now there's to be a rendezvous at seventeen hundred hours. No location was mentioned, so I guess it was discussed earlier. They're to bring an automobile with the three negotiators, and a helicopter with only a pilot. One person's to get out of the vehicle, unarmed and without body armor, and act as Dragon's hostage so he'll know there's no tricks. He told them to send 'Gordy,' so I suppose he meant his old friend Gordon Tower. Next the four of them go through with the second exchange. Then after Dragon's been taken out in the helicopter and arrives at his destination, if everything's like he wants, he'll provide the third item."

One coffeepot, and one set of formulae, Link thought. What was the third item?

"That's all." She took a deep breath. "Unless you can find him, he's going to get away with it, Link. Ansel Turpin's going to get away clean."

"Have you told any of this to Frank yet?"

"Should I?"

"Yeah. No matter what, Frank's one of the good guys."

"Just a sec." She was offline for only twenty seconds, then returned. "Frank's still out and they're not giving his location. Probably still in Washington."

"Don't press it and try to get more information, Erin."

"I don't think there's going to be any more. It's three o'clock out there, so they'll rendezvous in two more hours." She was even more downbeat. "Anything about your friends?"

"No. Turpin's my last hope to find them alive."

"Talk with Joseph Spotted Horse. Maybe he can help."

Why not? Link thought. He was getting desperate, and the old man had an uncanny view of what was going on.

He drove the Yukon, head hanging outside the window until he picked up the dog and man's tracks, and followed where they'd trekked along the side of the dry lakebed. They'd likely proceeded to the back side of Millionaire Mountain, which was adjacent to the Carson River where they were headed.

He drove on, thinking about what Erin had said, wondering where the rendezvous would be held and what Ansel Turpin had demanded in exchange for the secret to America's new future. Safe passage, of course, but what else? And then there would be more testing and experimentation, and Dan Roper had told him how dangerous that could be.

He slowed and bumped over ruts and rocks, backed up and went around gullies.

A dust cloud billowed far off to his right, and he watched the hermit's vintage weapons carrier passing in the distance. He was obviously in a hurry, and traveled a more hospitable route. The old man knew the desert paths—should because of all the time he'd spent prospecting and searching—but it seemed odd that he'd drive that fast.

Headed directly toward the NEL study site?

A mental image returned, of the first time he had seen the old man in the Misfits Saloon. Eyes sweeping the room as if he missed nothing. Just like . . .

Suspicion arose that he immediately dismissed as ridiculous. It came back, became a possibility. He turned toward the dust plume and accelerated, smashed into and across a shallow ditch and continued. Bounced over a small rise, and stopped before a ten-foot deep arroyo.

It might be smarter to go back and around.

Yeah, but he might lose him. Link gunned the engine, nosed the vehicle over, and began sliding down the embankment, trying to keep the wheels straight but feeling it slip sideward out of his control. He grasped the wheel tightly and braced himself as the Yukon began to tip over.

It rolled, slowly at first, then faster. Crashing onto side, roof, then onto the other side and—teetering precariously—smashing over and rocking on the wheels. Now upright at the bottom of the arroyo, engine stalled, windshield spider-webbed with cracks.

Link turned the switch, heard the starter grind. "Come on," he encouraged, hoping it was only disrupted fuel flow and nothing terminal. The engine sputtered, caught. He drove forward, bobbled over a few large stones, and took out a few clumps of dry sagebrush. Thinking of the hermit who came and went. Who had had difficulty getting around when he'd arrived, supposedly from a fall. Just as Ansel Turpin had been disabled by a gunshot in St. Petersburg. Arrived last year, when Piers Jergen and his colleagues had come to work at NEL.

Ansel Turpin was many people, and one of those was the hermit.

Was he headed for the rendezvous with the senior official and FBI agents?

The Yukon sped along the arroyo bottom, smoothed by years of flash-flooding and water runoff. The sides became less steep, and he angled up the right one—the Yukon was airborne for several feet as it plunged over, and then he was back on the desert surface, bouncing mightily.

The ancient weapons carrier had drawn far ahead, still creating the plume of foglike dust. He accelerated, careening over obstacles and hoping there'd be no more arroyos as deep and dangerous as the one he'd left.

Finally Link intercepted the nondescript roadway his quarry traveled, now only a quarter mile behind the hermit, and accelerated again. Passed through an open gate of the NEL perimeter fence, wondering if the rollover had damaged the rifle in back. Probably not, since it was in the case. Turpin-as-hermit would be armed and dangerous, but he *must* take him alive. Only he could tell him where Gary and Shelby were held in their cage with the rabid fox.

Link continued in the dense fog of suspended dust, only vaguely seeing the road ahead, and then the stone pillars on right and left as he drove into the mountain hollow.

He braked hard. Almost crashed into the halted weapons carrier in the midst of the pall of dust, slid past it, fishtailing, and came to a stop.

There was no time for idle thought. The hermit was obviously close. He looked back, saw the rifle case near the rear door where it had been tossed, started to crawl back, and looked out.

The hermit stood a dozen paces distant, staring

through the swirling dust with a penetrating look, hefting a weathered and ancient .30–.30. The unkempt hair and beard were convincing, an apt likeness of a true desert rat.

Links opened the door and stepped out unarmed. Recognition came slowly because of the bandaged nose. Then the hermit's eyes widened.

"Shelby and Gary," Link said. "Tell me where they are and I'll go for them. I don't give a damn what you do with the coffeepot."

"I don't know what you're talking about." It was spoken in a high voice, and Link recalled Erin saying that Ansel was fearful of him.

Link heard the distant sound of a barking dog, glanced toward the narrow chasm that passed through to the south side of the mountain. When he looked back the hermit's expression had changed to a craftier one, the eyes intense, like those of a trained agent whose life was defined by careful observation. There was no more pretense.

"Time to die, Anderson." The hermit raised the rifle.

Link dove behind the Yukon and tumbled, heard the weapon discharge and the *spang* of a bullet penetrating metal. He was quickly up, running toward one of the old buildings. Feinted right, heard another shot as he dropped and rolled left. Behind the building, he was masked for the moment as he sprinted toward the chasm through the mountain. He entered the passage as a bullet ricocheted off stone, head high and so close his face was stung by bits of rock. He plunged farther, still running, the sheer sides closing until they were shoulder width.

He stopped at a fence, hidden from the shooter's view, chest heaving. Unharmed thus far, but his broken nose throbbed and the wounds in his back and leg were dancing with sensation. Link listened, heard nothing. He could go no farther, lest he draw Turpin to Joseph Spotted Horse.

A final shot boomed from far behind. Then the guttural sounds of the weapons carrier's engine starting, of gears meshing, then of the vehicle being driven away.

Ahead the dog began barking once more. Aristotle

appeared on the opposite side of the fence, bristling and showing menacing teeth. Next came Joseph Spotted Horse.

"I told him it was only you," said Joseph, but he was looking warily beyond Link as if he might be wrong.

Link could hear the diminishing sounds of Ansel Turpin escaping once again.

"Lincoln," Joseph said gravely. "We have discovered something very odd. At first I thought it was the old people talking from the mountain. Now I think it is your friends."

37

4:20 P.M.—Millionaire Mountain

Link smashed the end of the steel bar against the obsidian surface. Chips flew and a new gouge mark appeared. He struck again, and again, steadily. During the twenty minutes he'd been at it he'd made good progress for he knew that every second might be critical for his friends inside.

After Joseph had explained what he'd found, Link had hurried back to the NEL site. There he'd found the Yukon disabled—the reason for Turpin's last shot—and his rifle case taken. The cell phone had dropped from his shirt pocket during his escape and was not to be found. All that had stacked up against him, yet he'd been more excited than he'd been in days.

He'd found the heavy bar beside the NEL warehouse, and hurried back through the chasm to scale the fence and join Joseph beside the Carson River. Not much farther and he'd seen the small section of exposed black wall, and after a moment heard it for himself. *Tap-tap-tap*, pause, *tap-tap-tap*. Then periodically a faint and muffled female voice crying desperately for help.

Link continued slamming the bar into the glass wall. *Thunk—thunk—thunk—thunk*. Steadily chipping. He stopped, chest heaving, wiped a profuse collection of sweat from his brow with his hand and flung it away. Held his head back and took in a long, deep breath.

Got to keep at it.

Tap-tap-tap. The sound was now distinct. "I think it will not be much longer," Joseph said hopefully, peering at the chipped and battered wall.

A change came over the old Indian—at first a troubled expression, then his face contorted as if he was in severe pain.

Link reached out. "Steady." Then he recalled the unsettling emotion he'd experienced when shown the entrances to the mines, and wondered.

"I must leave," Joseph said abruptly.

"But are you okay?" Link repeated.

"I must go from here." Perspiration dotted Joseph's brow, and he spoke in a low voice, as if he did not want someone to overhear. "Voices in my head are too loud."

Aristotle looked at Joseph, whined as if in sympathy.

"Come with me, big dog. We will only get in the way here." Joseph hurried away, stumbling in his haste, Aristotle trotting along at his side, peering up as if concerned. "I will bring you help," Joseph called.

Link rested for only a moment, then went back to chipping at the wall. Thinking about Joseph's pained expression and abrupt leavetaking and wishing he'd praised the old man more for his find. If Gary and Shelby were inside as it seemed, the credit would be Joseph's. Certainly not Link's, for he'd resisted allowing Joseph to become involved.

Long minutes had passed when he drew the steel bar back and jabbed forward, hard, *Thunk*. The end of the bar was stuck.

"You're *through*!" came the excited female voice.

Link prised the bar, withdrew it. "Get back!" he shouted, waited for her to move, then thrust forcefully, battering at the small channel, widening it. Listening to the trill of laughter he was now sure came from Shelby. He was unable to restrain the grin growing on his own countenance as he pried and jabbed. The hole was three inches, then six, then a foot in diameter, but he continued relentlessly. At eighteen inches, he staggered, and then paused. His arms were leaden, and he was close to collapsing from sheer exhaustion.

"We can get through," she said, and he could see her ᷉eeking through. The face was dirty and streaked, oddly ᷉psided, but undeniably Shelby's.

"Thank God," Link croaked, drained of energy. Then, "Gary?"

"He needs medical help. Jergen stabbed him."

Link had guessed correctly. Turpin's father was the rabid fox. "Is he still a threat?"

"I killed him," Shelby said in a matter-of-fact tone, then began to push a hardly recognizable Gary Runyon into the hole. Link grasped his friend's rail-thin shoulders and pulled him the rest of the way through. He was filthy, and a blood soaked T-shirt was wrapped about his lower abdomen.

As Link deposited Gary beside the river in the shade of a cottonwood, Shelby crawled out. Like Gary she'd been savagely beaten. There were lumps and bruises, and her previously aquiline nose was knotted and twisted so severely that she breathed through an opened mouth, displaying a badly broken front tooth.

She crouched over an ashen faced and hardly breathing Gary Runyon and grasped his hand. "We made it, Gary. We *made* it!" She was filthy and bedraggled, and more lovely than Link had ever seen her. "We've got to get help for Gary," she cried.

As Link started to tell her that Joseph was already on his way, a soft voice spoke from behind them. "He won't need it."

Adam Russo's image stood a dozen yards distant. He held a heavy, stainless steel revolver aimed at Shelby, and mirror sunglasses masked his expression.

"Pull the old man out," said the imposter.

Link's inner rage simmered hotter toward the monster that had caused the suffering.

"Get him," said the soft-spoken man, "or I'll simply kill all of you and do it myself."

"Don't you plan to kill us all anyway?" Link asked him. "Ansel?"

Russo-Turpin kept the aim-point steady on Shelby and stalked forward. "You are an irritating man, Anderson. Always in the way."

Link did not dare to move, for the gun was placed against Shelby's temple.

"Come closer, Anderson," said the ex-agent. "Do not

make a wrong twitch or I will blow your playmate's head off."

Link took two tentative steps toward Turpin. Looked just beyond him and saw the steel bar and was wondering if there was a way to go for it when the pistol swept about in an arc. Hard metal smacked solidly into Link's head. He crumpled, feeling an intense spike of pain— and then numbness flooded through his limbs.

Turpin followed him, grasped his shirt, and pulled him up so he remained on his knees. "I beat you!" he gloated, then released his hold and chuckled as Link Anderson fell to the ground.

For a while there was nothing. No feeling at all. Then with awareness came intense pain. Link was flat on the ground, arms askew, head pounding so violently that it was all-consuming, overpowering the tickling sensations of blood draining from ears and nostrils. There was no doubt in his mind that his skull had been cracked, or that he was in the process of dying. It was not a tragic thought. He'd considered the option since Marie's passing, but he knew there were things left unfinished.

Link was behind the others, unobserved, but the violent blow to his head had drained away all energy, and the slightest exertion seemed beyond his capability. With great effort he was able to pull his hands up from his sides, but when he tried to rise to all fours the task was Herculean, and he fell back to the ground.

Gullible fool! he cried to himself. He'd allowed Turpin to come up on them.

Ansel heard his movements, and turned to stare in amusement as Link struggled to hands and knees. "I thought you were dead," Turpin said almost amiably. He held the pistol on Gary as Shelby struggled to pull Piers Jergen's body through the hole in the sphere.

"That's good," Turpin said then, and walked over to look down at the old man. He prodded the glass sliver protruding from his chest with his foot, but there was no movement from Jergen. "Yes, you really did him in," he said. "As I said before: Bravo, Shelby."

She stared with a morose glare.

Ansel Turpin glanced at Link, then at his watch.

"They'll be on time. Punctuality and unlimited funds are the only virtues of the man I'm about to meet with, Anderson. I really don't like him. On the other hand I detest your friend and employer, and since Frank Dubois is both of those things, I will not treat you or yours well."

Ansel was savoring victory. He walked to the cottonwood, where Shelby now knelt by Gary. "I really should enjoy Miss Admire's charms while you look on, since we were so rushed the last time. But she's looking a bit used and dog-eared at the moment, so I'll simply shoot her."

Turpin cocked his head, gave Link a smile, then pointed the pistol at Piers Jergen. "But first another Ansel rule. Don't trust anyone." He fired once into Jergen's abdomen.

Old Piers's back arched, and he squealed.

"See. Daddy dear was faking." He fired again. A bright rosette appeared on Piers Jergens's forehead, and matter spewed from the rear of his skull. The squealing stopped.

Link desperately tried to gather strength to attack. To stop him before he could kill again. But he was fading, the world about him growing dim.

Turpin raised the pistol. Aimed it directly at a point between Lincoln Anderson's eyes, took up the minute amount of slack with his forefinger.

Link tried to summon some small vestige of strength that had not been taken.

Ansel chuckled and shifted his point of aim to Gary Runyon, who lay quietly unaware as Shelby hovered, eyes pleading for mercy. "No. Please!" she cried.

There was a new sound, this one of rushing feet, and Aristotle bounded energetically into view. He was airborne when he smacked into Turpin's midsection and sent him sprawling backward into the river.

Ansel yelped with surprise, and turned the pistol on the huge animal. He fired twice, missing once, but blood blossomed on the dog's chest as Aristotle's massive jaws clamped onto the wrist, making a grinding noise as bone was crushed. The revolver dropped free, and Turpin's scream echoed off the mountain as he frantically pushed the animal away. Aristotle followed, but the dog was severely wounded and came slowly.

Turpin slogged to the riverbank, cradling his hand and moaning with pain. His jaw hung open and he was looking dazed, as if what had happened were impossible. Glanced once toward his would-be victims and reeled along the bank until he turned the corner and was out of their view.

Link slowly pushed to his knees, attempted to rise to his feet, and dropped back to all fours. With supreme effort, he placed a hand forward, wavered, and almost fell, then drew himself up, placed another hand, and continued to crawl. He came to a sapling, clutched at its base and grasped and pulled. He put one foot under himself and very slowly lurched to his feet, stood for an unsteady moment with bowed head, then staggered after Ansel Turpin with a single purpose chorusing in his mind. The monster must not escape.

He turned the bend, and just ahead Ansel Turpin was perched atop the fence. He looked back at Link, jaw dropping and blood draining from his ruined hand, then dropped onto the rocky earth on the opposite side.

Link continued doggedly, now clutching at the chain link. "I'm coming for you, Turpin."

"Too late," said the man before him, and he staggered into the narrow chasm, holding the bleeding hand to his chest.

While the fence rose little higher than his head, it seemed impossible that Link might climb it. He gouged a boot toe into the mesh, then another, and slowly began to scale the thing. With each new step he had to stop and rest, chest heaving at the gargantuan task. But finally he teetered and then pushed himself over. He fell to the other side harshly, and the jolt sent bolts of fire through his head of such excruciating intensity that they were paralyzing.

The numbness was slow to leave. He rolled over onto all fours and vomited. Then, as before, he crawled for the first few feet, until he arrived at the sheer mountainside. There he pawed and pulled, and finally regained his feet. "Turpin!" he cried hoarsely, but drew no response and when he called out again the sound was lost as the clip-clop noises of a distant helicopter became more distinct.

He staggered forward, wondering if he could possibly make it through.

"Let me help, Lincoln," said an almost spectral voice, and hands circled his waist and held him up, and walked with him.

"I thought you were gone," Link gasped.

Joseph Spotted Horse sighed. "I should not have left you. We did not go far, that big dog and me. Then there was the shot."

They emerged into the open, and saw, only fifty yards distant, Ansel Turpin standing beside the weapons carrier, bleeding hand held slightly aloft, wearing a stern expression.

A dark limo was parked a dozen feet away, and three men had just emerged. One was black—Gordon Tower. Another was the Secretary of Energy. He spoke with Turpin, but the distance was too great and the approaching helicopter too noisy for Link to overhear the words.

As Link and Joseph continued forward, Ansel Turpin turned and pointed. His face was distorted by emotion. Hatred or agony? Link wondered.

Gordon Tower came closer. "We'll wait here," said the special agent, and winced as he observed the side of Link's head where blood had drained and matted.

"Turpin's killed too many people to let him escape." Link said in a croaking voice.

Tower regarded him without expression. "Ansel Turpin's dead."

"That's him, Gordon."

"Maybe. Or maybe it's Dr. Adam Russo."

"You know who it is."

The agent didn't react.

The Secretary of Energy had pulled away the tarpaulin. The coffeepot's metallic surface gleamed in the bright sunlight. He stared, then looked up at Turpin and smiled.

"He'll get away," Link said.

"Maybe. You don't look so good."

"I'll stop him," Link said, and started forth.

"Can't let you do that." Tower stood in his way, held a hand to restrain him.

They watched as Ansel Turpin walked toward the helicopter. Just before he entered the opened rear hatch, he turned and stared toward Link. He smirked then, and boarded.

"I know about the formulae and the coffeepot. What was the third item?" Link asked.

"A chart showing just how much radiation it takes to kill a human, how long, all that. Actually it was the first thing he gave them."

"Jesus," Link whispered. That was what the deaths in the valley had been about.

"The second thing traded is the coffeepot there, all primed and ready. The last deal's straightforward. Cash and carry for the formulae."

The pilot from the helicopter deplaned and walked briskly away.

"Turpin can fly the thing," said Gordon, and Link remembered that Erin had told that to Frank. What else had Frank asked her? Oh yeah. What was Ansel's state of mind?

"Look at the car," Gordon encouraged, and Link turned. Two more men emerged. One was Dr. Dan Roper, who immediately walked over to the coffeepot in the bed of the weapons carrier. The other was Frank Dubois, who laboriously transferred himself into a wheelchair.

"What's Frank doing here?" Link asked. He looked at the helicopter cockpit, where Ansel Turpin stared wide-eyed at the man he despised. He slowly clamped his mouth shut, and a look of angry determination spread across this face.

The helicopter's engine surged. The big rotor blade thrashed, popped a few times as the blade tip went supersonic. The aircraft lifted straight up.

"Keep an eye on the chopper," said Gordon Tower.

"Guess you didn't know about your boss making all those telephone calls this morning. After he talked to the congressional committee, Mr. Dubois made a few calls to the bureau, then he met with a gentleman who lives in a big white house a few blocks from there. Told him about all he knew, and how it would really sound bad to the press and the public. Say what you will about them, those boys in Washington are willing to deal. Especially when it comes to saving their butts."

"But Ansel Turpin just got away."

The aircraft had risen to an altitude of more than a thousand feet and now was hovering over the side of the mountain.

"That's what it's all about. Look at the chopper, Mr. Anderson. You and I know who's at the controls, all alone in that bird. And down here he just saw Mr. Dubois and you, two people he does not like one bit. Now *also* in the cockpit is the remote control he took with him."

Link looked over to where Dan Roper had just placed a metallic cloth over the coffeepot.

"Yeah," said Gordon Tower. "With the lead shield over it, there's no way it can be set off, but our buddy up there doesn't know that. See, the only thing that's going to happen when he presses the first button is—"

The flash was tremendous. All eyes were glued onto the burning fuselage as it fell through the sky, hit and tumbled on the side of the mountain, and disappeared on the other side.

"I guess they won't get the formulae," said Link.

"Probably not," murmured the special agent. He motioned his hand at the shrouded coffeepot. "And who knows what they're going to find in that thing. One of Ansel's old rules was never to trust a thief. I sort of doubt he gave them everything they wanted."

A wave of mixed fatigue and nausea swept over Link. The exhaustion and the fractured skull caught up with him, and Gordon Tower had to help Joseph Spotted Horse hold him erect.

"Lay him down over here," he vaguely heard. "I've

already called for a med-evac bird." He recognized Frank Dubois's concern-filled voice.

"There are others," Link heard Joseph saying, but a veil had descended over his vision and he could no longer see clearly.

Epilogue

The sky was vast, and the aging Dodge pickup seemed to be moving at a snail's pace upon the endless landscape. Yet periodically a small, resonant shudder would tremble through the vehicle, and he'd know to slow down for he was pressing the speed limit.

He was tall and gaunt, with dark-hued skin due to a combination of sun and genetics. A Western hat was pushed back on his head, and he wore comfortable boots—a pair once left in the desert, plied with mink oil and massaged until they were as supple and pliant as chamois cloth.

The desert shimmered in his vision, and he squinted, although there was only the one pickup visible on the highway called the loneliest road in America. He tired easily, not yet fully healed, and decided that he should stop early tonight, lest he nod off while he was driving.

Time passed slowly, quietly, and after a period a passenger materialized. A woman with long, raven-black hair, wearing a tender expression.

A rush of warmth enveloped him. "I've missed you," he told her.

"I know."

He had a thousand questions. "Have you been very far?"

She nodded.

"I met your friend Shelby," he said. "She's happy now. A friend of mine is writing a book about everything that happened. His publisher says it's great fiction, and may even be a best-seller. Shelby's helping him with the technical details and fixing up their home."

"That's nice."

He hesitated "For a while she and I became close."

"Some things aren't meant to be."

There was so much to tell her, and to ask. It was like a dream, yet real. She seemed so . . .

A horn blared. Link blinked, swerved so abruptly the tires squealed as he pulled back into his own lane. He felt foolish as the semi swept by.

When his breathing rate had returned to normal, he glanced over to where she'd been.

It wasn't the first time he'd spoken to Marie, nor the first time he'd imagined she had responded—but this one had been the most real. He was still not sure whether it had been Marie, or just his wanting to see and speak to her so badly.

Twelve weeks had passed since the confrontation at Millionaire Mountain. Since Gary and Shelby's rescue. Since his skull had been shattered. They'd flown him to Reno, then to Johns Hopkins Medical Center in Baltimore, where surgeons had battled to keep him alive in spite of the despondency that settled in.

There'd been a succession of visitors. His stepparents, Erin Frechette, Frank Dubois and his family. Other close friends. All acting upbeat, trying to keep him from sinking into a permanent abyss, all realizing there would have been no way he'd choose to live if he knew he could find Marie. But as Joseph Spotted Horse said, who could know such things?

He had been released from the hospital two days ago, then had ignored his friends' and family's pleas and flew out to get the pickup.

Link took a sip of bottled water, tepid from sitting so long in the warm cab, then looked across to where she'd appeared a few minutes earlier.

"Where are you, Marie?" The note she'd left him long ago, telling him to go on with life after she was gone, was in his shirt pocket. Hardly legible from the many times he'd unfolded it. Memorized it.

Stop it. The words were angrily spoken, and startled him. It took a moment to recover, then he wondered. Had it been her voice?

I said stop it!

Link pulled to the side of the road, continued until he was out of the way should a truck come by, and shut off the engine. Then he sat and stared at the empty seat, trying to sort it out.

Thoughts came in a rush.

Marie told you to get on with your life, then you tried to will yourself to die. She would have hated that. She'd have thought you were a quitter.

He felt anguish but knew it was the truth. "I miss her."

She's not the problem—you are, Lincoln. He was too shaken to note that both *L* sounds were clearly pronounced, as Marie had done when she was upset with him.

He pulled her note from his pocket.

Put it away!

It was still folded when he placed it into the glove compartment.

It would be best if you threw it away.

Link shook his head. "I can't." He waited vainly for a response until reality returned and crept over him. He had been holding the discussions with himself.

The cell phone buzzed in his pocket. The sound was startling.

He fumbled it open. "Anderson," he said.

"Erin here, pardner. What's your location?"

He remembered the last sign. "I'm on Highway Fifty, not far from a town called Eureka."

She paused, and he heard paper crackling as she looked it up on a map. "You're sure a long way from nothing," she said.

"I'll head north on Highway Ninety-three, and spend the night in Battle Mountain."

"I see it here." She hesitated. "When will you be back?"

Link turned options over in his mind. His intent had been to return to the wilderness for a while. Decide whether he shouldn't tell Frank Dubois to find a replacement for him.

"I'll be in Boudie Springs tomorrow night," he said.

"How about I have a Learjet waiting for you there the next morning?"

He smiled and shook his head at her stubbornness. But of course, friends were like that. Not wanting you to get down or feel sorry for yourself.

"I should stop by and see Joseph Spotted Horse. See if he still wants to visit New York."

"Take the Learjet. Frank says you ought to get back into the cockpit or you're going to forget everything he taught you. And he has a new project he needs to talk with you about."

"You're not going to give up, are you?"

"Nope." She paused. "I've never been there where you are. What's it like?"

He closed the glove compartment and started the engine. "A bit desolate."

"Lonesome?"

"Not now," he said.